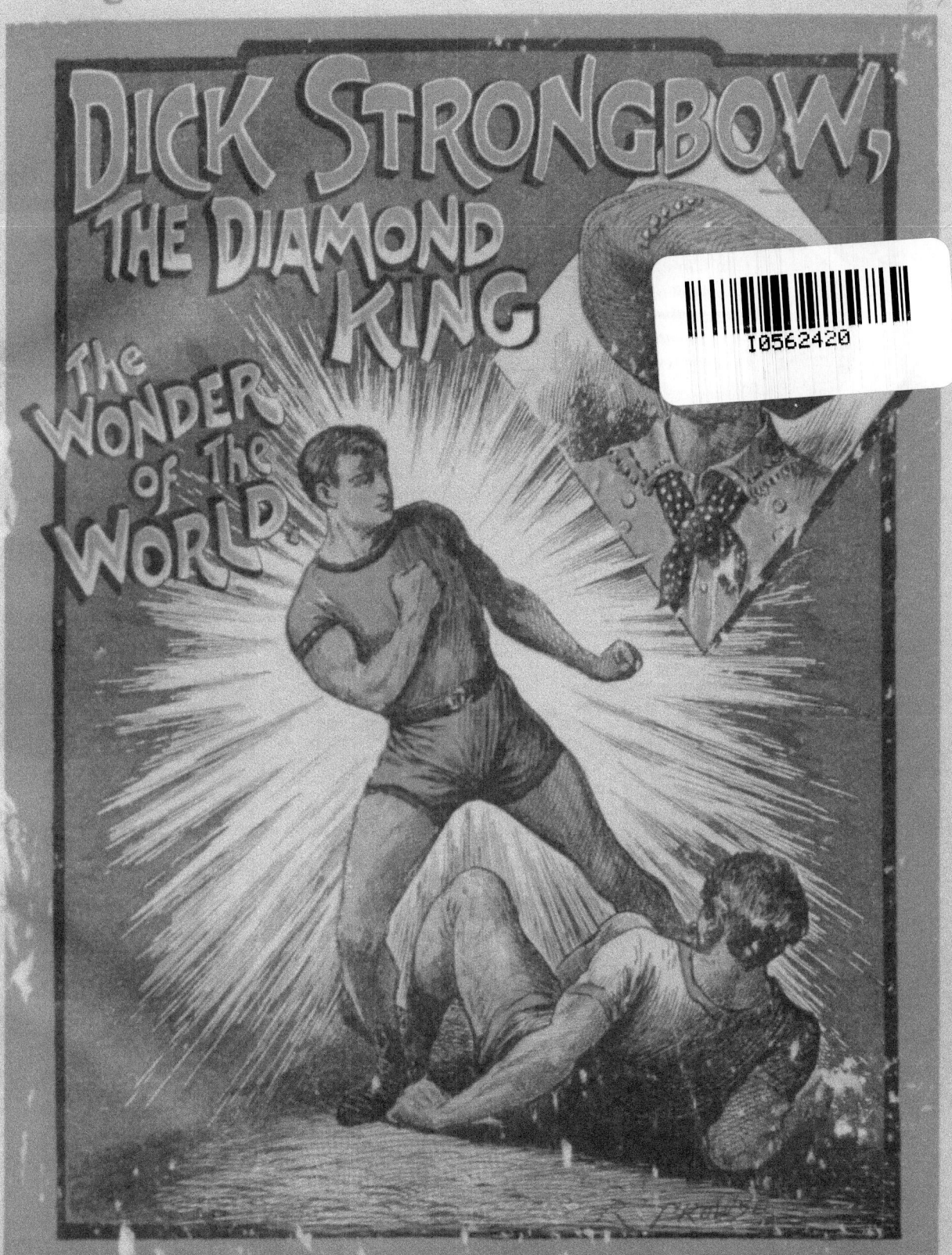

DICK STRONGBOW, THE DIAMOND KING

The WONDER of THE WORLD

Nos. 1 & 2.

Price One Penny.

DICK STRONGBOW,

THE DIAMOND KING.

CHAPTER I.

ONE HUNDRED POUNDS.

 ADIES and gentlemen, the feats I am about to perform, no other man on earth can do. If anyone here thinks he is able to accomplish them let him step up and try. If he succeeds here is a hundred-pound note for him."

Thus spoke Joe Grub, known to the public as "Ajax, the strongest living man." He was addressing a well-filled place of entertainment, Parbole's Theatre of Varieties, London.

He was a big, thickset man, a veritable giant, with an impressive display of muscle about his limbs. His attire was that of the ordinary acrobat.

Standing by him was a smaller man, also in professional attire—a stunted, ill-favoured specimen of humanity, who was evidently intended to be a foil to his gigantic and somewhat well-favoured master.

His everyday name was Reuben Perks, his professional name was Pan.

Part of his duty was to imitate his master, and by a series of failures excite the laughter of the audience.

"A hundred-pound note !" cried Ajax, flourishing the flimsy piece of paper above his head ; "fresh and crisp from the Bank of England. Is there anyone here who means to try and win it ?"

"I will," answered a quiet voice on the left side of the hall.

Ajax was engaged in folding the note, preparatory to placing it in an envelope, to be afterwards fixed in the slit of a wand which stood upright on the stage.

For many nights the note had been placed there, and the challenge issued, without anybody offering himself as competitor against the Strongest Living Man.

But now, unexpectedly, some daring spirit was in the field, and every eye was turned in the direction of the voice to see who it was.

Leaning against the side of the hall, with his arms folded, and with an air of composure which all the staring did not disturb, was a young fellow, apparently about twenty years of age.

Beyond his being very good-looking, there was nothing remarkable about his appearance.

He was of medium height, with well-squared shoulders, and of good proportions. That was all. Pan stared at him sneeringly. The lip of Ajax curled with contempt.

"Did you speak, sir ?" he enquired, with mock politeness.

"I did," was the reply. "I accept your challenge."

The audience laughed—some gaily, others derisively. Pan's face expanded into a grin of aggressive malevolence.

His feeling was that this interloper might possibly get all the laughter, and so shut him out from his part of the programme.

"Go on, master," he said. "Don't waste your time with a baby."

"It IS nonsense," replied Ajax. "Ladies and gentlemen, I will now begin my performance, and—"

"Am I to come upon the stage or not ?" demanded the youth, in an impulsive and fiery tone.

"You can if you like," replied Pan, "and make a fool of yourself."

"Let him walk up," said Ajax, in an under tone.

"If he comes up," cried Pan, "I claim the right to kick him down again, if he fails."

"You shall do it—if you can," returned the youth. The audience roared with delight.

Whatever happened they would get their share of the fun.

Many were disposed to think that it was an arranged thing, and that another foil to the mighty Ajax about to be introduced.

As much was said by two or three as the young fellow climbed upon the stage.

He turned his face in their direction, and quickly gave them the lie.

"I am an utter stranger to these men," he said, "so don't talk nonsense. I don't mind telling you wiseacres that I came here to-night to win the hundred pounds. I want it badly."

Something in this reply tickled his listeners immensely. Probably they thought that they wanted the note also.

But the youth was not jesting. There was a grave earnestness in his tone that left little doubt of his meaning what he said. He wanted this note.

Not simply as the majority of us would feel the need of it, but for some purpose out of the ordinary course of life.

Again, as he stood erect upon the stage, the audience saw nothing in him to give promise of great strength, such as Ajax possessed.

"There's not much in HIM," said one.

"Why, he's only a hobbledehoy," remarked another.

Then they settled down to see him fail, and to witness his ignominious expulsion from the stage by Pan.

Ajax, with an easy smile on his face, began his usual feats, and the young stranger, with his hands upon his hips, watched him closely and critically, but without displaying any signs of astonishment or doubt of his ability to do the same.

First, the Strongest Living Man took a pair of huge dumb-bells, raised them slowly, and beat them together over his head.

Then he held them out at arms' length, and gradually lowered them to the ground.

Loud applause followed this undoubted exhibition of great muscular power.

His next feat was to lift two enormous weights from the stage, and carry them around as the milkman bears his pails.

More applause and a few jeering suggestions to the young fellow followed.

Pan, with an imp-like action, danced about in front of him, snapping his fingers derisively.

But no notice whatever was taken of Pan by the young stranger, which had an exasperating effect upon Pan. It made him absolutely furious.

"I'll kick you half across the hall!" he hissed.

"Get out of the way, you mannikin!" calmly replied the youth.

What answer Pan would have made to this is uncertain. It was checked by Ajax, who had just performed a third feat of strength, calling upon the stranger to show him what he could do.

"If you can do what I have done," he said, "I have nothing more to show you."

"Try it, you whipper-snapper!" hissed Pan, "and I will get ready for the kicking."

No answer was vouchsafed him.

Advancing to the middle of the stage, the young fellow with great deliberation began to pull off his coat.

CHAPTER II.

WON.

AT once the audience settled down to witness the farce of a failure; but as the stranger removed his coat and rolled up his shirt-sleeves exclamations of wonder and admiration were heard all over the hall.

There was no mistake about the matter. That quiet young stranger had extraordinary muscular development about the arms.

"Knotted ropes," was the comment of a critical man near the stage, and, indeed, the arms of the aspirant for the hundred pounds had that appearance.

Upon Ajax there fell a sudden chill, and Pan's brow was darkened with a savage frown. With no apparent effort the young fellow took up the dumb-bells, lifted them above his head, clashed them together, twirled them about, and, unruffled, replaced them upon the boards.

For a moment the audience was dumb, and not a movement was heard.

Then, as if by one impulse, the throng burst into wild applause.

Apparently unmoved by this demonstration, the stranger went on with the feats, did them with the greatest ease, and, walking to the wand, took the envelope containing the note out of the slit, and thrust it into his trousers' pocket.

The uproar was tremendous. Some clapped their hands, others stamped their feet—a considerable number jumped up, waving their hats and handkerchiefs.

The noise was deafening.

Ajax, pale with dismay, stood back, staring at the victor dumb and helpless.

For all his strength he was a terrible coward, and dared not act upon the promptings of his heart to stop the young fellow and prevent his bearing away the prize.

The same desire was on Pan, but he had more courage than his master.

Getting in front of the youthful victor, he shouted to him that he had not fairly won the prize; that the tricks had not been properly performed; and he should not "rob his master" by taking the note away.

The patience of the youthful competitor was now exhausted.

He waved his hand for Pan to get out of the way; but the man was demoniacal with anger, and continued to bar his way, heaping all sorts of epithets upon him.

Suddenly the youth pounced upon him, twisted him round, seized his waistband, and hoisted him in the air as if he had been a doll.

Pan kicked and cursed; but he was helpless in that mighty grasp.

The roaring of the audience was now like that of a tumultuous sea. Everybody had risen, and, led away by excitement, shouted until they were hoarse.

The youth, after twisting Pan this way and that, looked round for a place to deposit him.

At first he seemed inclined to pitch him into the thick of the audience ; but the possibility of injuring others doubtless deterred him.

Then he looked at the stage-boxes—one was occupied and the other was empty.

Into the latter he pitched the helpless Pan, seized his coat, and, disregarding the uproar, leaped from the stage and stalked from the hall.

The audience made way for him as they would have done for a quick-travelling battering-ram. Much respect is shown to a giant's strength. The applause followed him to the door.

But he seemed blind and deaf to it all, walking with his eyes fixed ahead and his teeth set—a grim, terrible figure, in spite of his youthful beauty.

In the vestibule he stopped for a moment to put on his coat, and while he was thus engaged a man came panting out of the hall and rushed up to him.

"Excuse me, sir," he said ; "but may I have a word with you ?"

"Yes," was the reply. "Who are you, and what do you want ?"

"I am a journalist," said the man, "and the record of what has happened to-night must go into the papers. It will cause a sensation."

"Very well," said the young fellow ; "put it in. I don't know that it will affect me in any way."

"But I must know something about you," said the journalist. "Will you kindly give me your name ?"

"Call me Dick Strongbow," said the athlete, and, with a wave of his strong arm, implying that he had no more to say, he strode out of the vestibule and disappeared in the busy street outside the hall.

It was all over with Ajax. He had been matched, and more than matched, because Dick Strongbow had performed his feats more easily than he had ever done, and he was the Strongest Living Man no more.

He staggered rather than walked from the stage, to the unmusical accompaniment of the hisses of the changeable audience.

Only a few minutes ago he had been applauded to the echo, and now he was a fallen man—despised, laughed at.

And, what was equally painful, he had lost his hundred pounds.

When he reached the wing of the stage the curtain was dropped, and somebody in pity, seeing his half fainting condition, brought him a chair.

He sank into it, and it was fortunately a strong one, or his great weight would have broken it down.

"Don't let anybody come near me for a minute !" he gasped ; "but get me some brandy."

A Lion Comique, already dressed for his part, ran off for some, and different members of the artists and assistants gathered around him.

Among them was Mr. Parbole, the proprietor of the hall.

He was a short man, with a big black moustache, with waxed ends—the beau ideal of a music-hall manager.

At that moment he looked white and depressed, and when the Lion Comique had brought the brandy, and Ajax had swallowed it, he asked if he could have a few words with him in private.

"You can say what you require—in public," groaned Ajax. "I know what it is. You want my engagement cancelled."

"It's no good to you or me now," replied Parbole. "There's little chances of your drawing money, unless—"

He stopped and looked curiously at Ajax, who groaned again and wiped his eyes.

"Unless you can get hold of this young fellow and arrange some matches—on the cross. If you could persuade him to let you lick him next time, and then take your chance of being licked afterwards, there would be money in it."

"He ain't a pro," moaned Ajax.

"He can be made one," replied Parbole.

At that moment the journalist who had spoken to Dick Strongbow appeared on the stage.

He was desirous of knowing how Ajax took his defeat, and one glance at him was sufficient to give him matter for at least thirty lines.

The next morning all the public would read that the Strongest Living Man had been "completely overwhelmed by his defeat, that he had shed tears," and so on.

"Where's your man Pan ?" he asked, having made the requisite mental notes about Ajax.

"He's down by the stage-door, cursing and grunting and rubbing his sore places," said a stage carpenter standing hard by.

"Has he any bones broken ?" asked the journalist.

"He says he hasn't," replied the carpenter.

"That's a pity," muttered the journalist, with a disappointed look. "I thought I should have made half a column out of his condition in the hospital during the different hours of the night."

Ajax got slowly upon his feet.

"Don't you think, Mr. Parbole," he said, "that I could go on for a bit ?"

"Finish your week, if you like," was the answer ; "but you run the risk of being chaffed, and you won't draw an extra sixpence."

"Can't it be kept out of the papers ?" asked Ajax.

The journalist laughed softly.

"No," he said, "it is too big a thing. Think of what a line 'The Defeat of the Strongest Living Man' will make on the bills ! Sorry I can't oblige you."

Ajax walked mournfuly away to an adjacent dressing-room, where he slipped on his every-day clothes over his performing dress.

A glance round told him that Pan had been there to perform that office before him.

He found his assistant just outside the building, standing well within the shadow of the stage door.

"I thought you were gone home, Pan," he said, feebly.

"You thought nothing of the sort," snorted Pan. "Why on earth didn't you stop that fellow at his tricks ?"

"How could I ?" asked Ajax.

"How could you !" said Pan. "Couldn't you have said he wasn't doing them fair, and pinched him somewhere ? A dig in the small of his back would have done it."

"I didn't think of it," murmured Ajax.

"You DID," hissed Pan, "but you hadn't the pluck to do it. Hasn't it been done before to men who seemed to be getting near the mark ? Yah ! you were afraid of him."

"I don't think I was."

"You were. You are a lily-livered duffer—and if you say you are not—look here—*I'll hit you.*"

Ajax was big and strong enough to have smashed Pan with two fingers, but, arrant coward that he was, he caved in before his ferocious assailant.

"Don't get violent, old fellow," he said. "I couldn't help it. The whole thing was sprung upon me. I was too astonished to do anything except stare at him."

"What do you think Gabrielle will say?" demanded Pan. "She will cut up rough over it."

"I don't think I'll tell her to-night," gasped Ajax.

"If you don't I will," growled Pan.

By this time they had got into a neighbourhood where the houses were private, and of the middle-class in point of respectability.

In a quiet thoroughfare Ajax lodged with Gabrielle—h s wife. Pan had a room in the same house, and generally had his meals with his master.

As a rule they had supper together.

In a room on the first floor Gabrielle was awaiting them.

She was a little spare-built woman, of the fair-haired, blue-eyed sort—well suited to the stage or the circus with a little paint.

In her private domain she had a faded look—"washed out" is the general expression—and she was decidedly slovenly in her dress.

She glanced at the two men in a quick way as they entered the room, and noted the dejected appearance of Ajax.

"What's the matter," she demanded, shrilly. "You've not been missing your tip, have you?"

"No," groaned Ajax; "I did everything as well as ever, but—"

He stopped short, and Pan finished the sentence for him.

"He's let a boy—a cub—lick him," he said, "and never did a thing to stop him, but just stared at him in a goggled-eyed way."

"And the note—the hundred-pound note?" screamed Gabrielle.

"*It's gone!*" whined Ajax.

Gabrielle, with a wrathful exclamation, sprang up and gave her huge husband two boxes on the ears—one on either side of his head.

Good sounding smacks they were, and, like a big looby, he began to blubber.

"That's right, missus," said Pan, with a grin. "Give it to him; he deserves it. Let him have another."

But further marital chastisement was cut short by the ringing of the bell, followed by a short rat-tat on the front door.

"Who's that?" asked Pan. "Nobody ever knocks like that for the landlady."

He hurriedly left the room, and Gabrielle and Ajax stood silently listening.

They heard the door open, and a strange, deep voice speaking to Pan.

Then the door closed, and both the men were heard to saunter slowly away.

It was fully a quarter of an hour ere Pan re-entered the house, and came bounding up the stairs. His eyes, as he came into the room, were blazing with a strange light.

"Now, Joe," he said, addressing Ajax by his ordinary name, "see if you can't screw up an ounce of pluck. You are wanted for a particular job."

"What is it?" asked Ajax

"It's something," said Pan, "that will square accounts with that fellow, *and get you back your money.* Gabrielle, it's entirely out of a woman's line. Get us a bit of supper, and after it me and Joe are going out for an hour or two."

CHAPTER III.
GONZALO.

WHEN Dick Strongbow left the music-hall he hurried along through several well-lighted thoroughfares, and eventually reached a quieter neighbourhood, not far from Vauxhall-bridge.

Turning into a street, dimly lighted and stamped with the seal of that semi-poverty which is so hard to bear, he walked briskly to a house at the lower end.

The door opened to his touch, revealing a passage lighted with a small benzoline lamp, standing on a bracket fixed to the wall.

Dick, walking with a light tread, as if he feared to disturb the house, passed down the passage to the back room on the ground floor.

Softly entering, he found a common dip candle alight, with a perfect little mop of a wick, showing that it had been burning unheeded for some time.

The furniture of the room was of the poorest description—a rickety table, two common chairs, and an apology for a bed, in which a tall, gaunt man was lying seemingly asleep.

Although the night was cold, there was no fire burning in the poor little grate, and the rusty fender and poker exhibited no signs of recent use.

Dick walked on tip-toe to the bed, and gazed earnestly for a moment at the features of the man.

"Gonzalo," he said, in a whisper.

The eyes opened—big, dark eyes, that had once shone with the light of intelligence, but were now dim with suffering.

A faint smile of pleasure flickered about the drawn mouth as the man replied—

"Ah! is it you? Where have you been?"

"To Parbole's Theatre of Varieties," replied Dick.

"So," replied Gonzalo, with sudden fire, "they have seen you? Well, well—"

"I have made a little money to-night," said Dick. "I saw a bill with an announcement, from a fellow who calls himself Ajax, offering a hundred pounds to anyone who could perform his feats. I spent my last shilling to go in—"

"And—and you did them?"

"Yes—easy; they were not much for me to do."

"He paid you the money?"

"I helped myself," said Dick, with a quiet laugh. "See here—a hundred-pound note. I took good care they did not bamboozle me out of it. Now you shall want for nothing. You will soon be well again."

"Do not think of me," said Gonzalo, in a hollow

voice; "it is too late. Never mind that. Come, don't give way."

"My only—my best friend!" said Dick, with a choking sob, "why did you allow yourself to fall into this state? Why did you not send for me before?"

"I would not have sent for you now," said Gonzalo, "but to tell you of certain things you ought to know."

"It is horrible—terrible," said Dick, with a moan, "to think that I was idling at a German university while you were starving here. How you must have needed the money you were spending on me—and I not to know it! You never told me—"

"My boy," said Gonzalo, "you are my sister's only child. I have done my best for you. I trained and developed your wonderful strength. It will gain you a living any way, *and may help you to avenge a bitter wrong*. I gave you the education of a gentleman in case—"

Gonzalo stopped short, with a catching in his throat. Dick put his arm under his head and raised it.

"Do not talk too much now," he said. "Tell me all, whatever it may be, to-morrow."

"There will be no morrow for me," said Gonzalo, slowly. "The stroller is played out. I've been failing for years, and when I came here no manager would look at me. Never mind that. I tried to earn a little, and there was something put away which kept you at the university. You may want your education one day."

"It will be useful, I suppose," said Dick, gloomily, "but I've no taste for books."

"No—no; not for books," said Gonzalo, "but to help you fill your true position in life—*when you find it*. I think you will one day."

"I thought I was a stroller's son," said Dick. "I have never denied it."

"Ah! they used to sneer at you about it," said Gonzalo.

"*Once* while at the university they did so," said Dick; "but I took the sneerer up in my arms—it was in a café—and threw him clean through the window into the street. After that they let me alone."

"They did not dream of your hidden powers," said Gonzalo, with another faint smile.

"To tell the truth," said Dick, "I am *afraid* to use my strength. I feel if I were to strike anyone that *half a blow* from me would dash the life out of him."

"Husband your strength," said Gonzalo. "Use it wisely. It will not last for ever. If you can do nothing else to gain money practise it on the stage. The world will wonder at you—"

"If you wished me to take to the profession," said Dick, "why did you educate me? It is not wanted. It is a waste of time."

"I tell you," said Gonzalo, "that it may be wanted. Your mother was a stroller, but your father was *not*."

"Who was he?"

"I don't know. He was a reckless, handsome man, but he had a high bearing. His strength was great—you inherit it from him—and he was always performing some mad feat. But I cannot tell you of these things. You will hear of them by-and-bye. Go to Jacob Morelle, 47, Dane's Inn, here in London, and tell him you come from Gonzalo for the packet left in his hands seventeen years ago."

"Will he give it to me?"
"He will."

Dick had been so absorbed in the unexpected nature of the conversation that he had failed to note the rapidly growing weakness of his companion.

Now it was forced upon him by his falling back in a state of collapse. Only faint gasps showed that he still lived.

"What a fool I am!" thought Dick, in anguish. "I have brought in nothing with me. Gonzalo—Gonzalo—uncle—friend!"

Once more the dark eyes opened, and now there was a light in them which had not been there for many days.

It was brighter than that of the wretched candle with its heavy wick burning on the table.

"You can do *nothing*," he said.

"I did not think you were so bad," sobbed Dick. "I arrived here this morning, almost penniless, and found you, as I thought, ailing somewhat and in want. I left you for a little while to earn something somehow. I succeeded. A hundred pounds are in my pocket and you—"

"A million would not save me," said Gonzalo. "I am past all want. Have been so for days; but I bore up until you came. Good-bye, don't forget, Jacob Morelle—Morelle—Jacob—he will—"

And then the bright light in his eyes suddenly vanished, as if a dark curtain had fallen over them, and Gonzalo the stroller was—dead.

Dick, kneeling down by the bedside, gave way for a few moments to feelings akin to the agony of despair.

This man had been his only true friend from his childhood. They had been to each other what a father and son ought to be, and Dick had never known a mother's love.

She died when he was an infant, but left a portrait of herself in professional attire, that gave to Dick some idea of her.

But of his father he knew absolutely nothing. He left no portrait. Gonzalo had rarely spoken of him, and then only in a brief fashion.

Until that night he had given Dick no idea of his father, and the boy had never shown any curiosity on the subject.

His unknown parent had been an impalpable being, and Gonzalo filled his place.

And now Gonzalo was dead—dead!

Dick could not quite realise it as he arose from his knees and stared blankly round the dismal room.

But it was so—a glance at the face, with its half-closed eyes and fallen jaw, told him all was over.

The seal of death set upon a human face cannot be mistaken.

And now all that remained to be done was to find his faithful friend a last resting-place.

The money earned to give Gonzalo bread would have to be spent upon his grave.

"And I," thought Dick, "am alone in the world, with these strong and dangerous arms of mine—what was it Gonzalo said?—*to avenge a wrong*."

And then he fell into a train of thought, speculating in a dreamy way on many things, until he began to single out the fact that there were certain things to be done for the dead man which he ought to do.

He knew nobody, not even the people of the house; but help must be sought, and he was thinking how he should proceed when a startling cry fell upon his ears—

" Fire !—fire !"

He leaped to the door, and, without turning the handle, by sheer strength, involuntarily used, tore it open. The passage without was filled with smoke and flame, barring his exit from the room.

CHAPTER IV.

ARSON.

THE first thought of Dick on finding himself in such a position of peril was of the window at the back of the room.

There was no time to spare, for he was already surrounded by smoke, and a few moments of such an atmosphere would choke him.

He tried to raise the sash, but it was jammed fast, the cords being rotten and broken.

With scant ceremony he put his shoulder against the woodwork and forced it through into the small backyard that belonged to the house.

But there, beyond the chance of a little purer air, he was not much better off.

The only means of exit was by a small door that led into the kitchen of the house, and in there the fire was already raging.

He cast a glance upward, and saw that he was in a kind of shaft, formed by the blank walls of the closely-built surrounding houses.

Death was certain if he stayed there, and what other chance had he of escape?

Could he possibly break down the wall between the front and back rooms, and escape by that way?

He knew such buildings were flimsy structures, and it was worth the trying, especially as it was his only chance of life. Luckily he had closed the door on discovering the fire, and beyond the smoke that rushed through its ill-fitting joints, he had nothing for the moment to fear.

Taking out his handkerchief, he hastily tied it over his mouth, and sprang back through the broken window into the room.

The candle had now guttered down, and could only be dimly seen in the smoke that had gathered around and was stifling its flame.

Brushing past the table, he dashed at the partition.

It was a thing of lath and plaster, and yielded instantly.

The front apartment was filled with smoke, but here, as in the other room, there was as yet no flame.

Outside a mob was gathering fast, roaring and shrieking—

" Fire—fire !"

Dick felt comparatively safe now ; but it suddenly flashed upon him that poor Gonzalo was lying dead, and, unless rescued, his body would be given over to the flames.

He could not leave, even in death, one who had been so faithful to him, so back he went again, breathing a little through his handkerchief, and, raising the body with the spare bedclothes in his arms, made for the front window.

For a wonder the sash was movable, and when he threw it up and appeared with the dead Gonzalo

in his arms, a roar went up from the mob that seemed to shake the very houses.

The greater part of them were rickety enough to be brought down by any considerable atmospheric disturbance, but shouting, fortunately, was not sufficient for the work.

There was no intervening area, and Dick stepped into the street.

A score hands were extended to help the " sick man," as these volunteers called the remains of poor Gonzalo ; but Dick cried out—

" You cannot help him. He is dead. Show me some place where I can decently lay him !"

" Here—my house—my house over the way," cried half-a-dozen voices, and a lane was made for him to pass through.

As he was crossing the narrow road the rattle of a coming fire-engine was heard, and there was a general stampede to get out of its way.

Dick was borne along for a distance with his burden like a straw upon a rushing river, and now as the flames burst from the door of the burning house he cast a hurried glance around him.

Two faces near him he instantly recognised.

He had only seen them once before, and under very different circumstances, but he knew them both.

They were the faces of Ajax and Pan.

A terrified look was on the former, while the latter expressed the utmost malignance, mingled, as Dick thought, with disappointment.

He saw them one moment, and then they were gone.

It was no time to reason on their presence or to endeavour to interrupt and question them.

First of all a temporary resting-place must be found for the body of poor Gonzalo.

The door of a house was opened for it, and a man in labourer's attire bade Dick enter.

" Put the poor fellow in my room, sir," he said. " I'm a single man, and he's welcome to my bed as long as he wants it."

His room, a very poor one, was on the first floor, and there Dick laid the body of his friend upon the bed.

Then, hurriedly thanking the man for his courtesy, he hastened out to give such help as he could to extinguish the flames.

Smart work had been done with the engine, and, the water being turned on, a copious stream was pouring into the burning house.

The fire was already sinking under its influence ; no outside assistance was needed.

Dick waited until only smoke and steam remained, and then pushed his way to the front with scarce an effort, until he came to a line of policemen, who were keeping a clear space for the firemen.

" Can I pass through ?" he asked.

" No," was the abrupt answer.

" But I have only just escaped from the burning house."

" That's nothing to us. You can't pass."

Dick could easily have tossed them aside, but he refrained.

" I will wait and see your superior officer," he said.

Up and down the street a number of the inhabitants, in a panic, had been hauling out their little household goods—for they were not insured, and the loss of them by fire would be their ruin.

Now, however, the firemen were calling out that all danger was over, and the people were replacing their things.

By-and-bye an inspector came along the line of policemen, and to him Dick said a few words.

"I've just escaped from the burning house."

"Well," said the officer, "do you know how it happened?"

"No; I opened the door of one of the lower rooms and found the passage in flames."

"Who else was there in the house?"

"I know of nobody but a dead man—a friend of mine."

This strange reply drew many eyes upon him, especially those of the officer, who said—

"Let that man pass through."

"It's only a lad, sir," said one of his men.

"What's that to you?" replied the officer. "Let him pass."

So Dick passed through, and the officer, eyeing him up and down, said—

"I shall want to know something about you. Keep here for a moment."

Then he crossed over to the shattered doorway of the house, through which a fireman, with a lantern in his hand, was peering.

"Well," he said, "what do you make of it, Mr. Ingersoll?"

"Arson," was the answer; "the passage is full of burnt straw."

A few more words were hurriedly exchanged, and the police-officer went back to Dick.

"My lad," he said, "we can't talk here. You had better come with me to the station. It is close handy."

"Why to the station?" asked Dick.

"Well, you had better come quietly," was the cool reply. "There doesn't seem to have been anybody but you alive in the house, and we shall ask you to explain how the passage came filled with straw."

"With straw!" exclaimed Dick.

"Yes, my lad; odd, isn't it? Now, don't be a fool. Come quietly."

Just for half a moment Dick looked as if he would resist, and had he done so it would have been rough work for that collected inspector; but he saw that it would have been folly and, putting his hands into his pockets, he said he was ready to go.

CHAPTER V.
WHO DID IT?

DICK was not unkindly treated at the station. The inspector took him to his private room, and "put him through his facings," as he called it.

Dick told him his story in brief.

How he had heard of his friend Gonzalo's sickness and had come over to see him, working his way from Berlin because he had no money.

"And have you none now?" asked the inspector.

"Only a hundred-pound note," replied Dick.

"A hundred-pound note!" exclaimed the officer. "And where did you get that from?"

Dick told him, and he listened incredulously until the youth took off his coat and exhibited his wonderful muscular development.

The astounded officer took refuge in a whistle.

He listened to the rest of Dick's story with a different air, and seemed much impressed by that part of it relating to the breaking through the partition of the house.

"And I came here of my own free will, you know," said Dick, in conclusion, "for I could have picked you up like a child, and tossed you over my head."

"I should like to see you do it," said the officer, who was a very powerful man.

Dick instantly pinioned his arms to his side, and carried him in a state of helpless astonishment round the office, holding him at arms' length as if he had been a doll.

"My lad," said the inspector, when Dick had quietly dropped him into a chair, "I'm glad you did not rough up. I believe your story, but I must keep you here. If you want a sleep take it in my arm-chair before the fire."

This was what Dick did, after giving as clear a direction as he could where the body of Gonzalo was lying.

The officer told him that there would, under the circumstances, have to be an inquest.

"And for form's sake I think I shall have to take you before a magistrate to account for this note."

"It is easily proved how I won it," said Dick.

He slept in the inspector's arm-chair that night, and awoke in the morning to find himself famous.

Not only the story of his music-hall triumph, but a fairly true account of his adventure in the burning house had been seized by the reporters in time for the papers.

Everybody interested in athletics were enquiring after this wonderful youth.

Mr. Parbole was sent for, and recognised him as the winner of the hundred-pound note, so that after all there was no need of his being taken before a magistrate.

He was set free, and, accompanied by the now admiring inspector, went off to an adjacent inn, where the inquest was to be held.

There was an enormous crowd, far more interested in the living Dick than the dead Gonzalo, and the room was crowded almost to suffocation.

When he gave his evidence there was a breathless silence, and the busy reporters took down every word, for it would make splendid copy.

It seemed that at the time there was nobody in the house, and the facts pointed to arson from the outside.

The straw had been stolen from a carter's stables adjacent, and the front door being unfastened, as it usually was, access was easy.

The question was—Who did it, and why?

On this point no evidence was offered.

In Dick's mind a suspicion arose that Ajax and Pan had something to do with it, and he had seen them *after* the fire, as we know; but he dismissed it as incredible.

How could they have known he was in that house?

Like many others, they might have been in the neighbourhood, attracted to the spot by the cry of "fire." On what grounds could he accuse them of having originated it?

The theory of the police was that it was an act of malice on the part of one of the lodgers of the house, of whom there were nearly a dozen.

They all owed rent, and one of them, thinking the place was empty, might have looked upon it as a short way out of his difficulty.

It was a poor theory, but it served, as no better was advanced.

Gonzalo two days later was buried, and Dick paid for a piece of ground and a monument to be put over him, with the simple inscription—" Gonzalo a true friend."

Then, and not until then, Dick turned his attention to his own affairs.

First of all he went to Dane's-inn, and failed to find the Mr. Jacob Morelle Gonzalo had spoken of.

Nobody seemed to know anything about him, or had even heard his name before.

"I've been here seven years," said one of the occupants of the chambers, "and never heard of such a person."

"It was a delusion of poor Gonzalo's," thought Dick, as he walked sadly away; "he had got some odd fancy into his head. He was always a bit romantic, and worked up some imaginary yarn about my being the son of some big man. Hang it! I wish he had never got it into his head and put it into mine."

Well, there was Dick with about sixty pounds out of the hundred left in his pocket, and not a friend in the world.

What was he to do?

To live he must labour, and he had a pair of strong arms and a wonderful, if unobtrusive, general physique. With such things he felt he could make a name, if it was not exactly the name he had once aspired to.

"I'll make some money by my strength first," he said, "and then think of higher things. And for the present I will stick to the name of Dick Strongbow."

CHAPTER VI.

ROLLING IN THE MONEY.

ARBOLE was in the seventh heaven of managerial delight. Not only had he found out the young stranger who had defeated Ajax, but he had engaged him, and a most successful performance had also been gone through to a crowded house. Dick Strongbow was up and Ajax was down—snuffed out, relegated to a back seat, from which he would have some difficulty in advancing himself.

Parbole and Dick were in the latter's dressing-room, and it was as much as the manager could do to keep from hugging him.

"You are a wonderful young man," he said, "and not fully developed yet. Really a wonderful young man!"

"And now," said Dick, "we must come to the money part of the question. This was to be a test performance. Does it look like success?"

"It does."

"How much a night, then, am I to have?"

"H'm!" said Mr. Parbole, "we had better say ten pounds a night."

"Not enough," replied Dick.

"Twenty, then?"

"That's better, but still not enough. Say two hundred a week for a month."

Mr. Parbole thought a moment upon the extreme probability of other managers making as good or even a better offer, and, with a bit of a wrench, said—

"Agreed. But, excuse me, I did not expect to find you so tight a hand in money matters."

"Perhaps not," replied Dick; "but I want to make a little and have done with it."

Having now dressed, he shook hands with the manager, bade him Good-night, and strolled away.

The stage-door of the music-hall was in a narrow thoroughfare at the back of the building, on one side of which was a blank wall.

It was not much used by the public, and the lighting was defective. The street was also ill-paved.

Dick, on emerging from the doorway, saw a man skulking under the shadow of one of the houses close by, who raised his arm as if to strike or throw something at him.

Instinctively Dick suspected mischief, and sprang forward to see who it was.

Then the arm of the man made a sweeping motion, and a small bottle whizzed by Dick's head.

It struck the wall behind him, and shivered into a hundred pieces. Quick as lightning the man swung round, darted down the street, keeping in the shadow, and vanished. Whither, it was difficult to tell.

Dick, seeing that pursuit would be in vain, went back to the wall, and having found where the bottle struck, examined the moisture running down, and found it was vitriol.

"Oh! so it was you my friend, Pan. Just as I thought, the moment I saw you," he said, grimly. "Very good. We shall meet again some day, and then I will settle with you."

Dick had comfortable lodgings, not far away, and, undisturbed by the recent attempt to do him a lasting injury, he went thither, and after supper took a turn with the huge dumb-bells. Apparently refreshed thereby, he went to bed.

The next morning he went out for a walk, and we record this simple fact as it brought him into contact with one who was destined to be his companion for many a day afterwards.

In a thoroughfare near Westminster-bridge he came upon a very ordinary sight in London—a brewer's man lowering a load of beer into the cellar of a public-house.

But this was not all.

The brewer's man was in a very excited state, owing to the conduct of one of those certainly very troublesome imps—street urchins—who, as a rule, are half starved but cheerful, imperfectly dressed in rags, but bold and defiant as lords.

The particular imp in question was "bucking" from one barrel to another with the agility of a stage acrobat, laughing at the brewer's man, who was alternately ordering him off and aiming futile blows at him.

"If I only gets hold on you," he was saying, "I'll powderise you. Get off them barrels, will you?"

The boy was lying along one, grinning like a monkey, enjoying himself thoroughly at the man's expense.

Dick had a strong sense of humour, and the scene rather tickled him; but an impulse came over him to play a trick upon the urchin.

Stepping up lightly, and unperceived by the boy, he grasped the barrel in both hands, and hoisted it like a toy in the air.

"Now, you young rascal," he said, "what shall I do with you?"

The brewer's man had not too much breath at his command at any time—now absolutely he had none.

All he could do was to stare at Dick, and wonder whether he were waking or dreaming.

As for the boy, he instinctively clung to the barrel as a cat clings to anything in a moment of peril; but he was scared half out of his senses.

Dick held the barrel for a few moments in the air, then lowered it, and took the boy in his strong grasp, holding him out at arm's length.

"Now," he said, "will you ever play tricks upon this man again?"

"I—I don't think so," replied the boy.

"Very well," said Dick, as he put him on his feet. "Now be off."

Nodding to the brewer, he walked away in the direction of the bridge, across which he sauntered, stopping at the north end to look at the steam-boats.

Casually looking backward, he saw the boy hovering close by, staring at him open-eyed.

"I've fascinated the little beggar," thought Dick, with a smile.

Resolved to test the matter, he walked on to the Abbey, and, by the great door, suddenly wheeled round.

There was the boy again, about a dozen yards behind him.

"Come here," said Dick.

"You won't smash me if I do?" pleaded the boy.

"I won't hurt you a bit," answered Dick. "Why should I?"

The boy saw he was kindly smiling, and came slowly towards him.

"Now," said Dick, "tell me what you want."

"I'm only a looking at you," said the boy. "You are the strong man, ain't you—him as beat Hay-acks?"

Dick laughed outright. It was amusing to find that his fame had socially come down so low.

"Yes," he said, "I am the new strong man. But how came you to know anything about me?"

"I heard 'em talking about you when they was coming out of Parboil's. I never sees nothing, but I hears a lot."

"But how came you to guess that I was the strong man?"

"'Cause they said you was young, and not fat, nor stout, and as strong as half-a-dozen lions."

"You are a sharp boy," said Dick. "Where do you live?"

"Anywheres," replied the boy.

"Where does your father live?"

"Ain't got one—nivver seed him."

"But you have a mother?"

"Maybe," said the boy, "but I ain't seen her for years."

"What is your name, then?" asked Dick.

"Muffins," said the boy.

"That's a nickname."

"I ain't got no other as I knows on."

"Well, Muffins," said Dick, after a moment's thought, "I suppose you are honest?"

"I niver nicks nothing," answered Muffins; "but I begs a bit."

"I suppose you must of necessity," said Dick. "Now, I'm thinking of taking a boy into my service. Would you like to come?"

"Service—what's that?" asked Muffins.

"To wait on me—work for me," said Dick; "go on the stage with me."

"Oh! wouldn't I just like it," said Muffins, with a gasp. "But I ain't got no clothes."

"I'll find all that is wanted," said Dick. "You are a sharp boy, and a bit of a comedian in your way."

"Am I?" said Muffins. "If you say so, it's true; but I don't know what a comelian is."

"You will know by-and-bye," said Dick. "Now come along with me. First of all you shall have something to eat. Then we must find a bath-house, where you can be washed, and after that we will see about the clothes."

"Washed!" said Muffins, with a grin; "that will be a treat. I ain't been washed for—lor'! years, not properly, 'cept when I've been in the river. It's too cold now. But I can't believe it—you, the strong man, going to feed and clothe me?"

"It's all true," said Dick. "And I'll try to make a good boy and a man of you."

"I can't believe it!" said Muffins, clasping his head. "Nobody ever did anything for me afore, 'cept kick me, set dogs on me, and throw water over me. It's too good to be true!"

And ejaculating and muttering to himself like one utterly amazed, he followed Dick, who went in search of a place where he could get some food for his protégé.

There were two reasons for his taking this youngster under his wing. First of all he wished to do a kindly action, and, secondly, it flashed upon him that Muffins might be made into as good a foil for him as Pan had been to Ajax.

It would give zest to his performance to have the lively young imp burlesquing the feats of his master, and he was sure the boy could do it very well.

He was naturally a jester—a born comedian—too good to be wasted on the antics of a street boy.

So he took him in hand, and thus secured one of the most faithful and devoted followers ever possessed by man.

CHAPTER VII.

MUFFINS.

ICK made no reference to anyone of the attempt to throw vitriol in his face, but determined to keep a sharp look-out for his cunning foe.

Ajax apparently had totally disappeared.

He was not heard of in public, nor did any of the people that Dick now mixed with ever set eyes upon him, and the same may be said of Pan.

Dick, however, felt sure that he would soon come again into contact with one or both of them.

Meanwhile, Muffins was introduced upon the stage, and was a tremendous success.

He was attired in a tight-fitting scarlet dress, which gave his spare form a very impish look, and his face, garnished with paint and a moustache, and lighted up with a natural drollery, was so humorous that the audience roared with laughter as soon as he appeared.

Dick usually came on alone to receive his ovation, and then Muffins, after a short delay, darted on the stage, looked around as if in search of somebody, and, espying his master, twisted his moustache and took up a defiant attitude.

He turned up his nose at Dick's feats of strength, and when he paused for the usual rests made mighty demonstrations of excelling him.

In addition to being a born comedian, he had picked up several feats of tumbling agility, and the way he rolled and turned about with the dumb-bells and weights in his futile efforts to lift them made the audience scream with delight.

So successful was the whole show that Mr. Parbole, in an effusive moment, declared that Muffins deserved two pounds a week for himself, and, what was more, he should have it.

The first night he received his money, which was paid immediately after the performance, Muffins was so excited that he could not control himself.

Dick was talking to the manager, and the boy, finding behind the scenes was hot and stuffy to him, although it was anything but that to cooler people, went out by the stage-door alone to get a breath of fresh air.

Dick had warned him not to do so, but in the excitement of the moment he forgot all about that. All he thought of was that he felt "choky," and wanted to breathe more freely.

Dick, after a chat with Parbole, looked round for the boy, and not seeing him, asked where he was. One of the men said he had gone towards the stage-door.

Dick was not given to weak fears, nor was he troubled much by presentiments, but it flashed upon him that some ill had befallen the boy.

He rushed to the door, and opening it, looked down the street.

Not a living being was in sight.

"Muffins!" he cried.

There was no answer.

In a tremor of anxiety, Dick dashed back to the wings to make further enquiries.

He could at the moment only imperfectly do so, as there was a ballet being performed, and everybody was busy.

He worked his way about looking for Muffins, and at last came again to the man who had seen him go towards the stage-door.

"Are you sure you saw him?" he asked.

"I'm not likely to be mistaken," replied the man. "He was skipping and singing as if he hardly knew what to do with himself, and he was a-jingling some money in his hand."

"Where can I get a lantern from?" asked Dick.

"I'll find you one as soon as the scene is over," replied the man.

Before the ballet was finished everybody about the stage had heard that something had gone wrong with Muffins, and when the curtain fell quite a little crowd gathered round Dick.

"What's the matter," was the general question.

"I don't know," answered Dick; "but the boy has vanished. He went out by the stage-door."

"Oh! he's only gone to buy some toffee," suggested the Lion Comique, with a grimace.

He was rather envious of the popularity of Muffins.

"Here's the lantern, sir," said the man, appearing with one in his hand.

Dick took it, and followed by some half-dozen men, who for the time were at leisure, returned to the street.

A very brief examination of the pavement brought out evidence of Muffins having fallen into the hands of an enemy.

Close to the stage-door there was a small pool of blood, and in the gutter lay one of the two sovereigns—the first money he had ever earned or been able to call his own.

"He has been knocked down and robbed," said Mr. Parbole, who was of the party.

"But it is not an ordinary robbery!" replied Dick, between his set teeth. "Where is he? They have murdered him, and carried his body away!"

No more traces of the missing boy were found, and sending for the police did not mend matters.

They had very little to guide them to the authors of the outrage.

Dick now spoke out very plainly.

He believed that Ajax and Pan were concerned in the outrage.

But beyond his suspicions, there was nothing to go upon.

Enquiries were made, and it was discovered that until the noon of that very day they had lived in an adjoining street.

Gabrielle—Ajax's wife—went away days before, to Paris, it was said, where Ajax was engaged to perform.

"And I'll go to Paris," said Dick, "as soon as the week is ended."

Mr. Parbole, in an agony, remonstrated with him.

He offered him double the pay, but Dick said—

"No; I've got to settle about that poor boy first. I must know what has become of him."

In vain the manager pleaded; he even shed tears. Dick was firm.

"I can't let money stand in the way," he said. "I

DICK STRONGBOW, THE DIAMOND, AND WONDER OF THE WORLD.

Hoisting the terrified man in the air, Strongbow hurled him at his dumbfounded foes.

mean to get at the bottom of this mystery. More than that, I'm going to spoil Ajax's game in Paris.'

He went home with a heavy heart.

With all his strength he could not lift himself out of the well of grief into which he had been plunged.

Although Muffins had a short time before been only a ragged outcast, Dick had taken a strong fancy to him.

Under the poor exterior of the lad there was a heart sound and strong.

He was naturally bright, honest, and grateful—three things that will go far towards making the humblest youth liked by those around him.

And in the Theatre of Varieties, as Parbole's place was called, the boy was a great favourite.

They nearly all liked Muffins. The Lion Comique was the only exception. He was a bit jealous because the laughs he raised were not quite so loud as those created by Muffins.

Now that the boy was supposed to be murdered, even the Lion Comique could feel somewhat kindly towards him.

As for the ballet-girls, some of them cried about Muffins ere they went to rest. Strange as it may seem to some people, they had tender hearts, like other women.

Dick did not go to bed that night.

He spent hours in wandering about, not exactly aimlessly, but without any very definite idea of what was likely to come out of it.

About one in the morning he found himself upon one of the bridges that span the Thames.

A host of night prowlers had gathered together and were looking over the parapet at the dark river below.

Dick drew up behind them, and listened to what they were saying.

" I don't think they'll get her to-night," one said ; " but she'll more likely be about London-bridge when the tide turns."

" How did she do it ?" asked another.

" Oh ! just stepped on the top of the bridge and jumped," was the reply.

" Hallo—they've got her !"

" No, it ain't a woman !" cried a third, " See the light of the lantern on the face o' the body. It's a boy."

Dick's heart gave a great bound within him, and, as the host of night prowlers ran off towards the flight of steps at the end of the bridge, he followed them.

" What if it's poor Muffins ?" he asked himself ; and then he felt sick to the very depths of the soul within him.

CHAPTER VIII.

NOT MUFFINS—THE DESERTED ONE—A CRY FROM THE CELLAR.

HERE was to this bridge, as to every bridge in London, one or more flights of steps for the use of the public, and down one of these Dick Strongbow hurried in company with the motley crew of night-prowlers. At the bottom, near the stone landing-stage, was a boat, in which were three men.

One held a lantern aloft, and the other two were raising the form of a boy in their arms. The poor lad was drowned—dead, past all human aid.

By his ragged attire it was manifest that he was some poor, homeless waif—one of the many thousands of friendless children who help to swell the grand total of the population of London.

But it was not Muffins.

Dick's heart was touched by the sad spectacle of the friendless child drawn out of the cold river ; but he could not help feeling glad that it was not his cheery little attendant.

Assured of this, and feeling that he could be of no service, he turned away, and with a light, quick step reascended the steps.

Not Muffins !

It was something to know that ; and his heart was much lighter than it had been for hours. But the mystery of the boy's disappearance was not cleared up.

He wandered about all that night, here and there, aimlessly and strangely troubled.

Sometimes it seemed to him that an invisible hand was trying to force him in a certain direction ; but he persuaded himself that such a thing was ridiculous. London was again waking up for the day when he went home, and, having snatched a few hours' sleep and rested, set out again, with the restlessness once more upon him.

And now he went in the direction of the street where Ajax and Pan had recently lodged.

It was a commonplace thoroughfare enough, and, at one end, in a poor, neglected condition.

Two or three shops were in a dingy state, and one with a cellar-flap in the pavement, recently occupied by an oilman, was closed.

He was attracted to this particular shop—why, he knew not—and was standing near the flap, with his eyes wandering over the faded shutters and the half-obliterated name of the late occupier, when a faint moan fell upon his ears.

A quick glance around showed that it came from nobody near him. The nearest living beings, indeed were two small boys playing at some childish game.

" Was it fancy ?" he asked himself ; and the question was answered by a repetition of the sound.

This time he was sure that it came from under his feet, beneath the cellar-flap.

Stooping down, he listened intently for a few seconds, and heard the moan for a third time.

Immediately his strong fingers were inserted between the two portions of the ill-fitting flap, and he found that it was secured beneath.

The youth seized Pan's waistband and hoisted him in the air.

With a resistless tug he pulled it open, fairly tearing a chain out of the steps below.

At that moment a man in a paper cap and wearing a white apron came out of an adjoining house.

He stared first at the flap, and then at Dick, who was preparing to descend.

"Hallo! mister," he said. "What are you doing there?"

"Somebody is groaning below," replied Dick, "and I am going to see who it is."

"That's all stuff," said the man. "The place hasn't been opened for three months."

"Anyway," returned Dick, "I am going down below."

"Look here!" said the man. "I'm caretaker of these premises, for the boys always damage empty houses, scratching off the paint and breaking the windows, and I don't think I can let you prowl about the place."

"My friend," said Dick, quietly, "I am Strongbow the strong man. If you don't wish to get into trouble you had better not interfere."

The man's eyes opened wider than ever, and as Dick descended he contented himself with advancing to the top of the steps, and, in a stooping position, stared into the gloomy cellar below.

In a few moments he received what he called "the biggest staggerer he ever had in his life," by the reappearance of Dick Strongbow with a boy in his arms.

"Run for a doctor!" cried Dick, hoarsely. "Quick—I'll pay you."

The man darted off, and Dick, with the boy in his arms, sat down on the top step.

It was poor Muffins, pale as death, with a wound, covered with congealed blood, on his forehead. He was gagged, and both arms and legs were bound with bits of rope.

Dick's first care was to remove the gag and then the bonds. Poor Muffins, whose eyes were still full of intelligence, opened his mouth and tried to speak —but only indistinct sounds came forth.

"Don't try to talk," said Dick, hurriedly; "you can tell me all about it presently, my poor boy. What a base, brutal, cowardly thing to do!"

Fortunately, a "poor man's doctor" lived hard by—he kept a shop, giving advice free, and charged very little for medicine—and was soon on the spot, accompanied by the man in the paper cap.

He had brought something by way of a restorative with him, and, having administered a few drops, he said—

"Bring him along to my surgery. I can attend to him better there."

The "surgery" was a little room behind the shop, with an old sofa, a couple of chairs (one for patients who wanted a tooth extracted), and a few professional-looking bottles on a shelf.

Poor Muffins was laid upon the sofa, and after a little skilful care was able to say a few words, which he addressed to Dick—

"I am all right, sir," he said. "Not much hurt."

"Well said," cried the doctor, cheerily. "A boy like you will get through a very serious illness."

Turning to Dick, he said in an undertone—

"This is a very strange affair. Can you explain it?"

"I can only make a guess," answered Dick, grimly; "but it is near enough for me."

"Ought we not to send for the police?"

"They can do nothing. The perpetrators of this outrage are now across the sea. Muffins, old boy, how are you?"

"Better," said the boy. "I think I can get up, if you help me a bit."

"It is not to be thought of," said the doctor; "and you must not talk until you have had some refreshment—a little soup I would recommend."

The man in the paper cap knew where it could be got, and Dick gave him some money, bidding him hasten.

Then he sat by the sofa, and very little now was said until the soup was brought and Muffins, evidently by a great effort, had swallowed some of it.

He was much better after that, and by-and-bye had some more.

Then the doctor said he might talk, and tell them how he came in the cellar.

The story he told was very short; but it was clear.

On emerging from the stage-door of the Varieties Theatre with his money, he received a blow from an unseen hand, and immediately lost consciousness.

But he came round in a little while, as he supposed, and found himself in the cellar, gagged and bound, just as Dick discovered him.

Close by stood Ajax and Pan, the former white and quaking, and the latter furiously urging him on to kill the boy.

"But Ajax said as he daresn't do it," continued Muffins, "and began to blubber like a child. Then the man Pan, as I've knowed by seeing him come out of the Varieties, went on awful, and says at last— 'Well, leaving him here to starve by inches will suit me; but, mind you, if anything happens I'll make you dance for it.'"

"Then they looked at me," said Muffins, in conclusion, "and I'd got my eyes close enough, so that I could only just see 'em, making believe as I was dead, and they went away; and there I've been ever since, trying to holler, but couldn't for the gag in my mouth, and not able to get up, as I was tied so tight."

"Just as I thought," said Dick, in a quiet, intense tone. "I put it down to those two villains."

"And you say they are now across the sea?" said the doctor.

"Yes," returned Dick, "and I don't want any fuss over this matter. I can settle it myself. If you will accept this fee," he gave the doctor a five-pound note, "I shall be glad of your silence."

It was the biggest fee the doctor had ever received by a long way.

His eyes glistened with pleasure.

"As far as I am concerned," he said, "you may reckon on nothing being said about it."

The man with the paper cap had to be settled with, and a sovereign more than satisfied him.

"There is one thing I should like to know," said Dick, "and that is, how they managed to fasten up the cellar?"

"I don't suppose they ever unfastened it," replied the caretaker. "The fact is, there's a window at the back of the house—you go up the court to it—which I've left unfastened to go in and out. I reckon that they saw me do it, and so picked on this place for their purpose."

"I think you have hit it," said Dick; "and now, as my young friend is better, I shall be glad if you will fetch a cab, so that I may take him home."

CHAPTER IX.

AJAX IN PARIS—THE SENSATION OF THE HOUR
—ANOTHER CHALLENGE—ACCEPTED.

"AJAX — the great Ajax — Chief of Giants— Monarch among Men."

This is a translation of the headline of a huge poster, seen and read by thousands on the walls of Paris.

Ajax was performing at the chief circus, the Hippodrome, the home of French equestrian art.

An athlete must be good indeed to get an engagement there, and among the greatest if he satisfies the tastes of his critical audience.

Ajax had been performing for five nights, and as a rocket when ignited leaps up towards the stars, so had he soared above the other performers in the arena.

It was not as an exhibitor of feats of strength alone that he suddenly became famous, but he had come out as a wrestler.

Two successive nights some of the best wrestlers of Paris had pitted themselves against him, to be raised up like children and hurled down upon the sand by sheer strength.

One morning a knot of men stood outside the Hippodrome, staring at a poster depicting Ajax holding at arm's length two men, one in each hand. Behind were a number of spectators, overcome with astonishment.

" It cannot be true ! It is not possible !" said one.

" Ah ! you should see him as I have," said another ; " he stands thus, like a rock. He defies the world. A fool comes against him, and then see this Ajax raise him as we do our little ones, and throw him down as if he were a dog."

" Is it so ?" eagerly asked half-a-dozen voices.

" It is," continued the narrator, " and he who was so mad as to strive with the mighty, the peerless Ajax, lies breathless—he cannot rise, he cannot even curse, but looks at his conqueror with eyes as big as oranges, thinking, ' Thou art wonderful, thou Ajax. I was mad to stand up before thee.' "

The narrator had got thus far, and was preparing to expand upon the theme, when he saw two men approaching.

Immediately he changed colour and drew back.

" Not a word," he said, breathlessly ; " stand still. He comes. If he breathes upon us we must fall."

Standing with their backs to the hoarding, they stared hard at the giant Ajax, who, with Pan, was approaching the Hippodrome, to enquire if there was any competitors for a throw in the coming evening.

They were in private attire, of course ; but it was the physique of Ajax that betrayed his identity.

He saw that he was recognised, and passed the little crowd with the haughty indifference of autocratic greatness.

When they had gone by and were turning down a side entrance that led to the stage door, an approving murmur of voices followed him.

" You see," said Pan, " they have taken to you— booby."

" I wish you would be more polite, Pan," returned Ajax. " Somebody might hear you."

" I must let out somewhere," grinned Pan, " and as long as there is money in you, I'll keep dark before the public. But what a great man you would be if you had a heart in that huge carcass of yours !"

" I've got one," said Ajax with a sniff ; " I couldn't get along without it."

" I mean the heart of a *man*," returned Pan, " and don't you bandy words with me, unless you want me to fire up before these people here."

Ajax muttered something in the way of expostulation, and the pair entered the Hippodrome by the performers' door.

Passing down a passage and through the stables, they entered the ring, where a number of the performers in their every-day apparel had assembled.

It was difficult to say what their particular line was, judging by outward appearance, for the clowns —there were three of them—were talking seriously together, and those who seemed the most lighthearted were the performers of romantic feats on horse-back, such as the shipwrecked sailor, and the soldier who fights gallantly against a score imaginary foes and dies upon the battle-field—that is, the saddle-board upon the steed he is riding.

Strutting about, with an air of importance and a show of vivacity, was a little man not unlike a dancing-master, neatly dressed, except in regard to his watch-chain, which was a huge one, with a bunch of seals attached.

This was Monsieur Pablo Fanque, the ringmaster.

Quickly espying Ajax, he came forward, holding out both his hands with effusive joy.

" Ah ! *mon ami*," he said, " you man so strong— it is well. How is Madame Gabrielle ? Is it that she thrives in health ? Do you keep good stomach for your food ?"

" Oh ! he's well enough," replied Pan, answering for him. " Two pounds and a half of steak and half-a-dozen eggs for his breakfast. He and his stomach are very good friends to each other."

" It is you of ze jest, Monsieur Pan—you go him well," said Pablo Fanque, expanding his face with a smile.

" I have to eat," said Ajax, " or I couldn't do my tricks."

" It is so," replied the ring-master. " Ze bif-stek is your standpoint. You get on him and you are strong."

" Are there any acceptances of my challenge for a wrestle ?"

" No," replied Pablo Fanque ; " you dash too much—you frighten zem. It is nearly kill for some. Jules Garteaux, of last night, is inside ze bed still. Zey rub him all night vith oils. He make much groan."

At this moment an attendant came up and presented a letter to Pablo Fanque.

The ringmaster, with a bow, asked forgiveness for reading it, and drew aside for that purpose.

" Didn't I tell you so, Ajax ?" said Pan, in a low tone. " You've been too rough with 'em. Why didn't you drop 'em more gently."

"And then they would come again," said Ajax.

"Yes, and you would cut it," rejoined Pan. "But half the good business is over if you have nobody to wrestle with. These French frogs don't care for feats of strength. They want excitement—a contest."

"Rejoice with me!" said Pablo Fanque, advancing again. "Anoder is to accept your challenge—he is ready."

"Who is it?" asked Pan.

"Ah! I know not," said Pablo Fanque, twisting his body. "He is secret—vat you call him—anomalous?"

"Anonymous," corrected Pan.

"So—much ze same; but you Englese is diffee-cult—so much zat is like. See here—his letter."

He handed it to Ajax, who read, in a bold, clear hand, the following few but expressive words. They were written in French, but we give the translation.

"I accept the challenge of Monsieur Ajax. His hour of performance I know. I shall be punctual.—GRIP."

"Don't you know who he is?" asked Ajax.

"Grip? No," replied Pablo Fanque. "But what mattare—eh? It is no more zan anoder fool to kiss ze sawdust."

Pan took the letter unceremoniously from his master's hand and scanned it closely, but could make nothing of it.

"I reckon," he said, "it is some fool who hasn't seen you, or it is a joke."

"I'd rather know who he is," said Ajax, uneasily.

Pablo Fanque had gone again. He had a way of buzzing about at all times, and Pan could again speak his mind freely.

"What *does* it matter, you bundle of cotton-wool," he said, "whoever it is? Tackle him, and pretend to make a struggle of it, or, as you are a living man, the business will all be over in a week."

A new feat of strength was to be attempted by Ajax that night.

A board about ten feet long had been prepared by cutting a hole in the centre just big enough to put his head through.

The board would rest upon his shoulders, and four men on either side stand above.

Ajax proposed to make the attempt to carry them across the ring.

The eight men were there to rehearse it with him, and, having pulled off his coat, a well-fitting pad was placed upon his shoulders.

Then the board was put on, steadied, and the men, one by one, got into their places.

"Messieurs," said Pablo Fanque, "stand fast."

Ajax began his journey steadily, gradually increasing his pace as he went along. Half-way across the ring he broke into something like a run.

The other side of the circus was reached, and the eight men, accustomed to tricks of all sorts, joined hands and simultaneously jumped down.

"Bravo! bravo! Good!" cried the lookers-on, enthusiastically clapping their hands.

Two attendants relieved Ajax of the board. His face was flushed from his great exertion; but some of the colour was the offspring of joy.

"Monsieur Ajax," said Pablo Fanque, "who shall exceed you—who shall approach? It is good

for zis Grip zat he not see you now. Let him come in and kiss ze sawdust. He vill not vant ze suppare after zat."

CHAPTER X.

THE SIGHT IN THE ARENA—A CROWDED HOUSE —ENTHUSIASTIC RECEPTION OF AJAX—GRIP.

LONG before the hour for opening the doors there was a crowd outside the Hippodrome. Not only were the seekers of the cheaper parts of the house in great force, but also those who were going to occupy the boxes.

The name of "Ajax" was on every tongue. And when the doors opened the rush was prodigious.

There was much screaming and expostulating—likewise some outside compliments were exchanged; but nobody was seriously hurt, and in a very short space of time the huge house was packed from the ring to the top of the gallery.

Pablo Fanque was in a state of overpowering excitement. He was like the proverbial "cat on hot bricks," never still a moment in the dressing-room, but skipping about, asking questions without waiting for an answer, passing compliments, laughing and cackling for very joy.

He had great faith in his figure and believed it was generally admired. What a vast crowd would that night be able to look upon him as he gracefully performed his duties as ringmaster!

The joy he felt was not shared by the company generally.

There was too much "Ajax" in the air. His successful rivalry was a little overpowering, and, in addition, he was an Englishman.

"How could perfidious Albion send them such a giant?" they asked each other.

"See," said one, "he makes candles of us. He snuffs us out."

The clowns were positively savage. They were sure that the audience were bent on serious business that night, and would be in no humour for their antics and jokes.

In an undertone they breathed threats against him; but as Ajax could have pinched their weazen forms between his finger and thumb, they took good care to do so out of his hearing.

He arrived early at the circus and dressed at once. With an hour to spare, he and Pan lounged about the "Green-room," as we may call it, giving themselves airs before the lesser lights of the company.

The band began to play, and one of the men was summoned for a ring act with a lady.

It was a performance generally much appreciated; but that night it fell flat.

With a dark face the male performer returned to his fellows, and a whisper went round that their forebodings were more than fulfilled.

The "Merry Clowns" went in turns to the ring to come back filled with wrath and despair.

While they were uttering their best jokes, the word "Ajax" was rattling round, above, and below like the patter of distant rain.

Oh! it was too bitter, too hard to bear, and they would kill him—one day.

Pan was in the seventh circle—we won't say heaven—of malicious joy.

He understood their looks, if he did not catch what they said so softly to each other, and it warmed his heart as wine does the breasts of better men.

Ajax was triumphant, too, but not entirely happy.

He was continually on the watch for the coming of the anonymous Grip, who, however, did not put in an appearance.

As the time passed the spirits of the cowardly giant rose.

After all, it must be some fool jesting with him.

His non-appearance would, in the end, be a pecuniary loss by-and-bye; but he would escape a possibly dangerous opponent.

At last his turn came, and a number of attendants went out to make a lot of demonstrations, part of them needless, preparing the ring for the contest.

Everybody now was wondering why this mysterious Grip did not come.

Pablo Fanque, who had an eye to the more exciting business, kept popping in and out enquiring for him.

"It is a joke—a sale, as you English say," he said to Ajax. "Bring me ze fool and I kick him."

The band struck up a martial strain, and Ajax, as he strode towards the ring, followed by Pan, cast a look backward.

"It's all right," said Pan, with a savage grin; "he isn't here. You can go on with your tricks without being in a blue funk all the time."

The entrance of Ajax into the ring was the signal for such an ovation as he had never received in his life before.

The French, when they get excited on a subject, fairly go mad upon it, and their enthusiasm knew no bounds.

It was a long time before the people quieted down and Ajax could begin his feats of strength.

Being in the mood to applaud, the audience gave each an ovation, second only to that which he received on entering the ring.

The board trick fairly brought down the house, and, as it was the last on the list, nothing now remained to be done but to read the accustomed challenge, and declare that nobody had ventured to come forward and accept it.

This was the task of Pablo Fanque, who had been in the ring during Ajax's performance, and he came forward with one of his graceful bows to perform it.

"To all the world!" he cried. "A challenge from Ajax, the mighty. A wrestle for the best two out of three falls. Who accepts the same?"

No answer.

"I ask three times," cried the ringmaster, in his native tongue, "and if there is nobody to meet Ajax he is the World's Champion. Once—who answers?"

Not a sound, save the rustling of a few dresses, was heard.

"Who will meet Ajax? Twice."

The silence was profound.

"Who DARES to meet Ajax? Thr—"

"I DO!"

The voice that answered was heard all over the Hippodrome, and every eye was turned towards the curtained entrance to the ring.

There stood a quiet-looking young man in athletic attire.

Dick Strongbow!

And the people laughed—much as they had done on his first appearance at Parbole's Theatre of Varieties.

But their laughter fell like the cries of mocking fiends on the ears of the wretched Ajax.

Aghast, he stood staring at Dick Strongbow, who slowly advanced across the arena, calmly surveying the howling, derisive mob.

Pan went up to his master and hissed in his ear—

"Wake yourself up. Try and be a man. If you think you can't throw him fairly—foul him."

"What am I to do?" feebly asked Ajax.

"When you go to get your hold," said Pan, "turn your thumbs out and dig him in the small of the back. It will make him helpless for a moment at least. Then throw him, and fall upon his chest. Dig your elbows into it."

"I—I—I'll try," said Ajax.

And now Dick, who was in his professional attire, was standing in the middle of the ring with his arms folded, and there was a dignity in his bearing that gradually softened down the scoffing howling of the audience.

So rapidly did it subside that in less than half a minute there was complete silence.

Pablo Fanque and a clown were in the ring quietly looking on—wondering what the whispering of Pan could mean, and why Ajax's face was blanched with fear.

"I am ready!" cried Dick, and his voice sounded like a clarion through the vast place. At the entrance to the ring a little knot of the company had gathered to witness the struggle.

The muscular appearance of Dick's arms and legs were approvingly criticised, and the general opinion was that Ajax had a tough job before him.

"Get on, you cur!" hissed Pan.

Ajax, by an effort, recovered himself a little, and took a hasty glance around him.

Hushed was every sound.

Every eye was fixed upon the giant or his antagonist.

Rubbing his hands together, Ajax slowly advanced until he and Dick were within two feet of each other.

Pan followed him up closely, hissing like an ill-regulated steam-engine in his fury.

"Ajax," said Dick, quietly, "tell your man to stand back."

"He won't go," said Ajax, miserably.

"If he does not retreat at once," replied Dick, "I will pitch him out of the ring."

Pan heard what he said, and, knowing how likely he was to keep his word, retreated, frowning, to the side of the ring.

"And now one word," said Dick, fixing his eye upon Ajax; "no tricks. You understand? Fair play."

"Yes," returned Ajax.

"Lay hold!" cried Dick, throwing up his arms.

Then they closed, and every spectator held his or her breath, awaiting the issue of that truly dreadful grip upon each other.

Ajax made one effort for victory; then, feeling the iron arms of his antagonist closing about him, he gave in.

"Let me breathe!" he gasped.

Dick drew Ajax forward, quickly locked his heel behind the giant's, and with a tremendous effort threw him.

He went down with a thud that was heard by all assembled. An instant's silence followed, and then every voice was heard.

The men shouted, some of the women screamed, and the members of the company, leaping in the air, clapped their hands.

Pan rushed forward, and, staring at his fallen man, uttered a fearful imprecation, and then began to tear his hair.

Ajax lay quite still, as if he were dead, but Dick bending over him, saw that he was breathing.

"Get up, man," he said; "surely one fall is not enough for you? It is to be two out of three."

"I give in," dismally replied Ajax, and Dick, drawing back, indicated by signs that the struggle was over, and he had won.

But this did not by any means please the audience.

They could not understand so great a man giving in at once, and they shrieked for him to get upon his feet and renew the struggle.

Ajax did indeed get upon his feet, but not to renew the contest.

Slowly he arose and carefully felt his limbs, while the spectators shrieked with laughter, and Pan, in his rage, ran round the ring like a maniac.

Pablo Fanque remained literally calm under these trying circumstances.

It was true that Ajax—called the peerless and unapproachable an hour before—had suffered ignominious defeat. But was there not one here to take his place?

The fact of his having come to the circus in proper professional attire showed that he was in all likelihood open to an engagement.

Therefore Pablo Fanque was calm.

Dick walked from the ring, gracefully but quietly acknowledging the plaudits of those around, and Pablo Fanque hurried after him.

Ajax, with dejected mien, slowly followed to the jarring music of hisses and groans.

Pan, nearly beside himself, favoured the audience with a contemptuous gesture that raised the wrath of the audience.

If he had not promptly disappeared evil consequences might have come of it.

How had the mighty fallen!

Ajax, on reaching the men's dressing-room, was hailed with mocking laughter, which he had not the courage to resent, but began with all speed to put on his outdoor attire.

Pan, boiling with rage, did the same; and they were nearly ready to start when Dick Strongbow—also attired to leave—appeared.

He came up to the pair, and looking sternly at them, said, in a low tone—

"You will leave Paris to-night."

Ajax had no answer to give him, but Pan began to bluster.

"You've beaten him once, but it doesn't show it's all over," he said. "Why should we go?"

"That poor boy of mine has been found," said Dick; and then Pan quailed as if he had been as great a coward as his master.

CHAPTER XI.

VICTOR AND VANQUISHED—PARIS IN A FLAME OF ENTHUSIASM.

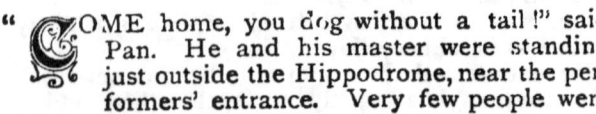

"COME home, you dog without a tail!" said Pan. He and his master were standing just outside the Hippodrome, near the performers' entrance. Very few people were about.

Ajax leant against the wall, and passed the back of his hand across his eyes.

"I'm done for now," he said. "Must get away within twenty-four hours—so he told us. Where are we to go to?"

"You leave that to me," growled Pan. "I'm your manager, ain't I? What a big booby you are!"

"What will Gabrielle say?" moaned Ajax.

"Something like what she's said before, and that won't mend matters. Come along!" snarled Pan.

Hissing and biting his finger-nails, Pan led the way, and Ajax, with the air of a broken man, slouched behind him.

In silence they threaded a number of streets, and presently stopped before a big house.

It was one of those buildings let out in rooms, with a concierge, or gatekeeper, who kept an eye on those who went in and out, took care of keys when necessary, received parcels and letters, and so on. The man in charge of this particular place was a little ferret-faced fellow, with small piercing eyes. Ajax was in his eyes a monarch among men, and as yet he had learnt nothing about his defeat.

"Ha! my master," he said, "you shall be early to-night."

"Yes, I am early," muttered Ajax. "Is my wife in?"

"No, monsieur. She started for the Hippodrome an hour ago, and, by my life, behold—she comes!"

Ajax looked round with a frightened face, and saw his better half bearing down upon him like an eagle swooping on its prey.

There was no need for him to tell her of his defeat.

"I must get upstairs," he said, hurriedly.

Snatching the key from the hand of the concierge, he hastened up to the first floor.

Pan remained behind to have a word with Gabrielle.

"Steady, mistress," he said, as she came up; "the least said the soonest mended."

"He gave in like a whipped dog," she replied, furiously. "I saw him do it."

"Well—well, he had to give into the same man before."

"Because he is such a cur!"

"Ah! how you women talk. As if a man could help another gathering strength!"

"I must see him," said Gabrielle. "Don't stop me, Pan, or I shall fly at you like a cat."

"Don't do that, mistress," said Pan, drawing aside. "I have a rough side to me, remember, and I am not afraid of you."

She hurried upstairs, and Pan followed. The concierge stared after them with his two small eyes like fixed stars.

Ajax was standing by the stove warming his hands as if he were cold.

The action was simply mechanical, for there was no charcoal, the common fuel of Paris, in it. When he saw his wife, he cast his eyes around for a place of refuge, and found none. For the lack of anything better to do, he placed his huge form against the wall, and stood there, a very good imitation of a lubberly schoolboy who expects a thrashing from a comrade.

"Beaten again !" screamed Gabrielle.

"He was too much for me," whined Ajax.

"Go at him again," cried Gabrielle.

"No ; I dare not."

"But you shall—I will send the challenge for you. Why, if you only FELL against him, down he must go."

"I tell you," said Ajax, "that it can't be thought of."

"What do you say to that, Pan ?" asked Gabrielle, facing round towards the satellite.

"It's right enough, mistress," he said. "It can't be thought of."

"This from you ?" exclaimed Gabrielle, in utter amazement.

"Yes, mistress, and we have to clear out from here to-morrow."

"Clear out ?" she murmured, with a bewildered look on her face. "Why ?"

"It's not a woman's business," said Pan.

"It's mine," insisted Gabrielle ; "out with it. What is it, Ajax ?"

"It wasn't me," muttered Ajax. "He would do it."

"Do—what ?"

"The—the boy."

"Hold your tongue, you fool !" said Pan, between his teeth. "I tell you it is not a woman's affair."

"I will know what it is," said Gabrielle, resolutely.

"All right, master," said Pan, drily. "Tell her."

"It was the boy—Strongbow's boy—Muffins," stammered Ajax. "He—he—"

"You killed him !" shrieked Gabrielle. "I can see it in your face. Oh ! you pair of cowards. You dare not touch the man, but it takes *two* of you to destroy the life of a boy."

"We didn't kill him, mistress," said Pan.

"You would have done it," said Ajax, anxious to make out a good case for himself, "if it hadn't been for me."

"What did you do with him ?" said Gabrielle. "Out with it."

"He was bound and gagged," roared Ajax, "and left in the cellar of an empty house to die."

"Oh ! you monsters," cried Gabrielle—her woman's hatred of a cruel crime perpetrated on the young dominant in her wrath. "Ajax, you are my husband and I shall be the mother of your child. In a little while it will see the light—but, hark you ! you shall never see it."

"Gabrielle !"

"I mean what I say. Out with you, the pair of you, and never let me see your faces again."

"Oh ! Gabrielle, my wife," moaned Ajax. "Anything but that. Don't cast me off."

"Out with you !"

She pointed to the door and cast a quick glance from one to the other.

Frail in form and with a beauty that was like a faded flower, she was nevertheless imposing—magnificent in her wrath.

Even Pan shrank from her eye, and was the first to move towards the door.

"You'll find it hard to get along without us, mistress," he said.

"If I cannot get along without you I will DIE," she said. "Go, or I will call in the gendarmes and place you under arrest."

They dare not linger longer, but slunk out of the room, and Gabrielle closed and locked the door behind them.

While this scene was being enacted, another of a different nature could have been seen in a room not far from the Hippodrome.

Seated at table, partaking of supper, was Dick Strongbow and Muffins.

The boy looked none the worse for his recent adventure, and seemed the picture of health and happiness.

"I wish I could have seen it, master," he said. "When that Ajax went down I must have split my sides with laughing."

"I would have pleased you," replied Dick, "but it would have spoilt the final business. Had they been aware of it they would have defied me and stayed in Paris."

"So they think I'm dead," said Muffins, delighted. "I wonder how they'd feel if they saw me. Perhaps they would think it was my ghost. Ha, ha!"

"Well, Muffins," said Dick. "I shall know to-morrow if they are gone. If they go, I shall introduce you to the Hippodrome people. I am engaged there for the next fortnight with wonderfully good pay, provided I can conquer all comers."

"You'll do that, master," said Muffins, rubbing his hands. "Nobody can touch you."

"Well, we shall see," said Dick. "In addition to my strength I have had a good training in foreign wrestling tricks at the German University. I hope I shall be a match for all who come against me."

And this hope was fulfilled.

Tempted by his lesser physique, a number of Parisian wrestlers came against him the next night.

He threw them all, and Paris was ablaze with his fame.

CHAPTER XII.

THE DAME AND HER DAUGHTER—RUNAWAY HORSES—A GALLANT FEAT.

MIDST all these scenes of excitement Dick kept the story of Gonzalo in his memory.

Whether it was true, or simply an hallucination on the part of the stroller, Dick could not shake it off.

He had a presentiment that one day Jacob Morelle would turn up—when or where he had no more idea than the man in the moon.

Very often he thought of the strange way he had been drawn towards the spot where poor Muffins lay bound and gagged.

There was something out of the common in it, but he could not ascribe it all to chance.

At the Hippodrome he was a great favourite, because he was modest under his overwhelming success.

There was some little jealousy on the part of the men because all the ladies of the ring, without mentioning some scores outside, were in love with him.

But they need not have been jealous. Dick kept his heart whole. One woman was to him exactly what another was, and no more.

On the fourth night of his performance he introduced Muffins, who met with a gratifying reception. Pablo Fanque said he was one of "nature's grotesques," and in private he offered the boy a fair salary to stop at the Hippodrome.

"I'll come to you when my master is DEAD," he said, "and not before."

"Ah! zen," said Pablo Fanque, "ven Monsieur Strongbow go, you shall say farewell to me."

Among other evidences of Dick's popularity were the bouquets showered upon him from the private boxes.

One night—it was about the seventh of his engagement—a family party gathered in one of these boxes, and they were evidently people of importance.

The father, a tall, handsome man, wore several decorations upon his breast, and the mother had the appearance of a proud, high-bred dame. Two young men, little more than youths, and a remarkably pretty girl, completed the party.

It was this girl Dick observed most, mainly because she took such a keen interest in him, insomuch that her mother was seen to whisper a few words of reproof in her ear.

The girl leant back, pouting a little, and confined her attention to Dick by simply keeping her eyes fixed upon him.

Among other feats Dick performed was that of taking a fair-sized pony in his arms and running round the ring with it.

Of course it was a docile, well-trained creature, but the feat was none the less remarkable, and it created uproarious delight.

He stopped opposite the box we have referred to, and, replacing the pony on its feet, bowed somewhat pointedly to the young lady.

Immediately afterwards the dame arose, and the party left the box.

As Dick was dressing, Pablo Fanque came to him, looking white and perturbed.

"My noble, great, unrivalled friend," he said, "it is wrong."

"What is?" coolly asked Dick.

"To single out one so high-born for your attention."

"Oh! indeed. I did it on the impulse of the moment."

"Ze impulse send ze Swedish Ambassador avay vary angry."

Dick said he was sorry; but it did not appear to trouble him much.

He really did not think he had done anything so very *infra dig*.

"But, of course, they only look upon me as a showman," he said to himself, with a tinge of bitterness; "but we shall see."

He was thinking of Gonzalo's story again all the way home. Muffins trotted beside him, and, seeing he was preoccupied, did not make any remark.

Some French *gamins*—of the same class as our street arabs—were in attendance on them that night.

Feeling somewhat jealous of the fame of Muffins, they vented their feelings by indulging in personal remarks.

Some were in French and Muffins did not understand them; but when it came to calling him "calf—ros-bif," he thought it time to resent their rudeness.

Turning upon the nearest, he gave him a blow in the chest which laid him sprawling, and one of his friends, trotting immediately in the rear, fell over him.

The rest fell back crying—

"Go—leetle strong man—boy—gi-ant—yah!"

"All right," said Muffins, standing in an attitude of self-defence; "if you want any more of it—come on!"

"Muffins!" called out Dick ahead; "where are you?"

"Why, licking some French tadpoles, sir," replied Muffins, as he ran up to him.

Dick was about to reprove him, when an uproar broke out at the end of the street, and the hoofs of galloping horses on the hard pavement reached their ears.

Two lamps, swaying to and fro, were also seen approaching, and some of the wayfarers were dashing into doorways, and other places of refuge.

"A runaway horse—or horses, Muffins," said Dick. "Get into the café. I must see if I can stop them."

"Master, they'll knock you down and trample on you!" said Muffins, in terror.

Dick did not answer him, but stepped into the road and fixed his eyes on the runaways, now getting into view.

There were two of them, wild-eyed, spirited horses, and the box seat was empty, the driver having jumped or been thrown off.

Something white was seen fluttering inside the carriage, and Dick guessed a woman was there.

Drawing a little aside, he waited until the carriage was almost level to where he stood, and then sprang at the horse nearest him.

He gripped the rein and struck the animal a blow on the head with his iron fist. It fell like a stone. Its maddened companion dragged it along for a few feet, and then fell also.

All danger from the runaway horses was over. A dozen men sprang upon the reins and held them fast.

Dick hurried to the carriage door and opened it. Inside were two ladies, in a half-fainting condition—the proud Swedish dame and her pretty daughter.

"Ladies," said Dick, "the horses have stopped. May I assist you to alight?"

The girl uttered a glad cry, and, springing up, laid her hand upon Dick's arm, saying—

"It was you who did it. You have saved us—I am sure of it."

"I knocked down one of the horses," replied Dick, quietly, "the other fell. But will you not alight and take a public conveyance home? Here is one. May I ask you where your coachman is?"

"The coward jumped the moment the horses ran away," replied the girl, contemptuously.

"May I ask to whom we are indebted for our safety?" asked the elder lady.

"Mother," said the girl, "it is that wonderful performer at the Hippodrome."

They had alighted now, and were moving towards a public conveyance which Dick had hailed.

The wondering crowd were all occupied with the carriage and horses.

As the girl revealed his identity, the mother sensibly stiffened, and, in a frigid tone, replied—

"He has done a brave thing, and he shall be rewarded. Lucella, you had better enter the carriage first. Monsieur—what is it?—Strongbow, you have earned my gratitude. You will not be forgotten. Will you tell someone that the horses and carriage are to be taken to the Swedish Embassy. Goodnight."

Dick uttered not a word in reply; but he raised his hat, and when the carriage drove off he told a gendarme who had arrived upon the scene where the carriage was to be sent to.

Then he sought Muffins, who had been watching the scene with his breast aglow with admiration.

"Come, my boy," he said, "let us go home."

"You speak as if you were tired," said Muffins, "and I don't wonder at it."

"I feel as if I had been hit—somewhere," replied Dick; "but it is nothing. I shall be right tomorrow."

But the blow he had received was not of the nature to be put right in a moment.

It was his pride that had been hurt.

"The young man is brave, and will not be forgotten," he muttered, as he strode along. "What do they take me for? How do these proud people think of such as me?"

He was very quiet indeed all that night, ate little supper, and went to bed early. Muffins was much troubled by the change in him.

"He's got a inside hurt somewheres," said Muffins, as he went to bed himself, "and I'm afeard it will stop his performing to-morrow."

Yes, the hurt was an inside one, near his heart; but he would be able to go through his feats as usual, although not with the same zest as before.

The next morning there came a letter, with a big seal, directed to "Monsieur Strongbow." It was from the Swedish Ambassador, and read as follows—

"*The Swedish Ambassador presents his compliments to Monsieur Strongbow, and encloses a slight recognition of the meritorious services he rendered to two ladies last night. Owing to the time of his office expiring to-day, which renders his immediate return to Sweden imperative, he is unable to call and personally offer his thanks. He trusts that monsieur did not suffer any inconvenience or receive any injury.*"

Enclosed was a cheque for a handsome amount; but in Dick's eyes it was gall and wormwood.

Sitting down, he wrote the following reply—

"*Monsieur Strongbow gratefully acknowledges the thanks of his Highness, the Swedish Ambassador, but as the 'meritorious services' he rendered were such as might have been performed by any man of courage, he sees no necessity for pecuniary reward. He therefore returns the cheque with the assurance that the eulogistic letter he received was an all-sufficient reward.*"

Having enclosed the cheque, he carefully sealed it and sent it to the Embassy.

"It is just as well for even him to know that Dick Strongbow doesn't do everything for money," said Dick, and after that he felt more at his ease.

CHAPTER XIII.

DICK AND MUFFINS IN SWEDEN—THE COMING REVELS—WHAT STRONG ARMS CAN DO.

"WE are going to Sweden, Muffins."

Dick made this remark to the faithful Muffins exactly one hour after his final performance at the Hippodrome.

All through his engagement his success was phenomenal, and on that last night the majority of the seats had been let at fancy prices by speculators who bought them up.

Dick could have had his engagement extended for a week or longer, but he said he had made other arrangements—nothing more—and so with many expressions of good will they parted.

"To Sweden, sir?" said Muffins. "Where's that, anywhere near America?"

"No; a little the other way," replied Dick. "A cold country. We shall want some thick clothing and furs. I am going to make quite a swell of you."

"Thanky, sir," said Muffins; "but 'scuse me, sir, are you going to perform there?"

"I can't say. Perhaps I may, perhaps not," replied Dick. "I have two reasons for going and I don't mind telling you one."

"Thanky, sir," said Muffins, gratefully.

"Two of your old friends have gone there," said Dick. "Ajax and Pan. I mean to follow them up and spoil them everywhere."

Muffins was not at all averse to this idea. He often felt as if he could do a bit of squaring himself with Pan, but he was not yet old enough.

Dick had now quite a nice little sum in the bank, and he could afford to travel awhile if he had a mind to. He meant, anyway, to have a run as far as Sweden—firstly, to harry Ajax, and, secondly, to —well, see somebody, just to look at her, and nothing more.

"So high above me," thought Dick, "but not proud. I wonder if I shall ever stand on a level with her socially? Of course, if Gonzalo's story—Oh! hang it, I must not dwell on that. There is no Jacob Morelle."

The next day he and Muffins started for the northern country. It was a long journey, and they broke it three or four times on their way.

Muffins saw strange countries and strange people, some of whom rather staggered him in their dress and language.

"I suppose they *do* understand each other, sir?" he said to Dick.

"Yes, of course they do," Dick replied.

"They must be uncommonly clever," said Muffins. "I couldn't tackle their crack-jaw languages anyhow."

At last they arrived in Sweden, and by that time they had donned their thick clothing and fur caps. Dick Strongbow wore thigh-boots, and Muffins had a pair that reached to his calves.

Dick, who, to the amusement of Muffins, seemed

to know all languages, made enquiries about an hotel, and they put up at one in a quiet street close to a large square

In that square was a palace, which Dick told Muffins was the residence of the king.

"Perhaps we shall see him before we go," said Dick, lightly. "They tell me that he very often walks among his people just like anybody else."

"With his crown on?" asked Muffins. "I should like to see that."

"I can't say anything about his crown," replied Dick, quietly smiling.

The waiters were talking about the king's birthday, which, it seemed, would be celebrated two days hence.

High revelry would be held at court, and all sorts of festivities going on in the town.

There were to be shows of all sorts, and some wonderful people had been engaged to perform before the king, among them a brawny man who gave his name as Jaxa, and his comic attendant, Nap, who had recently arrived from Windsor Castle, where they had been entertained by Britain's Queen.

Dick understood the language, and, of course, saw through the flimsy attempt of the strong man and his attendant to hide their identity.

Nap was Pan reversed, and Jaxa was a feeble distortion of Ajax.

Dick asked the waiter, simply as an interested traveller, about these men. How was it that the king knew of their prowess?

"All things English are welcome here," was the reply, "and they come from the queen's castle."

Dick knew that a lie had been told, and possibly a false testimonial fabricated, but he said nothing.

On his own account he determined to be at the court revels, and, as he had done before, bring the big, blatant coward down. But how to get there.

If he wrote to the king, asking for an engagement, it was not at all probable that he would get a reply Indeed, it appeared that all engagements were made, and the arrangement of the revels in the palace and city were complete.

But Dick did not despair.

After an early dinner he set out with Muffins for the palace—it was only a few minutes' walk—bent on making enquiries as to the possibility of his getting an engagement.

There was one peculiarity about the palace of the King of Sweden, and that was, it had no sentries around it.

Unlike every other monarch in Europe, he seemed to be in no need of being watched over, and it was a fact that the king was accustomed to go in and out just as any ordinary citizen goes in and out of his private abode.

The palace itself is a building of no particular order of architecture, but very handsome in spite of that, and Muffins, although now developed into a traveller, highly approved of it.

"I should think that the king ought to be happy there," he said.

"Perhaps he is," said Dick ; "but I do not aspire to be a king."

"Would you rather be like them?" asked Muffins, pointing to two men who were hovering about one of the entrances to the palace.

Dick looked at the men somewhat curiously, for they had a peculiar ook about them, an air of skulking, and their faces were dark and sullen.

They were attired in the rough winter garb of fairly well-to-do citizens of the country, but modest as the apparel was it had the appearance of being a disguise.

Dick did not like the look of the men.

"Those fellows are up to no good, Muffins,' he said.

"I've seen burglar chaps at home with the same sort of faces," replied Muffins.

"I'll keep an eye on them," said Dick ; "but don't let them see us watching them."

It was not Dick's habit to interfere with the business of other people, but his actions again seemed to be guided by an indefinite form of urging.

The unseen hand was again guiding him.

He passed the men with the air of a casual stroller, with Muffins close at his heels.

They cast their evil eyes at him, and muttered something to each other. What it was Dick could not catch.

As soon as he had passed he threw a quick glance over his shoulder, and saw a tall, handsome man in a uniform come out of the palace and descend the steps.

The two men drew back a pace, and each thrust a hand into the breast of his coarse jacket.

The officer, with a light, easy step advanced towards them.

They saluted as he passed, and the salute was returned ; but the moment he had gone by out came their hands from under their jackets, each grasping a revolver.

Their purpose was clear enough then. It was assassination, and the officer was to be their victim.

Dick uttered a shout of warning, and, dashing forward, sprang upon the foremost man.

The iron grasp was fixed upon the would-be assassin.

He was raised in the air even as he fired. His heavy body was thrown like a bolt from a huge catapult against his companion.

The pair were hurled to the ground, and Dick, springing forward, pinned each by the nape of the neck, and held them there.

Muffins, in an ecstacy of admiration, clapped his hands, and, forgetting his dignity for the moment, turned one of the "wheels" he used to indulge in when he was a ragged street arab.

Meanwhile the officer, who, seeing Dick rush by, had turned, and been a witness to the scene of attempted assassination and the way it had been foiled, had been considerably taken back.

It seemed to be more surprise than anything else that made him temporarily speechless. Recovering himself, he became instantly cool, and walked up to Dick.

"I thank you, sir," he said, in excellent English. "You have, by your resolution and promptitude, saved my life."

"I suspected these fellows, and watched them," replied Dick, quietly. "What shall I do with them ?"

"Let them go."

"Let them go ?"

"Yes, sir. Let the sting of disappointment and the whip of their consciences be their punishment," said the officer.

"As you please," said Dick. "Shall I disarm them first ?"

No. 3 READY MONDAY, JULY 18.

DICK STRONGBOW:
The Diamond King,
AND WONDER OF THE WORLD.

Dick drew Ajax forward, and with a tremendous effort threw him.

No. 3.   Price One Penny.

"Permit me to assist you."

The weapons were taken from the would-be assassins.

They were rapidly searched, and, no more being found, Dick LIFTED them up from the ground by their necks and placed them on their feet.

The officer looked at him curiously.

"You are very strong," he said. "Is it you who are to appear at the revels in the palace?"

"No," replied Dick; "but I should very much like to do so. It is a whim, if you like—I desire no pay."

He was still holding the two wretches by the neck, and their faces were a study. They were as helpless as babes in his grasp.

"Let those fellows go," said the officer, "and be assured that your wish shall be gratified. I will not at present offer you money for the services you have rendered me, for I am sure it would be distasteful to you."

"I thank you for that," said Dick, as his eyes flashed. "If you consider that I have done you any service, all I ask now is that I may be allowed to perform a few feats before the king, and in the presence of that man Jaxa."

"It shall be done," replied the officer. "Here, take this ring. It will pass you in on the day of the revels. You may go where you please about the palace. Show it when asked, that is all. I will myself introduce you to the king."

CHAPTER XIV.

DICK LOOKS FOR SOMEBODY—THE MORNING OF THE REVELS—A SPLENDID RECEPTION AT THE PALACE.

HE ring given to Dick was a big one, but it would only go over his little finger, owing to the size and strength of his hand. Carefully placing it th——, he returned to the hotel, and went out no more until the evening.

Muffins did not go out at all, for fear of meeting either Ajax or Pan. Dick desired that his appearance at the revels might be a complete surprise.

But as soon as night set in, Dick, well muffled up, went forth, and, having ascertained which was the fashionable quarter of the city, he did not go beyond it.

Of course it was round the palace, and a great many of the houses were lighted up for the reception of guests. Sledges and carriages of various descriptions were very numerous, and those who rode in them were wrapped up to their eyes.

It was bitter cold, but there was no snow.

Dick scanned the riders in the vehicles as they passed by, and although many of them were young girls he could not find one whom he could recognise as Lucella.

He stood awhile before some of the houses where the carriages stopped to set down guests, but such shadows as he saw upon the blinds were not known to him.

About eleven he turned back towards the hotel, walking slowly, wrapped in thought.

"It's both mad and foolish of me," he muttered. "Suppose I saw her a thousand times what good could possibly come of it? I am only a beggarly public performer, while she— Oh! it won't bear thinking of."

He had no dumb-bells or any of his appliances for exercise with him, and his usual practice before retiring to rest being out of the question, he went to bed.

The next day he spent in the seclusion of his hotel, hearing a great deal, but seeing a very little of the preparations for keeping the birthday of the king.

Occasionally, through the window, he saw some vans, very much like those of our showmen at home, go rumbling by, and there was a general holiday look about the people, old and young, as they hurried to and fro.

Muffins was, of course, anxious to be in the fun outside, but it could not be, and he killed the time by amusing the servants in the kitchen with some of his antics.

The morrow came, the day of revelry, and long before daylight the street was alive with vehicles and people on their way to the great square where the principal outside fair was to be held.

At seven o'clock Dick arose, and having put on his athletic attire, covered it up with his ordinary clothes and went down to breakfast.

Muffins, who had received instructions overnight, was already there with his scarlet dress under his everyday attire. Everything ready, except the paint for his face, and that was in his pocket.

At one o'clock the performances would begin in the palace, for the king was a man of early habits, and shortly before eleven Dick and Muffins started for the palace.

Contrary to the usual custom there was a guard of soldiers, under the command of an officer, at the main entrance, and as Dick advanced he was called upon to stop.

Dick held up his hand and exhibited the ring. The officer looked at it with an expression of profound surprise, and then saluted him respectfully.

"I will escort you to your apartments, sir," he said.

It was now Dick's turn to be surprised, for he had no knowledge of any particular room for his use, but on reflection he came to the conclusion that for each actor of the day a place to dress in had been prepared.

The officer ushered him through several passages, magnificently fitted up, and finally guided him into a chamber the like of which Dick had never seen before and Muffins certainly had not so much as dreamt of.

It was a small saloon, with rich furniture and splendid pictures on the panelled walls.

At one end was a huge hearth, where a wood fire was burning.

The mantel-piece was of marble, a master-piece of the sculptor's art.

"If you desire anything," the officer said, "you have but to touch this bell," indicating one upon an inlaid table, "and all your needs will be attended to."

Muffins was so terribly overcome with the gorgeousness of the things around him that he was quite limp, but Dick, of course, though charmed, was not by any means so painfully impressed.

"It seems, Muffins," said Dick, "that we have fallen upon pleasant places."

"Do anybody ever sit down on them chairs?" asked Muffins.

"Of course."

"Well, I dursn't do it, master."

The door now opened, and the officer whom Dick had saved the day before from the assassins entered the room.

He gave Dick a cordial greeting and nodded kindly to Muffins, who backed to bow gracefully, and fell over a foot-stool.

Apparently the officer did not see this little mishap, but went on talking quietly to Dick.

He brought with him a programme of the sports to take place before the king, in a covered hall in the centre of the palace, as he explained.

"Where do you wish to come in?" he asked.

"I desire to follow Jaxa," replied Dick, "and to attempt at his tricks, also some of my own. I likewise wish to wrestle with him."

"Good," said the officer, "but I fear you are too ambitious."

"If I fail to defeat him," replied Dick, with a smile, "my humiliation will fall upon my own head."

"It is so," answered the officer, smiling back. "You must excuse me now, as I have much to do. I shall see you anon."

"Pray accept my thanks for your courtesy," said Dick.

"It is nothing," was the reply, and then the officer departed.

Shortly after this a servant came in to announce that refreshment was laid in another chamber, and a dressing-room had also been prepared for "monsieur."

Dick kept totally calm under the pressure of their attentions, but Muffins was bewildered.

Was it real or a dream? Could it be possible that he, the ragged street-arab of old, was really going to dine in this fairy palace?

"Master," he said, as they were leaving the room, "please help me if I do anything wrong. I feel just as if I was going right off my head."

CHAPTER XV.

THE SCENE OF THE REVELS—AJAX AND PAN— ONCE MORE BROKEN ON THE WHEEL.

IN the centre of the palace was the great hall set apart for the sports which were designed to delight the king. As it was quite big enough to have served as a place of public entertainment, the centre permitted of an ample ring, like that of a circus, in which the exhibitors were to disport themselves.

At one end was a double throne for his majesty and his queen, and on either side seats for the nobility and their family were arranged.

For the lower lights of Swedish society, invited to share in the day's amusement, ample preparations had also been made.

By twelve o'clock the latter had arrived, at half past the families of nobles had taken their seats, and at one o'clock, heralded by a flourish of trumpets, the king led in his queen, with a train of aristocracy behind him.

And now the revels began.

The king who was known to be fond of horses was gratified by several feats of superb horsemanship as an opening to the day.

Then followed some excellent fooling by a number of clowns, and after that a troupe of Bedouin Arabs went through their agile, eccentric tricks, with which the world at large is now familiar.

Behind the scenes—that is, in a room outside the ring—were Ajax and Pan eagerly awaiting their turn.

They were timed for two o'clock to be in the ring.

On a trolly the huge dumb-bells, clubs, and other things were placed, and to give effect a horse had been harnessed thereto to draw it into the ring.

Pan was himself again.

Once more success promised to attend his master, and through the great athlete also fell upon himself.

Ajax, however, looked rather pale and nervous, and of course was reproved by Pan in his characteristic fashion.

"Now, you jelly of a man," he said, "try and pull yourself together. This king seems to be a soft, kind-hearted chap, and if you please him you will roll in money."

"I wonder what became of Gabrielle?" muttered Ajax.

"Oh! hang her," growled Pan.

"Hang you," said Ajax, with sudden ferocity; "she isn't YOUR wife."

"No, thank goodness," said Pan. "Now, time's up. I'll go and give out your challenge with the trolly. You can follow in five minutes."

A bell rang, and Pan signalled to an attendant with the horse to lead it into the ring, and he followed with no end of swagger upon him.

There was some applause as he entered, which he acknowledged with a gracious bow.

He next proceeded, with the aid of the assistants, to arrange the dumb-bells and clubs so as to make the most of them.

Lastly, with a bombastic air, he specified each trick as it would be done, and defied all nations and peoples to produce a rival to Ajax.

"He talks well," said the king to those around him. "Let us hope that his master will fulfil all the promises he has made."

And now the great moment for the entrance of Ajax arrived. Facing the king, on the opposite side of the ring was a splendid band, which by arrangement was to hail the entrance of the giant with a grand flourish of music.

Pan, with his one hand on his hip, grandiloquently beckoned for his master to enter. Ajax ought to have been on the watch and promptly obeyed the sign.

But he did not appear.

The band executed its flourish, and the inspiring sounds died away.

A dead silence followed.

"In the name of all evil things," muttered Pan, "what is the matter now?"

He was crossing the ring to see what had become of Ajax when that ponderous athlete appeared.

But where was the air of a giant among men? Was this the creature who had been declared to be without a rival in strength?

With a face as pallid as that of the dead, eyes staring and arms hanging loosely by his side, he staggered into the ring.

His fixed gaze was on Pan, and all others around him were as naught.

He did not see or think of them, and instead of saluting the king upon the throne he went by without so much as looking at him.

Murmurs of disappointment were heard on all sides.

"He has been drinking!" said one.

"He is an impostor!" said another.

Pan, with all things red before him in his fury, seized Ajax by the arm.

"What is it now?" he hissed.

"I've seen a *ghost!*" gasped Ajax.

'Whose—Gabrielle's?" demanded Pan.

"No; that of the BOY. *It's in the dressing-room.*"

Pan's face flushed for a moment, but he had no belief in ghosts, and his emotion was transitory.

"Face about and salute the king, and go on with your performance," he said. "You've been fancying things."

"I haven't," said Ajax.

"Face about, I say. Ah! that fiend here."

It was Pan's turn to be utterly confounded now, for Dick Strongbow, with Muffins close behind him, at that moment entered the arena. Immediately there was a silence on all things around.

Advancing to the centre of the ring, Dick saluted the king, but with his eyes more on the palsied Ajax than upon his Majesty, and in a clear, bell-like tone cried—

"Sire, I am here in response to a challenge from this man. I crave your royal permission to compete with him in the doing of sundry feats of strength and then as a wrestler."

A motion of the king's hand signified that the royal assent was given, and the leader of the musicians waved his baton as for the band to give another flourish. It was right heartily given.

Then Dick, calm and cool, drew a little aside and bade Ajax begin his performance.

But the wretched man could do nothing. His heart was as water within him. A horrible feeling of emptiness took away his strength.

He could not even lift the huge dumb-bells from the ground.

Pan was like some tortured fiend in his bitter anger. As for Muffins, if the presence of royalty and so many grand people had not kept him in awe, he would have laughed outright.

The assembly was not of the class to make any noisy demonstration of approval or disapproval, but the failure of Ajax excited their anger, and here and there faint sibilations were heard.

The king sat serenely in his throne. The only indication of his enjoyment of the scene was in his eyes, which quietly twinkled.

Dick, strong in elation, advanced, raised the dumb-bells with ease, and twisted and twirled them about as if they had been toys.

Then, without waiting for Ajax to make further effort, he went through all the feats that worthy usually performed, and, unruffled, drew back for his example to be followed.

But the huge coward could do nothing.

He did make one more effort to begin, but all his strength had vanished, as if scattered by the touch of a magic wand. With a groan he abandoned the attempt, and endeavoured to leave the ring.

But Dick quickly barred his way, holding out his arms as a challenge to wrestle.

Ajax sought to evade him, but Dick was not to be denied.

He sprang upon him, threw his arms around him, and threw the giant heavily down.

The usual reserve of that aristocratic assembly was broken down, and all, save the king, testified their delight with the waving of handkerchiefs and clapping of hands.

It was a triumph indeed, so complete, so crushing to Ajax, that all hope of even gaining a fragment of reputation in that country was lost.

Pan, whose control over himself in times of anger was limited, as we know, dashed at his master and gave him a fierce kick in his ribs.

"Get up, you dog!" he cried, "and come away from here."

And the dog, arising, with all speed followed him from the ring.

CHAPTER XVI.

AN INTERVIEW WITH THE KING—DICK'S REWARD
—AN INSPIRING LETTER.

UFFINS and Dick, having received a perfect ovation in the dressing-room from the other performers, dressed themselves, and in obedience to an intimation they received, through one of the king's attendants, returned to their apartments in the palace.

There they partook of refreshment again (excitement had made it needful), and sat down to await further commands from the king.

Presently an officer whom they had not hitherto seen entered the room, and announced that his Majesty desired to see Dick Strongbow alone.

"It is a great honour," said the officer, "and on yourself depends your future good fortune."

"It is little I shall ask for what I have done," replied Dick.

He followed the officer from the room, and was escorted through a number of passages and saloons he had not been in before.

Finally, a comparatively small room, fitted up as a library and smoking-room, was reached, and there Dick was left to await the arrival of the king.

He was not kept long.

Barely had the officer gone out by one door when the king entered by another.

An exclamation escaped Dick's lips.

His Majesty and the officer whose life he had saved were one and the same.

"I see you are surprised," said the king, advancing with a kind smile, "and I meant you should be.

I owe you much, and the jest at your expense is a small one."

"Your Majesty must forgive me," replied Dick, bowing low, "if for a moment I forgot the respect due to you."

"Strongbow," said the king, as he sank into a luxurious easy-chair, "I owe you my life, and I can never sufficiently reward you. But I have yet another favour to ask of you."

"A favour, your Majesty?"

"Yes. At present you have not spoken of it. That I attribute to your modesty. For my sake I wish you to preserve silence."

"On that subject, sire, I am dumb."

"I must tell you, Strongbow," pursued the king, "that it is a tradition among my people that the king is one of them—that he can walk here and there like the humblest, and no evil befall him. It has been so until the other day, when my faith in the truth of that tradition was rudely shaken. The faith of my people must, however, remain.

"Those two men who attempted my life," he went on, "were, I find, not of my nation. They belong to a band of Anarchists, who would destroy all authority, if they could. I, by reason of the simplicity of my life, was fixed upon as a mark for their demoniacal virulence. I let them go, as you saw, but they have been well cared for since. They will not trouble me again. Now as to your reward. Nay, no refusal. I am not bribing you to silence. I know you will be true to me."

Dick bowed.

"That boy of yours, now. He will not talk?" he said.

"No," replied Dick, "your Majesty may rely upon him. Besides, he does not know it is you whom the assassins attacked."

The king then asked Dick about his past life, and having learnt his history, asked about his plans for the future.

Dick had no particular plans save that whenever and wherever he met with Ajax he would humiliate and defeat him.

"It is the one purpose I have in life," he said, "and it is not a great one."

"You abandon all idea of endeavouring to find out who your father was?" said the king.

"There is nothing to find out, I fear," replied Dick, and the subject dropped.

Dick shortly after took his leave of the king and returned to his hotel, more than pleased with his day's work.

Pan and Ajax had disappeared.

He enquired after them before he left the palace; but all that was known of them was that they had pressed with all speed and taken themselves off.

Muffins was grinning over the ghostly fear of Ajax.

"Such a little ghost, master, to frighten such a big chap," he said, and then they had a hearty laugh together.

The king was as good as his word as to the reward.

In addition to the magnificent ring, he received an order on a Berlin banker for a sum equal to ten thousand pounds English money.

The reason for the money being made payable in Berlin was obvious. The king did not wish to excite curiosity by the payment of such a large sum to a stranger.

But there was yet another gift for Dick.

It came by post shortly after the present from his Majesty.

It was a small box containing another ring and a a scrap of paper, on which was scratched a few words—

"*I saw you to-day. You can be a great man, and a noble one, if you will only labour in another field. Do so, and one day we may meet again.* "L.""

These simple words set his whole frame aglow. He kissed the ring and placed it on his finger, next to that from the king. The letter he put away in an inner pocket near his breast.

"She is right," he said. "I ought to employ myself in worthier fields. I can do so now. But first to Berlin, and then—well, where kind fortune takes me. I did not see her to-day. Perhaps it is better so. If the 'one day' comes, it must be when I am worthy of her. Lucella, for the present, au revoir! We shall meet again."

CHAPTER XVII.

THE GERMAN CAFE—A BULLY CONFOUNDED—
THE CHALLENGE.

SWAGGERING into one of the cafés in Berlin, half-a-dozen students took possession of a table in a prominent part of the room.

Among them was one fellow of giant proportions, and somewhat repulsive in appearance, owing to the coarse expression of his face.

He gave an order to a waiter in an authoritative tone for some lager beer, and bade him hurry, if he did not wish to have his bones broken.

The German military student is in his own eyes a very important personage, and is inclined not to be trifled with by anyone weaker than himself.

He can be as brutal as any ruffian on earth, and very often is so.

Brawls and other forms of disturbances are common where these students are to be found. They do their best to create quarrels wherever they go.

The waiter, knowing his men, served them with all speed, and having been cursed as he was paid, shuffled away.

Before each student was a huge tankard of beer,

"Gentlemen," said the big fellow, "the usual toast. Our army—the army of the world."

"It is always Franz Muller's toast," said another.

"And why should it not be?" fiercely demanded Franz Muller, the big fellow. "I can choose my own toasts, I suppose?"

"No offence," said the other; "it's a right good toast, anyhow. But a little change wouldn't hurt us. Why not drink occasionally to the ladies?"

"I drink to nothing but sabre, gun, and lance," said Franz Muller. "Give me the music of the battlefield. There's nothing like it."

"And you have yet to hear it, Franz."

"Be silent or I will brain you with my tankard."

Franz Muller glanced fiercely at the other students, not one of whom was within easy distance of his size, and not seeing any pugilistic light in their eyes, growled something to himself and filled his pipe.

"I'm in the humour for a row to-day," he said.

"Then here is your match," replied one of his companions.

He nodded in the direction of an adjacent table, at which a quiet-looking young man had just seated himself.

It was Dick Strongbow, who had arrived in Berlin the day before, and had just been to the banker to get the King of Sweden's gift of money transferred to his own name.

Naturally, Dick felt in a very happy and contented frame of mind.

He was at peace with all around him, and desired to remain so.

Not so Franz Muller.

He glanced at Dick from under his beetling eyebrows, and with a sneer announced to his companions that it was "a drivelling Englishman."

"Go at him, Franz," said one by his side, "and let us see him drivel."

"Carl Yemitz is always good as an adviser," said Franz, "but he seldom does anything."

"If I don't, I never brag," said Carl Yemitz, quietly.

"Do I brag?"

"Yes; occasionally. You can't help it."

In a moment it seemed as if Franz Muller would assault his daring companion, but he thought better of it and turned his attention to the "drivelling Englishman."

Dick at that moment was about to light a cigar, a luxury he only sparingly indulged in, and had just lighted a long wooden spill.

Franz Muller had his pipe filled, and that also wanted lighting. Why not use the ready lighted spill of this "drivelling Englishman?"

Rising up and advancing a step or two, he stretched out his arm and took it from Dick's hand

"Thanks!" he drawled.

The next moment the spill was taken from his hand, the pipe jerked from his mouth, and an iron grasp was on his throat.

All this was done without any show of violence or excitement.

Quietly Dick held him, but so tightly that he was practically helpless, his companions looking on with amazement.

Having held him until the bully was on the verge of suffocation, Dick let him go, and he dropped back into his chair.

Dick, who still held his cigar in his left hand, without any sign of being ruffled, said—

"Now give me a light."

Franz Muller hesitated.

"If you don't," said Dick, "I will choke you outright."

Franz Muller, like a man in a dream, lighted a spill for him, and Dick, taking it from his hand drawled "Thanks."

The tone of voice and the manner were an exact imitation of Franz, and the other students broke into a roar of laughter.

"The fiends take such a grip as yours," said Franz Muller, glaring at Dick. "Who are you?"

"Why, a drivelling Englishman," serenely answered Dick.

"May I ask you a question?" inquired Carl Yemitz, with a smile. "I don't want to run the risk of your giving me a grip."

Dick, who was still standing by, quietly smiling, replied—

"Certainly. Why not?"

"Have you been in Sweden lately?" asked Carl.

"I have only recently come from there," answered Dick.

"Then you are the fellow who made such a sensation before the king?"

"I did a few simple tricks before his majesty."

"Who gave you a private interview afterwards. The Swedish papers say you are a nobleman in disguise, and, on my word, you look it."

Dick laughed. There was something rather attractive about this Carl, although he was not outwardly of the muscular order of men, but of effeminate appearance.

Franz Muller rose, and having rubbed his neck and gone through the action of swallowing something, said—

"It's time for me to be going. I've got an appointment to keep"

"Good-bye, Franz," said his companions, in laughing chorus. "You won't talk too much about this affair, will you?"

"Dare any of you talk about it?" asked Franz, fiercely.

"I for one," drawled Carl, "shall consult my own desires in that respect."

"And I!"

"And I!" chorused the others.

Franz Muller glared from one to the other, and saw in their contemptuous faces that his reign as bully was over.

They knew his worth now, and feared him no more.

With set teeth he strode out of the café, pausing one moment at the door to cast a malignant glance at Dick, who had taken possession of the seat he had vacated.

"It's odd that we never found him out before," said one of the students. "He talked a lot of what he has done, but he never tackled anything above a waiter until to-day."

"And what a failure!" said another.

"Gentlemen," said Dick, "I am sure that you had no share in the insult offered me just now, or I should not be sitting here. It is a good thing for that fellow that I am even-tempered, OR I MIGHT HAVE HURT HIM."

Dick put a slight emphasis on the latter words, but there was nothing of the braggadocia in his air.

The students laughed heartily, as they would have done at an excellent joke.

Dick was in good company, and the consumption of lager beer, a very harmless drink, was considerable.

The young Germans also smoked as if they were living factory chimneys.

Half an hour elapsed, and then there came swaggering into the café a fierce-looking officer in uniform.

He was a grey-headed man of about fifty, a regular fire-eater.

He came straight up to Dick, and saluted military fashion.

"Herr Strongbow, I belief?" he said.

"Yes," replied Dick.

"I come from Herr Muller," said the officer; "here is my card."

Dick glanced at it, and read—

"*Captain Gobmitch.*"

"Well," said Dick, "what is the meaning of this?"

"Will you please name a friend?" answered the captain.

"It would be difficult," said Dick, laughing, "as I am a stranger here, unless," he glanced at Carl, who responded quickly—

"With pleasure."

"Then make what arrangements you please," said Dick; "but it is hardly fair for a military man to challenge a civilian."

"And it is not fair for a giant to attack a weaker man," said the officer, fiercely.

"Pardon me," rejoined Dick, "he was the aggressor."

"He tells a different story," growled the captain.

"He was the wanton aggressor," said Carl, "and was most mercifully treated."

"It matters not," snarled the officer. "He sends you a challenge, and you accept it. It is so?"

Dick bowed.

"Then we can settle the rest," said the captain, "and if you will draw aside with me, Herr Yemitz, we will make the necessary arrangements."

They drew aside and whispered for five minutes or so, and then the captain strutted out again. Carl returned to the table.

"If you come with me," he said to Dick, "I will tell you what we have settled. Do you know anything of the sword?"

"A little," replied Dick, quietly. "I was educated at one of your colleges."

"Ah! then you took lessons. But you ought to have a little practice. Come to my quarters, and I will see how you can handle the steel."

CHAPTER XVIII.

MUFFINS IN THE PARK—AN INDIGNANT ATTENDANT—A DROP FROM A WINDOW.

MUFFINS had been left by his master at home in apartments in a street not far from the Kursaal Gardens, a popular place of public resort in Berlin.

He had permission to wander in the gardens for an hour or so, and, attired in a neat suit of tweed, he strolled about the hour of noon.

It was the time for the youth of Berlin to be much in evidence there. Troops of schoolboys were lounging about like old men, for the German youth is not given to lively disporting, but prefers stolid forms of mischief.

It was not long ere Muffins was espied and recognised as a foreigner. His spare form also led to the belief that he could be insulted with impunity.

Half-a-dozen young Germans gathered around, staring in their goggle-eyed way, but exhibiting no emotion on their faces.

"Hi! you English bullock," said one, suddenly.

He spoke our tongue fairly well. They cultivate languages with much assiduity in Germany.

"Hallo! you German sausage," replied Muffins.

The young German frowned, which made Muffins laugh. The frown deepened and was added to by a snarl.

"You be quiet," he said.

"Quiet yourself," returned Muffins.

"Put him down and rub his nose," cried another.

It may be here explained that German boys when they quarrel do not fight as our boys do at home.

They lay hold of each other, and he who can get the other down rubs his nose as hard as he can until he, in a manner of speaking, rubs him out of time.

Now Muffins, although he knew nothing of this mode of warfare, had, during his street career, been subject to many forms of assault, and was in a general way prepared to take care of himself unless the aggressor was a long way too much for him.

Therefore, when this German schoolboy, acting on the advice of his friend, closed with him, with the intention of treating Muffins according to the war code of Germany, he speedily found that he had tackled an experienced foe.

Instead of tamely submitting to be thrown, he wriggled like an eel out of the young German's embrace and hit out straight at his face.

It was a stinging blow the would-be "nose-rubber" received, and in an instant he was turned into a gory specimen of staggered youth.

His companions crying out, "Hi! hock. Ter Teufel," spread out as soldiers do from a bursting shell.

"Come on, the lot of you!" cried Muffins, dancing about and working his arms in approved pugilistic fashion. "Who wants any more? Come, don't *all* run away."

He rushed at two or three of them, but as they refused to fight he put his hands in his pockets and walked on.

The boys closed up behind him, he with the bleeding nose bringing up the rear, wiping his nasal organ and weeping.

"Hi—hi! English bullock—boy—cur!" they shouted.

Two or three times Muffins turned and tried to get at them, but with their bleeding companion as a warning, they at first kept out of his way.

Their numbers, however, increased. Other school-boys joined them, eagerly enquiring what was the matter; and on being told that the " Cur—English boy" had smitten Wilhelm so fiercely as to break his nose into bleeding, they also howled at Muffins.

Ere long dust and stones were gathered up and hurled at him, and prudence being one of the qualities of Dick's follower, he resolved on beating a retreat.

Not in an ignominious way, however, but with a deliberation amounting to defiance.

Old soldiers say that when a retreat is well carried out it is a moral victory, and certain it is that Muffins, as he slowly wended his way towards home, did not present the appearance of being defeated.

He kept his face to the foe, backing slowly, his hands clenched ready for action. His enemies howled, hissed, raved, and even spat at him, but they made no attempt to close for awhile.

At length, by the urging of some, the whole body, about thirty in number, decided to make a dash at him.

It was done, and Muffins, scorning ignominious flight, soon found himself in a whirlpool of screaming foes.

He hit out right and left, dealing out telling blows and receiving kicks in return.

Slates and books were used as weapons wherewith to assault him, and he was getting into serious trouble when assistance arrived.

It was in the form of one of the keepers or attendants of the gardens, an old soldier, armed with a very pliant cane.

Boys, as with many of our park-keepers at home, were his natural enemies, and it sufficed for him that a riot was going on.

It was not his business to enquire into the rights of it, but simply *to stop it.*

Accordingly, he went for the seething throng, and, using his cane sword fashion, soon fairly cut up the mob, until he reached Muffins, who, breathless, gory, and with his apparel rumpled and torn, was still full of fight.

"Cease! little pig," he said, seizing him by the collar.

"Let me alone," hissed Muffins, "or I'll be the death of you!"

"Ha! English—so!" said the keeper. "Come, now, to prison!"

Muffins gave one wriggle, and was out of the attendant's hands, leaving his coat behind him.

The man looked at the coat, then at Muffins, standing ten yards off, and gave vent to a grunt of astonishment.

"You give me my coat!" cried Muffins.

"Go to your home," said the attendant. "I follow, and take your name."

The German boys were all well scattered now, standing afar off and watching the scene with interest.

They expected that Muffins would be taken right away to prison—probably be hung, as all hard-hitting English boys, in their opinion, ought to be.

Muffins, without sharing this view, was beginning to wish himself well out of the brawl, and, feeling that his master alone could settle matters satisfactorily, he set out at a quick pace for home.

The attendant followed, and on their arrival at the lodgings Muffins found that his master had not returned.

"I will wait for him," said the attendant, ferociously.

He was disposed, like many of his race, to lord it over an Englishman whenever an opportunity offered, and accordingly he took possession of an easy-chair, and lighted his pipe just to show that he was a man of authority.

Dick Strongbow's rooms were on the first-floor front, so that Muffins, who stood by the window, had a view of the street.

Outside there was quite a mob of boys and men, waiting to see what the august garden-attendant would do to the Englishmen; but it was nearly an hour ere their curiosity was gratified.

Dick, coming home about that time, was somewhat astonished to find a mob of people outside the house, and a quick glance upward showed him the anxious face of Muffins at the window.

He understood at once that there was some link between the boy and the mob below, and hurried upstairs to get at the facts.

By that time the garden attendant had fallen asleep, and was snoring in the easy-chair.

In a few words Muffins gave his master a truthful account of the affair.

Dick felt very angry at the insolent behaviour of the German Jack-in-office, and one of his dangerous moods came over him.

"Open the window, Muffins!" he said.

Muffins did so with alacrity, half suspecting what was coming.

Dick seized the attendant by the collar of his coat, twisted him out of the chair, and grasped him further in the middle of the back.

"Teufel! what's this?" cried the startled man, as he opened his eyes.

He was being borne across the room by some power he could not see behind him. Before him he saw the open window, and wild alarm arose in his heart. One cry for help, and then all sound was frozen within him.

He was propelled through the window, lowered a couple of feet, and then dropped into the thick of the astounded crowd below.

For a moment there was silence, and then there arose a mighty clamour of voices, the word "Teufel!" being heard on all sides.

Dick closed the window, and took a seat at the table.

"Give me the pen and ink, Muffins," he said.

Muffins brought him writing materials from a side-table, and then stole to the window again.

The mob outside had broken up into groups, discussing the wondrous sight they had just beheld.

On the opposite side of the way the attendant was being carefully examined to see what damage had been done to his bones.

Apparently it was very little, for in a few minutes

This time the right breast of the German was pierced and he fell.

he, after looking at the window from which he had been so ignominiously dropped, strutted away with the air of a man who wished the public to think that such an affair was of everyday occurrence and beneath his notice.

CHAPTER XIX.

DICK MAKES HIS WILL—THE PLACE OF MEETING —"IT SHALL BE A DUEL TO THE DEATH."

ICK was engaged in writing about a quarter of an hour, and bestowed great care upon the work. He read and re-read it, corrected it here and there, and finally copied it out in a neat hand.

"Now, Muffins," he said, "come here. You see this paper?"

"Yes, sir," replied Muffins, staring hard at it.

"Can you guess what it is?"

"No, sir."

"Well, I suppose you cannot. It is my will."

Muffins had no idea what a will was, and turned an enquiring look upon his master.

"My will," said Dick, "leaving all my money and property to you in case I should be killed."

"Oh! master," cried Muffins, in sudden terror. "Don't talk of that."

"I don't think I shall be killed," said Dick, calmly; "but one never knows the chances in a duel. I am going to fight a German with swords. I tell you this so that in case of the worst you may know what to do. I am going now to a public notary, where I shall get this document witnessed and stamped. After that I shall give it to you, in case I should be slain.

"Oh! master—master."

"Muffins, I am only preparing you for possibilities. In case I am killed you will at once make your way home to England and go to Mr. Parbole, who will find a respectable lawyer for you. I leave everything I have to you, with instructions that you are to be educated and trained as I have been.

"As a final word," said Dick, "I advise you to sew this document in the lining of your coat, and keep it there. If nothing happens to me to-morrow morning, when I fight this duel, I may have a mishap another day. Wherever you may be, make for England, as I told you. This piece of paper will be worth ten thousand pounds to you."

Dick put on his hat and walked out, leaving Muffins to reflect upon the startling news he had had heard.

He was grateful to find how kind his master was; but he would not willingly lose him for twice ten thousand pounds.

"I'll kill whoever kills him!" said Muffins, between his teeth.

And then he shed a few tears; but when Dick Strongbow returned he was quiet again.

"Master," he said, "may I come and see the fight?"

"I think you had better not," replied Dick.

This was neither an assent nor a refusal; but Muffins said no more.

Quick-witted as he was, he saw his way to be present at the duel without disobeying his master.

A slit was made in the breast-lining of the boy's coat, and the will, duly attested and sealed, inserted therein.

Dick afterwards, in rather a clumsy way, sewed it up again, and then he had a quiet cigar.

"We won't talk any more about this duel, Muffins, until it is over," he said.

It cannot be too clearly understood that Dick was not in the least troubled on his own account. He had simply taken precautions necessary for the future welfare of Muffins in case of "accidents."

The boy, being no relation, could not inherit any of his property, except under a will. Without it, the boy, after his master's death, would be as poor as he was before.

Dick retired at a very early hour, the appointment for the meeting being at sunrise.

Muffins did not go to bed at all.

In his room he kept silent vigil, waiting for his master to move in the morning; and it was yet dark when the anxious boy heard him quietly dressing.

Dick shortly after went softly downstairs, and Muffins stealthily followed him.

From the staircase the boy saw the door open. A stranger to him was on the doorstep, waiting for Dick.

It was Carl Yemitz, with two swords wrapped in a cloth tucked under his arm.

"You are very early," said Dick, as they shook hands.

"Yes; there's nothing like being in good time in these affairs—the first on the field gets some moral strength."

They spoke in German, and Muffins did not understand them; but he guessed what was inside that folded cloth, and a sickening feeling came over him.

Sitting up all night lowers the nerves, and Muffins was not quite so composed as usual. To put it mildly, he was inclined to be "shaky."

Dick and Carl, walking as softly as a good pace would permit, went away down the street, and Muffins was soon upon their trail.

The boyish tricks of his earlier days, when he was a poor street-arab, served him now.

As he used then to watch and keep out of sight of foes, so he dodged now to keep out of sight of a friend.

But Dick did not once look round.

He and Carl lost no time in getting to a piece of waste ground behind the public gardens, and out of sight of the houses.

On one side was a fringe of bushes, which afforded an excellent place of concealment for Muffins.

Dick and Carl were the first on the ground, and the latter, drawing out a cigar-case, offered it to the former.

"I don't usually smoke so early," said Dick; "but it will serve to kill the time."

It was fully a quarter of an hour ere Franz Muller, Captain Gobmitch, and an army doctor, with a case of surgical instruments under his arm, appeared upon the scene.

Franz Muller assumed a swaggering air and

scowled like a brigand, but he was not quite at his ease.

Bows were exchanged, and the seconds drew apart to confer.

First of all the exact spot for the duel had to be chosen, which was not such an easy matter as it may seem, as a perfectly level space was not easily found.

Neither second would permit the other to select a portion of the ground which would give an advantage to a combatant, but after awhile this difficulty was got over.

Then the swords were brought out, measured and tested to see if they were sound. Last of all, the blades were wrapped up, and Franz Muller was given a choice of handles.

He selected one, and Dick, who had been calmly smoking all the while, took the other.

Then he carefully laid his cigar upon a stone, and, whipping off his coat, declared that he was ready.

Franz Muller was a little slower in his movements; but there was no pronounced delay, and at length the combatants faced each other.

Muffins, lying down among the bushes, held his breath. The feeling of excitement upon him was almost unendurable.

Dick knew nothing of Muller's swordsmanship, save a few words Carl Yemitz had dropped to the effect that he was considered very efficient in the use of it.

Franz Muller knew nothing whatever of Dick's capabilities as a swordsman until their swords crossed.

Then in a moment he knew he had a toe who was not to be despised.

When the swords touch there is what fencers call the "grip," which tells of the novice or proficient according to the nature of it.

The novice has a loose, uncertain touch, but the practised swordsman places his weapon firmly against the other, and in a winding style begins the preliminary play.

Dick's weapon seemed to be remarkably pliable; but that was the result of the working of his wrist, so strong in sinew, and the grasp of the hand, which closed upon the hilt like a band of steel.

Franz Muller was an expert swordsman, and had, in common with the usage of German students, fought several duels.

Many a scarred face to be seen in Berlin bore testimony to his prowess.

It is the custom with the Germans to aim at the face, and the first wound inflicted generally ends the fight.

But this meeting had been declared by Franz Muller to be a duel to the death.

The heart, then, would be the chief object of attack.

Both men, knowing this, began warily, and the supple steel flashed in the light of early morning like two bright lines of fire.

To and fro, with a terrible grating they moved, twisting, turning, playing this way and that with deadly intent.

A thrust.

It came from Franz Muller, swift and straight, but Dick parried it.

The movement on his part was hardly perceptible, but it was sufficient, and the German felt his weapon turned over so as to nearly twist it from his grasp.

The two seconds swerved, and the doctor, standing aside, watched every movement with keen anxiety.

Muffins from his place of concealment watched closely also, but, of course, understood nothing more than that serious results might follow a thrust.

Another thrust.

This time from Dick, and lightly given.

Franz Muller felt the prick of it upon his breast and wildly endeavoured to counter thrust.

Another thrust from Dick, and this time the right breast of the German was pierced, and he fell heavily to the ground.

Dick turned his weapon down, and, walking to the stone, picked up his cigar, and placed it in his mouth.

"I have not killed him," he said; "but I think that wound will suffice."

The doctor rushed over to the fallen man, and, kneeling down, unbuttoned his under-vest and tore open his shirt.

His experienced eye saw that the wound was dangerous, but, as Dick said, not necessarily fatal.

"I stop the duel," he said.

"Your interference is unnecessary," said Carl Yemitz, coolly; "Franz Muller won't stand up again."

Muller opened his eyes and glared at his old companion, thus showing that he was not so far gone as he pretended to be.

Captain Gobmitch turned away from him with an expression of disgust.

"Doctor," he said, "I will leave the patient to your care while I fetch a carriage to take him home. I think he ought to be happy that it is not his coffin I am going to order."

"I will do my duty," said the doctor, as he took some lint and a bottle of lotion from his case.

The captain, twirling his moustache, strode away, and Dick and Carl, arm-in-arm, walked off.

Muffins remained for awhile in his place of concealment, too much overcome with joy over the result of the encounter to be able to move.

It was not until his master was well away that he came out of his place of concealment and astonished the doctor by turning wheels right across the open space of ground, finishing up by jumping in the air and uttering a shout of delight that could have been heard half a mile off.

Having thus given vent to his feelings, he ran off like a hare in the direction his master had taken.

CHAPTER XX.

JACOB MORELLE AGAIN—NECESSARY DODGING—THE CUPBOARD TRICK.

FOR many years such a sensation had not been known in Berlin as there was when the story of the duel and its preceding events became known among the students.

Was it possible that Franz Muller, the strong bully and accomplished duellist, had been so easily overcome by an Englishman?

Then, in addition, the story of the attendant

It was called forth by the mention of the name of Jacob Morelle.

"I knew a man of that name five years ago," he said. "He was in Berlin, spending money like a prince. He was a social star for a whole season."

"What sort of a man was he?" asked Dick.

"Not a bad-looking fellow—say about forty,"

replied Carl. "But I did not like his face; it seemed to me both crafty and cruel. He gave out that he was going to Burmah to look after a ruby mine, which he said he had inherited."

"And you know nothing more of him?"

"Nothing."

Dick dropped the subject; but this short conversation opened up the old problem—the secret of his birth.

Was this the Jacob Morelle he failed to find, and, if he were, how was it that he, once a resident in a great place like Dane's Inn, had suddenly blossomed into a millionaire?

"Can it be that it was *my* money he spent so freely?" he asked himself again and again.

He could not shake off the idea that this Jacob Morelle was the man whom Gonzalo had trusted. If so, he had proved a traitor.

Dick's resolve was immediately taken. He would go to Burmah and try and find this Jacob Morelle. It would be something to do, and there was a prospect of adventure which he longed for.

He spoke to Carl at once upon the subject, and that lively young German was immediately on fire.

"To Burmah!" he cried, "and I will go with you."

"You?" said Dick. "But are you not a student for the army?"

"What of that—I can run away, I suppose? I have no taste for the everlasting drill and mechanical work here. We are not men or soldiers, but mere puppets. To Burmah—India—anywhere!"

So it was settled, but they reckoned without their host.

The next day Dick received a warning from the police authorities not to leave Berlin until the affair of the duel had been satisfactorily settled.

This touched the bumps of opposition in Dick's nature, and he decided to be out of Berlin in twenty-four hours.

His first step was to get some ready cash from the bank, and to arrange for the transfer of the rest to the Bank of England.

Then he got out a map, and marked the route he had to take.

His best course, he saw, would be to get into France, then down to Marseilles. There he could get a vessel outward bound.

He sent Muffins for Carl, and told him of his decision. Carl was of opinion that he would never get out of the country unless he adopted a disguise.

"Well, I will disguise myself," said Dick, laughing. "What do you propose?"

"We must go as a pleasant family—two brothers and a sister—one of us had better be the sister."

Dick did not like the idea, but as he was the one who would be especially marked, he gave his consent to put himself in petticoats.

"It is only for a few hours," Carl said.

He undertook to find the dresses, and bought them after dark. For himself and Muffins he had blouses, coarse woollen caps, wide trousers, and wooden shoes.

For Dick he bought a wig of coarse, dark hair, a homespun dress, huge white cap, and leather boots.

"There is a night train that will take us to the frontier," Carl said.

"But are you sure, old fellow, that you are not acting rashly?" asked Dick. "What will your friends say?"

"Be easy," replied Carl. "I have no relatives but a guardian, who will be glad to get rid of me. All I have in this world is about me."

He drew out a handful of gold and notes.

"This will carry me to Burmah," he said, with a smile; "after that I must trust to luck for a fortune."

"How is Muller?" asked Dick.

"Save for the brag you have let out of him, like wind out of a bag, he will be little the worse for the encounter," replied Carl.

The preparations for the journey were soon made.

Such luggage as they proposed to take they made up into bundles to be in character with the disguises.

The train, a night mail, started at ten o'clock. At nine the toilets of the trio were completed.

"It is half an hour's walk to the station," said Carl, "and we ought to go at once. Peasant people always get to the station early. Shall we start?"

Before Dick could reply a loud and peremptory knock was heard at the front door.

"That's official," said Carl.

"And possibly concerns me," added Dick.

They stood still listening, and presently heard the landlady shuffle to the door. The voice of a man reached them—

"Is the Herr Strongbow at home?"

"Yes; what is it?" asked the landlady.

"I am here to take him under arrest," was the reply. "The Herr Muller has suddenly become worse. His life is in danger. Which is the Strongbow room?"

"Up the stairs, first door on the right."

"What is to be done now?" asked Carl. "It is a serious thing to resist arrest."

"Put out the light," said Dick, "and you take charge of my bundle for a moment. Muffins, open that cupboard door. Now both stand ready to hurry out the moment I give the word."

The cupboard door was opened, and, the light being put out, only a faint glimmer came through the closed blinds from the street below.

With slow and solemn step the official, armed with a warrant for Dick's arrest, came stumping up the stairs and knocked at the door.

"Enter!" cried Dick

The man opened the door; but on seeing the room was in darkness, stopped short upon the threshold.

Dick, standing half behind the door, extended his arms, drew him in, and pinioned his arms to his sides.

"Silence," he cried, in German, "or you are a dead man. Dost feel how strong I am?"

The terrified man muttered something in reply. He did, indeed, feel Dick's strength, and it made him shiver.

CHAPTER XXI.

AN INSPECTOR ADOPTS A DISGUISE AGAINST HIS WISH—THE FLASK TRICK.

ICK raised the terrified man in his arms, carried him across the room, and thrust him into the cupboard, which was a deep one.

"Keep there," he said, "until you have my permission to come out. If you venture to open the door, you may be shot."

"Herr Strongbow, I will not move without your permission," gasped the man.

"Then you will not move in a hurry," muttered Dick, as he closed the door.

Walking softly across the room he re-opened it and motioned his companions to go out.

They did so, on tip-toe, and as there was a light below they could see their way downstairs.

In another minute they were all in the street, hurrying in the direction of the railway station.

Muffins, an inborn adventurer, was in a state of delight. Anything in the way of novelty suited him.

The world now was to him one grand, moving panorama of joyous and exciting events.

It was little more than half-past nine when they reached the station, and a long wait was before them.

"Let us hope our friend will remain in the cupboard," said Carl.

The office soon opened, and Dick took tickets for the train.

He spoke German as fluently as a native ; but he had not the patois of the peasant, and the clerk looked at him curiously.

"Is there a masquerade on to-night ?" he asked, with a smile.

"No," replied Dick, shortly.

"That's no woman," muttered the clerk. "I had better see the police about it."

The train was at the platform, and they took their seats in a third-class carriage at the top end of the train.

"Five minutes more," said Carl, looking out of the window at a clock.

It was an anxious time for all.

Carl, by running away from Berlin without a permit, would, if caught, assuredly be imprisoned, and the same fate certainly hung over Dick.

Muffins, as the associate of the law-breakers, might likewise get into trouble.

"Two minutes now," said Carl.

The passengers were taking their seats, the guard and porters bustled to and fro.

Luggage was being packed in the van with the usual disregard to the possibility of breaking anything inside the boxes and portmanteaux.

"One minute now," said Carl.

Hurry and bustle, a moving to and fro, and a banging of doors.

"We are off now."

The signal was given ; but instantly afterwards an authoritative voice was heard, crying—

"Stop the train ! Steady there. Halt !"

That the train was being stopped on their account our friends had good reason to fear, and the first thing Dick thought of was his attire.

He felt sorry that he had adopted it, and his first impulse was to remove it with all speed.

Under the peasant woman's dress he had his own clothes, but even this fact did not do much towards lessening the sense of degradation he felt. For his own sake he would never have adopted such a disguise.

But ere he could remove it, a railway inspector opened the door and thrust his head into the carriage.

He stared hard at the trio for a moment, and then, apparently satisfied, closed the door and went on to the next carriage.

"Drop the window, Muffins," said Dick, "I feel half stifled. As for this dress—off it comes."

"It's risky," suggested Carl, quietly.

"I can't stand it," returned Dick. "I feel as if all the MAN was taken out of me.

In half-a-dozen seconds he had made a bundle of it and cast it under the seat.

"Now I feel myself again," he said.

As he spoke the voice of some official was heard calling for the train to start, and, simultaneously, the inspector who had previously looked into the carriage, re-appeared.

He thrust his head and shoulders in at the open window, cast a quick glance round, and exclaimed—

"Ah ! what is this ? Awhile ago you were a woman, but now you are a man. I must stop the train and see to it."

He spoke in German, and Muffins, in blissful ignorance of his meaning, was laughing at the expression of his face, when a most tremendous thing happened.

Dick saw that if the train was stopped a second time, that he would indubitably get into trouble with the authorities. Strong as he was, it would be madness to fight against a host of officials.

He could do a lot of mischief, but in the end must inevitably be the greatest sufferer.

But he was not going to submit tamely to the authorities, and in self-defence took extraordinary steps for his temporary safety.

Like a hawk pouncing upon a sparrow he fell upon the official, pinned him by the arms high up near the shoulder, and by sheer strength drew him into the carriage.

It was done so quickly that the involuntary movement of the astounded official may be compared to that of a harlequin taking one of his familiar leaps in a pantomime.

Assuredly his disappearance from the platform was not observed by any of his fellows, for the train, having started again, proceeded steadily on, leaving the brilliantly-lighted station behind.

Carl was almost as much staggered as the inspector by such an exhibition of strength, but he was also amused, and joined Muffins in a hearty laugh.

Dick put the man in a corner facing him, where he lolled as limp as a doll, staring hard at the powerful youth, who coolly closed the window, and calmly addressed him thus—

"So long as you are quiet no harm will come to you ; but if you attempt to make the least disturbance at any place we may stop at I shall in a moment make a rag of you. Please take off your coat."

The man did not reply or make any movement.

He simply lolled in the corner in the precise position Dick had placed him, and stared with all his eyes.

"Take his coat off, Muffins," said Dick.

Muffins, with the glowing breast of one who is performing a meritorious action, speedily divested the limp inspector of his coat, just as if he were a nurse undressing a big baby.

Dick took off his own, and, folding it up, laid it upon the seat.

"Get out that dress," said Dick, "and put it on him. Give me his cap ; I must make a full-blown inspector of myself."

Without any resistance the man allowed himself to be transformed from an important railway official into a peasant woman.

Everything favoured the change, for he was close-shaven, and ugly enough to be a typical representative of the Teutonic market-woman.

Carl Yemitz went into fits of laughter and rocked about on the seat of the carriage with the tears rolling out of his eyes.

"It's the best joke out !" he said. "But you have forgotten one thing, Muffins ; give his trousers a roll up to the calves."

Muffins, as dexterous as a valet, complied with this request, and then the inspector sufficiently recovered to find his tongue.

"This," he said, "is an outrage our great Moltke will avenge. England can tremble."

"No doubt it will," replied Dick, "if ever it knows anything about it. But don't forget that I may not have done with you yet. It is just as easy to pop you out of the window as to pull you in, my friend."

"I beseech you to be merciful, mighty Herr," said the inspector, with a trembling lip.

"I tell you that so long as you keep quiet you will not be injured in the least," replied Dick, "and, furthermore, if you go with us in a quiet way you shall not go without your reward."

"Go—Herr—with you ! How far ?"

"To France."

"Save me ! I shall be a lost man."

"Well, you must go."

"Let it be so, great Herr."

Apparently he was very compliant, accepting the situation like a philosopher.

Presently the train stopped and he made an attempt to lower the window.

"Let it alone," said Dick.

"Herr, grant me permission to see whether we stop," pleaded the inspector.

"You will sit still and do nothing," replied Dick. "For the last time I warn you. The least movement on your part and I shall be compelled—for my own safety—to put an end to you. One grip with my finger and thumb, and it will be all over with you."

Dick did not mean all he said, but it was necessary to play upon the fears of their involuntary companion, and the effect of his words was all that could be desired.

"I give in—I yield," he said.

The train was brought to a standstill, and, in obedience to a sign from Dick, Carl and Muffins moved with him to the other end of the carriage.

The inspector was thus left to himself, it being Dick's intention in case of any rumpus, to disown him.

There were several passengers at the station, and one of them got in. He was a tall, lazy-looking man, of about forty, in farmer's attire.

He cast a glance round the carriage, and seated himself opposite to the supposed woman.

The wretched inspector closed his eyes and feigned to sleep ; but the farmer was not to be denied, he being of an affectionate disposition, and inclined to make himself agreeable to the gentle sex.

"Is it that you travel far to-night, fraulein ?" he asked.

No answer ; only the opening of half an eye on the part of the inspector.

"The lady a friend of yours ?" enquired the farmer, addressing Dick.

"Oh ! no," he replied. "I do not even know her name."

"Poor lonely child !" sighed the farmer. "I will protect her. It is hard to travel alone in the night-time."

He again tried the persuasive powers of conversation, but the inspector remained dumb.

At last the persecuting farmer tried something more seductive.

Groping in an enormous pocket of his outer coat, he unearthed a flask of goodly proportions, and proceeded to unscrew the top.

Immediately it was removed an odour of Hollands pervaded the compartment. The inspector opened both eyes a little.

With a slow, persuasive movement the farmer advanced the flask until it was within a few inches of the fair one's nose.

The hand of the disguised official rose up and grasped it.

"Ah !" exclaimed the farmer, "now we shall be friends."

The flask was placed to the lips of the official and tilted, once, twice, thrice, and then handed back to the owner.

He gave it a shake, and a hideous expression of dismay overspread his face.

"Der Teufel !" he exclaimed ; "it is made quite dry."

It was but too true. The harassed, thirsty inspector had emptied it.

And, to add insult to injury, he was feigning sleep again.

It was pretty nigh impossible for our friends to retain their gravity, but by making strenuous efforts they succeeded in keeping up a tolerable appearance of composure.

The farmer sulkily leant back in his corner, and feigned sleep also.

And so the train rattled on through the darkness, passing some stations and stopping at two or three, Dick keeping a watchful eye on the door.

But it was not opened. There was no addition to their party until the night was far advanced, and the train drew up at what was, no doubt, an important junction.

There were more people about than had been seen at any station on their way, and the platform on which were at least a dozen officials, well lighted up.

The sleeping inspector, who had been loudly snoring for some time past, now tried on a little trick he had possibly been contemplating all the way.

As the door was opened by a porter who cried, "All tickets !" he attempted to jump out upon the platform.

Dick was about to dash at him, when the necessity of his interfering was put an end to by the farmer.

He, too, had been feigning sleep, and nursing his malevolence against a supposed woman, who had the audacity to empty his spirit flask without so much as giving him a smile in return.

"No, my lady," he said, grasping the inspector's skirts, "you do not go until it has come to you to refill my flask."

"Let go your hold !" roared the inspector, in a deep, bass voice.

"Ha ! a man disguised as a woman," shrieked the farmer. "Robbery—murder, perhaps. Stop—help—all of you who are children of the Fatherland."

He held on to the inspector, who, in deadly fear of Dick, made frantic efforts to get away, and the pair fell out together.

The row on the platform was prodigious. A dozen officials surrounded the farmer and the inspector, who fought and struggled together like a pair of demons.

The farmer was very considerably half-mad over the way which he had been "taken in." That he should have his flask emptied by a man disguised as a woman was an outrage which he could never pardon until the offender had expiated his crime in prison.

The hapless inspector yelled out his explanation of the origin of his disguise, but nobody listened to him. The commotion was so great that the voice of that one man counted as nothing.

"Drag them both away," cried a man, who by his uniform was high in authority there. "We cannot have the train stopped by two midnight ruffians. Clear away there. Are all in? Go !"

And then the door was banged to, and the train moved on, bearing with it our three friends, who were speechless, and almost helpless, with laughter.

"All goes well, so far," said Carl, as soon as he could speak ; "it is a good omen. We are halfway out of danger of arrest."

CHAPTER XXII.

DICK HAS A CURIOUS DREAM—AWAY TO MARSEILLES—AJAX UNDER ANOTHER NAME—A BRIEF REIGN.

O further hindrance to the escape of our friends from German territory arose. In two days they were in Paris, and put up at one of the quiet hotels for the night, intending to take a day and night's much needed rest.

The night they enjoyed ; but the day in Paris was not to be. Casting his eyes over the papers on the following morning Dick came across a paragraph in one of them which put an end to any further rest then.

It was as follows—

" Ajax, the athlete who was ignominiously beaten at the Hippodrome by the renowned Stronghow, a short time ago, passed through Paris yesterday. He was accompanied by his attendant Pan, who, on being interviewed said it was their intention to proceed to Marseilles, with the object of shipping for some other country. He refused to give any further clue to their projected destination."

He showed it to Carl, who read it, and looked up at him with a smile.

"We are going to Marseilles, too," he said.

"Yes," returned Dick. "But after that, when do you particularly desire to go to Burmah ?"

"Any time—years hence will do."

"Good. Then, with your permission, I will keep upon his track. I have no particular injuries of my own to avenge, but I do not think that the score on account of Muffins is half paid off."

"I rather like the idea of dodging this lumbering giant about," said Carl.

Muffins was not at the table.

By his own choice, and in a really becoming manner as became his position of follower, he took his meals with the servants, among whom he instantly established himself as a star of small, but peculiarly brilliant, magnitude.

"To Marseilles, then, at once !" said Dick. "Garcon, a time-table, please."

The ready garcon placed one before him with the rapidity of a skilled magician who carries such things up his sleeve.

A reference to it showed that a train for Marseilles started in an hour, and by travelling all night they could get there about ten on the following morning.

It was not quick travelling from an English point of view, but it was "express" in France, and they could do no better.

At all events, Ajax could not have travelled faster, and, in all probability, had taken a slower train to save expense.

A few things necessary in the way of attire had to be purchased, and half-an-hour sufficed for that to be done.

A cabriolet took them with their limited luggage to the station, so that they caught the train in the nick of time, and away they went, light-hearted enough, and filled with delight at the prospect of further humiliating the wretched Ajax.

Dick certainly thought something about Jacob Morelle, but again his faith in unearthing that mysterious individual to his own advantage was on the wane.

Somehow he fancied that the past had better be left alone.

A faint idea of his father's wandering life had taken possession of him, having arisen from a dream.

It was, in the way of night visions, somewhat remarkable, and so vivid that he could not shake off the conviction that there "was something in it."

He dreamt it during the night he had spent in Paris immediately he fell asleep.

He saw himself wandering in a beautiful garden, seeking for a jewel which he fancied he had lost. It was very brilliant and valuable, that he knew ; but in this dream he could give it no definite shape, not being able to call to mind where he had seen it.

But he certainly had—that fact was keenly impressed upon him—and he wandered on and on down walks with magnificent flowers on either side.

Suddenly he saw lying on the ground, far down the path, something gleaming like a star of the first magnitude.

He sprang towards it with a cry of exultation, but ere he had gone far a man, springing from he knew not where, barred his way.

"Go no further !" cried the strange figure. "To touch that jewel is ruin."

The speaker was a stranger to him, and he was a man of noble presence and a magnificent physique.

Although they had never met before, Dick, in his dream, recognised the stranger as his father.

But, heedless of the warning, and eager to grasp the jewel, he pushed the man aside and ran on.

The jewel increased in size and brilliancy as he drew near, and every pulse in his skin throbbed audibly.

He reached it, touched it, and then in a moment it was gone, and in its place a most repulsive, bloated snake.

Aghast at the change he stood, and the loathsome reptile, with a triumphant hiss, thrust out its flattened head and stung him.

The moment after all things changed around him. The fair garden disappeared, and in its place was a sunless desert—a tremendous dreary blank, stretching round him on every side.

And now the reptile hissed, and dexterously threw its coils around him, binding his arms to his side. He made one frantic, futile effort to free himself, and then—awoke !

A heavy perspiration lay on his brow, and with a feeling of fear, hitherto an utter stranger to him, he struck a match and lighted the candle by his bedside.

A reference to his watch showed that he had slept half an hour, at the outside.

"What am I AFRAID of ?" he asked himself. "I know of nothing—but DISHONOUR !"

He lay awake for awhile, thinking of his dream, but soon became composed, and slept again.

In the morning the vividness of the dream had somewhat faded ; but it left its mark behind

He was now in no hurry to go to Burmah, or to find Jacob Morelle.

But nevertheless it was to be his destiny to meet that man at a time and place when he least expected it.

Meanwhile, we must go with him to Marseilles, where he arrived after a wearying journey, and at once sought for information concerning Ajax and Pan.

The giant athlete was sure to be a marked man, and Dick speedily learnt that he had been masquerading in sailor's clothes.

He announced himself as " Strongbow, the Victor over Ajax "—a piece of consummate, impudent fraud that no doubt originated with the fertile Pan.

Dick felt doubly exasperated over this imposture. Anything more likely to annoy him could not have been designed.

But the probabilities were that he had not been considered in the matter—the trick had simply been resorted to as a means of getting popularity, and possibly, making money.

Furthermore, it was ascertained that he would sail on the morrow in the Murat, a vessel bound for the Orange Free State, with a general cargo and a few passengers.

Dick got the name of the agent, ascertained that three berths were open to him if he did not mind a few inconveniences, and closed the affair on the spot.

The money was paid, and he promised to be on board at midnight.

"To-morrow, when we get to sea," he said, " I mean to give Ajax a pleasant surprise. Until then Muffins and I must be sick in our berths. Can't you show yourself and speak sympathisingly of your suffering friend ?"

"If I am able," replied Carl, with a grimace ; "but I am not sure that the beautiful sea will not put me on my back. I have never been afloat before."

As agreed, so the plan was carried out.

The trio went on board the Murat at midnight, partook of a hearty supper in the cabin with the captain, a genial old merman, who had seen much of the world, and then went to their berths.

In the morning Carl was up betimes, and attended to the two sick (?) passengers by smuggling a very fair breakfast to them, and at nine o'clock he imparted to them the good news that Ajax and Pan had come on board.

On the ship's books they appeared in false names, and Dick up to that time was only known as " Mr. Smith,' a simple and convenient cognomen for the occasion.

Ajax was attired as a sailor, and presented, indeed, a striking appearance.

As he strutted about the deck he was an object of awe to the diminutive French seamen, who took good care to give him plenty of room.

Presently he called for a chair, and one of the light deck-seats was given him. With a contemptuous laugh he took it in his hands and snapped it asunder, throwing the pieces into the sea.

"Hi ! captain," he shouted, " I want a chair—do you hear ?—a CHAIR !"

" Monsieur must endeavour to restrain himself. The usual chair for ze deck haf been given him !"

" Can I have a chair or not ?" roared Ajax.

" Monsieur shall have a chair," answered the captain.

A good strong chair was brought him, and in it Ajax sat at his ease, insistently puffing at his cigar in a demonstrative manner.

"Ah ! my friend," thought Carl, " make your hay while the sun shines. Your reign will soon be over."

He went down to Dick and reported what he had seen. Dick laughed quietly.

" We will let him have a day's fun," he said, "and to-morrow the extinguisher shall be put over him."

CHAPTER XXIII.

THE END OF THE USURPER'S REIGN—LOWER THAN EVER—A WAY TO DISPOSE OF MUFFINS.

HE passengers had a taste of Ajax's humour at the dinner-table that day. He took the last seat, grumbled that he was not helped first, ate enough for half-a-dozen people, and then asked, " what he had paid his money for ?"

Feeling sure that everybody was afraid of him, he acted like a bully and a cur, riding roughshod over people who yielded to him.

The captain yielded to him, but gave out signs that there would be a limit to his endurance. Pan, observing these symptoms, and knowing how soon his master would break away if boldly tackled,

DICK STRONGBOW:
The Diamond King,
AND WONDER OF THE WORLD.

He threw his arms around Dick, but the next moment he was on his back.

No. 4.   Price One Penny.

gave him a little advice when they went to bed in their double berth.

"Soften your antics before the officers of this vessel," he said, "and lay it on a little thicker with the underlings. They can't help themselves."

Ajax, a complete booby in his hands, obeyed him to the letter.

On the morrow he exhibited his oppressive bearing to the servants and seamen only. The offensive words he uttered, and the exasperating things he did, need not here be set down. By noon he had made himself thoroughly obnoxious to everybody.

Carl having reported these things to the invalids, Dick answered that he was quite well.

"It is time for me to get up," he said, "and drop down the usurping Strongbow, and put the real man in his place."

Muffins also "got well" at the same time, and, having dressed, followed his master on deck.

Carl Yemitz followed, and, like a spectator who anticipated enjoying himself, drew a little aside to watch the scene.

Ajax was on deck near the mainmast, railing at a seaman who "rudely brushed by him."

The man explained that the ship suddenly rolled, and so he accidentally fell against him.

"Confound you!" bellowed Ajax. "Is Strongbow the man for every fool to knock against?"

"Certainly not," replied Dick, who was standing close behind him. "Woe to the fool who tries it on with me!"

Ajax heard the voice, and in a moment the horribly *empty* feeling he had experienced before in the presence of Dick came upon him.

He staggered against the mainmast, and, turning round, stared at him with the eyes of a lobster which has had the ordinary interview with the boiling-pot.

Dick was quietly angry, and that form of anger is not to be trifled with. He walked up to Ajax, and took the helpless, dismayed bully by the throat.

Having favoured him with a "nip," he relaxed his hold a little, and said—

"So you are Strongbow, are you? Speak up, you lying ruffian!"

"No-o-o, I'm not," stammered Ajax.

"Louder! Let all on deck hear you."

"No-o-o!"

"That's better," said Dick, letting go of him. "And now kindly tell those around you *who* you are."

Some of the passengers and the captain had been drawn to the spot by the unwonted scene, and to them Ajax was desired to address himself.

"I—I—am Ajax!" he stammered.

"The man who was defeated by Strongbow?"

"Y—e—s."

"And who am I?" asked Dick.

"You—are—are—Strongbow!"

It was not without a struggle that the dismayed giant got out these words, which excited the utmost surprise in those around.

"Gentlemen," said Dick, addressing the captain and passengers, "this miserable imposter has told the truth against himself. I am Strongbow—and you need not think of this name with fear, for I am no bully to those who are physically weaker than myself. As for him"—pointing at Ajax—"if the feeblest among you stood boldly up to him, he would run away like a mongrel dog!"

"That's true, master!" said the delighted Muffins, who was standing near. "He ran away from me once! Ha—ha—ha!"

The expression on the face of Ajax as he glanced at the laughing boy was so ludicrous that the passengers roared with delight.

So did the seamen who watched events from afar.

And now another interested person appeared on the scene in the person of Pan, who had been below to get some drink for himself and Ajax.

As soon as he saw a little crowd collected he knew that something was wrong, and rightly guessed that his master had something to do with it.

Advancing quickly, he cried out—

"Hullo! what's this? Not all on one man, I hope? I tell you that you've got to think twice before you tackle the famous Stro—"

He stopped short, leaving the word uncompleted, for there, quietly and contemptuously regarding him, was the real Simon Pure, the genuine Strongbow.

"May lightning wither all on board," hissed Pan. "How came you here?"

"Better language," said Dick, "or you will be put under confinement—as things are, I doubt if either of you can be allowed to mingle with decent people again."

"Not at *my* table," said the captain, quietly, now speaking for the first time. "Zey can mess wif ze seamen or ze steward. Such conduct I nevare zee at my table."

"You hear," said Dick, "you two. Which do you choose—the seamen's mess or the steward's cabin?"

"Can we be put ashore?" asked Pan, violently.

"At ze end, not before," drily replied the captain; "ve do not stop on ze vay."

"Put me where you like," hissed Pan; "give us no food if it pleases you. Now, you blubberly booby, come out of it, down below you go. Hang all such mountains of cowardice, I say."

Followed by the laughter of the spectators the precious pair shuffled across the deck and disappeared below.

Dick then explained matters to the captain and two or three others around him, mainly for the purpose of finishing Ajax. He was no braggart on his own account.

He showed them the ring given him by the King of Sweden, and in response to a request from the captain, promised at a convenient time to give them an exhibition of his wonderful muscular powers.

"And you may rest assured," he said, with a smile, "that I shall not use them in any way, except to amuse."

They were all charmed with him, especially the captain who insisted on embracing him, and afterwards honoured Muffins with a hug, to the great astonishment of that young adventurer.

Then Carl was brought forward and, as the friend of Dick Strongbow, made much of—altogether a complete change came over those aboard the ship, and the voyage promised to be a very pleasant one.

Meanwhile, Pan and Ajax, shut up in their sleeping cabin, certainly not big enough to swing a cat in, reviewed the position.

"It seems to me," said Pan, "that it is Strongbow's game to hunt us to death. Now comes the question, what is to be done?"

"We can do nothing," wailed Ajax.

"*You* can do nothing," snarled Pan. "Is there such another lily-livered THING as you on earth?

I tell you something's got to be done, and, first of all, we'll sting him. That boy of his must be got rid of."

" I will have nothing to do with murder," whined Ajax.

"Wouldn't you like to kill him—out with it ?"

"Ye-e-s."

"But you dare not ? Speak up."

"No-o."

" *I* don't want *you* to do it," said Pan ; "that small job I'll take on myself, and do it in such a way that they may suspect much, but will not be able to prove anything."

"They'll prove it somehow," moaned Ajax.

"They won't—they can't," said Pan. "People, especially boys, often fall overboard, and, by all that is confounding, his Muffins shall go. There's no hurry—to-morrow, the next day—a week hence. Any time before we get into port. But go he shall— I *swear* it."

"Pan, you mustn't do it," said Ajax. "They are sure to suspect I've had a hand in it."

"Of course they will," replied Pan, "and what is that to me ? Let 'em suspect. And why shouldn't you be in it ? I want to kill the boy, ϗ do you. I'm ready to do it, and you are not. That's the only difference between us."

"Look here," continued Pan, dropping his voice, "how easy it is. By-and-bye it will be very hot. By day and night, too, everybody will want to be on deck. The boy, a street lad, to whom fresh air is life, will be sure to be there. He'll fall asleep alone one night, and then how easy to steal up near him. Watch your chance. Grab hold of him, and away he goes overboard."

"He'll wake up, Pan."

" I'll put you to sleep for good and all, if you keep a snivelling that way. It's easy to do it, and shall be done."

CHAPTER XXIV.

A QUIET NIGHT AT SEA—PAN FINDS MUFFINS ASLEEP—BUT NOT QUITE SO SOUND AS HE THOUGHT.

SWEET and soft was the balmy air. The Murat had been many days at sea, and was approaching her destination swiftly. All hearts were merry on board, save the two that beat in the breasts of Ajax and Pan. These worthies had been severely let alone by the other passengers, and partook of their meals by themelves.

By day they were very little on deck, but at night they would steal up and prowl about the deck, and woe betide them if they got in the way of any of the seamen.

A dab in the face with a mop or a kick would be sure to precede the words, " Get out of the way, will you ?" And out of the way they had to get.

That Ajax should endure that sort of thing is not to be marvelled at, for we know the stuff he was made of, but Pan's resignation was very strange.

Whatever his faults were, he had his share of brute courage, and, under ordinary circumstances, would not have endured an insult from a man of his own size. But he restrained himself because he was playing a deep game. He could put up with

a lot so long as he revenged himself in the end upon Dick Strongbow.

A daily witness of the devotion of the boy to his master, and Dick's kindly interest in him, there was evidence enough to assure him that a blow struck through Muffins would tell.

So he watched and waited for an opportunity to carry out his project—referred to in our last chapter—but without success.

Time was growing short, the long and weary journey was coming to an end.

If anything was to be done it must be done quickly.

Dick's popularity on board was unbounded, and Carl was only second to him.

The young German sang well, and the captain having a mandoline on board, he often discoursed sweet music, to the great delight of all hearers.

There were two ladies on board, the wife and daughter of a passenger named Lefrau. The girl's name was Aimée, and, if not exactly beautiful, she was pretty and vivacious.

A brother of Lefrau had left him a farm in the Orange Free State, and they were going out to it. If they liked the country they would settle there. If not they would sell out and go elsewhere.

For the present, we need only record that the Lefraus and Carl, in spite of the natural antagonism of the two races, were excellent friends. Aimée especially appreciated the young German's society.

To return to the main thread of our story.

It was a beautiful night, with sufficient breeze for sailing, but very warm. The sailors, in their characteristic way, declared that they were beginning to feel the hot breath of Africa.

In the cabin the passengers were partaking of dinner, and would soon be on deck. Muffins was already there.

He was moving about in a lazy, dreamy way ; but, finding that too tiring, threw himself down upon a pile of rope to the leeward of the vessel just to rest a bit.

He did not intend to go to sleep, but the drowsy god stole upon him and closed his eyes.

The men of the watch were all forward with their eyes ahead where they knew the land lay.

In the morning they expected to sight it, and the sailors' longing to get ashore was upon them all.

But there was one pair of eyes hard by that were not fixed upon the sea. They were the evil eyes in Pan's head, which was peeping up just above the companion.

He was looking at Muffins, who had dozed off, and was executing a variety of head movements, nodding this way and that, as sleepers in an uneasy position are apt to do.

After two or three jerks, which nearly woke him up, he settled out at full length on the rope, and went off sound and still. The wicked heart of Pan throbbed fiercely with exultation.

"At last !" he muttered.

Having cast a backward glance, and seeing the stairs clear, he stepped lightly up to the deck.

His feet had no shoes on. He could move about as quietly as a spectre.

The shadow of night had fallen upon the ocean, but the brilliant stars gave light enough for a tolerably clear view of the deck of the vessel from end to end.

Forward the men of the watch were still staring

ahead and whispering together. Muffins was drawing a long, deep breath, and now and then throwing in the softest of snores.

Pan, with body bent, crouching like a tiger approaching its prey, crept towards him.

All Pan's plans were laid. He knew what he meant to do, and exactly how it ought to be done, if success were to crown his efforts.

At last he was close up to Muffins, and with a swift double movement he had him fast. One arm was put round the boy, and a hand pressed upon his mouth.

Muffins awoke and found himself almost a helpless prisoner. The instant he was aroused his active mind was fully alive to his peril.

There is nothing in the wide world that can wriggle like an active boy. Muffins was a past master in the art, and proceeded to twist about in a way that was very embarrassing to his assailant.

It was all he could do to keep a hand over the boy's mouth and keep him from wriggling out of his arms.

Muffins fought, and kicked, too, with a ferocity beyond his years. Pan received several nasty stinging blows in the face, and the legs of Muffins worked like two drumsticks in the hands of an expert drummer.

But he held the boy in a deadly grip, and staggered to the side of the ship with the intention of casting him into the sea. And he would have done it too, but for the last resource adopted by the boy.

Abandoning the beating process with his hands, he fixed them in Pan's hair with the grip of mortal terror, and held on.

In vain did the villain endeavour to loosen his hold—the very effort to tear the boy's hands away added to the pain he was suffering.

"Let go, you little fiend!" he hissed, between his teeth.

It was an involuntary exclamation, and fatal to his project.

The words were heard by the men of the watch, and, turning, they saw the boy and man struggling by the side of the vessel.

In a body they swooped down upon Pan, dragged him back, and, despite his mad struggles, tore the boy from his grasp.

The commotion created was heard below, and the passengers came running up the companion, Dick Strongbow foremost.

A few words from the excited Muffins explained what had taken place, and a howl of indignation burst from the seamen. Then there they would have seized Pan and cast him overboard, but for the presence of their captain, and he, of course could not permit such a thing.

"He must be tried ashore for his crime," he said. "Put him down in the fore hold—it has little in it."

"I will put him there," said Dick, quietly.

He pinned the now quaking Pan by the arms and raised him above his head.

"Open the hatchway!" he cried.

The men were already at work upon it, and in half-a-dozen seconds it was thrown back.

Then Dick marched up to the dark opening and cast Pan down it as if he had been a bundle of offensive rags.

They heard him fall upon some packages below, and then he began to groan and curse.

"Where is his companion?" cried Dick.

Somebody said that Ajax was below, and Dick, followed by a sailor bearing a lantern, sought him in his cabin.

They found him huddled up close to his berth, quaking with terror. When he saw Dick he began to beg piteously for mercy.

"Do you know anything of this night's work?" demanded Dick.

"I begged of him not to do it," was the answer.

"Ah! you do know," said Dick, "and were too cowardly or villainous to warn us. Come out here and join your brother scoundrel."

"Have—you—thrown him into the sea?" asked Ajax, with his eyes standing out of his head.

"No; he is spared for a death more worthy of him," replied Dick. "Good seamen drown—knaves are hung. Come out, I say!"

Ajax, shivering, got upon his feet, and followed Dick from the cabin, up to the deck, where he was shown the open hold.

"Mercy!" he said.

"Go down!" said Dick.

Shivering like a nervous bather on the brink of a stream, Ajax stood still, fearing to take the plunge; but, Dick, who was hot with anger, became impatient, and hastened his movements with a kick on that part of his anatomy where such an assault is considered lawful.

He dropped with a groan upon the edge of the hatchway, his legs dangling over.

Thus he remained for a moment, and then one of the seamen gave him a push that sent him down.

"Close the hatches, and leave them to pass the night there!" cried the captain.

It was done, and then the passengers gathered in a circle to hear the further details of Muffins' story.

What the boy told them made it clear that a villainous and cowardly murder had been attempted, and loud and deep were their exclamations of indignation.

"What is to be done with them?" asked Lefrau.

"One of two things," replied the captain. "We must either take them back with us to be punished in France, or have them tried by the authorities of the Free State."

The latter was really the only course practicable and that was eventually decided upon.

How far it was successful in gaining a just punishment for the offenders we shall see later on.

CHAPTER XXV.
LANDING CARGO—THE FLAT-BOTTOMED BOATS—BOER JUSTICE.

"CAPTAIN," said Carl, in French, at breakfast on the following morning, "it is not quite clear to me how you carry on trade with the Orange Free State. It is fringed by a line of mountains near the shore, and it has, I believe, no port."

"Ah! so," the captain answered, "but it is easy. We anchor off the mouth of the Orange River, and flat-bottomed boats bring down hides, tallow, and other products of the country. All who go into the State return by the same boats."

"It is the first time I have heard of the trade," said Carl.

The answer was a shrug and a smile, which implied that the trade, if little known by the world at large, was not to be despised.

"We are watched for," said the captain, presently, "and the boats will arrive within a few hours of our casting anchor."

Land was sighted a few hours after this conversation, and just before sunset the Murat anchored off the mouth of the great river.

A gun was then fired, and it was answered by one from the rugged shore.

What a forbidding-looking country it was, with its tenantless coast, and an almost unbroken line of rugged mountains that sloped in some places right down to the sea, stretching away right and left.

In some places there were terrible cliffs, against the face of which the sea beat with restless, but apparently wasted, energy.

The gap through which the river flowed was wide, with shelving, almost precipitous, rocks on either side.

"It doesn't look promising," said Dick, as he walked the deck with Carl.

"Well, we can go back, if you think it will be better," replied our hero.

"No, let us see something of the Boers, if for nothing more than testing their pristine dealing qualities."

Muffins, who had fared very badly at the hands of Pan, had passed the day in his berth, with bandages dipped in arnica upon the bruises arising out of the ruffian's grip.

Before retiring to rest the two friends visited him, and found that he was going on well.

"There isn't much the matter with me, gentlemen," he said. "I am only a little bit stiff."

"Can we do anything more for you?" asked Dick.

"No, sir. You do more than I deserve or could wish for," replied Muffins. "I am very grateful, indeed, I am."

They left him and went to their berths, where they slept soundly all night.

Dick had a dreamless time of it, and when he awoke daylight was streaming through the porthole in his cabin. He got up, leaving Carl in the companion berth still asleep.

While dressing he heard the sounds of great activity above, and on going upon the deck found half-a-dozen burly-looking men talking to the captain in a guttural language that was supposed to be English.

Moored to the vessel were a number of big, flat bottomed boats, filled with bales, and with men prepared to pass them up to the deck.

They were a heavy-eyed, surly-looking set, and Dick was far from being fascinated with them.

They took no notice of him—not even so much as giving him "Good-morning."

Those on deck were very busy bargaining with the captain, who was showing them some samples of cutlery and cloth, which they handled and inspected with the keen air of judges and close bargain-makers.

Soon the business of clearing the boats was begun, and in an incredible short space of time it was done.

First of all the Boers' goods were shipped, and then the return cargo was passed down to the boats.

One was left clear for the passengers, and the captain had to explain he had two prisoners on board who were worthy of punishment.

The story of the attempted drowning of Muffins was told, Dick standing by quietly listening, and the Boers taking in the details with stolid gravity.

Dick was introduced as prosecutor, no reference being made to his great athletic powers, and was favoured with glances of cool, contemptuous indifference.

The Boers said they were willing to take the prisoners ashore and try and punish them ; but, of course, there were legal expenses.

"I will pay them," said Dick.

"No—first—once," insisted the Boers.

The sum they asked was equivalent to ten pounds in English, which Dick paid, merely stipulating that he should go in the same boat with the prisoners and be a witness to the working of Boer justice.

"So it be," said one of the Boers, a tall young man, built like an ox, who was smoking a cigar six inches long. He was called Jurand. "All go one boat."

The boat reserved for the passengers remained behind, the rest left, and, later on, in an hour or so, our friends were summoned to take their places in it.

Personal luggage was brought up and put into the boat, and then the Lefrau family, Dick, Carl, Pan, and Muffins, having taken leave of the captain and crew, took their seats in the lumbering river craft.

Last of all, both handcuffed, Ajax and Pan were put on board, and the boats were pushed off.

The tide had turned and took them slowly up the river. Four Boers accompanied them to work the boat, and among them was Jurand.

He acted as steersman, using a heavy oar, or sweep as it is called, and he was, in a rough way, the very prince of savageness.

He took no notice of the passengers, except now and then casting a glance of approval at Aimée, which excited the ire of Carl, who showed a strong inclination to get up and do his best to pitch him overboard.

But, acting on the whispered counsels of Dick, he restrained himself, and in gloomy silence the party proceeded up the river.

Ajax and Pan sat in the bow, hampered in their fetters, scowling, when they could do so without being observed, at Muffins and Dick.

The boat was moved along with two oars, worked in turns by the Boers, and the tide now being swift they made fair progress for six hours, and then, the river slackening its speed, the boat was turned towards the shore and moored fast to a tree growing near the water.

It was a wild country ; but on the slope of a broken hill, which, in Boer language, is called a koppie, was a log-house.

Jurand told them that his cousin lived there, and they could rest at his house, if they chose.

A general move was made in that direction, for sitting so long in the ill-constructed boat had a cramping effect.

Ajax and Pan were left behind, but not for long. Jurand had a talk with them, and after it he unlocked their handcuffs, and set them free, personally accompanying them up to the log-house.

He had taken a great fancy to Ajax, who was certainly blessed with an imposing figure, and Pan, noticing this, lost no time in making capital out of his master's prowess as an athlete.

At the same time, he took good care to say nothing about Dick Strongbow's gift of strength, and Jurand remained in ignorance of it.

The log-hut proved to be more extensive than was at first supposed. It contained at least half-a-dozen apartments, and the general room was large enough to accommodate all the guests.

It had fittings very much on a level with a tap-room in our own country, and it possessed an aroma which showed that it frequently received guests who were not averse to smoking and drinking.

Aimée and her mother found it unendurable, and preferred strolling about outside—Carl, as a matter of course, kept them company.

Jurand's cousin was a typical Boer—burly, small-eyed, and reticent to surliness.

He received his guests without any greeting, and put drink before them without being asked for it.

Then he held out his hand and said—

"Pay."

It was a simple way of doing business which rather tickled Dick, and he good-humouredly gave the Boer two or three pieces of silver, that evidently pleased him, if satisfied grunts mean anything.

The drink was some coarse spirits, not unlike Hollands, and one sip of it sufficed for the guests. Muffins, of course, did not touch it at all.

When Jurand appeared, accompanied by Ajax and Pan, Dick ventured to remonstrate with him.

"They are slippery fellows," he said, "and may run away."

Jurand did not even favour him with an answer, but, with a swaggering air, lit a big cigar, and ordered drink for himself and the "prisoners."

Dick took no further notice of the affair, but resolved to await his opportunity to show this Boer that he had made a mistake.

The fiery spirit put a little courage into Ajax, who, arm-in-arm with Pan, bye-and-bye strolled up and down outside the log-house.

Jurand announced that the boat would start again at midnight, and stop next at a place called Vraal, where it would remain for two days.

Mr. Lefrau said he could not stop there so long. He wished to go on to his destination which was fifty miles further up.

"A fair at Vraal," said Jurand, coolly; "all stop."

And then he leered at Aimée, as if he had uttered a joke of surpassing merit for her benefit.

Dick and Carl took an opportunity to draw aside, and hold a short consultation together.

"Carl," said Dick, "what do you think of things?"

"Trouble ahead," replied Carl. "I think that Jurand and myself will come in contact—have a meeting."

"It seems to me an awful country, and I am sorry I brought you here."

"Don't think of me. Perhaps it is not as bad as we think. Wait until we get to Vraal."

"We must watch over the women."

"Yes, and over that Jurand. He is a complete ruffian."

Luckily the two friends were armed. Dick disliked firearms, but he knew that the use of them was occasionally necessary, and both he and Carl carried revolvers of a small pattern, but very effective in a shooting sense.

We will pass over the time intervening between this their first halt and the arrival at Vraal. It was a miserable journey enough, but the night was warm and they all slept more or less. Before the tide turned again, they had arrived at the town.

It was shortly after sunrise when the boat was moored, and the word was passed for all to go ashore.

Vraal was not a very striking place, being a collection of wooden buildings of various sizes, straggling about on level land, around which were the jagged uninviting hills and mountains.

But Vraal, though in itself nothing particular, was alive with people.

Rude, springless carts were to be seen in every direction, and on patches of green hobbled horses were feeding by the score.

Boers, with their wives and families, had come in from the outlying farms, and were still arriving.

The men for the most part were on horseback, and the women and children in the carts.

It was no doubt a great day for Vraal. On an open piece of ground a strong platform, with a railing round, had been erected, of which more anon, and on several of the houses poles had been hoisted, from the top of which pieces of bunting fluttered in the breeze.

No attempt was made by Jurand to keep guard over the prisoners Ajax and Pan. They were allowed to go ashore and wander where they willed.

Again Dick remonstrated, and the answer of the Boer was—

"Orange *Free* State. Noting prisoner here. Go, be hang you!"

CHAPTER XXVI.

THE FAIR AT VRAAL—BASUTO VERSUS BOER— GONE AWAY—DICK AND JURAND.

ERE is no place for my daughter or wife," said Lefrau. "We shall go and see ze country."

"I hope it is safe?" said Dick, anxiously.

"As safe as *here*," replied the Frenchman, significantly.

Dick was not averse to the family going away for the time, as he had a shrewd idea that there might be a slight disturbance in the fair during the day, but he suggested that Carl and Muffins should accompany them.

"I can't leave you here alone," said Carl.

"Have no fear for me," replied Dick, quietly. "I wish you *all* to be away. Now, go, there is a good fellow. Watch your opportunity, and get off unseen."

Jurand, who plainly had no suspicion that any of the party intended to absent themselves, had gone away to one of the houses, outside which a number of Boers had assembled. Pan and Ajax followed him, both well primed with coarse spirits, and full of swagger.

"Now is your chance," said Dick to his friends. "Off with you !"

They begged of him to accompany them, but he refused.

"I have something to do here," he said. "It is not much, and you cannot help me. Your presence will only embarrass me. Go, I beg of you."

Muffins, always obedient, went off with the others, who tore themselves unwillingly away, one and all with a foreboding of approaching evil.

Dick, left alone, took up a position near a log hut, where he could see what was going on without being himself an object of attention.

Presently he saw about a dozen mahogany-skinned savages, tall, well-built fellows, with shield and assegai (a short, strong spear), arrive in the village.

For clothing they had nothing but a cloth about the middle, and for ornaments a feather or two, and a few beads.

These were Zulus, part of a host of refugees from Zululand, who fled from the tyranny of Chatka, the then ruler of that land.

The new arrivals selected a piece of ground near the platform and squatted down thereon, occasionally exchanging a few words with each other, but taking no apparent notice of anything or anybody around them.

A little later on another party of savages, darker skinned, and not quite so tall as the Zulus, arrived.

They looked like model athletes, and, beyond a short club and a knife in their waist-cloth, bore no arms.

They were Basutos, a portion of the tribe which inhabit the Malatea Mountains.

A stronghold from which neither rival tribes or the Boers have ever been able to dislodge them.

They settled down on the side of the platform opposite to that selected by the Zulus, talking together in a somewhat vivacious manner.

Dick watched the two tribes with great interest for awhile, and then had his attention drawn to a man who went about ringing a bell, and bawling something in a language he did not understand.

The meaning of it was, however, soon made clear by the flocking up of Boer men, women, and children, into the open space near the platform.

The fair was open, and the fun of the day began.

It was fun of rather a solemn description at first, mainly consisting of buying and eating cakes and sweetmeats, which were sold by men and women from baskets, stands, and trays.

Vendors of spirits were there in abundance, and all—even the children—drank. The savages alone did not drink.

And now the man with the bell got upon the platform to make another speech, which was short and to the point, judging by the signs of approval.

Then up sprang two savages—a Zulu and a Basuto, who had thrown aside their weapons.

Without any preliminary movements they closed at once, and struggled for a fall.

The quick way they twisted and turned prevented the contest being closely watched.

It ended in the Basuto being thrown with a violence that would have scattered the wits of a less hardy man.

But the Basuto was up again in a moment, and he and his antagonist leapt from the platform, to be instantly replaced by two others.

Thus the tribes contested, and in the end were about equal.

Now a Basuto, and then a Zulu fell, the difference in height making no appreciative difference in their respective powers.

The spectators uttered exclamations of delight when there was a fall, but there was no marked demonstration of approval or enthusiasm until some of their own young men appeared upon the platform.

Two lanky Boers, about twenty years of age, competed first, and one was soon thrown upon the back of his head, which successfully stood the shock. He walked off the platform apparently none the worse for it.

Other couples contested, some of them young, others in the prime of life, and settled the question of supremacy, and at last Jurand appeared upon the platform, accompanied by a huge Boer, whom he threw easily.

The demonstration of approval from the spectators showed that the victory was popular. Jurand was a well-known athlete among his people.

Instead of leaving the platform he proceeded to make a speech, challenging all there to compete with him.

The chief of the Zulus accepted the challenge, and was thrown.

Next a Basuto jumped upon the platform, and shared the same fate.

After that there was a pause.

"Who next ?" cried Jurand.

Dick, standing well back in the crowd so as to escape notice, then saw, somewhat to his amazement, the giant Ajax ascend the platform.

His appearance was hailed with a shout of surprise.

Jurand made another speech, the pith of which was that Ajax was the champion English athlete, and, having heard of the famous Vraal fair, had come so far to compete with him.

Dick could not grasp the meaning of all he said, but the trick about to be played was pretty clear to him.

He was not astonished to see Ajax, when he closed with Jurand, make a perfect sham of wrestling with him, and, finally, permit himself to be thrown.

That piece of humbug was no doubt the price of his being practically set free.

What a roar of voices !

"Jurand—Jurand !" was the cry from five hundred throats. Even the savages laid aside their phlegm and, dancing, uttered strange cries, waving their weapons over their heads.

The swagger on Jurand was now fearful to behold. It was a perfect burlesque ; but the Boers took it seriously, and shouted until they were hoarse.

While this was going on, Dick, in his irresistible way, forced himself through the crowd, and, ascending the platform, advanced towards Jurand, who stared at him with insolent surprise.

Dick extended his arms, as he had seen the others do, as a challenge for a fall.

"Away !" cried Jurand. "I kill you !"

"A fall," replied Dick, "unless you are afraid."

"Fool!" said Jurand, contemptuously. "I kill you"

A silence had fallen on the crowd—all being anxious to hear what was said.

Jurand, turning his face towards the people, cried out in the crude mongrel tongue of his people—

"An insolent Englishman asks me to kill him. Shall it be done?"

"Kill him!" shrieked the Boers.

"I will break his back," said Jurand, "as we crack the neck of a chicken."

Two of the spectators, and two only, knew better than that. Pan and Ajax, standing at the foot of the platform, exchanged glances.

"Let us clear out," said Pan. "Having settled that Dutch lubber he will be on to you and me."

Pan was no longer insolent when speaking of Dick. The way he had been handled and thrown down the hold of the Murat took all that nonsense out of him.

So they elbowed their way back through the crowd, and vanished from the scene.

Dick stood quietly in the middle of the platform awaiting Jurand, who, with careless ease, approached him, confident of victory.

He threw his arms around Dick, who gripped him hard, and the next moment was on his back with a hundred lightning flashes before his eyes.

Such a fall, and so speedily brought about, took all his breath away, and that of the spectators for a moment also.

Jurand did not attempt to get up, so Dick, inserting two fingers under his waist-belt, raised him, carried him to the side of the platform, lifted him over the rails without any show of exertion, and dropped him among the crowd below.

A wild scream from the delighted savages rent the air.

Basutos and Zulus leaped upon the platform, and, uniting in their joy, danced and capered round Dick, screaming and leaping into the air.

A murmur of anger was heard among the crowd.

What did this defeat of their champion athlete mean?

Could it be possible that it had indeed been accomplished?

Somebody cried out "foul play," and the cry was taken up.

Men shouted and produced their weapons. A call was made to go up and kill this daring, cunning Englishman.

In terror the women and children fled.

Jurand, not quite recovered from the shock of his fall, was assisted through the crowd.

"Shoot him," he said, between his teeth. "He spat poison upon me, and took away my strength."

The lie served, and there arose cries of "Shoot him," "Hang him," "Death to the poisonous dog of an Englishman!"

And Dick, what of him?

With folded arms and a contemptuous smile on his face, he stood on the platform prepared for the attack.

And gathered behind him were the Basutos and Zulus regarding the seething crowd with knitted brows and eyes that flashed fire.

One bold man and a score of untutored savages against a hundred Boers, armed to the teeth. The odds were very great, but the battle is not always to the strong in numbers.

Whether it was so in this case our next chapter will tell.

―――

CHAPTER XXVII.

DICK CLEARS THE WAY—EMBARRASSING FOL-LOWERS—BASUTO AGAINST ZULU.

FURIOUSLY raged the crowd of Boers, who were as ignorant and superstitious as the English people of the middle ages.

The assertion of Jurand, that he had been overcome by unfair, that is, un-canny means, aroused the fanatical blood in their veins, and the cry of "Kill him—shoot the man-witch!" was heard by those near the platform, while those behind shouted and yelled like maniacs.

All the women and children had fled, and were in hiding in the houses or elsewhere near the village. They knew by experience the danger of a riot among those semi-savages, the Boers.

Dick's eyes flashed fire, and all that was combative in his nature was aroused. He had no weapons but his strong arms, but he was not afraid.

The Basutos and Zulus, who had rallied round Dick as men of all ages have rallied round heroes, danced about him, twirling their weapons and uttering wild cries of defiance.

The Boers were the natural enemies of both tribes, and the half-stifled hatred of the savages, fanned by their enthusiastic admiration of Dick, burst into a flame.

But Dick did not desire to see the simple savages fall victims to their suddenly inspired reverence for a stranger.

Alone he would do better with that mob.

Parting the circle of savages with his resistless arms, he walked up to the hand-rail of the platform, and, resting his hands upon it for a moment, stared defiantly at the surging crowd.

"Why don't you shoot, you curs?" he cried in a voice that rose above the tumult.

In reply several shots were fired; but with an imperfect aim.

Dick heard the bullets whistle by, and a smile passed across his face.

"They are all afraid, and cannot shoot," he said.

His hands closed upon the rail before him.

It was stout and strong, and three ordinary men could not have loosened it; but with no apparent effort he tore it up, and, breaking off two of the supports, made for himself a huge, roughly-shaped club.

It was a terrible weapon in the hands of such a man, and when he leapt through the gap he had made to the ground, the crowd swayed back like the Red Sea from the rod of Moses.

A swarthy torrent of savages poured down after him, shrieking and whirling their spears and clubs

"Are you ready?" asked Phil Norton. "Yes." was the fierce answer of both.

ripe for a fight with the Boers, hungering for their blood.

"Clear the way there!" shouted Dick, as he swung the heavy piece of rail over his head.

"Shoot him!" yelled some of the more daring Boers, valiant because they were at the back of the crowd.

A rush was made to close in upon him, and the Boers nearest to him begun to yell and cry like frightened children.

But they would have closed in upon Dick against their will unless he took action to save himself.

He wished to avoid bloodshed, but they would not let him.

Once they fairly closed in upon him he would be as a man in a strait-waistcoat, and his own safety demanded energetic action on his part to gain his freedom.

Like a beam swayed to and fro by steam power he swung the broken rail, dashing down the Boers right and left, until a panic seized them all as one man, and, breaking away in all directions, they ran for their lives.

Flushed, and with eyes that literally shot fire, Dick walked straight out of the village, or town as they called it, taking the road Carl Yemitz and the others had traversed that morning.

And still the excited savages kept in close attendance upon him.

They danced behind and before him, ran round him as he walked, leaped in the air, and prostrated themselves before him.

The latter form of adulation was rather embarrassing, as the thing was occasionally done so suddenly that Dick was in imminent danger of being tripped up. Altogether, he would rather have gone on alone, for it was not quite clear to him how his admiring dusky attendants were to be got rid of.

As it was of the utmost importance that he should rejoin his friends without delay and warn them of the change affairs had taken, he turned aside from the road and climbed up a hill which gave him a good view of the country.

Just then he cast a glance back at the scene of his recent exploit, and saw the Boers running about like ants whose underground home had been destroyed by the introduction of a spade.

Some were gathering their women and children together, or harnessing their horses for immediate departure.

All the signs indicated that the fair had been broken up.

Superstition and terror were sending the Boers away to their homes.

With a smile upon his face he turned in another direction, and about a mile off he saw a man and a boy strolling about in an idle sort of way.

He had no doubt it was Carl Yemitz and Muffins.

If it were them, what had become of the Lefrau family?

He closely surveyed the country around, but could see nothing of them.

From speculations concerning their fate he was aroused by a sudden outburst of discordant cries from the savages, who were about twenty yards away.

To his surprise they had divided themselves into two bands—Basutos and Zulus—and ranged themselves in battle order.

The two lines of men were only a few feet apart, and the needed frenzy of the savage warrior was being worked up by dancing and gesticulating at each other.

Some of their movements were directed at Dick, who was soon able to interpret what it all meant.

The two bodies of savages, antagonistic as races for many years, *were about to fight for him*, either to be their leader, their friend, or their captive.

Dick would liked to have stopped the fight, but he saw it was a matter in which his strength would be of little avail. He could only have successfully interfered by killing them all.

With loud war-cries the two bodies of savages suddenly closed, and in a moment became a mass of fighting men.

"I can do nothing to serve them," thought Dick, "not even by waiting to see who are the victors."

So he quietly walked down the hill in the direction of the distant figures, leaving the dusky warriors to fight it out.

For awhile the riot of the fight raged furiously, but the cries soon began to slacken, and presently ceased.

Dick, looking back, saw about a third of the Zulus running away to the right, closely followed by a portion of the victorious Basutos.

He watched the scene curiously, for the Zulus were the finer race, and the assegai was assuredly a more deadly weapon than the club.

Why did they fly?

The question was answered by the Zulus themselves, who, as one man, suddenly pulled up, and, wheeling round, faced their pursuers.

The Basutos were about twenty yards behind, and they too stopped.

The peril of their position was apparent to them.

In point of numbers they were one more than the Zulus, but that was of no great matter.

Up went the arms of the Zulus.

The deadly assegais were poised, the aim taken, and the weapons thrown.

Down went every Basuto but one, transfixed by the keen-pointed weapons of the Zulus.

The one man who had escaped, simply because there was no foe to kill him, bounded away and vanished among the broken ground.

It was a matter of moments—all done while one could have counted five with moderate speed.

Dick was startled by the suddenness of the whole thing, and he could not help asking himself why the Zulus had not hurled their weapons at first.

We will answer the question for the benefit of the reader.

At close quarters the Zulu does not care to part with his assegai; nor is his aim so sure as at a moderate distance. And, again, as in this case, he will, as a rule, only throw it as a last resource to kill a foe and save his own life.

If he has two or more of his potent weapons in his possession, then, indeed, he will be prodigal in the use of them.

Dick had had enough of savage company for one day, and at once put a clump of bushes between himself and the Zulus.

Before emerging from this cover he looked out carefully, and saw they had disappeared.

"It is a strange dramatic finish to the morning's

work," he said. "I have begun my life here with something stirring, and now to see if it is Carl and Muffins that I saw from the hill."

CHAPTER XXVIII.

A NIGHT UPON THE HILLS—BOER SHARP-SHOOTERS—A DROP FOR THE BOERS.

S Dick approached nearer he saw that it was indeed Carl and Muffins, and furthermore that they were alone; but seeing Dick they altered their sauntering pace to a quicker one and speedily joined him.

"Where are the Le-fraus?" asked Dick.

"Well, we've parted for the present," replied Carl, rather sadly, "and I hope you will agree with what I've done."

"I am sure it was for the best."

"Well, I meant it to be so. The fact is, I haven't quite liked this country. I thought it better that they should go."

"But where have they gone, Carl? You haven't told me yet."

"Ah! friend Dick, so vivacious and so impatient. We Germans are slower—and now to my story. As we were moving about we met with a young Boer driving a conveyance *away* from the fair. He was going in the direction of Lefrau's destination, but, of course, would not go half the way. He said it would be easy enough to get there, and he would pass them on."

"You asked him to do it?"

"Of course. He seemed surprised to see us here, and, for a Boer, was not a bad sort of fellow. He told us he had no taste for fairs, and preferred the quietude of his farm, so it flashed on me hat his cart would be safer than the boat."

"But how about the luggage?" asked Dick.

"That will go on," said Carl. "The young Boer assured me that Jurand would not steal it. There is one good thing about these people. Despite their roughness they are neither thieves nor brigands."

"Your luggage will have to go on too," said Dick, grimly.

"How's that?" asked Carl.

Dick gave him the outline of the events of the morning, speaking in German because he did not wish to alarm Muffins.

But that astute young gentleman had learnt to understand the nature of things spoken of in that language.

"Master," he said, "please tell me what's happened? I'll promise you I won't be afraid."

So Dick told him, making matters lighter than they were, however, and Muffins, as he promised, showed no fear.

But they all felt a little grave.

The facts of the case were not to be shirked.

There they were, in a strange land, without any means of subsistence, and practically at war with the inhabitants, for it was a sure thing that the Boers, as soon as their first alarm had, in a measure, subsided, would send out the fiery cross against them.

Dick knew something of Boer life, and the fact that they were superb marksmen with the rifle was also known to him. Attempts to kill him off would be sure to be made as soon as opportunity offered.

"We must find some place to pass the night in," he said. "When in doubt about what to do there is nothing like sleeping upon it. I have half a plan in my mind, but it requires maturing."

"There is a place that may serve us for shelter for the night," said Carl; "it is about two of your English miles from here, and, luckily, we have some food."

Muffins carried a small parcel of refreshments, part of which had been brought from the village, and the rest purchased of the young Boer, who was taking home from the village liberal supplies for his farm.

Having found a spring and a secluded nook, the trio sat down and made a hearty meal.

"Food," said Carl, taking out his cigar-case, "puts a heart in a man. Things do not look so black as they did half an hour ago—in fact, they appear rather rosy. And now let us aid digestion with a smoke."

Muffins felt quite envious of his master and Carl as they sat with their backs to a big stone, contentedly smoking and chatting in an undertone. As a street boy he had often had a whiff from a cast-away end of a cigarette or stump of cigar, and he felt as if he would have liked one now.

"There's drawbacks to being so 'spectable," he sighed; and then he gave himself a blow on the head. "What a fool you are, Muffins! As if you wasn't having the life of a *king* with such a master. Blessed if I'd change *with* a king, or a queen, or any of our bloated 'stocracy. Who wants to sm—?"

Dick and Carl were considering what they would do. They were in sore need of a rifle each, with ammunition, for there was a prospect of their having a lonely life among the hills for a time.

With a rifle in a country which abounded with game they could not starve.

"And we must eventually do one of two things," said Carl; "either go south to Natal, or return to the coast on the chance of picking up with a vessel, like the Murat."

"Again I say we must sleep on it," said Dick.

They remained where they were without interruption until the day was almost gone, and then Carl undertook to guide Dick to his promised place of shelter.

It was a tumbledown old hut, which had once been occupied by some humble farmer.

Part of his rude furniture, mainly in a broken and rotten condition, was there still.

But the table, fixed in the floor, which was only beaten earth, remained sound, and there were two or three rickety stools to sit upon.

The place consisted of two rooms, and a stable at the rear.

In the latter was some hay, which had been kept dry by the airiness of the place.

The position of the hut was peculiar, it having been built on high land on the edge of a deep gully, at the bottom of which was a narrow water-course.

It was the dry season then, and no doubt in the rainy one the water-course was very much swollen.

Our friends had a look at it before going in, and Carl remarked that it would be an ugly place for a fellow, who, not knowing his way, rushed out of the hut and dropped into it.

"He would stand a good chance of hurting himself," said Dick, drily.

As there was nothing alarming about the place to keep them awake they went to rest at once, with the object of rising early with the sun and starting which ever way they decided to go.

The soft hay offering the best resting-place, they lay down upon that, and, being pretty well tired out, soon fell asleep.

Dick slept dreamlessly for awhile, and then suddenly awoke, to find himself in darkness and strange voices talking somewhere near him.

It was not without an effort that he succeeded in bringing his mind to bear upon his real position; but having succeeded in doing so he proceeded to locate the speakers.

They were in the living room of the hut, where the table and stools were.

Rising softly, he walked to the closed door, and now through one of the small chinks between the planks he could perceive the reflection of a faint light. As it flickered he judged it was from a small fire burning on the hearth.

The speakers were two in number, and in the language adopted by the Boers—a strange mixture of English, Dutch, and some native dialect—they were talking over the prospect of some "rare sport."

One said he could pick "him" out like a blessbok, and the other vowed he would riddle the "brute" with bullets.

They also talked of going to a certain point on the hills which would give them an extended view of the country round. From there they could scout and mark down "their man."

Dick had to supply the place of many incomprehensible words by putting in some of his own, so as to get at their meaning, but he did it correctly as events justified.

Who "him" and the "brute" were they did not make clear at first, although Dick shrewdly suspected that he was the object of their amicable intentions.

Before long all doubts on this point were set at rest.

They began to talk of the fair, then of Jurand, and, last of all, of Dick.

He was the "strong man," the "spell-maker," who was to be brought down like a blessbok, a species of deer that ran wild about the country, and scouts had been sent out in every direction to seek him out and shoot him.

Dick had had some experience of braggarts, and he was pretty sure that the two blatant Boers were made of stuff that could easily be scared. So he opened the door, and walked softly in.

They were seated at the table, eating some of the coarse bread and milk-cheese, of which Dick had seen abundance at the fair.

They were cutting it up with huge clasp-knives, which they employed as dangerous shovels to put the food into their mouths, escaping cut lips and tongues by a series of miracles.

Leaning against the wooden wall, in a corner of the hut, were their rifles, apparently first-class weapons. Hanging on a big nail were two cartridge-belts, containing about fifty cartridges in each.

Dick regarded the men quietly for a few moments, measuring them up.

They were young fellows, tall and raw-boned, with evil, cruel faces, such as are common in countries where perpetual war with others goes on.

Stepping into the room, Dick placed himself between the men and their rifles, saying, quietly—

"Good evening, gentlemen."

They started from their seats, and stared at him with eyes that "bounced" out of their heads. They recognised him, having probably been a part of the crowd round the platform in the morning.

"I have to thank you for your kind intentions towards me," said Dick, "but—"

They waited to hear no more. He simply raised his powerful arms as if to arrest them, and with a howl of terror they made for the door.

As the foremost pulled it open Dick heard the roar of a stiff night wind that was blowing. They darted out without looking behind them, and Dick, striding up, contemptuously kicked the door to.

"Not an ounce of grit in the pair!" he muttered. "Ah! is that you, Carl?"

The young German was standing in the doorway, yawning and stretching his arms, still heavy with a tendency to sleep.

"I heard some sort of a row," he said, "and came out to see what it was."

"We have had visitors," replied Dick; "two Boers. But they were in such a hurry to get away that they did not wait to be introduced."

"I suppose not, if you pressed them," laughed Carl.

"See," said Dick, "they have left their rifles behind. It is very kind of them."

He put some scattered sticks together, which the Boers had brought in with them, and by the blaze created the rifles were examined. They were first-class weapons, worth fully ten pounds apiece.

"This is a find," said Carl. "But how about your bashful guests? Perhaps they have only gone for some of their friends?"

"I do not think they will come back again," said Dick, easily.

And they did not return.

Neither Carl nor Dick went to rest again, and, by the early return of daylight, Dick found that he had slept longer than he thought.

With the first indication of the coming day Muffins was aroused, and, after a look out to see if anybody were about they all went out of the hut.

"The hills are not safe for us," said Dick, "and so I propose that we follow the track of the river—inland. We can breakfast as soon as we are under cover."

He had one rifle and Carl had the other. Around their shoulders they had slung the cartridge-belts, and Muffins stared at them in utter amazement.

"Master," he said, "had you them guns yesterday?"

"No," replied Dick; "some kind friends left them last night for us."

"I'm glad of that," said Muffins, relieved. "I was beginning to fancy that I couldn't remember."

As they were moving off Muffins, with boyish curiosity, walked to the edge of the gulch and peeped over.

One glance he cast down, and then with a short, sharp scream staggered back.

"Muffins!" exclaimed Dick, "don't make that noise."

"Master !" gasped Muffins, "there's two men down there, all of a heap, and quite still."

Dick and Carl stepped to the edge of the gulch and looked down.

There, indeed, were two men lying just as they had fallen.

Dick's visitors of an hour or two before !

In their hasty retreat they had rushed out, and, forgetting the dangerous pitfall, both had plunged headlong down, meeting with almost instant death.

Dick was moved by this gruesome spectacle.

After all they had done him no harm, and were young fellows who simply took upon themselves an office which they believed to be a right one.

They had set out to shoot one who "bewitched" and defeated their athletic champion, afterwards displaying strength that was passing that of an ordinary man

The first impulse of poor humanity anywhere—if they meet with anything they do not understand, and which appears to be dangerous—is to get rid of it by any means, fair or foul.

"It is a bad accident for them," said Dick, "but good for us. If they had not fallen down there, they would by this time have brought a host around us. It is a ghastly sight. Let us get away from it on to the river."

CHAPTER XXIX.

DICK TAKES POSSESSION OF A BOAT AND B SSES THE SHOW—A HUMBLED BULLY—THE MINERS' CAMP.

N with all speed, taking a bee-line, the trio made for the river.

The ground being broken, and here and there covered with trees and bushes, was all that could be desired to screen them from casual observation, and within an hour they were by the water's edge.

A glance at the river showed that the tide was on the turn, and would be shortly flowing inland. It would then be just the time for Jurand to start with his boat—if he started at all that day.

A project, which for coolness and daring was fully worthy of Dick, entered his head. Why should he not go with it—or *take* the boat if those who owned it objected to his company?

He mentioned it to Carl, who unhesitatingly approved of it.

"Boldness will carry the day," he said. "Let us go."

They had a little food left, which Carl divided, and they ate it as they walked along by the river.

There were huge trees growing rather close together on the banks, and they were safe from peering eyes inland.

The wood. as Dick knew, ran right up to the town, and the boat was moored to a tree on its outskirts.

By this time they had finished eating and partaken of a cool drink from the river ; they were near the town, and Dick, bidding Carl and Muffins wait for him, went forward to reconnoitre.

Keeping out of sight by stepping from tree to tree he succeeded in getting to a spot where he could view both the town and the spot where the boat was moored.

Nobody was stirring about the town, but in the boat, which was still moored, were seven men—Jurand, Ajax, and Pan, and four Boers whom Dick had not seen before.

They were re-arranging the luggage, and evidently preparing to start.

In a few minutes they would be ready.

Dick lost no time in getting back and apprising his friends of the state of things, and all three immediately raced for the boat.

They reached it as Jurand was casting off the rope, and without so much as a "by your leave," leapt in.

Had they dropped from the clouds, and, perhaps, some of the men thought they had done so, the Boers could not have been more astonished.

Jurand, Ajax, and Pan were like men scared into a speechless state, and could only stand and stare.

Dick drew in the rope, tossed it down, and said to the men—

"Out with your poles, and get her into mid-stream so that she may feel the tide !"

They obeyed in a mechanical sort of way, and Dick walked up to Jurand.

"You know me ?" he said.

Some strange words in Dutch burst from Jurand's lips ; but that was all.

"Give up your arms," said Dick.

Jurand made no effort to do so, and Dick spared him the trouble by taking them from his belt.

"Go and lie there," said Dick, pointing to the upper part of the boat.

And Jurand went and laid down—like a dog.

The boat was now in mid-stream, going slowly with the tide.

It was evident that this mode of progression would not serve them for long.

The next thing was to disarm Pan, Ajax, and the other Boers and bid them join Jurand.

Dick, Carl, and Muffins sat in the stern of the boat, the first named steering.

So they glided away out of sight of the town, unseen by any of the inhabitants, who had, after all, spent the night in carousing, from which they had not yet recovered.

"You are not to come this end of the boat night or day," said Dick, "nor until I bid you."

The Boers did not answer, they sat like figures of wood.

Ajax groaned and Pan snarled.

"Seven of us, and all give in to HIM," he hissed, "I believe you Dutchmen are right. He's more'n mortal."

All the drink and provisions were at Dick's end of the boat, and he was in no hurry to serve them out.

On glided the boat for awhile, but every mile the tide had less force, and at last Dick, seeing a pair of sweeps on board, ordered Jurand to fix them and put two men to work.

"You can settle among yourselves who is to do it," said Dick; "*but it has to be done!*"

Jurand, in a dumb, distraught fashion, put in the pegs for the sweeps, and motioned to two of the men to go to work.

They obeyed him, and the boat went on at an increased speed.

On, up the silent river, with shores that gave out no sign of human life.

Of animal life there was abundance.

When open spaces were reached they saw vast herds of deer of various species roving about—a sight to gladden the heart of that born slaughter-man, the lover of "sport."

Once they saw a puff of white smoke in the distance, and a deer fall from the unerring aim of some Boer wandering across the country.

But they did not see the man, and presently the banks were covered with trees again.

The morning was half-spent before Dick served out food to the seven men. His purpose was to cow them, and cowed they were.

One by one he bade them come down the big flat-bottomed boat and receive their rations—food, but not drink.

For the latter he gave one of them a tin dipper, and significantly pointed to the river.

When Pan came up Dick favoured him with a few words for his especial benefit.

"Pan," he said, "you are a small man, and, like all little curs, are given to snarling. Now, do not let me see you show your teeth again."

Pan lowered his eyes and crept back, drawing short, sharp breaths. Inside him raged a volcano, and he dared not show a spark of fire.

The booby-like appearance and bearing of Ajax sent Muffins into a fit of laughter, which extracted from the eyes of the cowardly giant a faint flash of anger.

By-and-bye the men were changed at the sweeps, and Ajax and Pan set to work.

Pan remonstrated with Jurand, who, however, insisted, and a word from Dick settled the business.

To work they went, tugging at the sweeps, blistering their inexperienced hands, Pan reviling Ajax in the minutest of whispers, and Ajax groaning in a minor key.

"Muffins, you are almost avenged," thought Dick

At noon they halted for a rest, and the seven other men lay at the head of the boat, silent and sullen.

Among other provisions on board there were some tobacco and cigars, which Dick and Carl tested the quality of, regardless of the scowls of the lawful owners thereof.

On again, by-and-bye, up the silent river, mile after mile, halting anon for another meal, until night was at hand.

Then Dick had the boat put in near the shore, and told his seven "captives" that they were at liberty to land and stretch their legs.

This was an offer they availed themselves of with suspicious alacrity; but Dick was not alarmed.

As soon as the last was ashore he picked up one of the sweeps and pushed the boat off.

"We shall be on the opposite side until to-morrow morning. Until then, adieu!"

His mocking tones excited almost ungovernable ire in the hearts of his hearers.

Pan threw himself down upon the ground and clutched the soft earth to keep back a torrent of violent language that rose to his lips.

Dick made light of the sweeps, working the pair as if they had been ordinary ones, and with powerful strokes, fairly *driving* the boat across the river.

At this point it was about three hundred yards wide, and very deep. If the party of exasperated ruffians had a desire to attack them, they would hardly have ventured to swim across. But Dick was quite easy on that score.

"I thought we might as well have a quiet night," he said.

"But do you think those fellows will turn up in the morning?" asked Carl.

"They can if they choose," replied Dick, laughing; "but I assure you it is not my intention to have them here again. Indeed, I do not intend to travel much farther by water."

"So?" said Carl, in a true German enquiring way.

"It is too slow—too monotonous," replied Dick. "A few miles further up we will land. As the sun is going down you may prepare to sleep."

When darkness came he feigned to go to rest with the others, but as soon as they were asleep he quietly rose up, unmoored the boat, and pushed out into mid-stream.

Then he took the sweeps, and slowly and steadily pulled up the river.

A strange, impressive figure, pulling strongly, steadily, silently. No sign of flagging or fatigue. On—on, past dense woods, black as ebony to the eye, and dimly limned against the starry sky; past open spaces, where the pattering of a thousand hoofs told of startled herds of deer who came down to the river to drink. On—on! for two hours without a rest, and then he turned the boat to the shore, and drew in the sweeps.

His companions still slept, nor were they awakened by the slight sounds which were unavoidable in mooring the boat.

Without disturbing them he lay down close to Carl, and, having lit a cigar, prepared to watch awhile.

"In a strange land," he said, "a foe may be anywhere."

The view ahead looked darker here than anywhere he had observed on the journey, and by watching closely he made out that a large hill or mountain was before him.

He was led to think it was not a cloud, because the shape did not vary, and its opaqueness never diminished.

Once he thought he saw a faint light as if a star had made an effort to struggle through mist; but he was not sure. It did not appear again.

It was about two in the morning when Carl awoke and sat up, with the startled air of a man who awakes and finds himself in a strange place.

"Don't be alarmed, Carl," said Dick; "everything is right."

"You have been watching, old fellow?" he said.

"It was just as well."

"Then I must take my turn."

"Thanks. I can put up with an hour's sleep."

Dick lay down and slept, and when he awoke he found it was daylight, and there was Carl and Muffins staring about them and wondering how on earth they came there.

Dick lay quiet for a few moments enjoying their

amazement, and then, sitting up, he, too, had a look round, and asked—"What place is this, Carl?"

"How can I tell?" replied Carl. "I have never been here before, and I don't know how we came here at all."

"Muffins," said Dick, shaking his head at the boy, "this is your work?"

But Muffins needlessly owned that he had nothing to do with it. At length Dick laughed outright.

"I took a turn at the sweeps," he said, "feeling I wanted a little exercise. I have brought you a few miles from our dear lost friends. Ah! as I thought, a mountain."

He was looking ahead where, about a mile away, a sweeping mountain rose up to the sky.

The river ran round its base and down upon its bank. At the limit of his vision, Dick saw some dark specks moving about.

"Men there," he said, pointing ahead.

Carl took a steady look in the same direction.

"There was nothing there ten minutes ago," he said; "it looks as if it is a community waking up."

"Master," pleaded Muffins, "may I go and see what they are?"

"But suppose you get into trouble?" urged Dick.

"I can dodge 'em, whoever they are," replied Muffins. "I've been a dodger all my life."

"Well, go," said Dick. "It is only fair you should have an opportunity to distinguish yoursell."

"And please, master," said Muffins, with a sly look, "may I have a wepping—a rifle or a revolver?"

"What for?" asked Dick. "To enjoy yourself with?"

Taking a revolver from his belt he handed it to the boy, saying—

"Remember, it isn't a toy. Don't draw it to look at, but keep it in your pocket until you want it to protect your life."

"All right, master," said Muffins. "I ain't been with you all this time without learning how to act when in peril. Thank you; I'll be careful."

And slipping out of the boat he walked proudly away, feeling himself every inch a man.

Muffins had never felt of so much importance before. He was entrusted with a mission which had a spice of danger in it, for it was very probable that the men moving about on the bank of the river might be dangerous foes.

With his hand upon the revolver in his pocket he went stealthily along, just a wee bit nervous, but rather anxious for some formidable foe to leap up so that he might exhibit his powers as a marksman.

"I would bring him down like a sparrer," thought Muffins, with all the confidence of one who is picturing to himself an heroic deed.

The boy was no coward, but he was only a boy after all, and not one of the monstrosities of gory fiction, who, single-handed, "hold the world at bay."

At the same time we are fully aware that many boys have done plucky things, and a determined youngster has often given no end of trouble to a grown-up man.

There was plenty of cover for Muffins, almost up to the very spot where the men had been seen. The wood acted as a screen for the boy, and a veil to him. He had no idea of the nature of the people he had come to spy upon until he was comparatively close to them.

_____

CHAPTER XXX.

MUFFINS DOES A BIT OF SCOUTING, AND MAKES A DISCOVERY—A SNEAKING SORT OF FELLOW —A LUCKY STONE.

THE sudden cessation of the wood gave Muffins a view of a remarkable scene.

For some distance up the slope the ground was like a giant rabbit-warren, but the holes were dug by men.

These men were presumably civilised, for they wore clothes and hats which had been made in a civilised land. The material and cut were of the class suitable to trappers and gold-diggers, and their wearers were evidently of the rougher order of humanity.

Muffins could hear their voices as they moved to and fro talking and calling to each other. He could not catch the words, but they sounded very much like English in his ears.

"I don't see I've any cause to be afraid of them," he thought, and his first impulse was to go up and make himself known in a friendly manner, as a traveller who, in a casual way, had just dropped down upon them.

His next thought was, "Would master like me to do it?" And not being sure on that point, he abandoned the idea.

He was about to return, when he saw a man approaching the wood in a very peculiar manner. He was creeping along, and taking advantage of every obstacle to keep himself out of the sight of those he was leaving behind him.

"Some chap running away," thought Muffins, "been ill-treated, perhaps. I'll protect him."

The notion was good and ambitious. Muffins had all the aspirations of a hero, but at present lacked the necessary physique.

His ideal of heroism was Dick Strongbow—a very good model to found himself upon.

"I am getting strong," he said, feeling his muscle, "so here goes to save the poor fellow."

It was a bold idea, but Muffins meant it; having had a rough time of it in his early days, he was ever in sympathy with the oppressed.

But as the man drew near, Muffins began to lose his friendly interest in him.

He was very far from being an agreeable specimen of humanity.

There was a hang-dog look about his face, the lower part of which was covered with a ragged beard. His clothes were covered with earth stains, and in a belt a knife and two big revolvers were stuck. In age he might be forty—perhaps a little older.

Muffins would have retreated with all speed; but for a burning curiosity which took possession of him.

Why was the fellow approaching the wood in that stealthy manner?

There was nobody after him, no signs of his being missed or wanted in the camp, and if he was simply some prisoner making his escape he was now near enough to the wood to break into a run and get clear away.

Muffins wanted to know what his object was, and being as good at hiding as he was at dodging, he crept under a thorn-bush, and, rolling himself up into a small compass, watched for the arrival of the man.

He was not long in getting into the wood, but when there did not penetrate far.

All he did was to get behind a tree, dig a small hole with his knife, put something into it, cover it carefully up, and return by the way he came.

Muffins came out of his hiding-place and saw him dodging his way back until he was within hail of the rest of the men. Then he straightened himself up, lit his pipe, and strolled back to the camp, if it may so be called, in the most casual manner.

"Well, he's a rum 'un," thought Muffins.

Curiosity being still in the ascendant, Muffins determined to see what this man of strange demeanour had so carefully hidden. So he, with *his* knife, dug a hole, and brought to light a stone.

Muffins turned it over and over in his hand, wondering why the man should have taken such pains to hide it. In size and shape it was like a small hen's egg, and differed from ordinary stones by being tolerably clear. It *felt* uncommonly hard, too, in an indefinite way.

"It's a lucky stone, perhaps," said Muffins, "and I don't think it belongs to him. It's findems keepems with a thing like this."

He put it into his pocket, meaning to ask Dick on his return if he might retain it. If his master objected it would, of course, be put back again.

He lost no time in returning to the boat, where he found all ready for a start.

"Jump in, Muffins," said Dick. "I've an idea what those fellows on ahead are."

"Here's your breakfast, Muffins," said Carl; "you can eat it as we go along."

"I've found out what the men are, master," said Muffins. "They ain't savages, but navvy chaps, I fancy. They are digging holes about the hill."

"Yes, yes," said Dick, who was at work with the sweeps, "I know. They are miners. We shall find some friends among them, perhaps. Anyway, we have nothing to fear."

Muffins was very hungry, and fell upon his breakfast with the appetite of a growing young wolf. For the time he forgot all about the "lucky stone" he had taken possession of.

Long before they reached the mining-camp the boat was seen, and about a score of men flocked down to the side of the river. There were no signs of hostility nor of friendship, but simply of curiosity.

They awaited the coming of the boat, and made no movement nor uttered a sound, until Dick, with a dexterous use of the sweep, brought his cumbersome bark neatly to shore.

Casting his eye over the men, Dick saw that they were of varied nationality—English, French, Americans, and Boers—and not, as a whole, very prepossessing.

"Sit quiet a moment, Carl," he said, "while I speak to them."

One of the group—a tall, powerful man—stepped out to meet him, but there was no cordiality in his air.

"I shall be glad to know," said Dick, "if we can rest here for a day or so?"

"Rest here for a day or so?" repeated the man, in English. "Well, I don't know."

"Surely you cannot object," said Dick. "We want nothing we cannot pay for."

"Hang your pay!" replied the man. "It isn't that. We want to know why you've come?"

"We are bound for Natal," said Dick. "Travelling to see the country."

"Ye-e-es," said the man, slowly; "just to look about you. Well, come ashore, and we'll talk it over."

There was an air of constraint about the man which was not very pleasing, and the rest of the fellows were exchanging sullen whispers.

Others of the community were coming in, too, and they all scowled at the newcomers.

The appearance of things was rather ominous.

"It seems to me," said Dick, "that we are not so welcome as we should like to be, and so we will go on."

"No—no," said the other; "we can't allow that." As he spoke the other men drew up nearer. "You've got to land and stop with us awhile. *Mates, see to the gentlemen's luggage.* You needn't fear, sir. We are above stealing."

He was dry and caustic in his manner, but he evidently recognised in Dick one who was educationally his superior.

His men moved quickly down to the boat, and took possession of it.

"Step out!" they growled to Carl and Muffins, who glanced at Dick, and, on receiving a sign from him, obeyed.

Their luggage was then taken out, the poles and sweeps also, and the boat made secure.

There was a high-handedness about this proceeding which Dick felt very much inclined to resent. Had he been alone he would have done so, but there were Carl and Muffins to be considered.

For their sake it was better to yield to the pressure of circumstances, and bide a time for putting matters right.

"And now you have fairly taken possession of us," said Dick, "will you kindly tell us why you have thought it necessary to do so."

"Two minutes' talk will do that," was the reply. "Just follow me."

CHAPTER XXXI.

THE MISSING DIAMOND—CHARGE AND COUNTERCHARGE.

MOTIONING for the men to disperse, the leader of the band, as Dick judged the tall fellow to be, led the way to a "dug out" at the foot of the huge hill.

It was a hut formed by cutting away the earth, and fixing up a few planks, with a roof over all.

"It's rough," he said, "but it's the best I've got to ask you into. There's seats enough, I know."

Such seats as there were consisted of tubs and boxes. The table was simply a few planks nailed together and fixed upon four legs. The chimney was a hole in the roof. Altogether it was very primitive.

DICK STRONGBOW:
The Diamond King,
AND WONDER OF THE WORLD.

As Mullins got his head and shoulders out of the hole the rock came down with a crash.

No. 5.   Price One Penny.

"First," said the host, "let me know who you are?"

Dick gave him their names, and told him they were simple travellers, bent on seeing a little of the world.

The narration was listened to quietly by the man, who said it was "near enough."

"All I want to know is, are you prospecting?" he added.

"For what?" asked Dick.

"Gold—diamonds—anything!"

"No."

"On your honour?"

"As I live."

"That's satisfactory," said the other, with a sigh of relief. "I thought you were agents for some of them confounded company-makers, who collar a place, send down a lot of plant, and turn a mine into a sweating shop. I'm downright glad we ain't got any need to hang you."

Dick opened his eyes a little at this, and the other laughed.

"Yes," he said; "we should be bound to hang you if there was need of it. Howsomever, it's all right; but you can't leave us."

"Why not?" asked Dick.

"Because it's the rule here. Having joined us, you've got to stop until there is a general move. This is the Green Mountain Diamond Mine, worked by a party — captain, Phil Norton; that's me. When we've got enough we shall make a start in a body—all fair and square—no playing any low-down tricks on each other."

"And how long may I have to stop?" asked Dick.

"Can't say. Months, anyway—maybe a year," was the reply.

"And suppose I say I will not stay?"

"Then we shall keep you here. It's a question whether you will stop dead or alive; but stop you must. We've got to keep this place close. If the general body of Boers got hold of it they'd be down in a jiffey, and make short work of us."

"And what are we to do—sit still and see you grow rich?"

"Oh! no, Mister Strongbow; you can mark out a claim and go to work. We've lots of picks and spades and washers, which belonged to some of our party."

"And may I ask what has become of them?" put in Carl.

"They've—departed," said Phil Norton, slowly; "some because they couldn't keep their hands from picking and stealing, others because they showed a tendency to rove."

There was a moment's silence after this. Even Dick felt as if he—to use a homely phrase—"had brought his pigs to a pretty market."

It was Carl who asked the next question, and he did so in the manner of a man who wishes to assist in a flagging conversation.

"What sort of luck have you had?"

"Good!" said Phil Norton, emphatically. "We've all got a fair lot of stones; I've one in particular that is a fortune "—he opened his waistcoat and put his hand into an inside pocket—"a fortune. I hardly know the worth of it. Why—why, where the fiends IS IT?"

He turned his pockets inside out, then tried all the others in rapid succession, a wild expression of dismay gradually springing up and deepening on his face.

He stopped, stared about him, and then frantically tried all his pockets over again.

"I've been ROBBED!" he shrieked; "it wasn't a dream—there was a man in my dug-out last night."

He strode to the door of his hut, put his hands to his mouth, and sent forth a clear, piercing cry —the Australian "cooey."

"Coo-o-o-o-o-o-o-ey!"

It could have been heard two miles away, and to every man on that hill-side it was as clear as a trumpet-blast.

They had for the most part just began the labours of the day, but, on hearing the cry, they cast down their picks and spades, abandoned their washers by the river, and came hurrying up to the dug-out.

Phil Norton stood in front of it, a few yards from the door, erect, very quiet, but ghastly pale. Dick, Carl, and Muffins had come out and stood just behind him.

Not a word did Norton utter until every man belonging to the mine—there were at least fifty— had gathered in front of him.

The mass of faces was a study—all were eager to know why they had been summoned, most of them thinking that the strangers had to do with it.

Mutterings were heard to the effect that Phil ought to have strung 'em up at once, and had no palavering about it, and one, a lowering-looking fellow, whom Muffins recognised as the man he had seen in the wood, said, aloud—

"Look at 'em! They're mighty cheeky over it. A bit of rope will bring 'em down a bit."

"You mean hoist 'em up a little," said another.

There was a general laugh at this little joke, but it was instantly checked by the stern voice of Phil Norton.

"Silence!" he cried. "I've not sent for you here on account of the strangers. They're right enough, as far as I know. It's another matter altogether. I've been robbed of the King of Diamonds."

A general shout of dismay followed this announcement. On every face there was a look of dismay.

"Robbed!" repeated Phil Norton, "by a man who was in my hut last night. I half woke up, and saw him sneaking around, but fancied I must be dreaming. I know now it was a reality. Now comes the point: Who's got it?"

A dead silence followed this question. Not a man stirred.

"If it's a joke," said Norton, "let the joker stand out and say so. As I live, I'll forgive him."

Again there was a silence.

"It's clear to me now," said Norton, "that it is a deliberate robbery. Did anybody see the thief prowling around?"

Again there was no answer, save an indefinite one.

"We generally sleep too sound to notice anything at night," said one of the men.

"I've got something to say," said a sturdy little man, stepping out of the crowd; "but I can't say that it proves anything."

"Out with it!" said the men, impatiently.

"You all know," said the man, "that me and Josh Craker share the same dug-out. Well, I woke about the middle of the night, and not hearing him breathe—for a good snorer he is in general—I struck a match to have a look at him: but he wasn't in his bunk."

"Stand out, Josh Craker!" cried Phil Norton.

Then the man whom Muffins had seen in the wood stood out, his shifty eyes gleaming with malice.

"All I've got to say is," he said, "that Ben is a liar, or he dreamt it."

"Was he there in the morning?" asked Norton of Ben.

"Yes."

"And did you see him come back?"

"No; I didn't think no harm of it, and went to sleep again."

"I say," said Josh Craker, violently, "that you are a liar. Come now, I'm ready to be searched. Search us both; do what you like with me—I'm honest."

"It is useless to search anyone," said Phil Norton, "for it isn't likely the thief would be such a fool as to keep the King about him. The question is—which of you two are lying?"

"Why, Ben, of course," replied Josh Craker. "He stole it, and is trying to put the job on me."

"If I was such a liar as you are," said Ben between his teeth, "I'd hang myself."

"You needn't do it," returned Craker, with a forced laugh, "as someone will do it for you."

"One of you two did it, that's clear," said Phil Norton, resolutely, "and I want to know which it is. Look here! if you don't make it clear which it is within an hour I'll hang you both!"

"The best way is to fight for it," suggested one of the men. "Let's have one of them orgeals by battle."

"I want my diamond, anyway," said Phil Norton, whose face was ghastly pale. "If the right man is killed I shall never know. Dead men cannot speak."

"I'm ready to fight," said Josh Craker, with a villainous gleam in his eyes. "With bowies, or I'll go him three throws. He who gets two to be hung."

"Knives then!" said Ben, furiously. "I'm not going to have the job put on me. I've allers run straight."

"A ring—a ring!" cried the men, and in a few seconds one was formed round the two suspected men.

Dick and friends kept outside it, but Phil Norton stepped inside to see fair play.

The two men pulled off their coats, rolled up their shirt-sleeves, and tightened their belts.

Eager expectancy was in the eyes of their comrades.

A fight was always interesting to them, especially on such an occasion as this.

The old superstitions were ripe in them. They had faith in the ordeal by battle, believing, in a rough way, that justice was sure to outstrip strength or skill.

Of the two men, Josh Craker was much the taller and stronger.

He was also known to be an expert in the use of the bowie-knife, having used it in several frays with the skill of a Spaniard handling the stiletto.

"Are you ready?" asked Phil Norton.

"Yes!" was the fierce answer of both.

"Then go at each other," said Norton.

At that moment Muffins plucked Dick Strongbow by the sleeve, and, in a breathless way, asked—

"Master—what is the King of Diamonds?"

CHAPTER XXXII.

MUFFINS TO THE FORE—LYNCH LAW—A FAILURE —TROUBLE AHEAD.

FAIR play in the fights of the rougher class is an element that is rarely absent—especially when it is an arranged thing—and whatever may have been the individual opinion of the miners about the identity of the guilty party, they were bent on seeing that both combatants had it.

The men stood a few feet apart, eyeing each other without moving for a moment or so, and then began to advance with a slow toe-and-heel movement. There was no haste visible; an impetuous dash might have been fatal to him who indulged in it. They had to approach warily.

As they drew nearer a dead silence fell upon the miners, who, under the excitement of the time, held their breath.

They saw how the combatants clutched their weapons, slowly drawing up, and watching for the opportune moment for striking.

Suddenly the circle of men was broken, and Dick Strongbow strode into the ring.

"Stop!" he cried; "this fight must not go on."

A yell of execration burst from the miners, and there were cries of "Shoot him!" But Dick, undaunted, again cried out—

"This fight must not go on!"

Phil Norton held up his hand as a signal for the men to keep quiet, and, accustomed to obey him, they became still.

The two combatants stopped and eyed the daring stranger who had ventured to stop a miner's fight with wonderment.

"Mr. Strongbow," said Phil Norton, quietly, "it isn't usual for strangers to interfere in these matters."

"But I have a right to do it," replied Dick.

"Why?"

"I know the thief."

This reply caused the utmost amazement among the miners.

Ben looked at him enquiringly.

Josh Craker became ghastly white.

"There he stands!" cried Dick, pointing at Craker. "Let him deny it if he can."

"I DO deny it!" roared Craker. "What do you know about it?"

"Nothing personally," answered Dick; "but I have somebody here who does. Muffins, come into the ring!"

Muffins stepped into the ring with the air of an important witness, who felt strong in having nothing but the truth to tell, and being determined to tell it.

"Before you all," said Dick, "I am going to ask a few questions of this boy. You shall hear his answers. Muffins, did I not send you this morning to see what sort of people were camped here?"

"You did, master," replied Muffins.

" And you came ?"

" Yes, sir."

" How far ?"

" To the edge of the wood."

" What did you see there ?"

" I saw a man come sneaking up and bring something in the wood."

" Will you kindly point out the man ?"

" There he is," said Muffins, extending a finger towards Josh Craker.

A rumour of mingled suspicion and execration was heard among the men around. Josh Craker, in a loud voice, cried—

" Here's another liar ! I ain't been out of the camp this morning."

" You weren't to be found first thing," said Ben.

" Silence, all of you," said Phil Norton. " Now, Mr. Strongbow, go on with the boy."

" I can tell you the rest myself," said Dick. " After that villain," pointing at Craker, " had buried the something he went away, and my boy here, after he had gone, dug it up again. It was what he thought was a lucky stone and he put it into his pocket. On his return to the boat I cut short his report by telling him that I was coming on here, so he forgot all about that stone until just now. I ought to tell you that he is a poor, ignorant lad, whom I have taken into my service, and he had no idea of what an uncut diamond would be like. It has only just flashed upon him that he may have found the lost stone. Norton, is this the jewel you have lost ?"

Dick held up the lucky stone, and the miner, with a cry of joy, took it from him.

" My own—my beauty !" he said, exultingly. " It's the real thing. Heaven reward you both !"

" I tell you it's a lie !" shrieked Josh Craker. " They stole it between them, and want to plant it on me. Why, you—"

He sprang at Dick, aiming a blow at him with his bowie-knife, which, if it had taken effect, would have killed him right away.

But Dick stepped lightly aside, and, pinning him by the arms, put on the " iron grip," and held him fast.

He made one frantic struggle to get free, and then sank down helpless.

" Don't hold so, master," he groaned. " YOU'LL SMASH MY BONES."

" As for our being guilty of stealing the diamond," said Dick, looking round at the astounded miners, who were marvelling at the easy way he held Josh Craker, " is it likely that we should have come here afterwards to put it on this brute ?"

Not even the most prejudiced mind could gainsay this reasoning. The guilt of Josh Craker was sufficiently proved for so rough a court of justice.

" Put the ropes round him," said Phil Norton, " and let the lots be drawn."

They bound him fast, and he was thrown upon the ground like a sack of weeds.

Then a bag was brought out, and a number of stones were put into it—six white and the rest a dark colour.

There was but one for each man, leaving out Dick, his two friends, and Phil Norton.

This bag was passed round, and each man took one, which he put into his pocket without looking at it.

When this had been done, the prisoner, reviling them one and all, was carried up to a dug-out near htat of Phil Norton, and thrown in.

The door was made fast, and the men went away to their work.

The relieved Ben, who had spent much of the time while this was going on in wiping the perspiration from his brow, now went up to Muffins and took hold of his hand.

" My lad," he said, " you are true grit, and as such alone I'd respect you. But you've laid hold of my heart tight by saving my life, for, as sure as there's a sun shining at this moment, that ere Craker would have killed me. I'm no match with him in a bowie fight, and I knowed it. My lad, as I said, you've got me tight !"

Then he kissed Muffins' hand, and walked away, leaving the recipient of his expressed gratitude quite overcome with astonishment.

Phil Norton shook hands with Carl and Dick warmly and at some length. At first he seemed to have some difficulty in speaking, but presently he said, tenderly—

" You've given me back my fortune," he said ; " and a big fortune for a man like me. You'd got no need to do it, for you could have held your tongue and said nothing. You would never have been so much as suspected. You are strangers, but my heart is hot towards you. I can't pay it all back, but I'll try and give you a bit of it some day "

" It was only common honesty," answered Dick. " As for the boy, as I told you, he had no idea he was carrying anything valuable ; but if he had known it would have been just the same. He is as honest a lad as ever breathed."

" He's a young nobleman," said Phil Norton. " Come here, my lad, out with your hand ! It's one a man is proud to grasp. Long life and good luck to you !"

" By-the-way," said Dick, " I did not quite understand the drawing of those stones just now."

" Well, in the first place," Phil Norton said, " Josh Craker's got to be hung."

Dick nodded.

" I reckoned so," he said ; " and I don't think it's a case for my interference."

" Then there were six stones white in the bag. The men who drew them are to be his executioners."

" Again I understand that. But why did not the men show them ?"

" It's just this way," said Phil Norton. " We made the arrangements from the first. It's not to be known who drew them yet. At midnight the six who drew the white stones will get themselves up in a particular way, and with a bit of linen, with two eyeholes in it, over their faces, they come to the dug-out and take the prisoner away to the hanging-tree. Not a word will be said—nothing to show each other who they are. Nobody will ever really know who was in it or who wasn't—save that each man will know about himself, and he'll keep it to himself, which, I reckon, is about the best way of doing such things."

" I suppose there is a penalty for speaking of the matter ?" suggested Dick.

" The penalty is the same as that for stealing," said Phil Norton, drily.

" But suppose a man gets a white stone, and doesn't choose to come ?" suggested Carl.

" Well, it might happen," replied Norton, " but it

hasn't come about yet. When it does, we may find a means of getting at him."

He left them alone for awhile, and Carl and Dick talked over their position.

That Carl hankered after staying for a time at the Green Mountain Diamond Mine was evident, and Dick saw no objection to it.

"We have started well," he said, "and it may be, Carl, that the fortune you seek may come to you here."

"Then let us mark out our claim and go to work at once," cried Carl.

The sight of the big diamond had fired his ambition, and Muffins, when he learnt the value of it, opened his eyes and breathed hard.

"Worth thousands of pounds," he said, "and I fancied it was only a lucky stone!"

"It may prove a lucky stone to you," said Dick.

As the miners had marked out their claims close to each other, our friends had to choose a spot just outside the ground at present being worked.

There was really little to guide them in their choice, and having staked out a plot about thirty yards square, they began to work.

Phil Norton sent them some tools—picks, spades, and a "rocker," or rather a small trough, on a stand, loosely fixed, so that it could be rocked to and fro.

Its use was to wash the soil away from the stones, and out of the latter the diamonds were picked when there happened to be any.

According to what they heard the men all round had, up to the present, met with fair success. Some very good ones had been found, and small stones were plentiful; but up to the present there had been only one of the size of the King of Diamonds brought to light.

"But these things don't lie about alone," said one of the miners. "We are bound to find its mate sooner or later."

Dick and Carl preferred to make their own dug-out, and the former, having borrowed an axe, cut down some small trees in the wood.

Having lopped their superfluous branches from the trunks, he shouldered them one by one and carried them up to the spot which had been selected for their "dug-out."

As each of these trunks would have given two ordinary men a tough job, and Dick carried them with ease, the miners began to marvel among themselves what sort of visitor they had among them.

Not a word had as yet been said about Dick's great natural strength, and the amazement of the miners was a source of amusement to him and Carl.

When the night came round they had their dug-out almost ready, and a few blankets having been lent them, they decided to sleep there.

Muffins, who had passed a day of excitement, digging spadesful of soil, and washing them for diamonds, was rewarded in the afternoon by finding one the size of a small bean.

Phil Norton told him that it was probably worth several pounds—say thirty when cut; but he was not to be sure until it was examined by an expert to see if it had any flaws.

Muffins was so excited when he lay down that he could not sleep for hours, but when at last he did get off it was only to be aroused, almost immediately, by a fearful scream.

He started up on his rough couch, and after awhile could faintly see Dick and Carl sleeping soundly.

Muffins was wondering whether he had heard the scream or only dreamt it, when he heard the tramping of feet, and then he remembered the events of the day. Was this the hour for the execution of Josh Craker, and did that scream come from him?

With a saddening feeling in his heart he got up and went softly to the opening of the dug-out, where there was at present no door.

Then he saw that indeed the hour of the doomed man had arrived.

By the light of the stars six men, masked and disguised, were made visible.

In a rough, unceremonious way they were carrying along a man—gagged and bound.

It was the most awe-inspiring sight the boy had ever looked upon, and, shuddering, he crept back to his blanket and rolled himself in it over head and ears, as if he could by that means shut out all thoughts of the dreadful scene.

But it was not to be driven away, and he lay there thinking of the doomed man until he heard the sounds of returning footsteps.

Then he knew that all was over—the decree of Judge Lynch had been carried out, and the thief and liar had met with his reward.

But Muffins could not reconcile himself to the idea of the man deserving so horrible a punishment for his crime.

"It's dreffull—dreffull," he said. "I can't bear to think of it, and I had something to do with it."

It was therefore with a feeling of considerable relief he heard that it was discovered in the morning that the hanging had by some means been imperfectly carried out.

When a party of men were sent down to the wood to "do the burying" of the executed man they failed to find the body.

The tree was there, and the rope with its noose was there, but Josh Craker was gone.

The tidings of this miscarriage of justice caused something like a commotion in the camp, not so much on account of the escape of the culprit as the probability of his spreading abroad the existence of the mine, and bringing down a host of Boers upon the place.

A post of observation was at once made high up a hill, from whence a view of many miles of country could be obtained, and arrangements were made for a prompt retirement towards Natal, if too big a force should be brought against them.

"Against a small one," said Phil Norton, "we will stand our ground; but to attempt to fight a big one would end in our all being murdered, and the proceeds of our labour pocketed by men who have no right to them."

"The position begins to get exciting," Carl slowly afterwards remarked to Dick, who said—

"I for one should like to have another go at the Boers. If Jurand is a fair sample of them, they are a hateful, overbearing, braggart race. But until they come let us work, and see what fortune the earth has in store for us."

PART II.

CHAPTER I.

THE BIG FIND—BETTER STOP NOW—JUST TWO OR THREE MORE—THE FALL OF THE ROCK.

"ANOTHER big 'un, master !"

Thus shouted the boy Muffins, faithful servant of Dick Strongbow, as he tilted the washing-cradle, and picked out a stone about the size of a pigeon's-egg.

Dick and his friend, Carl Yemitz, paused in their work to look down in the direction of the speaker. They were digging under an overhanging rock on the outskirts of the Green Mountain Diamond Mine.

It was a fair-sized band of men, in point of numbers, working there, and good luck had fallen upon all, but not as it had done upon these three.

For fourteen days only had they been at work, and a vast fortune had been unearthed by them.

It did not come at first, for the lower part of the claim proved to be barren. But presently they lighted upon two or three good-sized stones, and, working their way up, they found a nest of them.

And such a nest !

It was under the overhanging rock, and the first spadeful of earth turned out by Dick Strongbow brought to light a diamond which Phil Norton said was worth a thousand pounds.

Phil was the original leader of the band of miners, but his supremacy was not destined to last.

He knew that he would have eventually to yield to Dick Strongbow in wealth, in strength, in qualities that make a commander—in everything.

Phil Norton was a wise man. He did not mean to injure his head by hurling it against a stone wall.

There were few men in the world who could approach Dick as an athlete. Those who have read his previous doings know what he was, and every day saw an increase in his marvellous muscular power.

The work of a miner was child's play to him.

He could dig with one hand, thrusting the spade into the ground as a warrior would thrust his sword through a sack of straw, and turn the hard earth up as if it were froth of the sea.

It was a feat he often did when called upon by the admiring miners.

Dick was not at all vain of his powers. He did everything in a quiet way, without demonstration.

He could begin work at dawn, and labour on till sunset, without showing or feeling the least fatigue, and the men rightfully called him "The Wonder of the World."

It was not the first time the title had been bestowed upon him. It seemed natural to call him by it, and he *was* a wonder.

Sometimes the men, when they got together after dark to smoke and chat, would enter into little contests of feats of strength. There were strong men among them, but they always barred Dick, even if he offered to do with two fingers what they performed double-handed.

"You ain't a common man," they would say, "and we can't stand up against you. Why, if you were to exhibit yourself in some of the big cities you could make a fortune that way."

Dick winced a little at this. It was the only subject that touched his pride ; for he had, as we know, exhibited in London, Paris, Stockholm, and Berlin—crushing his rival, the big, cowardly Ajax.

There was no reason why he should have been ashamed of having exhibited, that he could tell, but there was something within him which was antagonistic to it.

"You were born to do greater things than simply exhibit yourself as a strong man," he thought.

Well, there he was at the mine, hidden away from the world, save and except the few men with him.

And of these men he had, without any unseemly pushing forward, become a ruler. Phil Norton, once their chief, had voluntarily yielded the post to him, saying—

"I give in to no man unless I see he is better than myself. I look on you as a man worth ten like me."

How Dick ruled over these men we shall soon see. And now let us return to the part of our story with which the chapter begins.

"Another big 'un, master !"

Dick laid down his spade and walked down to the boy, who was standing by the rocker, his face quivering with excitement. Between his finger and thumb he held up a stone about the size of a pigeon's egg.

Carl Yemitz, the young German, and Dick's devoted admirer and follower, came down also, and they stood side by side, looking at the newly-found prize.

"Carl," said Dick, drawing a deep breath, "it is the biggest of all."

"And yours," said Carl, readily.

Dick looked doubtful, but Carl insisted on the point.

"It was agreed," he said, "that we should each in turn take the stones as they turned up. It is no fault of yours that you have the best of the luck."

"No," said Dick, thoughtfully ; "but I get more than my share."

"And don't Muffins and I do well also?" asked Carl, merrily. "Have we not enough here," smiting his breast, "to gladden the hearts of most men ?"

Muffins assented to this declaration with a glad grin, and thrust the big diamond into his master's hand.

"I wish it was as big as a house !" he said.

Dick took the stone, and, opening the bosom of his shirt, produced a small leather bag.

It was hung round his neck and secured by a strip of hide.

As he opened the mouth he disclosed the fact that it was already half-full of stones of various sizes.

"The king of the lot," he said, as he dropped the jewel in.

At this moment Phil Norton, tall and strong, if somewhat rugged in appearance, came sauntering up.

"I heard the boy shout," he said. "Is it more luck?"

"Yes," said Dick; "here—peep into the bag. There it is—the top one."

"What a beauty!" said Phil Norton, with glittering eyes. "Why, your claim is regularly peppered with diamonds."

"We get the best ones from that hole—under the overhanging rock."

"Yes, it looks a likely place," said Phil; "but don't you think you had better prop up that lump of stone."

"It looks solid enough," said Carl Yemitz.

"Oh! it's solid enough," said Phil Norton; "but solid things will come down now and then."

He said no more, but sauntered off to his own claim, about fifty yards off.

Carl and Dick walked up to the rock and closely inspected it.

"Well, as you say, Carl," said Dick, "it *looks* solid enough, but we have made a pretty deep hole under it, and it might come down. We had better look for a prop or two."

There were some odd pieces of timber lying about a hundred yards away, and they proceeded in that direction to pick up two or three suitable pieces for props.

Muffins was left alone, and as the rocker was empty he had nothing to do but await their return.

He, too, looked at the rock, and smiled as he thought of the possibility of its coming down.

"Norton wants to scare master away from the claim," he said. "I'M not afraid of its coming down."

There is no more miserable creature on earth than a boy who has nothing to do, it being a necessity with all of his class to be up to something, or just die.

Muffins had his full share of juvenile restlessness, and, after casting a quick glance at the retiring figure of his master, he seized a spade and jumped into the hole.

"It may be my luck to dig out another big 'un," he said, "and it's my turn for a stone."

He thrust the spade into the ground, close under the rock, and loosened some earth. Taking up a spade, he began to fill the basket used to convey the soil to the rocker.

Muffins worked with a will for a few minutes, until the basket was quite full.

Then he drew himself upright, and wiped the perspiration from his brow. Having exerted himself considerably he was a bit pumped out.

Standing in the hole, he could just see above the edge of it, and he was about to look out to see what his master was doing when he saw the huge mass of rock above him move a little.

It could not have been more than a quarter of an inch; but he saw it, and an overwhelming terror laid hold of him.

Was that rock about to fall and crush him?

It must be remembered that he was but a boy, and this temporary loss of nerve was very pardonable. He was absolutely helpless.

The rock moved another inch, and some of the soil at its base began to crack and open out.

Now, indeed, the great peril of his position was forced upon him.

The rock WAS coming down.

He tried to turn round to climb out of the hole, out his body only swayed to the left, and, staggering, he fell upon his side.

"Master—master!" he hoarsely screamed.

Another shifting of the rock, with some breaking up of the earth. The eyes of the terrified Muffins stood out of his head.

"MASTER!" he yelled.

"What is it, my boy?" asked somebody, running up.

It was not his master, but Carl.

"The rock's coming down!" gasped Muffins.

"Come out at once!" cried Carl.

"I can't!" groaned Muffins. "I'm reg'lar limp I'm done."

Carl cast a hurried glance at the rock, saw it shift, and, with an exclamation of horror, was about to jump into the hole, when the voice of Dick Strongbow was heard.

"Don't jump, Carl; it is instant death. I am here."

He dashed up to the edge of the hole, and, planting his legs firmly, raised up his arms to the rock now gently coming over.

"Muffins! Come out!" he cried.

Muffins heard the inspiriting voice, and it brought back his strength.

Turning over on his hands and knees he crawled out.

Only just in time, for as he got his head and shoulders out of the hole the rock came down with a rush.

Dick caught it on the palms of his hands, and, for a moment, he was bent back.

Every fibre in his body quivered.

Carl, horror-stricken, sprang aside.

"The boy!" cried Dick, gasping. "Where is he?"

"Out, master," screamed Muffins; "safe!"

Then Dick let go, and staggered back as the rock, with an ominous thud, fell upon the "lucky lode," as the miners called it, completely covering it.

The exertion necessary to hold it up, even for that short space of time, had been tremendous.

It taxed to the utmost the wonderful powers of Dick Strongbow.

He reeled back half-a-dozen paces, and fell to the ground.

CHAPTER II.

THE SCOUTS UPON THE HILL—A MEETING.

CARL sprang to his side, and threw his arms around him. Muffins, pale with remorse over the fact that he had been the cause of doing his master an injury, drew up to him, trembling and sobbing.

The miners, many of whom had witnessed the scene from afar, came tearing up, one after the other, shouting with excitement, and gathered round.

"Give him air !" said Carl; "he will be better in a minute."

"I am better now," said Dick, looking quietly up. "I do not think I have injured myself in any way; but"—here a faint smile flitted upon his face—"it is the biggest thing in the way of feats of strength I have yet done."

Phil Norton, who had come up nearly last, pushed his way through to the front.

"I didn't think it would have come down so soon," he said, "or I wouldn't have gone away; and to think that you held it up ! Why, there isn't ten men here who could have done it together."

"There isn't ten men here who would TRY it," said Ben Chadder, the humourist of the camp.

He was not exactly a champion joker, but such little witticisms as he uttered served to raise a laugh in season.

The miners laughed now readily enough, because Dick had got upon his feet, and was stretching his limbs to see if any of the muscles were injured.

"No damage done," he said, cheerily; "but I certainly did feel as if my arms had been forced right out of their sockets."

The miners clapped their hands, and dispersed again to their work, talking over the new feat in glowing terms.

Dick was more than ever their hero.

"Master," said Muffins, gently, "you'll never forgive me for being such a FOOL."

"Don't say another word about it, Muffins," replied Dick; "it was nothing but what any man would have TRIED to do."

"The very thought of it overpowers me," said Carl, with a shudder.

"Come and see if it has closed up our luck," said Dick.

They examined the fallen rock and saw that it had wedged itself into the hole "like a cork into a bottle," Carl said, and was apparently immovable.

But Dick did not think so.

"We can dig away the earth from the lower side," he said, "and start it with a lever. Once it goes it will roll like a ball into the river."

"There is only one man who would attempt such a thing," said Carl; "but YOU will do it."

"I will rest to-day," replied Dick, "and to-morrow we will commence the work."

The day was almost done, and, gathering up their picks and spades, they strolled off to their "dug out"—a crude shelter, made by cutting away a part of the hill, hollowing it, and fixing up some wooden walls and a roof.

Carl and Dick threw themselves down upon the turf outside and lit their pipes. Tobacco, moderately used, is a great soother of perturbed feelings, and half-a-dozen whiffs dispersed what little excitement remained in their bosoms.

Resting on his elbow, Dick glanced up at the huge hill sloping high above him.

It was green to its very summit, save in places where the rugged rocks peeped through.

His eyes wandered from place to place, until they rested on the top, which was smooth, and shaped liked the end of an egg.

"It is a peculiarly-formed thing this," he said to Carl.

"It is," replied Carl, lazily, "but I hope you won't blame me for that."

Dick laughed.

"There isn't much at present to blame you for," he said, "except that you are in no hurry to go after your sweetheart, Aimee."

"I am satisfied that she will be true to me," replied Carl, "and that we shall meet again when the right time comes. Why, what is the matter with you, Dick ?"

"Don't move, Carl," said Dick; "keep your eyes fixed upon me. There is somebody on the top of the hill, peeping over, and, I fancy, looking down. His head is only a small black dot."

"You are sure it is a head ?"

"Yes; and now it is gone."

"It can't be any of our men," said Carl, with a glance in the direction of the miners, "and not being one of them—"

"It is some enemy," interposed Dick—" Jurand, Ajax, Pan, or Josh Craker."

"Hum !" said Carl.

"And being probably one of the four," continued Dick, "the chances are that he is not alone."

"Muffins," cried Dick, "go and ask Mr. Norton to step up here."

Muffins, who was killing time with a solitary game of "knuckle-down," with stones for marbles, abandoned that pursuit and hurried off.

Three minutes afterwards Phil Norton was squatting by the side of Dick, listening to his story.

"It is just what we might have expected," he said, "and I reckon there is a strong body of them."

"On what grounds ?" asked Carl.

"Three weeks ago we hanged Josh Craker for stealing," said Norton—"at least, he was not hanged properly, for the work was hurriedly done, and he got away. What has he been doing all this time ?"

"Looking about for a place of safety," said Carl.

"He has been looking up a party to attack us," returned Norton. "It takes time do it in this lone, scattered country, but I feel sure he's gone through with the job. Now, what we've got to do, in the first place, is to make no fuss about it."

"Certainly not," assented Dick.

"If it is an enemy we shall see or hear something of them at night," said Norton. "Unless they are very strong they won't attack us by day. We must give up our easy way of living, and act like men upon the war-path. Chief, we are in your hands."

"I suggest sentries or scouts at night," said Dick.

"Good !" replied Norton.

"And that we divide ourselves into a series of watches, to take in turn that duty night and day."

"Right !"

"And that the watches be arranged at once, each with one of their number in command, whose duty it shall be to go round at intervals, and see that every man is safe at his post."

"Yes, that's business."

"Well !" said Dick, "then that's settled. Now, all must be done in secret. As soon as it is dark let every man quietly assemble here."

"I'll pass the word round," said Norton, rising. "And, before I go, I'll tell you that since I've been sitting here I've seen TWO heads pop up over the hill. There's no doubt we've got enemies around, and their scouts have come to see if we are expecting them."

With a quick movement Dick Strongbow dashed the heads of the two Boers together, whilst Muffins was also busy.

He left them, and returned to the claim which he was working with two other men. He laboured there for a little while, and then threw down his pick, stretched his arms like a tired man, and yawned.

In a deliberate manner he filled his pipe, and sauntered about the camp, stopping now and then to speak to one of the miners.

Ostensibly he discussed their work with them, but he was in reality calling an "emergency meeting of the men," at Dick's dug-out, as soon as it was dark. They were told to come alone, and quietly, not even smoking, lest the glow of their pipes should be seen by an enemy prowling around.

The precise cause of the meeting being called was not imparted to them. All they were told was that "important business was on hand," and the general opinion was that some criminal or traitor was to be brought to book.

The general work went on until sundown, and was then abandoned.

Every man went to his dug-out, two or three generally living together, and prepared their evening meal. It was very simple, and there was not much cooking to do. Before night came they had eaten their fill, and, apparently, retired to rest.

But when it was dark they stole out one by one, and, like shadows, glided up to where Dick and Carl awaited them.

Muffins squatted down on the ground at his master's feet in a state of pleasurable excitement. Anything dark and mysterious was just to his fancy.

It was as strange a meeting of men as ever gathered together under the blinking stars. In the faintest of whispers the probability of the presence of an enemy being near was made known, and the men were divided into six watches—five in each.

Dick alone remained out, he being their commander. On him would devolve the duty of being watchful at all times.

It was done under half an hour.

The order of the different watches was settled, and the first five men, with revolver and knife, ready for defence, departed in different directions.

Two went up the great hill, bearing away from each other at an angle of forty-five, two more started from the mine right and left, and the fifth was appointed to parade along the bank of the river.

Carl was the captain of this body of watchers, and as soon as the rest of the miners had scattered and gone away to rest for the night he took leave of Dick.

"I shall keep on going round until my time is up," he said. "You get some rest while you can—Muffins, too."

"I wish I might go with you, Mister Carl!" said Muffins.

"You would only be in the way!" replied Carl, kindly enough. "Not to-night, at any rate."

Muffins heaved a little sigh of disappointment. He bitterly wanted to go.

It would be splendid to prowl about in the dark, looking for an enemy, and perhaps cover himself with glory by shooting somebody.

Muffins, unknown to his master, had bought a pair of revolvers of a miner who had a double set, and these somewhat dangerous weapons were stowed away in his trousers pockets, loaded and ready for action.

In obedience to a whisper from Dick Strongbow,

he followed him into the dug-out, and lay down in his particular corner to rest.

But not to sleep. No! Muffins was in a state of burning excitement, and had never been so wide-awake in all his life.

"I sha'n't be here long. I can't keep still," he thought. "If master would only go to sleep I could have a little turn outside. I wouldn't go far, but I should just like to look around a bit."

———

CHAPTER III.

MUFFINS GOES FORTH A SCOUTING—CARL MAKING HIS ROUNDS—THE DEED OF DARKNESS—CARL IN TROUBLE.

ERE long Dick Strongbow was sound asleep. The work of the day and the tremendous feat he had performed combined to produce a weariness he had not often felt. Sound repose came to him as a recuperative boon.

Muffins continued as watchful as when he first lay down, and his restlessness increased.

In his heart he had all the spirit of a born adventurer, and the gift had been fostered by his varied and, of late, romantic life.

He lay on his back picturing to himself the lone scout watching for the foe, all their senses on the alert and their blood coursing with excitement swiftly through their veins.

They were all heroes in his eyes, and he longed to be one of them.

"Why shouldn't I?" he asked himself. "One more on the look out wouldn't matter, and master didn't positively say I wasn't to go."

Muffins called to mind at least one other occasion when Dick Strongbow had not been "positive," and Muffins had done as he pleased with subsequent commendation. Why should he not repeat the experiment?

"I feel as if I'd GOT to go," he said.

He sat up in his humble bed, and listened to the breathing of his master. Dick was drawing the steady breath of a strong man, and was evidently deep down in the realms of sleep.

"I'll go," muttered Muffins; and, rising, he went softly to the door of the dug-out.

It stood ajar, and, having pushed it open wide enough, he wriggled out and stopped for a moment, holding his breath.

It was an exciting time, and everything was so still that he could hear his heart go "thump—thump," as if it were knocking against his ribs.

Above and around the camp was still, and away down he could see a faintly luminous broad band, which was the river, reflecting the light of the stars. Those far-off, bright luminaries were not so brilliant as usual, for there was a light mist in the air gradually settling down, undisturbed by the wind, into dew upon the ground.

Muffins had no definite plan in his head, but,

after a little thought, he decided upon going a little way up the hill and then he would work his way round to the river.

Adopting a stooping attitude, and in the steeper places crawling on his hands and knees, he wended his way up the great hill until he was about a hundred feet above the level of the workings, when he stopped for breath.

Not a sound could he hear.

He felt, for the moment, as much alone as if he had been in a deserted world.

The place he had chosen to stop at was near one of the rocky projections on the face of the hill—a large stone, which he could see faintly outlined in the gloom.

It was about half-a-dozen yards away, and in approaching it he had acted the part of a perfect scout, and had not made the least noise.

Suddenly the stillness was broken.

It was the slightest possible sound, but it made Muffins prick up his ears, for it came from some place close by—from behind the big stone near him he judged.

It sounded in his ears like a suppressed yawn.

Muffins, with a fast beating heart, stretched himself out at full length upon the ground and listened.

Another sound broke the stillness.

It was that of a man's voice, speaking in the lightest of whispers, but half-a-dozen words fell upon the boy's ears.

" Isn't it about time to move ?"

" Yes," said another voice ; " but first look to your arms."

A slight rattling of steel and the click of a pistol or rifle-lock followed, and then came a rejoinder—

" All right."

Muffins made himself as flat as possible, with his face turned a little sideways, so that he could see ahead of him.

Out from behind the rock crept a man, tall and rather lean.

He wore a broad-brimmed hat, and his general attire was that of the Boers whom he had seen when he first arrived in the Orange Free State.

Nay, more. He thought it was Jurand, whom Dick Strongbow had wrestled with at the fair held at Vraal, where he completely and ignominiously defeated him.

That the young Boer hated Dick with his whole heart on that account was, of course, to be expected ; but surely he had not dared to come thither alone for the purpose of revenge ?

As this speculation passed through the mind of Muffins another figure emerged from behind the rock.

Then another and another, until there were six in all.

Whether their heavy boots were muffled or not Muffins could not see, but certain it was that beyond the speaking at first they made no noise.

Like evil spirits prowling about under the cover of darkness they glided down the hill-side in the direction of the camp.

Muffins got up as soon as he dare, and with the feeling on him that now he must distinguish himself or never, carefully took out the two revolvers he had provided himself with, and went upon their trail.

.   .   .   .   .   .

Before the scouts were sent out a watchword had been decided on. It was "Diamond King ;" and

Carl had furthermore announced that his approach towards any of the men was to be from the right.

" If anyone comes from the left," he said, " shoot him down, and THEN ask who he is."

As the men were to keep their faces in an outward direction from the camp, and Carl would go round in one direction only, these arrangements could be easily carried out.

He made his first round without any hitch, and found all the scouts on the alert. He stopped a short time with each, exchanging a few whispers and watching with them.

Nothing occurred to give rise to any alarm, and in due time his second round began.

First of all, he went to the man who was on duty by the river-side. He found him standing upon the bank, stooping down and peering into the stream.

" Anything wrong ?" he softly whispered.

" Nothing certain," replied the man, in the same tone ; " but I fancied a short time ago I saw something like a boat."

" Coming this way ?"

" No ; it simply crossed the river. But it might have been nothing but fancy."

Carl remained with the man for nearly half an hour, but, boat or no boat, it did not appear again, and he passed on to the next man.

This scout was placed on the outskirt of the workings, about a hundred yards from the river, and, consequently, some distance up the side of the sloping hill.

He had nothing to report, but Carl remained some time with him also, and then went up the hill to a third scout.

This man's post was on a projection of the hill, from the summit of which he could hear the slightest sound, and also command the best view of the land the darkness permitted.

Carl exercised the utmost caution, and silently approached the spot where, an hour ago, he had left the man alive and well.

Now, as he drew near, he failed to see the man at his post.

There was the projection, dimly seen, but plain enough to reveal the fact that the scout was gone.

This discovery startled Carl, and he cast a quick glance around, to see if he were on the lower ground.

The limited range of vision did not reveal the man, but as there was a possibility of his being on the other side Carl moved forward.

He had but a few yards to traverse ; but he had not covered more than half the distance ere he discovered the scout.

Not standing on the projection, but lying in the shadow at the foot of it—upon his face.

What did that mean ?

Was he unfaithful to his trust and sleeping ?

It seemed barely possible ; but sentries and scouts had slept at their posts before then, as Carl knew, and seeing nobody else near he went boldly up to the man.

Yes, there he was, lying on his face—sleeping his last sleep.

And upon his back was a broad stain, caused by the escape of his life's blood from a terrible gash there.

His shirt had been cut open by the force of a downward blow, leaving a long opening, exposing the wound beneath.

All this Carl saw as he bent down over the man.

It was a ghastly discovery, and removed all doubts about there being a foe in the neighbourhood of the mine.

"A stealthy, cruel, crafty enemy!" muttered Carl. "How did they get at him?"

He stooped again over the man, and the next moment a heavy weight fell upon him and he was dashed to the earth.

Before he could see who it was he knew that a man had thrown himself prone down from the projection above.

The moment after his fall a strong hand pinioned him by the back of the neck, forcing him down with his face to the earth.

In this position his mouth was as useless as if it had been gagged.

He could not cry out, and he was furthermore secured by a second man precipitating himself upon his legs and holding them down.

"Finish him!" whispered this second man.

"I can't," replied the first. "I've dropped my knife. Lend me yours."

CHAPTER IV.

CARL SEES DEATH—A TIMELY SHOT—THE COMING FOE.

EATH seemed to be near Carl Yemitz. In his heart he bade adieu to Dick and Muffins. With a pang he thought of Aimee, and then braced himself up to meet his end as became a man.

"Lend me your knife—quick!" again said the fellow who held him down by the neck.

"You are in a mighty hurry," replied the other. "It's stuck a bit, and won't open. There it is."

Click!

Carl heard the ominous sound as the blade sprang upright.

He knew the sort of weapon it was by observation—broad and strong, and pointed like a dagger. The Boers all carried such a knife, which they used in cutting up the deer they shot upon the plains.

One blow from it—well directed, as he knew it would be—and all must be over.

"Good-bye, all!" he thought.

But his hour had not arrived.

As the knife was raised by the murderous Boer, the report of a revolver broke in upon the quietude of the night, and the man, with a yell, let go his hold. He rolled over on his side, execrating the unseen hand that had laid him low.

The second man jumped up, and half-a-dozen others, who had also come from above, uttered so many cries of surprise.

A second shot was fired as Carl leaped to his feet.

He literally FELT the bullet whizz by him, and had a narrow escape of being killed by his rescuer.

The pellet of lead struck one of the Boers behind him in some vital part, and he fell without a groan.

Carl lost no time in acting on the aggressive.

He had his arms ready, and, whipping out a revolver, he supplemented the two previous shots by one of his own.

A third Boer fell.

It was a matter of half-a-dozen moments.

Taken wholly by surprise in their turn, the band of ruffians lost their heads, and did not make even a feeble attempt to defend themselves.

They fled like a herd of startled deer, breaking away and scattering right and left, the darkness favouring their retreat.

Carl did not attempt to follow them.

It was, indeed, practically impossible to do so over the broken ground and under the cover of night.

But the wounded man on the ground demanded some attention, as he still possessed the power of doing harm and might be dangerous.

Carl accordingly stooped down and deprived him of his weapons, two huge, old-fashioned pistols and the knife he had borrowed.

"Are you going to finish me?" snarled the Boer. "If so, be quick—no torture."

"I shall neither torture nor kill you myself," replied Carl, coolly. "Keep quiet; you do not appear to be much injured. If you give any trouble I may hurt you a great deal."

Hitherto Carl had no time to look for his rescuer, but he now peered about him, and asked who it was that had come to his aid.

"It's me, Mister Carl," replied a voice.

And Muffins, in a state of delicious excitement, came out of the shadow of a big stone.

"You!" exclaimed Carl. "My dear, good, brave young friend, how came you here?"

"I couldn't rest," replied Muffins; "I did so want to be in it. I shot two of 'em, didn't I?"

"You did," said Carl, "and you will shoot me if you don't mind. Put away your revolvers now. I think we are safe from further attack. On my word, you should he proud of what you've done to-night, Muffins."

Voices from below now reached them. The miners had been aroused by the firing, and the whole camp was alive.

Apparently they did not quite comprehend what had happened, as there was no move at first made in the direction of the scene of the encounter.

"Get up, my friend," said Carl to the wounded Boer.

"Lame—shot in leg," muttered the man.

"You had better get up," said Carl, quietly.

Growling, the Boer slowly got upon his feet, and, by the direction of Carl, limped painfully down the slope.

The first shot fired by Muffins had hit him in the knee, and the wound was decidedly painful, if not dangerous.

As they drew near the camp the voice of Dick Strongbow was heard, demanding who they were.

"It is all right," sang out Carl.

"Are you alone?"

"Don't say I'm with you, Mister Carl," pleaded Muffins.

"I have a prisoner with me," answered Carl.

So they came down, the prisoner foremost, and he was immediately seized and bound.

"Who is he, Carl?" enquired Dick.

"I don't know," replied Carl. "He is one of about half-a-dozen who amiably intended to put me out of the world."

Muffins had not come forward with Carl, but hung back in the gloom.

Proud as he was of the feat he had performed, he wanted, before showing himself, to hear what Dick thought of his absence.

"Muffins is missing," said Dick, "and I am afraid he has got into trouble. Has anybody here seen him?"

"Two people," replied Carl; "myself and this worthy gentleman here," pointing at the prisoner. "I owe Muffins my life, and our friend may thank him for his wound."

Then Carl briefly told the story of his rescue, and Muffins was called upon to show himself, which he did, and received a most gratifying reception all round.

It is true chance had put him in the way of doing a bold thing, but the fact remained that he had bravely availed himself of his opportunity.

In this respect he was like hundreds of other heroes. The moment for action arrives, they seize it, and a reputation is made.

Phil Norton dubbed him there and then "The Little Wonder," and Ben Chadder, who had the credit of being the camp poet, gave out two lines of impromptu praise—

"*Who is it here that smit them Boers—the ruffians?*
Why, our young pride and glory—by name, Muffins."

This poetic outburst, if committed to paper and sent to a first-class magazine, might not have been immediately accepted.

It is decidedly under laureate mark, but Ben, like many other local poets, was a genius in the eyes of the small circle around him.

"That's good, Ben," said one of the men, "them lines go straight to the point without any high falutin' bosh leading from nothing up to nowhar. The whole thing's put in a word or two—you get it all at once. It goes home to the heart like a bullet."

This was the general feeling, and the poet was complimented by being asked to put his two-lined ode to paper, so that the miners could one and all get it by heart.

Meanwhile Dick, Carl, and Phil Norton had drawn aside to discuss the situation.

It was undoubtedly serious.

Phil knew the Boers too well to think for a moment that the small party which had attacked Carl had come there alone.

He was sure that it was a scouting party in advance of a considerable force.

"I don't say that the Boers are cowards as a body," he said, "because they ain't, but they're cautious and economical. They don't waste powder or shot, or themselves if they can help it. You won't find much dash about 'em, but they come on slowly and steadily—feeling every inch of their way. It's my opinion we shall have to budge."

"I don't like that," said Dick.

"No more do I," replied Phil, "but what's the use of stopping if it's only to lay down our lives? If there's a big number of 'em, it would only be suicide to stop."

"That's true," said Dick, thoughtfully. "Now I wonder if the prisoner would tell us the truth if we asked for it."

"No," replied Phil, "but all we've got to do is to go by contraries. I'll just hear what he's got to say, shall I?"

"Do—there's a good fellow."

The prisoner was under the care of three men, who guarded him closely.

Phil had a short conversation with him and then went back to Jack and Carl.

"He says there isn't another Boer within twenty miles," he said, "so that we may reckon there is a big party of 'em close handy. We shall have to move."

"Without a fight?"

"What would be the good of it? This is just the place where they could box us in—and provisions are running short. Hunt we couldn't. Come, Strongbow—you are a plucky fellow, but you must be prudent."

"Is there any hurry for a few hours?"

"No, for as I was saying, the Boers move slowly, but we ought to be ready to start at any moment."

"What about the prisoner?"

"Leave him to me," said Phil Norton; "he shall have miner's justice—no more. A life for a life it is, and don't forget that there's one of our men up yonder who's got to be paid for."

No further alarm took place that night, but not a man cared to sleep again.

One and all passed the time in disposing of the results of their mining labours about their persons.

Some stitched the diamonds up in belts, several secured them in inside pockets, which were sewn up, and others—like Dick—simply placed their wealth in a bag and hung it round their necks.

The majority were not sorry to go, for they had gained a modest competency, and were anxious to enjoy it in a more favoured and civilised region.

But many objected to the Boers taking possession of the field.

It was still rich in places, and the hole under the rock in Dick's claim was considered to be a veritable diamond mine in itself.

It was now closed over, hidden away by the fallen rock, as it never had been before—sealed up against all marauders as it seemed.

"If we have to leave for the time," said Dick to Carl, "I shall certainly come back to it—one day."

"It is miserable to have to cut it from these Boers," said Carl.

"We are not gone yet," replied Dick, quietly. "I've a plan or two in my head which I think will work."

When the morning came many an anxious eye scanned the big, green hill and the country round; but no indications of the presence of an enemy could be discovered.

The first care of the miners was to bury their comrade, who had been murdered at his post.

He was quite a young fellow, of genial disposition and generally liked.

The miners felt very bitter against his assassins; but they said very little as they laid him in his grave.

The two Boers were buried also, some distance from him.

Whatever the men may have felt towards the living, they had no spite against the dead.

For the living there was no mercy, and shortly after the prisoner taken overnight was led away into the wood and did not return.

Dick Strongbow asked no question about him. The miner has a certain idea of justice, and is not to be moved away from it.

He who comes to kill must expect to be hanged if he is caught.

The rough pioneers of civilisation do not profess to give time for the criminal to reform his ways.

Dick had been busy all night maturing a plan for getting away, if an overwhelming force should present itself. It was not possible for a handful of men to fight against a horde of sharpshooters.

"But I shall not go yet," he said to himself, "whoever profits by what we leave behind us, it shall not be Jurand, Ajax, or Pan.

He had a shrewd suspicion that these three would all be found in the force arrayed against him, and possibly Josh Craker too.

With the latter he could leave the miners to deal; but the former required his especial care.

He called the men around him at an early hour, and asked them if they were prepared to accept him as their leader still. If they did they would have to obey him in all things, no matter how contrary to their wishes his orders might be.

The answer was an immediate "Yes." And some asked to be sworn. But Dick said—

"I take your word. It is enough. He who would break his word would ignore his oath."

CHAPTER V.

THE BOERS IN HIDING—THE MINERS GONE—A DANGEROUS SLEEP — A RAPID FIGHT AND FLIGHT.

NOTWITHSTAND- ing the apparent absence of a foe, a force of two hundred men were within easy distance of the diamond field. On the other side of the hill was a piece of dead level country, terminating in one of the dense woods scattered about the district. Right and left of this wood was rising land, and some few miles away the high Maluti Mountains reared their heads.

To all appearance it was uninhabited country; but in the district between the mountains there were many Boer settlements; and from these came the two hundred men—sharpshooters every one.

They had been gathered together by Jurand, the champion Boer athlete, who had succumbed to Dick Strongbow at Vraal, and with him were Ajax, Pan, and Josh Craker.

The two hundred men were hidden in the wood, and the quartette referred to above were on the outskirts of it early on the morning following the events recorded in our last chapter.

The ponderous Ajax, looking more gigantic than ever in the rough settler's dress he had adopted, reclined on the sward at full length.

Near him squatted Pan, with his restless eyes wandering here and there, and his teeth employed in that tell-tale pursuit—biting his finger-nails.

Jurand and Craker leant against the trunk of a mighty tree hard by.

"It seems odd," said Pan, "that none of them have returned. Where in the fiend's name have they got to?"

"So much hurry, you English," replied Jurand; "so little do. We go on—stop now—go—stop—but sure"

"Ah! yes," said Pan; "but sometimes you are cocksure, and it doesn't come off."

"You've got a tongue that is like a rasp," said Josh Craker. "Why don't you soften it a bit?"

"Do so—and copy your master," suggested Jurand, with a grin. "He is soft enough."

He nodded towards the mighty Ajax, whose face became suffused with a deep blush, just like that of a schoolboy who is jeered by his fellows, but he said nothing.

"Soft!" snarled Pan. "Putty is adamant to him; he hasn't any pluck in him."

"Can I help that?" demanded Ajax.

"Yes," said Pan, curtly.

Ajax opened his lips to reply, but he changed his mind, and said nothing.

Jurand glanced at him with contempt, and drawing out a big cigar from his pocket, lighted it and smoked awhile in silence.

"Somebody coming along at the double," said Craker, suddenly.

Following the direction of his outstretched arm, Jurand saw the form of a man coming towards them. In a few minutes he recognised who it was.

"It is Jules," he said.

Jules was a man of about thirty, a strong-built fellow, with rather a good face for a Boer.

It was quite calm when he strode up and saluted the party by touching his sombrero with his hand.

"You are alone?" said Jurand.

"Yes, at present," replied Jules; "but more shall come."

"All?"

"No—three dead. Two shot last night—one hanged to-day."

There was a sweet brevity about this style of telling rather a serious story that amused Pan. There was a broad smile on his face as he squatted down listening.

"Who kill?" asked Jurand.

"Pouterbrach, Shriever—Gobmert hung," replied Jules.

"And you kill none?"

"One."

"Ach!"

It was a satisfied kind of growl that escaped Jurand, but it was from his mouth alone. His face had no expression in it.

"Anything more?" he asked.

"No more; but they go—they are afraid. They pack up."

"Good!" grunted Jurand.

"Why don't you go at 'em boldly?" asked Pan. "You are two hundred, and they are thirty."

"You know the Strongbow," replied Jurand; "is he not a TERROR?"

"Good lord ! yes, but surely you can shoot him down ?"

"But if we should miss," said Jurand, "and he got a grip—ah ! it is the feel of being so HELPLESS in his hold. It is so horrible—it brings dreams."

"There's something in that," sighed Pan. "I've felt it, and I must say I know nothing like being gripped by him. It's just like—like—what it is."

"Another scout," said Josh Craker, who had been watching.

In a little time a second man came in, and he had a further report to make.

The miners were packing up their tools, and no doubt contemplated going.

By-and-bye the intelligence was further confirmed by a third arrival.

He brought the news that the miners were going UP the river, some on the bank, and some in the big flat-bottomed boat which had brought Dick and his friends to the spot.

Provisions were being put in it, and all the tools of the men. Probably in the afternoon they would be gone.

"To-morrow," said Jurand, "and the field will be ours."

"They will take some of it away with them," hinted Pan.

"Would you not let it it go ?" asked Josh Craker.

"No," replied Pan, with an oath ; "I'd have a go for the lot. Why, if you ain't lied, Craker, there's A MILLION going away with 'em. Isn't it worth fighting for ? And if you don't want to fight openly, isn't there enough to sneak around and pick 'em off ? I'd have that money, or money's worth."

"So would I," replied Jurand ; "but at the name of Strongbow my men quake—shake—he is, I say, a TERROR."

. . . .

That night the flat-bottomed boat glided not up but DOWN the river.

In it were Carl and half the men, and all the tools, save the rockers, which were big and awkward to carry, and others could be knocked up anywhere.

The men left behind shortly after made a move in the direction of the boat, under the command of Phil Norton. Dick Strongbow and Muffins remained behind for a little while.

Like the captain of a sinking ship, Dick was the last to leave, and he was in no hurry to go.

It went against the grain to retreat before any foe, but he knew there was no help for it. The position was untenable.

But he lingered on in the darkness, thinking of many things.

His mind went back to the days when he lived with the strollers—to Gonzalo, the gymnast, who hinted at his being heir to a name and wealth, and who left so little evidence to prove it.

Many things passed through his mind, one after the other, and, as he thought, Muffins, who had been heavy all day, fell asleep.

Dick soon heard his regular breathing, but he made no effort to wake him.

"Let him sleep for a few hours," he murmured ; "I am in no hurry."

Now, when a man begins to yawn, any one in his immediate vicinity is sure to follow suit. So it is with sleep.

In a few minutes a huge cloud spread over Dick's mind. He struggled feebly against it, murmuring—

"What does it matter ? I have plenty of time—" And then he, too, slept.

From dreamless slumber he was aroused by somebody shaking him by the shoulder.

Opening his eyes he saw Muffins, who, with a gesture, indicated the need of caution.

It was daylight, and the sky could be seen through the chinks in the dug-out. Then the full knowledge of his position flashed upon him.

"Some men outside, master !" softly whispered Muffins.

"How many ?" asked Dick, as he quietly rose up.

"I don't know, sir. I daren't look."

Dick slipped to the door and listened.

He reckoned by the voices that there were three men outside, speaking in the harsh, guttural tones of their country.

He had paid the penalty of having incautiously slept. His enemies were there.

In a moment his spirit was aroused, and he decided on immediate action. To hesitate was to be shut up like a rat in a hole, and perhaps shot down.

"Muffins," he said, "follow me, and when I give you the word, run for the nearest hiding place."

He drew himself up, squared his shoulders, gave the muscles of his powerful arms a little play, then he opened the door, and went boldly out.

Three men were there—two of them were peering through the cracks in the hut. They had heard whispering inside, and were endeavouring to find out who was there.

The third man was looking on, with the air of a man preparing to run in case there was need, to save his precious neck.

He uttered a loud cry as Dick appeared, and put his hand upon a belt round his waist, feeling for the ever ready knife.

The two men faced about, and Dick instantly grasped their throats, one in either hand. Then he dashed their heads against the rough wooden planks that formed the wooden walls of the dug-out.

At the same moment Muffins, with a fever of heroism flaming up in him, sprung at the third man, and performed a feat he long after remembered with joy.

In an ordinary struggle Muffins must have speedily been worsted ; but he was no ordinary boy, and had lived no ordinary life.

His old existence in the streets of London, when he was a poor, neglected, hunted waif, had given him a fine education in the art of overcoming those stronger than himself.

All things are fair in boyish warfare, so, instead of going at his foe in the usual way, he ducked down, bolted between his legs, and upset him.

The fellow, who was tall and awkwardly built, was thrown off his balance, and, pitching forward, fell upon his head.

It was a strong one, but it could not stand the shock, and every particle of the wits he possessed was scattered.

Senseless he lay upon the ground, and Muffins, who had fallen upon his hands and knees, got up with a face the colour of beetroot, and turned to give aid to his master.

But he needed none as regards the two men.

The force with which they were driven against the hut bewildered them, and when, without a visible effort, he opened out his arms, still grasping the men, and, with a quick movement, knocked their heads together, they had finished with the business altogether.

One might have counted five, no more, while these things were being done, then the rapid scene was over. But all peril was not past.

There had been witnesses to the scene.

About ten yards away stood Jurand, rifle in hand, but not at the present. As soon as he saw it was Dick Strongbow who had thus unexpectedly appeared from the hut, his heart became void.

Not a grain of courage was left in it.

And dotted up the hill-side, at intervals of about a score yards, were men descending one by one, with Boer caution. They, too, saw all, and although none of them knew Dick by sight, his powers made his identity clear.

"It is the Strongbow!" they yelled.

"Shoot him!" cried those above; but the men below began to turn tail.

Jurand instinctively raised his rifle to his shoulder; but his palsied hand refused to pull the trigger, and, with a groan, he dropped the weapon and fled.

Dick could have drawn one of his revolvers, and perhaps have shot him down, but he made no attempt to do so.

Much as he had cause to dislike the man, he could not shoot him like a wild beast in the back.

So he let him go, and with a smile of contempt upon his face he watched the rapid flight of the Boers.

There was one man, with more courage than the rest, about half way up the hill. He did not immediately fly, but, kneeling down, brought his rifle to the present, and took aim at Dick.

He was a crack shot among his people—a man who would name a spot on a running deer a hundred yards off, and hit it with an infallibility bordering on the miraculous.

A moment more and his bullet would have sped upon its deadly errand; but Dick, with two bounds, reached the spot where Jurand recently stood, and picked up the rifle he had dropped.

It was ready cocked, and Dick, raising it, fired at the man above him—almost without aim.

There are such things as lucky shots, and this was one of them. The bullet went straight to its billet, and this grand marksman of the Boers, spreading out his arms, fell upon his face.

"Master," cried Muffins, breathlessly, "shall I run?"

"Not yet," replied Dick, coolly; "it would only put heart into them—stand under the shelter of the dug-out. I will tell you when to go."

CHAPTER VI.

A LONG NIGHT OF ANXIETY—BEN GOES OUT SCOUTING—DISTURBING INTELLIGENCE.

ARL, with the men in the boat, acting according to Dick's command, glided down the stream for about ten miles, and then steered for the opposite shore.

It was a well-wooded piece of land, with a vast number of tall, straight pines, growing together in the almost mathematical regularity peculiar in that class of trees, admitting of free movement to and fro, and giving splendid material for constructing defensive works.

But, Dick, in choosing that spot, had thoughts beyond defence, as we shall see by-and-bye. For the present, all Carl had to do was to land the men and the things he had brought, then pull the boat across the river, and await the coming of the rest of the band.

This part of the programme was carried out without a hitch, and in about an hour Phil Norton and the rest of the men appeared.

It was very dark, but Carl, as soon as he had run his eye over the dim forms on the bank, missed Dick Strongbow and Muffins.

He asked where they were, and Phil Norton, in his turn, expressed his surprise at not finding Dick Strongbow there before him.

"I fancied he started ahead of me with the boy," he said; "but I am not sure."

Carl said no more, but at once embarked the men and had them transported to the other side of the river.

Then with Phil he once more crossed, and, having moored the boat, awaited Dick's coming.

We know from what transpired that they waited in vain.

We need say very little about the weary wait—the pain of hope deferred, the joy when a fancied footstep was heard, and the gloom when it was discovered that it was only one of the ordinary sounds of the forest—the cracking of a huge branch or the fall of a few rotten sticks.

How slowly lagged the time, but day returned at last and found the two men still watching and waiting.

On the other bank, in the shadow of the wood, the rest of the men were lying about, some sleeping.

"They must have passed the spot in the darkness," said Norton.

"Hardly," replied Carl, "for they would not go far from the water. Perhaps they have fallen into an ambush."

It was an uncomfortable thought, and for a few minutes there was a gloomy silence. Then came a suggestion from Phil Norton.

"One of us ought to go back and see," he said.

"Our orders were to wait for him here," returned Carl, "and we have but to obey."

"That's true," said Phil; "so we have nothing to do but to exercise our patience."

DICK STRONGBOW:
The Diamond King,
AND WONDER OF THE WORLD.

Dick Strongbow caught hold of the Horse and tossed the Boer out of the saddle.

No. 6.   Price One Penny.

Shortly after all the men on the opposite bank were up and stirring, and there was a feeling of general dismay when it was known that their leader and the Little Wonder—Muffins—were missing.

"I have an idea, Phil," said Carl; "one of the men might go up on the opposite side and have a look around. He needn't show himself; there is plenty of cover."

"Ben Chadder would do it safely," said Norton; "he is one of the best of scouts."

"The utmost caution must be exercised," said Carl, "for it was Dick's wish that the Boers should get it into their heads that he had gone the other way. To that end we did a bit of barneying yesterday when the scouts of the Boers were still skulking about."

"I call it a regular fix," groaned Phil.

"Well, Chadder must go," said Carl; "but he must be cautious."

They pulled the heavy boat across the stream, and Chadder received his commission in whispers.

It was not a personally dangerous business, but it wanted a man who knew how to get about without being seen.

On that side of the river there were several gaps of open country, across which only an expert at scouting could hope to get without being seen by an enemy on the look-out.

Of course, there was the possibility of there being no watchers abroad; but the probability was the other way.

"It's only a few miles as the crow flies," said Chadder; "but I shall be obliged to go inland here and there. It will take me two hours."

He went away through the undergrowth, and the two hours passed in a waiting of growing hopelessness.

The men had gone further into the wood, and Carl and Phil, with the boat, lay under the shadow of a huge willow tree.

Not a sound reached them to announce the coming of those they watched for, and Ben Chadder had not returned.

Another hour passed, and then Carl began to feel that, with or without orders, he ought to go back to the diamond field in search of Dick.

"I am sure now," he said, "that something has gone wrong with them."

"And supposing YOU don't come back?" said Phil Norton. "Shall I come after you?"

"No," replied Carl, sadly. "You will still have your men to look after. Things will be as they were before we came to you. Wait for me until night, and then, if you hear nothing of us, act as you think proper."

"But you will come back?"

"Not unless I find something of Strongbow and Muffins."

They shook hands as friends do at parting, and Carl, slipping ashore, glided away into the wood.

"One on each side of the river," muttered Phil. "Surely they will find them."

Carl had been gone about a quarter of an hour when a slight commotion on the opposite side of the river attracted Phil's attention.

He glanced across to the spot, and saw Ben Chadder had returned, and was talking low, but in an excited manner, with two or three men.

It was a heavy boat, even when empty, for one man to pull across a river; but Phil Norton—in a fever of sad apprehension—pulled with might and main, and speedily reached the opposite bank.

His coming had been marked, and Ben came down to join him.

"What news, Ben?"

"Bad."

"Have you seen anything of the captain?"

"No, and I don't think you will ever again," said Ben, passing a hand across his eyes, "or of that Wonder boy either. The Boers have got hold of the mine."

"Confound 'em!" muttered Phil Norton.

"They wasn't there when I first got near the place," said Ben. "I took up my post close to the bushes—you know 'em—and squinted across the river. Lor! how d esarted the place looked. Well, arter awhile I see's the Boers on the top of the hill—more'n a hundred strong—and they come down in a body, just swooping upon the place.

"I see Josh Craker among 'em, conspicuous like," continued Ben, after a short pause. "He was walking behind with a big giant of a fellow, who, I reckon, was that Ajax we've heard on. They were ready for work, all of 'em, armed to the very eyes, and when they got down they went from one dug out to another, and looked 'em through."

"They found nobody?"

"Not a sign of a livin' creetur'. After that they had a look at our diggings, and took up handfuls of earth; but they hadn't any spades, and couldn't go to regular working. But, of course, they will do that by-and-bye. They acted just as if they had come to stay."

"They've got the captain," groaned Phil—"our 'King o' Diamonds,' our EMPEROR. Ben, he was our emperor, born to rule, and to rule well. Look ye here, most of us have got enough to live on, but we ain't goin' to sneak away without avenging the cap, are we?"

"I, for one, won't," replied Ben; "I'll have a man for him and two for the boy."

"Get the fellows quietly together, and put the question to 'em," said Norton. "Them as don't like to stay needn't. We don't make it compulsory."

Ben went off to the men, and Phil Norton, a prey to the keenest anguish, walked slowly up and down.

In five minutes Ben came back again, and Phil saw the answer written upon his face.

"They will all stay?" he said.

"Every man," replied Ben.

CHAPTER VII.

ALL RIGHT WITH DICK—THE BOERS IN FALSE SECURITY—ATTACK AND VICTORY.

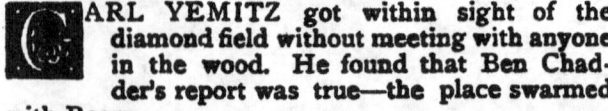

CARL YEMITZ got within sight of the diamond field without meeting with anyone in the wood. He found that Ben Chadder's report was true—the place swarmed with Boers.

The whole band, under Jurand, had, as a matter of fact, taken possession of it.

They were not working in the ordinary sense—for, as we know, they had no tools—but they were engaged in turning up the earth with their big knives, and eagerly examining it.

Among others he saw Ajax and Pan in one of the holes previously dug, scraping, as it seemed, like a a pair of rabbits in a burrow. The diamond hunger was upon them all.

They had no scouts about, no watch was kept. All were busy in seeking for the most precious of precious stones; but, apparently, they had, as yet, found nothing.

With the simple means at their command this was not to be wondered at; but, having got possession, it would be only a question of a short time ere they had better fortune. Half-a-dozen men despatched for tools could get them there in three days.

"It would not be a difficult matter just now to put them to the rout," muttered Carl, half-aloud. "It would be worth trying, if only to avenge my brave friend Dick."

"Is there any need to avenge him?" asked a quiet voice, close to his ear.

The shock of surprise was very great, for it was Dick's voice. Carl hardly dared for the moment look around, for fear of finding that it was the offspring of fancy.

A hand, the same strong hand he knew so well, was laid upon his shoulder, and turned him gently round.

There, indeed, was Dick Strongbow—and Muffins also.

They were both smiling, and there was no change in them, save that Muffins looked a little fagged.

"It IS you, Dick," said Carl, drawing a deep breath.

"Certainly; why not?" replied Dick, jauntily. "Surely you did not think I had been worsted by that crew?"

"We hardly knew what to think. It is so many hours since we saw you."

"We are both to blame, Carl—that is, Muffins and myself. I was stupid enough to fall asleep last night; but there—this is not the time to tell the story."

"I ran the wrong way," said Muffins, dubiously, "and master and me have had to go miles round to get here."

"We had a brush with some of those fellows this morning," said Dick, "and when I cleared them off I told Muffins to run. He ran, as he says, the wrong way, which compelled us to hide awhile. After a time I saw the Boers return in force, and we made a wide detour round the back of the hill, and were on our way to the trysting-place when I saw you coming along this way. We just followed up to see if you meant to tackle those fellows alone."

"I felt as if I should have liked to," said Carl.

"Well, we can give them a bit of surprise," returned Dick. "They evidently think we have been scared away. How long will it take you to get the men here?"

"Say an hour and a half, Dick."

"They will come, of course?"

"Gladly. Half a word from you would bring them from the other end of the world."

"Bring them here," said Dick, with glistening eyes. "I can't stand this intrusion on our property. I will wait here with Muffins, and, by-the-way, don't forget to bring us something to eat—we want it."

With joy in his heart—after a short chat on the plan of attack—Carl set off at a smart pace, humming an air, for a weight, which had been like that of the Atlantic on his breast, had been lifted up.

Dick and Muffins stood just within the wood—the former scanning the ground before him, to decide upon the way to advance and the method of attack.

He was half ashamed of himself for having retreated at first, but prudence whispered it was for the best.

Had he remained with his men at the mine he would have been at the mercy of Boer sharpshooters, who could have been posted about the summit of the hill.

But now, if in a moment of fancied security he could pounce upon them and give them a sound drubbing, a scare might set in.

"I must make myself a TERROR to these swinish fellows," he thought.

Personally he was already so to a great extent, but he must increase the feeling if he was to hold the mine in security.

They were two hundred, and he had but thirty men. Great odds these.

But in history you will find that many small bands of men have not only stood their ground against mighty odds, but as aggressors in battle have been victorious.

The news that Carl took back with him was hailed with suppressed enthusiasm.

But for the need of caution the men would have tossed their hats up, and made the air echo with their shouts.

But Carl desired them at the outset not to be demonstrative.

"We are going to pounce on these self-assured fools," he said. "Caution and obedience from you all is absolutely necessary."

He then told them that Dick's plan was as follows—

Half-a-dozen men were to remain on the opposite side of the river, and, under the guidance of Ben Chadder, to make their way up-stream just beyond the mine, and, from the cover of some bushes on the bank, open fire upon the Boers.

The attention of the usurpers of the mine would be drawn in that direction, and then Dick and the rest would attack them from the other side.

"The time for you to open fire," said Carl, "is half an hour before sundown. We shall have daylight to do all we want to—if successful—and if defeated —which I don't think of for a moment—darkness will come on speedily to cover our retreat."

"There is one thing I should like to point out," said Phil Norton, "and that is, ammunition is running short with us."

"The Boers have a stock with them, no doubt," replied Carl, quietly.

Carl had observed, while watching by the wood, a number of small bales and packages piled up near one of the dug-outs.

This was, of course, the luggage and ammunition of the camp, which, in their feverish haste to get at the diamonds, the Boers had not undone.

Ben Chadder would rather have gone with the main party of attack; but the orders of his leaders must be obeyed, and, having chosen half-a-dozen men, he started.

The rest crossed the river, and, under the leadership of Carl, wended their way to where Dick and Muffins were eagerly awaiting them.

They kept back out of sight of the Boers, no man

speaking. As there was nearly an hour to spare, the rations they had brought with them were served out.

Dick and Muffins having been all day without food were in sore need of it. A hearty meal set them both on their legs again.

And all day long the avaricious Boers had been digging with their knives and clawing with their hands, but found little to reward them.

A few small precious stones came to light, which only served as a stimulus to their exertions.

Ajax and Pan, inexperienced at the labour, found nothing.

The day was almost done when Josh Craker came up to the hole in which they had toiled, and stood on the verge of it, looking down with a dry smile upon his face.

"What luck?" he asked.

"Accursed luck," replied Pan, wiping the perspiration from his brow with an unsteady hand. "I don't believe it is a diamond mine at all."

"Isn't it?" said Craker. "Look here!"

He held up a fair-sized stone between his finger and thumb. Ajax and Pan looked at it curiously.

"Uncut," said Craker, "this is worth forty pounds. Jurand will send for tools to-morrow. We shall all be rich in a week."

He laughed, and his laugh was like the croak of a raven. Ajax and Pan, sitting down, with their heads about level with the ground, looked at his prize curiously.

"Where did you find it?" asked Pan.

"Over on the other side of the field," replied Craker; "just where that big stone lies. It looks as if it had only just fallen down. This beauty was close to it. I reckon there's something under that bit o' rock, and I mean to be at it to-morrow."

Many men are going to do so much on the morrow, and it is never done.

For Josh Craker there was to be no to-morrow.

The place where Ajax and Pan were working was at the upper end of the field—the farthest away from the wood where Dick Strongbow and his men were awaiting the time to attack.

Josh Craker stood up against the evening sky, a conspicuous figure for the watchful eyes of Ben Chadder, who was on the other side of the river nearly opposite him.

Ben owed a deep debt to Josh Craker, and here was an opportunity to pay it in full.

So, the time of action having arrived, he covered him with his rifle and fired.

The report rang out sharply on the evening air, and the busy throng at once stopped work.

Ajax and Pan, with terror-stricken faces, saw Josh Craker open out his arms and bend towards them. There was death in his eyes as he pitched down head foremost at their feet.

"A thousand fiends!" cried Ajax. "Who did that?"

Four or five other rifles sent out reports that echoed back from the hill, and the sounds were promptly followed by a chorus of cries and yells from the startled Boers.

"Down with you!" hissed Pan to Ajax; "if you don't want a bullet through you."

There was no need to have urged the big coward thus.

The firing had already caused him to sink down beside the dead man in a paroxysm of terror.

Pan, although not by any means so cowardly as his big companion, had no great liking for leaden bullets, and he crouched also. Thus were the living and the dead in ghastly company.

The Boers had laid aside their rifles while working, but they now made a rush for them.

But ere one was grasped there was firing of a more deadly nature from another quarter.

Twenty-five rifles poured out their leaden missiles into the thick of the scared Boers, and down went half-a-score of them, the dead to lie still, and the wounded rolling down the slope towards the river.

Then up from the cover of rock and bush sprang Dick Strongbow and his men.

He alone was a host to inspire terror.

As he raced towards the foe, with his men behind him, there were cries of "Strongbow!" started by Jurand, and taken up by his scared followers.

What are numbers in a panic?

Only a hindrance to action. There is no fighting power in a disorganised mob.

Bent on inspiring, once for all in the breasts of his foes, a lasting terror, Dick, with every nerve quivering, dashed into the thick of them.

He used no weapon but his own strong arms—matchless as yet in the athletic world.

To one man he gave a blow with his fist that laid him down upon the soil—dead. Another he seized and tossed into the air, a third he dashed to the earth as if he had been a ragged scarecrow.

Like some resistless missile—say a stone from a huge catapult, such as our forefathers used in warfare—he went straight through the whole body of Boers, parting them in twain.

Behind him came Carl and his men, using their weapons with deadly effect right and left.

Up the hill and down to the river ran the parted Boers. The latter plunged into the stream, and made an attempt to swim to the other side.

But, ere they were half across, Ben Chadder and his few followers appeared on the bank, and the Boers, screaming for mercy, turned back.

Some sank by the way, and a few, reaching the shore again, ran up the country for their lives.

"Let them go!" cried Dick Strongbow; "the fight is won."

So they allowed them to escape, and wisely, too, to tell the story of their defeat, and warn off others from attempting to dispossess Dick and his men of their own.

Yes, the fight was won, and the sun going down. In a few minutes darkness would descend upon the scene, and hide all that was ghastly in it.

Death on the battle-field is never pleasant to look upon.

There may be glory in victory, but there is ghastliness in defeat, and no man worthy of the name finds a pleasant subject to look upon in the slain or wounded.

Dick Strongbow, as soon as the fight was over, found that his tremendous exertions had somewhat exhausted him. He sat down upon a mound of earth, and glanced around him.

All he could see of his living foes were those who were already far away, fleeing for their lives, and the wounded in his immediate neighbourhood.

For the latter he had a thought in this moment of triumph, and he bade Phil Norton go round and see what could be done for them.

Four or five of his own men had also been injured, so there was a fair amount of work for an impromptu ambulance corps which Phil Norton promptly formed.

CHAPTER VIII.

MUFFINS MAKES A BIG CAPTURE—PAN AND AJAX GO INTO SERVITUDE.

 HERE was Muffins all this time? Well, not exactly in the fight, for he had been positively commanded by Dick Strongbow to keep in the rear. In the rear he kept, but not so far as prudence dictated, for when the Boers scattered he was sufficiently near for one to run against him. This was no other than Jurand, who aimed a blow at him with his knife which, if it had taken effect, would have made a big gap in Muffins.

But the boy ducked down, and escaped the amiable effort to cut—really cut—short his promising career.

After that Muffins walked right across the field, casting quick glances at the dead and wounded.

He did not like the spectacle any more than his master did; but, naturally, he felt elated at the complete triumph which had attended the bold attack upon the Boers.

Muffins had his revolvers with him, in his hand. He had not fired a shot, not even at Jurand; but that was owing to the rapidity of the events attending their meeting.

Jurand collided with him, aimed the blow, and ran off, all, as it were, in a moment, and Muffins was too much flurried to think of the weapons he carried.

Now with them in his hand he strolled about until he came to one of the holes, and there, hearing voices, he pulled up short.

He knew those voices, and this is what was being said—

"Keep still, you shivering fool, can't you? Your teeth are clicking together like the bones of a corner man of a nigger troupe."

"I—I can't he-elp it, Pan—" clicketty click. "I—I am so cold—" clicketty click.

"Cold, you cowardly brute? No wonder. You are HOLLOW. There's nothing in you. Stop it, will you?"

"I—I—I'll try—" clicketty click.

"In ten minutes it will be dark; then we can get off. If found here we shall be strung up. If I had such noisy teeth as yours I'd have 'em all drawn."

"Ajax and Pan!" thought Muffins. "What a find!"

His first thought was to make himself known, order them to come out of the hole, and follow him on pain of being shot.

It would have been a dramatic thing to march them before him into the presence of Dick Strongbow.

But they were two to one, and men against a boy.

They might run the risk of pouncing upon him, and take his weapons from him.

No—the odds were against him, so he softly stole away and hurried up to his master, to whom he imparted the news of his discovery.

In a moment Dick was on his feet, and, bidding Muffins show the way, hastened in the direction of the two skulkers.

He called for no assistance, but alone went to their hiding place, and presented himself to their terror-stricken gaze.

"Come out, YOU TWO!" he said, curtly.

Pan was almost as terrified as Ajax. Neither had an ounce of fight, or the least thought of resistance.

Quivering with fear, they came out from their hiding-place, revealing the form of the dead man below

"Who is that?" demanded Dick.

"He said his name was Josh Craker," replied Pan, sullenly.

"Goodly company for you," returned Dick. "Is he dead?"

"Yes; shot by somebody."

"Go on before. Don't try any tricks."

"Are you going to hang us?" asked Pan, with a quivering lip.

"Oh! mercy—mercy," cried Ajax.

"You deserve the rope," said Dick, "but I may possibly spare your lives. We shall see."

Dick had already a plan in his head for the further punishment of the two scoundrels, without descending to bloodshed or unmanly cruelty.

But ere he acted upon it he decided to consult Carl and Phil Norton.

The sun was down, and with a twilight so short that it was like the last flicker of an expiring candle, darkness would soon be there; but Dick was not going to pass the night in gloom.

With supreme contempt for his foes, he ordered fires to be lighted in convenient places, and before one of them he bade the prisoners lie down and await his pleasure.

Pan ground his teeth as he obeyed; but he dared not resist.

Neither he nor Ajax had anything in the way of weapons, and an attempt at flight would lead to their being shot down or speedily recaptured.

Dick, with a sense of the ludicrous, ordered Muffins to keep guard over them while he consulted with his junior officers, and a more congenial task he could not have set his youthful follower.

With a cocked revolver in either hand, Muffins squatted down a few yards away from the prisoners.

"I'd like you to know," he said, "that I'm growed into a crack shot, and if you attempt to bolt I ain't likely to miss you. I'd hit such a lubber as Ajax half-a-mile off."

"Don't chatter to me!" growled Pan.

"I'll chatter if I like," replied Muffins. "And don't you turn your nose up at me. Mutiny in this 'ere camp is punished with death. What, you will talk? You open your mouth again, and I fires!"

Pan lay back scowling, with such a feeling of rage in his heart that he felt as if he would have given up his own life if he could only first dispose of Muffins.

Ajax said nothing.

He simply gave in, accepting the position with the resignation of a hopeless and incurable coward.

What a spectacle !

Such a mountain of flesh, with a heart no bigger than a pea !

A monster nut, without anything inside it worthy of the name of kernel.

So they remained, one in sullen resignation, the other in abject fear, until Dick Strongbow came back. He had come to a decision with his friends about what was to be done with the two prisoners. Carl and Phil had, as a matter of fact, readily fallen in with his views.

"See here, you two," he said ; "your lives are to be spared, in the first place."

Pan looked up quickly, with flushed cheeks. It was evident that he had not expected mercy.

"But you will remain here," continued Dick, "as servants, and for your services will receive a small remuneration ; but you will have no share in the profits of the mine. The least attempt to escape will be punished with death. There will be no faltering, no extension of mercy. Too much has been shown you already. Muffins, you may come away."

Muffins got up grinning with delight. The humiliation of the precious pair was just to his taste. It exhilarated him like a draught of new wine.

"Behind you," said Dick, as he turned away, "is a dugout, which once belonged to Josh Craker. He shared it with another man, who left it when that miserable scoundrel got away. You will pass the night there, and do not venture out in the morning until you are called."

He left them with Muffins skipping behind him, and when they were out of earshot Pan turned upon Ajax and struck him in the face.

"A curse upon the day I first met you !" he snarled. "There is a blight upon your life that falls on all who are associated with you."

Ajax said nothing, but, wiping his face, got up and walked into the dugout.

Pan could not see his face. Had he done so he would have marked the restrained malevolence in the giant's eyes and called to mind the old proverb "That a worm will turn."

And, Ajax, as we know, was such a very big and strong worm.

———

CHAPTER IX.

A LUCKY TIME—BREAKING UP OF THE CAMP—RETURN OF THE BOERS.

 Y turns the miners were set to watch upon the summit of the hill for the possible return of the Boers ; but days passed and they came not.

Meanwhile, the others worked and reaped a wonderful reward for their labour.

Dick and Carl set to work to remove the huge stone that blocked the rich part of their claim, and by strenuous efforts, mainly on the part of the former, succeeded in removing it.

It was worth the trouble.

By far the richest portion of the field had fallen to their lot. A wonderful luck was theirs.

Every cradle full of earth had its sparkling jewel, big or little.

Two witnesses of their success viewed it with the bitterness of disappointed Peris shut out of Paradise.

These were Pan and Ajax, who were kept employed at the cradle, rocking and washing, first with one miner and then with another ; and over them Muffins was set to see that they did not purloin anything on their own account.

They had also to cut up wood, light fires, cook, and do a great deal of general waiting on all who chose to demand their services.

Very little rest was given them from morn till night. No Israelitish slaves toiling in Egypt ever had harder task-masters, and they deserved their lot.

Ajax had no thought of flight, but Pan entertained it in his mind.

He, however, could not see that freedom would be any service to him.

Whither was he to go?

To the Boers?

No. What he had seen of them was not much to his liking.

THEY also were hard taskmasters, and were not at all likely to waste any sympathy upon him.

As for the sparsely-inhabited country, it had few charms to tempt him to flee.

So he abandoned all thoughts of flight, and bided his time.

One day the scale of fortune might turn again in his favour, and then he would pay back all he owed —coin for coin.

The food of the camp was now entirely the flesh of deer, cooked in various ways, with a few herbs found around and in the wood.

Water was their only drink, and the diet sufficed.

The deer was obtained by watching by the river at night, first in one place and then in another.

Vast herds came down to drink, and a few shots fired into them in quick succession provided food for several days.

Thus a fortnight passed, and there were no signs of the foe.

But there were indications that the diamond field was giving out.

Stones of any size and value became scarcer and scarcer.

Even Dick Strongbow's lucky claim was now, in the eyes of men so rich, not worth the working.

But who cared?

All had done well, and some were more than satisfied, notably Carl Yemitz, Phil Norton, and Dick Strongbow.

The latter, thanks to his great luck and gift as a leader, had been dubbed the Diamond King.

One afternoon the labour in many of the claims was absolutely fruitless, and the idea of a general move was talked of.

Phil Norton broached it to Dick, and he was not averse to it.

"Why should we stay?" he said. "We have ousted our enemies, and we shall leave nothing worth having. Let us move by all means, and towards Cape Colony. We are strong enough to defend ourselves on the way."

"I hope so," said Phil. "So it is to be a move then, and when?"

"To-morrow morning," replied Dick.

Then Dick brought out something which he had kept hidden from them for a long while.

It was some whisky and wine, which he had brought up the river with him.

"I am no lover of strong drink," he said, "but once in a way a little does not hurt a man. Here is sufficient to be merry with, without going to excess."

To men of that class the gift at such a time was a boon indeed, and they prepared for a jolly evening.

First of all, as mining was to be abandoned, and their picks and spades, too burdensome and of too little value to carry, they were by common consent tossed into the river.

Not in contempt for such good friends as they had been, but to keep them from the Boers.

It would be desecration for them to be put to common use by such a race, and one by one they were thrown into mid-stream.

Each miner, as he cast his tools away, gave them a cheery good-bye, and when the last was thrown they formed a ring and danced like joyous school-boys on the eve of a long holiday, round the cradles, piled up in a heap, to form a farewell bonfire, and then they began to sing.

The usual watch upon the hill was abandoned, all joining in but Pan and Ajax, who squatted apart, gloomy and savage.

Like a good general, Dick left no arrangements for the morrow.

After the singing the division of ammunition and the examination of arms took place, and a few words as to the necessity of obedience to their leader were spoken by Dick.

Once more they vowed to follow him and obey him in all things, until the time came when they should reach a civilised place.

Then every man was to be free to go where he pleased.

Among them was one of the Boers who had been wounded in the fight a short time before.

He was the sole survivor. The rest died, and were buried by the river.

This man was not a bad sort of a fellow for a Boer, and, having been well treated, he had shown his good qualities, and worked with the best of them.

Such good fortune as he had met with he was allowed to enjoy, and with a few hundreds of pounds worth of diamonds in his pocket he was prepared to go anywhere with the band.

It was indeed a jolly afternoon, and a merry evening.

The cradles and other timber which had been in use made a big bonfire, and blazed brilliantly.

Dick, Carl, and Phil, reclining on the ground a little way apart, talked over their plans and their hopes.

They were all rich men, and the prospect of a life of ease and enjoyment was before them.

Muffins, too, having a fair share of the proceeds of the diggings, was rich enough to have visions of becoming Lord Mayor of London.

It was his intention, when he got into the civic chair, to give the usual dinner to the street-boys instead of the swells, "because they wanted it more;" but that would be in years to come.

Just then he had not the years nor the corpulency or such a dignified position.

The night deepened, and the bonfire went down. At an early hour Dick gave the word to retire.

"We must be up in the morning before the sun, and away, my lads," he said.

"I don't feel as if I wanted to go to bed," remarked Ben Chadder.

"But you've GOT to go," said Dick, quietly

And Ben went straight away.

So did the others, to rest, if not to sleep, and the fire got lower and lower, until it was nothing but a heap of red-hot ashes, casting a faint glow about fifty feet around.

It was shortly after the men had retired that it flashed upon Dick that no watch had been set that night.

In the excitement of "breaking up," the usual precautions had been forgotten and neglected.

Carl and Muffins had already fallen asleep, and, judging by the dead silence around, the majority of the others had also found unconsciousness.

Dick would not disturb any of them, but even at the last moment he felt it would not do to be lax in a needed duty.

"I will be sentry myself to-night," he said.

And, carefully taking down his rifle from the wall, so as to make no noise, he went out.

With a silent footstep he passed toward the outside of the camp, unseen and unheard by any of his followers, and, having got clear, began to make the circuit of the whole field.

His way lay up the hill, and he decided to go to the very summit of it.

So he went upward, with a light, springy footstep, his keen eyes singling out the rocky obstacles as he drew near them.

Up, up, to almost the summit of the hill, and then he suddenly stopped.

A faint murmuring sound had fallen upon his ears.

It was no more than a swarm of bees at a moderate distance would have made, but it was significant. He paused a moment, and then went on more stealthily than ever, until the very top of the hill was attained.

Then he heard it, louder and clearer. It was not one sound, but many.

Right and left there was the dull tramp of horses' hoofs, and coming up the opposite side of the hill were a number of men in a line on foot.

He could just faintly see them like a wall, advancing stealthily, as he felt sure, although the movement was not clearly perceptible in the gloom.

A mind much inferior to Dick's would have grasped the import of these things.

The Boers had come back in double, treble, perhaps ten-fold strength.

By luck or skilful design they had arrived at a time when everything appeared to be in their favour.

To the right was one body of horsemen, to the left another.

A third body of men, on foot, was coming over the bill.

In a little while—half an hour at the outside—the band of sleeping men below would be surrounded.

Who can wonder that even Dick for a moment stood aghast?

The night was not blacker than the immediate prospect before him and his friends.

Brave they might all be; but with such overwhelming numbers brought against them what could they do but fight—and die?

All this darted in an instant through Dick's brain, and then, turning on his heel, he, as quietly as he made the ascent, hastened down to his friends to give the alarm.

     .   .   .   .   .   .

Cautiously the Boers advanced until they had surrounded the camp on three sides. The river cut off retreat from the fourth.

All was silent, and, in a few moments, previously-appointed scouts descended from the foot party on the hill. They crept like wolves over the ground, and made no sound.

But there was no need for such caution.

The camp was empty.

With wondrous celerity Dick had aroused his followers, warned them to be quiet in their movements, and they were gone.

All, including the unwilling Pan and Ajax, had vanished.

As soon as this was known, there was a wrathful panic among the Boers; but they tried to console themselves with thoughts of having won the mine.

The night passed, and the morning came, and ere an hour's daylight had lighted up the earth, it was discovered that the prize was worthless.

Five hundred men went nearly mad on hearing this fact, and none were madder than the commanders of the two parties of horsemen.

Their names were Jurand and Gaff Dietrack. Jurand we know; Dietrack we have to learn something of by-and-bye.

"They have got away, but not far," they cried. "They must be found."

Leaving the foot party in charge of the worthless diamond field, the two parties of horsemen set out to scour the country. Gaff Dietrack went up stream with his men.

He had a powerful, swift horse, that soon began to outstrip the steeds of his followers. In his eagerness he made a race of it.

Instead of going forward in order, they were soon straggling, but still in sight of each other.

Gaff Dietrack's blood was heated with the thoughts of the diamonds these men had stolen away with.

As he rode on he saw a man ahead calmly watching his coming from the outside of a clump of trees.

He had never seen him before, and knew not that it was Dick Strongbow. But he was sure it was one of the escaped mining party.

"Give yourself up, you dog!" he cried, as he rode at him.

Dick waited his coming with folded arms, apparently yielding himself up, until the Boer's horse was close upon him.

Then he quietly stepped aside, and seized the reins with a tremendous grip with one hand, sharply stopping the horse.

The beast reared, but Dick held on, and with his disengaged hand caught a fore hoof, then, letting go the reins, he laid hold of the foot of the Boer and tossed him out of the saddle.

It was all done in a moment, witnessed by the amazed advancing Boers, and by some of Dick's friends, who were coming out of the wood to give him aid—if he needed it.

CHAPTER X.

TWO BOERS COME TO GRIEF—MOUNTS FOR CARL
AND DICK—PAN'S LATEST SCHEME.

ERROR, almost of a ludicrous description, was upon the face of the fallen Boer. He had a revolver in his hand, but amazement, combined with the shock of the fall, put that fact out of his mind, and he made no attempt to use it.

Dick was no stranger to the saddle.

From the circus people, with whom he had spent his early youth, he had learnt the art of riding, and as a vaulter on horseback he had few equals, even among the trained performers.

But he had never made a public exhibition of his acquirement, and for a long time it had been with him a neglected art.

But with some men a thing once learnt is never forgotten, and it was so with Dick.

His powerful grasp on the horse conveyed to the quadruped the indubitable fact that it was in the hands of a master, and it became as docile as a dog.

Calling out to Carl to secure the fallen Boer, Dick vaulted into the saddle and turned the horse's head in the direction of the main body of the foe.

There were about half-a-dozen hard by, and they were doing their best to rein up their steeds, for the simple presence of Dick was a terror to them.

Having got his horse in a line with them, he allowed the reins to rest lightly on his arm, and urged on the animal with his knees. In either hand he had a revolver ready for use.

It was ludicrous to see the men he was charging upon. In their fright they lost all sense of being supported by friends. Each only thought of himself and the probable result of an encounter single-handed with Dick.

Wildly tugging at the reins, they opened out so that only one man could be got at, and Dick, with reckless daring, rode straight at him, like a knight of old in a tournament.

Seeing that the man was practically unarmed, for he made no attempt to use his weapons, Dick guided his horse so as to pass within a foot or so of him.

Of the moment occupied as he flashed past he made the best use, by striking the Boer in the ribs with his clenched fist.

The sound emitted by the blow was like that which might have been drawn from a muffled drum, and the breathless man, fairly shooting out of the saddle, fell heavily to the earth, where he lay without sign of life.

Dick wheeled his horse round and charged at another Boer, who, shrieking for help, dug his heels into his horse's side, and was borne away at a hand-gallop.

The rest of the Boer party, tailing off in the distance, had all more or less reined up, gaping and staring at the scene.

Had Dick been alone, they might have screwed up the courage to bear down upon him in a body, but behind him were his own men, who had formed themselves into a line, with their rifles ready to pour in a deadly volley as soon as the horsemen were near enough to receive it.

Dick did not carry his recklessness so far as to

"It is Gaff Dietrack!" cried the foremost Boer, as the man made an effort to rise.

proceed with his attack upon the Boers, but contented himself with catching the second horse, and riding back with it to his friends.

"A mount for you, Carl," he said.

Carl was busy keeping guard over the first defeated Boer, who was now recovering his consciousness. The man had, of course, been relieved of all offensive weapons.

"Give it to Phil Norton," sung out Carl.

"I'll take the next," said Phil. "Don't argue, for I WON'T have it."

Muffins, who had been standing behind the men —a position he had reluctantly taken up by the command of Carl—came through the ranks in obedience to a beckoning sign from Dick, and took the bridle of the horse.

It was not a handsome animal, but it looked sound and strong, and quite up to sixteen stone.

"Is our friend hurt much?" asked Dick, alluding to the fallen man.

"He's had his wits scattered a bit, that is all," replied Carl.

"Send him packing," said Dick. "We don't want to be bothered with prisoners, and we won't shoot helpless men."

The Boer heard his words and stared at Dick as if he could hardly believe his ears.

"Not shoot?" he said, slowly.

"No," replied Dick; "get away with you."

"Goot—kind," muttered the Boer as he began to limp away.

"And if your friend yonder isn't dead," said Dick, "help him up and take him with you."

Number two was not dead; but between the blow and the tumble he was in a very helpless state.

Dick and his followers watched him as he saw the released Boer help him up, and urge him to come away.

Their mounted friends had gathered together in a body, about a quarter of a mile off, evidently holding a perturbed consultation.

"He'll get him along," said Phil Norton; "but it will take time to get back to the others."

Before the two men had gone far the Boers, however, decided what to do.

Turning their horses round, they rode away, apparently abandoning the whole business.

The two men on foot went plodding along after them, a ludicrous, and at the same time pitiable, spectacle.

"They won't trouble us any more to-day," said Dick.

"Nor to-morrow," said Carl.

"We will wait and see what tale the morrow tells us," replied Dick, quietly. "I don't think they have altogether left us."

He motioned to the men to return to the wood, and, dropping from the saddle, he gave the reins to Muffins.

"Lead them both into the camp," he said.

The party had camped in a tolerably open space, about fifty yards in the wood.

There a fire had been lighted, and Pan and Ajax were preparing food—a stew—in the sole culinary vessel belonging to the miners, a huge iron saucepan.

Although they had been left to themselves, and knew the cause of the sudden movement on the part of the miners, neither of them attempted to flee.

Pan kept on at his work, stirring a thick savoury stew of deer-flesh, wild birds, and herbs, muttering anathemas on all things, and his own bad luck in particular.

"Why don't you bustle youself?" he said to Ajax. "Move round, you bundle of bounce and cowardice!"

"You always take the lightest job!" growled Ajax.

"And ain't I got a right to it," asked Pan, "being the weakest of the two? Fancy ME making stew for a lot like this! Oh! what would I give for a pound of arsenic to put into it."

"You are the most murderous chap I ever met with!" said Ajax, as he threw some dry sticks upon the fire.

"If I had your strength," growled Pan, "I'd carry out some of the things I hope and dream about; but "—here he shuddered—"having once felt HIS grip, I'm almost as big a cur as you are when I think of him!"

"Hush!" said Ajax, with a shiver. "Here he comes."

Pan went to work assiduously, stirring the stew, and Ajax ran here and there, picking up the rotten branches which had fallen from the trees.

Dick strode into the open ground, and without so much as looking at either of them walked up to the fire and picked up a burning stick to light his pipe with.

The rest of the party soon appeared, and the horses having been secured to a tree, the men stood about in groups talking together of the recent affair, mostly in an undertone, for Dick, they knew, had a deep objection to open praise.

Pan's evil eyes lighted up a bit as he glanced at the horses.

He had no need to inquire how they were obtained, for the chatting around soon let him into that secret.

Very little he cared about from wherever they came.

His thoughts concerning them looked ahead.

A born schemer, his mind was soon busy with a problem. Could these two horses be turned to his own account?

In a little while the stew was ready and the miners began their meal.

Pan and Ajax drew aside to wait, like good servants, until their masters had finished, before they ventured to eat.

Nobody had suggested they should ever do so, but in sheer terror of Dick they adopted this act of humility.

"Sit down, will you?" said Pan, when they had withdrawn out of earshot. "I want to speak to you."

"Some fool's scheme on, I suppose," grumbled Ajax.

"Don't you tack the word fool on to anything I do," said Pan, "or I'll be letting into you."

"And don't you touch me again," snarled Ajax. "Why not?"

"Well, I've had enough of it, and I shall hit you."

"You—hit—me!" said Pan, quite overcome with astonishment.

"Yes," said Ajax, with a feeble snigger. "I can do it, and I will. If you are violent I may also talk to Strongbow. He'll protect me."

"I'm a blarmed saint if ever I heard anything

like that," said Pan. "Have you been talking to him?"

"No," replied Ajax, "but I've had a word or two with Muffins, and he says he'll speak up for me."

Pan was obliged to lean back against a tree for support. He was, as he could not help admitting, "flabbergasted."

The position was so utterly absurd that he could have laughed outright but for the fact that it had a serious side for him.

If Ajax had complained to Muffins, and Muffins laid his complaint before Dick Strongbow, there was little doubt but that Pan would get into trouble.

"I'm done now," he said, "but for all that I must try and wake you up a bit. You can ride, I know, and so can I. There are two horses, and if we could manage to get away in the saddle—"

"Oh! dear," said Ajax, "I wouldn't think of it. Go away alone, if you like—"

"I would," snarled Pan, "but for leaving one of the horses behind me. There mustn't be half a chance of pursuit when I clear out."

"I dursn't do it," muttered Ajax.

"You've got to try," said Pan. "On horseback we could soon get to Cape Colony, and drop in amongst some of the right sort."

"I can't think of it, Pan."

"You must. Look here, you've got to do as I tell you, or I'm hanged if I don't go to Strongbow and tell him you've been putting it into MY head, and then do you know what he'll do?"

"No," groaned Ajax.

"Hang you like any other horse-stealer," said Pan. "And so you've got to go about as usual and wait for the word from me. The sight of those two horses has put a new heart into me. It seems as if they were sent here for our use. I call it quite providential."

And Pan grinned as if he had said a very clever thing, but Ajax only softly groaned and closed his eyes, as if to shut out the very thought of attempting to escape.

CHAPTER XI.

A NIGHT EXPEDITION—AJAX AND PAN ATTEMPT TO GET AWAY WITH QUALIFIED SUCCESS—A SPLENDID CAPTURE.

NIGHT had fallen on the land, and the camp was still. The tired miners lay in a circle, with their feet to the heap of hot ashes of the fire.

With the double object of keeping the heat in and preventing a telltale flame, clods of mossy turf, cut from a shady part of the wood, had been laid upon the top. By this arrangement it would keep in until morning.

It is true that the nights were warm, and in the open a fire would hardly have been needed, but a wood is always more or less damp, and a heavy dew was falling.

Precautions to escape chills and subsequent fever had to be taken, for Dick was as careful of the health of his men as of his own.

But five of the men were not asleep. Three of them were Phil, Dick, and Carl.

During the evening they had been in close conversation together, and the outcome of it was a resolve to attempt a very daring thing. Carl and Dick were to carry it out.

They waited until all the rest were apparently asleep, and then cautiously got upon their feet and stole away out of the wood.

A short distance away the two captured horses were tethered by the lasso-ropes which every Boer carries attached to the saddle. The hardy animals had made a meal of the coarse long grass around, and were lying down to rest.

Phil fished out the two saddles from some adjacent bushes, and stirring up the not too willing steeds, placed them on their backs.

"I won't hurt you," said Phil, as he patted one of their necks. "You are only going for a gentle trot around."

Dick and Carl got into the saddle, and with a "good luck to you" from Phil rode quietly away into the darkness.

Phil walked slowly back to the edge of the wood, and leaning against a tree, was getting his pipe ready for a smoke, when a shuffling sound close by fell upon his ears.

In a moment he became as still as an Indian scout who hears the footsteps of an enemy, scarcely breathing.

Somebody was coming from the direction of the camp towards the open ground.

It was Pan and Ajax, who, while feigning sleep, had not observed the departure of their leaders, and were now bent on making an effort to escape.

That is, as far as Pan was concerned. Ajax was a most unwilling sharer in the venture.

"Come on and walk quicker, can't you?" hissed Pan. "You are more like an elephant than a man. Fiend alive! what are you treading on now?"

"It was a dry stick," replied Ajax.

Phil heard their voices and recognised them. He guessed their object, but not exactly the full intention of Pan.

"Going to make a run for it," he muttered. "Well, I'll have a bit of fun with you."

He had with him the lasso-ropes by means of which the two horses had been tethered. At one end of each was a running noose.

Putting one of the coiled ropes over his shoulder, he got the other ready for a throw, and, crouching down, awaited the coming of Pan and Ajax.

They came up and stopped short within a few feet of him.

"Now let me see," said Pan. "I don't want to make a mistake. The horses were tethered about fifty yards straight from here. Listen. They are sure to make some sort of sound to guide us."

They listened for awhile, but heard nothing. An impatient exclamation escaped Pan.

"Hang the brutes!" he muttered; "they can't have got away."

"I should think so," replied Ajax, readily. "We had better go back."

"You are an idiot," was Pan's kindly recognition of this suggestion.

Again they stood still and listened, but not the slightest sound was heard.

"We must go and look for them," said Pan. "March on ahead—I can't trust such a skulker as you are."

Ajax had taken but one step forward when a short, sharp cry of pain was heard from Pan.

He turned in alarm, and saw his companion drawn back against a sapling-tree.

By his constrained attitude it was clear that he had his arms pinioned to his side.

Utterly bewildered, Ajax stared blankly about him until he heard something whirr over his head and settle down upon his shoulders.

"A snake!" he roared.

It was the rope, and nothing more.

Phil, hidden by the darkness of the wood, jerked it, and Ajax, yielding like a child, allowed himself also to be drawn back to a tree.

There the rope was passed two or three times round him and secured by an experienced hand.

Not a word was uttered, and when the work of securing him was completed his captor seemed to vanish away into space.

Nothing more was heard of him for awhile.

The only sound was a slight hissing emitted by the terrified, humiliated Pan, who in his heart put down his capture to Dick Strongbow, and was afraid to move or speak.

Ajax was the first to open his mouth and deplore the end of their attempt to escape.

"I knew something wrong would come of it," he groaned.

"What's done to you?" asked Pan, softly.

"Bound to a tree."

"So am I, but it's only a rope, and a man of your strength can snap it like a thread."

"I'm not going to try," mumbled Ajax.

"Why, man," said Pan, "haven't you snapped CHAINS across your chest, and are you going to let a few strands of hemp hold you?"

"It doesn't matter what I've done," sulkily replied Ajax, "I'm going to do nothing now."

"We've been bound here by Strongbow," said Pan, "and he's gone to get the men to hang us."

"I can't help it," groaned Ajax; "I've led such a life that I think I'd just as soon be hanged as not."

"Hanged!" exclaimed Pan, hoping to terrify him into doing something to get free. "Do you know what it means? Come, you can break your rope and set me free. Act like a man."

"I can't—I daren't."

"Think of what's coming. Fancy that rope round your neck, and you hauled up as helpless as a doll—choking—choking, your blood on fire, your eyes starting out, your life going. Come, be a man, and snap that rope."

"I'll try," groaned Ajax.

And try he did, but Pan, in his eagerness to frighten him into action, had overshot the mark.

The fearful picture of hanging drawn by Pan had made him helpless with fear.

The old limpness which he experienced more than once when he encountered Dick in days gone by had come over him.

"It's too much for me," he whispered; "I can't even strain it."

Pan opened his lips to favour his old master with one of his usual string of left-handed compliments, but was checked by the sight of a flash of light in the distance.

It was followed by another and another, and after a few moments the sharp rattle of rifle-firing was borne down to him on the night air.

"What's that?" he cried. "Who's fighting yonder?"

The flashes of light had been seen by another— Phil Norton, who, standing a few feet away from the prisoners, had been an amused listener to their talk.

He knew the portent of those flashes, and hurried back to the camping-ground.

"Up, lads!" he cried; "you may be wanted."

His clear voice startled the sleepers, and, like men accustomed to the experiences of a hardy life, full of peril from foes, they were awake and alive to their position in an instant.

Muffins, who had been sleeping very soundly, was aroused also, and, jumping up, saw the men gathered around Phil Norton.

"Boys," he was saying, "the cap'en and Carl have gone to have a look around with the hope of lighting on them Boers, so as to borrow a few horses from 'em. It 'pears to me they have hit on 'em."

"Hurrah!" cried the miners.

"Don't shout yet," said Phil. "I can't tell you what luck they've had; but there's firing out yon, and that's how I know they've hit on 'em. Follow me; we've got to be ready for action if we're wanted."

In a body they followed him to the skirts of the wood, where they got a view of further indications of a lively time ahead.

Right and left flashes of light leaped out of the darkness, and the sharp rattle of the reports, assisted by the echoes, put an end to the stillness of the night.

"Anyway," said Phil, exultingly, they ain't got the cap'en yet. The Boers don't waste powder and shot on the empty air."

"I hear some horses coming, Mister Norton," shouted Muffins.

"Are you loaded, lads?" cried Phil.

The miners, who slept with their weapons ready loaded by their sides, answered in the affirmative.

"Wait for the word from me," said Phil. "If it's the Boers coming, we'll give 'em a warm reception. Fire low. If you bring the horse down you've done for the man. Silence!"

In the stillness which followed his command the thud of the hoofs of the approaching horses could be plainly heard. The sound increased each moment in volume.

"There's fifty of 'em at least," thought Phil.

Louder and louder grew the sound, and Phil, straining his eyes, endeavoured to make out the approaching horsemen.

He had little doubt in his heart that it was the Boers, for the horses were coming on well together.

"Dick and Carl went out to stampede their cattle," thought Phil, bitterly, "and failed. Ready, lads!"

"Phil Norton, ahoy!" sang out a cheery voice.

"Dick Strongbow, by Jingo!" yelled Phil. "Cap'en, ahoy!"

"All right there?"

"All right."

"And all right here. Stand away a bit. We've got half a hundred horses with us."

"By George!" cried Phil, amazedly. "Stand back, lads; loose horses are dangerous in the dark."

As the men retreated to the wood the voice of Dick was heard calling upon Carl to rein up. A few moments of wild movement of horses followed, and then came comparative stillness.

"Give me your rope, Carl," Dick was heard to say; "we must put their heads together. They can't bolt then."

After a brief delay Dick came riding to the wood, and, dropping out of the saddle, called for Phil Norton.

"Here," said Phil.

"Glorious fortune has come to us," said Dick, gleefully. "We dropped upon half a hundred horses tethered in a circle together—heads inside."

"Boer fashion," said Phil.

"Just so," returned Dick. "So we loosened two of the lariats—Carl took one, and I the other—and here we are with a horse for every man and some cattle to spare."

"Any harm done?"

"No."

"But how did you get away untouched? The Boers are like cats, and can see in the dark. And they can shoot as well as they can see."

"There were several circles of horses," said Dick, "and somehow a second lot broke away and took a direction wide of us. It was that lot the Boers favoured with their attention."

"We are in luck," said Phil; "but it's not our luck, it's yours. It's the luck of the Diamond King."

CHAPTER XII.

TRESPASSERS—THE LONE HORSEMAN—THE NEWS HE BROUGHT—DEAD MAN'S PASS.

FIFTY horses with saddles and lasso-ropes or lariats, as they are more often called — complete. What a haul! What splendid fortune for the band of men under Dick's command!

With horses to ride the men thought nothing of the many miles they would have to travel, and this great boon they owed to their plucky leader and his friend Carl.

No more sleep was to be thought of that night, save for the trio whose wakefulness had resulted in such a splendid result for all.

Dick, Carl, and Phil lay down for an hour's rest, and as a proof of the excitement caused by the success of the night's adventure, it may be stated that Pan and Ajax were completely forgotten.

The miners were enjoined to keep an eye on the captured horses, and they carried out their instructions by going out in a body and hovering near them all night, ready to put a stop to any dangerous, restless movement. But the horses were tired out, and needed no watching.

Accustomed to being tethered, they lay down and rested or slept until the morning came.

Phil was awakened by a roar of laughter, and, rising, as Carl and Dick were coming out of their sleep, he saw Muffins running in towards him.

"What's the matter?" asked Phil.

"Pan and Ajax!" gasped Muffins. "The men are having games with 'em."

"I had forgotten the beggars," said Phil.

He told Dick about the attempt of these worthies to escape, and then, for the first time, the full extent of their intention was made clear to him.

"They meant to steal the horses," said Dick. "Well, they shall ride away from here—my way—not their own."

He paid the wretched captives a visit. The men had been up to tricks with them, chalking their faces and putting grass into their hair, to make more hideous what a night's unrest and terror had made sufficiently repulsive.

With his own hands Dick let them loose, boxed their ears, as if they had been naughty schoolboys, and told them to go back to their work.

It was a relief to both to find they were not to be hanged, and they went readily, not dreaming of a treat Dick had in store for them.

He cast his eyes over the open land and saw no sign of the Boers. In two or three places, about a mile away, there were small dark mounds, which he rightly guessed to be dead and wounded horses, which the Boers had unintentionally shot when firing in the night.

All the rest had disappeared.

An hour later his own party were ready to move.

After two of the poorest brutes had been picked out for Pan and Ajax, and the next worse selected for pack horses, to carry the few camp necessaries they possessed, lots were drawn for choice of the remainder.

This was speedily carried through, and the men mounted.

Muffins had a quiet horse, which just suited him, for the boy had yet to learn the art of riding But he took kindly to it, and MEANT to stick on, which is half the battle of learning to ride.

Carl and Phil then mounted, and only Dick, Pan, and Ajax remained.

"Get up, you two," said Dick; "not that way—with your faces to the horses' tails, please."

"But how are we to guide 'em, master?" asked Pan, in dismay.

"You will be attached to the pack horses," said Dick; "it's that way, or you will be left behind on the trees yonder."

The significance of this hint was not lost upon the precious pair. With as much readiness as the novelty of getting the wrong way into the saddle permitted, they mounted, and their gallant steeds were attached to the pack horses.

These in turn were taken in charge by two of the men, and the cavalcade started.

About three miles of open country lay ahead of them, and then there were hills and broken ground, which might to a great extent impede their progress.

But Phil Norton said there was sure to be a trail to guide them, as the Boers were in constant communication with Cape Colony.

He and his men had come thither on foot over

the hills by a route impassable to horses, but he had no doubt of the existence of a tolerable bridle-road.

During half their journey across the open ground they saw no sign of the foe, but everyone had his eyes about him, and a keen look-out was kept.

Presently a solitary horseman was seen moving slowly along the horizon.

That is, he seemed to be going slowly, but a horse at that distance would be obliged to gallop to make movement discernible to the eye.

It was going in their direction, moving parallel with them, making for the hilly country.

"A scout going to give the alarm," said Phil.

"To whom?" asked Dick.

"I don't know," answered Phil. "There are not many inhabitants hereabouts."

"I do not think we need trouble about him."

In a little while the horseman disappeared, and as he did not come again into view, the possibility of his being a harmless rider, ignorant of their existence, was entertained.

"At any rate," said Dick, "I see no reason why we should trouble our heads about him."

Half an hour afterwards they struck the hills, and once more the good luck of Dick Strongbow was made evident.

After a short survey of the ground they came upon a distinct horse-trail leading into the hilly country.

"This is the Boers' road to the Cape Colony," said Phil, "or one way, at least. By to-morrow afternoon we ought to be on British soil."

.   .   .   .

We must take a more rapid flight across that broken country than Dick Strongbow could do, and carry the reader to a small piece of land about five miles on the south side of it.

A fertile spot, an oasis in a rather broad desert of hill and stony ground, about two miles wide and one deep, with a stream running through it—a fair amount of sheltering wood, but mainly grass-land.

Comparatively small as this spot of fertility was, quite a considerable number of men were camped thereon, without tents, however.

Horses could be seen tethered in every direction, nibbling the refreshing grass, and down by the stream rough men were busy with rather a womanly pursuit—washing their clothes.

But they had to perform this labour because no women were there to do it for them.

There was little mirth among them, for they were, as a body, heavy-limbed, beetle-browed men, who exchanged remarks in guttural tones, in which the words "gold" and "diamonds" were frequently heard.

Nearly to a man they were of Dutch breed, but here and there a dark-skinned Basuto or Zulu moved about with the freedom of their race, and obeyed the orders of the Boers with a dignified silence, bearing patiently the insults put upon them.

This party was from the Orange Free State, taking advantage of the lonely nature of the country to trespass upon and prospect a portion of British soil.

The fertile patch of ground gave them provender for their horses ; with their rifles they provided food for themselves.

It is part of the Boers' nature to prospect on land that does not belong to them, and these men were hunting around for a piece of land that might give them gold or diamonds.

Their cupidity had been aroused by the stories which had reached them of the success of the English in Cape Colony, and as that land had once been theirs, they hated the lucky possessors with their whole hearts.

They talked of little else but rich mines, much as the Jews of old used to converse in the Wilderness of the Promised Land.

"Our turn will come," said a tall, bearded man, leaning on his rifle. "The good luck won't always be with the thieves."

"They are everywhere!" growled another. "I'd like to have them shut up in a pen with a chance of shooting all—ALL!"

There were four men and a Basuto in the group. They were at the upper end of the pasture-land not far from the mountain.

Wearily they turned their eyes towards the hill

The road they came by could be seen between two steep precipitous risings of rocks and stones.

They were half regretting that they had left their farms on what promised to be a wild-goose chase.

No luck had attended many days and weeks of search.

An exclamation from the Basuto, and his outstretched arm, drew their attention to the coming of a horseman down the road.

The man was feebly striking his horse with his lariat, and the jaded beast could hardly respond to his call.

Both were almost pumped out, and as the horse staggered along the men hastened to meet them.

A messenger coming in this style must bring news of importance.

The man and steed got clear of the mountain road, and on reaching the grass-land a little momentary life was put into the horse. It broke into a feeble trot.

But only to cover about two hundred yards, and then stagger and fall.

"Ach!" exclaimed the spectators, "both are dead."

They ran up to give assistance, and at the same time the man made an effort to rise.

"It is Gaff Dietrack!" cried the foremost Boer.

"So—it is me!" gasped Dietrack. "Give me drink—I am going!"

One of the men pulled out a flask and put it to his lips.

He emptied it at a draught, and then in a few moments, with assistance, got upon his feet.

"What of my horse?" he asked.

"Dead, master—much dead ; all gone," replied the Basuto, who had made a rapid examination of the animal.

"So good a brute!" said Gaff Dietrack—"it is a pity ; but I had to ride hard all the way."

"What brings you here?" asked one of the men.

"I came to overtake—to find you," replied Dietrack. "While you are poking around others have been clearing out the State of diamonds."

"Ach! so? Who is it?"

"There are thirty of them, most English, or British. What does it matter—English, Irish, Scotch—any of the accursed breed?" replied Gaff Dietrack. "They come—enough!—each man a walking mine. They must bear hither through Dead Man's Pass. How easy to block it—to stop them—to pick them off! There are two hundred good men to follow up."

"Two hundred! Hein! it is too many to share."

"There is enough for all—more than enough; the chief has a large fortune alone—all have much. Lose no time. To the Dead Man's Pass! Stop them, if you are men!"

He tossed his arms up in his excitement, his eyes blazing, his hands trembling.

His fervour roused the others out of their natural phlegm.

"Call the men together," pursued Dietrack; "lose not a moment. Lend me a horse and I will go with you. More drink!—food by-and-bye."

"Here is some meat," said one of the men, taking out a package, wrapped in linen, from his breast; "it will put life into you."

Dietrack seized it, tore off the wrapper, and ate some pieces of meat as if he had not had food for a month.

He "wolfed" it, as the saying goes.

The Boers left him and ran for their horses, shouting to their companions to get their steeds and gather together.

Hearing the cries, the other men ran in from all sides. The news spread. The excitement was intense.

There was a brief time of maddening haste, getting to their horses, putting on the saddles, looking to their arms, and mounting.

A horse, belonging to one of the party who was unwell, was found for Gaff Dietrack. He took the command, and away they went pell-mell to block the Dead Man's Pass and to kill the men who had been appropriately called "walking mines."

·   ·   ·   ·   ·   ·

Meanwhile Dick Strongbow and his men rode steadily on, through desolate passes and between towering hills, guided only by scanty signs of others having passed that way.

Sometimes they came to a spot offering them two roads, and they had to judge by appearances which was the better one.

Phil was the best authority on the subject, and he guided them aright.

Here and there the road was so rough that they had to get off their horses and lead them, the poor beasts blundered about so badly.

Pan and Ajax were always compelled to remount in their first humiliating position.

"With your backs to all honest men you shall enter the colony," said Dick.

Night came, and they halted by a trickling rill that dribbled down the mountain-side, forming a small pool below.

Here there was some water for the horses and scant herbage to crop—better than nothing.

So they rested during the hours of darkness.

As soon as there was sufficient light in the morning they resumed their way. The roughness of the path increased, the hillside became more precipitous. They rode through valleys where gloom was dominant by day and deeper darkness held sway throughout the night.

"Here," said Carl, "in this spot some curse surely rests."

In two or three places they came upon the bones of horse and man mingled, sad relics of wanderers who had perished in that home of sterility.

The influence of such a ride could not be lost even upon men accustomed to a hard life. Gradually the cheerful chatting ceased, until all were riding along like dumb men.

But for the clatter of the horses' hoofs, or an occasionally startled neigh from one of the animals, the band might have been taken for spectres.

At last they came to something even worse than this.

It was a pass in which the rocks above overhung so as to almost meet.

A little more leaning, and they would have made a tunnel of it.

"Ah!" said Carl, breaking silence, "it looks like a road to the River Styx. I should not be surprised to find Charon, Death's grim ferryman, waiting for us at the end."

"It seems like the home of Death itself," replied Dick; "but we are not children, and bogies have gone out of date. Still, I like not the appearance of the place, and before you enter I will explore it alone."

"One go—all go," said Phil Norton.

"No," resolutely replied Dick, "I have a fancy for scouting work, and will go alone. Await a signal from me before you come on."

Then alone, sitting easily in the saddle, but watchful for some danger, which he instinctively felt was near, Dick rode into Dead Man's Pass.

CHAPTER XIII.

THE AMBUSCADE—A FIGHT IN DEAD MAN'S PASS—ANOTHER ROUT.

"RIDE on—hurry up, or you will be too late!" Thus spoke Gaff Dietrack as he urged on the Boers. Stimulated by avaricious thoughts Dietrack was himself again—strong, dogged, determined, and filled with hatred of Dick Strongbow and his successful followers.

On rode the party, their horses, accustomed to broken country, making light of the rough road.

Now and then one of the animals would slip and fall, throwing its rider; but, as a rule, they were up again in a moment.

A man was, however, disabled, getting his leg broken in one of these tumbles.

Regardless of his groans and cries, they rode away, leaving him to get on as well as he could without assistance.

On either side of the road the rugged, precipitous sides of the mountains rose higher and higher, and by-and-bye began to lean inward.

This was the other entrance to Dead Man's Pass, and here the Boers dismounted.

Leaving the horses in charge of two of their number, the rest hastened forward with Gaff Dietrack at their head.

"We are in time," he said, exultingly; "the English robbers and their crew are at our mercy."

The way was now literally paved with pieces of rock which had fallen at different times from the overhanging masses above.

The road darkened, for there was now an almost

continuous roof of rock over their heads. At intervals there were openings above.

It was like travelling through a tunnel, with a shaft for light and air every hundred yards or so.

At last the point Gaff Dietrack aimed at was reached. They were in time. The party of miners had not yet arrived.

Rugged rocks lying here and there formed excellent opportunities for ambuscade, and a few yards away was the narrow, low-arched entrance, with the full light of day beyond it.

This was the very heart of Dead Man's Pass.

Gaff Dietrack disposed of his men so that they could, if necessary, fire a volley; but to each man especial directions were given.

"As soon as they appear," he said, "we must make sure of two-thirds of their number."

To one he said, "Aim to the right," to another, "Aim to the left," and so on.

With his directions fully carried out, a party of horsemen riding up the pass outside must have suffered severely.

But one little matter marred the whole arrangement—the miners did not advance in a body.

About a quarter of an hour after the Boers had been posted in ambuscade a solitary horseman was seen approaching.

It was Dick Strongbow, who had passed through a short tunnel-like road, and now reached open ground.

Seeing that there was yet another ugly bit ahead, he came along coolly, to see if there was any danger about.

"A brave man that, anyway," said one of the Boers.

"It is Dick Strongbow," said Dietrack. "Now, be steady. Bring HIM down—riddle him! Every man aim at his heart?"

"But he is only one," urged a Boer, as he sighted his rifle.

"He is a regiment—a host; you do not know him," said Dietrack, hotly. "He can toss men about like straws, snap them in two like sticks, squeeze their heads off their shoulders with his finger and thumb. Kill him—riddle him! Hush! he is near."

Now, the Boers in their excitement had overlooked one thing—the acoustic properties of a covered way.

Dick, who had keen ears, heard a murmuring of voices as he drew near, and the nature of the danger ahead became apparent to him.

"The question is, how many are there?" he asked himself.

Prudence whispered to him to beat a hasty retreat, but one of his dogged moments was upon him, and, stooping a little in the saddle, he rode boldly into the dark tunnel-like place.

At the same time the gleam of two or three of the rifle-barrels caught his eye, and instinctively he threw himself flat on the side of his horse, so that his head was level with its neck.

Then came the volley, almost like the firing of one rifle.

Down fell horse and man.

"GOT HIM!" shrieked Gaff Dietrack; and, eager to have a chance of plundering the dead, he was the first to rush forward.

But Dick Strongbow, although he had fallen with his steed, was unhurt. The horse was fairly riddled about the head with bullets, and was out of its misery, but Dick, by the practice of the old Indian trick, had escaped.

For once in his life he played the spider, shamming death until Gaff Dietrack was upon him.

Then he sprang up and seized the startled Boer by the throat, gave him one nip, that utterly bewildered him, and then used him as an offensive weapon to upset the others advancing.

With tremendous force he hurled Dietrack at the foremost, and down they went as if struck by a thunderbolt.

Quick as hands could grasp he seized these fallen men, and hurled them one after the other at those behind.

It was a tremendous, overpowering exhibition of muscular power, and completely staggered the Boers.

Cries were heard—

"It is not a man, but a fiend. He is no living creature, but the genii of strength!"

Terrified out of all cool or collected action, they began to retreat, falling here and there over the rough stones as they tried to run.

Dick had done a great thing, but he was not mad enough to think that he could, single-handed, annihilate all these men, so he wisely resolved on taking advantage of their confusion to retreat.

So occupied were they by their own fears that they did not see him going until he was well out of the cave.

Gaff Dietrack, who was a man of leather, recovering from the confusion engendered by the rough treatment he had experienced, was the first to observe that Dick was walking away.

Rising, with an effort, to his feet, he rallied his followers with cries, calling upon them not to let one man go away and laugh at them.

"Shoot him—shoot him!" he shouted.

Dietrack had dropped his own weapon, and had to look for it.

The others had to reload.

By the time one was found and the others refilled with cartridges Dick was almost out of sight, and in a moment vanished round a bend in the pass.

"Follow him!" cried Dietrack.

The Boers lingered a little while, thus losing a few precious moments, of greater value than they thought at the time; but, urged on by their leader, they gathered courage and went in pursuit.

Now, Dick, although he walked quietly when in sight of the Boers, as soon as he got round the bend broke into a run.

He knew he would be followed, and he wished to make preparations to receive his enemies with all the honours they deserved.

Ahead of him was the narrow, overhung part of the pass which he had traversed first.

At the other end his friends, he believed, were awaiting him.

To reach them and return in force so as to meet the Boers on equal ground was his object.

"Have I sufficient time to do it?" he asked himself.

He feared not, but to his joy he saw that his orders had been disobeyed.

Out from the gloom of the narrow way rode Carl and Phil in hot haste.

"We heard the firing," said Carl. "and thought something had happened."

DICK STRONGBOW:
The Diamond King,
AND WONDER OF THE WORLD.

With a crash the door was forced clean off its hinges.

No. 7.

Price One Penny.

"Something has happened," replied Dick; "back with you. One good ambuscade deserves another. Where are the men?"

"Following slowly to see if they are wanted. Where is your horse, Dick?"

"Dead, poor brute! Ah! here are the fellows. Halt! there."

A few words of command and the men were back under cover, ranged in a double line, to give the Boers a welcome.

Rifles ready and everybody cool—the first row of five lying prone, the second kneeling, and the third erect.

Howling and shouting, the Boers, with Gaff Dietrack leading, came round the bend at a heavy trot.

When Dick gave the word, fifteen rifles, all that could be brought into use, belched forth their deadly fire.

Gaff Dietrack leaped up a foot in the air, and pitching forward, fell upon his face.

Half of those behind him fell also.

At that short range the bullets could hardly fail to kill, and of all who fell not one survived half-a-minute after he reached mother earth.

Those who escaped turned tail and fled, wildly shouting for help, utterly oblivious in their terror of the fact that no help was near.

A second volley from the followers of Dick, as the Boers reached the bend, dropped four more of their number, and the rest got away.

After a wild scramble through the darker parts of the road they eventually reached the spot where their horses were in waiting.

A few words to the men in charge of them sufficed to urge all that survived to scramble into the saddle and ride away to the oasis on the borders of the mountains.

Gaff Dietrack was dead.

Overwhelming defeat had fallen upon the attacking party, and a band of desperate men, headed by "a giant with the strength of a wild ox," was advancing.

Such was the tidings they took back with them, and immediately there was a stampede of all who remained of the band.

Boers and natives rode or ran away, and when at dusk Dick Strongbow and his followers emerged from the mountain-pass they found the pasture deserted.

CHAPTER XIV.

CAPETOWN—THE DIGGERS' SALOON—THE FREE-HANDED STRANGER.

INTENSE excitement reigned in Capetown. Tidings of a great discovery of diamonds had been brought by some ragged, half-starved Boers, who declared that the lucky finders were coming in literally laden with the precious jewels.

On the outskirts of the town was one of the favourite resorts for loafers, gamblers, and gentlemen of that ilk. It was known as the Diggers' Saloon.

Its company was in a general way so rough that a forewarned stranger, if he went there, took with him the familiar brace of revolvers, and carried them in a place handy for immediate use if required.

Too often he discovered that the precaution was not needless, but a stern necessity.

If he met with a quarrelsome frequenter, he generally had to "shout," that is, stand drinks all round, or take his chance of being shot.

As a rule, the habitués played fair.

If one of their number tried to take a rise out of a new comer, and got laid out for his pains, there the matter was allowed to end.

They carried their fallen friend into a shed and laid him down until somebody was kind enough to bury him.

This task fell, as a rule, upon the landlord, who had to do it in self-defence.

In that climate the dead soon make their presence objectionable, and some sort of interment is imperative.

With a spirit worthy of a great public purveyor of amusement, the landlord of the Diggers' Saloon had put aside a portion of his garden as a burial-ground, a "quiet corner," where some score of rough mounds told their tale of past encounters.

Of course tombstones were considered superfluous, and even a wooden cross would have been looked upon as a vanity. So there was nothing to give any information about the individuality of the departed.

In no place was there a more idle gang than there was in the Diggers' Saloon.

The class of men who frequented it were not fond of work of the ordinary kind, but preferred a short route to money-making.

Diamond-finding was, in their eyes, one of the few desirable pursuits by means of which daily bread was earned.

Among the frequenters there was a tall man of fifty or so—a grizzled, dangerous man—a hard drinker and ready fighter.

A wonderful shot when sober, and a fair one when in liquor.

He was an Englishman, and despite his rough exterior, was, in comparison to his fellows, a very courteous man.

The tone of his voice was good, and he was evidently well educated. He was also given to talk about the "legal rights" of people, and was fond of expounding the law on any subject to those who obeyed no law but that which was agreeable to them.

Report said that many years before he came from England with a lot of money, which he spent freely or lost in gambling with sharpers, to become a sharper in his turn, as other flats have done.

Sometimes he was called "Gentleman Jim," at other times he was "the Lawyer;" proper name had he none.

On a particular day—the exact date does not signify—he was standing in the bar with half-a-score loafers, and the talk ran on the rumours afloat about the discovery of diamonds.

Among the company was a Boer named Hebran, who was one of the purveyors of the exciting news.

"We have heard such yarns before," said Gentleman Jim, "and so often it has turned out nothing but lies."

"I do not lie," replied Hebran, fiercely. "I

have seen the diamond field, and the men who skinned it."

"Well," said Gentleman Jim, "I'll believe you when I've seen the men and TESTED THEIR POCKETS."

There was a general laugh at this, for "testing" meant rifling in some way, and that was a pursuit very much to the taste of the listeners.

"You won't find it easy to test some of them," said Hebran.

"Indeed ?" said Gentleman Jim, slowly.

"No. I can speak for one man," replied Hebran, "who will make rags of you."

A dead silence followed this audacious remark.

Nobody had ever come to that saloon who could "make rags" of the Lawyer—the coolest, quickest, and one of the surest shots in the colony.

"If you were not a beggarly Dutch cheese," said Gentleman Jim, with his hand gracefully resting upon his hip, "I'd make rags of you for that suggestion."

"You are not man enough," replied Hebran.

In justice to the Boer, we must point out that he was a stranger to the place, and did not know the man to whom he addressed these objectionable remarks.

As he spoke he thrust his hand into his pocket, but he never drew it out again alive.

There was a quick tigerish movement on the part of Gentleman Jim, a turn of the wrist, a sharp crack of a revolver, and then Hebran tumbled in a heap by the side of the bar.

The landlord, who was arranging some bottles on a shelf at the back, did not so much as turn his head, as he enquired—

"Have you settled him ?"

"The usual place," replied Gentleman Jim, coolly, "just between the eyes."

"Put him away, gentlemen," said the landlord.

Four of the loafers picked up the dead Boer, and Gentleman Jim, with the air of a sporting man who had just performed a successful feat, ordered drinks round.

Ere they were served the four bearers came back again, and, without any remark about the victim, partook of their share.

"If the story's true, lads," said Gentleman Jim, "we've got to keep an eye for the coming of the lucky ones. I don't see why they should not share a bit with us. Eh ?"

Another laugh followed this humorous suggestion, and no more drink being forthcoming, some of the idlers lounged outside.

Before them was a wide, roughly-kept road, leading into a vast tract of country, poorly populated in comparison with home places, but still inhabited according to colonial notions.

About two miles away there was a cloud of dust, with some imperfectly defined forms of horse and man in the thick of it.

A riding party was approaching, and the news being conveyed inside, there was a general movement out of the bar to survey the approaching riders.

"A party of settlers coming to market," said one.

"Too many of them," replied Gentleman Jim, sententiously. "It may be the lucky ones, boys. They're pretty strong."

"Too many for you," said the landlord, who had come out with the rest.

"We shall see." said Gentleman Jim.

The party of horsemen came along slowly, their steeds fagged, for they had travelled far that day. Their riders were, as the reader will readily guess, Dick Strongbow and his followers.

As they drew near they looked somewhat ragged and forlorn, the result of a long and weary march through a poorly-occupied country.

Dick and Carl rode at the head, and, seeing the party outside the saloon, drew rein.

"Where is the nearest place for us to put up ?" asked Dick.

"Here is as good as anywhere, sir," replied Gentleman Jim, suavely. "There is a capital bit of grass at the back for the horses, and as for food and drink for yourselves you could not do better."

"Shall we halt here, Carl ?" Dick whispered.

"Why not ?" was the reply. "It will be just as well to get some decent clothes before we go into the town."

"Can you sleep us all ?" asked Dick, addressing Gentleman Jim.

"The landlord can," he answered, with a smile. "The fact is, it is not my place, but I live here, and am so well treated that I am always anxious to say a good word for it."

A bow from the landlord revealed his identity, and to him Dick now put a question.

"Can you sleep us all ? There are more than thirty of us."

"I don't think so," was the reply, "unless some of you can put up with a shed."

Here two or three of the men made a remark to Dick, and a short whispered conversation took place among the travellers.

The men wanted to go on to the town. They had reached a civilised place, and wished now to go their own way, as originally arranged.

It was only natural, for some of them had wives and families in other lands, and, now that they were rich, wanted to return to them.

Finally, it was arranged that they should go on, and only the following members of the party remained behind—

Dick, Carl, Phil Norton, Muffins, Ajax, and Pan.

The two last had no voice in the arrangement. Dick said they would have to remain yet awhile, and there was an end of the matter.

Then came the leave-taking, warm, but hearty, as became men of hardy natures.

A grasp of the hand, a kindly wish to one and all, and away they rode, each bent on going his own particular way and making what use he pleased of his store of diamonds.

Dick and the rest dismounted, and the loafers, taking their cue from Gentleman Jim, were very civil and obliging.

They offered to take the horses round to the grass-field and to give them some water, and the offer was gratefully accepted.

Dick still had some money about him, having had no use for it since he landed on the coast.

It was a mixture of French and English, but he knew that it would serve.

His first care was to give orders for the obliging loafers to be supplied with a moderate quantity of drink, as a recognition of their services, and then, after a moment's hesitation, he invited Gentleman Jim to dine with him.

"We are all strangers here," Dick said, "and I

shall be glad if you will give us some information about the country."

"Consider me at your service in everything," said Gentleman Jim.

At the end of the bar was a public saloon, capable of holding fully a hundred people. Behind this was a smaller apartment, and into that the landlord ushered his guests.

Gentleman Jim did not go in with them. He said he would join them when dinner was ready. Meanwhile materials for a wash and brush up should be sent to them.

He remained behind to give a few general instructions to the landlord.

"Two of the party are gentlemen," he said, "and as such will want different treatment to that generally bestowed upon your guests. Give them a clean cloth and knives and forks. For meat, you had better twist the necks of half-a-dozen fowls, and perhaps that wench of yours can make some sort of a pudding."

"I wonder who the big fellow is?" said the landlord.

"Don't waste your time in wondering," returned Gentleman Jim, "but just bustle about and let us have dinner sharp."

"Here's two of 'em coming out again," growled the landlord.

Gentleman Jim cast a glance up the saloon, and saw Ajax and Pan sullenly walking towards him.

"Put the whisky and some glasses on the bar," he said, "and leave these two to me. Then run out and tell the boys not to hurry back for five minutes or so."

———

CHAPTER XV.

AN EVIL COMPACT—A DINNER—IS IT THE MAN? —TRYING THE DOOR.

AN came into the bar with the mighty Ajax behind him.

Both had a sullen, discomfited air about them.

"Have a drink with me, gentlemen?" said Gentleman Jim.

"Don't GENTLEMAN us, please," said Pan. "We are only servants—flunkies to that squad in there."

"Indeed!" exclaimed Gentleman Jim. "I should not have thought it. But servants or gentlemen, have a drink."

It was a thing neither could refuse, and they named the ubiquitous and too-popular whisky.

The stuff supplied to them was strong enough to eat holes in iron, and it soon loosened their tongues.

In a quarter of an hour they had told Gentleman Jim many things about Dick Strongbow and his recent adventures, which interested him keenly, but they only let him into a knowledge of part of the truth.

They said nothing about our hero's enormous muscular strength, but they did not forget to laud that of Ajax.

In him Gentleman Jim saw one who would very probably become a useful tool, so he made much of him and trusted they would be friends.

He let them know that he was boss around there, and could at a pinch gather a hundred men around him.

A little later on these three, villains each one, had entered into a compact, the nature of which will be apparent as our story proceeds.

"I have only to tell you this much," said Gentleman Jim, when it was settled, "that I will not bind you by oath or even by your word. If you attempt to betray me your doom is sealed. There is no place in this country where your lives will be safe from me."

"It's all right," replied Pan; "we will be true to you. The moment you began to speak I saw a chance for what I had been longing for."

And then they shook hands to seal the compact.

Dinner was shortly afterwards announced by the landlord.

Ajax and Pan were told they could have what they required in the saloon, and Gentleman Jim sauntered into the inner room.

As he passed through the doorway he saw Carl and Dick talking together, and two words from the lips of the latter fell with great distinctness upon his ears—

"Jacob Morelle!"

He immediately stopped short, and his cheeks blanched to a dull leaden hue. He grasped a chair hard by, and stood there staring at them with wild, terrified eyes.

Carl was facing him, and saw these evidences of a strange and overpowering emotion.

"I fear," he said, "that you are unwell?"

"No, it is nothing," replied Gentleman Jim, rousing himself. "I occasionally get a slight attack of indisposition. It is a matter of digestion, that is all."

He smiled in a wan way, and took a seat pointed out to him. He faced Carl.

The table was laid for five, and Muffins sat opposite his master.

A dish of boiled fowls, with accompanying vegetables, was put upon the table, also some bottles of Cape wine.

They talked, as strangers do, for awhile of general matters, but by degrees Gentleman Jim led on Dick to talk about his early life.

"You were not brought up to the rough life of a settler?" he said.

"No," replied Dick. "I spent my early life with some circus people. My mother was a celebrated equestrienne."

Why he should name this he could not tell, but it was out, and Gentleman Jim was fully entitled to enquire further.

"And your father, too, I presume?" he said.

"No," answered Dick. "He lived with them, but was not of them. I have every reason to believe that he was well-born. My uncle, my mother's brother, as good as told me so."

"Indeed?"

"Yes, and dying, he informed me that he had left a packet with a man in Dane's Inn, London, which would let me know all."

"And the name of that man?"

"Jacob Morelle."

Gentleman Jim helped himself to a glass of wine, drank it off, and then said—

"And this Mr. Moselle—Morelle. What had he to say for himself?"

"Nothing," replied Dick. "I could not see him. I could not find the man. On making inquiries at Dane's Inn, nobody seemed to know anything about him."

"Ah! then I can guess at the root of that business," said Gentleman Jim, with a laugh.

"You think he is a myth?" queried Carl, who had been casting keen glances every now and then at the guest.

"I am sure of it," said Gentleman Jim. "These strollers are romantic people, lovers of mystery, and they put a halo round you which was not warranted by facts. This Gonzalo you speak of doubtless dwelt upon it, and in the semi-delirium of his last moments he—"

"I assure you," said Dick, "that he was quite collected, and was at no time in his life given to romancing."

"But surely your father, Mr. Strongbow—"

"My father's name—that by which he was known—was not Strongbow."

"But yours is?"

"I call myself Dick Strongbow, and that must suffice now, as it has done before."

Dick spoke politely enough, but his manner made it perfectly clear to Gentleman Jim that any further pumping would be distasteful.

With ready discretion he put on an air of indifference.

"It's no affair of mine, of course," he said, "and if I give you a piece of advice I do not intend to be impertinent. If I were you I would bother no more about Jacob Mo—Mo—Morelle. That's the name, I believe?"

"It is," replied Dick, "and I have such a firm conviction I shall one day meet the man, that I do not intend to abandon the hope of coming across him."

"When a man gets hold of a conviction of this nature," remarked Phil Norton, "there is generally some foundation for it."

Gentleman Jim laughed, and drank off a glass of wine.

"I am not going to quarrel with you about it," he said, "but I have met with so many mysteries without any bottom to them, that I am not at all inclined to believe in your success."

The subject then dropped, and general talk saw out the dinner. A second supply of wine and some cigars finished the entertainment.

"I am sure you are tired," said Gentleman Jim, as he rose from the table, "and stand in need of a good long sleep. You can put up with a rough bed, I hope?"

"After having had nothing better than the hard ground for many days," returned Dick, "I think we can."

Muffins had talked very little during the dinner, and while the men were smoking, he fell asleep in his chair. No leave-taking in his case was necessary.

Gentleman Jim went out, Carl politely escorting him to the door. He closed it, and stood there listening until the footsteps of the retreating man had died away.

"Anything wrong outside?" asked Dick.

"Much that is wrong has just left the room," Carl replied. "Dick, did you not observe anything peculiar about that man?"

"He seems to be a decent sort of fellow," replied Dick, carelessly, "and disposed to be helpful to us."

"But when he came in first—his sudden indisposition?"

"Yes, that was queer."

"He heard what you were saying. You were talking of Jacob Morelle."

"But why should that upset him?"

"BECAUSE HE IS THE MAN," said Carl, in a clear, thrilling whisper. "Steady, Dick—don't say anything to give a clue to a possible listener."

Dick was looking at Carl and Phil with the intensity of one startled and utterly dumfounded, but not a word escaped him.

"The man," said Carl, "and no other. I saw it in his face. Don't worry yourself about the strange chance that has brought you together, but accept it as a fact."

"But if he is Morelle," said Dick, "why did he not say so?"

"Oh! thereby may hang a tale," returned Carl; "anyway, we won't try to get at the bottom of the affair to-night. A good sleep will not do any of us harm."

He opened the door and looked forth Pan and Ajax had disappeared, and the bar was half filled with a rowdy lot of noisy men.

"The door of our bedroom is close by," he said. "I suppose we shall find the place ready."

"Rouse the boy," said Dick; "he is to sleep in the same room with us. Carl, you have given me a bit of a shock, and I feel as if I can't rest until—'

"Dick, you must rest. You won't get anything out of that man by questioning him here. We must entice him into a quiet place and force it out of him. Leave that until to-morrow."

Carl woke up Muffins by the simple process of lifting him out of his chair and giving him a shaking.

"Stand up, Muffins!" he said. "Now see how well you can walk."

Yawning and stretching, Muffins followed his master, Phil, and Carl into the saloon.

A small lamp was burning on one of the tables, evidently intended for them. The saloon was apparently not ordinarily used by frequenters.

The door Carl had spoken of was only a little way down. Taking up the lamp, he opened it, and they passed into a fair sized room, in which were three iron bedsteads with tolerably clean linen.

"I think," said Carl, "we had better fasten the door. Some of that rowdy lot might take it into their heads to pay us a visit."

There was a strong bolt to the door, which he pushed into the socket and tried. To all appearances it was strong enough to keep out intruders.

"Now tumble into bed and sleep," he said.

They got into bed with all speed. Muffins, who was to sleep with Phil Norton, especially exhibiting alacrity in this respect.

Carl and Phil did not intend to sleep for awhile if they could help it, and all sleep had fled from Dick's eyes.

After the lamp was put out they laid down, silent, but very watchful.

From the outside came a loud murmur of voices mingled with the rattling of glass, and then there would be a few angry words, but beyond these elements of rowdy life they had nothing to disturb them.

After a time the landlord was heard calling out that it was time to close, and in a little while the bacchanalians departed—some talking loudly and others singing.

The last speakers heard with any distinctness were the landlord and Gentleman Jim.

Judging by what he heard, Carl concluded that they were making up a bed for the latter in a corner of the room where our friends had dined.

And then, in a little while, absolute silence fell upon the place.

All this time the three friends had lain awake, each hoping and believing that the other was asleep.

But all three men were as open-eyed and clear-headed as if they had slept for hours.

This state of things could not last much longer.

They had felt the hardships of their recent rough life, and that day they had travelled a long way, when the worn-out state of their horses is considered.

Gradually sleep began to descend upon Carl.

He struggled against it at first ; but its sweet soothing influence was not to be denied, and at last —he slept.

How long ?

It might have been hours or only a minute. No dreams gave him a clue to the flight of time.

He sank into oblivion slowly and came out of it suddenly, to find himself in total darkness, and his mind marvellously clear.

A creaking, straining sound fell upon his ear.

He located it instantly. It was in the direction of the door.

Somebody was trying to quietly force his way in.

Old travellers are always prepared for emergencies, and Carl's revolvers were ready by his side.

He took them up and with one in either hand waited the development of events.

Creak—creak—creak.

Yes, there was not the least doubt about it.

Some expert hand at house-breaking was trying to force the door.

CHAPTER XVI.

DICK GOES MORE THAN HALF-WAY TO MEET THE ENEMY—AJAX MAKES CONFESSION—THE SALOON AT DICK'S MERCY.

FOR a little while Dick Strongbow, who was also awake, lay still, listening, so that there might be no doubts about the nature of the creaking sounds.

As far as the strength of the door went, he knew that an ordinarily strong man could easily force it ; but, for very good reasons, the person or persons now endeavouring to enter the room wished to do so quietly.

That somebody was endeavouring to do so there was not the least doubt.

"Carl !" whispered Dick.

"Yes ?" came back the soft response.

"Do you hear anything ?"

"I do—somebody trying to get in. I am ready for them ; I have covered the door with my revolver."

"Put it down," said Dick. "They are trying to break in, and I am going to astonish them by breaking OUT."

As Dick stepped quietly out of bed Carl did the same, and in a few seconds both had slipped on their clothes, except their hats.

Creak—creak !

The operation of cautiously breaking-in was still going on, and now Dick could see the door was bent a little inward, for through a crack a light in the outer saloon was visible.

"Don't stir, Carl !" was Dick's final whispered injunction.

Then he drew a deep breath, bracing himself for a great effort, and dashed at the door.

With a crash it was forced through, carried clean off its hinges, and down it went, with a man underneath it.

A few feet away Dick saw Gentleman Jim, standing with a lantern in his hand.

Behind him was Ajax, in an attitude expressive of mortal terror.

No other person was visible, and beyond the light thrown by the lantern the saloon was shrouded in darkness.

For one moment only Dick saw Gentleman Jim. The next instant the lantern was hurled at his head, and went out in its flight.

Dick threw up his arm, warding it off, and rushed at his assailant.

But the darkness was now complete, and Gentleman Jim eluded him, leaving Ajax to receive the rush of Dick Strongbow.

The lubberly giant went down with no more resistance than would have been offered by a figure of pasteboard, and Dick, carried forward by his impetuosity, fell over him.

"A light, Carl—quick !" he cried.

Carl was already engaged in lighting a match, and as soon as its feeble glare made things around partially visible, Dick saw that Gentleman Jim had escaped. The man who had fallen under the door had also got away.

"There's the lantern," said Dick ; "light it, old fellow."

Carl picked up the lantern, and having refixed the candle, which had been jerked from the socket, put the match to the wick.

"Now," said Dick, "we can have a look about us. Wake up Phil and the boy. It won't do to stay here. I reckon we have got into a den of thieves."

A somewhat violent shaking was needed to rouse Muffins and Phil, for both were sleeping the sound sleep of tired travellers, and while Carl was making them sensible to their position, Dick turned his attention to Ajax.

"Get up," he said.

"Are you going to hurt me ?" whined Ajax

"No, if you answer me truthfully."

"I will tell you all I know—indeed I will.'

Ajax got up, with a watchful eye on Dick, fearing a blow from his powerful fist, but Dick had always kept his word, even to arrant rogues.

"Stand there," he said.

Ajax took up a position in front of him. He bore a strong resemblance to a naughty boy at school, summoned by the master for punishment.

It struck Dick so, and an involuntary smile passed across his face.

"You meant to rob me to night," he said.

"THEY did," replied Ajax. "Pan said he would settle me if I didn't join in."

"And, perhaps, you meant also to murder me."

Ajax hesitated a moment before replying. Then he faltered out—

"Pan and Gentleman Jim said it would be better TO QUIET YOU ALL."

"Had the landlord a share in this business?" asked Dick, sternly.

"He knew something was going to be done," replied Ajax, "and had only left us a moment when Pan began upon the door."

"Why Pan? You were the stronger of the two."

"He said I should be sure to bungle it. We had to get in quietly."

"And Gentleman Jim, was he not expert enough?"

"Oh! he sort of bossed us."

"I see," said Dick; "a case of mind over matter."

Phil and Muffins now appeared, dressed in a fashion, the boy distorting his face in the most wonderful manner with a succession of yawns.

"Where does the landlord sleep?" asked Dick, abruptly.

"In a room behind the bar," replied Ajax.

Bidding Ajax remain where he was, and Carl, Phil, and Muffins to follow him, Dick threw up the flap of the bar and strode to a door immediately behind it.

Opening it unceremoniously, he entered the room, Carl following with the lantern. It was seen the landlord was not there.

"Bolted!" said Phil.

"It seems so," replied Dick, "and we ought to lose no time in getting away. Ajax!"

The giant came creeping out of the dark saloon, meeting Dick as he returned to the bar.

"I saw a lot of loafers about here to-day," said Dick, "where are they?"

"Gone down town, where they hang out," replied Ajax.

"You are sure?"

"Yes. Gentleman Jim said he did not want so many to share in—in what we were going to do. Besides, he told us they could not be trusted, but would be sure to get drunk and blab about things that would get us all into trouble."

"That sounds all right," said Dick, in an undertone to Carl.

"I think so," was the reply. "Hullo! Muffins. What now?"

The tired boy, standing just behind Carl, had fallen asleep and tumbled against him.

"I beg pardon, sir," he said, as he woke up, very wide-eyed, and just a wee bit frightened. "I feel as if I couldn't keep my eyes open."

"One thing is clear to me," said Dick. "We have this place to ourselves, and I would pull it down or fire it, but for the fact that it would give a handle to our enemies. Now, the question is—Where are we to go?"

"The town is all asleep by this time," said Phil. "There seems nothing for it but the open air. We have camped out before, and one night more will not hurt us."

Dick walked to the outer door of the bar, which he found ajar. By that way Pan and Gentleman Jim had, doubtless, made good their escape.

Stepping outside, he found all still, and overhead a sky brilliant with numberless stars.

Away to the left lay the lights of the town, which had an inviting look; but Dick decided to wait until the morning ere he showed himself among strangers.

At the same time he saw no necessity for sleeping in the open air, feeling convinced that he had succeeded in giving not only Gentleman Jim, but the landlord, a scare which would keep them away for a few hours.

He accordingly proposed that all should return to their beds except Ajax, who was told to lie down in a corner of the saloon, "like the dog he was," and stir out of it, until he had permission, at the risk of his life.

He laid down submissively, without demur, while Dick shut the front door and put up a wooden bar by which it was ordinarily secured.

Then they all went back to rest, and, strange to say, soon slept.

Dick was the last to close his eyes, for his brain was heavy with thoughts concerning the man who bore the name of Gentleman Jim.

CHAPTER XVII.

DOWN TO CAPETOWN—AJAX IS REPRIEVED— DICK'S PLANS.

 ALM and bright, with a refulgent sunshine, was the morning when Dick opened his eyes to find himself alone in the room in which he had slept.

Springing up he cast a hurried glance around him, and was beginning to wonder what had become of his friends when he heard a movement in the saloon.

Immediately after Carl presented himself.

"We let you sleep on, Dick," he said, "while we had a look round."

"What's the time?" asked Dick.

"About seven, I reckon," answered Carl. "Muffins has got the breakfast ready."

"Here?"

"Yes, there is plenty to eat and drink, and it would be folly for us to begin the day on an empty stomach. I have, however, one piece of news for you that you will not like."

"Ajax gone?"

"No; but the horses are."

"Well—they were not our own property exactly," said Dick, easily, "and I don't see that we have much cause to grumble, nor do I think we shall need them again."

Muffins was not an expert at laying a table, and in the eyes of a head-waiter of a fashionable hotel would have appeared a bit of a muff; but he had done his best to prepare a suitable breakfast, and those whom he served were satisfied.

Even Ajax was well supplied, and partook of a hearty meal alone in the bar.

In half an hour all were ready to start for the town.

"I suppose I needn't wash up," said Muffins, with a grin.

This office having been declared unnecessary, the party set out for the town, where the day was now begun, and the streets alive with busy men.

Capetown is a big place, having fully thirty thousand inhabitants, a considerable proportion of whom come under the head of "rough," which does not necessarily mean dishonest.

But it has its share of knaves and low dens, mainly on the side near Table Mountain, which rises majestically on its flank.

In front of it is Table Bay, where there is generally a fair amount of shipping.

As Dick and his friends descended to the town, they looked upon a picturesque scene, which, after their travels through lonely lands, was especially refreshing to the eye.

The party would have passed into the town almost unheeded, for men of the digger class abounded there, but for the presence of the giant Ajax.

His enormous proportions naturally attracted the attention of the wayfarers, who stopped to stare at him and to exchange remarks, more or less audible to Dick and his friends.

"I think we had better get rid of him," said Phil.

"Just what I was thinking," replied Dick, "but with a different purpose in view to yours. He will always be easy to find."

Turning to Ajax, he said—

"Here we part company. You are in a civilised place, and can easily earn your living. Go back to your old game and exhibit your feats of strength. You have no cause to fear that I shall come and spoil you. Only, one thing you must do."

Dick paused, and looking steadily at him, said—

"If you should by chance hear anything of the person calling himself Gentleman Jim, you must send the information to me."

"Where am I to send it?" asked Ajax, feebly.

"Direct your letters to me at the post-office for the present," said Dick. "Do not attempt to betray me or to deal falsely with me in any way. This is the last chance I will give you. Run counter to me again and I WILL PAY YOU IN FULL—you understand?"

"I do," said Ajax, hanging his head, "and I mean to do exactly as you tell me."

"You must," said Dick, quietly. "Here is a little money for your present needs. Now go about your business. I should think that you would be able to get an engagement at one of the places of entertainment here. Take another name."

"I'll do my best," said Ajax, wearily; "but I wish you had killed Pan last night. Had I not known him I shouldn't be what I am now."

"That I can well believe," said Dick. "But we must part now."

Ajax turned away, strange to say, sorry that Dick had got rid of him.

He had one hope, and that was that Pan and Gentleman Jim had fled up the country and would trouble him no more.

When Dick left him he was standing in a broad street, apparently one of the leading thoroughfares of the town.

There were several places of amusement in it, and a little distance down he observed a huge canvas in the front of a building, on which was inscribed—

ROYAL MUSIC HALL.
CONSTANT VARIETY.
The best hall in the town!

"I might do something there," he muttered, and walked over to the building.

It was not so gorgeous an erection as we have at home; but it was a place of mark in the colony, and the proprietor, a Jew, was a big man in the town.

He was at that moment standing by the main entrance—short and stout, much bejewelled and watch-chained, and wearing a shiny hat very much on one side.

"Can you tell me where I can find the proprietor of this place?" asked Ajax.

"And where may *you* come from," asked the Jew, "that you don't know ME, Ichabosh Beldan, Esq.? S'help me, I've come to something to be asked where I can find *myself!*"

"I beg your pardon," said Ajax; "I've only just come into the town."

"From the emigrant ship?"

Ajax nodded.

"And vhat may you vant vith *me?*" asked Ichabosh Beldan.

"An engagement as a strong man. I can do things that no other man can. Dumb-bells of three hundred pounds are toys to me. I can snap strong chains on my chest, bend a stout poker on my arm, and a score other things. Yes or no? If you don't want me I can go elsewhere."

Ajax could be bold enough in dealing with a little man like the Jew, and his sharp, decided way was not without effect on Ichabosh Beldan.

"Come in and let me see what you can do," he said; "I'm bound to get novelties for the Royal. Come in, I say."

While Ajax was thus making arrangements for himself Dick Strongbow was also making his arrangements for a stay in the town.

The first thing to be done was to get some ready money by selling two or three of the smaller stones in his possession.

There was no difficulty in doing this, as dealers in precious stones abounded. Dick selected a shop which looked as if it was one of the best, and entering, found a man about fifty seated behind the counter.

"What will you give me for these?" asked Dick, placing three stones upon the counter.

The dealer took them up and carefully examined them.

Dick, watching him closely, saw a satisfied look dawn upon his face.

"You did not get these stones at the fields," he said.

It was a wonder Mumms did not shriek out—for he recognised the unfortunate victim.

"No," replied Dick; "I found them in the Orange Free State."

"H'm! What part?"

"That," said Dick, "is my secret for the present. Do you buy?"

"I will give you twenty pounds for these stones."

"You mean a hundred."

"My good man, I should lose by the transaction.'

"This," said Dick, picking up one about the size of a small nut, "is worth more than I ask for the three, and you know it. Will you buy? I am not going to waste my time in bargaining."

"Ninety pounds," said the dealer.

Dick took up the stones and was walking out of the shop when he was hastily called upon to stop.

"Here is the money," said the dealer, "and if you have any more to sell, I'll purchase them."

"I have more," replied Dick, "but shall not part with them just yet."

Having got possession of a fair amount of ready money, he bought some general necessaries in the way of clothing, and having looked around a bit, selected as a place of temporary abode an hotel bearing the appropriate title of the Koh-i-noor.

But to find Gentleman Jim—that was Dick Strongbow's main object now.

He did not trouble himself about Pan, or his lost horses, or the saloon-keeper, but concerned himself with Gentleman Jim alone.

The suggestion from Carl that this man and Jacob Morelle were one and the same had become almost a conviction with himself.

On the morning after his putting up at the Koh-i-noor he was reading the town morning paper, when his eye lighted upon the following paragraph—

"A DESERTED SALOON.—The infamous den which for a year past has been run just outside the town by Tim Doohley was yesterday found deserted by Private Fenley, of the Mounted Police. Judging by the appearance of the interior, one of those scenes of violence for which this unhallowed spot has been notorious was recently enacted there. But the exact nature of it, in the absence of Doohley, cannot be ascertained. There are no signs of bloodshed, and the police are of opinion that the landlord and the gang which frequented his place have cleared out, and for good reasons have gone up country— probably to the diamond fields. Anyhow, the town is well rid of the gang."

So far all was well.

Dick saw that there was no prospective trouble to himself about the saloon business, so he could give all his attention to the one now absorbing subject on his mind, the discovery of Gentleman Jim.

That he had gone up country Dick did not believe for a moment. He was in everything a town man. There was nothing of the hardy adventurer or pioneer about him.

So in Capetown he must look for him.

Carl, Phil, and Muffins went out that day to look about them, but Dick remained at home, writing various memoranda and making arrangements for his future course of action.

In the evening his friends returned with the information, amongst other matters, that some men were pasting up bills advertising a new attraction at a music hall. They brought one with them.

It was attractive and arranged as follows :—

MORE NOVELTY! MORE NOVELTY!

ICHABOSH BELDAN once more to the fore.

THE STRONGEST MAN IN THE WORLD

Has been engaged to exhibit his unapproachable feats for a few nights only.

PANJAXICUM,

The giant, a man of marvellous muscular power, will this night perform the following feats, challenging rivalry and defying competition :—

He will bend a poker by simply striking it on his naked arm.

Snap a strong chain by expansion of his chest.

Toss enormous weights in the air, catching them as they fall.

Support a man at arm's length, raising him from the ground.

Wrestle with any man.

And in other ways exhibit his prodigious strength to a startled audience.

NO EXTRA CHARGE

Except to a few seats reserved for the *élite* of Capetown.

Come early to prevent disappointment.

A great rush expected.

"What a foolish fellow it is," said Dick, "not to be able to think of a better disguise than this; but he has done just what I hoped for—secured an engagement, and announced himself in such a way that he will surely bring his friend Pan back to him."

"Is it Pan you want?" asked Phil.

"Gentleman Jim will be in Pan's company," replied Dick, "and that is the man I want. I shall be at the Royal Music Hall to-night."

"Do not go alone," urged Carl. "Take me for company."

"I am not afraid of the fellow."

"Granted—but prudence is not unworthy of the bravest."

Then Phil wanted to go, and Muffins too, so it was settled they should make a party of it, and Carl went off to the Hall to engage four of the seats reserved for "the élite of Capetown."

He was successful in his object, and at eight o'clock the four fellow-travellers found themselves seated in the second row of the Royal Music Hall.

It was a big room, oblong square in form, with a stage at one end and a gallery at the other, and the success of the new engagement was evidenced by its being crowded in every part.

There was nothing very royal about the place, and the company was scarcely of the class one would expect to find at the Italian Opera at home. The majority of the men were of the working class, with a considerable sprinkling of loafers, and a few women.

The less said of the latter the better. One does not care to be hard upon even the most depraved of the sex, and therefore their looks and bearing may be left to the imagination of the reader.

A more noisy assemblage of men Dick had never seen gathered together, and he could not help thinking what a fearful scene a general riot in the place would be.

The possibility of such a thing taking place led him to look around to see what chance there would be of getting safely out in case of a general row, and it was not without a feeling of uneasiness for his friends that he saw two ways only were open.

One was by the main entrance under the gallery, the other was by mounting the stage, and so get out the same way the performers would take when making their exit.

While he was thinking over this state of things the musicians put in an appearance.

There was a long-haired, foreign looking gentleman, in a seedy evening rig-out. He took his seat upon the stage, in front of a well-worn piano.

The next was a stout, watery-eyed man, with a battered cornopean, the instrument having apparently been at one time used as a weapon of assault or defence in a free fight.

In addition there was a fiddle and a man with a bass viol, the latter a full-sized instrument, taller than the performer upon it, and HE was a tal man.

The first part of the entertainment was one of the modern so-called comic songs, with the usual objectionable matter accentuated by the license of the place—flavoured, in fact, and spiced to suit the audience.

An enthusiastic reception was accorded this doubtful performance, and the recognised repetitions followed.

Then appeared a man who walked, danced, and ran about upon a barrel, doing everything with it, in short, except getting inside it.

One of the audience did indeed suggest that he should jump through the bung-hole, but he was first howled down, and then violently ejected, as an unseemly jester who had exercised his wit at the expense of consistency.

After this three or four other forms of variety entertainments were got through with varied success, and then Ichabosh Beldan, in evening attire, diamond studs, enormous watch-chain, and his fingers covered with rings, appeared upon the platform.

He was hailed with a burst of applause, mingled with jesting queries about the object of his putting in an appearance.

"What are you going to do, old Ninety-percent.?"

"What's the price of pigs?"

"How about that shiny tile of your's, Ichy? Who paid for it?"

These questions were interlarded with suggestions that he should "stand upon his head and let 'em see the soles of his new patent boots," and that he should "raffle his watch-chain at a shilling a head."

One man asked him why he "didn't let the missus show herself, too?" adding that she IS a beauty, but you ain't, Ichy, and nothing can make you one."

With a dignified bearing that was intended to awe the audience, but only excited the laughter of the ribald spirits of the company, Ichabosh Beldan waited for the warmth of his reception to subside, and the audience having in the course of ten minutes worked off their superfluous vocal steam, he was allowed to proceed.

"Ladies and gentlemens," he began, "I have this evening the honour to interduce to you the—"

"That'll do, Ichy," said a drunken digger in a front seat. "We knows what's coming. Bring in your chain-breaker and let me smash him."

"Why don't you cheese it, Butterflick?" cried out someone in the gallery. "You are much too drunk to fight anybody but a baby."

This insinuation, or rather bold assertion, excited the ire of Butterflick, who stood up, faced about, and called on his asperser to come down and have it out with him.

"Not me," said the culprit. "I've paid my bob to see the chain-smasher, and not to sit on you. Your bounce ain't worth tuppence to nobody."

This contemptuous recognition of his challenge so excited Butterflick that he began to give the audience some very flowery specimens of digger language, and Ichabosh Beldan, stepping back to the wings, gave an order of some sort to an invisible person there.

"As I suspected," thought Dick, "there will be a shindy."

Turning to Carl, he bade him, in case of a row, see to Muffins, and take his cue about retreating at a fitting time from him.

Phil also received similar information, and Dick again turned his attention to the stage.

Four burly-looking men now came in and stood by Ichabosh Beldan, who, with calm severity, asked Butterflick if he meant to behave himself or be "led out by the ear."

Butterflick, who was not so drunk as to be quite insensible to the whisperings of prudence, said "that he would be mum until he saw what that Panjaxicum was made of; but if he was a fraud, like many other stars that had been run on that stage, he might expect to be made a mop of."

Ichabosh Beldan signalled to his chuckers-out to retire, and proceeded with his oration.

It was very eulogistic of Ajax, and the effect was heightened by the bringing in of sundry heavy weights, one after the other, in a barrow, the same being deposited with considerable thumping and rumbling upon the boards.

Ichabosh Beldan drew aside, and the band executed a wild flourish to herald the appearance of Ajax, who stepped with stagey majesty from the side and bowed to the audience

Catching sight of Dick, he turned pale ; but on a sign from our hero his confidence was restored.

A stout poker was handed to him with much ceremony by Ichabosh Beldan, and with one blow Ajax bent it upon his arm.

Then he straightened it by the same means, and enthusiastic applause testified to the satisfaction of the audience.

He next snapped a very fair-sized chain across his chest by inflation, and afterwards tossed the weights about in a manner that was really wonderful and dexterous.

Loud acclamations brought a flush of pleasure to his cheek, and he stood forward boldly to issue his challenge for all or sundry to come and wrestle with him.

Just for one moment he looked at Dick, with his eyes expressive of apprehension ; but seeing he made no movement Ajax was comforted.

Then was heard the voice which had previously resounded in the gallery.

"Now, then, Butterflick, are you going to do anything for the honour of Old Sally, or do you mean to lie down and let the stranger walk over you?"

Uprose Butterflick in his wrath, pulling off his coat with a jerky action.

"Old Sally," he said, "can look arter her own honour, and I'm a-going to look arter mine."

Dashing his coat violently down upon the seat he had vacated, he climbed upon the platform, there being no footlights, and confronted the mighty Ajax.

He was a big, muscular man this Butterflick, but he was no match for Ajax, if he could keep a heart in him.

As a matter of fact, Ajax saw no reason for fear and was bold as brass.

"What's it to be?" asked Butterflick; "two chucks out of three?"

"Yes," replied Ajax.

Then they cautiously approached each other, and, after a little preliminary fancy work, closed.

Butterflick made one effort, no more, and then was thrown upon his back with a violence that dispelled all the fumes of drink within his head and instantly made a sober, repentant man of him.

As he did not make any immediate attempt to rise, his friend in the gallery endeavoured to stimulate him with a few kindly words.

"Up agin, Butterflick!" he cried, "and let us see what you look like after your second chuck."

"I'll chuck you," growled Butterflick, "when I get over this. All right, mister," to Ajax, "I give you in best. I've got a feeling of general bust on me."

It was a happy moment for Ajax, and Dick did not begrudge it him. After all, the big lubber had been mainly the tool of a more venomous spirit than he had within him. He had been guilty of a great many things that were to be condemned, but he had suffered. To a certain extent he had paid the penalty of his evil-doing.

After a judicious rest, Butterflick slowly arose, hobbled to the edge of the platform, and descended with a gingerly care that excited the derision and laughter of the observers.

On getting back to his seat he addressed the audience as follows—

"You laugh—you catwollopers—you do. Why? Because you've seen a man try to do more than what's in him. It's only fair you should give me a laugh, as a square deal between us. Come up, some of you, and see what YOU can do."

There was no immediate response to this vicarious challenge, and it seemed that all the wrestling was over for the evening. But suddenly the audience were startled by a voice at the end of the hall.

"I'll have a try."

All eyes were turned in the direction of the speaker, who was seen to be making his way through the crowded hall.

Dick Strongbow watched for his coming and presently saw him. It was Pan.

It was clear that he had, as Dick surmised, been all the time in Capetown, but why he should risk a fall with his old master was not at first quite so obvious. But ere long Dick got at the truth.

He was bent on bullying Ajax into defeat.

He relied upon the giant's want of pluck, intending to terrify him in some manner, and when he was upset by weakness to throw him.

When Pan got upon the platform his appearance was hailed with a burst of derision, to which he responded with a gesture of contempt.

Advancing to Ajax, with his malevolent eyes fixed upon him, he hissed out these threatening words—

"Throw me, and you are done for. Gentleman Jim and his pals are at the back of the hall, and they mean to lynch you."

But Ajax did not look alarmed.

His recent success had put something like courage into him, and he also felt increased confidence from the presence of Dick Strongbow.

There was likewise another emotion at work within him.

He hated Pan with his whole heart, and he resolved there and then to avenge all past injuries by punishing Pan for his temerity.

THE WORM HAD TURNED.

Pan saw it, and as he moved a little aside, with a sickening sensation of fear, his eyes fell upon Dick Strongbow. The sight of him completed his confusion, and he would have turned tail and fled.

But Ajax would not let him go.

Stepping forward, he threw his huge arms about him, exclaiming—

"You've got to wrestle, and it won't be my fault if I don't KILL YOU."

Pan was, as we know, not an absolute coward, and he made one bold bid for liberty from the strong grasp of his old master.

It was a vain effort.

He felt himself lifted from his feet, the hall and audi seemed to turn right over, and then he was thrown.

The spectators had sunk into a state of breathless silence. Then the crash of Pan's fall was heard all over the place, and half the rough men there shut their eyes.

The fallen man did not stir. A woman screamed.

Then every tongue was loosened, and a chorus of fierce cries was heard at the end of the hall.

Up sprang a man into a prominent position upon a counter that served as a bar.

All could see him, and three-fourths of the audience recognised in him a man who, for years, had been a terror to many of them.

It was Gentleman Jim.

"It was no wrestle!" he cried, in a voice of thunder. "That fellow put the grip on too soon. The man has been murdered. At him, boys! A life for a life!"

CHAPTER XVIII.

THE RIOT IN THE MUSIC HALL—GENTLEMAN JIM HAS HIS EYES CLOSED AND OPENED AT THE SAME TIME.

"ARE Gentleman Jim's gang !" shouted a stentorian voice.

It was Butterflick who gave out this note of warning, and, as a preliminary to defensive operations on his own account, he laid hold of an empty wine-bottle by the neck and held it ready.

The gang under Gentleman Jim had the advantage of organisation, while the audience were only so many disunited atoms.

Discipline in its crudest form is an effective thing, and on this occasion, as upon others, it soon began to tell.

The gang, in wedge form, with Gentleman Jim at the head, began to force its way up the hall, amidst shouts and cries of terror from the men and shrieks from the women.

Blows were exchanged, none of them child's play and some very serious, and blood soon began to flow down the faces of many, who did not need this addition to their ordinary repulsive expression.

Acting on an old course of proceeding, the gang not only assaulted the audience, but began to rob. Watches, scarf-pins, and purses were appropriated with marvellous celerity, the victims vainly crying aloud for the police.

The police indeed were there, three or four of them at the entrance of the hall, but these were completely powerless to stem the tide of disorder.

All they could do was to dispatch one of their number for reinforcements, and this was promptly done.

Meanwhile, Dick Strongbow had been estimating the danger of the position of himself and friends. First of all he thought of Muffins.

Taking him up as if he had been a feather-weight, he lifted the boy upon the stage, at the same time telling him to go behind and get out of the place as soon as he could.

Then he turned to Carl and Phil and advised them to follow him.

"I can't do it," said Carl.

"For the sake of the boy," replied Dick; "they would murder him, if they laid hold of him. I can take care of myself."

Carl still hesitated, but Phil Norton volunteered for the service.

"I'll see the boy home," he said, "and come back again. It isn't far."

He jumped upon the platform, now clear of all but the fallen Pan.

The musicians, Ajax, and Ichabosh Beldan had fled, the latter having taken refuge in a cupboard in his private office at the back of the stage, where he was hurriedly engaged in removing his jewels and concealing those valuables in his boots.

What a scene it was that Phil Norton for the moment gazed upon !

In the centre of the hall was the gang, a compact mass of determined ruffianism, breaking its way through the seething, terrified audience.

He understood their movement thoroughly. To avenge Pan was merely a pretext; their real aim was violence and robbery.

There are some men who revel in scenes of bloodshed—and their appetites grow on what they feed on. Thus it was with Gentleman Jim and his gang.

They were drunk with the lust of cruelty.

Seizing Muffins by the arm, Phil hurried the half-dazed boy out by the wings—the way being indicated by a small stream of actors and assistants making their way to the stage door.

Outside there was almost as much noise and riot as within.

The news of a row at the Royal Music Hall had spread with lightning rapidity, and streams of night-birds were hurrying up from either end of the street.

Several cabs were in waiting for the chance of a customer, but their drivers, seeing that a dangerous row was on the board, were making preparations to drive off.

Phil stopped a cab and thrust Muffins into it.

"Take this boy to the Kohinoor Hotel," he said, "and wait till I come. You shall be well paid for your trouble."

"All right, governor," said the man, "I'll take care of your young 'un."

He lashed his horse, crying, "Hi—hi !" and the advancing mob broke away to let him pass.

Phil waited a few moments, watching, until he saw the cab turn into a side street. Then he felt satisfied that Muffins was safe, and he could return to the Hall.

To the stage door he hurried, and finding it open dashed in. All the company had fled by this time, and he met with nobody on his way to the stage.

As he drew near it the popping of firearms fell upon his ears. The more dangerous forms of fighting had begun.

When he came in sight of the rioters he felt like a man who suddenly comes upon a whirlpool. The confusion was chaotic.

Butterflick and two or three more men on the stage were busy hurling all the movables at their enemies.

The bass viol had gone, and pieces of it had been utilised for warfare. The piano had been bodily overturned below and formed a stepping-stone to the stage.

Pan had disappeared.

Phil took in all these things at a glance, and then he looked about him for Dick Strongbow.

He was still near the seat he had occupied, and beside him was Carl. Both had their eyes fixed upon the gang.

Suddenly Dick made a forward movement, and it seemed as if he went through everything like a steam-plough. Two seconds sufficed for him to stand face to face with Gentleman Jim.

Of all men Gentleman Jim had certainly not expected to find him there. That much was made evident by his start of surprise, and the sudden collapse of his onslaught on those about him.

He had been wielding a life-preserver with deadly,

effect, and he certainly raised it in a half-hearted manner to strike Dick, but in a moment it was wrenched from his hand.

Then our hero struck him between the eyes, not with all his might, for that would have killed him, but with sufficient force to promptly render them temporarily useless for seeing purposes.

He fell heavily, like a dead man, and Dick passed over him, shouting to Carl—

"Take care of him, and leave the rest to me."

Soon Dick was in the midst of the gang, and he scattered them like water.

Men in the gallery, who witnessed the scene, said that he was like a man endowed with super-natural strength, and bearing a charmed life.

The desperate men could not retreat, for the people they had so brutally assailed had closed up behind them, rallying at last—to act on the defensive and the offensive too.

Packed in so close together, the use of the revolver was dangerous, but some of the foremost had fired into the thick of the gang.

And now Gentleman Jim's followers were using their weapons too. It was their turn to be the weaker side, and they had to fight for liberty and life.

Dick swept in among them, using his appalling strength without stint or thought of mercy.

He treated them, as they fully deserved, like wild beasts.

Five hundred men in the gallery, and from various points of vantage in the hall, were witnesses of his prowess.

They looked on, wondering and cheering wildly.

Some of the gang he favoured with an old feat of his, tossing them in the air ; others he struck down with a force that sent them to the ground as if they had been hurled from the clouds.

Revolvers were pointed at him and fired by the terrified bullies, but where the bullets went no man knew. Not one touched Dick.

And now high above the uproar was heard a voice that was like the roar of the ancient Brazen Bull.

"Don't let one man do all the work. At 'em, boys !"

Then there was a closing in upon the gang, and the few remaining upon their feet were knocked down and secured.

The cries began to subside, the fight was over, but the excitement was still intense. A number of police officers appeared at the door, and spread themselves across the hall.

"Not wanted now," shouted a score of voices, but the policemen, in a line, began to press steadily forward.

They seemed to know exactly who they wanted, for members of the audience not connected with the gang were allowed to pass between them and go out quietly.

When they came to one of the body of assailants, they placed the handcuffs on him and he was put into a corner of the hall.

Some of the insensible ones were dragged there and laid upon the floor, to recover as well as they could, but three of their number would never speak again.

Of the audience two were dead also—one a woman, who had been knocked down and the breath of life trodden out of her.

The number who had received injuries of one sort and another was very great, but they were mainly of the class that a little sticking-plaister and rest would put right.

By the time the police reached the spot where Dick had brought confusion upon the gang, he had drawn aside and was standing quietly, a mere spectator of the scene.

Hard by was Carl, keeping a grip upon Gentleman Jim, whose eyes were quite closed up.

He was too well known to escape the police, and they at once made for him.

Carl looked at Dick enquiringly.

"Let them have him," said he ; "in prison I shall at least know where to find him."

"I want to know why you came here," said Gentleman Jim, as Carl pushed him over to the police.

"To stop your little game," was Carl's reply.

"I don't mean you," said Gentleman Jim, impatiently, "but that Dick Strongbow—the fellow with the iron fist."

"I came with the hope of finding you," replied Dick.

"And having found me, what then ?"

"Wait and see."

"I can wait, and you will have to wait a long time before you get anything out of me," said Gentleman Jim, with a sneer. "Blind as I am, I can see through your game, but you will live and die AND NEVER KNOW WHO YOU REALLY ARE. I've got the pull of you there, my young shaver. Now, gentlemen of the police, I am at your service. Be so good as to give me a hand, as I have got a short-sighted fit upon me. Dick Strongbow, BASTARD, *au revoir.*"

CHAPTER XIX.

GENTLEMAN JIM GOES TO PRISON—A DAY OF VISITING AND DEPUTATIONS.

IT was well for Gentleman Jim that he was blind and surrounded by the police when he hurled that insult at Dick, for assuredly, had he been otherwise situated, he would quickly have repented of his temerity.

Dick's face paled a little with wrath, but he made no reply to the dastard taunt.

"I may have to trouble you to attend the police-court to-morrow," said one of the police. "Where can I find you ?"

"At the Kohinoor," replied Dick ; "you have heard my name from that rascal's lips."

"It is an alias," said Gentleman Jim.

"I grant it, JACOB MORELLE," retorted Dick, "and before I have done with you I mean to extract my right name from you."

"Perhaps," said Gentleman Jim, drily.

The police led him away, and Dick having no further interest there, left the place, accompanied by Phil and Carl.

They found that order in the streets had been in a measure restored, the people being forced back and a space left clear, as if there had been a fire.

Having struggled through the crowd, they made their way to the hotel, where the cabman who had taken Muffins home was waiting.

Phil gave him a sovereign and received an avalanche of thanks in return. In the vestibule of the hotel they found Muffins in tears.

Muffins was very indignant. He did not like being sent home "just as if he was a baby," and didn't know how to take care of himself. He did not think that he was getting a fair show.

"It's my doing," said Phil, consolingly, " but the next time there is a certainty of your being knocked on the head I'll let you have your own way."

Dick ordered supper, and desired it to be something good, for they all had need of it.

"I don't know that it is wise to use my full strength," he said to Carl, "for I always feel so pumped out after it."

He made this remark as he sank back into a chair in their sitting-room, and indeed he did not look very well.

But Carl knew that it was not physical exhaustion which had made this change in his appearance.

It was the deadly insult thrown at him by Gentleman Jim. The sting of it had gone in deep, and left a poison behind.

"Dick," said Carl, quietly, "I don't want to touch upon a delicate subject, but that man is a liar. He will prove himself one, too, before we have done with him."

"Carl," said Dick, "you speak as a friend, but I cannot feel as you do. Gonzalo never told me my full history, but wrote it out, and reserved the reading of it until after his death. There must be some reason for that."

"Not the one that blackguard hinted at," said Carl. "No, my dear fellow. You may be easy on that score."

Dick was, in a measure, comforted by Carl's assurances, and when supper was served he was as merry as any of them.

The rest of the evening was, indeed, rather jolly, and Muffins forgot his grievance of "having no show," enjoying himself to his heart's content.

Dick's name was on every tongue the next morning. The daily paper had a long account of the riot, by "its special reporter," who had been there and seen it all with one eye, although he did not say so.

The second optic was closed up early in the riot.

Dick's name figured strongly in the reports, and there were at least half a dozen narratives by "Eye-Witnesses of the Scene," all of whom spoke of him as a marvel of strength and courage.

There was also an account of an interview with the proprietor, Ichabosh Beldan, Esq., who, according to his statement, had acted, like a true captain of a sinking ship, by being the last to leave the stage.

He said nothing about hiding in a cupboard with his valuables in his boots until everything was quiet.

There was besides a short statement from Ajax, who "had left the scene" when he saw the police and "gallant Mr. Strongbow" had mastered the rioters.

Carl was reading these statements to his amused friends at the breakfast-table when a waiter appeared and informed Dick that a gentleman wished to see him.

"Is it one of the police force?" asked Dick.

"No, sir. He looks like a digger, and says his name is Butterflick," replied the waiter.

Dick remembered the name and the man, as indeed the others did, and with a smile he desired Mr. Butterflick to be shown up.

Mr. Butterflick was accordingly shown into the room, and a glance at him sufficed to inform the company that he had got himself up for the occasion.

He was in his go-to-meeting clothes, his very best, consisting of a red shirt with big black spots, a blue check necktie, white leather breeches, and high boots in a marvellous state of polish.

A broad hat he doffed as he came into the room.

"Morning, Mister Strongbow," he said. "I hope you'll excuse me coming in at this time, but it's Bill Butterflick's game to be first on the job."

"I have no doubt of that," replied Dick, politely. "Have you had your breakfast?"

"No," replied Butterflick, "and at the present moment I don't feel as if I could eat any. To tell the truth, me and a few others got to drinking your health last night, and we kept at it so long that it's kind o' drove away our appetites. I don't mind a brandy-and-soda, though, my tongue being a bit leatherish."

Dick ordered the brandy-and-soda, and desired Mr. Butterflick to be seated.

"As I said," he observed, "I like to be first on a job, and perhaps you can guess the job I'm on?"

"No, indeed," said Dick.

"H'm! I should ha' thought you'd ha' jumped at it," rejoined Butterflick. "Arter what you did last night it's only nateral that a few deppytations should wait on you."

"Deputations!" exclaimed Dick, opening his eyes.

"Yes," said Butterflick. "We boys know pluck when we sees it, and although we don't count much on a man's mind, not being bothered with too many brains, we thinks a lot of muscle. Moreover, we've got a whisper of who you are. You've got the name of the Diamond King, ain't you?"

"Yes; it was given me by some friends—in jest, I should say," replied Dick.

"Jest be blowed!" said Butterflick. "And now I've got a great favour to ask of you—may I just feel your biceps? I want to get a touch of the arm that can do the things I saw done last night."

"Well, if it will give you any satisfaction—yes," replied Dick, laughing; "but, of course, I cannot be expected to grant the same mighty favour to all comers."

"Give it to me," said Butterflick. "Now let's touch."

Dick bent his arm, and Butterflick, using both hands, made a vain effort to span his biceps.

"It is a treat," he said. "And to think that I should be the first to receive the favour! I'm the proudest man in Capetown to-day. I ought to tell you that Panjaxicum was one of the party as drunk your health last night, and when he got pretty ripe he up and admitted that you'd chucked him orfen, but wouldn't do it last night out of kindness."

"That's a pity," said Dick. "Letting out so much may spoil him as an exhibitor of strength."

"Not that," said Butterflick. "He's chucked ME, and that's enough for Capetown. May I just feel them 'ere biceps again?—and then I'll be off."

He was allowed that pleasure, and then he finished his brandy-and-soda with a sigh.

"If I had an arm like that," he said, "I wouldn't change with a king who ate diamonds for his dinner ; but you've made me a happy man—and remember this—if Bill Butterflick can ever do anything to serve you, he's on the job. Good-morning !"

They let him get well away before they laughed over the interview, for the man was evidently in earnest, and did not seem to be a bad sort of fellow.

"It would be a pity to hurt his feelings in any way," said Carl, "but I could hardly keep my countenance when I looked at him examining your arm."

Butterflick was not the only earnest man on the subject. The greater part of Capetown was in a state of serious admiration of Dick's prowess.

Everybody who was anybody, and a great many nobodies, lost no time in waiting upon him.

Reporters were well to the fore—all in a state of thirst to get his full history out of him.

It was a day of visitors and deputation-receiving. One thing he was spared—he was not required at the police-court.

The prisoners had been briefly examined, and remanded for full enquiries into their antecedents.

It was a mere matter of form, as their antecedents were well known.

One of the visitors was a tall, lean man, with a humorous face, who gave the name of Dabster Brown.

He asked if Bill Butterflick had been there, and was very wroth when he learnt that he had been absolutely the first to call.

"Just like him," he said, "taking all the front seats."

"You are the man who was chaffing Butterflick from the gallery last night," said Dick.

"I am," replied Dabster Brown, "and when I do chaff him I've got the sense to have a few rows of people between us."

"But you may meet another time."

"Oh ! Butterflick don't remember chaff ; he forgets and forgives."

Dabster Brown departed, leaving behind him additional testimony of the natural worth of Bill Butterflick.

Late in the afternoon Dick got tired of visitors and would see no more.

Then a mob gathered outside and cheered themselves hoarse, and two or three born orators came to the front and gave impromptu lectures on "Pluck and muscle."

As the darkness set in they took to singing songs more or less eulogistic of brave men and Dick Strongbow in particular.

The police moved the people on now and then, but they came back again to sing louder than ever, until the lateness of the hour and a general hoarseness terminated the vocal festivities.

"It seems to me to be a lot of excitement about nothing," said Dick, as he, Phil, and Carl sat enjoying a last cigar.

"People everywhere go mad at times about something," replied Phil. "Music, circuses, quack doctors, anything. Here strength is king. Every man wants it, and they look upon such muscles as yours as they would upon enormous diamonds. That's how I take it."

"And the right way too," said Carl. "They are very earnest and honest, and that is something."

CHAPTER XX.

GENTLEMAN JIM IN PRISON—DOGGED AS A MULE—BUTTERFLICK AS ORATOR—STARTLING NEWS OF AJAX.

 OURNFULLY meditating sat Gentleman Jim in a cell within the prison of Capetown. On his face there was an expression which none of his rough companions had ever seen there.

It was a look of dejection and despair.

Strange to say, he never bore any resemblance, save in his attire, to the class he had mixed with for many years, but looked like a man of birth and breeding who had fallen upon hard times. He had a very clear idea of the lot in store for him.

His gang was broken up ; some were dead, others crippled for life, and the rest laid by the heels.

As the leader of a body of men long notorious, and who for years had succeeded in evading the law, he knew that all the punishment the judge could give would fall upon him.

"I shall get a lifer at least," he muttered, as he rose up and paced to and fro in his cell.

He took off his hat, and in a paroxysm of helpless fury cast it upon the floor.

"And I have to thank HIS son for it. What strange mishap has brought us together—or WAS it to be ?"

He paused, and drawing out a handkerchief, wiped his forehead, then resumed his walking.

"His son," he muttered, "and like him, too, although I never noticed it until it was too late. Had I seen it at once I would soon have put a hundred miles between us ; but now he has laid me by the heels."

Footsteps without cut short his meditations. There was the rattle of a key in the lock and the door was thrown open.

"A visitor to see you," said the turnkey, gruffly. Dick Strongbow entered.

Gentleman Jim knew who it was without turning towards him. Who else had he to expect ?

He had not a friend in the world, and only one enemy who would trouble to come and see him.

"I have an order for a private interview," said Dick to the turnkey. "Would you like to see it ?"

"No, sir ; I know it is all right," replied the man.

He backed out, closing and locking the door. Dick and the prisoner were left to themselves.

"Jacob Morelle," said Dick, "I have come to see you for the purpose of bringing you to reason, as much for your sake as my own."

"I am not Jacob Morelle," was the answer ; "and I have nothing to say to you."

"In vain you deny your identity," said Dick. "You betrayed yourself when you, like the hound you are, lied about my birth."

"What I said was—"

"Repeat the lie, if you dare."

The tone of Dick's voice was awe-inspiring. Gentleman Jim, or rather Jacob Morelle, as we shall in future term him, stopped short.

DICK STRONGBOW:

The Diamond King,

AND WONDER OF THE WORLD.

Butterflick counted ten and then fired with fatal effect.

No. 8.   **Price One Penny.**

"Say I am the man you name," he said, after a pause, "what then?"

"You have a paper which concerns me," replied Dick, "left in your charge by Gonzalo, the acrobat."

"Again, say it is true—what then?" asked Morelle.

"I want that paper."

"You cannot have it. I destroyed it accidentally with other papers."

"But you know the contents?"

"No; they did not interest me that I know of. The man, unsolicited, left the paper in my charge."

"By the desire of my father."

"I know nothing about that, and did not know your father."

"I have come to you, once for all," said Dick, "and you lie to me. It is enough. I shall not come again. You are throwing away your one chance of getting a mitigated sentence for your crimes. You will not tell me anything?"

"No," was the dogged answer.

"That will do," said Dick; "the hour of grace is past."

He tapped at the door, and the turnkey opened it.

Outside there was a view of a passage, and beyond that another open door.

What possessed Jacob Morelle to make a dash for liberty we cannot say, but make a run for it he did.

Plunging at the turnkey, he upset that phlegmatic official, only to be grasped the next moment by Dick, who seized him by the collar of his coat and threw him back into the cell.

It was far from a gentle action, and Jacob Morelle lay for a few moments upon the ground in a stunned condition.

The turnkey got upon his feet, and they waited a few minutes to see if he would recover without assistance.

This he did after a short time. Opening his eyes, he stared at Dick for a moment, and then recovered himself sufficient to sit up.

"Your father was a strong man," he said, bitterly; "but he was a child to you."

"Indeed!" replied Dick; "and yet you say you are not Jacob Morelle and never knew him."

A shade of anger passed across the face of Morelle.

It was followed by a look of set determination.

"What I have said I have said," he retorted, "and you won't get any more out of me."

Dick walked from the cell, and the turnkey followed him.

"I shall report his attempt to escape," said the officer, "and the governor will perhaps put him in irons."

"It is hardly worth while," replied Dick; "but do as you please."

He left the prison, and outside was joined by Carl, to whom he related in a brief form the result of the interview and the attempt to escape.

"He will say nothing," said Dick, "and I suppose I shall have to live in the dark all my life."

"I would not let it worry you," replied Carl. "You must try to arouse yourself, and get it off your mind. Brooding eternally on one subject is not good for any man."

"By-the-way," said Dick, "have you heard anything of Pan?"

"Not a word," answered Carl. "He must have stolen away during the riot, and if I know the man, he will give Ajax a return somehow for that fall."

"Ajax will have to take care of himself," said Dick.

They crossed the street and entered a square, in the centre of which was a small fountain, which apparently had not played for years. It was one of the corporation failures of Capetown.

Neither Dick nor Carl would have taken much notice of it but for there being a host of men around it and a man standing upon it "orating."

It was Bill Butterflick, and he was holding forth on the proud position which the friendship of Dick Strongbow gave him.

They stopped for a few moments to listen, keeping out of sight behind the outer portion of the listening crowd.

"Look ye here," Butterflick was saying, "I am a man who tells the truth when I says that Dick Strongbow is my pal. 'Butterflick,' he says, 'you've got the heart of a man in you.' 'I hope so,' I says, humbly enough. 'Keep it there,' says he, 'for my sake. I may want you one day,' says he."

"What for?" asked one in the crowd.

"What for?" exclaimed Butterflick. "I'll give you what for if you put fool's questions to me. What for! As if any man wouldn't know what for!"

"I don't," said the querist; "and I should like to hear what it is."

"I'm hanged if I tell you, then," said Butterflick, with the air of an insulted magnate. "If you want to know what Dick Strongbow's business is you go and ask him. Do you know what he would do to you?"

"No, nor you either," was the reply.

"He'd fix his eyes on you," said Butterflick, with a contemptuous sneer, "and make you feel like a humming-bird that's lighted unbeknown within six inches of a rattlesnake. Then he'd walk to the fireplace, pick up the tongs, and with 'em carry you to the winder and drop you into the street. He wouldn't condescend to touch a man of your pattern with his hands."

"Let us go, Carl," whispered Dick, laughing. "I can't stand butter even when it is laid on in this style."

"Stop a minute," said Carl, "the stupid fellow has been drinking, and there's a lot round who are going to make a set at him."

This appeared to be the case, so Dick stopped a bit, and it was well for Butterflick that he did so.

A number of the audience began to chaff him, asking what he was paid for puffing the "fighting swell," at which Butterflick got indignant, and gave the nearest offender a crack on the head.

A rush was made at him, and he was tumbled into the dry fountain with half-a-dozen men on top of him.

Dick began to push his way through the crowd to go to his assistance, and was almost immediately recognised.

A cry of "Strongbow" was raised, and the crowd opened out in marvellous quick time. As for the half-dozen men who were pommelling Butterflick, they scrambled out of the fountain and bolted for their lives.

No greater tribute to the potency of a name could have been paid.

Dick laid hold of Butterflick by the waist, and lifting him out of the fountain, stood him upon his feet.

"You foolish fellow!" he said. "Why do you get yourself into trouble about me?"

Butterflick's nose was bleeding, and his assailants had furnished him with a first-class black eye, but his whole face lighted up with joy when he saw who it was that had rescued him.

"The Diamond King—hurrah!" he shouted. "Whoop, lads! here's at some of you."

He charged at the nearest of the scattered crowd, and held his own in gallant style.

A general stampede took place, and Butterflick chased a man across the square.

Dick and Carl saw no need to remain, and laughing heartily, walked away.

They reached their hotel, and found Phil Norton in the sitting-room. There was an anxious look upon his face.

"Have you heard the news?" he said.

"No," replied Dick. "What is it?"

"Ajax has been shot as he was walking along the streets," said Phil. "They've carried him to the hospital, and they say he won't live till the morning."

"Pan's work," said Dick.

"Maybe," replied Phil; "but nobody seems to have seen it done, and Ajax is not able to say where the shot came from. He's asked for you. He says he's got something particular to tell you. It's about that man they call Gentleman Jim."

CHAPTER XXI.

POSITION OF AJAX—THE PRISON ON FIRE—AN EXCITING SCENE.

FEW people can look upon the near approach of death with equanimity, and certainly to a man with the disposition of Ajax the King of Terrors was doubly terrible.

It was apparently all over with him.

The bullet from an unseen assassin's hand had gone through his lungs, and no mortal aid could save him.

It was hard, very hard, he thought, just as he got a chance of doing better in the world than he had done for a long time.

He lay on a bed in a corner of the chief ward of the hospital—a huge form, striking to the eye, and none the less so for his white face and despairing eyes.

By his side sat a nurse who had just come in.

She measured out a small quantity of medicine from a bottle, and raising his head with one hand helped him to drink it.

"There is a friend of yours outside," she said; "do you feel strong enough to see him?"

"What's his name?" asked Ajax, feebly.

"Strongbow, the handsome young man all Capetown is talking about."

"Yes," said Ajax, "I should like to see him. I asked the doctor to send for him."

So the nurse went out and soon returned with Dick, who sat down in the chair she had vacated, and said—

"This is a bad business, Ajax."

"It is," replied the giant, "but I don't see that I can wonder at him. I mixed myself with the wrong people. I've done it all my life. But I was a good friend to Pan. I took him off the streets starving."

"Did you?" said Dick; "that was kind."

"Yes," returned Ajax, "I was a friend to him, and he has repaid me by shooting me like a dog. I didn't see him when he did it, but I am sure it was his work."

"I don't know the particulars," said Dick, "and I ought not to trouble you to tell me."

"There isn't much to tell," said Ajax. "I was walking along a quiet street, thinking over my recent good luck, when I heard a report, and at the same moment felt as if something had stung my chest. I fancy the shot came from a doorway near, but I don't know. I just tumbled down and lay there till they picked me up—done for."

"I hope it isn't so bad as that," said Dick.

"Oh! yes it is," replied Ajax, "the doctor tells me so. It may all be over with me to-morrow. Oh! how horrible. But I must speak to you about two things. First, I've got a wife somewhere, and a child. The latter I've never seen, for she left me vowing that I should never set eyes on it, and I never have and I never shall. I love it, and I've pictured it to myself a thousand times lying in its mother's arms, cooing and laughing as the little things do. If ever you meet them you will be kind to them, won't you?"

"I will do my best to find them," said Dick, "and if I succeed neither shall ever want."

"You've got a heart in you," said Ajax, "bold as a lion's and as tender as a woman's. If I had had one like it I should not be lying here now dying like the cowardly dog I am. Well, you don't want to hear about that. The next thing is Gentleman Jim. That man knows more about you than you do about yourself."

"I think so myself," returned Dick.

"I don't know exactly what it is," continued Ajax; "but when he was drinking with us he let out a little. It may give you a clue. He said that—"

Ajax stopped, and a spasm of pain crossed his face. The nurse, who was standing a little way from the bed, came up to him.

"You must not talk, I fear," she said.

"I must," replied Ajax; "it is now or never. Dick Strongbow," turning his face to our hero, "Gentleman Jim said you would like to see the old place at Warlingham—it was when he was half-drunk, you know. 'At Warlingham,' says he, 'they would give him a welcome if they knew he was the son of—"

Ajax stopped again, a ghastly hue overspreading his face.

The nurse motioned for Dick to move out of the way, and gently raised the suffering man's head.

"You can do no more good here," she said, and Dick softly left the room.

.   .   .   .

"Fire!"

It is an awful cry, let it be heard at any time of the day or night.

"Fire! Fire!"

It was shouted in the streets of Capetown, and taken up and carried from mouth to mouth, until the dread word was heard in the furthermost corners of the city.

"Where?" was the next word on every lip.

"At the prison."

Of all places in the world a prison is the most terrible place for a fire.

As we hear of it we think of the prisoners in their cells, shut and locked in, helpless and despairing, beating the doors, and vainly striving to escape through prison bars.

From every quarter ran the people, some keeping in the track of fire-engines, hastening towards the scene of danger.

As a wild mob swept past the Kohinoor Hotel, Dick Strongbow, at dinner with his friends, asked what was the matter.

"A fire at the prison, sir," the man answered.

Dick sprang to his feet. A fire at the prison !

It concerned him nearly, insomuch that Jacob Morelle was there, and might possibly make good his escape during the inevitable commotion.

"Carl," he said, "we must go there."

In the haste of the moment the usual precautions for the safety of Muffins were forgotten. He was neither advised to remain at home nor was anybody told off to look after him.

In a body they tumbled out, and, Dick leading the way, they mixed in the throng hurrying up the street.

Dick's blood was at fever-heat. He was alarmed about Jacob Morelle, who might possibly escape from the prison or perish in the flames. The recent disappointment, arising out of Ajax not making a full revelation of what he knew could be made, had made Dick doubly anxious.

They had to traverse a considerable portion of the city, and, owing to the crowded nature of the streets, their progress was much impeded.

Every step they took put fresh obstacles in their way, and nearly half an hour had elapsed ere they came in view of the prison.

Before it was an open space filled with a vast concourse of people, kept back from a too near approach to the prison by a double line of police.

One end alone of the prison was on fire ; but the flames rose high, showing that the conflagration had got a firm hold.

Something was wrong with the water supply, for as yet but two of the half-dozen engines assembled had been able to get to work, and the jets they cast upon the flames were not so potent in their extinguishing effect as they might have been.

Scattered about the crowd were many people who had friends in durance vile, and they were raising cries for the prisoners to be brought out.

Dick, in his resistless manner, worked his way through the crowd, but his friends, not possessing his muscular powers, were not so fortunate.

One by one they were cut off from him and from each other, and were pushed here and there as the excited mob swayed to-and-fro.

Dick worked his way amongst the crowd until he came to the cordon of police, and there prudence bade him stop short.

He had a clear view of the chief entrance, with its sombre gates, which were closed.

There was no appearance of the officials being abroad, save on the roof of the governor's house, just inside the gates, where there was a solitary man in uniform directing the men with the hose.

That the fire gained ground was evident. The most inexperienced among the spectators could see that much, and the cries to "Save the prisoners !" grew loud and louder.

But to their demand there was no response.

Suddenly Dick found himself projected forward by the pressure of the mob behind. The cordon of police was broken, and the mass poured into the space just without the prison gates.

Order was at an end, and chaos set in.

In vain did the police endeavour to keep back the crowd, even with the assistance of the firemen.

Hard knocks did little to deter the forward rush of the people. The most advanced remained there because they could not retreat. The hindermost did not care a straw for that which they did not feel.

All efforts tending to the subjugation of the fire was stopped. The engines could not be worked in the thick of a crowd. The hose was trodden upon, and a great part of it destroyed.

"Open the gates there !"

It was the roar of a hundred voices that first made this demand, and the cry was taken up by the excited masses.

Inside the prison all was now still.

The man had disappeared from the roof of the governor's house, and no other took his place.

What was going on within no man could say, but the general inference was that the authorities were doggedly resolved to let their prisoners die a dreadful death rather than set them free.

"Make way, there."

The crowd parted, shrieking and yelling, as a tumbril, on which was the trunk of a tree, was urged forward.

Like the Juggernaut car it was propelled onward, and was almost as destructively cruel in its course.

Men and boys were thrown down and the wheels of the heavy vehicle went over them, crushing out their lives.

On—on it went, propelled by the arms of fifty strong men, right up to the prison gates.

With terrific force it struck just where there was a wicket-door, which it dashed off its hinges, the top of the tree penetrating several feet into the courtyard beyond.

Dick, in the midst of the maëlstrom of men, saw it done, and he also caught a glimpse of the interior. In front of the gates were half a score men in uniform, armed with swords and revolvers.

What were they against so many ?

Dick, with all his strength, was powerless to help them. The tree was drawn back, and the mob, mad with excitement dashed for the opening.

A number of them were wedged for a moment in the doorway, but pressure behind forced them through, the foremost to be cut down by the men in uniform.

But as water is spurted through a crack in the side of an aqueduct, so was the mob sent into the courtyard.

Numbers prevailed, and some ready-witted knave having drawn the bolts of the gates back, a flood of humanity poured in.

The scene that ensued defies all description.

To seize the gaolers and wrench their weapons and keys from them was the work of a moment. Men expert in dealing with locks found the right keys, unfastened the doors, and the prison was in the hands of the mob.

Dick had got as far as the gate, and then he remained close to the wall, sturdily defying the efforts of the stream of men to dislodge him.

He cared little for the release of the prisoners save in the person of one man, and him he determined to seize, at all risks, as soon as he appeared.

From the interior of the prison came sounds of further resistance, but it soon ceased, and men with startled faces began to appear, making good their retreat.

Some were in prison garb, others in their ordinary attire. The former had been convicted, but the latter were awaiting their trial.

All were in a state of bewilderment, not knowing what to make of the tumultuous scene.

Dick saw many of the released men pass by, but Jacob Morelle was not among them. By-and-bye there came another cry—

"The mounted police are coming!"

A panic ensued, for men on horseback are dangerous beings to encounter. The mob outside had already broken away, and the men inside began their retreat.

Dick went with the stream, as he had, perforce, done before, and was borne backward away from a line of mounted men, who were using the blades of their sabres, and occasionally their sharp edges, with an unsparing hand.

He saw them break their way through the crowd and reach the open gate, where they formed in line, completely blocking it up and barring the exit of those within.

Many prisoners had escaped, but a considerable number of their rescuers were made captive in their place. On the morrow the magistrates would be busy sentencing the rioters and prison-breakers.

"He will not get away now," thought Dick. "Unless he has already lost his life I shall see him again."

And now the police on foot, having reformed, were clearing the open ground, and those who had no taste for a broken head hastened to get out of the way.

Dick accompanied the rest, and did not turn until he was where there was a comparative calm in the crowd.

Then he looked back, and saw the engines had got once more into play, and were pouring an increased body of water on the fire.

CHAPTER XXII.

ESCAPE OF JACOB MORELLE—ON THE TRAIL.

HANKS to the vigorous treatment of the police, mounted and on foot, the more rowdy part of the crowd had become subdued.

There was still plenty of talking and some shouting, but the demon of disorder had vanished.

Dick was now anxious about Carl and the others. He had been an eye-witness to the unceremonious treatment of the mob by the police, and the possibility of his friends being injured flashed upon him.

He reproached himself for having in his excitement allowed himself to be so far carried away as to lose them.

About Muffins he was particularly anxious, for, in addition to the ordinary danger of such a scene, he knew that the spirit of adventure, which was very rampant in the heart of that youth, might lead him into mischief.

After awhile he came across Carl, who was also engaged in looking for those he had lost.

"Where's Phil and Muffins?" asked Dick.

"I haven't seen them for some time," replied Carl; "but I should think they are safe."

Together they had a good look about the crowd, but failing to find either, decided to go back to the hotel.

There was evidence that the fire was rapidly being got under, and would not extend beyond the one wing of the prison where it first broke out.

Neither Phil nor Muffins had returned to the hotel, and very reasonable fears were now felt for their safety. In half an hour or so Phil put in an appearance, and dispelled all apprehension on his account. But where was Muffins?

Leaving Dick and the other two to speculate anxiously upon this subject, we will devote ourselves to the task of tracing out the movements of the missing boy.

When he got separated from his friends he might very reasonably have given way to a feeling of alarm, but he was an old hand at getting into mobs, and took things very coolly.

As a street arab, he had many a time gone to a fire in London, just as people with money do to a play, and enjoyed himself as much—perhaps a little more.

A little squeezing and bundling about in a huge assembly of people did not hurt him. He ignored it, and devoted his energies to getting into a good place to see what was going on.

Of course, he got into a place of danger—boys always do on the least provocation—and narrowly escaped injury.

But for his superb dodging powers an irate policeman would have broken his head with his truncheon.

"Whoop, there! would you?" he cried, as he dashed under the officer's arm. "Why don't you hit one your own size? Call yourself a man, do you?"

Then he was borne onwards to another part where commotion reigned, and was battered about like a shuttlecock until he got into a good position right in front of the part of the prison on fire.

He was just in time to be one of the witnesses to a remarkable scene.

The chief body of flame was inside the wall of the prison, the wall itself being intact, but close enough to be presumably too hot to be touched.

Suddenly a man appeared on the summit, seemingly leaping right out of the flames, which, of course, he did not do. He came from some place in advance of them.

After standing still for a moment, looking down upon the crowd, he walked coolly along the summit of the wall until he came to a buttress with three projecting ledges, about twelve feet apart from each other.

From ledge to ledge he rapidly jumped, like a

cat, escaping a fall in a most miraculous manner, and finally dropping down upon the ground.

A rush was made for him by several policemen but he broke through them all, and ran towards where Muffins was standing.

"Let the man go!" shrieked the mob; "he's earned his liberty."

Admiration for daring, which is in all of us, prompted this cry, and the police were only moved by a sense of duty in endeavouring to recapture him.

They made no real effort to overtake him, and, darting into the crowd, he was practically free.

But Muffins recognised the man. It was Jacob Morelle.

Although he did not know the full history of the man's life, he was acquainted sufficiently with matters to feel that his escape would be distasteful to Dick Strongbow.

Anxious to serve his master, he resolved to follow the man, see where he hid, and by acquainting Dick with his hiding-place, do something towards preventing his ultimate escape.

Here again his early training stood him in good stead. He could easily wind in and out among an ordinary crowd. Not for a moment did he lose sight of the escaped prisoner.

Through the crowd down to one of the low quarters of the town, Muffins keeping close to the houses, as Jacob Morelle did also, until they came to a narrow turning.

And there Muffins lost his quarry.

It was—at least, just there—a very quiet part of the town. Only two or three people and a skulking dog were in sight.

At the bottom of the street was a general shop, dimly lighted, but down the turning where Jacob Morelle had disappeared all was darkness and silence. Muffins went down that turning warily.

It was just possible that he had been seen by Jacob Morelle, who might be skulking in a doorway ready to pounce upon him as he passed by.

Keeping close to the wall, Muffins felt his way along, step by step, taking a peep at each doorway ere he showed himself in front of it.

In this cautious way he passed three houses, and then a very serious accident befell him.

In the wall of one of the houses was an opening like that which is ordinarily used as a way into a cellar. It had neither window nor door, although it was big enough to pass through.

Muffins, when opposite it, trod upon some vegetable substance, a piece of orange-peel, or something in that line, and slipping up sideways, fairly shot into the hole to the extent of three parts of his body.

He made a frantic clutch at the footway to save himself, but there was nothing to hold by, and down he went.

He fell eight or nine feet upon damp, soft ground, at full length, and for a brief spell of time was in a chaotic mental state, which prevented him doing anything but lie still and feebly wonder what had happened.

But having no limbs broken, he soon recovered sufficiently to get upon his feet, and his first clear thoughts were directed towards getting out of the place.

He tried to get at the opening above, but it was too high to be reached by jumping or climbing.

The wall under it was quite smooth

Nor did there appear to be anything in the cellar-like place to aid him.

He groped in vain in the dark for something suitable to mount upon, and found nothing but a few handfulls of rotten straw.

"What a beastly fix to be in!" he muttered; "but perhaps it's an empty house, and I can get out by the front door."

There was a door to the cellar, as he soon found on the other side, opposite the way he involuntarily entered. It was not locked, nor did it appear to possess a fastening of any description.

Stepping softly outside, he stood still for a time listening.

At first he could hear nothing, but soon his ears detected a humming sound, which seemed to come from the top of the house.

"There's people here," thought Muffins, "but if there's nobody downstairs I may get away. If I'm catched—" His blood ran cold at the thought.

Whatever the people might be, discovery could not fail to i a very awkward thing for him.

If they were of the wrong sort they might kill him, and honest people would certainly take him for a thief.

But stopping there could not help him. He had to get out somehow, and having groped about and found a flight of stairs, he slowly began the ascent.

He held his breath and screwed his courage up, but it was impossible for him to avoid feeling a bit shaky.

Every nerve was strained, and his listening powers were in full exercise.

About a dozen steps brought him to another door, and this was simply secured by one of the old-fashioned latches, which are raised by pressing on a spoon-shaped piece of iron with the thumb.

Muffins exercised the utmost caution in lifting it, but it clicked in spite of him, and as he pushed the door open somebody above called out—

"Is that you, Busker?"

As it was not Busker, no answer was returned, which did not appear to satisfy the individual upstairs, for he called out again—

"Is that you, Busker? Everything is right. I've squared things for you."

Muffins was now in the passage meditating on the advisability of making for the front door and clearing out that way.

Had he done so on the instant he might have got safely off, but he hesitated.

And he who hesitates is lost, or gets into some sort of unpleasantness.

The precious moments were gone, and the idea of flight that way had to be abandoned.

A light flashed above, and a man was heard coming swiftly downstairs.

"I'll see who it is," he said to somebody he had left behind him; "it was the cellar-latch, I'll swear."

Muffins was in a fix indeed.

A retreat to the cellar would lead to discovery, and if he went to the front door and found it fast, the man would see him ere he could return.

In his dilemma he looked hurriedly round for some place to hide in.

Already the approaching light had in a measure dispelled the darkness, and he made out a door at the bottom of the passage.

To this he glided, and to his joy found that it opened into a back room.

There was some furniture in it, and a fair-sized window without blind.

In one of the houses a few feet away a lamp was shining, and it cast sufficient light into the apartment for him to see about him.

In a corner was an old-fashioned upright eight-day clock. It was not going, and being about as big as a cupboard, it flashed upon Muffins that it would be a good place to hide in.

Anyway he had no time to debate on the subject, for the man was already in the passage, and judging by what he called out, was examining the cellar door.

"It's open," he said, "and somebody's come up this way."

"I'll come down and help you to look for him," replied the other.

Muffins was just getting into the clock when the answer came back.

It accelerated his movements, for he recognised the voice of Jacob Morelle.

Thus by a series of mishaps and chances he found himself under the roof of the same house with the man he had been tracking.

Perhaps he too, by design, had entered by the cellar. If so, it was indeed a marvellous thing that Muffins should have accidently found out the same way.

But life is full of chances, and Muffins, not being a philosopher, did not endeavour to reason out what had befallen him. His prevailing thought was to get into a place of safety.

He got into the clock, and a few minutes later the men entered the room.

The interior of the clock became illuminated, and Muffins, looking up, saw that the WORKS AND FACE WERE GONE.

It was simply a shell he was in.

"There's nobody here," said Jacob Morelle, impatiently. "Have you a cat in the house?"

"Yes," was the reply.

"That accounts for it. The beggars can raise a latch like that as well as you or I."

He pulled up a chair and sat down, while his companion put the light upon a bracket fixed to the wall.

"Haven't you a blind to that window?" asked Morelle.

"No ; but there's shutters."

"Close them."

While the other man was busily engaged in doing this the cellar door was heard to open, and a hurried footstep sounded in the hall.

"That's Busker," said the man. "Halloo, there ! We are in the back room."

The door was opened, and a gruff voice said—

"We've got a subject. Is the front door undone ?"

"All but the latch," was the reply.

"Right."

The man ran down the passage, and Muffins heard the front door open. There were footsteps, heavy and slow, like men carrying something weighty.

The perspiration ran off Muffins' face in little streams.

"What are they bringing in ?" he asked himself.

"Why, you've got him in a sack," said Jacob Morelle.

"'Bliged to put him in one to get him along,"

was the answer ; "he's quiet enough, for he's got a double dose of the drug inside him."

"Couldn't you make him QUITE quiet,' asked Morelle's companion, "before you brought him here ?"

"It wasn't safe to do it," was the answer, "nor could we get his money without running risks. He's got it sewn up in a belt that is STITCHED round him. So we shoved him into a sack and brought him along just as if he was a pig for the market."

Muffins listened to these remarks with a sensation of horror the like of which he had never before experienced.

By standing on tiptoe he could manage to peep out of the opening from which the face of the clock had been removed, and the impulse to do so was too great to be resisted.

"I'm not going to have a hand in this," said one of the new arrivals.

"All clear out but Busker and me," said Jacob Morelle ; "we can do what is necessary. Catch hold of the sack. Now pull. What a weight the fellow is !"

Then on the table, in the middle of the room, Jacob Morelle and Busker, a ruffian of the first water, laid the form of a burly man, made unconscious by some vile drug, which had been treacherously administered to him.

It was a wonder Muffins did not shriek or cry out, for he recognised the unfortunate victim.

It was Bill Butterflick !

CHAPTER XXIII.

MUFFINS FINDS AN UNEXPECTED ROAD TO LIBERTY—BILL BUTTERFLICK HAS REASON TO BE GRATEFUL.

VERY rarely has it fallen to the lot of one so young as Muffins to be in such a terrible position.

Apart from his own peril he had the awful prospect of being a witness to a cruel, heartless murder.

Endowed with a considerable amount of natural courage, his heart revolted at the idea of doing nothing to save the unfortunate Butterflick.

But what could he do?

As ill luck would have it, he had come away from the hotel without the revolvers he was so proud of. Carl had, in fact, taken them away from him for fear of accidents.

Busker and Jacob Morelle were holding a conversation together in an undertone.

Not that they thought there was an atom of need for caution, but the nature of the crime they meditated had a subduing effect upon them.

Muffins shifted a little in his place of concealment, and in doing so slipped from a narrow ledge on which one of his feet was placed.

He fell.

And although his fall was only a few inches, he made a mighty effort to save himself, and in so doing upset the rickety old clock-case

Over it came, and fell to the ground with a crash that broke it into a dozen pieces.

The weight of it jarred the room with sufficient

violence to throw the lamp from the bracket, and it shivered to atoms upon the floor.

Luckily it was at the same moment extinguished, leaving the room in darkness.

Muffins, whose hearing was at its keenest, and his mind in full activity, lay quite still for a moment or two, thinking it better to put the onus of the fall upon the clock.

It was the best thing he could do, for neither of the men knew exactly what had happened, and, their hearts beating wildly with sudden fear, they made for the door.

After a short struggle for supremacy one of them got it open, and they bolted from the room.

"What is it ?" cried one of the men outside.

"Clear out," was the breathless answer of Jacob Morelle.

There was a sound of the front door being hastily opened, a scrambling of feet, and the band of villains were gone.

Muffins saw it all in his mind's eye, and the sense of relief he felt almost overpowered him.

There have been cases in which men, reprieved from a sentence of death, have succumbed to the sudden reaction.

"Joy sometimes kills—grief never," says the sage.

A swimming in the head was the first result to Muffins, but he soon got over that. It was followed by a feeling of lassitude, approaching helplessness.

He felt utterly tired and worn out, just as if he had been running a race.

"I must not lie here," he muttered, and, raising himself, he struggled to his feet.

A soft moan escaped Bill Butterflick, accompanied by a slight shifting of his feet.

The shutters being closed, Muffins could not see him. The place was in utter darkness.

Nor did Muffins at first see how he could help the man. He was much too heavy to carry away, and if he remained there awaiting his reviving, Jacob Morelle and the rest might return.

One thing only could he do, and that was to get out of the house as soon as possible, find a member of the police force, and tell him what he had witnessed.

Groping his way to the door, Muffins found it ajar, and peeped into the passage. It was dimly lighted up, the front door being open.

In a moment the boy was out of the house.

One glance up the street and another down showed that it was quite deserted. Then off he went, as fast as he could, to the main thoroughfare.

A policeman was soon found, to whom Muffins gave an outline of the story.

"I can't go down there alone," said the man. "You see that red lamp yonder. That's the station. Ask for the inspector, and tell him what you've told me. If it's lies, don't go near him, for he'll make you smart for it."

Muffins had no fear of the inspector, and he soon put that austere individual into possession of the facts.

Three men of the reserve were despatched with Muffins to give what services they could to Butterflick. Accompanied by the policeman Muffins first addressed they went to the house, which the officers seemed to know had a bad name, and found the door open.

They turned on their lanterns and entered.

"He's in the back room, at the bottom of the passage," said Muffins.

Yes, Butterflick was there, sitting up and looking about him with the expression of an owl. They spoke to him, but he only stared and put his hand to his head.

"A case of drugs," said one of the men. "Come, mister, see if you can't stand upon your feet !"

It was as much as he could do, but with assistance he moved along in a mechanical way.

When they got him as far as the street the fresh air revived him a little, and he began to expostulate with them like a drunken man.

"You—leave—alone—go's well—you—"

"All right," said one of the men, soothingly. "You are as lively as a kitten. Come and have a cup of tea with me and the missus."

As two men sufficed to get him along the other two remained by the door of the house to await the coming of reinforcements and to help them search the place.

"You've dropped on the worst place in Capetown," said an officer to Muffins, "and if there isn't a public testimonial got up for you for doing what you've done there ought to be."

Muffins modestly disdained any desire for a public recognition of the affair, then went back to the station and gave his name and address.

Butterflick was put into an inner room in a chair before a fire, where a chop for the inspector's supper was cooking.

"We'll have the doctor for him," they told Muffins. "He'll be as right as a trivet in the morning. You had better have a man to see you home."

Muffins thought it would be just as well, for he had in his excitement lost all count of the way he came.

So he and a stalwart policeman went back to the Kohinoor Hotel, where Dick Strongbow was found in a state of restlessness about him.

Carl and Phil Norton were out looking after the missing one. Dick received Muffins as a father would a son, and when he heard what had kept him away so late had, of course, no word of reproof for him.

"This man, Gentleman Jim as he is known to you," said Dick, "must be found. I will give five hundred pounds for his capture."

"Consider it done," said the officer. "Don't put any bills out, but leave it to us. He doesn't know the boy has bowled him out, and it's ten to one if he or some of the gang don't come back to the old shop."

"You mean the house ?" said Dick.

"Yes," replied the officer; "it's been notorious for years. Everything that's bad has been done there. It's a regular crib for the worst of 'em, and as with us so with them—there's no place like home. They'll come back and look at it, if they do nothing else."

"Take him alive," said Dick. "I don't give the reward for a dead man."

"All right, sir. Good-night," said the officer, and off he went with five hundred prospective sovereigns in his mind's eye.

It was now midnight, but the hotel was not closed, and Muffins being hungry, Dick ordered supper for him.

While he was engaged in partaking of a meal which only a boy dare venture on, for fear of aggravated nightmare, Carl and Phil were heard outside.

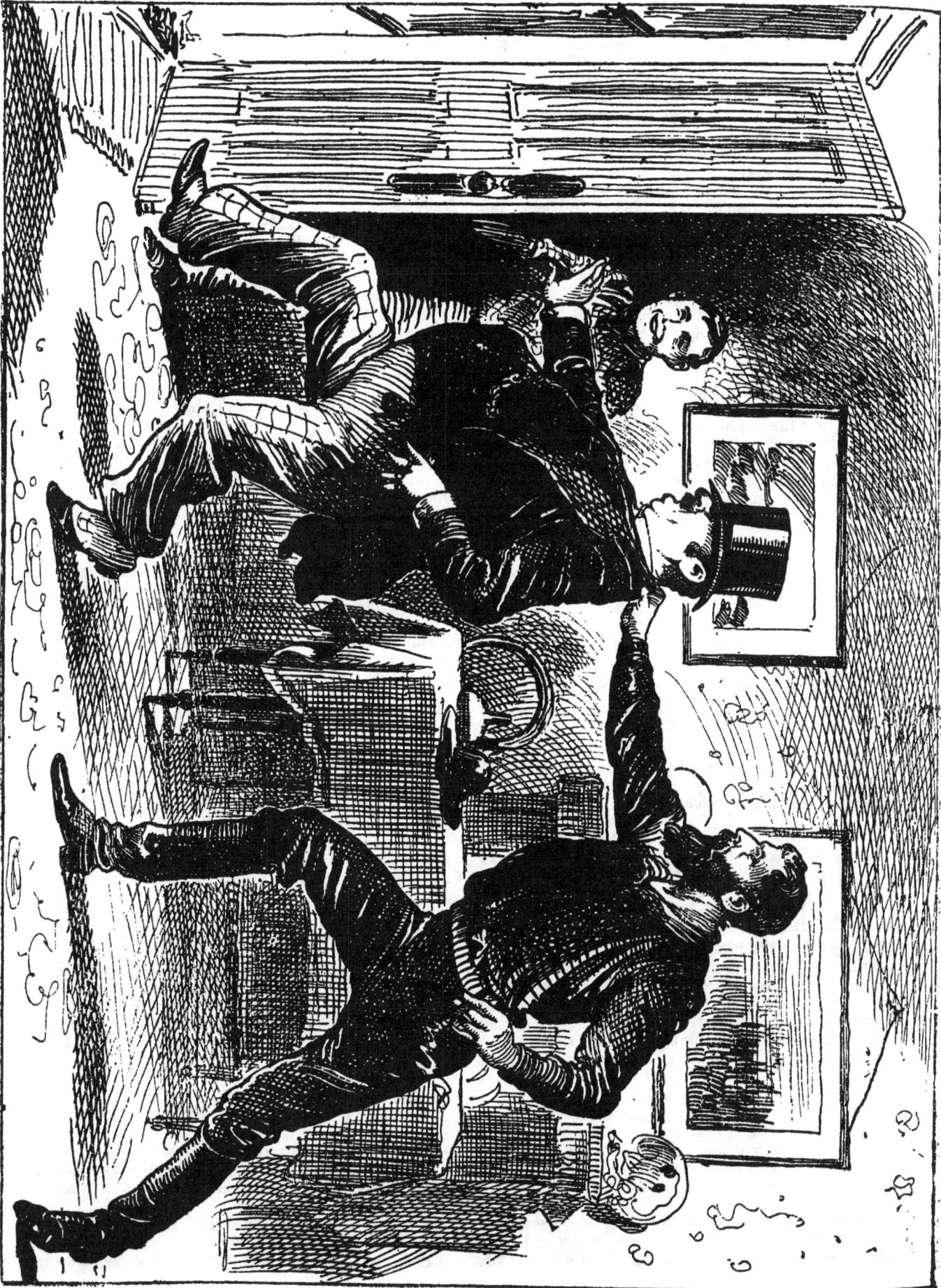

"Oh! don't, I'm a-smothering," gasped the victim of these forcible attentions.

"Get under the table, Muffins," said Dick, and Muffins dived down.

"We can't find him anywhere," said Phil Norton, as he entered the room, "nor hear anything about him. The young fool's been and got into mischief."

"He wants a spanking," said Carl.

"I'd give a hundred pounds to know where he is," said Phil Norton.

"How much?" asked Dick.

"A hundred pounds."

"I think I could earn the money by guessing."

"I'll bet you don't," said Phil, "and put the money down?"

"Well, say we bet fifty—just in a friendly way?" said Dick.

"Done!"

"Done. He's under the table."

"Dern it! so he is," growled Phil, stooping quickly down, and peering beneath it. "Come out of it, you young catamount! Where have you been?"

"Of course, it's no bet," said Dick, laughing. "No man has a right to bet on a certainty. Now, Muffins, tell them where you have been."

And this Muffins did.

Having heard his story, Carl voted him a wonderful boy, and Phil Norton said he was born to be a hero, and would die famous.

CHAPTER XXIV.

NEWS OF ROUGH WORK IN THE MOUNTAINS—DICK STRONGBOW DOES SOMETHING NOTABLE.

E will now pass over a fortnight with a few words. It was a time of waiting and watching without any news of the whereabouts of Jacob Morelle.

Dick and his friends, as well as the police, were always on the alert, but the cunning villains eluded the vigilance of them all.

Butterflick was busy too.

It took him about three days to fully recover from the effects of the drug, and when he learnt the particulars of his narrow escape from being murdered, two feelings took possession of him.

One wa· a deep feeling of gratitude towards Muffins, which he gave vent to in a series of presents which he considered suitable to a boy.

Among other things he purchased a bowie knife, an old cavalry sabre, and a set of fencing foils, all of which Muffins prized, but they were put away as somewhat unsuitable for present use.

The second emotion in Butterflick's heart was a lasting hatred for the men who had drugged him.

"I treated 'em, strangers as they were, like princes," he said. "'Name your drinks and have all you want,' I ses. 'If you go on till I tell you to stop,' I ses, 'you will go on for ever.' And them to go and pizen a chap for his money. I only want to meet 'em, anyhow and anywheres."

Finally he gave up drink altogether, and became a teetotaller, so that he could keep clear-headed and out of harm's way.

But he did not go bragging about it, telling people how good he was and how bad he had been, or indulge in any cant whatever.

"I'm keeping sober," he said, "to make sure of my men when I meet 'em. I shall know their faces, hang 'em."

Some of the time Dick spent in disposing of his diamonds and banking the proceeds. Ere half were disposed of he found himself a rich man.

The others also, Muffins included, were practically independent gentlemen for life.

As soon as Jacob Morelle had been secured and induced, or compelled, to satisfy Dick Strongbow's demand, they all proposed to go back to the old country and make the best of their fortunes.

Carl and Dick had each a fair one in their minds, but under the circumstances they could only wait and hope.

A fortnight had passed, as we have said, without any news of the whereabouts of Jacob Morelle, when tidings came of him from an unexpected quarter.

A short distance from Cape Town there is a famous mountain which bears the name of the Lion's Head.

There are several paths around it which travellers use, and at various times it has been infested with robbers, mainly lonely, desperate men.

For some time, however, it had been free of marauders—thanks to the vigilance of the police—but now again there were men of evil living upon the mountain.

One evening a man with half a dozen wounds about his head and body came staggering into Cape Town.

He told a story of being waylaid on the mountain, robbed, and left for dead.

The party which assailed him consisted of about half a dozen men, one of whom he could particularly describe.

From the description he gave, there could be no doubt about that man being Jacob Morelle, or, as he was still called in Cape Town, Gentleman Jim.

The papers were full of the affair on the following morning, and all sorts of suggestions were given for the capture of the "brigands."

Dick Strongbow, when he saw the account of the affair, resolved to set out at once in pursuit of the band.

With Carl Yemitz, Phil Norton, and Bill Butterflick, he started within two hours for the Lion's Head.

Muffins was left at home, with strict instructions not to wander far away from the hotel.

He obeyed this injunction with ill grace—and as events turned out it was fortunate that Dick afterwards relented and took the boy with him.

Butterflick knew the Lion's Head very well, and as they marched thither he suggested a plan for the capture of the robbers.

"Most of the thieving work," he said, "has been done on the south side, where the road runs round a cliff, with a steep pitch down of five hundred feet on the other side. They lets a man get half way, then show up at either end. He's trapped, you see, and it's a case for him. Now, I'll go along that path and let them nab me."

It was not quite clear what good would come of this arrangement, not even when he explained that at one part he could "gammon" the thieves by pretending to throw himself over the cliff.

"There's a nice little ledge where I can drop on," he said, "and they'll come up to see what's come of me. Well, now's your time. Pick all off but Morelle, and then you have him."

Dick Strongbow pretended to fall into the arrangement, the success of it depending entirely upon the marauders, if still about, selecting that spot for their operations.

The Lion's Head is an excellent mountain for stealing on a foe, and is also available for hiding.

It is very rugged, and has many caves, principally produced by the action of springs. One of these caves, Butterflick said, was of considerable extent ; but nobody ever went into it, as it was haunted.

"Whereabouts is it ?" asked Dick.

"On the south side, about a thousand feet up, away on a side path."

"We will take a peep at it on the way," said Dick.

"What's the good o' that ?" asked Butterflick. "I tell you that there ain't a durn critter in Cape Town, man, woman or child, tinker, tailor or soldier, thief or policeman, who will put a foot into it."

"Just as a matter of curiosity, I should like to see inside it," said Dick.

"Bad luck'll come of it," replied Butterflick, solemnly. "No man ever so much as peeped into it any time these twenty years without getting into trouble before he was a day older."

"I shall not ask anyone to run the risk with me," said Dick.

"Oh ! durn the risk," returned Butterflick. "If you go, I'll follow ; but it's a waste of time, and, may be, a waste of life will come of it."

They were all amused at his caution ; but there was in them, as in all of us, something that can be touched by a superstitious suggestion.

Carl, being a German, was most impressionable, and next to him was Muffins, who believed in ghosts because he had seen them in pictures outside the theatres.

Phil Norton was not so impressionable, and Dick least of all.

It seemed to him that the legend of the Spectre's Cave, as Butterflick called it, would be known to Jacob Morelle, who was just the sort of man to laugh at the idea of ghosts, and if he could induce his companions to go there that would be his hiding-place.

To the Spectre's Cave Dick would go at all risks.

As they traversed the mountain-road a sharp look-out was kept in every direction for signs of human life, but no living creature—save a few mountain sheep—were seen.

"Yon's the point I told you of," said Butterflick, pointing to the right and high above him. "There's the cliff on one side and the precipice on the other. Lively looking, isn't it ?'

"And the road to the Spectre's Cave ?" asked Dick.

"Lower down. We can't see where it branches off until we come to it."

The party had not come without creature comforts, and after two hours' walking they halted to refresh.

Before this was done Dick enjoined them to be as quiet as possible, and if they talked at all to speak in whispers.

The way was now very lonely, and for the most part shut in by rocks that stood on either side.

Here and there in the windings they got a glimpse of the plains below, with Cape Town and the sea beyond, but of the path above they could see very little until they came to it.

"What could be handier for picking a fellow off ?" said Butterflick. "Why, a man posted up there— Look out !"

He sprang to his feet as the sharp crack of a revolver was heard, followed by the ping of a bullet striking the rock behind him.

Dick looked hurriedly about him, but could see nobody. Butterflick was already on the move.

"Gentleman Jim," he said. "I saw his head up yon. Be ready to pop at him if he peeps again."

"Let me come to the front," said Dick.

The way was narrow just there, and Butterflick's burly form nearly filled it.

"No," he said ; "let 'em have a pop at me and you fetch 'em down. I don't mind a bullet in me. I carry two now—one in the right thigh and t'other somewhere near my ribs— Whoop !"

A head and hand appeared above a rock ahead. In the hand was a revolver.

Dick's sharp eye saw the head, and, raising his weapon, he fired.

A howl of anguish followed, and the revolver fell from the fingers he had shattered.

Howling with anguish, a man danced into sight.

It was not, as he hoped, Jacob Morrelle, but Busker, at the sight of whom Butterflick uttered a shriek of triumph.

"My bird !" he shrieked. "Don't touch him."

Busker tried to flee, but the anguish arising from his wound was so great that he hardly knew what he was doing.

He blundered forward a few paces and fell

Butterflick pounced upon him and pinned him to the ground.

"Give a man a chance," Busker howled.

"I will—just the sort of one you gave me," replied Butterflick, aiming at his head.

"One moment," said Dick. "I don't like killing a man in cold blood."

"I'm hot enough, I can tell you," replied Butterflick. "He is my bird. There—now for it. If the captain says you are to have a chance, I'll give you one. Run. I'll let you have a start of ten feet."

Busker was glad of anything in the form of grace, and started off.

Butterflick counted ten paces, and at the tenth fired with so good an aim that the man threw up his arms and fell backward.

Busker was not dead, but lay huddled on the ground, glaring like a wounded wild beast.

Dick went up to him, sorry for the dying wretch.

"Are you alone here ?" he asked.

"Can't you see I am ?" was the sullen reply.

"I mean have you any companions on the mountain ?"

"Perhaps I have—perhaps not ; anyway, they ain't just here."

"Tell me where they are ?"

"Where you won't find 'em. If you get it out ot me, what's the good ?"

"You shall have such care as we can give you, and if you recover you shall not be interfered with."

A faint smile crossed Busker's face.

"Did you ever know a man who could keep a secret ?" he asked.

"Very few," answered Dick.

"THEN HERE'S ONE," said Busker, ferociously ; "I'm booked, but I'm not soft. You don't get anything out of me. Go forward and get your throats cut for your pains. I'd like to have a hand in it, but I can't."

He stopped short, his face suddenly whitened, and with a gasp he fell back—dead.

"There was good stuff in the fellow," said Dick, "but it has been misapplied. Somehow I always feel sorry when a man of his stamp comes to grief so suddenly. It doesn't give him a chance."

"He wouldn't have taken one if it had been given to him," replied Butterflick. "I'd a right to bring him down, and I did it."

"I do not blame you," said Dick, quietly. "I was only speaking of the courageous quality of the man ; he had it in no small degree."

The road now inclined a little to the left, and there was not such good shelter for a foe as there had been ; but they were none the less watchful.

Suddenly Bill Butterflick pulled up short.

"See them two rocks yon ?" he said.

Dick nodded.

"Between 'em is the road to the Spectre's Cave."

"But I see no road overhead," said Dick, " nor any signs of one."

"It is because it goes down for a bit, and winds round until there's a way up again. It's about as nasty a bit o' travelling as you could wish for."

"I will go first now," said Dick.

CHAPTER XXV.
THE WAY TO THE SPECTRE'S CAVE.

HURRYING on ahead of all, Dick reached the narrow way and plunged into it.

His fearlessness made him indifferent to all personal danger.

The road sloped down, and a short way from the entrance wound round to the right. The clean-cut surface of the rocky sides showed that it was the work of man.

Dick trusted a great deal to the terror-inspiring nature of his presence. It had served him before in an extremity, and he believed it would serve him again.

So, regardless of the fact that he was outpacing his friends, he hurried on.

Higher rose the walls of rock above, until there was thirty feet above him.

The width of the passage was less than six feet, and, as it twisted to the right or left every few yards, he could not see far ahead.

A shout from the rear checked him.

He turned to see what it meant, and the next moment a huge piece of rock from above came crashing down.

Obeying a natural impulse, he stepped back a few paces, and looked above him.

Another rock fell.

But the hand that rolled it over was invisible.

In rapid succession a number of big stones followed, blocking up the way and piling themselves one upon another, some bulging out in such a way that climbing over the mass was next to impossible.

Whoever was doing the work did it rapidly and well—but it is probable that they had begun it too soon.

The intention, doubtless, was to shut the whole party in.

And it was furthermore clear that Dick and his party had been watched ; their movements, and perhaps their words, spied upon, and preparations were made to make them prisoners.

If all had been shut in it is more than likely they would have perished.

Dick could not do impossibilities.

With all his strength he could not stop these falling stones, nor attempt to dislodge them.

And now he was in imminent peril of being crushed if he remained where he was.

His one chance of safety lay in going on and alone seeking such shelter as the Spectre's Cave afforded him.

What effect this act of the hidden enemy might have upon his friends he could only guess at ; and whether they would be strong enough to cope with the enemy without him was a matter of surmise also.

He could not help reproaching himself for the rashness which had put him in such a fix.

The very next turning brought him into sight of the Spectre's Cave—the mouth of it bee-hive shaped, and about seven feet high.

All was as dark as pitch within, and in no case would it have been inviting to a stranger.

As things were, it was a place which few men would have ventured into alone ; but Dick, when he fairly pulled himself together, was utterly without fear.

Simply taking the precaution to have a revolver cocked and ready for use in his right hand, he boldly entered the cave.

.　　.　　.　　.　　.

While Dick was going through this ordeal his friends had almost as rough a time of it.

In the first place, Butterflick, who was a few feet in advance of the rest, had a narrow escape of being crushed with one of the first stones that fell.

Then as the others showered down the whole party had to beat a retreat.

They could not help Dick, and their own safety demanded a prompt retirement from the narrow, cliff-lined path.

We cannot put on record exactly what Butterflick said in this emergency. He was a man who had lived a rough life, and rough words came naturally to him.

If what he said had possessed annihilating powers the operators above would have been transformed into impalpable dust.

On getting to a more open spot they looked about for some traces of the foe, but nobody was in sight. But they could hear the stones still thundering down.

To Carl the position was insupportable, and the grief and bitterness of Muffins and Phil Norton may easily be imagined.

None of them knew whether Dick was dead or alive.

He made no signs of existence, and it really seemed as if he had come to an untimely end.

"If dead," said Carl, "we will avenge him. Follow me!

He began to climb up the masses of rocks piled above them, and the rest followed.

A professional climber would have found it none too easy work, and to our inexperienced friends the task was arduous.

About that particular spot the mountain seemed to be mainly a mass of piled up stones of various sizes.

Here and there some huge rock rose up or projected at an angle which barred their way, and in some cases they could not climb over, but had to work their way round.

This meant delay, and fully twenty minutes elapsed ere they stood upon the spot where the stones had been hurled over into the path below.

The work had ceased, and nobody was in sight.

In vain they looked around for some sign of the recent presence of man.

There was none.

And to make things more puzzling just then, the side of the mountain was fairly smooth, and no hiding-place for a man was visible in the neighbourhood.

"Well," said Butterflick, "what do you think of this?"

"I can't think at all," replied Phil Norton.

"It is a puzzle," said Carl.

"Is master DEAD?" asked Muffins, with a sob.

Phil Norton was standing on the edge of the precipice, peering over. He could see nothing of Dick below, and just there the mouth of the Spectre's Cave was not visible.

What could they do?

Without a rope it was next to impossible to descend, even if they had been disposed to go below.

As far as they could see, nothing would be gained by venturing on such a course.

Butterflick's face was a study.

All that was superstitious in him was in full activity, but he hardly liked to give it vent.

At last it burst from him.

"I said so," he muttered. "Nothing but disaster and death could come of going to the Spectre's Cave."

"I won't believe in ghosts," said Phil Norton, resolutely.

"I am not inclined to," said Carl; "but where the deuce are the fellows who have been rolling down these stones?"

Muffins said nothing.

He did not feel himself competent to judge either way, but the balance of his faith was with Butterflick. Still, the boy would not believe Dick Strongbow was dead.

He had such faith in the powers of his master that he could not conceive anything mortal getting the better of him.

Of course, if spectres were brought to bear, it darkened up matters a bit; but even an ordinary ghost would, in the opinion of Muffins, have to go down before Dick Strongbow.

"Come on," said Carl. "We will follow the course of this path, and get a peep at the cave."

"I'll not look at it," replied Butterflick. "It's bound to bring further trouble. Not that I care, though. Go ahead!"

He settled his hat upon his head, and with a set face started off with the rest, keeping close to the edge of the precipice.

A short journey brought them into view of the cave.

It was fully a hundred feet below the eminence on which they stood—a very black spot in the rocks below.

"That's it," said Phil Norton, "and it looks like an old mine shaft. Have a look at it, Butterflick. Don't be funky, man."

But Butterflick kept his back resolutely to the fatal spot.

"In anything that a man may do I'm with you," he said. "But I don't see the use of throwing away my life for nothing."

"Hush! What's that," cried Muffins.

The boy was kneeling down, with his head on one side—listening.

He motioned with his hand for the others to keep still. They remained quiet for a while, and then a dismal sound uprose from below.

A groan from the Spectre's Cave.

CHAPTER XXVI.

MUFFINS MAKES A DISCOVERY—DOWN IN THE SPECTRE'S CAVE—JACOB MORELLE HAS A GREAT LOSS.

SOMETHING must be wrong there," muttered Phil Norton, and they all peered anxiously into the depths below. To get down, save by falling, seemed impossible.

A rope would have been of service to them, but they had nothing that would serve as one in their possession.

A sense of helplessness was on all the men, and they stared around them in silence.

A cry from Muffins aroused them from a state of mental lethargy.

The boy had wandered a short distance away, unperceived by the others, and was kneeling on the ground making efforts to raise a big stone about three feet in diameter.

"He's found something," cried Butterflick, exultingly.

"There's a hollow place under here," replied Muffins, "and I heard scampering below."

"That's enough," said Butterflick. "Stand clear. I'm the man to hoist this 'ere thing up."

It required an effort, for the stone was very hard and solid, but Butterflick was a strong man, and he rolled it back after a bit of a struggle, disclosing a flight of steps cut out of the solid rock, leading below.

Few men would have cared to risk leading the way down such a place, but none there thought of hesitating.

It was a fair struggle for first in, and Phil Norton won.

"Clear the way," said Butterflick; "pop a shot ahead before you start."

It was not a bad idea, and Phil fired a shot down below, with the result that a howl was heard, and the scampering of feet followed.

"Whoop—hurrah!" cried Butterflick, "we've got 'em."

"Nearly, but not quite," said Carl, quietly.

The opening was narrow, but as soon as they got inside they found the steps widen out so that two could walk abreast.

But the darkness of the place was its great drawback.

It was like going down into a well, with the prospect of being potted by somebody below; but they boldly descended, going slowly simply because they had to feel their way.

"Clear the way," said Butterflick again. "I hear some of the vermin scuffling ahead."

The report of two revolvers fired by somebody in front made them all involuntarily duck their heads, which, as Phil Norton said, was "a fool's trick," for no man ever yet successfully dodged a bullet.

No harm was done.

Butterflick felt one go by unpleasantly near to his left ear, but a miss is as good as a mile, and he thought no more of it.

Promptly the firing was returned, but the enemy in front seemed to have cleared out, as there was no responsive groan or sound of movement whatever.

In a few moments they were all slightly inconvenienced by the smoke, but there was a strong upward draught and the way down acting as a flue, it was soon gone.

Half-a-dozen more steps brought them to level ground.

Looking above, they could see the way they came faintly illuminated by the waning daylight, but ahead all was black as pitch.

"I don't know as this isn't a trap," muttered Butterflick.

"Not that," said Phil Norton. "They have locked themselves in. Didn't you notice that iron handle fixed in the stone? You bet they meant to hide. Hush!'

A wild shriek resounded through the cavern—the cry of one in mortal terror or agony.

It was followed by an appeal for somebody to "Let go!"

"I've got you now," replied a second voice, "and I will have the truth out of you."

"Dick Strongbow, by jingo!" cried Phil Norton.

"Master—dear master!" roared Muffins, running forward.

"Steady there!" cried Carl. "There may be pitfalls. Who's got a match? A light from one would be better than nothing."

They had to speak loud to make themselves heard, for the piteous cries for mercy were renewed, filling the cave or passage with resounding echoes.

Every sound made was indeed more than quadrupled, the rocks bandying them to and fro, like the exchange of firing between enemies.

Phil Norton had some matches, and lighted one.

By its flare they could see that they were in a tunnel about fifteen feet high, and just ahead of them was a chasm, from falling into which Muffins had just mercifully escaped.

It was a rent right across the floor of the place, going deep into the mountain.

A stone kicked into it by Butterflick went tumbling down with the impressive intonation which the fall of a solid body into a deep place invariably gives out.

But provision had been made for crossing the dangerous gap in the form of a broad plank placed close to the left-hand side of the wall.

It required some nerve to make use of it, and only those thoroughly acquainted with the place would have succeeded in doing it in the dark.

That the man who fired at them had done so was clear, so Phil, having lighted another match, signalled for the others to come.

Carl offered Muffins a hand, but a boy who in earlier days used to excite the ire of policemen and the terror of the public by scampering along the parapets of the London bridges did not want any assistance.

"I am not afraid," he said, and trotted over.

The width of the chasm was not great—not more than half-a-dozen feet, and the plank was a stout one.

There was, however, some elasticity in it, and the vibration caused by Muffins hurrying over sent a thrill through the spectators.

"Go easy!" muttered Butterflick. "Old Sal always used to say that when she got into a tight place."

Before the match had expired they were all over, standing together listening for some further signs of the presence of Dick Strongbow.

The cries for mercy had sunk down to a low muttering or sobbing, and the voice of Dick was no longer heard.

Once more the superstitious fears of Butterflick came to the fore.

"It's the spectres mocking us," he said.

"Your grandmother!" replied Phil Norton; and, putting his hands to his mouth, he sent out the long piercing cry of the Australian aborigine—

"Coo-o-o-o-o-ey!"

Long before the echoes of the most far-reaching sound ever uttered by the human voice had ceased the answer was coming back—

"Coo-o-o-ey!"

"Come on!" cried Phil; "steady! I've some matches left, and will lead the way."

He struck the third match, and by its feeble light, which he had to preserve by shading with his hand, they hurried on.

The way was a crooked one, and they had taken a dozen turnings before a most welcome sight burst upon them.

It was Dick Strongbow, with Jacob Morelle pinioned by the arms.

On the ground lay another man insensible.

Hurried exclamations of joy were exchanged, and the next moment they were in darkness again.

"Hang the matches!" growled Phil; "they don't last a minute." Here he struck another. "I would give a pound or two for a decent-sized candle."

"You might find such a thing hereabouts," said Dick Strongbow. "It seems to me that this place has been recently inhabited. Speak up, Jacob Morelle—is there such a thing as a candle hereabouts?"

"There's a lamp yonder—in the niche!" gasped

Morelle. "Don't grip me like that; it takes my breath away. Save me! what strength you have."

The niche he alluded to was a short distance away, and there a lantern was found, with a lot of other odds and ends, such as men living in a place like that would gather together.

Phil lighted the lamp, and by its light the arms of Jacob Morelle were secured with a strap Butterflick had round his waist.

Dick then explained what had happened to him since he entered the cave.

He had not stepped far in it ere a man sprang upon him—one of the town gang with whom Jacob Morelle had recently associated.

He had no idea of the style of man he had attacked, but he speedily found out.

Dick struck him once, and he went down like a felled ox.

"He is lying near the mouth of the cave," said Dick. "I have heard him groan two or three times."

"And he was the derned ghost that skeered us," growled Butterflick. "If ever old Sal hears o' this she'll get the laugh o' me."

After felling the man who attacked him, Dick quietly waited to see if there were any more like him in the neighbourhood.

It seemed there was not, for Dick was interfered with no more.

He waited and waited until he decided that the man was alone, and was moving forward to gauge the size of the cave, and, if possible, find another way out of it, when the firing of his friends and Morelle and his companion reached his ears.

Then he guessed that Carl and the others had by some means found their way into the cave, and were advancing to his aid.

He hastened as well as he could to meet them, and soon came upon Morelle and the other man.

He heard Jacob Morelle bid his companion to keep by the wall and take the first turn to the left.

Although he spoke in an undertone, every sound had its echo. The place, in fact, was a very good whispering gallery.

"Strongbow is in the gully," Dick heard Morelle say. "'Ware him, my lad. If he gets hold of you—Ugh!"

Dick grasped him with one hand, and with the other he hit out in the dark, fortunately striking down the other man.

Then he "put the grip" on Jacob Morelle, who uttered the wild shriek of helplessness which Carl and his friends had heard.

That awful clutch had invariably the effect of taking all the nerve out of a man, and Jacob Morelle, bold as he was under ordinary circumstances, lost his head.

He shrieked for mercy like a woman, and it was not until Dick relaxed his hold a little that the paroxysm of fear partly subsided.

"Don't do that again," he pleaded. "I'd rather you shot me down like a dog."

It was not Dick's intention to kill the man. He wanted him to live, at least for awhile, for a purpose which the reader will understand.

The question now was, what was to be done with the prisoner?

With regard to the two men he had knocked out of time, he proposed to leave them to recover as best they could; but with Jacob Morelle it was another matter.

If taken back to prison he would be in the hands of the authorities, and the end Dick had in his mind's eye might be defeated.

But what was he to do with the man?

"I'll keep him for the night at least," he thought.

And drawing Carl aside, he gave him a few whispered instructions.

Carl in turn spoke a few words to Butterflick, telling him to return to Capetown, and procure sufficient provisions for a day's stay upon the mountain.

"Not here!" exclaimed Butterflick, aghast.

"No, you will find us outside," said Carl, "on the openground, near the steps that we descended by."

The whole party moved forward, and having lighted Butterflick over the plank bridge, they told him to get away.

Then Carl, with the lantern, crossed over, Muffins next, and Phil Norton behind him.

"Now," said Dick to Jacob Morelle, "it's your turn."

The man was strangely altered during the last few minutes.

Occasionally he had looked at Dick, and shuddering, turned away. An overwhelming dread of the Diamond King had taken possession of him.

He stared vacantly at Dick, and muttered a few unintelligible words.

"Go on," was the imperious request of the man who had cowed him.

Jacob Morelle went forward, stepped upon the plank, and stood still. He looked back at Dick then at the dark, awful depths below.

There was no mistaking the meaning of his gaze. He was, in a vague, wild way, comparing a grave in the bowels of the earth to being Dick's captive.

A moment more and his decision would have been made for the former, but the iron hand grasped him by the shoulder and pushed him forward.

"Over—quick!" said Dick, between his teeth.

But a sudden desperation seized the man. He would not move.

"I wish to die!" he cried, and threw himself off the plank.

But Dick held on, although he fell on his knees upon the plank, and so for a moment they remained, one kneeling and the other swinging over the dark abyss.

An exclamation of horror burst from the witnesses of this terrible scene, and Carl made a forward movement to assist his friend.

"Back!" cried Dick. "I shall do better alone."

Jacob Morelle was quiescent now.

The desire to die had gone, and in its place was a helpless terror. He had not the power to groan or utter a sound.

The dead weight of a man is a dead weight indeed.

Those who doubt this assertion had better test the truth of it by trying to raise a limp man from the ground.

No other known living man could have done the feat that Dick now performed.

Once, twice, thrice he swung the helpless Morelle to and fro, and then tossed him out upon the other side of the abyss.

"Hold him!" he cried, and, rising, he stretched himself in a way he always did after performing some deed that required his full muscular powers, and then steadily crossed the plank.

There was no need to hold Jacob Morelle.

As he fell, so he lay, and when Phil called upon him to rise he did not stir.

"Raise him up and get on," said Dick.

They lifted him up, and between Carl and Phil he walked along in a feeble, mechanical way, neither looking at anyone nor speaking a word.

Along the narrow way, up the steps, to the outer air they walked.

Night was at hand now, and already a few stars were shining in the east.

"A warm, still night," said Phil Norton; "it won't hurt any of us to sleep out."

Dick did not answer. He was looking curiously at Jacob Morelle.

They walked to a spot where the sloping ground was tolerably smooth, and then Dick bade Morelle sit upon the ground.

He did not answer by word or look, but when Dick gently pressed his shoulder he sat down, staring into vacancy.

"Morelle," he said, "you are not well. Here—drink from this flask."

There was no meaning in the eyes of the man he addressed. He did indeed look at the flask, but made no attempt to avail himself of the offer.

"Drink," said Dick.

But Morelle turned his head aside, and in a low voice began to sing.

It was the burden of a song such as a boy would know—one he had, perhaps, been taught in his early days by those who loved him.

They stared at him, all but Dick, wonderingly.

An ashen hue had overspread Dick's face, for he saw that he had captured the man to lose the chance of getting from him what he wanted.

"What ails him?" asked Phil Norton.

"Only this," said Dick, with a groan, "he has gone mad!"

CHAPTER XXVII.

RETURN TO CAPETOWN—BUTTERFLICK IS EN-TRUSTED WITH A CHARGE, AND COMES TO GRIEF—OLD SALLY.

RUSHING in its effect was the shock the terrible announcement gave to all of them Apart from the sympathy they must have felt, even for an enemy, they furthermore real-ised all it meant to Dick.

Horror, dismay, and a vague sense of being in a manner responsible for the calamity was upon them all.

"We must take him back as soon as we can," said Dick, "but the poor wretch seems to be tired out."

Jacob Morelle now stretched himself upon the ground, and was composing himself to sleep, just as a child might have done.

And sleep came to him, as it comes to those who are sinless.

"It is horrible," said Dick. "I never reckoned on this."

"I do not see how you can rightfully blame your-self for it," said Carl. "The fellow has led a wild, reckless life, and sooner or later the settlement with Nature comes."

"Perhaps he will get over it," suggested Phil Norton.

"He may," said Dick; "but I do not think so. However, let him rest. We will see what to-morrow brings forth. Muffins, my boy, you must be tired out. Try to get some sleep."

"Yes, master," replied Muffins, obediently.

He laid down, but the excitement of the last few hours had roused his brain into abnormal activity, and sleep was far away from him.

So he amused himself by watching Phil Norton seated beside the sleeping Jacob Morelle, killing time by examining his revolvers, and Carl and Dick walking slowly to and fro.

They were talking together in a low tone, but he could hear what they said.

"I rather expected to find Pan with him," said Carl.

"Pan—ah! I had forgotten him," replied Dick. "The thought was a natural one on your part."

"He may be in the cave for all we know, Dick."

"It matters little, Carl. He plays but a minor part in the drama of my life, and whether he is off or on the stage is of little moment to me."

"A man of his character is always dangerous."

"No doubt; but he has had a lot of malice taken out of him by Ajax."

"Ah! Ajax—I suppose he is dead?"

"No; I think he will live. For all his fancy he did not look to me like a dying man."

For a time there was silence between them. Carl took out his cigar-case and offered it to Dick.

"Have a weed," he said; "it will help to compose you."

Dick took one, and they lighted up, smoking awhile without speaking.

"Suppose the worst has befallen that man," said Carl, indicating Jacob Morelle, "what will you do?"

"I must first find an asylum," replied Dick.

"And then?"

"I must wait until he recovers or dies."

"Not here, in this country, surely?"

"Yes, Carl, on the spot, as it were, in case he might want to see me. I think he will one day."

"And I will wait with you," said Carl.

"No," answered Dick. "I cannot consent to such a sacrifice. You have given your heart to Aimee Lefrau, who must not be made to suffer in my cause."

"She would think little of me if I deserted my friend—and such a friend!"

"But I will not permit it. The time has come when you must think of yourself. You are no longer poor, and all the happiness that health, wealth, and an honest woman's love can give awaits you. I will not hear another word about further sacrifice from you. On our return to Capetown you must write to her."

Carl apparently acquiesced. If silence is to give consent, he may be considered to have con-sented. But occasionally a dumb assent is a form of negative.

DICK STRONGBOW:

The Diamond King,

AND WONDER OF THE WORLD.

Dick laid hold of him with that deadly grip of his.

No. 9.   Price One Penny.

It was during this silence that they heard a scuffling footstep on the steps, and Phil Norton rose to his feet.

The head of a man appeared at the opening, and after a hasty glance round, the whole of one of the ruffians whom Dick had stunned came into view.

The fellow seemed to be still half dazed, for although he looked in the direction of the party he did not appear to see anyone, but went off down the mountain side, occasionally stopping to feel his limbs, as if he feared one or more of them was broken.

"Let him go," said Dick; "he is not one of the class we have to fear."

They watched for a time for the other to appear, but he came not.

No sight or sound of him was ever heard on earth again, for he had, after recovering from the blow he received, wandered into the cavern and fallen into the deep abyss that divided it in two.

Down into a depth which no man had ever plumbed, amid the dark horrors of the bowels of the mountain, he found a grave.

. . . .

"I stand by it," said Butterflick, "the cave is haunted, and although it was not hurtful to us it was fatal to Gentleman Jim and his pals."

As Mr. Butterflick gave vent to this opinion he cut off a plug of ham—a thumb-piece, as he called it—and put it into his somewhat capacious mouth.

He had returned laden with provisions, morning had come, and Jacob Morelle was awake.

Awake, but there was no change in him, except that he was more ghastly in appearance in the daylight.

In addition to the scattering of his wits, sudden old age had come upon him.

The day before he had been a grizzled, hardy man of fifty or so. Now he looked seventy.

His hair was white, his form bent, and a score of deep seams had been added to his furrowed brow.

They gave him food, and he ate it—drink, and he drank it; but he uttered never a word.

Daylight brought with it other discoveries, in the form of long iron bars, which Jacob Morelle and his companion, or companions—it was not certain whether he had one or two—had used to prize out masses of loose rock and block up the narrow way below.

"If you live for a hundred years, Strongbow," said Phil Norton, "you will never have a narrower escape than you had last night."

"I suppose not," said Dick, calmly; "but life is full of risks, seen and unseen, and it is useless to dwell upon those we have escaped."

They started down the mountain, but had to go slowly, for Jacob Morelle walked feebly, and frequently halted like a child to pick some wayside weed or flower.

All were disposed to humour him. There was no hurry now. The slow progress was only part of the necessary waste of time Dick was prepared for.

We pass over the plodding journey of the day. There was nothing in it we need put on record. Night had come again when they reached Capetown.

Dick's first care was to find a lodging where Jacob Morelle could be taken care of for the night, and Butterflick, whose knowledge of the town was extensive and a little peculiar, found what he wanted.

Furthermore, he undertook to sleep in the same room with him and see that he did not get away.

To make things sure, the door was locked and Dick took away the key with him.

The room in which Morelle and Butterflick were accommodated was in a quiet street, where poverty, or next door to it, was much in evidence.

People living there were always glad to take in lodgers and ask no questions.

Weary with the few days' outing, the rest of the party went off to the Kohinoor Hotel, where they had some light refreshment and went to bed.

To bed and to sleep, with a soundness that is twin sister to death.

Unconscious of everything around them, they remained until the morning, when Bill Butterflick appeared at the hotel.

The hour was almost nine, and the busy life of the day had partly begun. Butterflick, on entering the hotel in a great hurry, bounced against an old gentleman, begged his pardon, cannoned off on to a waiter, whom he upset into the umbrella-stand, and bolted upstairs to Dick's sitting-room.

"Drunk again," was the mental comment of the waiter as he gathered himself up.

Butterflick was not drunk, but he was in a state of mind almost as distressing.

Not finding Dick in his sitting-room, he rang the bell, and when the waiter appeared, asked where he slept.

"Mr. Strongbow's number is ninety-six," replied the man, "but I don't think you ought to disturb him."

"I'll disturb you if you try to stop me," cried Butterflick. "Out of my way there. You—up—I'm on the rampage—I'm off—I won't take anything, even from old Sally just now.'"

As the waiter only scaled about eight stone, he made way for the bulky Butterflick, who strode upstairs to Dick's room.

He held Dick sufficiently in awe to remember that he ought to knock before going in, and he did so.

Aroused from his sleep, Dick drowsily bade him enter.

All the rush suddenly evaporated out of Butterflick, and he entered the room with a meek, dejected air. In a moment Dick was fully awake.

He realised what had caused this early visit.

"Jacob Morelle has got away," he said.

"Levanted some time in the night," replied Butterflick, "by the winder, and out by the backyard. To stop my running after him if I woke, he stowed away my clothes up the chimbly. Luckily there wasn't much soot in it. Fires ain't orfen used in bedrooms here."

"And how have you got out of the room?" asked Dick.

"By the winder too," groaned Butterflick. "There's a water-butt a few feet down under it. It bore his weight, but the lid gave way and let me in. I started wet up to the waist, but I've run myself almost dry. Knock me on the head, cap'en; I ain't fit to live."

"I won't blame you," said Dick; "it was my fault. I never thought the poor demented creature would think of escaping."

"But was he—what do you call it—demented?" cried Butterflick. "In my belief he was shamming."

"Hardly possible."

"Ah! cap'en, you don't know what Gentleman Jim can do. The games he's been up to in the colony would make your hair curl. Shamming swell or beggar, parson or rough, it was all the same to him."

"But you did not think yesterday that he was shamming," said Dick.

"I didn't," replied Butterflick. "I'm a baby at some things, but I'm good at finding out things arter everybody else knows 'em. He wouldn't have look in old Sally—not he."

"After all," said Dick, "he may not be shamming, and in that case will be easily found again. Don't distress yourself, Butterflick. I am sure you did your best to keep him safe."

"Thank 'ee, cap'en," said Butterflick, gratefully.

"By-the-way," said Dick, sitting up in bed, with twinkling eyes fixed on Butterflick, "who is the lady you so often speak of?"

"Oh! Sally, you mean?" said Butterflick, with an embarrassed look.

"Yes; old Sally, of course."

Butterflick had a look round the room ere an answer came slowly from him.

"She's a lady—as I knowed years—ago—as I kind o' got acquainted with, and, in due time, married. I was happy enough for a week, and then I cut and run."

"From where?"

"Australey. I emigrated from England there when I was a boy of twelve. My father was a Cornish miner."

"And how long is it since you saw your wife?"

"A little mor'n seventeen years," said Butterflick.

"That's a long time," said Dick. "And have you not forgotten her?"

"Forgotten her!" said Butterflick, with an indescribable look. "No, a man as had had the ferlicity to be married to old Sally wouldn't forget her while he kept his noddle straight."

"Was she old when you married her?"

"Lor! bless you, no, cap'en. Not more 'n twenty-two, and a widow. She was a relic o' Mike Parsons, who only survived the joy o' married life a month. He might, I fancy, ha' been alive now if he had done what I did—cut and run in a week."

"She was peculiar, I suppose?"

"Well, she was—old Sally," said Butterflick. "When I runned I was almost bald, and I had a chip or two about the cheeks and eyes as spoke of nails. Our 'umble cottage home rained rollin'-pins as it seemed to me, and there wasn't a corner in the place that she didn't keep summat handy for me—from the fryin'-pan uppards. I've orfen spoke of her as a woman o' mark, and the boys ha' got hold o' her name, and they kind o' chaffers me about it. Dabster Brown is uncommon free on the subject."

"I suppose you are not likely to see her again?" hinted Dick.

"Lord help me! I hope not," exclaimed Butterflick, with terror in his eyes. "You see—a woman like that's got everything her own way. She can lay on, and if you are a man you CAN'T hit back again. You've got to give up your work, stand chipping, and all the rest of it, unless you want to dergrade yerself by hammering her, and that won't do."

"I suppose not," said Dick. "Well, Butterflick, as you are here, you had better stay and have some breakfast with me. We must talk over what is to be done."

<hr />

CHAPTER XXVIII.

TWO LETTERS—DICK HAS AN OFFER—BUTTERFLICK SQUARES ACCOUNTS WITH AN OLD PAL.

SANE or mad?" muttered Dick, as he went slowly downstairs.

Notwithstanding the fact that he had spoken lightly to Butterflick, the disappearance of Jacob Morelle was a heavy blow.

It seemed hardly possible that any man could be such a consummate actor as to play the part of a lunatic so well.

On the stage it would be easy enough to a man of talent, but he would have the make-up," the foot-lights, and the associations of the place to aid him.

Jacob Morelle, if shamming, had played a part for close upon twenty-four hours, the greater part of the time in full daylight, without betraying himself.

It was incredible.

"I can't believe it," said Dick, "especially as his condition can be fully accounted for. Thousands of men, going through what he did, would have mentally succumbed."

There was a note from the hospital for Dick. It came from the doctor, and it referred to Ajax.

"Better, but still in a very dangerous state," was the substance of it.

Dick was not sorry to learn that there was a chance of Ajax getting the better of his injury.

The strong, true-hearted man does not find a pleasure in utterly destroying a rival who is an inferior.

Up to a certain point Dick followed Ajax and punished him; beyond that his dislike of the man did not go.

Shortly after Dick appeared in the breakfast-room the others came down, and breakfast was served.

Butterflick was still bowed down with grief; but he ate like a man whose appetite never failed him.

Dick, to keep his mind from being worried about Jacob Morelle, led him on to talk about old Sally, and some striking passages of his brief but exciting matrimonial career were put on record.

"She'd got a spring on her—a 'lasticity of foot-step, as them writer chaps put it," he said, "the like o' which I ne'er seen in anything short of a mad bull. She was a injyrubber woman, and the way she'd get round you, laying on with the leg of a chair, or mebbe a copper-stick, was surprisin'."

"Was she a big woman?" asked Phil Norton, innocently.

"Big?" exclaimed Butterflick. "Not she—a Tom Thumb sort o' a woman. She had to jump up to lay hold o' my hair; but she was 'lastic, and could ha' skipped right over me if she had a mind to."

This interesting conversation was interrupted by the entrance of a waiter with a letter on a salver.

It was for Dick, and addressed "Professor Strongbow."

"What may this mean?" said Dick, as he opened the envelope.

Inside was a letter from Ichabosh Beldan, and it ran as follows—

"*Mr. Ichabosh Beldan, proprietor of the Royal Music Hall, will call upon Professor Strongbow at half-past ten o'clock, with a view to engaging his services as a Strong Man. It is to be hoped that Professor S. will arrange to be at home, as Mr. Ichabosh Beldan is a busy man, and has no time to fritter away in waiting.*"

Dick was at first disposed to be angry with this epistle, which had a leaning towards the impertinent, but cast off the feeling, and laughingly read it aloud.

"I don't know on what grounds this gentleman thinks I am likely to make a public exhibition of my strength," he said. "Nobody has given him any encouragement, I suppose?"

They all declared they had not, but Carl pointed out the fact that the papers had made much of Dick's display of strength on the night of the riot in the music hall.

"I had forgotten that," said Dick; "but even that does not give this fellow a right to pen a letter of this description. I shall not be here at half past ten—but I will leave word that I cannot see him."

"May I ax the favour o' being the bearer of that message?" asked Butterflick. "I know old Ichabosh well—have done so for years. I can put the matter straight, so that he won't trouble you any more."

Dick had no objection, and breakfast being over, he had a short consultation with Carl and Phil, with the result that they went out together.

Muffins was left at home with Butterflick, and he was not sorry, for he had got it into his head that the interview with Ichabosh Beldan might have some fun in it. A verification of this idea was soon given him by Butterflick.

"Muffins," he said, "we've just got twenty minutes to prepare for the reception of the magnate, Ichabosh Beldan, Esquire, of the Royal Music Hall. It's an opportunity I've wanted for a long time. Put an easy-chair there for me—now shove the table back so as to have a clear run to the door; Ichy, may want it. That's a box of cigars you have over there, isn't it?"

"Yes," replied Muffins; "Prueba's—full size—big ones."

"That's the sort; hand me one," said Butterflick. "Do you think you could tackle one yourself?"

"No, I'm afraid not—they are very strong,' replied Muffins, dubiously.

"I want him to feel when he comes into this room that we are as good as him, and better," said Butterflick, "and there's an independent look about a cigar in the mouth that nothing else can touch. Swells on the stage allus smokes in the drawing-room—seems to show that they got the true blue blood in 'em, and are a cut above the common mob. You can tackle a cigarette anyhow?"

"I'd rather not," answered Muffins; "master says that smoking stops a boy's growth, and saps up his strength."

"Somebody's coming upstairs," said Butterflick, hurriedly; "that's Ichy's voice. Stand there, easy, with one hand on your hip, and 'a don't-care-a-d—for-you' look in your eye. That's it, steady does it."

Butterflick, with a big cigar in his mouth, threw himself down in the easy-chair, stretched out his legs, and sent out a column of smoke as Mr. Ichabosh Beldan was ushered into the room by a waiter, who announced him and retired.

He stared at Butterflick and Muffins, and then with a frown put his hat, which he was carrying in his hand, upon his head again.

"I expected to see the professor," he said.

"There ain't no professors here," replied Butterflick, "unless you are one—professed old humbug and thief."

"Who are you that dare to address me in this way?" demanded Ichabosh.

"An old pal o' yours, Ichy," said Butterflick, rising, "although I never introduced myself to you before. It's only when you come your insolence to a MAN that I'd die to serve that my blood is ris. Ichy, I spotted you six months ago, but I never blowed. Why should I? Half of us you robbed is dead and gone, and the living are scattered."

"I tell you I don't know you," said Ichabosh Beldan, backing.

"Don't lie," growled Butterflick, "you know me. Bill Butterflick of the Old Sally Mine, from which you levanted with all the property you could lay your hands on. You was knowed then as Aaron Shemivitch. Oh! I see you know me now."

"Butterflick," said Ichabosh Beldan, abjectly, "you'll never go and blow on an old pal. It couldn't do no good, and as long as you live there's a free stall for you at the Royal."

"Catwollopers seize your free seats," said Butterflick. "If I wants a seat I can pay for it, as I've done afore. I want to know two things. Fust, why a man like you have got the imperence to think that our cap'en would be part o' your show, and next, what yer mean by wearing your hat in the presence of two gentlemen in their special private room?"

As he spoke he removed the offending tile with a round arm blow that sent it flying to the further corner of the room.

It was a high hat of exceptional stiffness, and its removal and fall was not accomplished without some commotion.

"Butterflick," said Ichabosh Beldan, hoarsely, "you don't treat an old pal fair. I looked for better things from you."

"Ba—ah!" said Butterflick, snapping his fingers under the other's nose, "you are a rippercrit. Pick up your hat and cut it, and don't you so much as think of again making imperent offers to the cap'en."

Ichabosh Beldan, breathing hard, crossed the room, and by diving under the table succeeded in recovering his lost chapeau.

"Put it on your head," growled Butterflick.

"Excuse me, I don't wish to be impolite—I—I—"

Butterflick snatched it from him, banged it on his head, the hind part before, and forced it over his eyes.

"Oh! don't, I'm a-smothering," gasped the victim of these forcible attentions.

Butterflick's answer was to get behind him, and with another bang force it further on. It thus became, in the most painful manner, firmly fixed upon Ichabosh's nose.

"Door, Muffins," said Butterflick. "Go on, Ichy,' seizing him by the collar, "forward—landin' sir— now you are by yourself—mind the stairs—whoop ! there he goes ! Below there—gentleman with a tile loose coming down."

CHAPTER XXIX.

DICK GOES OUT FOR AN EVENING—A RUN OF LUCK—A GRATEFUL GAMBLER.

NOT a word could be heard of Jacob Morelle. Every enquiry that could be made without exciting attention was indulged in without result. It was a very puzzling business altogether. On returning to the hotel in the evening, they found that Butterflick had gone out, leaving Muffins at home.

He had left a short, characteristic letter behind him to explain why he had gone.

" *Ime getten on with drink, having given Ichy a start ; and I donte want a boy to see me in licker. Ime orf.*"

"He doesn't say that he's gone for good and all," said Carl.

"I hope not," said Dick; "I rather like the fellow. He's a bit of a rough diamond."

Muffins did not know anything about it, except that Butterflick had spent the day drinking his own health, after the confusion he had heaped upon Ichabosh Beldan.

That worthy, it seemed, had not hurt himself seriously by falling downstairs, and having been got out of his hat with the assistance of two waiters, he had gone away humbled and abased.

"His nose was swollen up like a big plum," said Muffins, laughing heartily. "Oh ! dear, I never shall forget it."

"And I daresay Ichabosh will remember it," remarked Phil Norton, drily.

Dick Strongbow was in a restless frame of mind, and after supper strolled out alone.

As he did not ask Phil or Carl to accompany him, they remained at home.

Night is the liveliest time in Capetown, and the bigger part of the inhabitants keep late hours.

The days are hot, and at noon all who can conveniently do so take a rest. After sunset it gets cooler, and then is the time to be out and about.

It is a place of freedom, and things are done there which would not be permitted at home. Saloons where gambling is carried on more or less openly abound.

Dick strolled about the streets, heedless of whither he was going, eventually entering one which may reasonably be called "shady."

Every fourth house was given up to some sort of amusement, and feeling thirsty, Dick entered a place which by its outward appearance showed that it was a drinking saloon.

It was a small affair apparently, with a bar, which was, however, deserted. The majority of men who entered passed through a green baize door at the upper end.

Experience told Dick that beyond it was a gambling-room.

He was no gambler in heart, but he was not averse to a friendly game of anything he understood, and it occurred to him that he might possibly get some information bearing upon the subject which most interested him.

Men who frequent these places have a pretty good knowledge of everything that is going on, and have a habit of freely conversing among themselves. It was just possible that he might hear of something which would help him to find out what had become of Jacob Morelle.

Having drank a glass of claret, he sauntered down to the green baize door, pushed it open, and found himself in a square apartment, in which were at least a hundred men.

They were quiet enough, being engaged for the most part in gambling.

On the right hand was a *rouge et noir* table, around which was a group of eager players.

Dick, having watched the game for a few moments, put a sovereign on a number.

The croupier, a thick-set fellow of the prize-fighting type, was the only man speaking—in an ordinary tone.

"Make your game, gentlemen," he said, " while the ball is rolling. At any time before it stops you can plank your money down, but when it don't roll any more you've got to pick up your winnings or stand your losings. It's a game for men who've pluck, and there's a fortune for a bold heart whose willing to risk a sov. Thirty-one—red is the winner this time, gentlemen, and there's only one coin on it. Yours, sir !"

Dick was the only winner, except those who had simply backed the red, and as he calmly took up his money many an envious eye was cast upon him.

"Just like the luck of the young 'uns," said a grizzle-headed man with a hungry look; "they always win."

"That's the devil's art to lead 'em on," said another, "and when a young 'un has got the thirst he runs everything against him."

"I'll leave five pounds on the red," said Dick, "and stroll round."

"All right, sir," replied the croupier, "your money is safe. We play fair and square here. The ball is rolling—mark your game, gentlemen. This is a players' night, gentlemen. The bank is out of luck. Put your money down any time while the ball is rolling. Red again !"

"I'll follow the young'un !" cried the grizzle-headed man.

Some did, but others with ideas of their own did not. Dick, indifferent to whether he won or lost, quietly strolled about, until a loud cry from the gaming-table attracted his attention.

"The red six times running !" yelled the grizzle-headed player.

Dick walked up to the table and found six hundred and thirty pounds awaiting him.

He was not greedy, but he did not care to play any more, and scraping up the notes and gold, carelessly thrust them into his pocket.

"Go on, young 'un," said the grizzle-headed man.

"Not at present," said Dick, quietly.

The croupier said nothing.

It was all the same to him, for he felt sure that Dick would come back again, if not then, to-morrow or another day.

The grizzle-headed man, however, could not leave off.

"I'll have another shot at the red," he said, "and then stop."

He left all his winnings on that colour, and the ball was sent round again.

At first it travelled quickly, but it soon began to steady down.

Every eye was upon it. The watchers held their breath. Slowly the end came, and at the last it looked as if it would be red again, but the ball, after balancing itself for the infinitesimal part of a second between the two colours, settled upon the black.

"What did I say?" yelled the grizzle-headed man. "The luck goes with the young 'uns. That clears me out."

"You must be quiet, gentlemen," said the croupier, "or you can't have the game called. The ball is rolling again. At any time, until it stops, you can put your money on. It's a fortune to a man with pluck, but faint heart never broke the bank. Black, gentlemen, wins. Number twenty-seven, and no backers."

Dick had left the table and taken a seat close by. An attendant came up and asked him if he would take anything to drink?

"Nothing now," he said.

"There's nothing to pay, sir."

"That makes no difference to me. I would rather pay for anything I have if I wanted it."

The man went away, and the grizzle-headed player took the vacant seat beside Dick.

"You know when to leave off, sir," he said. "I don't."

"I assure you," replied Dick, "that there was no calculation in the matter. I did not play for the sake of gain."

"I wish I could say the same," was the grim reply; "but I can't keep away from the table. I've lost all to-night."

"Try your luck again," said Dick, with a smile, handing him a five-pound note.

"I say, you are a good fellow," said the other, with a grateful stare. "Would you mind doing me another favour?"

"What is it?"

"Tell me what to back."

"I know nothing about the game."

"All the better. Shall it be black or red?"

"Try black," replied Dick.

The inveterate gambler went back to the table and put down the note on the sombre colour. Black won.

He left his winnings there, and once more the ball rolled on black again.

The lucky player looked back at Dick.

"Shall I go on?" he asked.

"No," said Dick, absently; "try red."

The man tried it, and red won. So it did a second and a third time.

"What shall I do now?" asked the exultant winner.

"Give it up for the night," answered Dick.

"And so I will," said the player, as he gathered up his winnings. "Blessed if I wouldn't like to be guided by you for a twelvemonth."

All eyes were now fixed upon Dick, and two or three men were whispering together.

They were of the roughest types in the room, men who hang about such places, living in a way only themselves know exactly how.

Dick was a stranger to them, and they were speculating on the chance of taking "a rise out of him."

"He's a young 'un and alone," said one, "and he can't know what to do with all that money. We ought to ask him to lend us a trifle."

Dick at that moment rose up and walked to the green baize door. Half-a-dozen of these fellows followed him.

He went into the bar, and was going out of the place when they called upon him to stop.

"I say, guv'nor," said one, "you will stand something to wet your luck, won't you?"

"Why should I do so?" asked Dick, eyeing the party with no particular favour.

"Because it's always done," was the answer.

"I am afraid the rule will be broken to-night," said Dick. "I don't know you, and I am not in the habit of treating strangers."

He walked slowly down the bar, but ere he reached the door three of the men got in advance of him.

The barman became suddenly interested in the placards behind the bar, and apparently saw nothing of what was going on.

"You've got to shell out," said one of the men. "It isn't much—a pound apiece will do."

"I assure you," said Dick, severely, "that I do not intend to give you a farthing. As far as I can judge you are a set of arrant scoundrels, and any tip to you would be thrown away. Let me pass."

"You don't go until you part," they said.

A signal was passed to the party behind, and one of them pinned Dick by the arms.

With no visible effort Dick broke from his grasp, and, facing about, struck the fellow down.

The green baize door opened, and the grizzle-headed man came out of the gambling-room.

"Here—hi! What's up?" he cried. "Get out of it, young 'un. They'll maim or blind you."

The five remaining men went for Dick, and the grizzle-headed man shot one of them down.

"I'll stand by them as stands by me," he yelled, "if I die for it."

He was getting ready for another shot, when Dick, by his movements, showed that his further aid was unnecessary.

With a force that astounded the recipients of his defensive attentions, he thrust them in a heap against the wall, which was a flimsy wooden partition, and fairly drove them through it.

On the other side was a supper-room, in which a number of persons, sexes mixed, were partaking of refreshment.

The astonishment of these persons and of the grizzled-headed gambler and the barman was ludicrous.

As for the worthies in a heap upon the floor among the ruins of the woodwork, they were half-stunned, disabled, and dismayed.

The crash of the partition had been heard in the gambling-room, and stopped the play.

A stream of men came pouring out, eager to ascertain what had happened.

Dick, contented with what he had done, sauntered out before any explanation could be given.

At first a clear idea of the nature of the catastrophe could not be obtained. There were more talkers than witnesses. A babel of voices filled the bar.

But at length the facts were got at, and as some

there had heard of Dick Strongbow's deeds at the Royal Music-hall, his identity was made clear.

The man shot was seriously wounded, and was taken away to the hospital, while the grizzled-headed player seized a fitting opportunity to disappear.

But the roughs who had received a well-merited punishment were in a very serious state of mind.

They said little then, but, having left the house, they gathered together in the streets, angrily discussing the affair.

"He stays at the Kohinoor," said one; "it's closed by this time, and while he's ringing for the night porter we can shoot him down. Come on, lads. There's half a score dark corners near the hotel where we can drag him and ease him of his plunder."

Furious at being foiled—as such men always are—and smarting from the rough treatment they had experienced, they hurried off in the direction of the Kohinoor Hotel.

———

CHAPTER XXX.

DICK RECEIVES A TIMELY WARNING—THE PARTY IN AMBUSH GET INTO MISCHIEF.

NCONSCIOUS of the arrangements made for his demise, Dick, on leaving the hotel, sauntered along through the streets, which were now being darkened by the closing of some places which had the grace to close their doors at such a comparatively early hour.

The little excitement of the evening's adventure had done him good.

He could not help laughing as he recalled the astonished looks of the ruffians when they were being forced through the partition.

The alarm exhibited by the supper parties had also a ludicrous side to it, and he was obliged to stop two or three times to give full vent to his merriment.

"I wonder what sort of a rough I should have made!" he thought. "Brutality allied to my strength would have done some memorable deeds."

Finding himself in the neighbourhood of the hospital, he bent his steps thither to enquire after Ajax.

It was, of course, an unreasonable hour, but there would be a porter on duty who could enlighten him about the condition of the giant.

A short walk brought him to the hospital, and the information he desired was easily obtained.

Ajax was a little better, but not progressing well.

"The doctor says that what he wants is a HEART," said the porter. "A man with courage can pull through where a coward would die ten times over."

"That's true enough," replied Dick; "but don't forget that a man hasn't the making of himself, and if he hasn't a heart, he must put up with the deficiency."

The porter laughed in the style of a man who hears a rather humorous truism for the first time, and Dick, turning away, bent his steps towards his hotel.

He felt in an easier frame of mind all round. In the adventure he had gone through he found the anodyne he needed.

Unconscious of impending evil, he reached the entrance to the street in which the Kohinoor Hotel was situated, and there he encountered a man whom he recognised as his grizzle-headed gambling acquaintance.

"I've been watching here for you," he said, "hoping you would come this way home."

"It is very kind of you," replied Dick, somewhat drily; "but I assure you I—"

"Oh! I understand,' said the man; "you don't think it necessary for our chance meeting to grow into lasting friendship."

"I do not put it so offensively," said Dick, good-humouredly. "The fact is, I have little time to form new friendships."

"Just so," was the answer; "and I do not intend you to be burdened with me. I'm not a man worth cultivating. But you did me a good turn to-night, and I am grateful."

"That is a good trait in your character, although I did little that I can boast about."

"Look here, Mr. Strongbow—you see I know your name—gratitude is a poor thing without action to match, and I'm here to act. There's a plant got up against you to-night."

"A plant?" exclaimed Dick. "Where—and by whom?"

"Yonder, near the hotel, by the gang you upset in the saloon," said the man, looking behind him uneasily. "They're a rough, determined lot, and didn't take their punishment kindly—naturally enough. I dursn't show in it, for if I did I might as well order my coffin. But I can warn you not to go home to-night."

"Well, what is the plant?" asked Dick. "And how is it to be worked?"

"I got at the particulars," said the man, "by dodging around and listening. When you get near your hotel a sham beggar will come up to you and begin a piteous yarn. Of course you'll bite for a moment—so they reckon—and then the gang, hiding in dark doorways and such like, will spring out and shoot you down."

"And after that?"

"They will drag your body away somewhere and clear your pockets out."

"Thank you," said Dick, as he moved forward; "whatever I did for you has been amply repaid. Good-night, my friend; you are indeed a worthy fellow."

" But, save us !" exclaimed the man. " You are not going on, are you ?"

" I am," said Dick.

" Then you don't believe me ?"

" Oh ! yes. I am sure you have told the truth ; but now that I have an idea of what is contemplated I shall go on. I have a trick in dealing with fellows of this class. Come and see how it is done."

" They would spot me," said the man, trembling.

" Well, come on behind and watch from a distance," returned Dick. " How many skulkers are there, do you say ?"

" About a dozen, Mr. Strongbow."

" A goodly number—and all armed, of course.'

" With something — bowies, six-shooters, or clubs."

Dick smiled, and with a friendly nod sauntered on —the gambler, with his grizzly hair fairly on end, followed at a distance. He had seen one manifestation of Dick's enormous strength, and he wondered what form it would take now.

The street was very quiet. One man only passed Dick on the way. He was the worse for drink, and thickly muttered a " good-night " as he rolled by.

The shops and other houses were now closed, and for the most part wrapped in darkness.

Here and there an upper window was dimly lighted up, where someone was going to bed, or perchance it was a sick chamber.

At the hotel Dick could see, long before he reached it, that the gas in his private sitting-room was burning.

Possibly Carl was sitting up for him, although he had expressed a wish that he should not do so.

Walking slowly, and apparently indifferent to things around him, Dick approached the hotel. Without any visible movement he scrutinised the doorways and passages he passed.

Near the hotel he detected two men skulking in a doorway.

The story told by his grateful acquaintance was undoubtedly true.

Half-a-dozen pa es from the hotel the beggar put in an appearance. He came out of the shadow of the porch, hobbling with a stick and bent almost double, as if in pain.

" For the love of all good people," he whined, " give a poor fellow—"

Dick laid hold of him with that deadly grip of his, and the appeal ended in a wild shriek for help.

Dick utilised the man as a means of calling the attention of the hall-porter to his return by dashing the yelling wretch against the door with a force that made it rattle again.

He cried out no more, but lay in a heap, silent and still.

" Come out, you skulking hounds !" cried Dick, facing around.

They had all witnessed the fate of their fellow-conspirator, and knew that the ambuscade was what they called " blown upon."

The fate of the sham beggar filled them with terror, and dashing out of their hiding-places they sought safety in flight.

Ere they had got far several shots from a revolver were fired in rapid succession, and half the gang came tearing back again just as the door of the hotel opened, throwing a flood of light across the street.

This started them off again, all but one man, on whom the glare fell, and he paused a moment, too bewildered to know which way to go.

He who hesitates is lost, and Dick with three strides was upon him.

A knife he carried in his hand was wrenched away with a force that made that hand useless for evermore, and a blow on the side of the head stretched him senseless upon the ground.

In the doorway of the hotel stood the hotel porter, looking on with bewilderment. Aroused from a doze in a chair, he could hardly believe that he was not dreaming.

" See that the police take care of these two fellows," said Dick, as he stepped over the prostrate sham beggar. " An attempt has been made to rob me. Ah ! Carl, my dear fellow, waiting up for me ?"

" I have been uneasy about you," replied Carl, as he descended the stairs, " for a reason. I saw somebody pass here to-night."

" Not Morelle ?"

" No, indeed ; but Pan. I was seated by the window, enjoying a cigar. The room being hot, I had turned down the gas, so I was almost in darkness. He stopped on the other side of the way, looked up, and shook his fist with all the old venom."

" Pan !" said Dick, contemptuously. " I do not count him at all."

" Treachery does a deal of mischief at times," said Carl, " and many a good man has been shot down by a cowardly ruffian in ambush. You are very late."

" And you have been anxious, like a good fellow."

" The police are coming up, sir," said the porter ; " will you see them ?"

" I may as well, I suppose," said Dick.

There were three officers, fine strapping fellows. One stepped into the road to look at the prostrate man there, the others came up the steps and halted by the form of the beggar.

" What's the matter ?" they asked.

Dick in a few words explained that there had been an attempt to rob him. He had thwarted it thanks to a friendly intimation he had received.

" From whom ?" asked an officer.

" A stranger," said Dick.

The officer turned over the form at his feet, and the light of the hall lamp fell upon the face.

" It's Ramping Joe," he said.

" He won't ramp any more," said the other officer, " for he's as dead as anything. You've killed him, sir, and Capetown ought to be grateful to you. There lies all that's left of one of the most cowardly, cruel, treacherous scoundrels that ever breathed."

Turning to the roadway he called out to the third officer—

" Who have you there ?"

" Bos Barker," was the reply. " He's snuffling a bit and will soon come round."

" There's two dead and one seriously wounded down the street," said the officer to Dick. " You don't know who's accountable for that ?"

" How should I ?" asked Dick, evading the question.

" It's like as not they shot each other," said the officer, " and it doesn't matter. They're a bad lot, and the mourning won't be very deep for 'em. We may want you to-morrow, sir."

" Very good," said Dick ; " I am at your service. Good-night."

"Stay there until we finish the game," said Dick. "If you attempt to get down I will sweep the floor with you."

"Good-night, sir."

"I expect my grizzly friend is accountable for the casualties below," muttered Dick, as he ascended the stairs with Carl ; "he utilised the occasion to pay off an old score."

"Who is your grizzly friend ?" asked Carl.

"I will tell you about him to-morrow," answered Dick ; "I am too sleepy now."

CHAPTER XXXI.

PAN AT LOW WATER MARK—HE MEETS AN OLD FRIEND — THE GRIZZLE-HEADED GAMBLER AGAIN.

RAWLING about in a narrow street on the east side of Capetown was Pan — broken — dejected — penniless — miserable.

The avenging sword had fallen upon him and severely smitten him.

In addition to his other miseries he had lost the pluck he undoubtedly possessed in the old days. Dick Strongbow had done much to shake it out of him, and Ajax had done the rest.

That the born coward should have been strung up to do such a thing was the bitterest pill of all. He could not swallow it willingly.

It stuck in his throat, and from the moment of his fall he had never in his waking moments ceased to think of it.

He escaped from the music-hall in the confusion by creeping into one of the side boxes, where he lay cursing until Dick was gone.

Then he crept out and limped forth, a cowed and beaten man.

The supposition that he had since been with Jacob Morelle was incorrect.

He had not set eyes upon the man up to the moment when we find him broken down in the narrow street.

Had he proved the man of old, he would soon have found a way, by violence or chicanery, to get possession of some money, but the dare-to-do was all gone out of him.

Ajax had never been more abject than he was now.

A score of times during the past two days he had had opportunities of getting money from men who were either the worse for drink or easily cowed and robbed, but in every case he hesitated until the opportunity was lost.

"What's come to me ?" he asked, ruefully. "It's a second childhood—worse, for children have courage of a sort, and I have none. Not an atom left."

He had hungered all day, and tasted no food. Now he was driven to the last resource of the destitute—to beg.

He stopped by a small general shop, and looked in at the window.

There he saw several forms of coarse food displayed, and after a moment's hesitation he entered.

A woman was standing behind the counter, and she looked at him with no very great favour as he walked in.

"What do YOU want ?" she asked, curtly.

"Food. Give me some," he replied, in a tone so abject that he positively did not know his own voice.

"Food !" she said, roughly. "Go and work for it. There are too many idlers and loafers in the town, and there is plenty of honest labour waiting for them to turn their hands to."

"I really haven't the strength to work," he pleaded.

"Lies !" she said. "Get out of the shop."

He hesitated, and tried to summon up courage to bully her.

To all appearances she was alone, and it seemed that it would have been easy work to frighten something out of her.

But while he hesitated she came round the counter, BOXED HIS EARS, and turned him into the street.

He was staggered by this summary mode of treatment, and as he crept down the street he stared about him, asking if it were not all a dream.

HIS ears boxed by a woman !

Yes, it was so, and he had not resented it. Not from any sense of manliness, but because he dared not.

"Was there ever a man so transformed as I am ?" he groaned.

"I think I can introduce you to another," said a voice in his ears.

He turned and saw an old man, whose features he fancied were familiar, but he knew him not.

"Don't you recognise me ?" asked the other.

"No," said Pan.

"I am Jacob Morelle."

"Impossible !'

"It is true," said the other, with a wan smile. "I, too, am transformed out of all—or nearly all—likeness to what I was but a few short hours ago."

"Have you any money ?" asked Pan. "I am cleaned-out—starving—and I can't talk to you until I have something to eat or drink."

"Come over here with me," said Morelle.

He crossed over the road to a public-house on the opposite side of the way, and Pan noticed that his step matched his appearance. It was that of an old man on the verge of senility.

They entered the place, and found the bar almost empty.

There was a man drinking by himself at the bar, another asleep upon a form close by, and a girl in attendance, that was all.

Morelle ordered some drink first, and after a dram Pan was ready for food.

Some cold meat was obtainable, and with a plate of it and a piece of bread he sat down in a corner, where there was an empty barrel that would serve as a table.

The two men sat down together, and Jacob Morelle watched Pan as he devoured the plain food before him, saying nothing until the keen edge of his appetite had been taken off.

"I feel better now," said Pan, breaking silence. "You know my story. Now tell me yours "

Much of Morelle's story we know, and little remains to be told.

From the time when he was held by Dick over the abyss in the Spectre's Cave up to the hour when he found himself sleeping in a room with Butterflick for a companion his mind was a perfect blank.

"What happened between I don't know," he said ; "but I must have received a terrible shock that stupefied me or put me into a frame of mind such as I have read of, when a man is ANOTHER BEING FOR AWHILE."

"It seems odd," said Pan. "And you don't know how you came to be there with Butterflick ?"

" No ; but it was enough for me that I was there, and I got up softly. The fellow was sleeping, and I could have killed him, but I thought it was dangerous."

"Say you hadn't the nerve," said Pan, gruffly.

"That's it," said Morelle. "I got out by the window, and slipped away. I've had a look at myself in a glass ONCE since "—he stopped and shuddered—"and I don't want to see myself again."

"You are twenty years older," said Pan, candidly, "and I've gone back to babyhood. Both changes we owe to that Dick Strongbow, and I'd like to see him lying dead in a ditch."

There was something of the old venom in his manner of uttering this amiable aspiration, but the old fires were extinguished; it was but a feeble flicker

"I don't want to see or meet him again," said Jacob Morelle ; "if I do I feel I shall tell him something that I want with all my heart to keep from him."

"It's about who and what he is ?"

Jacob Morelle nodded.

"I suppose you can tell me," said Pan, in a wheedling tone.

"No," replied Morelle, "for then there would be two geese to cackle the secret. I must get away from here and back to the old country."

"What for ?" asked Pan, opening his eyes.

"I don't know," said Morelle, "but I feel that I must go."

"Is there any money hanging to what you've got to tell him ?" asked Pan.

"Yes, but not much," replied Morrelle. "THAT won't matter to him now. He's independent of it All I could lay hands on I spent or brought away with me."

"And that paper left in your care by Gonzalo," said Pan, "you destroyed that ?"

"No," replied Jacob Morrelle.

"Have you it in your possession ?"

"I have not. That is at 47, Dane's Inn, Strand."

"What, all these years ?"

"As far as I know, unless the place has been pulled down. I left it behind me in a secure place, because I could not keep it. But don't bother me any more about it now. All I want is to get back again."

"And I'd like to go too," said Pan ; "anywhere to be out of HIS way. Couldn't we work our way over ?"

"We could try. Some of the ships that come here have to go back shorthanded."

"I should make a poor sailor," said Pan, grimly. "I don't think I dare go aloft to save my life."

"If you went aloft you might lose it," retorted Morelle. "But there's other work than that to do aboard. I'll have a look around to-morrow."

"And to-night—is there anywhere for me to sleep ?"

"I know of a snug den where we can be quiet enough."

Then they rose up, and, after a final dram, went out together.

The man who had been drinking alone in the bar did not so much as look at them, but the moment they were gone he emptied his glass and followed.

It was the grizzle-headed gambler, who felt himself so deeply indebted to Dick.

"I don't know what all your jaw means," he muttered, as he reached the street, "but I heard enough to let me know that you have wronged Strongbow somehow, and I'll just see you caged for the night, and then go and give him the tip."

CHAPTER XXXII.

BREAKING THE PLEDGE.

HY is it that shipowners still stick to the word "sail," when they mean a certain vessel will steam away at a given date ?

It must be because there is a stronger flavour of the sea in it than could be got out of any other word.

Whatever the real cause may be, all ships sail, and none are announced as about to steam.

In the " Capetown Argus " there were the usual advertisements of a mixed nature, as Dick Strongbow, running his eye over it, had the pleasure of noting.

The " Argus " is the representative paper of the colony, and it gives a prominent place to all things appertaining to communication with the outer world.

Therefore was it set up in bold letters that " The fast clipper Archimedes would depart on the eleventh CERTAIN, and those who desired berths had better secure the same to prevent disappointment."

Just beneath it was the further announcement that the popular liner Cygnet, mail steamer, would depart on the fourteenth, with first and second class passengers only.

Now these two announcements were made interesting to Dick by means of a letter he had just received.

It was a short letter, written in a cramped hand, and ran as follows—

" RESPECTED SIR,—*The two parties have taken berths, second class, on board of either the ship Archimedes or the Cygnet, but, as they have done it under false names, I can't say which it is.— Your obedient servant,*
" SIMON STARK."

The writer of the letter was the grizzle-headed man, who, by keeping a strict watch on Pan, had discovered this much.

He had seen Pan go into the shipping office and come out of it with two tickets in his hand.

Burning with zeal, Simon Stark went into the office and asked the clerk what ship the gentleman who had just gone out had booked for.

" Do YOU want to book for any vessel ?" asked the clerk.

" No," replied Simon.

" Then hook it," was the polite rejoinder.

Foiled thus, he left the office and wrote the above letter to Dick Strongbow.

As for Jacob Morelle, he had vanished again, and was possibly hiding away disguised.

Now Dick's position was this.

He shrewdly guessed that Jacob Morelle intended to return to England, and the best thing he could do would be to follow him there, and by some means get the truth out of him.

Failing that, he could lay him by the heels, and, once in the hands of the home authorities, he was not likely to again escape.

But by which ship would he go ?

The Archimedes sailed first, but she was the slower vessel, and the Cygnet was timed to arrive in the port of London two days before her.

If Morelle and Pan went by that, well and good. Dick could follow in the Cygnet, and await their arrival.

" I must take berths on the Cygnet," he finally decided.

Meanwhile four days intervened between then and the departure of the Archimedes, and much might happen during that time.

Ajax had so far recoved from his wound that he could get up and walk about a little.

But he was very weak, and the doctors said he would never again be able to appear as a strong man.

He did not tell him so, but Ajax knew it, and he said as much in a letter he sent to Dick."

" *I am broken down*," he wrote, " *and I shall only be fit for a servant's place. If you want a faithful one, try me. At least, let me go back to England with you. I want to get somewhere where I can be at peace.*"

Muffins was deputed to call upon him with a message to the effect that when Mr. Strongbow went back to England he would take Ajax with him and endeavour to find him suitable employ-ment.

Butterflick accompanied Muffins to the hospital, by way of volunteer body-guard.

" I feel just as if you was my son," he said. " If such a boy as you had come to me and Old Sally, he would have acted as ile on the waters of domestic confliction."

" Mrs. Butterflick has no children, then ?" said Muffins, with a sly glance at Butterflick.

" Not as I knows on," replied Butterflick, gravely. " It is to be hoped she didn't ; if she did—well, Lord forgive me for a villain who runned away from his family."

The possibility of his having run away and left a crowing little one behind him troubled Butterflick for a few moments, but he soon brightened up.

" I can't help it if it is so," he said. " One o' these days I may meet the young 'un, and then I can square accounts with him. HE'LL understand by this time why I runned away from his mother. I'll bet he's had some prime spankings."

This idea had a laughter-creating effect upon Butterflick, who was grinning still when they reached the hospital.

Ajax was in the hall, where it was cool, walking slowly up and down with the aid of two sticks.

It was a pitiful sight to see such a massive man almost as helpless as a child.

He was very glad to see them, and Muffins was certain he saw tears in his eyes as he shook hands with him.

" Tell Mr. Strongbow," he said, " when he had received the message, " that I am grateful, and one day I hope to do something to repay him."

They talked to him for a time, and then took their leave.

As they were passing down the street, Butterflick drew his hand across his mouth and smacked his lips.

" How do you feel, Son Muffins ?" he asked. " I'm a bit dry."

" It's warm," replied Muffins, " and a bottle of lemonade would not hurt us."

" Lemonade is a beneficial drink—to young 'uns," said Butterflick, in a dreamy kind of way ; " but somehow it don't seem to do grown men a power o' good. It's weak stuff, and, as far as I can make out, don't pan out well as a stimerlant."

Now Butterflick, as we know, had been a tee-totaller since his adventure with Busker and the rest of the gang, and with one exception up to that moment had been staunch.

Here, however, was a sign of breaking away.

" I think you had better wait until you get back," suggested Muffins.

" Just one glass—it wouldn't hurt," said Butter-flick. " Here's a house ; I'll be in and out in a moment."

Muffins did not feel called upon to play the part of the good boy in the story-book, who would have intervened his frail body between Butterflick and the public-house and refused to let him pass.

Muffins was not of the impertinent breed, and never consciously took liberties with his elders.

So, instead of endeavouring to keep Butterflick up to teetotal mark by juvenile resolution, he simply said—

" If you will, you must ; but don't be long."

It was a corner house they were standing by, and Butterflick, faithfully promising to be out again in the moment specified, went in.

Muffins walked quietly up and down, awaiting his return ; but the minutes passed and he came not.

It was really not a serious matter, for the street was a highly respectable one, and Muffins had nothing to fear.

A number of business people and a variety of vehicles were passing to and fro, and not even Jacob Morelle would be mad enough to attempt any violence at that hour.

So far, well ; but it was rather aggravating that Butterflick should not keep his word.

After waiting a quarter of an hour Muffins pushed open the door and peeped in.

To his astonishment he could see nothing of Butterflick.

The only person in the bar was a quiet, elderly-looking man, reading the paper.

Behind the counter was a stout woman, the land-lady.

" Go away," she said to Muffins ; " we don't serve boys here."

" I am looking for a friend of mine, that's all,' replied Muffins ; " a stout gentleman, who talks rather loud."

" He went out by the other door," replied the landlady.

Muffins was more than astonished to hear this—he was staggered.

Butterflick gone, and by the other door, without so much as taking the trouble to look for Muffins!

It was hardly what he expected from a father to his son, even though the latter was only adopted.

"He can't have forgotten me," thought Muffins, "for he hadn't time to muddle his head with drink. What does it mean?"

Not being able to imagine a solution of the mystery, he did the wisest thing under the circumstances, and went back to the hotel.

Carl and Phil Norton were at the doorway, smoking and chatting. They asked after Butterflick, and Muffins told the story of his disappearance.

"It's the oddest thing I ever heard of," said Carl. "You say he hadn't time to get drunk?"

"No," answered Muffins; "and I am not sure he had any drink at all. The landlady simply said he went out by the other door."

"I don't see how we can help him," said Phil Norton. "Perhaps he will soon return."

CHAPTER XXXIII.

BUTTERFLICK AND HIS YARN—PAN AND MORELLE LET OUT THE SECRET OF THEIR MOVEMENTS—SIMON STARK, AGENT.

OURS passed, and Butterflick did not return. Dick Strongbow came back from a visit to the shipping office late in the afternoon and heard the account of his disappearance with mingled feelings.

"It's the drink," he said. "Not having had any lately, one glass upset him. He's what they call 'broken out,' and will wander from one public-house to another until he is half mad. We shall have him back here in a fine state."

It was not a pleasant prospect, truly; and Dick made up his mind if Butterflick did come back in a state of intoxication to let him know that it was time for their acquaintance to cease.

"I think I can put him out without troubling the people here," he said, in his quiet way.

He was very angry with Butterflick, and at six o'clock, when dinner was served, he took his seat at the head of the table with knitted brows.

A plate was laid for Butterflick, and Dick had just ordered the waiter to remove it, when Butterflick himself walked in.

Instead of being the worse for drink he was as sober as a judge, and looked almost as wise as one—in fact, wiser than some judges we have at various times set eyes on.

"I'm glad you've come home, Muffins," he said, "but I guessed you would be all right in the middle of the day."

"I am sorry to find you cannot be trusted," said Dick.

"Now, don't you get humped with me until you hear my story," returned Butterflick. "You think I've been drinking, don't you?"

"You went into a place to drink."

"I did; but as soon as I gets in I sees somebody going out, and in a moment I knew it was that chap Pan."

"Sit down and have some dinner," said Dick, softening at once; "you can talk while you eat."

"And I CAN eat," said Butterflick, "for neither bite nor sup has passed my lips since breakfast this morning."

The waiter had left the room, and Dick having helped Butterflick to a liberal supply of cutlets, the much-maligned man went to work eating and talking together.

"I had no time to give Muffins the tip," he said, "for Pan was hurrying off as hard as he could, and I had all I could do to keep up with him. I followed him smart to a house down on the sea side of the town, and saw him go in. Nearly opposite, on a bit of open ground, was an upturned boat and a few odds and ends, which I gets behind, and watches. I knowed by the build o' the houses there was no back way out, and I'd only to watch and wait; and I was right."

Here he was compelled to stop a moment to dispose of a whole cutlet, which, in the excitement of talking, he had put into his mouth, bone and all.

Having satisfactorily performed this feat he went on.

"Hour after hour I waited and not a bit of the varmint did I see. I was just beginning to think he'd got away somehow without my seeing him, when out he comes and that Jacob Morelle with him.

"And would you believe it," said Butterflick, looking round, "but they both of 'em comes right over to where I was, and, squatting down the other side of the boat, put their pipes on. Then they begins to talk as free and easy like as if they were Lord Chamberlains in the Queen's front parlour.

"'That was a good idea o' yours, Pan,' says Morelle, 'taking them tickets.'

"'It was,' says Pan, 'and they'll be after us in no time.'

"'And it was better still to offer to pay the passage back of two poor devils,' says Morelle, 'and give em our clothes to wear.'

"Then they both larfed," said Butterflick, solemnly; "larfed as if a good joke had been got off. The rest of their talk was about going back to up-country to see if they couldn't work something there, but they didn't make up their minds where it was to be, except that it was to be as far away from Capetown as possible. With your leave I'll now finish my dinner," said Butterflick, in conclusion, "while you talk over what is to be done."

Dick said very little, while Carl and Phil discussed the position. Both were of opinion that the immediate arrest of Morelle and Pan was desirable.

"There is no hurry," said Dick. "I propose to take berths for us all on board the Archimedes, and they are sure to hear of it. The next move will be to lie close until the vessel sails."

"Expense isn't any object to you," said Carl, "or to us. Taking berths on the ship will completely blind them."

"I will do it to-morrow," replied Dick, "but there will be no need to make a song about it. I am going out for an hour."

He left them to themselves, Butterflick progressing satisfactorily with his dinner, and the rest talking over the way Morelle and Pan would find themselves sold, until ten o'clock.

Then Muffins, yawning, went away to bed, and the others descended to the billiard-room to while away an hour.

It was past midnight when Dick returned, and without attempting to give any account of himself he sat down beside them.

"The dodging about of those fellows has upset his plans," said Phil.

"Perhaps he may upset them," said Carl.

"How?" whispered Phil. "He can't drag Morelle on board and take him away to England. As for forcing anything out of him, I don't think it can be done."

"Boys," said Dick, "I'm a bit in the dumps. I feel as if I wanted a ROW with someone. Here, let us have a game at pool."

One of the tables happened to be unoccupied, and they took possession of it. A tall Yankee sauntered up, and, in nasal tones, asked to join them.

"We are three friends together," said Dick.

"What of that?" asked the Yankee. "This is a public room, and I think I've a right to join you. Snakes! the pride there is in these Britishers."

"I'm no hand at the game," said Phil; "you three play. I would rather look on."

Carl was an expert, and Dick, during the idle hours he had spent at the Kohinoor, had picked up a knowledge how to play.

He had plenty of nerve, and cared little whether he won or lost.

It was not so with the Yankee, who was one of those gentlemen who live upon what they can pick up.

He hoped to find greenhorns, and was himself, in a measure, taken in.

Of course Dick and Carl played an honest game, but it was much too good for the sharper, who found himself going the losing way.

"You play well," he said, "too well for me. Quite professional."

He was in the act of putting his cue up as he said this, just like a man who finds he is the hands of men who are too sharp for him.

"What do you mean by that?" asked Dick.

"Jest what I sa—ay," drawled the Yankee; "this game may be good for you, but it is very bad for ME."

"Do you think I care about your beggarly money?" said Dick, as he twisted the Yankee round and flung the coins in his face.

The hand of the Yankee disappeared behind him, with the intention of securing a revolver in a certain secret pocket there; but Dick, in a moment, was upon him.

"If you attempt anything in that way," he said, "I will squeeze you to a pulp."

He put just a HALF GRIP on the man, and that was enough. A pallor overspread his face, and, with a gasp, he cried—

"Lor'! what a grab you've got. Let go!"

"Not until I've taught you a lesson not to be so impudent," said Dick.

He looked round the room to find a place in which to deposit the quaking man, and saw nothing but a broad mantel-piece that would suit.

There were a few ornaments upon it, but, using the Yankee as a brush, he swept off what there was at one end, and plumped him down upon the marble.

Then he took the revolver from him and said—

"Stay there until we finish the game. If you attempt to get down I will perform a feat that is much talked of in your country but seldom performed. I will sweep the floor with your body."

Then he and Carl went on with another game.

The marker and Phil were the only other persons in the room, and neither of them attempted to interfere. Phil would not, and the marker knew better.

"I don't know who you are," drawled the Yankee, sitting composedly enough upon the shelf, "having only just arrived at this infernal hole; but all I can say is that I'd like to show you through the States at half profits. I'd run the risk of all expenses."

Dick could not help smiling. It was a very characteristic speech—cool and business-like under very trying circumstances.

"And what would you show me as?" asked Dick.

"As a man who would make a limp doll of John L. Sullivan," the Yankee replied, "and pulp anything ever born under the Stars and Stripes. I feel just as if you'd FLATTENED ME OUT."

"Let me assist you to descend," said Dick, advancing towards him.

"Thanks," replied the Yankee; "with your permission I'll get down myself."

"I won't hurt you."

"You mayn't mean to, but you're a human vice and don't know how hard you squeeze."

"Well, shake hands," said Dick.

"Will you go easy?" asked the Yankee, with a doubtful look.

"Of course I will. Let it be a touch and let go, to show that there is no animosity existing between us."

Dick touched hands with him and let him off easy as desired. Then the Yankee ordered a drink.

"I feel as if I want it," he said, with a sigh. "When you laid hold o' me all my inside went out of the heels of my boots."

"You had better have something with me," returned Dick, and he ordered a bottle of champagne.

"A giant and a prince," said the Yankee, when the glasses were filled. "Here's luck to you."

"If I could only get you to the States and keep you dark," continued the Yankee, meditating, "what a game we could work together. 'Ezekiel Smurch's Unknown will match himself against any living man for ten thousand dollars,' would read well in the papers, and what a rush there would be to get on—Sullivan and a score of others, with their asses of backers. I wish you would think it over."

"I assure you that it is not at all in my line," replied Dick, with a smile.

"I'm sorry," sighed the Yankee. "I feel like a man who is within an inch of a fortune and can't touch it. Good-night."

"Good-night."

"I hope you feel better," said Carl, as the door closed upon the disappointed Yankee.

"I feel as well as ever I did in my life," replied Dick.

CHAPTER XXXIV.

PUZZLING MOVEMENTS OF DICK—DEPARTURE FROM CAPETOWN—NOT EXACTLY WHERE THEY THOUGHT.

N the following morning a paragraph appeared in the "Argus," of which we give a verbatim copy—

"DEPARTURE OF MR. DICK STRONGBOW. — The inhabitants of Capetown will hear with regret that this famous gentleman, whose deeds have rivalled the feats of the mythical Hercules, intends to leave us. It is his intention to go up country in search of further adventures, so congenial to his disposition. It is only natural that one endowed with his enormous strength and unrivalled vitality should find the comparative repose of our business place irksome to him."

"How on earth did these people get hold of your intentions?" asked Carl, who read the paragraph aloud as he and Dick were having a morning cigar together.

"I have given notice to the hotel people," replied Dick, "that we intend to leave on the night previous to when the Archimedes puts to sea."

"Was that necessary?"

"I thought it was polite at least. They might be able to let our rooms."

"Morelle will read it and guess that we have bowled him out."

"He may, or he may not. I can't help it."

Dick smiled, as if he thought it was a matter of indifference what Morelle read, or in what way he succeeded in following his actions, and, flicking off the ashes of his cigar, said he was going to see Ajax.

"Of course you will not take him with you?" said Carl.

"I intend doing so," replied Dick.

"Really!" returned Carl. "You are in some things a most inscrutable fellow, and do the strangest things."

"But I generally come out right in the end," answered Dick.

Preparations for their departure were now begun.

Boxes were packed, and, beyond a kit for each—small but useful—everything was to be sent away.

Dick said he would find a storing-place for them, and engaged Simon Stark, with whom he held two or three secret conferences, to remove the packages one by one.

Accustomed to obey him in all things, and rely upon his judgment, his friends asked him no questions, but did exactly what they were desired to do, and no more.

All moneys, save a moderate amount, that would suffice for a year's travel, were, through a banking agency, transferred to England.

This was a wise step, all agreed, as it left them practically free men, without any anxiety.

A compact was entered into, and written and signed, that if any of them died or lost their lives the property of the rest was to be divided among the survivors.

An exception was, however, made in favour of Carl, who desired to leave a third of his possessions to Aimee Lefrau, the charming French maiden to whom he had given his heart, despite their antagonistic nationalities.

It appeared that she was with her father on a farm in the Transvaal, which would shortly be sold, as the jealousy of the Boers did not admit of its being worked to advantage.

As soon as possible the Lefrau family would return to France.

"I hope one day to meet her," sighed Carl; "but one cannot tell."

An offer from Dick to release him from his bond of friendly service he refused with some heat.

"As if I COULD leave you with your work undone!" he said.

The eventful night came at last, and shortly after dark Ajax came in a cab to the hotel.

It appeared that he did not exactly know where he was going, save that it was with Dick Strongbow, and that sufficed for him.

He could walk with one stick now, but he was sure that as long as he lived he would never be a professional strong man again.

"The doctors tell me," he said, "that some sinews have been cut through that will keep me weak, but if I live quietly I shall be all right."

About ten o'clock Dick said it was time to go.

The bill was brought in and paid, and, with their small kits strapped to their backs, they went down to the hall.

The proprietor and all the servants were there to see them off and wish them "God speed."

A cab was waiting at the door for Ajax. Simon Stark was on the box.

"It is just as well to let him go ahead," said Dick

Carl made a wry face, and looked doubtful.

"Morelle, I suppose, has started," he said.

"Two hours ago," answered Dick. "I have, through trustworthy agents, kept an eye upon him, His every movement is known to me."

No more questions were asked.

Ajax got into the cab and was taken away. Adieus were exchanged with the hotel people and the party set out on foot.

Carl expected Dick to make at once for the open country, but instead of that he faced in the direction of the sea.

Leading the way, he went down to the harbour, where a boat was in waiting.

"What's the meaning o' this?" asked Butterflick.

"I am going to visit a vessel," replied Dick; "please do not talk until we get on board. I will then explain my future movements to you."

Wondering more and more, they got into the boat, and two sturdy oarsmen pulled them out to a huge vessel lying at anchor.

There they seemed to be expected, for an officer was on the passenger ladder waiting to escort them on board.

He did not give them a word of greeting, but led the way, first to the deck and then to the first-class saloon.

It was quite empty. The few passengers who had come on board had gone to their berths; the main body would not be there until seven in the morning.

"Are all the second-class passengers on board?" Dick asked the officer.

"Yes, sir," was the reply, "and in their berths. It's our rule to have the second-class lights out at ten o'clock.'

He asked if they required anything, and, being answered in the negative, left the cabin.

"Perhaps you know what all this means?" said Dick to Butterflick.

"I must say that I am floored," replied that undoubtedly amazed man.

"It means this," said Dick, "that you were taken in that day when you saw Pan.'

"Me taken in? How!"

"Pan or Morelle must have seen you, either before or after you got behind the boat, and they came out for your especial edification."

"Hanged if I see what you mean!" gasped Butterflick.

"They came out to where you were," returned Dick, "to gull you."

"Do you mean to say they talked lies?"

"I do."

"I'm blessed."

"So you may be in some things, but not in the acumen that makes the true detective. Their plan was to send you back to me with a cock and bull story about their going up country, and all the time they meant to go somewhere else."

Butterflick took his hat off, laid it on the table, and gave his head a good rubbing.

"Old Sally used to say I was a natural fool," he cried, "and I begin to think that she may have been right. Gulled me, did they? But let me ask you, Richard Strongbow, how you know THAT?"

"I guessed it," said Dick, serenely, "and I ascertained exactly what they intended to do. At ten o'clock to-night they started disguised, certainly, but not in a way to deceive Simon Stark. He reported their every movement by messengers. Hark! there is Ajax. He has travelled round the town in a cab, and been brought here late, on the chance of Pan and Morelle not having retired."

"Retired!" exclaimed Butterflick. "Where to?"

"To their berths, my friend," said Dick. "The two rascals, confident of having done you, and me through you, are now sleeping, or trying to sleep, on board this craft, the Archimedes. If they are informed of their error before they reach England, and in all probability they may be, it will then be too late for them to get away. I now consider that I have fairly snared my bird."

CHAPTER XXXV.

A GAME OF HIDE AND SEEK—MUFFINS PLAYS A BIT FOR HIS OWN AMUSEMENT.

LYING in his bunk Jacob Morelle, on the following morning, was reviewing his position. The result was not entirely satisfactory to himself.

He had spent the best years of his life in a manner that was not creditable, and only for a brief time profitable.

After paying the passage-money of himself and companion, he had a very few pounds left.

But why did he take Pan with him?

Of what possible use could such a man be?

That Morelle had a use for him was certain, for he was not a man to be governed by generous impulses.

Whatever it was will, of course, be made clear.

Meanwhile, let us listen to his muttered reflections—

"Do I hold the trump card? I think so. After all, I can work him on THAT tack. If the old place is to let, it's a sure thing; if not, I may be able to find my way into it. Yes, I do hold the best card. Clear as day, with time to act and think—aye! I've got the upper hand, after all."

There were eight berths in the cabin he occupied, but only two were taken.

Very few people were going back from the Cape.

Pan had a berth opposite it, and Morelle, looking across, saw that it was empty.

"What a restless brute it is!" he muttered. "Does he never sleep?"

The door of the cabin opened, and Pan came in with a cup of coffee in his hand.

"I thought you would like it," he said. "There's a drop of brandy with it to take off the roughness."

Pan spoke lightly, but he had a troubled look upon his face, which keen-eyed Jacob Morelle instantly detected.

"What's gone wrong?" he asked.

"Everything, I should say," replied Pan. "Ajax is on board; I've just seen him walking up and down, with a stick, on the upper deck. Fancy that hulk of a fellow travelling first-class!"

"Perhaps Strongbow has sent him home for his health," suggested Morelle, as he sipped his coffee.

"If he had," answered Pan, "do you think he would have travelled first-class?"

"But is he travelling first-class, as you say? Perhaps as an invalid he has privileges."

"It isn't that," said Pan, gloomily, "and I am surprised that a man like you can't see what it means."

"You think that Strongbow and the rest are on board also?"

"I do. I'll bet my life on it."

"Not a very valuable thing as a stake, if you have not hit on the truth," said Morelle, drily.

"It's valuable to ME," with a faint imitation of his old snarl.

"Did he see you?"

"No."

DICK STRONGBOW:

The Diamond King,
AND WONDER OF THE WORLD.

With all his strength Muffins hurled the melon at Pan and hit him full in the face.

No. 10.   Price One Penny.

"Then we've got one thing in our favour left. It is possible they don't know we are on board."

"It is we who have been made fools of," Pan said "We didn't take in Butterflick that day."

"You mean Strongbow," said Morelle. "He's the head—the real head of the party."

"I've given up all idea of getting over HIM," returned Pan. "I'd like to scuttle the ship and send all on board to the bottom."

"It would take a better man than you to scuttle an iron steamer, even if you could get below to try on the job. Well, we must do something. Either show a bold front or lie close."

"A bold front to HIM," sneered Pan. "I'd like to see you do it."

"I'm pretty well certain he doesn't know we are on board," said Morelle, "for if he knew our movements wouldn't he have had us arrested?"

"Yes, that's just possible," said Pan, brightening.

"Well, then, don't you be uneasy. It's not a difficult matter to keep out of sight of the first-class passengers in these vessels. The upper deck is their place and the lower one ours."

"But haven't they the privilege of going anywhere they like?"

"Certainly; but they don't often avail themselves of it. We must keep constantly on the watch, and clear out as soon as we see any of them coming."

Now, as the reader knows, Dick Strongbow and his friends knew perfectly well who were on board with them, but, acting on Dick's advice, they shammed ignorance. There was not the least indication that they were on the look out for anyone, but for all that sharp eyes were ready to detect anything of interest to them.

Two days elapsed, and nothing was seen of Jacob Morelle or Pan. In their hearts, Butterflick and Phil Norton began to think that Dick, after all, had been outwitted.

By-and-bye, Carl began to think so too, and he ventured to express his fears to Dick.

"It would be a sell," he said, "if they have gone by the Cygnet after all."

"They are here," said Dick, easily; "but I dare-say they have found us out and are skulking."

Muffins put an end to all doubts about the subject in an accidental way.

Like all boys, he hated to be confined to a certain space, however extended, and he soon found the upper deck too cramped for him.

The other passengers were few in number, and not particularly sociable. They were mainly commercial men or traders of some sort, who were doubtful about the social status of the Strongbow party, and so held aloof.

Dick was not troubled by their reserve. It only made him smile; but Muffins was disgusted.

"A stuck up lot!" he said to himself. "I'd like to see master chuck 'em overboard."

Perhaps the offending passengers were not exactly worthy of such condign punishment, and it is just possible they were not bad people in the main.

Well, Muffins took to roaming about the ship generally, and he soon had the pleasure of seeing Pan dodge away out of his sight.

He also caught a glimpse of Jacob Morelle, who also vanished like a ghost at cock-crow as soon as Muffins came into view.

"What a lark!" thought Muffins. "They are afraid of ME. Master has knocked every bit of nerve out of 'em both."

He was so tickled with this idea that he was at last reconciled to the narrow limits of the vessel.

Indeed, he would have liked them to be narrower, just for the fun of the thing.

Without saying anything to his friends he now began to devote his spare time and his youthful energies to chevying the foe.

Whenever he could do so he was prowling about the lower deck, and naturally kept Pan and Morelle confined to the narrow limits of their cabin.

They, on their part, surmising that their presence on board was not known—a belief strongly induced by the liberty given to Muffins to go where he pleased—were more than ever bent on remaining undiscovered.

It was a very funny position all round, and gave great joy to Muffins.

But to Pan and Morelle it was not exactly unadulterated bliss.

CHAPTER XXXVI.

MR. PARDIGGLE BROWN—HIS WIFE—THAT BOY MUFFINS—GALLANTRY OF BUTTERFLICK.

IEF among the passengers, in their own estimation, were Mr. and Mrs. Pardiggle Brown, who made themselves both heard and felt by all on board.

Who Mr. Pardiggle Brown was, or what he had been, was not exactly known, but everybody was made to feel that he had got some money.

He was one of the "attic born and gutter bred" breed. Wherever he went he made himself objectionable.

A man may have been born in an attic and yet be a gentleman, and being reared in the gutter does not always make the company of a person objectionable. All depends on the disposition of a man.

Now, Pardiggle Brown was a braggart. He was not only a great man, but a wonderful one. He had the first seat at the table, and he thought it was his right to have the pick of everything.

For Dick Strongbow he felt the deepest mistrust.

He despised the other men of his party, and he loathed Muffins.

Muffins did not care, and when he was not hunting Pan and Morelle he was worrying Pardiggle Brown.

If he saw him making for a particular camp-stool Muffins would glide rapidly forward and take possession of it, as he had a right to do, being a first-class passenger.

On failing to get there first he would sit down beside him, which would ensure the rapid retreat of Mr. Pardiggle Brown.

Next to Muffins, Pardiggle Brown loathed Butterflick, who WOULD be friends, and declined to see that he was not wanted.

As for Mrs. Pardiggle Brown, she talked much about her "pa," and kept her nose in the air, which suffices for a description of her.

One morning—the vessel was ten days out—Butterflick came on deck, and was astonished to see a deadly struggle going on between Pardiggle and Muffins.

Near them was a camp-stool, upset.

"Here! what's the row?" asked Butterflick.

"Steady, governor! He's only a boy."

"He's a fiend, and I'll murder him!" hissed Pardiggle Brown.

"No you won't!" said Butterflick. "You don't murder my son, if I know it."

"Your SON!" said Pardiggle Brown, as he let Muffins go. "Why don't you keep him in order, then?"

"What's he been doing?" asked Butterflick.

"I was about to take that camp-stool when he came up and seized it," said Pardiggle Brown.

"There's lots more about," hinted Butterflick.

"I suppose I can have my choice?" said Pardiggle Brown, swelling out. "Do you know who I am?"

"Not 'zactly," replied Butterflick; "but I think any fool can measure you up with a two-foot rule. Look y'here, if you so much as lay a finger on my boy again, I'll tar and feather you!"

Mrs. Pardiggle Brown had a moment before arrived on deck. With an angry face she listened to Butterflick's threat.

He happened to catch sight of her the next moment, and, taking off his hat, he made a polite bow.

"I beg pardon," he said. "I didn't know a lady was present. I never forgot myself even with Old Sally, who was a human eruption; but really, ma'am, you might try to put an ounce of manhood in that husband of your."

"Pardiggle," said Mrs. Brown, "have you been quarrelling with this person?"

"He's been walloping the boy," explained Butterflick.

"Speak, Pardiggle!" cried Mrs. Brown, ignoring the explanation of Butterflick; "answer me?"

"I have had words with him," replied Pardiggle Brown, sulkily.

"Oh! indeed," said Mrs. Brown, with lofty scorn; "if my pa could have forseen this hour he would have forbidden our union."

"Your father would have been in the union if I had not kept him out of it," replied Brown.

"WHAT!" screamed Mrs. Brown; "my PA in the union?"

"Your pa, as you call him," said Pardiggle Brown, "was the most shuffling old humbug I ever met with, and I believe he was only a travelling fiddler."

The precious pair were now quite absorbed in themselves, and forgot everything else. Oblivious of the arrival of the rest of the passengers of the upper deck, they went at it hammer and tongs.

"A travelling fiddler!" gasped Mrs. Brown—"a TRAVELLING fiddler—oh! ah!"

"He played the fiddle worse than any man I ever heard," continued Pardiggle Brown; "he scared even the cats. He drank, too."

"And to think that I should have been lured into a union with YOU," said Mrs. Brown, looking up and down the podgy form of her husband.

"If I wasn't took in by you I'll be jammed," said Pardiggle Brown. "I knowed you hadn't a penny for I had to pay for your wedding trosser, but I thought you had blood. Your father said the noblest blood ran in his veins, but when I gave him a smack on the nose for calling me a purse-proud upstart I thought it was very poor stuff."

"Oh! you—you—" began Mrs. Brown, and then, unable to stem the murderous torrent in her heart, she went for him.

They closed, and Brown, forgetting sex and everything else, hit out as if his wife had been a man.

But suddenly he found himself in an iron grasp, and heard his wife scream loudly and fall upon the deck.

Pardiggle Brown stared through his hair, which his wife had pulled over his eyes, at Dick Strongbow.

He was quite subdued by the sense of being held by a resistless hand.

"You had better go below," said Dick. "What could have induced you to so forget yourself?"

"Where's my wife?" asked Pardiggle Brown, fiercely.

"I've got her," cried Butterflick, who had raised her in his arms. "Lor'! how like in speerit she is to my old Sally. Purty creature!"

It was lucky he finished off with this expression, for being compared to "old Sally" would of itself have brought Mrs. Pardiggle Brown out of her faint.

As it was, she still lay passively inanimate, or apparently so, in Butterflick's arms.

"You put my wife down," said Pardiggle Brown, with a miserable assumption of hauteur.

"You get out of it," said Butterflick, "and I'll see to her. She wants more devotion, she does. You don't know how to treat this purty creatur'. I calls her a bit o' china—she wants delicate handling."

She certainly was as like china as paint could make her.

Butterflick deposited her in a big lounging chair, and put her feet upon a stool. Then, to the huge entertainment of the rest of the company, excepting her husband, he proceeded to fan her with his broad hat.

"She'll come round directly," he said, "and then I would recommend a cup o' tea, with a 'spicion of cognac to keep her from going off again. Oh! I can't make out how a MAN—if he is one—can so serve a purty creature like this."

Butterflick's manner was all that could be desired, but there was a lurking twinkle in his eye as if he were enjoying the whole thing.

Mrs. Pardiggle Brown now thought it was time

for her to come back to consciousness, which she did in the usual way of sufferers on the stage.

First she sighed, then slowly opened her eyes and stared wildly around her.

Her next move was to faintly ask, " Where am I ?" and finally, with a little scream, get upon her feet.

It was now time for her to burst into tears, and she did so, pumping them out copiously. Butterflick offered her his arm.

"You are kind o' agitated, ma'am," he said; "allow me to escort you to the cabin."

Mr. Pardiggle Brown glanced at Butterflick, as he escorted his wife from the deck, and then glared round upon the passengers.

If he expected to freeze anybody up he made an error. They were all in a melting state with laughter they could not quite conceal.

"Somebody shall pay for this," he cried, and then with a glance at Muffins he departed on the trail of his wife.

CHAPTER XXXVII.

A CHANGE AT SEA—THE GREAT STORM—BATTENED DOWN—BURSTING THE HATCHES.

 GREAT changes are matters that those who spend adventurous lives are always prepared for, and when, after a spell of sunshine and balmy breezes, the sky became cloudy and the wind gusty, the officers of the Archimedes were not disturbed.

"We shall get some dirty weather," they said, "but perhaps before the worst comes we may be clear of the Bay."

Dread Bay—bearing the name of Biscay—famous in song, and the watery tomb of thousands of gallant seamen.

Natural enough for the officers to wish they were clear of it ere the worst came.

It was a north-west wind they had to battle against, and the engineer was ordered to put on full steam.

He sent word to the captain that his engines would not be quite safe at full pressure; but the answer was, "Go on at all risk."

He who serves well obeys without demur, and the Archimedes forged ahead, with the rising wind to check her full progress.

Darker grew the sky, leaden-coloured became the waves, and on the horizon the two were so mingled that it was difficult to tell where one ended and the others began.

A sudden silence fell upon the ship.

There was no more singing or laughter, no exchange of merry jest, no words of animosity.

A sense of common danger was over all.

A brave man can appreciate the gravity of a perilous position without being afraid, and so it was with Dick Strongbow.

He knew by the captain's manner that there was danger ahead, and the Archimedes, a vessel past its prime, could not battle with a big storm like a more modern vessel.

Every hour it was clear that the wind blew harder.

It seemed at last that it could not exhibit additional force, but it still increased, ravening like ten thousand wild beasts eager for prey.

Over the huge waves went the Archimedes, apparently with great speed, but the fact was the sea was too strong for her, and she was making very little headway.

And what was more, she was drifting slowly but surely towards the Spanish coast.

It is true that land was several miles away, and if the gale would only abate the lost way could soon be regained.

But the wind would not abate. Steadily it increased in force.

It was now dangerous for the more fragile passengers to walk about the upper deck. The captain advised all to remain below.

But Dick Strongbow protested.

He said the stifling air would kill him, and he was not afraid.

"Is there nothing I can do?" he asked.

"What can you do against such a sea?" answered the captain.

The second-class passengers were already ordered to keep below, and to assure their absence from deck they were battened down.

The first-class passengers were warned that a like fate would be theirs in a few hours.

"We must have the decks clear," said the captain to Dick. "I rely upon you to assist me in this matter. Do your best to keep order below."

Dick saw that he was right, and promised to do as he wished.

All that night the gale continued, and the Archimedes fought it out with the furious wind and tremendous sea.

The change of circumstance was practically so sudden and complete that some of the passengers could hardly realise it.

Mr. Pardiggle Brown and his wife, who had been living in a state of domestic nagging, forgot their petty animosities and sat beside each other, hand in hand, in a corner of the saloon.

The others lounged about, walking being next to impossible.

How the ship rose and fell—how she heaved and rolled !

Sometimes it seemed as if she was rising in the air like a rocket, bow foremost; at another time she threatened to go down to the bowels of the earth.

Then came a roll to the right or left, as if she meant to turn turtle and end the whole business by sinking.

Butterflick, with Muffins by his side, sat smoking and thinking.

Now and then he spoke a word of encouragement to the boy.

'"These gales are common enough, and a good ship has nothing to fear."

Or, "We must be 'most through the Bay now, and arter that it's only a pleasure trip home;" but there was little that was consoling in his voice.

They all ate or drank as usual, although some of them showed a considerable falling off in their appetites.

The first night they went to their cabins to sleep at the proper time, the second night they were later, and the third night they decided not to go to bed at all.

"The crisis is near," said Dick; "it must be. To-morrow the worst will be over. Let us sit up and hail the change for the better with thankfulness."

At midnight somebody without any apparent cause proposed that they should shake hands all round.

The proposal was immediately assented to.

"For my part," said Butterflick, "I think it's a nice thing to do; anyway, it will pass the time."

He and Pardiggle Brown shook hands with a fervour very much at variance with their recent strained conditions.

Mrs. Brown wept as she held Butterflick by both hands, and dried her eyes, poor woman, utterly oblivious of the fact that she was washing off a deal of the youthful paint which lay upon her cheeks.

Muffins was not exempted from the handshaking, and after it was over they sat down silent again.

The fierce throb of the engines, the pulse of the vessel, had been going on for days.

It had become part and parcel of their daily life, but now as the hand-shaking continued it suddenly ceased.

They all missed it instantly, and a look of alarm leaped into their faces.

Boom!

A huge wave had struck the vessel with a force that threatened to dislocate every joint.

Those who were standing upon their feet staggered forward or sank upon their knees.

Boom!

A second blow, harder than the first, and the vessel was heaved over almost on to her beam-ends.

She righted herself slowly, and there was no indication of her going on.

The engines were dumb.

"What's the matter?" asked Carl of Dick, in an undertone.

"I fear the shaft is broken," replied Dick; "but do not say so."

"We are shipping seas."

"Undoubtedly. But steady, Carl. The crew will give us full warning, and the hatches will be opened when we have to take to the boats."

"Suppose they go away and leave us?" asked Carl.

"They would hardly dare to do so," replied Dick. "I will go up and see if I can hear them moving about. Let all remain quiet here until I return."

He crept up the stairs, and planting himself against the closed and fastened companion, listened intently for any sounds upon deck.

There was the roar of the storm and the striking of the sea against the vessel's side, but no footsteps, no words of command.

It is true that both might be drowned by the contention of the elements, but Dick did not like the appearance of things.

He beat upon the companion-door with his strong fist, but all he did was to bring the alarmed passengers up immediately behind him.

There was no response from the deck.

"Stand back!" he cried to those below him. "We shall all stifle here."

"Save us!" cried some of the more timid.

"Carl, take them back," said Dick; "we shall smother in this hole."

Carl, Butterflick, and Phil all lent a hand to draw the passengers back, but they clung to each other and shrieked and yelled for mercy.

The air was stifling, and in a few minutes some at least would have been asphyxiated.

"We must have air," thought Dick. "Better to drown than die in this stifling air."

He placed his back against the door and his feet against the opposite panelling, then put forth his whole strength.

For a moment there was resistance, and then, with a crash heard above the storm, the doors burst asunder, and he fell out upon the deck.

Boom! Another wave struck the vessel.

He looked up and saw a huge hill of water come on board and fall upon the deck with a crash that was like the rending of a mountain.

Then a torrent of water was swept across the deck, and he was carried, like a cork, to the vessel's side.

There he managed to grasp a stanchion, and held on, but it required all his strength to keep himself from being swept into the sea.

The water passed away, and, dropping down upon the deck, he cast a look around him.

The only light to aid him came from the cabin below.

But by its aid he could see that the captain's bridge and the funnels were gone—a sure sign of the vessel being a wreck.

Probably all hands had been swept overboard.

His friends on the staircase had all been washed down again by a resistless rush of water, and were now floundering about knee-deep in it, the weaker calling for help.

"We are all doomed," thought Dick; and, like a strong man, he prepared himself to meet the end calmly.

It was hard, very hard, to be cut off in the flower of his youth; but wailing and moaning would not help him.

Bending down, he shouted out—

"Rouse up, all of you—the next wave will drown you like rats in a hole!"

And as he gave this warning the vessel struck heavily upon a rock and heaved over upon her side, so that the deck was almost as upright as a wall.

CHAPTER XXXVIII.

THE OUTCOME OF THE WRECK—A MIRACULOUS PRESERVATION.

ERILOUS in the extreme was the position of the Archimedes, and Dick, clinging to the broken hand-rail of the companion, momentarily expected her to divide in two, or break up altogether. Of the fate of his friends he knew nothing, for now the howling of the wind and the fierce beating of the waves upon the doomed vessel drowned all other sounds.

The lights below, too, had gone out, and all was darkness there.

"Is this to be the end of all?" Dick asked himself, bitterly.

He felt for his comrades deeply, but he was not afraid.

The truly brave, especially if they have lived honourable and just lives, have no fear at the supreme moment, when death hovers over them with his dart. They may regret leaving the world behind them; terror has no share in their emotion. In a few moments he became somewhat reassured.

The angry seas struck the vessel with tremendous force, but they did not break her up.

And the water had no hold upon her almost upright deck, gliding off in an instant, as it were.

Some waves seemed to leap clean over her, but the general effect was that of a broken cascade—a rapid fall of water, a check, more water, another check, and so on.

Dick soon saw the true position of the vessel, and gathered hope from it.

She lay on her side, as we have previously described, hard and fast upon some rocks, close in shore, most probably, although it was too dark to make sure of that.

In her position the seas struck her rounded bottom, and so lost four-fifths of their force.

Thus there was the possibility of the old vessel holding out until the storm had abated.

But Dick felt he must know the fate of his friends, and for this purpose he would have to go below.

Dick had to slide down what had been the wooden sides of the staircase, and take his chance of what he dropped upon below.

Down he slid, and immediately found himself in the midst of a mass of struggling humanity, from out of which issued a scream of alarm.

Matters were quieter down there, and the cry was heard clear enough.

Dick shouted back at his loudest—

"Who is here?"

Back came a roar from Butterflick, whose voice would have shamed the Bull of Bashan.

"The cap'en, by Old Sally! Hoo-roar!"

"Keep still," cried Dick; "we are safe at present. Who has a light? I am wet through."

It was Carl Yemitz who answered now—

"I have—I will strike one."

After a short delay the small flame of a match flickered up, and Dick saw a spectacle that drew a smile from him, despite the perilous nature of their position.

There were Carl, Muffins, and four of the passengers in a corner, holding on to each other.

Near them was Butterflick, gallantly supporting Mrs. Pardiggle Brown in his arms.

Brown himself was lying like a limp doll in the midst of half-a-dozen overturned landing chairs.

Everything was upset, lopsided, and chaotic.

Before the match went out Dick espied one of the lamps, which had been put out by the shock when the vessel struck, but still hung against what had been the ceiling of the saloon, but was now, owing to the position of the Archimedes, the wall.

Carl saw it, too, and, having lighted a second match, cautiously approached Dick, picking his way among the debris. Between them they got the lamp ignited and fixed so that it would burn.

Its light had a weird effect upon the scene, but it was better than darkness, and there was a feeling of something like relief all round.

Talking with freedom was impossible, so Dick did not attempt it.

By signs he informed his friends that their position was not hopeless, but they must remain where they were, and keep as quiet as possible.

Such adjuration was scarcely necessary to his friends. Ajax was wonderfully quiet, when his nature is considered.

By the loss of physical strength he seemed to have gained an amount of moral courage that was quite up to the average.

The pounding of the sea upon the vessel went on, but she held together, and hope grew stronger in the hearts of all.

Every now and then an extra creak or a groan from the maltreated vessel would cause a general anxious look round, but she was still in one piece.

Philosophers say there is the ludicrous element in everything. It was certainly in that saloon, and it was to be proved in the person of Pardiggle Brown.

This hapless gentleman, overcome with terror and wedged in among the ruins of the furniture, lay helplessly staring at Butterflick, who kept his arm about Mrs. Brown, notwithstanding the fact that the lady had quite recovered consciousness.

And she did not seem to mind it a bit.

On the contrary, she frequently looked at Butterflick and smiled upon him.

Then she would look at her husband with a frown.

It was quite clear that she looked up to Butterflick and down upon Pardiggle Brown.

What a time of torture it must have been to that wretched man; but like all things it came to an end.

Signs were not wanting that the storm was abating, but all night long the seas kept up a remorseless pounding upon the Archimedes.

It was a marvel, a miracle, that she did not go to pieces.

But the dawn came, and as soon as it was visible through the open companion Dick crept up to take a look about him.

To his utter amazement, he found that they were close in shore—on the shore indeed—and with a receding tide would be left high and dry.

And the tide WAS going out as fast as the still stiffly-blowing breeze would permit.

To the right and left stretched the coast of Spain, and as far as Dick could see there was no inhabitants near the spot.

But that, he knew, might be deceptive, for in no

part of Spain are there any wide, sterile wastes to land.

Over the sloping hills by the shore, or away to the left among the rich woods, inhabitants would be sure to be found.

He went back with the joyful news, and bade them go up one by one and look about them.

Words cannot describe the thankfulness of all.

There they were, the most helpless part of those who had left Capetown, saved from a premature death, which, sad to think, the captain and all, or the greater part, of the crew had suffered.

Some of the men might be in hiding forward, as Dick knew, and there were two certain men in whom he was interested—to wit, Jacob Morelle and Pan.

He wondered what had become of them, but took no steps to discover.

At any rate, they would not run away just yet.

Down sank the wind—out went the tide.

As the water receded the thankfulness of the wrecked ones increased, and when at last there was little or no water about the vessel, they came out of their hiding-place, one by one, and with shouts of joy leaped upon the wet sands below.

Butterflick, gallant to the last, bore Mrs. Pardiggle Brown in his arms, but losing his foothold as he descended the steeply sloping deck, precipitately delivered himself and his burden upon the wet sand, where they lay in very undignified positions until their laughing friends helped them up.

Pardiggle Brown was positively the last to come out of the cabin, and he alone did not seem happy, but gloomily and steadily slid down to the sands, and in a stiff, stilted fashion walked up to Butterflick.

"Sir?" he said.

"Sir to you," replied Butterflick, who was filling his pipe.

"For all your gross insults you shall suffer," said Pardiggle Brown; "you hear, sir—suffer!"

"Why, Heaven help you for a fool!" exclaimed Butterflick, "what have I done? You ought to be thankful to me for saving your pretty wife. She might have died but for me."

"Died? He—ahem—oh!" coughed Pardiggle Brown. "I tell you that I will make you suffer."

Here he stopped—coughed, choked, and grew very red in the face.

Butterflick, in the most friendly manner, patted him on the back to ease him.

"Hands off, villain!" cried Pardiggle Brown; "don't tempt me to murder you."

Mrs. Brown stepped forward and took her husband by the arm.

"If you don't want that man to EAT you, come away," she said. "I call it very unkind of you after he has saved my life. But for him you might now be a widower."

"I'll give a fiver to be one this moment," said Pardiggle Brown, savagely. "But let me alone. I'll say no more just at present; but a time will come—ha! ha!—a time will come!"

— —

CHAPTER XXXIX.

TWO FOOLS IN HIDING—HARD TIMES—QUIET CAMPING.

WHAT about those two fellows?" asked Carl, in a whisper to Dick.

"If drowned, they must remain where they are," Dick answered; "but if alive, they will skulk in their cabin until they see a chance of getting away. "I do not think there would be much difficulty in finding them. Now, Carl, get these people ashore, and Butterflick and myself will see about getting something out of the vessel for breakfast."

"Oh! yes," said Carl, laughing. "It occurs to me, now that I am safe, that eating is a pleasure and a necessity of life."

The morning was warm, and the bright sun having cleared the clouds away, the little party were almost as happy as the members of a picnic.

But they could not shake off a feeling of pain as they thought that all save themselves had perished.

At least, the passengers thought so, but Dick was not sure.

He had a conviction that Morelle and Pan were alive.

The Archimedes lay upon the sands like some stranded, antedeluvian monster, more impressive in its ruin than it had been in its time of usefulness.

Although the gallant vessel had held together, she had suffered many a wrench, and in the store-rooms which Dick and Butterflick visited to get provisions, doors were wrenched and jammed, and the contents of the great cupboards tossed about and mixed together in a jumble that seemed to defy restoration to order.

And here Dick's great strength came into use.

He tore open resisting doors, pulled out heavy chests, disentangled all sorts of things, and in an hour had sent ashore provisions for a week.

Muffins—once more in his element—Phil Norton, and two of the passengers acted as light porters, and by ten o'clock all the necessaries of a good breakfast were ready on the higher part of the beach.

Muffins made the coffee, and Butterflick, who called himself for the occasion the "champion rasher-cooker of the universe," attended to the bacon.

There were potted meats also, biscuits, butter, cheese. and light wine for those who fancied it—in short, all that mortal could desire.

The breakfast party were watched by two hungry, bitter-minded men.

Morelle and Pan were not drowned.

Afraid to come out of their cabin, and unable to get at any provisions, which were all kept aft, they lay upon the side of the companion with their heads raised just high enough to see what was going on ashore.

"Nice, ain't it?" growled Pan. "The luck is always with HIM."

"It's no use talking," returned Jacob Morelle,

surlily. "They may make a move directly, and then we may get out of this hole."

But there was to be no moving on the part of our friends that day.

The fact was, excitement and want of sleep had exhausted some of the passengers. Pardiggle Brown and his wife, as soon as the strain, born of danger, was over, became very low and unable to exert themselves at all.

All had need of a rest, and it was decided to rig up a tent or two and make themselves as happy as they could under the circumstances.

This arrangement necessitated a visit to the ship for some pieces of canvas, trunks, and tools.

Jacob Morelle and Pan hid away in the second-class saloon, both in a state of fear and trembling.

But they need not have distressed themselves.

It was not the intention of Dick Strongbow to visit them. The game he was playing was something very different.

Muffins did, indeed, come to the door of the cabin, which, of course, was in an horizontal position, and looked in casually.

He saw the outlines of the forms of the two hide-aways under a heap of blankets, and had a mind to go in and give them a kick.

But the daring idea was cut short of execution by Phil Norton calling for Muffins.

"None of your skulking, youngster," he cried; "come and help with these things."

"I am only looking to see if there are any rats about," replied Muffins.

"They deserted the ship long ago," said Phil.

Muffins went away, and, after a lapse of time, when the sounds of people moving about the vessel had ceased, the two men came out of their hiding-place again.

Hot, thirsty, dusty, and hungry, they would have given something handsome for food and drink, but without going on deck, and, by that means, to the saloon, they could get nothing.

There was, of course, the ordinary means of communication between the two decks, but the doors were jammed tight and wanted a Strongbow to open them.

It appeared as if they would have to wait until night to be released from their unpleasant position; but shortly after noon Pan saw a chance of beating a retreat.

The whole party had disappeared, apparently, within three rough tents which had been erected.

He reported this to Morelle, who growled out—

"Taking a siesta, I suppose. I hope they will enjoy it."

"I say, governor," said Pan, "can't we get away now. If we could slip down—"

"Wait a bit. If nobody moves in a quarter of an hour we can try it."

No sign of movement was visible, and at length they plucked up heart to creep out and go to the first-class saloon in search of food.

They found a bag of biscuits and a bottle of wine. The latter they drank at once, and having filled their pockets with biscuits, prepared to start.

"Eat as you go," said Morelle, "and do as I tell you. There's a ridge of rocks a hundred yards higher up, and if we can only get to them unseen we are safe."

The rocks he alluded to were such as we often find at home—notably on the south coast.

On the shore side was a sloping hill—sand and earth mixed—and on the summit of that hill a broad belt of trees, many of them bearing fruit.

On that wood Jacob Morelle fixed his eye. That was a haven for him and Pan.

"Sharp's the word now," he said. "Drop down and run for it."

They slid down the vessel's deck, tumbled off upon the sands, then sprang up and ran.

Morelle kept his eyes in the direction of the little encampment, but saw no signs of their movements being observed.

The rocks were reached safely, and they lay down among them, panting, to take a rest.

CHAPTER XL.

OUT OF THEIR RECKONING—THAT MELON— THE SPANISH VILLAGE—WRECKERS.

A VERY common thing it is for people to be out of their reckoning. They conceive a certain plan, perfect the arrangements, and proceed to carry them out, with a full conviction that success will attend their labours. But lo! in the flowing tide of prospective success, something unexpected crops up, and ruin and confusion is the result.

Now, not one of the movements of Morelle or Pan outside the saloon of the vessel had escaped observation.

One of the very quiet party ashore had an eye on them throughout.

When they lay down behind the rocks, Muffins and Butterflick, acting under orders, were keeping in a line with them higher up, to mark the road they took.

"The bare direction will suffice," said Dick; "having found out that, come back here."

The pair of scouts gained the wood, where they found oranges of an inferior description growing wild, also prickly pears and a species of pumpkin.

The latter were green and round, and about the size of a football.

The vines on which the fruit grew had climbed the trees and spread about in every direction, looking very picturesque.

Muffins regarded them contemplatively, but not with the eye of an artist.

"I'd just like to give 'em one," he murmured.

Taking out his pocket-knife, he cut off a melon—large, round, and very ripe.

"Are you going to eat THAT, my son?" asked Butterflick.

"No, dad," answered Muffins, "not yet."

They crept to the edge of the wood, and, from the friendly shelter of the vine-covered trees, looked down below.

Pan and Morelle had just rested, and were preparing to resume their way.

The next moment Muffins tripped head foremost into the marble basin and Butterflick followed his lead.

They cast an anxious look backward, but not aloft, thereby showing that they had no suspicion of the presence of Muffins and his "dad."

Then they began to climb the slope, Pan foremost, on their hands and knees.

"Draw back a bit, my son," whispered Butterflick.

"Go on, dad," murmured Muffins.

Butterflick walked back on tip-toe, and placed himself cautiously in a very retired position, where the vines grew thickest.

But Muffins did not immediately follow.

He waited for Pan, who was coming up active as a cat, and when he was within a few feet of the top he straightened himself up and looked sideways in the direction of the little encampment.

That was Muffins' opportunity, and he readily embraced it.

With all his youthful strength he hurled the melon at Pan and struck him full in the face.

He uttered a loud yell as it burst and bespattered him with its juicy seeds, and, falling back, rolled upon Morelle, whom he bore down to level ground again with a rush.

"What's the matter?" cried Morelle.

"I'm shot!" gasped Pan.

"Shot, you fool! It's only a ripe melon fallen from the trees" growled Morelle. "Get up with you."

He got up himself, then, taking the lead, scrambled up the slope.

Having reached the summit, he awaited the arrival of Pan, who sulkily followed him.

Meanwhile Muffins had joined Butterflick, where, well concealed from observation, they essayed to suppress their laughter, and, after a great struggle, succeeded.

"How was I to know it was a melon?" snarled Pan. "It struck me like a cannon-ball."

"You have become a regular cur!" tartly answered Morelle, "and I'm a good mind to turn you up. Wipe off that mess from your face and coat. It doesn't look pretty."

Pan pulled out his handkerchief, and, grumbling like a bear who has been worried by a hive of bees, proceeded to remove the evidence of Muffins' handiwork.

"Who'd ha' thought it could do it?" he said. "It gave me such a knock that I thought I was done for."

"They are heavy things," said Morelle. "Are you ready to go on?"

"Yes; but where to?" asked Pan.

"We must go into the country and work our way to Madrid," replied Morelle. "No law but that of Spain can touch us there. After all, the wreck has not been a bad thing for us. I can work my business as well from there as in England—perhaps better. I know the point to start from. Come on."

After debating a moment about the exact way to take, Jacob Morelle started off at a left angle with the two worthies in hiding, who made no attempt to follow them.

They had ascertained all, and more than Dick desired them to do. Their scouting had been completely successful.

Having waited a reasonable time to let Pan and Morelle get well away, they started back to the camp, Muffins in high glee, and Butterflick complacently rejoicing in the performance of "his son."

"You've got grit in you," he said; "a ready wit, a fairish strong arm, and a good aim. I couldn't have done better myself."

"I don't think we will tell master," said Muffins; "he might be angry with me. You see he told us to keep out of sight, and it was running a risk."

"It was," said Butterflick, gravely.

The members of the camp were still lying close when they returned. Dick, Carl, and Phil were smoking under a piece of canvas hanging over two branches of a tree, and falling to the ground, forming a crude sort of tent.

The report given, as described, was considered more than satisfactory.

"We must get rid of our 'friends,'" said Dick, "and get away to Madrid as soon as possible."

By "friends" he meant the passengers, of course, but he would not desert them at an unnecessarily early period.

It was desirable to get their luggage from the ship if it could be done, as in the evening he and Carl decided to go in search of help.

"It is possible" said Dick to Butterflick, "that some wreckers may put in an appearance. If not too strong in numbers keep them off"

"I'll wreck 'em," said Butterflick, simply.

Leaving the camp was a matter that gave rise to some anxious remarks from the passengers. They all looked up to Strongbow—relying upon him as children do upon a strong and able father.

They begged of him not to be long away, and Dick promised to be back early the following morning.

"Help or no help," he replied, as he waved his hand as a farewell.

On leaving the shore, the friends had to ascend a piece of rising ground and pass through a fair-sized grove of trees. This brought them into view of the open country.

To their gratification they found that the agriculturalist had been at work there, and dotted about in different places were small tenements from which smoke was ascending.

About three miles away they saw a cluster of houses—a village, it seemed to them—and towards it they directed their steps.

After a walk of a quarter of an hour they came to a narrow road running in the direction they desired to go, and presently encountered an aged peasant hobbling home with the aid of his staff.

"Your servant, senors," he said, in Spanish.

"Yours," replied Dick, in the same language.

"Friend," said Dick, "we are strangers here—wrecked, and would find an inn. Is there one hereabouts?"

"There is one at Santa Josef," was the reply.

"About how far?"

"Two English miles from here."

"A good one?"

"As good as the rebels have left us, senor. I pray that you be no friend of Don Carlos?"

"I am neither his friend nor foe," commenced Dick, smiling.

"It is well, senor, that you do not name him," said the old man, "and if it is put before you, say, 'I know him not—who is he?' That will ensure you a welcome."

Dick took a piece of silver from his pocket and

gave it to the peasant. He stared at it as he had stared at them, as a thing he had not dreamed of seeing.

"Senor," he said, "you must be a prince in disguise."

"I know not what I am," said Dick, under his breath.

He and Carl saluted the old man again, and hurried on.

By-and-bye they passed a cottage standing at the road-side. It was flush by the road, and two little children were playing at the door.

On seeing the strangers they began to scream, and a man and woman came hurriedly out.

The man was about thirty—a well-built fellow, but coarsely dressed, and, like the majority of his countrymen, presented an unwashed appearance.

His wife was handsome, too, and held a babe to her breast.

"Senor," the man said, "whither do you come and whither go?"

"We are making our way to the village of Santa Josef," replied Carl.

"For whom? Is it the Don?" demanded the man, slipping into the road with a threatening air.

"Hang your Don," said Dick, who did not like to be "bounced" by any man; "get out of my way."

"I must know who you are," said the Spaniard, whipping out a stiletto. "Stand!"

Dick sprang upon him, and, grasping his wrist, twisted the weapon out of his hand.

The man writhed in the strong grip of Dick, who held on for a few seconds and then let him go.

"Don't play any tricks with me," said Dick; "I am a stranger here, wrecked upon your confounded coast, and I am only seeking help for those who were saved with myself."

"Senor," said the Spaniard, with his wrist tightly pressed between his knees and his face screwed up with pain, "you have the fiend's grip on you. I have lost the use of my right hand."

"If you cannot put it to a better use than to threaten strangers," said Dick, "you had better lose it. Stand out of my way."

The man drew aside, and Dick was about to pass on when the woman cried out—

"I pray that the saints may give me such a hold as you. He shall not then strike ME again. It is good for you, Lara, to have met your match."

"He is a match for all Spain," growled the man, as he leant against the wall and rubbed his wrist to restore its lost circulation.

"Confound the fellow," said Dick, as he and Carl hastened on, "why did he put me out? I am not often irritable, but to-night I feel so."

"After last night," said Carl, "you want rest."

They saw no more people until they came in sight of the village, a straggling lot of houses, mostly of the poorer type.

But there was one of some pretension half way down, and opposite it was the inn.

About half a score people were about, and they all stared at the two friends, who hastened on without giving them greeting, seeing that, for the most part, they were scowling.

By the door of the inn stood a portly man smoking a cigar.

He saluted them, but did not get out of the way to let them pass.

"We are strangers here," said Dick—and here we may as well say, once for all, that he generally conversed with the people while in Spain in their native tongue—"and we need refreshments."

"Strangers have come here before," said the man, "and have brought nothing but ruin and misery."

"You think I am a Carlist," said Dick, with a smile.

"I think nothing," was the surly reply.

"I want some help," said Dick. "Myself and some half-score English people have been wrecked on the coast."

The eye of the landlord lighted up quickly.

"A wreck!" he said. "Has the vessel gone to pieces?"

"Not yet. She lies upon the shore."

"And the captain and crew, senor?"

"All drowned. Only a few of the passengers survive."

"Come in, senor," said the landlord, bowing low; "refresh yourself, and rest here to night. Your friends—will they not come on too?"

"They are camping near the wreck," said Dick, as he entered the inn, "and I have promised to be back on the morrow with help, to get out our baggage, also to remove the cargo—"

"Ah! the cargo, senor?"

"And stow it away in safe custody until we can communicate with the owners."

"Senor, my house is yours," said the landlord, bowing lower than before.

He ushered them into a room, the best in the house he said it was, and nothing even then to brag about.

The furniture was poor, and the walls bare; a small window at one end imperfectly lighted it.

"A fowl or something to eat as quick as you can," said Dick; "meanwhile a bottle of light wine."

"Senor, I fly to obey," replied the landlord, and vanished from the room.

"Mighty civil all of a sudden," said Carl.

"Too much so—but never mind. We will wait and see what it means," replied Dick.

"I suppose," said Carl, "that it means he finds we are not so black as he expected."

"More than that."

"Indeed?"

"Yes. Hush! here he comes."

"Senor," said the landlord, as he came in with a bottle and glasses, "I have here a rich and rare wine, such as our nobles drink."

"I have no doubt it is good," said Dick; "by the way, have you a resident magistrate here?"

"Yes, senor," replied the landlord; "but he is away at present."

"A gendarme then—any man in authority?"

"Senor, they are all away, but will be here to-morrow."

"To-morrow will do," said Dick, easily, "thank you. Have you any good cigars?"

"Senor, I have the pick of Havannah."

"Let us have some."

The landlord left the room, and Dick walked to the window. Carl knew by his manner that he was in some way disturbed.

"Dick," he said, softly, "you suspect this fellow?"

"I more than suspect," answered Dick; "I am convinced that he contemplates looting the Archimedes. Every Spaniard is a born robber, a wrecker, and an innate thief."

CHAPTER XLI.

THE DINNER—PRETTY VIARDOT—A REVELATION —A QUIET DEPARTURE.

OR a brief space of time the two friends remained silent, each busy with his thoughts on the position they were placed in.

Wreckers, like highwaymen, are not murderers unless their nefarious pursuits are interfered with; but if any rash man ventures to endeavour to guard or protect his own, his life is taken as the penalty of his audacity.

"If we were by ourselves," said Dick, "we should know exactly what to do; but the question is, how will the others show in a fight?"

"Pardiggle Brown, for instance," suggested Carl, with a smile.

"And the rest," continued Dick; "they are not men accustomed to fighting, and small blame to them if they do not show up well in a row."

"Had we not better go back at once?"

"No, Carl; that would raise their suspicions. These fellows will probably muster strongly, and what we want to do is to SURPRISE THEM!"

"But after the first surprise, Dick, may they not return in greater force?"

"I hope to SURPRISE them out of all idea of robbing the vessel," replied Dick, quietly.

A Spanish girl now entered the room with a cloth upon her arm.

She was pretty and graceful, and the bow she bestowed upon the guests was worthy of a duchess.

"Senors," she said, "I hope I do not intrude."

"No, indeed," replied Dick, with a pleasant smile.

As the girl proceeded to lay the cloth she glanced at Dick more than once from under her eyelashes, and the aspect of our stalwart young friend appeared to be pleasing to her.

On Carl also she bestowed a glance of approval, but it was not like that she gave to Dick.

The table was soon ready, and the girl retired, lingering for a moment at the door as if she wished to say something.

But Dick and Carl were whispering together by the corridor, and she went out without speaking.

A few minutes elapsed and she was back with their dinner, which she placed upon the table.

"Will you need any more wine, senors?" she asked.

"Another bottle of this stuff won't hurt us," said Carl.

"Very well," said Dick, and gave the order.

The girl was some time ere she re-appeared with a bottle in her hand, and Dick observed that under the swarthy colour of her cheeks there was a strange paleness.

She closed the door softly so as to make no sound, and placed the bottle upon the table.

"Senor," she said, softly, bending down so that her lips almost touched Dick's ear, "drink none of it."

"What do you mean?" asked Dick. "Is it drugged?"

"Give me your word that you will not betray me," said the girl, glancing from one to the other.

She held out a slender brown hand, and Dick, without any hesitation, took it in his own.

"I give you my word," he said, "that whatever you impart to me shall be held sacred."

"For your friend too?" suggested the girl.

Carl rose up and held out his hand. The girl gave him her disengaged one.

"Hear me, then," she said, "and like true gentlemen, as I'm sure you are, never let my uncle know what I reveal."

"Your uncle is the landlord?" said Dick.

He is. I am an orphan, and he and his wife— m aunt—make me their slave; but I wish not to tell you that, but of things that concern yourselves. The wine is drugged so that you may sleep soundly all night, while my uncle and his friends visit the wreck."

"To steal what they can."

"They will pick it clean, and leave nothing more than a hawk would leave on the bones of a sparrow."

"Aptly put, my pretty girl," said Dick, "and now, my dear, what is your name?"

"Viardot," she answered.

"Is not that an Italian name?"

"It is. My mother was an Italian, my father a Spaniard. You promise me?"

"You may trust us even to die ere we betray you," said Dick.

The girl gave their hands a gentle pressure and let both go.

"I must not remain here," she said, "lest the suspicions of my aunt should be aroused. She does not care for me to wait on young men, as she wishes me to marry— But that is of no concern to you. Senors, I leave you."

She curtseyed, and, drawing back a pace, gave them a final hint.

"Empty the bottle, as if you had drank it. The window is handy, and if you are cautious the wine may be poured out safely."

Then she vanished, and the two friends began their dinner, being hungry, and of the temperament to take things coolly.

"The old rascal!" said Dick. "I would like to twist his neck. The first bottle is not quite empty."

"About a glass apiece in it," said Carl, holding the bottle up to the light.

"That will serve for dinner. Now, Carl, all we have to do is to get our dinner over and retire to our room at once, pleading drowsiness. I don't know where that room is, but it is sure to have a window in it, by means of which we can get to the ground; then, under cover of darkness, we can be off and away to prepare a surprise for our host and his friends."

"I leave all to you," said Carl, "and as a preliminary punishment for the rascal let us make a hearty dinner."

While they were partaking of it their host was in the village visiting house after house, exchanging a few words with the men when at home, and leaving a message where they were away.

From this labour he returned just in time to see his guests come out of the public-room yawning and stretching their arms.

"Show us our chamber, my good fellow," said Dick; "we are tired, and the air of this place seems to make us drowsy."

"It is very strong, senor," replied the fellow, "and generally overcomes strangers. This way, senors."

It was now as dark as it would be that night, and

a lamp was burning in the bar. Taking it up, and calling to Viardot to bring another, he took it from her, and, walking backwards, escorted his guests upstairs.

"The chamber," he said, "is at the back of the house, senors, so that you may be quiet. Sometimes we people are restless, and are alert the greater part of the night. Behold it—a goodly resting-place."

It was a fair-sized room, with two beds constituting the main part of its furniture—a chair or two, a washstand, and some pegs to hang clothes upon, constituted all the rest of the fittings needing reference to.

"A bolt to the door," said the host, "although you need not fear robbery here. We are all honest men in Santa Josef."

"I must say," said Carl, with a frightful yawn, "that I have rarely seen a face like yours on which honesty was so indelibly branded."

"I am rejoiced by your eulogy, senor."

"You are quite welcome. Good-night."

"The repose of the angels be yours, senors."

He closed the door and walked away. They waited until the sound of his footsteps ceased, and then Carl drew the bolt.

"It is not the sort of thing that would keep YOU out, Dick," he said.

"But I mean to keep those Spanish thieves out," returned Dick. "First, we will put the bedsteads against the door. Walk softly."

He lifted the nearest up bodily, as if it had been a chair, and placed it so as to act as a barricade. Then, bidding Carl lay hold of the foot of the other, he placed it crosswise on the first.

"That will do," he said; "now put out the light."

Carl turned down the lamp and blew crosswise into the glass, not downwards, for he knew that many an explosion had been caused by that mode of extinguishing.

At one end of the room was a window, to which Dick softly walked, and, pushing aside a heavy curtain hanging before it, looked out.

The night was fine, and, in addition to the light cast by a brilliant array of stars, there was the cold radiance of a rising moon, revealing the inn-yard in all its dirt and disorder.

On the opposite side a man was just moving away, after having, as Dick surmised, been watching the windows to see when the light was put out.

He came across the yard and entered the house by the back way.

"It is early to move," said Dick, "but I think we may venture now. The more time we get the greater and more effective will be the surprise."

The window was an old casement, opening upon hinges.

Having pushed the curtain away and looked at it, Dick perceived that it was very rusty, and if opened wide would be sure to creak.

As it was of such simple construction that it could be lifted off, Dick adopted that expedient, opening it a few inches and raising it with a finger and thumb, as if it had been made of pasteboard.

He placed it on the floor, and leaning out of the window discovered that a stout vine growing against the wall offered an easy means of descent.

A word of caution and he was out and going down without a sound. In two minutes they were in the inn yard.

"Careful now," said Carl, "is there a dog here?"

"The Spaniards," replied Dick, "are not fond of dogs."

Only one way out of the yard was visible, and that would bring them into the main street of the village. The question was, could they get out without being perceived.

A sound of footsteps and a faint murmur of voices reached their ears where they stood.

The wreckers were mustering.

No time was to be lost.

Walking silently in the rotting straw, strewn all over the yard, Dick went to the gate and looked out.

Halfway down the street about a score of men had gathered together.

The majority of them were armed with old flint-muskets, almost as long as themselves, and some had such weapons of offence as a scythe, a hammer, or a club.

"We must get ahead of them," said Dick. "Ha! I see a byeway leading from the road. It bends towards the top of the village."

"But we have to cross the road."

"Let us go boldly," said Dick. "They may not see us."

"And if they do?"

"Well, we will still get ahead of them SOMEHOW."

Walking swiftly and lightly the two friends crossed the road, and paused a moment to mark if they had been seen.

But there was no movement, no sound from the group of men, and with joyful hearts they hastened down the narrow path, which appeared to run almost parallel with the main street.

"We have forgotten to pay our bill, Dick," said Carl, grimly.

"I mean to settle with the landlord by-and-bye in full," was the significant reply.

CHAPTER XLII.

BUTTERFLICK DISTURBED—A NIGHT BATH—IN A DILEMMA—SEAWEED APPAREL.

"OTHER 'em. I can't sleep."

"What's the matter, dad?"

"Hinsects, my son, hinsects," said Butterflick, with considerable emphasis. "The place is alive with 'em."

"I've got some matches," said Muffins. "Shall I strike a light?"

"Do so, my boy," replied Butterflick. "Drat 'em. These creatures want old Sally among them."

Butterflick and Muffins were sleeping under a tent of their own. Like the others, it was little more than a sheet of canvas stretched over the boughs of a tree.

Muffins felt in his pocket for a match, and while he was getting a light he could hear Butterflick vigorously slapping himself, and uttering suppressed anathemas on his tormentors.

"Why, dad, look here!" said Muffins, holding the

atch down to the ground. " You've been lying on
a nest of soldier ants and broken it in."

"I've got 'em all over me," said Butterflick ;
"and, stars ! they do bite. Hang 'em !"

Slap—slap !

"You had better go outside, dad, and take off
your things and shake 'em," said Muffins. "There's
no sleeping here to-night—the little beasts are
all over the place."

They were indeed. Thousands upon thousands
of the ants, which are the most pugnacious of their
breed, were out and about, burning to avenge their
ruined city.

Butterflick had broken the top of it in, and ruin
had come upon the colony.

"I'll go down to the beach and have a wash,"
said Butterflick.

"All right, dad."

Butterflick set out, but he had barely been gone
a minute when Muffins was startled by the sudden
appearance of Carl and Dick.

"Is that you, master?' he gasped.

"It is," replied Dick. "Move quick, and wake up
everybody. There is little time to spare. The
tide is out, I think ?"

"Yes, master."

"Let all get on board at once," said Dick.

"We hoped to have been here an hour ago," said
Carl to Muffins, "but lost our way. Look alive,
boy ! Ask them to go as quiet as possible. Tell
them there is little danger if they make no noise."

"I understand, Mister Carl," said Muffins.

Dick hurried off to the vessel, and Carl went to
watch for the arrival of the wreckers, whom he
knew would soon be there.

More than half the night had sped away, and in
an hour or so daylight would be advancing.

Mr. Butterflick, to get his needed wash, had to
go beyond the Archimedes, which lay in the same
position as before.

The tide being out there was nothing more than
damp sand around her.

Unconscious of any peril Butterflick took off his
clothes, and leaving them on the dry part of the
beach, which was, of course, higher up than the
vessel, walked out to give himself a bath to cool the
bumps raised by the ants, which bit as viciously as
miniature scorpions.

He found the dip in the sea an immediate relief,
and in other ways delightful.

The night was warm and the water only just
agreeably cool, so he kept on disporting himself like
a merman for a long while, until aroused by a shouting in the direction of the stranded vessel.

Looking up he saw two people running towards
him—a man and a woman—and he had no difficulty
in recognising Mr. and Mrs. Pardiggle Brown.

Here was a fix.

Butterflick could walk in the sea where it was
shallow, but he was no swimmer, and a jump into
deep water would end in his being drowned.

"Hallo ! Don't come this way," he roared.

"His voice. My protector," he heard Mrs.
Pardiggle Brown shriek. "Oh ! save me."

"Goodness. woman ! Don't come here," yelled
Butterflick. "I've nothing on."

He looked wildly about him for his clothes, but
they were far away on the dry sand.

The only thing that could possibly help him was
an adjacent heap of seaweed.

He made a plunge at it, and grasping an armful,
proceeded to clothe himself as well as he could
with it.

"Don't come here, I tell you !" he roared. "I'm
a bathin'—that's what's the matter."

"Murder—brigands—thieves !" cried Pardiggle
Brown, who was now within a score yards of
Butterflick.

Mrs. Brown was hobbling and panting up about
the same distance behind him.

" Brigands ?" said Butterflick.

The report of half-a-dozen muskets in the direction
of the Archimedes fell with startling suddenness
upon his ear. Shouts and sounds of a desperate
struggle followed.

"A fight, and I not in it," cried Butterflick.
"Here, where's my clothes ?"

Dropping half the seaweed, in which he had
enveloped his body, he dashed off in the direction
of the shore, passing Mrs. Pardiggle Brown.

The moment she saw the unhappy condition he
was in she threw up her arms, uttered a wild scream,
and flopped down upon the wet sand.

"Brown, you brute !" she said ; "you shall pay
for this. It was your intention to deliberately
degrade me."

"It's all your fault, you hag," replied Pardiggle
Brown ; "if you had only got up and gone at once
to the vessel with the rest we should have been
safe. But you would tidy your hair, and get your
improver straight, and—"

But we will leave them to wrangle it out, and
follow Butterflick, who rapidly lost all his seaweed
apparel, and when he reached the Archimedes was
as naked as a newborn child.

A desperate fight was going on upon the sands
just outside the vessel. Firing had ceased, for all
were at close quarters, and it was just as easy to
shoot a friend as a foe.

He saw Dick, without anything but his mighty
arms, breaking through the mass of Spanish men,
howling like fiends. Carl, Phil, Ajax, and even
Muffins were busy.

Butterflick had no time to look for his clothes.

He had to go into the fight as he was, or lose his
chance.

So he went as he was.

Springing upon a man near him, who was carrying an old flint musket as if it were too heavy for
him, Butterflick first of all struck him between the
eyes, and then wrenched his weapon from him.

"Hurooh ! I'm in it," cried Butterflick.

"A wild man !" burst from the lips of the Spaniards,
as the naked Butterflick rushed into the fray.

Their confusion was almost complete at this time,
and he settled the business.

They broke away and began to run, howling for
mercy.

Half their number lay groaning on the sands,
among them the landlord of the inn at Santa Josef.

He lay stretched out, with his eyes feebly blinking, but giving no other sign of life.

The victorious party—Dick excepted—pursued
the flying would-be wreckers, but not to kill.

When they got hold of one, they knocked him
down, or belaboured him until he implored them to
be merciful.

In their flight some ran over the little pile of clothes
left by Butterflick, kicking them in every direction.

The first thing he found was his waistcoat, then

his shirt, his boots, and his coat, but his nether garments he could not find anywhere.

"Some derned thief have stolen 'em. I must make the weskut do for the present."

So he put his legs through the armholes and buttoned it behind, which really was as good a thing as he could do under the circumstances, especially as Mr. and Mrs. Brown were coming back, and the dawn was breaking in the eastern sky.

Dick Strongbow, meanwhile, was looking around to see what damage had been done.

His own party had suffered very little, but the wreckers had had a rough time of it.

Half a score of them were lying about in various stages of confusion or complete insensibility.

Two, on being assisted, managed to rise, and were by Dick directed to get back to the village of Santa Josef, and return with some sort of ambulance, a cart if nothing better could be got, for their less fortunate friends.

"They have had a lesson they are not likely to forget," he said, grimly.

Meanwhile Mrs. Pardiggle Brown had arrived upon the scene with her husband, who was in a sulky mood.

"I wish to know," said Mrs. Brown, "how long I am to remain here subjected to the awful spectacles I have seen to-night."

"It is a matter of necessity, madam," replied Dick, sternly. He had no patience with the woman, and her paint, and airs, and mincings.

"Matter of necessity !" she exclaimed. "Necessity for a man to go about in—in a child-like simplicity of attire, his body garnished with sea-weed, and nothing else ?"

"Really, madam—" began Dick; but ere he could say more Butterflick advanced from the rear.

"It's all right, cap'en," he said. "You see I got a lot o' them creeturs giving me the nip all over, and I went out for a wash when this lovely lady and her husband came along and see me. I did the best under the circumstances."

He stopped short as all the company burst into a roar of laughter after looking at his toilet arrangements.

Mrs. Pardiggle Brown uttered a shrill scream, then, after looking about for somebody to support her, and finding nobody, she spun round twice slowly and sank upon the sands as little girls do when making "cheeses" with their dresses.

"Butterflick, what are you doing, man ?"

"One o' them varmints have boned my breeches, and until I gets another pair I thought I'd make the best o' the weskut."

They all roared again, except Butterflick and Mr. and Mrs. Brown.

It was no laughing matter for the former, and as to the latter, one was in a state of sham collapse and the other as sulky as an owl.

"Well," said Dick, as soon as he could speak calmly, "a waistcoat is better than nothing for the moment. As soon as we can get at our boxes we will find you another pair of inexpressibles. Meanwhile, let us see what we can do for these rascals. They hardly deserve any care, but it is as well to be merciful to the meanest foe."

CHAPTER XLIII.

ARRIVAL OF THE SPANISH GOVERNOR—PAULO THE ATHLETE—A TRIAL OF STRENGTH.

IT was evening, within an hour of sunset, when a Spanish gentleman on horse-back, accompanied by half-a-dozen mounted gendarmes appeared upon the scene.

Up to that time no help for the injured had been sent from the village; but they had been well cared for by our hero and his friends.

The clatter of swords and heavy horse-trappings was heard before they came in sight, and Dick, accompanied by his followers as a body-guard, went out to meet the coming friend or foe.

He could not, of course, tell exactly which it was; but, if a foe, he was determined not to be made a prisoner of.

As the two parties neared each other Dick raised his hat, and the Spaniard, reining up his horse, courteously acknowledged his salute.

This was a hopeful beginning, and Dick, bidding his followers remain where they were, advanced alone.

"Whom have I the honour of addressing ?" he said.

"I am the governor of this district," was the reply, "and my name is Don Sebastian de la Tourville. Your name, senor ?"

"Dick Strongbow."

"English ?"

"Yes."

"And what doing here ?"

"We were wrecked upon this coast," said Dick, "and sought help in the village of Santa Josef to save the cargo and protect the vessel. The help they gave us was to play the part of wreckers, and endeavour to rob us of everything."

"As I suspected," replied Don Sebastian; "the knaves and scoundrels ! The tale they told me was very different—no matter what it was, I know they have lied." He stooped down and held out his hand. Dick grasped it.

"You have among you a man of giant strength," said Don Sebastian. "Which is he ?"

"I have a reputation of being stronger than most men," replied Dick, with a smile.

The Don's eyes while speaking had rested on Ajax, who was one of the party in the rear.

"You !" he exclaimed, turning his gaze upon Dick. "I should not have thought it. But of course they would exaggerate. I have here a man," turning to one of his followers, "who is said to be the strongest man but one in Spain."

"Indeed !" said Dick. "I congratulate him."

"He is up to all forms of wrestling," said the Don, lowering his voice. "I do not propose it, but would you like to try conclusions with him ?"

"With pleasure," replied Dick.

The eyes of the Don sparkled. He was evidently a lover of sport, and here was an opportunity to gratify it.

"Just one fall," he said, eagerly; "or more if you will."

"I am ready," replied Dick, quietly.

"Paulo," said the Don, turning to one of the horsemen, a man of powerful build, "the English-man will try a fall with you. He of whom we heard so much in the village."

"I have little love for wrestling with boys," replied Paulo, with a contemptuous glance at Dick's smooth face.

"You may take my word for it," said Dick, "that I have wrestled with men and have come off victorious."

"If you will—you must," said Paulo, descending from the saddle, "but I warn you that I have a rough hand."

"So have I, at a pinch," answered Dick, calmly.

"Senor," said the Don, as he dismounted, "your defeat is certain, but I like your face, and would spare you humiliation."

"Am I to yield without a struggle?" asked Dick.

"No—but the spectators may as well be few," said the Don. "Choose one of your friends to stay here. I will dismiss my men. It will be enough, and more than enough."

"It is kind of you," returned Dick.

Turning to his friends, he bade all but Carl go back to the camp.

At the same moment the Don dismissed his men, who went away with disappointed faces, one of them leading the governor's horse.

"Now we are by ourselves," said the Don, with a smirk of satisfaction. "My brave athletes, will you strip for the struggle?"

"No," replied Dick; "but Paulo may do as he pleases."

"I? By the saints, no," retorted Paulo, with a curl of his lip. "I am ready, if you are."

The Don whispered a few words to Paulo, bidding him be as light of hand as he could with the "English youth."

Paulo answered—

"Don Sebastian, if I kill him I cannot help it. My strength is so great, and it is not always under my control."

From which it may be gathered that he meant to do all the injury in his power, and Dick might prepare himself for the worst.

A whisper was also exchanged by Dick and Carl.

"What will you do with him—give him an easy fall or one to remember?"

"Carl, the fellow is a burly bully and nothing more. Besides, I have to make my mark here for the sake of us all, and his fall must be like that of a tower brought down by an earthquake."

"Do not kill him?"

"Kill him—no. He shall have the full length fall—even from head to heel—it shakes, but it will not kill."

"I am waiting," cried Paulo, with a swaggering air.

"Ready here," said Dick.

The Don and Carl exchanged bows and drew aside together.

Paulo and Dick drew up to each other.

"Catch hold," said Dick, opening his arms.

"Bah! this is child's play," hissed Paulo. "I am made a fool of"

And with an angry exclamation he threw his arms about Dick.

He would have thrown him at once, ere Dick could get a hold, but our hero was too quick for him.

The strong arms were round the burly body in a moment—closed in that awful clasp that had taken the strength out of many before.

Paulo felt it, and, like a whiff of smoke borne away by a high wind, all his bravado vanished.

"Senor," he gasped, "one moment. I—"

And then he was down, full length, with all created things around him performing a chaotic dance Inside him was a surging mass of humiliation, helpless fury, and mortal terror.

And the Don—what of him?

For a moment he looked at his fallen follower, scarce crediting his senses. Then he raised his eyes to Dick, who exhibited no signs of unwonted exertion, and exclaimed—

"Marvellous—marvellous! Are you really a mortal man?"

CHAPTER XLIV.

PAULO THE DEFEATED—A LOVELY PLACE.

"RISE, Paulo!" said Don Sebastian, advancing.

The fallen man looked at the speaker with lack-lustre eyes, but made no reply.

"You have crippled him for life, I fear," continued the frightened Don, addressing Dick.

"No; he will be all right presently," answered Dick; "I was careful not to break any bones."

Paulo now got into a sitting position, feebly and slowly. His eyes were fixed upon Dick.

"You have leagued yourself with the evil one," he said, with a hiss.

"No, indeed," replied Dick, smiling. "Strength in my opinion comes not from evil. Let me give you a hand."

"You will not grip me again?" said Paulo.

"Why should I?" asked Dick.

"Senor," said Paulo, as Dick raised him "I have a favour to ask of you."

"If reasonable, and within my power to give, consider it granted," replied Dick.

"It is this—let what has passed here now remain a secret outside."

"I am not given to bragging of every paltry feat."

"No, senor; but you have a right to talk of such a fall as you have given me," said Paulo. "I, who fear no man but Carrugia, the King of the Arena.

"Don Sebastian," continued Paulo, after a pause for breath, "I know you have no great love for Don Carrugia. He is arrogant, he is popular, he is the darling of the women."

"Yes—yes," interposed the Don, hastily; "say no more on that head."

It was evidently a sore point with the Don, and there was a constrained smile on Paulo's face as he proceeded.

"He comes—this Carrugia—to Orveito in two days' time to show his powers and strength in the arena. His great feat is to seize a bull by the horns and hold it fast. It is a feat that taxes all his strength, and it exceeds all I can do. But he,"

DICK STRONGBOW:

The Diamond King,
AND WONDER OF THE WORLD.

"Grand! Bravo! Good!" shrieked a thousand voices.

No. 11.   Price One Penny.

pointing to Dick. "Ah! what a child he will make of the bull."

"I cannot say that I have ever taken the bull by the horns," said Dick, "but if there is any fun to be got out of it I will try. Who is this Carrugia?"

"A maestro," said Don Sebastian; "the hero of the bull-fight—proud, arrogant, vicious. Lower him and I will give you a thousand ducats."

"Money I do not need," said Dick, "but I have no objection to pit myself against this mighty man of Spain."

The spark of emulation was fired in Dick's breast. Like Alexander, he wished to be the conqueror of all, so a compact was made.

The issue of the encounter between him and Paulo was to be kept a secret, and the latter, for a time at least, was to be left to tell his own story concerning it.

Don Sebastian de la Tourville was in a state of high glee.

His admiration for Dick was genuine, and a feeling of honest friendship was born within him.

He brought out his cigar-case and offered it to Dick and Carl, and then the whole party went on to the camp.

There the Don was very gracious to all, and afterwards inspected the ship.

"It shall be closely guarded," he said, "until I can send men to remove the stores to a place of safety."

For this purpose his horsemen were summoned, and desired to give up their horses to Dick and his companions. It was the Don's intention to leave the passengers behind for awhile, and send them conveyances to bear them to Orveito.

"Where you will find hospitality," he said, "and get time to make your arrangements to return home."

They were aghast at the idea of losing Dick's protection, but he assured them all was well, and promised to look them up at Orveito.

Then he, with his followers, and the Don and Paulo, rode away to Santa Josef.

Their entry into that village caused the utmost consternation to the thievish inhabitants.

Seen approaching from a distance, with every sign of a good understanding, all the men who had taken part in the attempt to rob the vessel hid away, so that there were only women and children to greet them.

Viardot, the pretty Spanish girl, was one of the first to welcome them with smiles, and Dick explained to the Don the part she played in bringing confusion to the would-be robbers.

"She is very pretty," said the Don, "and what is more, will make a man a good wife. Senor, if I can read a woman's eyes, you have only to whisper a word to win her."

"Don Sebastian," said Dick, gravely, "I have no heart to give."

"Is it so?" returned the Don; "then poor Viardot I say I. If you should ever be heart-free, you never need be ashamed to espouse her, for she has good Spanish blood in her veins."

"And yet an innkeeper's daughter?"

"Senor, this is a distracted country. The quarrel about the throne has dragged many a noble down, and raised up scores of parvenues for the time. Don Carlos has the scum of the country with him."

"He seeks the throne?"

"Yes; but he will not get it. He can only destroy what belongs to us; he can build up nothing for himself. But enough of HIM. Yonder house is mine, although I am seldom there. May I ask of you to partake of my hospitality?"

The house he pointed at was the one mansion in the village to which we have made brief reference before.

It was nearly opposite the inn, and the outside had a very blank appearance, not at all inviting to the English strangers.

But when they rode under the gateway into a square they saw that it was a very delightful abode.

The house on the inside formed three-fourths of a square of beautiful Moorish architecture, and stretching away on the open side was a splendid garden, such as could only exist in a sunny clime.

The richest flowers, the noblest plants and ferns, and the choicest fruit were there in abundance.

Cool fountains played in every nook, and slung between the trees were numerous silken hammocks, to lie in and idle the hours away.

The clatter of the horses' feet brought half-a-dozen attendants, mostly negroes black as night, the others swarthy half-castes.

They all wore white clothes, with rich scarves about their waists, and silken turbans on their heads.

Not a word escaped their lips, but after a low obeisance to their master and visitors, they held the stirrups as they dismounted, and then led the horses away.

"Hang me!" said Butterflick, "if I don't think I'm a-dreaming."

"It don't seem exactly real to me, dad," replied Muffins.

A similar feeling, only in a lesser degree, was upon all.

Barely had the horses disappeared when more attendants came from the house, and at a signal from their master proceeded to prepare a table under a verandah of filagree stone-work, shady and cool.

"You would like a bath this hot day," said the Don; "permit me to show you the way."

He escorted them through the house to a small inner court, where there was a huge marble basin, filled with water as clear as crystal, a constant supply being kept up by a fountain formed of carved allegorical figures in the centre.

Around this place were small dressing-rooms, which he invited them to enter.

"I am so seldom here," he said, "that things may not be in order. If aught is deficient, please forgive me."

"It is a splendid place," replied Dick, "and you have given us a royal welcome."

"Excuse me for a while," said the Don. "After the bath I will join you at the table. You will be able to find your way, I trust."

And with a graceful bow he left them.

———

CHAPTER XLV.

GLORIOUS TIMES FOR THE ADVENTURERS—A GARDEN INDEED—SUSPECTED TRAP TO CATCH DICK STRONGBOW.

LTHOUGH he had seen many beautiful places in the world, Dick had never been in such a charming place as this, nor had anyone there. Muffins, Butterflick, and Ajax did nothing for a few minutes but rub their heads and look at each other. Dick aroused them by bidding them prepare for a bathe.

"I had a dip this morning," said Butterflick; "but I can put up with another cooler. Lor'! if old Sally could see me now. Ajax, old man, don't be quite flabbergasted."

"It is fairyland!" said Ajax, with a gasp.

They entered the dressing-rooms, which were small, but they found all they could need there, and more.

There were short bathing-dresses, towels, brushes, perfumes, and boxes of cigarettes to smoke as they resumed their attire after the bath.

In a sort of haze Butterflick took off his clothes and put on a pair of silken drawers.

When he emerged he found that Dick and Carl were already swimming in the cool water, and Muffins was about to plunge in.

"My son," he said, "be careful. It looks shallow, but it may be deep."

"There is only about three feet of water at the upper end."

Ajax and Phil Norton now joined them, and those who could not swim kept at the upper end.

Dick, Carl, and Phil disported themselves like sons of Neptune at the deeper end.

The refreshing bath over they dressed again, and went back to the verandah. The Don and a well-spread table awaited them.

Dick and Carl were naturally refined, and their education had made them all that could be desired.

Phil was a bit rough, Ajax embarrassed, while Butterflick and Muffins could have done with a little more polish.

But the Don treated them all with the courtesy he would have shown to the highest in the land.

And thereby he showed the breeding of the true gentleman.

It is true that he talked more with Dick than all the rest, but it was clear that he had been deeply impressed by the exhibition of the young fellow's amazing strength.

Dick frankly gave him an outline of his life, which the Don listened to with deep interest.

"You are an extraordinary man," he said, "and you have a wonderful story."

Excellent meats, pastry, fruit, and wine made up the repast, to which all did justice, and afterwards they divided into parties to stroll about the garden.

Dick paired off with his host, Phil Norton with Carl, while Muffins, Butterflick, and Ajax went together.

Such walks, beds of flowers, charming little corners, fountains, and general beauty, none of them had before seen in so small a space of ground.

"Muffins, my son," said Butterflick, "these Spaniards know how to live, and they've got the climate to grow anything. Let us sit here and try to picture what your mother would think of it."

"My mother?" said Muffins, opening his eyes. "I never knew her."

"I relude to that dear far-off creetur, Old Sally," said Butterflick. "Ajax, I believe you are married."

Ajax hung his head.

"I have a wife somewhere," he said, in a low voice.

"A tartar?"

"No; but a woman of spirit. She left me justly. I had done the wrong thing."

He looked askance at Muffins, who favoured him with a forgiving smile.

"Don't think any more of it on my account, Ajax," he said.

"Any children?" asked Butterflick.

"There may be one," replied Ajax, huskily; "one was expected at the time we—we parted."

"It'll all come right, old man," said Butterflick, smacking him on the back.

"Thank you," returned Ajax, "and I hope it will be the same with you."

"It's right enough as it is, thanky," said Butterflick, rising. "Come off, there."

Muffins, true to the instincts of his years, was walking round the marble edge of a fountain.

"Oh! it's all right, dad," answered Muffins gaily.

Then the next moment his foot slipped, and in he went.

"Save him!" yelled Butterflick, as he made a plunge forward.

In his haste he also precipitated himself over the edge of the fountain and immersed his head and shoulders.

As it was only about eighteen inches deep he was soon out again, spluttering and glaring about him with a wrathful eye.

Muffins, accustomed to small disasters, was already out upon the walk, wringing his clothes, and apparently rather amused than otherwise by the accident.

"I see," said Butterflick, "that if I don't keep a tight hand over you I shall have a lot of trouble. Come here and take a spanking."

"Not until to-morrow, dad," answered Muffins. "It's all right. If I run round a bit I shall soon dry myself."

"I'm bound to give you a spanking," growled Butterflick. "As Solomon says, 'Spile a rod rather than a child.'"

A race then ensued round and round the fountain, Muffins keeping ahead of his irate parent, who presently stopped, blowing like a whale.

"All right, my lad," he said; "it's one to you now. Another time it will be one to me."

Passing his hand over his clothes, he found they were already getting dry, and his momentary irritation subsided. He bade Muffins come and shake hands with him.

"No games—honour!" said Muffins.

"Honour!" assented Butterflick.

Then Muffins came up, and a shake of the hand reconciled father and son.

A pleasant hour or two followed, and presently they were attracted by the sound of a guitar and a sweet woman's voice.

Hastening in the direction of the sounds, they found Dick and the others listening to Viardot, who was singing a Spanish song as she slowly walked to and fro.

The pretty face, the sweet music, the charm of her manner, the hour, the still air—all aided to complete the beauty of a scene which no pen can do justice to.

The roughest there was touched, and as the sun went down and Viardot, having finished her song, courtseyed gracefully and went away, there was a silence of a minute's duration, none caring to speak.

Don Sebastian was keenly watching Dick's face, which was tinged with a shade of thoughtfulness.

There was eagerness in the look of the Spaniard, which showed that he was anxious to know what Dick thought of the girl and her singing.

"Very pretty," said Dick, at last.

"Viardot or her song ?" asked the don.

"Both," said Dick ; "and they harmonise with this delightful place. Don Sebastian, I have not slept so much of late as I should like. May I have your permission to retire ?"

"Senor, your chambers are ready," said the Don.

Again he looked at Dick, and a faint smile flickered about his lips.

Carl cast a quick glance from one to the other, and a shade of anxiety deepened on his brow.

To him it appeared that the Don was setting the girl, for some purpose of his own, to captivate Dick.

If so, on Dick alone would depend the success or failure of the project.

To speak to Dick would be the very worst thing he could do—that Carl knew.

If you wish a man to fall in love with a pretty girl, warn him against it, and he will be sure to think about her, and so tumble into the pit.

"I don't like it," thought Carl, "and I am beginning to wish that we had never come here."

It was, indeed, the Don's suggestion that Viardot should come and sing to them.

He told Dick that she was famous in the neighbourhood for her voice and tasteful singing, and Dick expressed a desire to hear her.

Hence the scene we have described.

One other had a suspicion of the design on the part of the Don, and of all men in the world it was Butterflick.

As they were going into the house he fell behind with Phil Norton and, choosing a fitting moment, when the Don was telling a humorous story, he whispered to him—

"The Spanish Don is putting that girl up to set her cap at the cap'en."

"You may leave Dick Strongbow to take care of himself," replied Phil Norton.

"I don't know that he can," sighed Butterflick. "The strongest of us go under to the weakest of women. A pretty face is the worst man-trap out, and, once it lays hold of you, there you are—a fixture."

"Well ! you can't interfere," said Phil, "unless you are burning to get into trouble."

"I'm cool on that," said Butterflick, as he entered the house, and the subject dropped.

CHAPTER XLVI.

AT ORVEITO—HEAVY BETTING ON THE BULL-FIGHT —A SCENE IN THE STREETS—THE BOASTFUL MATADOR.

RVEITO is an old town, where all the traditions of Spain are reverenced.

There the ancient sports of the kingdom are more firmly fixed than in Madrid itself.

Thrice in the year, or oftener if it can be arranged, there is a bull-fight in a grand old arena, built on the model of the Coliseum as to interior, with seats for many thousands.

The words "bull-fight" and "Carrugia" were on every lip, had been upon every tongue for weeks past, and the day was come for a display on an extra scale.

Half-a-dozen young bulls, wild and vicious, had been obtained, and were kept caged, in waiting for the hour when they were to be set free to be tortured, driven mad, and in turn to wreak their vengeance on helpless horses, or perchance a minor matador or two.

The chance of his venting his wrath on the chief matador, Carrugia, was very small, for the hero of the arena was quick of eye, sure with the death-dealing rapier, and as strong as the bulls he encountered.

We may here state for the benefit of the uninitiated reader that the fighting bulls of Spain are not so big as the bulls we see at home.

They are about the size of a heifer, but are very strong and nimble, and not by any means despicable antagonists.

It was night-time in Orveito—the eve of the bull-fight—and in the chief hotels a number of Spanish dons had assembled.

There, too, were our friends with Don Sebastian. Dick held aloof from the other Spaniards, but the Don went among his fellow countrymen, who were wagering on the events of the morrow.

It seemed that there were two or three other aspirants to perform the feat of seizing the bull by the horns, and the betting for the most part was upon their prospect of success.

Heavy odds were laid and still offered that not one of the new men succeeded in performing the feat.

Don Sebastian quietly took all the wagers, backing one to do it.

Some of the Spaniards, in their grave way, rallied him upon his being rich, and wanting to get rid of his money.

"I always had a fancy for taking odds," he said, quietly, "and I care not if I lose a ducat or two. I have two thousand more at my bankers I am anxious to dispense among you."

"I will lay eight thousand to two," said a foppish-looking youth.

"Ten to two are the odds," answered the Don.

"But I have so heavy a book now that I do not care to risk more."

"Eight to two be it then."

"They say that an Englishman will try what he can do to-morrow," said a haughty-looking man with iron-grey hair.

He was one of the richest nobles in Spain—famed in his youth for his wild living.

"One has had the temerity, I believe," said the Don, lightly.

"Ah! these Englishmen," said the other; "what audacity they have! They think they can go anywhere and do everything. It will be rare fun to see this bold fool tossed by the bull."

"The best of fun," assented the Don; "but he has only himself to blame."

"What is his name?" inquired the fop. "Smith, I should say."

"No," said the Don, drawing a paper from his pocket. "I have it here—Nemo; a strange name."

"It means no name."

"Perhaps he hasn't one?" suggested the haughty Spaniard. "I will lay a thousand ducats that if he goes within a metre of the bull he will be tossed."

"Odds wanted," said the Don.

"Two to one."

"I take you, and now my book is full."

He closed it as he spoke, and after lingering awhile to exchange a few words with his more intimate acquaintances, sauntered out.

"Tourville has gone mad," said the fop.

"It is a dispensation for our benefit," said the haughty Spaniard; and then they all laughed.

The man credited with madness did not leave the hotel, but went upstairs to the second-floor, where, in a quiet room, he found Dick and Carl together by the window.

The lamp was turned down, and they were watching the moving crowds in the street below—a gay and interesting spectacle.

"Senor Strongbow," he said, "how do you feel to-night?"

"Well as ever I did in my life," replied Dick.

"No weakness, no fears—pardon me—no doubts about the morrow?"

"None. For me to doubt is to be beaten, and —believe me, I have no desire to boast—I have never yet been conquered."

"I have been frank with you," said Don Sebastian, "and told you that I mean to make money out of your victory; but that is not the greatest thing it will bring to me. I want Carrugia—the haughty matador—the overbearing snob, to be humbled—crushed—as he will be if he has to take second place to any living man."

"I will do my best," said Dick.

"And your best will suffice to do him," said Carl.

"In return," continued the Don, "or, in advance, as I may say, I have had our police-officers set to watch for the two men you seek. I have news of them."

From his pocket he drew out a paper and handed it to Dick.

"Peruse it at your leisure," he said. "From it you will learn that yesterday they were eighty miles south of here, and are really on their way to Madrid."

"I thank you," returned Dick, "and I assure you that I am amply repaid for the service I hope to perform—WILL perform for you to-morrow."

"I am yours to command in all things," said the Don, rising. "Excuse me if I make my stay short. I must not let it be known that you and I are acquainted. At present nobody knows that you and the daring Englishman, as they call Senor 'Nemo,' are one."

He laughed pleasantly, and, saluting them, retired.

"Do you like the Don?" asked Carl, a minute after the Spaniard had gone.

"I think so," answered Dick. "He seems to be a good sort of fellow."

"A clever man," rejoined Carl.

"It is to our mutual interests to serve each other."

Outside the window was a small balcony of stone. Having turned the lamp quite out, the two friends carried their chairs outside so as to watch the scene below from a better vantage ground.

Carl alone smoked.

Dick was saving himself in every way for the morrow.

A motley scene it was—a moving panorama of romantic life.

The pretty girls, with their short dresses and mantillas; the swaggering cavaliers, the priests, and beggars, all helped to make up the show, illuminated by the light from the cafés and the sprinkling of lamps in the street.

Above was a sky of deep blue-black, bespattered with stars, shining at their best, for the moon had not yet risen.

The scene was entrancing—a beautiful dream.

The tinkling guitar, not in one sense the choicest music in the world, but appropriate to the clime and the hour, was heard on every side.

Rich baritone voices sent forth fragments of song, that rose clearly above the loud murmuring of the throng.

Then suddenly a scream and a surging of the crowd on the opposite side.

"What now?" cried Carl, springing up. "A fight?"

At first they could see little, but in a few moments the crowd parted, and four men, bearing the body of a young, handsome fellow, came slowly across the street.

Following close was a fragile girl, weeping bitterly.

An old Spanish story, truly.

Love, hatred, and the deadly stiletto.

As the young fellow walked with his sweetheart, whispering soft nothings to her, a rival came out of the thick of the crowd and stabbed him in the back.

All was over. He was dead, and there would be one spectator less at the bull-fight on the morrow.

Will the girl be there?

Who can tell?

Spanish women love lightly and forget easily. The temptations of the arena may be too much for her, and she may be there with another lover.

The author of the cruel, treacherous deed had gone undetected.

The surrounding people had been too busy with their own affairs to heed him.

Or, perchance, if one saw the blow given, he would hold his tongue, for fear of the stiletto of some friend of the murderer.

"I don't care to sit here any longer," said Dick; "the whole thing is spoilt by that tragedy."

He entered the room, Carl followed, and Dick bade his friend good-night.

"You are somewhat hipped, Dick," said Carl.

"No, not exactly that," replied Dick; "but I

confess I was deeply moved by the sight of that poor young fellow, dead in the arms of his friends. The strongest man cannot digest cold steel."

"True," said Carl; "but let no thoughts of harm to you spoil your rest."

Dick smiled.

"It is not fear I feel," he said as he left the room.

Carl did not emulate his example, but, having put on his hat and lighted another cigar, went down to the hotel bar. It was full of the revellers, mostly young men, who were crowding round a tall man.

His face was one of the handsomest Carl had ever seen; but for all that it was not a pleasant one.

It looked cruel, and there was a haughty curl of the lip that was repellent to Dick's friend.

Addressing a Spaniard near him, Carl asked who the man was.

"And who are you," exclaimed the Spaniard, "not to know the matador Carrugia?"

"I am a traveller, and have but just arrived," explained Carl.

"Ah! that accounts for it," returned the Spaniard. "He is a great man, this Carrugia; he has not his match on earth."

"So I have heard," replied Carl.

He drew up nearer to Carrugia, who was talking loudly, to hear what he was saying.

"What do I care if Don Sebastian backs the Englishman for a million ducats?" he said. "The end will be the same—he will have to pay. Bet on me all you have—grow rich on my success—if you can find fools enough to lay against me."

"We shall all know the result to-morrow," thought Carl, as he turned away. "I wish the day was over."

CHAPTER XLVII.

THE MORNING OF THE BULL-FIGHT—MR. AND MRS. PARDIGGLE BROWN ARE EARLY AT THE SHOW—MAD JEALOUSY.

AIR woke the morn, and ere the eyes of dawn were fully open half the population of Orveito were in the street.

Once more the scene is gay—not so romantic as at night-time, but more vivid in colour, thanks to the sunshine.

There is less love-making, although many a dark eye sparkles benignly under the shade of the mantillas, and the roystering youths leer back in answer.

Early as it is, many are already on their way to the arena to secure a good seat in the cheaper places.

For the better class there is no hurry. The nobility and monied people have secured theirs long ago.

From out of a second-class hotel come a man and his wife—Mr. Pardiggle Brown and his spouse.

They are reconciled. There is no Butterflick to arouse jealousy, and all is peace between them.

"Pardy, how long shall we have to wait?" asked Mrs. Pardiggle.

"Some time," he replied, evasively; "I don't quite know how long."

"I don't understand the talk of these people," said Mrs. Pardiggle Brown; "when I say anything to them they talk gibberish and grin—that's all."

"They mean well, my love," replied Mr. Pardiggle.

The place for the bull-fight was on the outskirts of the town, and they had to ask a good many questions of Spanish men and women ere they got there.

Here and there they found somebody who imperfectly understood them, and the directions they received were not so clear as rapid locomotion demanded.

But they got there at last.

It was a huge stone building of circular form, with many minor entrances, which were closed to the public, and one main entrance, which was open to anyone who had money to pay for a seat.

Already a stream of people was pouring in, and Pardiggle Brown guided his wife into the stream.

They went on with it to a pay-place, where a very ferocious-looking Spaniard was taking the money.

"How much?" asked Pardiggle Brown.

"Pay and pass on," replied the man in Spanish.

"Have you any ducat seats?" asked Brown.

He held up two ducats, and the man offered one ticket.

Pardiggle Brown shook his head and held up two fingers.

The receiver of money contemptuously drew back the single ticket—a red one—and gave him two blue ones in its place.

Then they were pushed on, and passed into a dark, cool passage.

"Now, I wonder where we go with these?" said Pardiggle Brown.

A little further on they came to an opening where an attendant and a gendarme were standing, the former to take the tickets and the latter to oust any person whose manners were obstreperous.

Pardiggle Brown held up his tickets, and the attendant pointed with his hand to signify that they were to go higher.

On they went. Soon they found a staircase and another attendant, who, on seeing the tickets, motioned them to go higher still.

"Brown," said his spouse, "it's as bad as going up the Monument."

"I can't help it," he growled. "You would come."

On they went—higher and higher—four, five, six staircases—followed by some of the lower order of the populace—Mrs. Pardiggle Brown panting, her husband puffing and blowing behind.

At last they came to the open air again, being allowed to pass through a doorway, when they found themselves at the very top of the building, in a part evidently set apart for the rabble of the place.

"And do you think I am going to stop HERE?" said Mrs. Pardiggle Brown.

"I am not going down again," replied Brown, doggedly, sitting down.

"But look at these people."

"They are all right. They are the same as you see painted in the pictures."

"But what a horrid smell of onions!"

"It isn't onions—it's garlic."

Mrs. Brown, disdainfully sniffing, sat down and opened out her skirts, so as to have as wide a seat as possible all to herself.

But much space was not allowed her.

The people passed up and rapidly filled the place.

Then came an attendant, who made them sit close, so as to make room for more.

"Brown," said his wife, "I shall go down again if you will not."

"All right," he replied, "do as you please. Once up these stairs is enough for me."

She was a woman, and therefore a determined being. Rising, she signified to the people that she wished to go out, and they politely made way for her.

Pardiggle Brown, left alone, sat with an owlish expression of face.

He did not like the people around him, and he very much objected to being alone.

Such a jibbering, gesticulating, howling rabble he was never before mixed up with.

The seats below, separated from those above by a high barrier, and nearly all the opposite side of the arena, were as yet unoccupied.

These seats were numbered and reserved, save one space round a raised seat, to be occupied by the ruler of the sports. This space was what a betting-ring is to our race-course, and would presently be filled with the Orveito sporting fraternity.

An hour passed and Mrs. Pardiggle Brown did not return.

Her spouse sat sweltering in the sun, watching for her appearance in one of the open spaces below in vain.

Another hour and yet she was not visible.

"She's gone home," thought Pardiggle Brown, "and the best place for her. Oh! hang this garlic. It's strong enough to curl the bristles of a hair-broom."

The lower classes of Spain are always redolent of this strong-savoured vegetable, and when its odour is accompanied by a fusty smell of old clothes it is almost unbearable.

But Pardiggle Brown had come to see the bull-fight and he would not budge.

The whole place rapidly filled—thousands of people from the town and country were arriving, all bent on enjoying a day's "sport."

In the betting-ring a great gathering assembled, and the wagering on different events must have been very heavy, for pencils and books were on every side, and all in use.

Pardiggle Brown watched the scene for awhile, amused and interested. Then suddenly the colour forsook his cheeks.

Below, in a front seat, near the betting-ring, sat Carl, Phil Norton, Muffins, Ajax, and Butterflick.

Close to the latter, evidently enjoying her position, was Mrs. Pardiggle Brown.

A terrible cry burst from the lips of her agonised husband.

It was a compound of despair and an exclamation of mad fury.

The people near him started with terror and looked at his wild countenance.

He stood up waving his arms.

"Let me pass," he cried, "or I shall murder somebody!"

They could not understand his words, but they grasped his meaning. He was taken bad, and wanted to get out.

Without the slightest hesitation they made room for him to leave—doing so in a bit of a hurry perhaps—and, scrambling out, he disappeared.

"Poor fellow!" said an old Spanish woman; "it is the sun. It has stricken his brain and driven him mad."

CHAPTER XLVIII.
SCENES IN THE ARENA.

THE hour had come, and with it, punctual almost to the moment, a score of handsomely-dressed young Spaniards entered the ring.

These were the matadores, who with darts would torture the bull, and with a fluttering red scarf draw him from his prey. Barely had the shouts which greeted the arrival of the matadores shown a tendency to subside when half-a-score mounted men, padded about the legs and sitting in high saddles, appeared.

And now into the arena strode the director of the ceremonies, who is of the same importance at a bull-fight as a ring-master is at a circus at home.

He wore a black mantle, a turned-up broad hat with a white feather, velvet breeches, silk stockings, and pumps.

Having by sign marshalled his men in a row, they, at a given signal, bowed to the royal box, which in this case was occupied by some high dignitary from Court. Then in a body they retired, and two horses, each with two riders, entered.

The men rode back to back, and were armed with stout staffs to beat off the bull, who almost immediately came snorting into the ring from a side entrance.

The animal was not in a condition to do serious damage to anyone, for his horns were tipped with balls of lead.

By the shouts of laughter from every side it was evident that this was the comedy part of the entertainment. The serious part was to come after.

As soon as the bull saw the horses with their double riders he made a dash at the foremost, and, ignoring a couple of hard blows from the men, he dashed himself against the horses' flank, and bowled it over.

Down went the riders, rolling in the sand, to the great delight of the spectators, who roared and clapped their hands with delight.

The bull, having prostrated one of his enemies, was so far content, and made no effort to do further injury in that direction.

But he had his eye upon the other riders, who had withdrawn their horse to the opposite side of the arena, jeered at by the public.

The bull pawed the ground, snorted, and bellowed—then it charged.

Vain was the attempt of the horsemen, who seemed to be mere country louts lured into making fools of themselves, to get away.

The bull came up behind the horse like an express train, dashed into its rear, and fairly hoisted its hind quarters in the air.

Both riders fell over the horse's head, and the shrill screams of laughter from the lookers-on were deafening.

The horse rolled over upon its side, and, as before, the bull seemed satisfied.

After trotting up and down a bit, glaring at the spectators with its fiery eyes, and surveying the high barrier round the ring, as if speculating on the chance of getting over it and putting an end to their laughter, it quickly made off by the way it came, and was seen no more.

The horsemen got up, assisted their steeds to rise, and led them away, bowing with mock solemnity in acknowledgment of the derisive cheers they were favoured with.

And now came the serious part of the day's business, or pleasure, as we suppose it must be called.

The laughter subsided, and the loud talking dwindled into murmuring, as every eye that commanded the main entrance to the arena was fixed upon it.

Enter the matadores with half-a-dozen single horsemen, all looking very earnest, knowing well that no child's play was before them.

They spread about the arena, and finally faced one of the main entrances, by which the bull would enter the magic circle.

The gate presently opened, and a compact, short-legged, fiery little animal dashed out.

The matadores and mounted men separated immediately, banners fluttered, and the bull, snorting with rage, charged at them pell-mell.

Here and there dashed the bull, the matadores twisting and turning out of his way, and, in the extremity of danger, leaping the barrier.

At last the bull got a victim—a horse.

The horns of the beast, not shielded like those of the first bull, but bare and sharp pointed, were plunged into the side of the horse and a deep gash made.

The rider quickly dismounted and fled.

What a shout arose !

The ghastly sight of a horse staggering about with the blood pouring from its side roused the onlookers to a pitch of enthusiasm.

The matadores became excited and more daring.

They drew nearer, fixing darts in the bull's back and sides, fluttered their scarves in his eyes, and one, more venturesome than the rest, leaped over the beast's back as he was rushing at a flying assailant.

The horsemen now departed, the wounded horse staggering away to lie down in some corner and die.

A few minutes later all the other men, at a given signal, made for the barrier, and, leaping it, left the bull alone.

And now the supreme moment of this, the first real fight of the day, had come.

The bull, left to himself, walked about the arena, stopping every moment or two to paw the ground and bellow a defiance to all mankind.

The time for the appearance of Carrugia had arrived.

He entered the arena without weapon of any sort, or banner, or dart, and, with seeming disregard of the bull, bowed to the applauding audience.

The bull saw him instantly, and stood a little while staring at him intently, as if marvelling at his temerity.

Then down upon the daring matadore he bore.

Carrugia waited calmly until the bull was within a foot of him, then stepped aside.

The bull, knowing that it had missed its aim, pulled up short, and wheeled round to charge again.

That was Carrugia's opportunity.

Ready to take advantage of the moment of turning, he sprang upon the bull and seized it by the horns.

At the same moment another matadore ran into the ring, and while Carrugia held the bull he drew a sharp knife across its throat.

The applause was tremendous—deafening. It was bull-fighting in excelsis—a feat unparalleled.

And yet there were several people who looked on with a smile of contempt, notably two familiar to our readers—Dick Strongbow and Carl Yemitz.

They were standing in the right-hand corner of the betting-ring, and behind them was Don Sebastian de Tourville, who listened eagerly to their comments.

"What think you of that, Dick ?" asked Carl.

"A clever trick," Dick answers. " He seizes the bull at a moment when it is overcome with surprise, for an instant only I grant, but it is long enough for the man with the knife to come in and do his work."

"You can do better than that, Dick ?"

"I hope so."

Don Sebastian touched him upon the shoulder.

"My dear senor," he said, "I have made an arrangement that will please you."

"Thanks," replied Dick ; "and it is—"

"The next bull is yours," said the Don. "You would not care to appear at the fag end of the day."

"I am ready," said Dick. "There is no time like the present."

"Come with me," said the Don, "but walk as if you were not in my company."

The Don sauntered back to the top of the ring, and left by a small side door.

It led into a passage, where they found Paulo awaiting them.

"Senor," he said, huskily, to Dick, "you will not fail? You cannot—"

"I hope not," answered Dick ; "but it is as well not to be sure until it is all over. I am quite new to this sport, if sport it is."

Paulo was in a state of feverish excitement, so was the Don, but the latter restrained himself, and was outwardly cool.

"I am taking you to the dressing-room of the matadores. You will find them inclined to snub you and be rude, perhaps. But I beg of you to pay no heed to them until after the meeting with the bull."

"Are they so very terrible ?" asked Dick, with a smile.

"No ; but Carrugia is not the man to throw a chance away," replied the Don. "If he suspects what is in you he may inspire some of his followers to use the knife on the least pretence, and at least disable you."

"I will be cool," said Dick.

"There is the dressing-room of the matadores," said the Don, pointing to a door on the right. "Paulo will introduce you. For the present, senor adieu."

————

The sight behind lid was a most exhilarating one.

CHAPTER XLIX.

DICK IN THE ARENA—AN EXCITING SCENE—PAR-
DIGGLE BROWN AN INVOLUNTARY MATADORE—
CARRUGIA'S THREAT.

ICK STRONGBOW received a very scanty greeting as, accompanied by Paulo, he entered a square stone chamber lighted by means of gratings on two sides of it.

Lounging about, smoking cigarettes, and chattering, were a number of matadores, probably a score.

Senors," cried Paulo, "the Englishman !"

They turned their eyes upon him, but gave him no greeting. Some of them as they looked away again laughed cynically.

It was ridiculous to think that this young, fair-haired man could emulate the deeds of Carrugia.

The signal was now given for the second fight, and the matadores, tossing away the ends of their cigarettes, hurried off.

Paulo and Dick were alone.

"It is a pity," said the former, "you have no dress for the arena."

"Dress would not help me," replied Dick. "How shall I know when I am wanted ?"

"There will be a cry for the toreador ; but you need not wait for that. Come and see the bull."

They left the room by another door, and Paulo ushered him down a passage, at the end of which was a wide entrance to the arena, barred by a heavy grating.

A few matadores had assembled there to look on, amongst them Carrugia. He stared for a moment at Dick and smiled scornfully.

"Senor," he said, "it is to be hoped that you have settled your worldly affairs."

"Why ?" asked Dick, quietly.

"They have a strong bull for you," said Carrugia, "and if it tosses a man it will kill him."

"Do all who are tossed die ?" enquired Dick.

"Not all, if there are matadores to save them," said Carrugia, "but you are so confident that you will not need any assistance."

"Pardon me. I am not confident—in speech, at least," said Dick ; "but I do not ask your help. Let it be a matter between the bull and myself."

"When you have held the horns for a time," said Carrugia, "the knife-bearer can give him the coup-de-grace."

"I decline help of any sort," said Dick.

At this moment a loud shout from the spectators was heard, and the matadores were seen flying over the barriers.

The bull was left in the arena alone.

"It is a magnificent bull," said Paulo, "stronger than the other."

"When it has killed the Englishman," retorted Carrugia, "I will avenge him."

The latter words were spoken in a mocking tone ; but Dick heeded them not.

The grating was drawn a little aside to enable him to enter the arena, and, having handed his hat to Paulo, he went forth.

As he came into view of the vast audience a sudden hush fell upon them.

Outside his friends, including Don Sebastian and Paulo, not a living creature had any sympathy with this daring young man, who had thrust himself forward as a rival to the great Carrugia.

But all were interested.

Their savage Spanish blood was aglow, and they looked eagerly for a scene in which their love of the horrible would be gratified.

The bull, standing in the centre of the arena, glared at Dick, lashing his sides angrily with his tail.

Suddenly the voice of a man was heard, crying—
"At him, Toro !"

It was Carrugia who shouted out the encouraging cry from behind the gate.

It was taken up by the majority of the vast multitude, and "At him, Toro !" was heard all over the place, like the roaring of an angry sea.

The bull, as if inspired by the cries, lowered its head and rushed straight at Dick.

He stood his ground, with his legs planted sufficiently far apart to give him the firmest of footholds, while hand and eye were ready for action.

Some of the colour left his cheeks, but not from fear. The moment was an exciting one.

On his coolness and strength his very life depended.

It was scurvy treatment that had been meted out to him. The strongest bull had been provided for his downfall, and as it thundered towards him he knew that he would require all his strength to save himself from destruction.

To stop the bull in its full career was more than mortal man could do. One part of Carrugia's trick he was obliged to resort to.

He stepped aside as the chief matadore had done, so that it passed harmlessly by, and as it turned to renew the attack he seized it by the horns.

The bull made a grand effort to regain his liberty, and the struggle that ensued roused the spectators to frenzy.

There was nothing like it with Carrugia.

He simply caught hold of the bull, and another matadore rushed out and instantly cut its throat.

But see this Englishman—how he holds on !

Mark what he does.

"He is dragging the bull !" shrieked a thousand voices. "Grand ! Brava ! Good ! See ! Brava !"

Dick was roused, and exerted all his tremendous power. He dragged the bull by the horns half way towards the centre of the arena, and then, by an exercise of strength that made every sinew crack, he suddenly jerked the fiery animal on one side and threw it.

For one moment all was black before him, and he felt as if he was about to die.

But he did not even fall.

The black mist cleared away as quickly as it came, and he looked down upon the bull lying on its side—panting, beaten, cowed, subdued.

It did not even make an effort to rise, but lay there with scared eyes fixed upon the man who had overcome it so completely.

Dick placed one foot upon its body and looked in the direction of his friends.

He saw them all wild with delight, shouting and waving their hats.

And in the betting-ring there was chaos.

Don Sebastian had heavy bets with several of those who were, as they now found out, too ready to lay the odds, and many would be absent on settling day.

But for that he cared little. Anyway, he had made a tremendous haul.

Dick bowed to the audience, and having patted the prostrate bull upon its flank, he backed slowly to the gate.

It was opened by Paulo, who grasped both his hands, heaping all sorts of blessings upon his head.

Carrugia was nowhere to be seen, but the other matadores had gathered in a group, and were staring at Dick overcome with awe.

The audience was still in a state of ferment, but yet another treat was in store for them.

For as Butterflick, standing on his seat, was waving his hat and supporting Mrs. Pardiggle Brown with one of his manly arms, a wild-eyed man suddenly climbed up and stood at his side.

"Villain," he said "your hour is come!"

It was Pardiggle Brown.

After a lot of searching about he had found his faithless wife and Butterflick.

By some means he had got possession of an old Spanish sword, with which he now threatened Butterflick.

"Die, villain!" he screamed.

Butterflick let go of Mrs. Brown and grasped the daring would-be assassin by the wrist.

"Brown," he said, "you are a fool Do you think I care tuppence for your wife 'cept as a friend?"

"You shall die!" yelled Brown, wildly.

He looked so determined that Butterflick was driven to a course of action which at any other time he would rather have avoided.

He hoisted Pardiggle Brown over the barrier and dropped him upon the sanded arena.

At that moment the bull got upon his feet.

Very few of the amazed people who saw Pardiggle Brown in the arena, with a drawn sword in his hand, knew how he had got there and why.

But it was enough that a man was there, and they cried—

"At him, Toro!"

The bull had had two-thirds of its vice shaken out of it by its fall, but there was sufficient of the old spirit left to cause it to resent the intrusion of Pardiggle Brown.

In obedience to the cry of the audience it went for Pardiggle Brown.

"Run, you fool!" yelled Butterflick.

But Pardiggle Brown did not move.

The fact was he could not.

He held the sword out straight before him, quite unconscious of what he was doing, and gave himself up for lost.

The point of the weapon met the throat of the beast, snapping the blade off at the handle.

Then up he went—somewhere near the top of the amphitheatre, so he believed at the time—and with a rush came down upon the soft sand, after which he remembered no more for awhile.

When he came to he found himself in the matadores' room, with Dick and Paulo, who had just given him something to drink.

"You are better now?" said Dick.

"I must be," he replied, "for I thought I was a dead man. Where's the bull?"

"The matadores have lured it out of the arena," replied Dick.

"Who picked me up?" asked Brown.

"I did," said Dick, with a smile; "the brute for some reason won't hurt me. If you can walk now we will go back to our friends."

"I feel as if I'd been taken to pieces and badly put together again," said Pardiggle Brown; "but I can walk."

"They have a third bull out," said Dick, "but I have no liking for the sport, and intend to return home as soon as I have got my friends together."

"My wife!" gasped Pardiggle Brown.

"Oh! she is all right, I daresay," said Dick. "We found her on the way home this morning weeping, and I induced her to come back with us."

"Oh! it was you?"

"Yes; and I asked Butterflick to take care of her. He said he did not care much for it, not being a lady's man, but would do his best."

"I've made an ass of myself, that's clear," said Pardiggle Brown, "and I'm very thankful for my merciful escape."

In the vestibule of the building, to which they adjourned, they found the rest of their friends, save Don Sebastian, who, until he got his money from those with whom he had betted, wisely did not show that he and Dick Strongbow knew anything of each other.

The meeting between Pardiggle Brown and his wife was very tender.

She was glad to see him alive and fairly well after his encounter with the bull, and he rejoiced to find that she was in such a loving mood.

They embraced and shed a few silent tears, which Butterflick observing, he was himself affected, and scraped a drop out of his eye.

"That's right," he said. "Kiss and make it up, and don't get to hammer and tongs again. What's the use of it? as I orfen said to old Sally. But, somehow, she WOULD see a use in it, and what's the consequench? She's as good as a widow, and I a widower, and neither on us can marry again."

Dick now announced his intention of returning to the hotel, and, having shaken hands with Paulo, he took Carl's arm, and they sauntered out.

The others followed, and Paulo remained behind in a delighted frame of mind.

His meditations were brief, for a few moments later Carrugia appeared, walking with a swagger that was mostly outside show.

"Ah! friend Paulo," he said, with a sneer, "you here—weeping over my downfall?"

"How have you fallen?" asked Paulo, in feigned surprise.

"Bah! I hate a fool's question," said Carrugia. "Have I not been outdone by an Englishman—a stranger who has never entered an arena before—and has not your master, the Don Sebastian, emptied the purses of the ring? I am down, and I fall because I have had two men to throw me. But how long shall this victor over me enjoy his fame, think you? Are there no daggers to lay him low? Is there no poison to stop the beating of his heart? Carrugia has his friends, who will serve him as he wills. So warn this puppet of yours to fly while there is yet time."

"I might warn him," replied Paulo, "but he would not fly; and you, Carrugia, be wary how you interfere with him. He is a leviathan among men, before whom such HALF-HEROES as you must bend the knee."

Carrugia started at hearing himself thus referred to, and put his hand upon his dagger, but, quickly recovering himself, he snapped his fingers in Paulo's face and walked away.

———

CHAPTER L.

DICK WILL NOT TAKE ADVICE—THE DON AND THE DUKE—VIARDOT.

BARELY had Dick Strongbow, accompanied by his friends, reached the hotel, when Don Sebastian put in an appearance.

The Spanish race is not usually demonstrative, and those of the higher classes especially cultivate a suppression of excitement in private life.

In the arena, during a bull-fight, it is another matter.

Then rich and poor, high and low, give expression to their feelings in a most pronounced manner.

No race on earth, not even the enthusiastic sons of the Emerald Isle, are more impulsively demonstrative.

The Don was in a most excited condition of mind, and, laying aside the phlegm of the Spaniard, he seized both Dick's hands and shook them warmly.

"My friend," he said, "you are a king among men."

"I am glad I am not," replied Dick, laughing, "for I would rather not be bothered with a crown."

"Especially a Spanish one," returned the Don; "it has a very precarious position on the head. Ah! my friend, you have done me a very great service."

He stopped and looked around, for they were in the public room, and he did not appear to desire any listeners.

But only Dick's friends were there, and they had walked to the windows to look at the passers-by.

"Years ago," said the Don, "I was an inexperienced young man, and I fell into the hands of what the English call gentlemen sharps. They fleeced me of half my property—a considerable sum—but I have got it all back to-day—ha! ha!—with interest. Thanks to you."

"I am glad to hear it," said Dick. "I owed you something for your hospitality and friendly feeling. Suppose we say quits?"

"I would like you to share—" the Don began, but Dick stopped him with a motion of his hand.

"I assure you," he said, "I have no need of it, nor any of my friends."

"You are generous, as well as strong and brave," said the Don. "To-morrow I gather in the ducats, and there is commotion in the breasts of some, who will find it hard to pay. But pay they must. Years ago they did not spare me. I will have no mercy on them now. Before I go let me ask you what you will do to-night."

"Probably stroll about," said Dick, "and watch the fun, if there is anything to be seen."

The Don stood for a moment silent, and his hesitation brought a slight smile to Dick's face.

"You wish to warn me against someone," he said.

"Yes," answered the Don. "Carrugia."

"Is it likely I should fear him?"

"Not as man to man, good Strongbow, but as one who has the daggers of a hundred assassins at his command."

"I have run too many risks in my life to shirk one now," said Dick.

"The risk is not only yours, but that of your friends," replied the Don; "if I know the spirit of Carrugia, and I think I do, his malevolence will aim at them all."

"Will he go so far as that?"

"Yes; down to the very least to all."

"And you would advise me to leave—to run away after a victory?" said Dick.

"No, not exactly to run away," replied the Don; "all I would suggest is that you incur no needless risks."

"For Carrugia, and his little army of assassins, THAT," said Dick, snapping his fingers. "We are few, but ere to-day we have fought many. Let but a scratch be given to any one of my party, and I will treat Carrugia as I would a rat."

"I see it is useless to argue with you," said the Don, "and will take my leave. All I can do now is to pray for your safety. At least you can with honour leave for Madrid the day after to-morrow."

"Yes, I can do that," replied Dick.

"Then all being well," returned the Don, "we will on that day go together. I shall have landed my *coup* and need no longer conceal that I look upon you as a valued friend."

They shook hands and the Don went his way, looking and feeling like a man who had wasted good advice upon an obstinate friend.

On leaving the hotel he bent his footsteps in the direction of the arena.

His reflections all round were very pleasant.

The sum of money he had won by Dick's prowess was enormous, and the men whom he had hit hardest were truly those who, years before, had taken advantage of his inexperience to plunder him.

In the return game he had come out by far the largest winner.

Presently he met a tall, haughty-looking man, whose high bearing alone proclaimed rank and title. On seeing the Don he stopped short.

"Tourville," he said, "you have played a trump card. Where did you pick up your wonder?"

"Ah! duke, you must put my good luck down to chance," replied the Don. "I saw him at Santa Josef and guessed there might be something in him. Besides, the odds tempted me."

The Duke of Seville—that was the title of the haughty Spaniard—smiled quietly.

"It is a pity you did not trust me."

"A secret known to two ceases to be a secret," replied Don Sebastian.

"True. But at least you might have left me out of the list of losers, for of a truth it will go hard with me to pay to-morrow."

"My bets with you, Seville, are nothing. As we are known to be friends, I thought it better to take your offers, or the others would have been suspicious. See here; I have already crossed them out."

The Don took out his book, and, opening it,

showed it to the duke, whose face lighted up with a smile.

"Tourville, this is good of you !" he said.

"To carry out my plans I could not betray my secret even to a friend," replied Don Sebastian; "but I need not plunder him. I know that the Carlist war has made you temporarily poor; could I be so mean as to take advantage of a friend in trouble ?"

"Tourville," said the duke, "one day I hope to be able to render you a service in return."

"You can do me one now," said the Don. "You have power, if not money. When this Strongbow gets to Madrid he must be received with all honour."

"It shall be done. When does he go ?"

"The day after to-morrow."

"The way is dangerous, and he shall have an escort."

"He would not accept it. With his handful of friends he has travelled far, met with many foes, and conquered them all. The protection, if afforded him, must be invisible."

"I will see what can be done," said the duke, thinking. "At all events, my dear Tourville, I will do my best."

They saluted each other and passed on. Don Sebastian met nobody else whom he knew until he came to the arena. The general public were now pouring out—the day's sport was over, and the people were hastening homeward to partake of an evening meal and then enjoy the final revelries in the casinos and streets. The Don stood aside, near the gate at which the matadores and their friends would come forth.

It was the practice of the bull-fighters to allow the spectators to get away ere they departed, to avoid any demonstration in the streets.

It was, indeed, so ordered by the authorities, as, in the case of rivalry, it often led to disputes and more serious forms of quarrelling.

On this occasion the Don knew that Carrugia would be in no hurry to show himself.

While he was waiting some of the men with whom he had made bets passed by, and they all honoured him with a scowl, which he responded to with a smile.

At length, as the crowd was thinning, somebody stopped close beside him, and, turning, he saw the girl Viardot.

She was simply attired, as usual, the only ornament she wore being an arum lily in her hair. Around her shoulders was slung a small, richly-inlaid guitar.

"Ah! my child," said the Don, "I have not seen you to-day. Where have you been ?"

"Inside, of course," she replied, "seeing all that was to be seen. Oh! he is great—wonderful."

"It is time that you forgot him now," said the Don.

"Why ?" she asked.

"His heart will never be given to a Spanish woman."

"Don Sebastian, are you a prophet that you can say so much ?"

"I am sure of it. He has other things in his mind."

"Another woman, perhaps," said Viardot, bitterly; "but what of that ? Women are truer than men, and yet they have been won from those they love. How much easier is it to win fickle man from HIS love ?"

"Child," said the Don, kindly, "you must forget him. He is not poor, as I thought, but rich, and if I mistake not has good blood in his veins."

"And what is in mine ?" asked Viardot, proudly.

"It counts for little in his country," said the Don. "Your uncle keeps an inn. They will look at that."

"They may," said Viardot; "but I'll not believe it of him. Don Sebastian, he has won my heart, and if he goes away never to return I shall die."

"I'll not hear such idle talk," said the Don. "You are young, and will never lack a friend in me."

"While I keep such beauty as I have," answered the girl. "Don, you have spoken like that before, when I was only a servant-girl at the inn."

"As you will be again, child, if you are wise."

"No—I have left it for ever."

"To go whither—to do what ?"

"To follow him through the world, if he should go so far—to prove to him what the devotion of a woman is—to die, if need be, for his sake."

"A romantic and foolish thought, child."

"It may be all that you say, but it rules me now. I must obey its promptings."

While they were talking thus the crowd had thinned so quickly that only a few stragglers remained, and the Don, seeing the gate open, pointed to it, saying—

"Here comes the pick of Spanish strength and manly beauty. Is there none among them whose love will suffice for you ?"

"None," the girl answered.

But she did not go away.

Standing beside Don Sebastian in an easy, graceful attitude, unabashed, and yet with a true modesty in her bearing, she watched the string of matadores and their following come forth.

CHAPTER LI.

DON SEBASTIAN AND THE MATADORE—A FRIENDLY WARNING—CARRUGIA SEEKS REVENGE.

FOREMOST was Carrugia, who walked along with as much swagger as he could muster for the occasion. His quick eye saw the Don, and with a bitter smile upon his face he saluted him.

"Don," he said, "accept my thanks. You have taught me how wise it is to be humble."

"It is a lesson we had all better learn without assistance," answered the Don.

Carrugia turned his eyes from the Don to Viardot, and recognised her with a look of pleased surprise.

"You here, my pretty village maid," he said; "and in such good company. I congratulate you."

"The company I keep is not your affair," answered Viardot; "and it will be better for you to keep a civil tongue in your head, or I will ask a friend of mine to chastise you."

"The name of that friend, I beg of you ?" asked Carrugia, politely.

"He is called Strongbow," answered Viardot ; "and he destroyed your reputation to-day. If you anger him he may to-morrow destroy you altogether."

The face of the matadore blanched. From a number of his followers, who had gathered around, were heard sounds of suppressed laughter.

"You are fortunate, fair lady," he said, "in having so many friends. It must be very pleasant and profitable."

The eyes of the girl flashed, and stepping forward she swiftly struck him upon the face with her open hand.

"Go away, dog !" she said.

The action took him by complete surprise, and the effect of it was to deprive him for a moment of both speech and motion.

Recovering himself he gave vent to an expression of anger, and thrust his hand into his sash.

Don Sebastian stepped between him and the girl.

"Pshaw ! man," he said. "Do not quarrel with a woman. Viardot, not even your beauty, which excuses a great deal, privileges you to strike Carrugia. You forget what is due to yourself, my child. Leave us, I beg of you."

The girl, with a smile of scorn upon her lips, passed her fingers contemptuously across the strings of her guitar and walked airily away.

Then Don Sebastian said to Carrugia—

"I am here to speak to you. Come with me."

They walked aside together, and the other matadores passed on, commenting on what they had seen and heard in a way not flattering to the deposed Carrugia.

The interview between Carrugia and the Don was very brief.

"Carrugia," said the latter, "I know what is in your heart, but there it must remain. You must not go beyond THINKING of assassination."

"Even a beaten dog longs for the last bite," urged Carrugia.

"But in your case he must go without it," said Don Sebastian, smoothly ; " if so much as the skin of Senor Strongbow or one of his friends is pricked by you or any of your gang I will have you, one and all, shot as brigands. That is all I have to say. You may now go to your friends, if you have any left."

"Don," said Carrugia, steadily, "if aught is done it will be done by ME, AND IT WILL BE DONE WELL. What matters if I am shot afterwards ? There is nothing left me to live for."

So saying he strode away with a quick step and disappeared.

And the Don, with a tinge of compassion for his fallen countryman upon his face, followed slowly, pondering as he went.

The night came on and once more Orveito was en fête.

It was a repetition of the night before, accentuated by additional people in the streets and the excitement of the day.

Once more there was the old drama of flirtation, love-making, rivalry, and hatred.

Many a quarrel was stopped by the friends of rivals, but tragedy was not absent.

Two young men and a girl, barely sixteen, were laid out in death by the too ready wielders of the knife or stiletto.

A commotion near the scene of crime followed each event, but it soon subsided.

It was little more than the casting of a stone into a pool of water.

Gloomily Carrugia stalked among the throng, hiding his face as well as he could with a broad straw hat, but here and there he was recognised and asked questions of a pertinent, not to say impertinent, nature. A fallen favourite meets with merciless treatment all over the world.

While in the zenith of his fame every vulgar mind worships him ; once down, their adulation is changed to derision.

He paid no attention to the jesters, save in one instance, when a man the worse for drink persisted in following him, calling out—

"Here comes Carrugia ! Make way for the man who was beaten by a cursed foreigner !"

On this man he turned and dealt him a blow that felled him to the earth, where he lay as if he had been dead.

"Is there anyone else who wants to feel the weight of the fist of a fallen man ?" cried Carrugia.

He was still high above the masses in strength and daring, and their only answer was to open out and let him pass.

The man whom he had knocked down was picked up by his friends and carried into a cabaret, to be restored with the aid of brandy or wine.

Carrugia wanted to meet with Dick Strongbow.

Not face to face, like a man, but unseen and unrecognised until he had plunged the stiletto he carried at his waist into his heart.

"After that," he muttered again and again, "they may hang or send me to the galleys for life."

He twice passed the hotel where our friends were staying—he had enquired all about that—and saw that they were out.

The few people on the balconies were not those he sought.

As he was going away on the second occasion he saw a face in the crowd moving up and down which he thought he knew

But he saw it so briefly that he could hardly tell whether it was a man or a woman's.

It just flashed before him for the infinitesimal portion of a second and it was gone.

"Where is that Strongbow ?" he asked himself.

At length he caught sight of the man he sought, seated outside a café of the better class.

Dick, Carl, and Ajax were at one table, smoking and drinking coffee, while Muffins and his adopted father, with Mr. and Mrs. Pardiggle Brown, sat near them.

Mr. Pardiggle Brown, after long reflection, had come to the conclusion that, taking things all round, he had rather distinguished himself in the arena than otherwise.

So he wore his hat very much on one side, and, with a big cigar in his mouth, was the image of self-complacency.

Mrs. Brown was happy too.

She had got her husband again, and was free, in a measure, to flirt with Butterflick, who accepted the glances and banterings with about as much emotion as a wooden figure would have exhibited.

Muffins was sufficiently occupied in watching the human panorama passing him.

With his elbows on the table, and his keen eyes never at rest, he took in everything and everybody.

Not even Carrugia was an exception.

The matador, as soon as he caught sight of Dick, drew back into the crowd, but the boy had seen him, and having heard of the possible violence which might be expected from him he was troubled.

Muffins bent over towards Dick, whispering—

"Master—master!"

"Well, what now, Muffins?" asked Dick. "Have you made any new discovery?"

"Perhaps he has found a senora worthy of his affections," said Carl.

"Eh! what's that?" asked Butterflick, dodging a playful dig with a fan which Mrs. Pardiggle Brown was about to favour him with.

"Muffins has fallen in love," said Carl.

"Nothing of the sort," replied Muffins. "I shouldn't think of such a thing. I'm not fool enough for THAT."

"Spoken like a true son of mine," said Butterflick, gravely. "If ever I hear of your going on that lay, I'll give you up for ever. What would your mother, old Sally, think of it I wonder?"

"I tell you I'm not thinking about such foolery," said Muffins, with a very stiff air; "I only wanted to tell master that I've seen Carrugia."

"Where?" quietly asked Dick.

"In the crowd to the right," replied Muffins; "he's just dodged back again."

"Ashamed of himself I should say," remarked Ajax. "I know what the feeling is to be utterly licked in a contest. It isn't nice, although," he added, with a sigh, "I'm not likely to experience it any more."

"Don't bother about Carrugia," said Dick, "he's nobody—now."

So they resumed their talk. Pardiggle Brown gave his hat a little more inclination, and his wife entered upon another course of allurement for the benefit of the immovable Butterflick.

Dick lighted a fresh cigar, and apparently Carrugia was speedily forgotten.

Nevertheless Dick felt that there was need of keeping his eyes open, and by assuming a carelessness which he did not feel he was able to quietly scan the crowd, especially that portion of it which passed in and out the café in two streams.

It was a hot night after a sultry day, and thirst was universal

The café inside was crowded, and the jingling of glasses and cups was like the tinkling of a thousand sheep-bells.

Dick's table was near the door, which was a wide one.

At least half-a-dozen people could pass in abreast.

The in and out streams were about three people broad, but varied occasionally, according to circumstances.

Presently it happened that more were going in than coming out, and there was a temporary block.

On the far side of the in-goers was Carrugia, walking with a slight stoop, and his hat drawn down well over his eyes.

His object was doubtless to get into the café unseen, and then come out behind Dick to carry out his fell purpose.

Dick, of course, was not certain about that, but with the warning given by Don Sebastian still in his ears, he could not give Carrugia credit for being there without a motive.

But there was another figure in the crowd which Dick did not see.

It was that of the girl Viardot.

She followed Carrugia into the café, and almost immediately after a commotion took place.

Voices rose high, and, as there would have been in any place in the wide world when a multitude had gathered together, there was an immediate press inward of people inspired by curiosity.

Such a chattering was heard that it was impossible to tell what was going on, but a cue was given by the appearance of Viardot being ejected by two waiters.

In a moment Dick was upon his feet.

"Let go of that lady!" he thundered.

"She has insulted a matadore," replied one of the men. "Who are you to interfere?"

Dick's answer was to seize the wrist of the hand by which he held the girl, and then he gave it a nip with his finger and thumb, which caused the waiter with a howl to let go of Viardot.

"Santa Maria!" yelled the man, "he has crushed my arm."

The other man looked keenly at Dick and also let go his hold.

"It is the English matadore!" he screamed.

And now the crowd around Dick and Viardot became so great as to separate them from Carl and the rest.

Several tables were overturned, and there seemed to be the prospect of a row approaching a riot.

Carrugia, a few paces away, was urging the crowd to attack Dick.

"He sent that woman to insult me. Not satisfied with having, by devilish arts, beaten me to-day, he seeks my life!" he cried.

It is natural for people to stick up for their own countryman, and the Spaniards began to scowl and curse and finger their knives.

The pressure around Dick became closer.

"Viardot," he whispered, "you must go away. I have friends near—let me make a way for you."

"Oh! let me remain," she said; "the gendarmes will soon be here. Carrugia means to assassinate you."

Dick's answer was to push aside some of the people near until he had cleared a path to Carl.

"Take care of her," said Dick, gently pushing Viardot to him; "I will be back in a moment."

"Don't go, master," cried Muffins.

The others cried out too; but Dick, heedless of their words, pushed his way through the crowd again and entered the café.

In truth he had need to do little pushing, for now that he was known few cared to attempt to bar his way.

And Carrugia—what of him?

He saw all that took place, and would have fled, but there was only one way out, and that was by the door.

He could not depart that way, so he must remain and face it out.

The people fell away from him as Dick advanced, and a ring was involuntarily made, in which he and Dick were left alone, with a few overturned chairs.

Dick had no weapon. The Spaniard's stiletto glittered in his hand.

Chivalry is not yet dead in Spain, and one of the

foremost men, drawing a long, keen knife, tossed it into the ring.

"Take it, senor," he cried ; "the fight should be a fair one."

"I thank you," replied Dick, without looking towards the man ; "but I do not need it."

CHAPTER LII.

A SCENE IN THE CAFE—FINAL HUMILIATION OF THE MATADORE.

ICK'S eyes were upon Carrugia, on whose face was a snarl like that of an angry tiger.

As yet he did not know exactly the power of his antagonist. He felt that he could kill an unarmed man easily.

"If you will not have a weapon," he said, "your death be upon your own head !"

And then he made his spring.

It was sudden and swift, so that he looked more like a tiger than ever.

But Dick was prepared for him.

He jumped on one side, and Carrugia passed him, to be seized the next moment by the arms behind.

Dick held him just above the elbows and pressed them in with a force that threatened to break in the ribs of the matadore.

He uttered a strange cry, the like of which few there had ever heard before.

It was the cry of mortal fear, which has an accent of its own, like no other sound on earth, and it is much the same no matter from what lips it springs.

His fingers opened a little and the knife fell to the ground. Then his head sunk forward and his legs relaxed, so that he would have fallen but for Dick's grip.

He had fainted away.

Dick held him up to be viewed by the people.

"You must find a better man than this to fight me," he said, and then, gently enough, he laid him upon the floor.

"When he comes round," he said, "tell him never to be rash enough to attempt to injure me again, or anyone connected with me. If so, his life will pay the penalty."

Then he motioned for the crowd to let him pass, and they moved aside, their eyes fixed on him wonderingly.

As Samson of old was a startling phenomenon to the Philistines, so Dick was to the Spaniards that night.

After he was gone they picked up their fallen hero, who in a little while gave signs of returning consciousness.

He opened his eyes, cast a glance around, and recalled everything.

A shudder of fear shook his stalwart frame.

"Where is HE ?" he asked.

"Gone," they replied.

He rose slowly from his chair.

"Let me go, too," he said ; "I have something to get over, if I can. I have known to-night what

it is to see death. I felt my life going out of me ; he could have crushed me even if I had been made of iron."

"He left a message for you, Carrugia," said one of the bystanders.

"Ah ! a threat, perhaps."

"No—a warning. If ever you think of doing him an injury again he—"

"I need not hear any more," said Carrugia ; "I shall never dare to do so. Let me pass—I am sick and I want to sleep."

He went from them with the step of one advanced in years, and was soon lost in the crowd.

Then there was a movement outside to get another glimpse of Dick.

But he was gone, and the seats occupied lately by himself and friends had been taken possession of by others.

And then those who had witnessed the scene scattered, to talk of Dick Strongbow, and spread his fame wider and wider.

.   .   .   .

Travelling in a straight line from Orveito to Madrid is not possible even in these days.

Railways have never found in Spain that encouragement they have met with in other Continental nations, and the consequence is that half the rich country does not know how the other half travels.

To put it in other words, half the Spaniards have never set eyes on the chief modern means of locomotion.

At the time we write of Spain was in a disturbed state.

Don Carlos had laid claim to the throne, and was seeking to win it by force of arms.

As a pretender he always took first rank, and really made a good show as a monarchical claimant and general.

Travelling from Orveito to Madrid was, perforce, carried on to a great extent by road.

The railway, such as it was, could not be considered safe travelling, as the Carlists had destroyed portions of the permanent way, and threatened to destroy more.

The safest mode of progression was therefore by diligence, and on the backs of mules.

As for the diligence, it had of late had so few passengers that when Dick Strongbow applied for seats for himself and party, he found that he had the whole vehicle at his service.

So far all was well.

In addition to his close friends, Mr. and Mrs. Pardiggle Brown had expressed a desire to travel with him, and he could not say nay to them.

"But I warn you," he said to them, "that we may be beset by Carlists, who will show you just as much mercy as you would get from brigands."

"That doesn't matter," said Mrs. Pardiggle Brown, cheerfully, "for you are quite a match for a hundred brigands."

It was pleasing to find so much confidence placed in him, but Dick was not anxious to prove that he could be a match for a hundred ruffians armed with rifles.

But he was not troubled with fears, and the Browns joined his party.

He and his friends took the precaution to be well armed, but Pardiggle Brown was requested to travel without any.

"Why ?" asked Pardiggle Brown, indignantly.

DICK STRONGBOW:

The Diamond King,
AND WONDER OF THE WORLD.

Don Timole lunged forward and pricked the Spaniard in the breast.

No. 12.   Price One Penny.

" Because you are more likely to shoot one of us than any enemy you may aim at," said Butterflick, " or, worse than that, you may bring down your lovely wife like a tom-tit from a pole."

The simile was not particularly pleasant, but " lovely wife " fairly fetched Mrs. Pardiggle Brown, who declared that her husband should not carry so much as a walking-stick for fear of his doing mischief

The diligence started from an inn near the arena, and the party had to be there by eight in the morning.

On putting in an appearance Dick was told that one more seat had been taken—an inside one—by a lady.

She was already in possession of it, he was informed, and Dick's curiosity was aroused.

Peering into the diligence, he saw a woman with her mantilla dropped over her face, apparently asleep.

Mrs. Pardiggle Brown was to be an inside passenger also, but the men elected to ride outside.

In addition to the driver there was a guard, and both of them wore a very gorgeous dress, such as the hero of " Fra Diavolo " wears upon the stage.

Each was armed—the driver with a rifle, and the guard with an old-fashioned blunderbus.

Both these valiant men had moustaches, which, in a case of emergency, would have served as black-ing brushes.

Neither of them knew Dick Strongbow, as they had not been at the bull-fight.

Nor had Dick entered himself by name, and he was, therefore, quite a stranger to them. Two horses of the boniest kind were harnessed to drag the heavy diligence, and at half-past eight, half-an-hour behind time, they started.

About a score of idlers gathered to see them off, and the guard played a farewell blast on a huge horn, formed of bent brass-tubing, which, if straightened out, would have been about eighteen feet long.

Orveito was soon left behind, and they went lumbering along a road, the chief charm of which was its roughness.

It was evidently not the work of the Romans, or of any experienced body of road-makers known to the world.

The guard exhibited his blunderbus, and talked mainly to Dick about its potency as a weapon.

According to his statement it could at one dis-charge, if properly aimed, sweep about two score men off the face of the earth.

" It is the terror of the Carlists," he said.

Nobody took much interest in it but Mr. Par-diggle Brown, who was awed by its bell-shaped mouth and enormous trigger.

Being anxious to know how it was loaded and fired, the guard proceeded to show him how it was done, and in the act of doing so let it off accidentally.

Fortunately, beyond singing the right whisker of Mr. Pardiggle Brown, it did no harm except to waste about five ounces of powder and fifty bullets of dif-ferent sizes and shapes, and startling the horses so that for two minutes they fairly galloped.

The driver called the guard a " pig," and the guard told the driver that he was " the son of a Seville ass," which exchange of compliments seemed to refresh them both, as they afterwards burst into song

At the end of ten miles or thereabouts they stopped at an inn to change horses, but here they met with a check.

The landlord came out, and, with tears in his eyes, informed the driver that the Carlists had the day before requisitioned all his horses.

He could do nothing until more arrived from a market town, whither he had despatched a trusted servant to buy some.

" Would not," he asked, " the senor and senoras alight and favour his humble hostelry with their company for a day or so ?"

Dick Strongbow said " No !"

" If," he added, " there are no horses here we must go on with what we have."

He was so firm, and so well supported by his friends, that the guard suddenly woke up to action, and, producing his blunderbus, he demanded horses of the landlord on peril of his being blown into bits so small that the eye of his wife should not find them.

And then, strange to say, the horses required were brought out.

They were, if possible, a worse lot than the first set, and the look of them would have given a London busman the heart-ache.

" We shall never travel five miles with that lot of brutes," whispered Carl.

" We must do the best we can," said Dick. " I think the fellow has given us the best he has."

They started in a little while, with the assistance of two ostlers and the landlord, who urged on the noble steeds with most fearful curses and sounding kicks in the ribs.

The horses shambled along, and the diligence rolled and creaked.

It was a most excruciating mode of travelling.

Muffins alone enjoyed it.

Anything in the way of novelty was good fun to him, and every roll of the ponderous vehicle created the ecstactic feeling experienced by the young people who get into a swing at a fair, and in the shallow, boat-like car, risk their necks by exciting upward flights.

The country became both sterile and lonely.

In a rocky sense it was picturesque enough, but in a verdant one it was uncommonly dreary.

Here and there they passed a hut which, the guard said, was the home of a peasant, but deserted.

" Everyone joins the Carlists, or runs away from them," he said, " unless it happens to be a man in a public position like myself."

" And what would you do, if you met any of them ?" asked Butterflick.

He put the question in English, and Dick trans-lated it.

The answer was, " Fight them—blow them into the company of the people in purgatory."

" I don't believe you would hit a elephant in a week !" said Butterflick.

" What did he say ?" asked the guard, who, of course, spoke his native tongue only.

" He says it would be a bad job for a regiment of them if they met you," Carl translated.

" It is so," said the guard, complacently, rubbing his stubby moustache.

The road now lay between two rugged hills, not exactly bare of vegetation, but nearly so.

Overhead towered masses of piled up rocks, which looked as hot as bricks in the kiln, and were indeed nearly so, thanks to the powerful sun.

It was glaring to the eye, and it was with a sigh of relief that the guard called their attention to a wood ahead.

"Two miles of trees," he said, "and most of them sweet chestnuts. The nuts are ripening, and almost fit to eat."

"I can't bear chestnuts," said Pardiggle Brown.

"Pardon, you say?" inquired the guard, in Spanish.

"He says he came to Spain especially to taste the chestnuts in their home," translated Carl.

"It's been a joy in store," said the guard.

The diligence now entered the wood through which the roadway had been made many years before.

But the trees still grew thick at the sides, and the wood appeared to be generally very dense.

Ere they had gone far the diligence suddenly pulled up.

The guard immediately began to shake all over, and to cock his blunderbus.

"What is the matter?" asked Dick.

"Brigands, replied the driver. "They have felled trees and blocked the road."

It was so, as a look ahead showed.

About a score of trees had been felled and tumbled about in a disorderly manner, so as to completely block the road.

The diligence could go no further.

CHAPTER LIII.

CARLISTS OR BRIGANDS—A VERY STRANGE DEN —HIS BIT OF A COTTAGE.

ERE was a predicament.

The driver had no need to pull up his horses. They were only too willing to stop on the least provocation. All the men descended to look at the obstruction.

That it had been deliberately cut down was clear enough, and the first natural thought was that it was the work of brigands.

But the driver was of a different opinion.

"It is only the Carlists," he said. "There's a lot of them in the neighbourhood, and they probably expect the arrival of some royal troopers."

"But I say," cried Pardiggle Brown, "where are the authorities, and the police, that this sort of thing is allowed to go on?"

"There is no real authority," said Dick; "as for the police, what could they do with this obstruction?"

"Can YOU do anything with it?" asked Pardiggle Brown.

"With a cross-cut saw," replied Dick, laughing,

"or some powder perhaps. After all, I am but mortal."

"Well, I call it a derned mean trick," said Butterflick.

"Isn't there any way round?"

The question was put to the driver by Carl, and his reply was that there were several ways round, but all were impassable from some cause or the other.

Here the voice of Mrs. Pardiggle Brown was heard.

"What are we stopping for?" she asked, from the window.

"Because we can't get on any further, my dear," replied her husband.

"That's a donkey's answer."

"If it is, my dear, it is a true one."

"I'm tired of this sort of travelling," said Mrs. Pardiggle Brown, "especially with a young person who hasn't opened her mouth all the way. I'd like ANYTHING better than this."

Bang—bang!

The desired change was at hand.

The rifles were only a short distance away, and bullets were heard to whizz overhead.

"Brigands!" said Carl.

"No, senor—Carlists," insisted the driver.

"I strongly suspect there is not much difference," said Dick, calmly.

Whichever they were, they soon made themselves manifest.

From all sides they came, a motley crew of ragged Spaniards, with a mixture of other races.

One of their number was, however, gorgeously attired, and he appeared to be the leader.

He came from the left, one of the foremost, a man of about thirty, attired in a velvet tunic, with a broad leather belt, in which several pistols were stuck. He wore high boots and a broad, flapping hat, with several feathers in it.

In his hand he carried a long, straight sword.

"Begorro!" he cried; "if ye're not about the funkiest lot I iver come across. Divil take it! ye don't understand a word of what I'm saying."

And then he began to rate them in Spanish, which, to put it politely, was not exactly of the best.

On nearing the party he doffed his hat and favoured them with a bow worthy of a Spanish nobleman.

"The top o' the morning to every mother's son of ye," he said. "Divil take it again, they don't understand."

"Pardon me," said Dick, "but we DO understand. We are real Britishers, except the driver and guard."

"Blessed be the powers if ye're not welcome then!" said the leader, grasping Dick's hand. "It's long since I heard the true language. And what may ye be doing here now?"

"We are travelling, and have been stopped by this obsruction."

"You don't say so? Then it's Don Timole Murphaleo as will give you a bit of his hospitality."

When Dick heard the name of the leader he burst out laughing; but Timole, cocking his hat over his left eye, regarded him with indignation.

"What be ye afther laughing for now?" he asked.

"Why, you are an Irishman, are you not?" said Dick.

"Divil a bit," was the answer; "as true Spanish as iver was born."

"But you speak like one."

"Ah! that's because I learnt the language in good old Dublin City, glory be to it, and long life to ivery one in the old counthry! Now let us see what we've here," he continued. "Any mail-bag in this diligence?"

"None, senor," replied Carl.

"Ah! the sharpers, to be stingy of sich things. But niver mind. What's that I see—a purty face at the window? Senora, it's myself that's your humble servant."

"Go away, you wretch!" cried Mrs. Pardiggle Brown, who had been thus tenderly addressed.

"Descend, my lovely creetur," said Don Timole Murphaleo, as he opened the door; "come and press the soft turf with your lovely little feet."

Mrs. Pardiggle Brown did as she was told, partly subdued by the compliments bestowed upon her, and partly because she did not know what else to do.

Don Timole peered inside the diligence.

"Ah!" he exclaimed, "is it another angel I see. Come down, my purty bird."

"She's Spanish and don't understand you," said Mrs. Pardiggle Brown.

"And isn't it a Spaniard I am myself?" demanded the leader. "Glory to the day when I picked up the swatest tongue in the world in old Dublin."

Then in Spanish he bade the other occupant descend, which she did, with the mantilla still over her face.

But it was only a poor disguise after all. Dick, as soon as he got a fair view of her, saw that it was Viardot.

"This lady," he said to the chief, "is a friend of mine."

He stepped to her side and she let her mantilla fall, revealing her pretty face.

"Begorra," said Don Timole, as he called himself, "a man could get along with many such friends. What's this you've left behind, my dear—a guitar? It's myself that can play on that same thing, and I'll sing to ye by-and-bye. Meanwhile we'll just, one and all, come to my bit of a cottage and rest a bit."

He gave out a few words of command to the men, who had been standing around motionless and silent, and they immediately closed in.

"Prisoners, by Jupiter!" exclaimed Butterflick.

"Resistance would be useless," whispered Dick; "let us go with him. I do not think any great harm will ensue."

The prisoners were marshalled two and two, the women being requested to walk together, and about half of the men formed themselves into a guard around them.

"The rest," Don Timole explained, "would remain behind to protect that same diligence from thaves."

"It's an absurd position to be in," said Dick, "but I don't see how we can help ourselves."

"Brigands or Carlists?" asked Carl.

"Not exactly brigands," said Dick.

"Fall in—march!" cried Don Timole, "and none of ye need trouble about your luggage. That will be brought after ye."

He led the way back for a short distance, and then turned into a path on the right, just wide enough to allow the cavalcade to proceed in the order in which they started.

Don Timole, in front, lit up a big cigar, and walked on briskly, with a jaunty step, occasionally flourishing his sword.

Once he broke into song—

"When first I saw swate Peggy,
'Twas on a market day;
In a low-back car she rode and sat,
Upon a thruss of hay."

"Ah! be jabers," he exclaimed, aloud, "it's that same song as will go well with the guytar, and there's a thrate in store for some of ye."

Nothwithstanding the annoyance arising from their position our friends felt amused.

The leader was so jaunty and gay, and his followers so solemn, as to make the contrast very ludicrous.

Now and then he would favour them with a bit of the language he had "picked up in ould Dublin."

"It's the swatest collection of pig-headed asses ye are!" he said, "with nivir a smile on your faces. Ye'd make good barbers' dummies ivery son of ye."

That was about the style of his powerful addresses, and even Mrs. Pardiggle Brown got a laugh out of them.

Half an hour brought them to open ground again, and there, right before them, perched upon a hill, was as extensive a castle as any of the party had ever seen.

This was Don Timole's "bit of a cottage," as he called it, and he pointed towards it with his sword, looking back upon the prisoners.

"It's there ye'll meet with hospitality as ye'll not forget," he said; "and, divil a bit, if ye're complaisant, and behave like gintlemen, will any harm come to any of ye!"

————

CHAPTER LIV.

WITHIN THE CASTLE—A DISMAL CREW OF CARLISTS—SEPARATING THE PRISONERS.

GRANDER scenery of its class would not have been easy to find.

The mountains, picturesque in shape, were of many shades and colours, owing to the different nature of the rocks, and on every point of vantage a tree or trees had been planted.

Near the wood vines grew in profusion.

The grapes were not ripe as yet, but the clusters hung thickly, waiting for the sun to make them wholesome food for man.

Wild flowers in every spot where their roots could get a hold added to the beauty of the scene.

But, strange to say, the castle, though but the work of man, dominated over all.

It was of such vast extent and had so many towers and high walls—arranged with an eye to true effect—that it was the first to engage the attention of the observer and hold it.

"My little cottage," said Don Timole, calling.

needless attention to it again, "and by the piper that made the lakes of Killarney still wid his music there's room in it for every pig in ould Oireland."

"It seems a mighty place," said Phil Norton. "Is it garrisoned?"

"Filled wid soldiers, do you mane?" asked Don Timole. "By the powers, it's got some in it, all friends of the true King of Spain, Don Carlos."

On hearing this all the prisoners breathed freely.

They had not fallen into the hands of brigands, but into the power of one of the armies of Spain.

"Is the Don Carlos there?" asked Pardiggle Brown.

"HE there! No," replied Don Timole. "It's not big enough for him—bless all the hairs of his head! Don't I tell ye it's MY bit of a cottage?"

With an indignant wrench of his body, real or feigned, he gave the word to move on, and the cavalcade proceeded up a path that led to the castle.

It was zigzag by design, and an invader approaching it would have to run the gauntlet of many places where a handful of men could hold the ground against a regiment.

The castle seemed to be very near, but it took them half an hour to reach its huge, heavy gateway, accessible by a drawbridge, which was down.

Don Timole, with the handle of his sword, thrice struck an iron plate upon one of the gates, and immediately both rolled back.

Having passed under an archway with a heavy portcullis suspended above, the prisoners found themselves in a courtyard, where quite a host of men were lying or hanging about.

They were fully as ragged and dejected as the lot escorting the prisoners, at whose arrival they made no demonstration whatever.

"What's the matter with the fellows?" asked Carl; "are they dumb?"

"I know what's the matter with 'em," said Butterflick.

"Well, what is it?"

"They're clemmed—half starved—but it don't show so much through their dark skins as it does with proper white people. Just look at 'em."

Butterflick had hit upon the truth.

Dick saw that the followers of the Spanish Pretender were indeed in a bad way as to food as well as clothing.

Their listlessness was the outcome of the weakness of semi-starvation.

Don Timole was the better fed man of the lot, but even he was not in exactly prime condition.

His cheerfulness acted as a cloak to his real condition.

"Rouse ye every man!" he cried, in Spanish; "glory to the arms of Don Carlos—another victory!"

Nobody responding, he showed his activity in another direction. Taking a short, knotted piece of rope out of his pocket, he gave the nearest Spaniard to him a smart cut with it.

"Dance, look lively, you garlick-loving spalpeen," he cried. "Is this the way to receive honoured guests? If you don't skip a bit on your own account, be jabers I'll make ye?"

His energetic words and the application of the rope caused something of a stir among the men, and at his bidding a number of them passed into the main building in the interior of the castle to prepare chambers for the guests.

"It's a bit of dividing I shall have to do," he said; "but, on the word of a jintleman, no harm shall come to any of ye without due notice. First of all, the ladies," he went on; "they must be attended to, bless 'em! Now, ye divils, some of ye escort these ladies to the velvet chamber."

"May I ask what all this means?" asked Dick Strongbow.

"All in good time, my friend," replied Don Timole; "you won't be siperated entoirely. Now, ladies, if you please."

They had to go, Viardot walking proudly and Mrs. Pardiggle Brown softly weeping.

The next three ordered off were Ajax, Phil Norton, and Brown, to whom was apportioned the amber chamber. Butterflick and Muffins were dispatched next, and Dick and Carl remained.

"Before I send you to the state apartment," said Don Timole, "I'd like a word or two with you two jintlemen. As for the driver of the diligence, all he's got to do is to enlist in the service of King Carlos."

The driver, who had been standing apart, made a sign of protest.

"Very well," said Don Timole, airily, "just as you like, my darlint. Not being for King Carlos ye must be against him, and in an hour ye'll be shot as a rebel."

This announcement had a startling effect upon the driver, who at once declared that he was ready to fight for King Carlos in preference to being shot.

"I'll deal with ye mercifully this time," said Don Timole, "and let ye off. Once with King Carlos always with him, for by Father Mathew—rest his bones!—if the other side lay hold of you, they will hang you right away."

Leaving the driver to digest this rather startling announcement, he motioned to Dick and Carl to follow him, and led them away into the interior of the castle.

A short passage brought them to a banqueting hall, bare of everything but an oak table.

It was entirely deserted, and did not present the appearance of having been recently used for a feast.

Crossing it, Don Timole opened one of half-a-dozen doors within a few feet of each other, and a second short passage brought them to a moderate sized chamber.

Here, some attempt had been made to make it habitable.

The furniture consisted of a table, half-a-dozen rough chairs, a low wooden couch, and a few cooking utensils. Light came through narrow slits in the wall, high up, near the ceiling.

CHAPTER LV.

SHORT OF FURNITURE—MUFFINS DOES A BIT OF
CHIMNEY WORK—UNEXPECTED FREEDOM.

HAT do ye think of this?" asked Don Timole; "isn't it iligant?"

"I suppose it is all you require," replied Dick, evasively, "and he who has that is well served."

"For all that," said Don Timole, taking a seat, "I can see you don't think much of it. Anyway, you've now got your eyes on every blessed bit o' furniture in the place. Sit down. Not that chair—it's got a weak leg. The two agin the wall are strong enough to bear an elephant."

They sat down, and Dick, who was beginning to have his doubts, proceeded to put a question to his host.

"Again," he said, "let me ask why we are brought here."

"It's me purpose to gratify you as to that," replied Don Timole. "Don Carlos is King of Spain, and his majesty is mighty short o' money. Be jabers! if an imp danced in his pocket he wouldn't just now-chip his shins against a shilling. It's meself that's his right-hand field-marshal. 'Murphaleo,' he says, 'it's your duty to get me money from somewhere, and if ye don't do it, make your will and lay in the drink for a wake, for, as sure I'm King of Spain, I'll make a corpse of you.'"

"And you look for money from us?" suggested Dick.

Don Timole nodded.

"How much?" asked Dick.

"If ye'll give an order on your London banker for ten thousand you can go—all of you."

"And how do you know I have so much?"

"It's not meself that knows it," replied Don Timole, with twinkling eyes, "but Don Carlos does. It's money we must have; and ye name's good. The Don knows what to do with a bit o' paper ye may sign."

"Why this is brigandage," exclaimed Carl.

"It's got a bit of a look of it," said Don Timole, candidly; "but ye mustn't put it on me. I came here to fight; but it's Don Carlos—a murrain—a blessin' on his name—that's the making of a thafe of me."

"If you object to it why don't you leave his service?" asked Dick.

"It would be a sure putting of my head into a rope," replied Don Timole; "for that baste of a usurper would show me no quarter. It's a poor look out all around, for it's roasted horse beans and sour grapes we're livin' on now in this bit of a cottage."

They sat looking at his smiling face for a few moments thinking he was jesting, but his eyes, always the most speaking part of a face, told them that he had uttered a solemn truth.

"Horse beans," he said; "and some as hard as bits of iron—it's mighty quare! As for a dhrop of whiskey, it's so long since I tasted it that I should have to drink hard for a fortnight to bring back the flavour of it."

"I should like a little time to think it over," said Dick. "Ten thousand pounds is a large sum of money."

"Ye'll have the note o' hand of Don Carlos for it," hinted Don Timole, with his head knowingly on one side.

"And what may that be worth?"

"Every penny, with interest, when he's knocked the usurper on the head."

"That won't happen to day, or to-morrow," said Dick.

"Well, you can have time, but not much," said Don Timole, "for if there's not something done soon I'm afraid my regiment will forget their bringing's up and turn cannibals. The first choice mossel would, of course, be that dainty creature who came with you."

"Is that a threat?"

"Divil a bit. It's a starn fact. There are six hundred men in this bit of a place, and not more'n handful of beans each left. It's clear to ye that they must eat something, and they'll go for the daintiest first. I'll show ye to your chamber, and leave you for an hour."

He escorted them from the room, through several passages, and finally deposited them in a place utterly destitute of anything in the way of furniture.

There was a huge fireplace, and a few slits in the walls for windows, but nothing else to relieve the monotony of the place.

"It's little throuble ye'll have to kape the place tidy," said Don Timole; "just a touch o' the broom and it's done for a week."

"But surely you don't mean to keep us here so long?" said Dick.

"It's not myself that's keeping you," answered the Don, "but the thrue king of Spain, Carlos by name, and glory to him."

"Every day," he added, "ye'll have a few hours for exercise, and maybe ye'll meet your friends and talk over the position—d'ye see?"

They did see, and the spectacle was far from pleasing, but they said no more to him, and with a sweeping bow he left them.

"Carl," said Dick, "if we had but known or guessed, we might not have given in so easy."

"It's a fix," replied Carl. "Prisoners on a fare of roast beans and sour grapes—ugh."

They examined the place, which did not take long, the chimney to the fireplace being the chief object of interest.

It was very wide right away to the top apparently, but it was so high that it was difficult to tell.

A number of iron bars were fixed in it to prevent escape by that way, and they were stout enough to defy even the vast strength of Dick Strongbow.

"It's about the most confounded mess we have been in," said Dick, "and really so absurd, which makes it worse. I wonder how the others are getting on?"

In a similar chamber immediately above were Butterflick and Muffins, also a bit in the dumps.

They, too, had nothing better than a chimney to examine, but, unlike that below, they could not see very far up. It did not run straight, but by a bend communicated with the main one.

There also were iron bars across, and any attempt to get out that way appeared to be futile.

"Muffy, my boy," said Butterflick, "if your mother, old Sally, knew of the predicament we are in, it would break her heart."

Muffins was not so much moved as he ought to have been to hear that his "mother's" heart was so tender.

He could not as yet accept her as his maternal parent, although Butterflick, by his curious process of reasoning, had given her that position.

"I wonder whether he was joking?" said Muffins, after a pause.

"He—who?" asked Butterflick.

"That Irish chap," replied Muffins, "when he talked about roast beans and sour grapes."

"If he wasn't it'll be serious to us," said Butterflick, "for I don't mind telling you, my son, that I'm getting a bit peckish. I could do with a nice steak now, with pertaties, gravy, and new bread."

"Don't, dad," pleaded Muffins. "I can't bear to think of anything better than a dry crust."

"Beans and grapes!" moaned Butterflick. "We shall be skellingtons in three days, and dead in a week."

"Dad," said Muffins, "I must do something to keep me from thinking of it. Will you give me a leg up the chimney?"

"What for, my son?"

"To see if there isn't a way out of this den."

"You may find one," sighed Butterflick; "but I don't think there is."

Anyhow, there was nothing like trying, so Muffins got his "leg up," and, laying hold of the lowest iron bar, pulled himself up between it and the wall.

There was just room for him to do so, thanks to his spare form; but a fat boy or a man would invariably have stuck fast.

"All right, dad," he said; "I can get along. There's daylight a little higher up."

"Don't go away too far,' said Butterflick, anxiously, "and lose yourself. In some of these old places the chimbleys is reg'lar maizes."

"You mustn't worry, dad. I shan't come to any harm," said Muffins.

He got the best of the first obstacle, and stood upon the bar. A second one impeded his way, and he wriggled past that to find himself opposite the opening leading into the main chimney.

The latter was, of course, that which Dick and Carl had inspected.

Muffins got into it without much difficulty, and sitting on a bar looked about him.

Which way should he go—up or down?

It so happened that Dick and his friend were silent at the time, so Muffins, unaware of their vicinity, decided to go higher.

The bars were so close together that he could stand upon one and grasp the next overhead. Wriggling his way upward, he presently came to another opening, similar to that he had passed through below.

From this came the sound of voices, and in one of them he recognised the tones of the Carlist leader, Don Timole.

Muffins crept along, came to another inner chimney, and, descending some half-dozen bars, stopped for a rest.

The twanging of a guitar now fell upon his ears. The instrument was evidently touched by an inexperienced hand.

"Shure, it's a lovely thing," Muffins heard Don Timole say; "the music of it goes straight to the heart. Shall I sing to you, purty creetur'?"

"Go away, you wretch!" replied a voice, not exactly indignantly, but with gentle anger.

"Old Mother Brown," thought Muffins.

"If you strike the strings in that way," said the sweet voice of Viardot, "you will break them."

She spoke in Spanish, which Muffins only imperfectly comprehended.

The reply of Don Timole was in the language he had picked up in Dublin City, glory to it.

"Faith, ye swate angel, it's the sthrings of my heart ye've struck and broken."

"Are you talking to me?" asked Mrs. Pardiggle Brown.

"Faith, and to no other—bless the roses on your cheeks!"

"Don't you know I'm a married woman?"

"I'll take yer word for it; but the king shall grant us a divorce, and we'll send old Brown to the divil."

Then he gave another bang upon the guitar and began to sing—

> "*Soft o'er the fountain,*
> *Lingering falls the southern moon;*
> *Far o'er the mountain,*
> *Breaks the day too soon.*"

"It's a lovely song," he said, stopping short, "and the hinder part of it's the swatest, only I've forgotten it, my honey. It's time for me to go, so I'll just take a kiss all round, for friendship's sake."

"Come near me if you dare!" cried Mrs. Pardiggle Brown, in tragic tones.

"It's the younger one I'll begin wid, sure then," said Don Timole, in an insinuating tone.

"I carry a stiletto," replied the girl.

"Was there iver sich unreasonable craythures," said Don Timole; "but I'll not leave ye both so coldly. Mrs. Brown, I expect ye to be more complaisant."

The sound of scuffling ensued, and Muffins, in his eagerness to see what was going on, dropped down to the hearth below.

The sight he beheld was a most exhilarating one.

Mrs. Pardiggle Brown had got possession of the guitar, and holding it aloft like a battle-axe, was about to strike, she having pinned the amorous Timole by the back of the neck with her disengaged hand.

Viardot had made for the door, which she was in the act of pulling open.

The next moment she would have vanished, but Muffins, seeing his opportunity, rushed out of his place of concealment and called to her by name.

She turned, and seeing who it was, smiled gladly and beckoned to him to come out.

He was soon by her side and she closed the door.

A bunch of keys were hanging from the lock outside.

She locked them in.

"Ought we to leave the old woman?" asked Muffins.

Viardot shook her head. She did not understand him.

Then she made signs indicating her desire to let out the other prisoners.

"Below," said Muffins, turning his thumbs downwards.

A stone staircase was hard by, and down this they hurried to the floor below.

"Dad's here," said Muffins, pointing to a door.

Viardot glanced at the lock, and quickly singling out the right key unlocked it.

Butterflick inside had his head up the chimney. He was calling for his lost child.

"Come down you little beggar!" he was saying, "or I'll give it to you for scaring me to death. Have you stuck fast or lost yourself? Come down!"

Muffins hurried across the room on tiptoe, and gave his anxious foster-parent a dig in the back.

"Here I am!" he said.

Butterflick turned round and stared at him as if he were a ghost instead of flesh and blood.

"Here, you know this lady," said Muffins. "She's got the keys. Let us find the others."

Viardot was beckoning them impatiently to come out, and down they hastened to the floor below.

The Spanish girl, seeing another door, tried two or three keys, and having found the right one opened it.

Dick and Carl were walking up and down the chamber, and the appearance of the party of rescuers was a complete surprise.

Viardot beckoned to them to vacate, and, short as had been their confinement, they had had quite enough of it, so they readily responded.

CHAPTER LVI.

ALL RELEASED—DON TIMOLE AND THE CARLISTS —A CLEARING OUT.

KEEP your heads cool, gentlemen," said Butterflick; "I'm blowed if mine isn't like a humming-top."

"Viardot," said Dick, "how came you to our assistance?"

The girl waved her hands towards Muffins, whose face was aglow with excitement.

"I went up the chimbley," he said, "and got into two other chimbleys, then into a room where the ladies were, and we've locked in the Irish Don with old Mo—Mrs. Brown, and she's hammering him with the guitar."

Two or three questions made the facts of the case clearer, and Dick's first thought was for the others in confinement.

"We must find Brown, Phil, and Ajax," he said, "and we can't leave Mrs. Brown with that wild Irishman. There's no harm in him in my opinion, but we must have her."

They returned upstairs, and Dick, taking the keys, opened the door of the chamber in which that august lady was confined.

They found her in a state of exhaustion with Don Timole, who was fanning her with his hat. He did not show so much surprise on seeing the party as might have been expected.

"'Sorry the day," he said, "that iver I made love to this faithful darlint. Let Brown be proud of her."

Strange to say, the arrival of her friends acted as a complete restorative to Mrs. Pardiggle Brown.

She released herself from his supporting arm and aimed a blow at him, which he dodged.

"Where are the others?" cried Dick.

"Right at the top, in the golden chamber," replied Don Timole.

"I presume," said Carl, "that you use the old names for these desolate dens?"

"Divil a bit!" replied Don Timole. "I named 'em all myself, and I found 'em just as they are. Confound 'em all!"

He was requested to accompany them, which he readily did, leading the way right to the top of the tower, where in a room of smaller dimensions they discovered Ajax, Phil, and Brown.

There was now for the first time a good deal of joyous greeting all round, Dick, meanwhile, keeping an eye on Don Timole, who, however, showed no disposition to run away.

On the contrary, he with coolness, and what Butterflick called "cheek," joined in the general congratulations, totally ignoring his share in their recent incarceration.

"It's a blessed moment for us all, he said, "and it'll be a shock to them bastes of Spaniards when they find we've circumvented 'em. May ivery mother's son of 'em live on beans for iver."

"You take things pretty much as they come," said Dick.

"It's as well," said Don Timole. "When I found I must be a Carlist, I jined 'em, and a mangy lot they are, rest 'em early in their graves! Perhaps, now ye're here, ye'll go quite to the top o' the tower—the view from there is very foine."

"You must not play any tricks with us," said Dick, sternly.

"Is it thricks ye mane," demanded Don Timole; "the only thricks I'll play is to show you out o' this place and go wid ye."

A few more stairs brought them to the top of the tower, which had a high parapet with embrasures.

The view from it was indeed very fine, and for a moment or two everything, including hunger and the possible dangers ahead of them, were forgotten.

Don Timole had seen it many times before, and he simply cast a glance around. As his eyes turned in a northerly direction he saw something that drew an exclamation from him.

"Begorra!" he said; "did ye iver see the like?"

"What is it?" asked Dick.

"Do ye see the little lines yonder—just on the level ground."

"I do, and they seem to be moving."

"It's moving they are, and they're royal troops, bad luck to 'em! for I didn't expect 'em till to-morrow."

"Then you are not prepared to fight them?" said Dick.

"Fight 'em, did ye say?" exclaimed Don Timole. "What! wid the straws of men I've got below? Ye could blow 'em all to Americay wid a fair-sized bellows. No—ye've only got to tell 'em

With whip ready Dick awaited the onslaught of the lion.

the royal troops are coming, and they'll be off like smoke. I'll give 'em the word, wid your lave, and then we shall have the castle to ourselves."

"And if found here?"

"Can't we all then be poor travellers, who've been waylaid and robbed by the Carlists; and won't the royal troops take care of us and feed us?"

"But you, my friend," said Dick, "may be known to them."

"I'll run the risk," said Don Timole. "I was only travelling wid ye. It's not needful for ye to own me."

It was impossible to withstand his insinuating manner, so as he proposed they decided it should be.

"Then stop here," he said, "and see how them same troops o' mine can be dispersed all over this beautiful counthry. It'll be like opening the door of an aviary."

He waved his hand, doffed his hat to the ladies, and dived down the stairway.

Strange to say nobody there thought it possible that he could play the traitor to them, except Pardiggle Brown.

"I don't like that man," he said; "he's got a leer in his eye that don't please me."

"He's peculiar," said Mrs. Brown, "but a perfect gentleman."

"Ah! I see," said her husband, with a sniff, "he's been making love to you."

"And if he has, is that anything rare?"

Brown did not answer, but turned away, once more troubled with that restless fiend—jealousy.

The others were watching through the embrasures for the promised exodus below—Dick and Viardot side by side.

"Chance," he said, "has once more brought us together."

"It was not chance," she said; "I came—because I MUST."

"You Spanish women are strange creatures," said Dick. "Why should there be any 'must' in this case?"

She turned her head away. Dick lightly laid a finger on her arm.

"Viardot," he said, "better for both if we had never met."

"You may think so," she answered, without looking at him; "but what of that? IT WAS TO BE."

"Ah! you believe in fate."

"In some things," she said. "There is the man for the woman and the woman for the man, and if it is to be, all the world cannot keep them asunder."

He would have endeavoured to reason with her for Dick was no fatalist; but at that moment a commotion in the courtyard below attracted the attention of all.

CHAPTER LVII.

THE HONOUR OF A MAN—SAVED BY A LOCKET—
A STRANGE RETURN TO AN OLD LOVE.

ROW and me not in it!" said Bill Butterflick. "This won't do."

"There seems to be more talk than fight," replied Carl Yemitz. "We had better wait awhile."

The commotion went on for awhile, and high above all sounds was heard the voice of the Carlist chief; but by degrees the talking subsided. Another brief delay, and he was heard reascending the stairs.

"Begorra!" he said, "I'll make the thafe smart for it. It's two gintlemen I want to make up the party."

"I should have thought there were sufficient of us," said Phil Norton.

"It's a party for downstairs, I mane," said the Carlist; "and I'll just ask the favour of your company, Mister Sthrongbow, and your friend the German gintleman."

"And what's to become of us?" asked Mrs. Pardiggle Brown.

"Be aisy, darlint," replied Don Timole; "it's not long ye'll have to wait."

"Before I go," said Dick, "I should like to know exactly what it means—no trickery my friend."

"Is it thrickery ye mane from ME?" was the indignant reply, "wid the best gintleman blood of Spain inside me. By the powers it's well I've got a party on, or it's calling ye out I'd be at for that. Ye come along—it's all square."

Dick and Carl accompanied him downstairs, the rest being desired to remain on the top of the tower "until called for," as Don Timole said.

Dick felt the easier because by this time he knew that the ragged band of Carlists had all bolted and left their chief to get along without them.

The royal troops also promised security.

They had arrived, and were assembled in the courtyard, or a portion of them it might be, for very few were in sight; but pacing up and down was a good looking man, who had a military bearing, evidently in command.

"Captain Granalo," said Don Timole, "permit me to introduce the jintleman I spoke of, Mistare Strongbow."

The Spaniard bowed, looking keenly at Dick at the same time.

"I have heard of you, senor," he said, in excellent English; "but I cannot see in your appearance a verification of what I have been told of your great strength."

"Shall I give you an example of it?" asked Dick.

"I shall be glad—not that I doubt you," replied Captain Granalo.

Dick turned to Don Timole, and taking him by the waistband hoisted him into the air.

"Divil take ye!" he roared. "What do ye mane by it? The saints preserve me, man! If ye drop me I'll be smashed entoirely!"

Dick put him down gently enough and addressed the Spaniard.

"I hope I have satisfied you?" he said.

"What little doubt I had is dispelled," was the reply.

"Manewhile," said Don Timole, "if ye'll get your friends together we'll proceed to business."

"There are four of us," said the Spaniard. "That will be enough. Go on—I will speedily follow you. The terrace behind the castle will serve."

Dick, Carl, and Don Timole started off.

To Carl the business on hand was quite clear, but Dick was somewhat puzzled.

"I don't understand all this," he said.

"It manes," said Don Timole, "that he's cast a slur upon my honour, and I intend to have satisfaction."

"Can't it be settled any other way?" asked Dick. "I hate duels!"

"By my faith, no!" answered Don Timole. "When a jintleman's honour is impugned he's got to stand up for it if he's riddled with bullets."

Don Timole walked on ahead frowning.

Carl put his hand to his mouth and whispered to Dick—

"It must be a very serious thing to impugn his honour. I wonder what was said to him?"

"What matters!" replied Dick. "Let them fight it out."

Captain Granalo soon followed, bringing with him two duelling swords. He begged the favour of Dick to act as his second.

"I am ready to admit that I was in the wrong," he said; "but that is not sufficient for a hot-headed Irishman."

"A what did ye call me?" cried Don Timole; "it's not ashamed I'd be if I was one of that same people, but wid the bluest blood as iver sparkled in this counthry running about me it's a mane insult of ye."

The swords were measured and found to be of the same length. Captain Granalo gave his opponent a choice of weapons and took one.

Very little preparation for the fight was thought necessary.

Carl assumed that he was Don Timole's second, although not a word was said about it.

The moment their weapons crossed two things were apparent—Captain Granalo was a master of fence, but Don Timole knew nothing whatever about it, or at least nothing worth mentioning.

But he made up in vigour what he lacked in experience, and went through so many astounding movements that the Spaniard was fairly nonplussed.

He could make nothing out of the other's attack or defence, and stood on the latter himself, waiting to get a thrust.

But he never got a chance, and Don Timole after a series of wild antics lunged forward and pricked the Spaniard in the breast.

The effect of the thrust was very strange.

It was a violent one, and drove him back so that he fell; but it did not appear that the wound he received was a very serious one.

In proof of it he was up again in a moment, ready to renew the fight.

Dick Strongbow stepped in between.

"Surely," he said, "that will suffice?"

"I'm satisfied," said Don Timole. "It's not malicious I am, begorra! Shake hands, captain."

The Spaniard hesitated for a moment, but his better nature came to the front, and he assented with a smile.

"Such doubts," he said, "as I had were very natural; but the matter's over, and there's no more to be said."

"And now if it is to your liking," said Don Timole, "we'll go back and have something to eat. Ye brought good rations with you?"

"We are amply supplied," replied Captain Granalo, "and my work being done, by the dispersal of those ruffians, I shall return to Madrid."

"That is my destination, and of my friends also," said Dick.

"You have friends with you?"

"Yes, they are in the castle, awaiting the result of this meeting, the nature of which, I may say, they are ignorant of."

Dick and the Spanish captain walked on ahead. Carl and Don Timole fell behind.

"If it is not a ticklish subject," said Carl, "may I ask what our friend ahead did to offend you?"

"He impugned my honour," replied Don Timole.

"Yes, I know that," rejoined Carl; "but how? What did he say or do?"

"Ye'll hardly belave what I tell ye—the maneness of the crayture."

"I'll take your word, of course."

"Well, then, it's this," said Don Timole, with twinkling eyes; "he had the audacity to say I WAS A CARLIST, and talked of putting a rope round me neck and strangling me like a brigand. It's myself that said I'd make him ate his words, and, to the glory of old Dublin, he's done it."

Carl burst into an explosion of laughter, in which Don Timole did not, however, join, save in the matter of winking eyes.

Dick looked back and asked what was the joke.

"Too good to tell here," said Carl. "We must wait until we are together. It will go well with a glass of wine."

"Better wid a drop o' whisky," said Don Timole. "It was while I was studying in Dublin that I picked up a taste for the same. Sorry a dhrop have I had for months."

Dick and the captain were already good friends.

On the way back to the castle the former told the story of the capture of the diligence by the Carlists, omitting, however, to say anything which might get Don Timole into trouble.

After all he had not shown any remarkable animosity towards his captives, and as a peculiar specimen of humanity he was a bit of a study.

"You are safe now from further molestation," said the captain. "Don Carlos has fled. He made a start for England a week ago. It is kind of your country to give a home to every vagabond who chooses to land on your shores."

"Is the Don a vagabond?"

"Well—hardly. He is an adventurer—a gambler who has thrown the dice and lost. All we have to do now is to deal with the scattered bands of brigands he has left behind him. That is a matter of minor detail. You are safe, and in three days from this time we'll be in Madrid."

"There is one thing I should like to ask you," said Dick. "In the duel did you slip and fall?"

"No."

"Yet you were pricked, and are apparently unhurt."

Captain Granalo smiled.

"I have hung around my neck a locket, in which is the portrait of a girl I met two years ago. I loved her, and I bore away her image when she said 'No' to my wooing. It was well. That locket saved my life."

He drew it from his breast, and showed Dick where the point of the sword had made a deep dent in the side of it.

The locket was a broad, oblong square, and covered with ornamental work.

To the latter the gallant captain really owed his safety, for it had prevented the point of the weapon slipping off.

Had it done so he would have been a dead man.

"It is well to be faithful to your love," he said, "whether she cares for you or not. Would you like to see her face?"

"I am a bit curious," replied Dick; "certainly it will be interesting."

The Spaniard, after a little trouble, succeeded in opening the case. He handed it to Dick.

The face was, indeed, a pretty one, and he knew it well.

It was that of Viardot!

CHAPTER LVIII.

A SAFE ESCORT—MORELLE AND PAN IN MADRID —THE SHOT FROM THE WINDOW.

ERE was a discovery. Dick was amazed, as we all have been at times, to find how small a world we move in, though we roam all over its expanse.

Viardot, whom he had met in a remote village, brought by chance to the castle, whither comes an old lover to disperse a rebel band, and there they must meet again.

"Shall I tell him she is here?" thought Dick. "No, it will be better not. An unexpected meeting may bring about a happier result. Yes," he said, as he handed back the locket, "it is a good face—a pretty face, and one that a man, heart-free, might easily fall in love with."

The captain kissed the locket fervently.

"I adore her," he said.

And still Dick said nothing.

On their return to the castle, Carl went up to the top of the tower to bring down their friends, who had seen them depart, and were anxiously watching for their return.

They imagined all sorts of things but the truth, of course, and Carl's explanation to them was not entirely received as gospel.

His recommendation to keep the secret of the true character of their Irish-Spanish friend was not entirely to everybody's taste.

Mrs. Pardiggle Brown was especially hard on him.

"The impudent scoundrel!" she said. "He made love to me."

"The deuce he did," returned Brown. "And what did you do?"

"I hit him over the head with the guitar," she answered. "I am afraid, miss"—to Viardot—"that I broke some of the strings."

"They are easily replaced," replied Viardot.

"No good would come of splitting on the fellow," said Carl, "and I beg of you all to be silent."

They promised, but as Mrs. Pardiggle Brown could not be fully trusted Carl, whispered to Butterflick that he had better keep an eye upon her.

"If she attempts to let the cat out of the bag," Carl said, "stop her SOMEHOW."

"I'll do it," replied Butterflick, hurriedly, "even if comes to kissing her."

When they got to the bottom of the stairs they found Dick waiting for them.

"I wish to introduce you to the commandant of the royal troops, Viardot," he said. "He is in one of the apartments here."

Viardot, unsuspecting, allowed herself to be led across the courtyard to one of the doorways, through which they peered.

"He is in here," said Dick, turning to the right.

The captain was pacing up and down a small chamber which, like the rest in the greater part of the castle, was entirely denuded of furniture.

"Captain Granalo," said Dick, "permit me to introduce you to my dear friend—Viardot."

He turned and their eyes met.

An exclamation escaped the captain, and the girl uttered a cry, covering her face with her hands.

"May I leave you together?" said Dick. "I can see you are old friends."

"No—not yet," gasped Viardot.

"At least, I may touch your hand," said the captain.

She held it out and he raised it to his lips.

"I have been patient," he said, "and I will wait still. Hope will only die with my life."

He made no further effort to keep her there, and they went out together, Viardot with a strange light in her eyes.

She did not look at Dick nor at her other companions, but kept her eyes fixed on things ahead, and for hours after she was very silent.

But she took part in a picnic just without the castle where there was much merriment.

That most excellent turncoat, Don Timole, was particularly happy with his jests, but he gave Mr. Pardiggle Brown, who kept an eagle eye on him, a very wide berth.

Then they had a hour's rest, after which the march back began.

"Five miles from here," said the captain, "I have tents, which you can use, and there we will pass the night."

"We have some luggage here," said Dick, looking at Don Timole.

"Begorra," said that worthy, "it was myself that saved it from the thaves. It's in one of the rooms yonder."

It was routed out, and such things as could be taken were carried by the soldiers.

The rest was left under a small guard to remain there until mules could be sent to convey it away.

"I will undertake to deliver it safely in Madrid," said the captain.

A few miles on they came to a little encampment, which had been left in the care of a troop of soldiers.

There the tired travellers found themselves under canvas, and they divided according to the necessities of sex and association.

Viardot had her guitar, which she deftly put in order, and one of the last things Dick saw ere he went to rest was Viardot sitting outside her tent, softly playing an air and singing sweetly.

A short distance away Captain Granalo reclined upon the ground, listening with the wrapt attention of a lover who had loved long and was still true to her.

"He may win her yet," thought Dick, and then he sighed.

But the image of Lucella rose up before him, and softly humming an accompaniment to the Spanish girl's song, he entered the tent apportioned to him and went to rest.

．　　．　　．　　．　　．　　．　　．

Hie we on to Madrid before the travellers, as we have no longer need to keep them company for awhile, all perils of the road being past.

Madrid, the romantic, the beautiful city of gaiety and sadness, home of the brightest and darkest shades of humanity.

Of its history, as history is written, the world has read a great deal; but of its inner life in these modern days very little comparatively is known.

First, let us take a peep at its dubious side, among a maze of narrow streets, where poverty and crime have made their home.

In a one of these street, where the houses were high, so as to shut out the sunlight from its pathway save for one brief hour in the day, Jacob Morelle and Pan had made a temporary home.

They had a lodging in a house inhabited by mixed characters of both sexes, but they kept themselves apart.

The song of eve and the riot at night was nothing to them.

More than once during a fortnight's stay they had heard a desperate struggle on the stairs, or in some room below, accompanied by the oaths of men and the shrieks of women.

Once, on going out, they found a broad dark stain in the lower passage, still damp, which told of a life lost there, but it was not their business.

"If they choose to fight and kill one another it is nothing to us," said Morelle.

"Unless they take it into their heads to bring us into their rows," returned Pan.

"If you leave them alone you will be safe," replied Morelle.

They had a little money with them, some of which they had got, by the way, in a manner we need not put on record. It was not honestly earned, you may be sure.

Every man labours according to his notions, and he who has lived once by crime hardly ever gives his time to profitable labour.

Pan never went out alone. His old nerve was gone, and he was afraid of men and things that a year ago he would have treated with contempt.

Jacob Morelle had lost some of his old courage, but not so much as Pan, and he occasionally went out in the morning by himself, returning at eve.

He told Pan that he was seeing the marvels of the city, but Pan knew better than that.

He felt sure that his companion was abroad to gain information about Dick Strongbow, and one eve Jacob Morelle confirmed this idea.

He was later than usual when he returned about dusk, and the night prowlers had gone abroad.

It was dangerous for a stranger to traverse the locality at that hour, but the peril he had run did not account for the colourless face he brought home with him.

"Curse the fellow!" he said, as he threw himself down upon the wretched bed he slept on.

It was upon the floor, and there were no chairs in the room.

Two wooden boxes served as seats at the rickety table at which they took their meals.

"He has come?" said Pan.

"No—but he will soon be here," returned Jacob Morelle. "The city rings with his name. He has outdone the pet matadore—the darling Carrugia—beaten, crushed, annihilated him."

"Is he going to turn bull-fighter?" asked Pan.

"Do you think it likely?" asked Morelle. "No—he will simply come here as a hero. The men will envy and hate him, but they will bestow favours upon him. As for the women, they will worship Strongbow the mighty."

"He is a lucky fellow," growled Pan; "so young, with many years of joyous life before him. You and I are already on the wrong side of the meridian."

"Hold your peace, you hound!" said Morelle, fiercely. "Have you any wine in the place?"

"One flask."

"Give me some."

He ordered Pan about as if he were a slave, and Pan obeyed him like one.

For a drinking vessel they had an old tin cup, from which Morelle drank the wine, poured out by his servitor, with thirsty relish.

"Is it not a pity," he said, "that it should be ruinous to the nerves to pour such good stuff down our throats? A man drunk is happy. When the wine is going off he is a grovelling cur—a croaking, groaning, trembling creature!"

He filled his pipe and lit it. Pan did the same after he had taken a modest portion of the wine to himself.

The room was very dark, but they could see a little, thanks to the light in a room on the opposite side of the narrow street.

There was no blind to either windows, and they could see a woman passing to and fro, with a babe in her arms, which she was softly singing to sleep.

"Only think, Pan," said Morelle, "that you and I were like that little one once upon a time. What would the mothers who in anguish bore us, and in joy nurtured us, think if they could see us now."

"I don't know," growled Pan, "and I don't care."

"I was what the world calls well brought up," continued Morelle, in a dreamy tone; "my father was a gentleman and my mother a lady. I was an only son—a spoilt child."

"Very much so," returned Pan, drily.

"I don't know why I talk of these things to a dog like you," said Morelle, "unless it is that, like some people, I feel I must get a little weight off here," smiting his heart "by talking to somebody."

"If it's any consolation to you," said Pan, "I don't mind it, but at the same time I don't see the good of it."

"You could not see good in anything if you tried," retorted Morelle.

The mother had now got the child to sleep and was putting it to rest.

She had just laid it down in a box that served for its bed when a swarthy man entered the room.

He was of the ruffian type, and would have looked a villain in any garb.

He looked especially so in the ragged dress he wore.

The woman held up her finger for him to be quiet; but he began to curse and swear, and, finally, without any visible cause, struck her.

The woman fell insensible across the cot in which the tired child still slept.

The ruffian bent over her and listened to her breathing.

A savage grin spread across his face as he drew a knife from his waist.

Pan laid still, watching the scene with brutal indifference, but Jacob Morelle sprang to his feet.

"I can't stand it," he said. "If he dare touch her with that knife he is a dead man."

"Master," said Pan, "don't be a fool. You will have all the place on to us if you shoot."

"Clear out," said Morelle; "I'm going to do it, as I live. Away to the river! Meet me on the quay where we stood watching the boats yesterday. If I don't come in an hour you may reckon they have closed my history for me."

"Master—"

"Out you go—there's not a moment to spare."

Confounding the stupidity of his master, Pan hurried out of the room.

That the Spaniard meant to kill the woman was now clear.

In glancing round the room he saw that the window was open, and he came forward to close it.

It was one of the old latticed casements that opened outward like a door, and, having no catch, it had been blown back against the wall.

To pull it to him the ruffian had to lean out in a manner that brought half his body into the open air.

As he stretched out his arms Jacob Morelle drew a revolver, took steady aim at his head, and fired.

The aim was true, and the bullet shut out the light from the ruffian for evermore.

He fell dead upon the window-sill, lay there limp for a moment, then, sliding forward, pitched headlong into the street below.

"I have not done many good deeds in my life," said Morelle, as he walked to the table and took up the wine-flask, "but that is one of them."

CHAPTER LIX.

ARRIVAL OF DICK—AT THE SIGN OF THE GREAT TORO—A LION TAMER'S CARD.

 THE report of the revolver sounded with remarkable distinctness in the narrow thoroughfare.

Immediately there was a shouting of voices, a noise of opening casements, and a clattering of feet downstairs.

The weapon is an unfamiliar one to the Spaniard at home. He prefers in all his quarrels to trust to the deadly, silent knife.

As the inhabitants rushed into the street they espied the dead man lying doubled up where he had fallen. They picked him up and exchanged cries of anger and amazement when they discovered who it was.

He was a leading ruffian in the neighbourhood, a terror to the community at large, and even to those with whom he associated.

As they gathered thickly around him Jacob Morelle slipped out of the doorway, and, keeping close to the wall, glided rapidly down the street.

Ere he had gone far he heard cries of "the accursed Englishmen," in Spanish, and looking back he saw them pouring into the house he had recently occupied, bent on vengeance.

They had hit upon the nature of the tragedy, and were thirsting to take a life for a life.

"It is well we cleared out," he muttered.

But although he had temporarily made his escape he knew that Madrid would no longer be a place of safety for him.

The Vendetta would be established against him, and in a hour a hundred ruffians would be seeking him.

"I did not reckon on that," he muttered, as this contingency flashed upon him; "but it's my luck. Clear out is the word again."

It was more than a quarter of a hour's walk to the appointed spot.

As he hurried he covered the distance in a little over ten minutes.

Pan was awaiting him with marked impatience.

"I've been listening to the chatter of some of the people here," he said. "I can't understand all they say, but I made out one thing. Your *bête noir* has arrived."

"It doesn't matter who has arrived or who hasn't," replied Morelle. "We must get out of this. I spotted that fellow, and they've spotted one of us as the man who did it. They were swarming into the house as I came away."

"How did they fix it on you?" asked Pan.

"He was leaning out of the window when I shot him, and he fell into the street," replied Morelle; "they found him at once, and I suppose his being shot blew the gaff. The blackguards use the knife themselves, and they know we are English."

"You had better have left him alone," growled Pan. "No good ever yet came of interfering between man and wife."

"It was the child that did it," said Morelle; "he could have killed the woman ten times over if there had been no youngster in the room, and I should not have raised a finger."

"Well, you've done it, and that's enough," returned Pan. "Where to now?"

"Come further away," replied Morelle, "and I'll think it out."

. . . .

And thus once more, at a moment of triumph for Dick, the great enemy of his life was in trouble.

Captain Granalo, unknown to our hero or his friends, had sent a messenger forward to say that the man who had lowered the colours of Carrugia was coming.

A great crowd assembled at the northern entrance to the city, and the utmost excitement prevailed.

When Dick appeared, riding in a carriage with Carl, Butterflick, and Muffins, a murmur ran through the crowd—

"Which is he?"

But there was little or no applause, owing to the uncertainty of recognition.

Nor could it be expected in another sense.

Dick had cast down a popular idol, and those who had worshipped at the Carrugia shrine could hardly be grateful.

Behind them came another carriage, in which were the Browns, Phil Norton, and Viardot.

Don Timole was not one of the party.

For some reason he did not give—let us assume that modesty was at the root of it—he decided to walk in by-and-bye.

Captain Granalo and his men received a great ovation.

Acting on the advice of the gallant captain, our friends drove to an hotel that overlooked the river. It has changed its title two or three times, as the politics of the people changed, but the owner had settled down at last to the sign of the Great Toro, which did not clash with the sentiments of any class.

The telegraph had prepared for their reception, and the party was received with much courtesy.

"What I like this country for," said Pardiggle Brown, "is that every waiter here seems to be a grandee. You seem to want to wait on them, and not them on you."

"Them may be your sentiments," said Butterflick, "but they ain't mine. I ain't proud, and I'd just as soon wait if I couldn't do anything else, but when I've got the money, and can pay for it, I likes to be waited on. It gives a chap a bossy feeling."

"A feeling you should never show," said Phil.

Dick and Carl inquired into the nature of the arrangements made for them, and expressed their satisfaction.

They ordered dinner, and went up to their room to attend to little toilet matters.

The captain was invited to join them at the festive board, but he pleaded duty and left them.

Dick was the first down in the dining-room, when a bowing waiter came up and said—

"Senor Strongbow—is it you?"

"Yes."

"A card, senor."

Dick took it from the tray on which it was presented, and read—"Wampa, the Monarch of Lion Tamers."

"What is the meaning of this?" asked Dick, in Spanish.

"He is at your service—to see you," was the reply.

"Not to-night," replied Dick; "ask him to come in the morning. What in the name of all that's ridiculous does the fellow want with me?"

―――――

CHAPTER LX.

WAMPA'S CHALLENGE—AN AMBASSADOR'S HOME —LUCELLA.

 ERILY," said Carl, with a smile, as he stirred his coffee at breakfast on the following morning, "there has been little time lost by this Wampa in seeking your acquaintance."

"I don't quite see what the fellow wants," replied Dick.

"I think I know," said Carl.

"And I, too, can guess," put in Phil Norton.

"And guess wrong, perhaps," returned Dick, "so we won't puzzle our brains. He will be here soon, and then we shall see what his majesty wants."

The Pardiggle Browns, with Muffins and Bill Butterflick, had breakfasted early and gone out in a hired carriage, to get what Butterflick called "the gography of the town."

Dick and his two lieutenants were, therefore, by themselves.

They finished breakfast, and lighting their cigars, awaited the coming of the mighty Wampa.

Shortly after the attendants had cleared the table he was announced.

As the door was thrown open he came swaggering in—a tall man, inclined to stoutness, of a true Spanish cast of countenance, made somewhat coarse by free living.

His dress was similar to that of a matadore, but garnished with many additional silver buttons, and on his breast he had quite an array of medals.

One of the most striking things in his appearance was his hair, which was thick and long, and, save that it was as black as a crow, was like a lion's mane.

He greeted the trio of friends, who rose to receive him, with a condescending wave of the hand, and glanced from one to the other, as if seeking the man he wanted.

As a matter of fact he did not know Dick, and was unable to single him out.

"Which you senors," he asked, in broken English, "am ze great matadore."

"I fear," replied Dick, "that none of us can claim to that proud title; but I am Strongbow."

"Oh! you," said Wampa, eyeing him calmly. "Ah! not so great, so much to fear. How shall it be zat you beat my cousin Carrugia? Was he in ze drink?"

"I am not prepared to discuss anything concerning Carrugia," replied Dick, quietly. "If you came for no other business but to talk about him our interview is at an end."

"So," said Wampa, knitting his eyebrows, "you can be rude—pert—to me—Wampa?"

"My good fellow," said Dick, "I have no desire to be rude to you; I simply want to know what brought you here."

Dick spoke very civilly, in the quiet tone of one who is not desirous of a quarrel. Wampa's lip curled.

He thought he had a man to deal with over whom he could crow if he chose.

"Carrugia," he said, "is my cousin—of family mine I come to challenge you.

"Nonsense, man!" interposed Dick, sharply; "I am not going to fight the whole family. Carrugia sought his defeat, and as he is down there is an end to the matter as far as I am concerned."

"Not for me," said Wampa, nodding his head. "I gif you a challenge—come see me with my lions. Say then you do the same or no. If you do, you brave—if not— Poof! you are nothing."

"Really," said Dick, "I don't know that I am interested in your performance, or that I desire to emulate it."

"You will not come then?" said Wampa.

"I do not say that," said Dick. "Where are you performing?"

"At the Grand Cirque," said Wampa, "to-day, at three, in ze daylight. Wampa want no glare of light to make daze his lions. You see all—you will come?"

"Yes," returned Dick.

"I go, then," replied Wampa, rising.

He went out without any further ceremony, leaving the room with such a swagger upon him that Carl and Dick could hardly keep from laughing.

"Another novelty," said Phil, as the door closed

"If I had been you, Dick," said Carl, "I should have cut him short."

"Why?" asked Dick, laughing. "He came here to air his grievance and to scare me; but he does not know his man. I am in the secret of many of the tricks and traps of these men. Do you know what he will do?"

"No."

"He will at once get out bills to say that I, who defeated Carrugia, will attend his show this afternoon; that will be a draw for him."

"No great harm in that."

"No; but when he gets me there he will challenge me to enter the den of lions, and if I refuse—"

"As you will, of course," said Phil.

"If I refuse," repeated Dick, "he will then make a mighty hubbub out of the fact that he can do greater things than the man who defeated Carrugia."

"Ah! I see," said Carl. "On the ruins of his cousin's reputation he seeks to build another story to his own."

"That is how I read it."

"And will you play into his hands, Dick?"

"Yes—and no. Wait and see what I shall do."

"For goodness' sake," said Phil, "don't think of turning lion-tamer."

Dick laughed pleasantly.

"All I will say to that," he replied, "is that I know the tricks and the trade of lion-tamers, and this fellow amuses me. Let us go out for a stroll."

Dick lit another cigar, and they sauntered out. A guide was offered them by the host, but they refused his services for the present.

They were strangers, and as such attracted some attention, but not much, for none they met thought for a moment that the quiet-looking young man was the conqueror of Carrugia, the pride of Spain.

By making a few discreet enquiries they found

their way to the Grand Cirque, and found that it was a fair-sized circular building of stone, evidently long associated with entertainments for the public.

Along the walls there were a host of old bills, torn in places by the boys and idlers, who are as mischievous in one country as they are in another.

These placards related to all sorts of performances except bull fights, for which the building was not adapted.

A young Spaniard, smoking a cigarette, seeing the "foreigners" scanning the bills, undertook to explain.

"You look at old ones," he said, in Spanish; "they are nothing. This of Wampa is the only one to see."

"Wampa is a very great man," said Dick.

"A king," replied the Spaniard. "He looks at a lion, and it becomes a cat—a toy in his hands. It crouches here and there—licks his hands—it is a dog."

He laid the end of his cigarette on a projecting stone, produced a piece of paper and a pinch of tobacco and deftly made another, which he lighted with what was left of the first.

"Wampa," he said, "is the only man in the world before whom a lion will lie down."

"Indeed," said Dick.

"The only man," repeated the Spaniard. "It has never been done before, except when the lions are drugged—made drunk. He is very great."

"And does he draw?" asked Carl. "Do the people rush to see him?'

"Well—no, not as one would expect," was the reply. "The people doubt—they say he makes his lions drunk too—that he stupefies them. But how should it be so, when they caper about like kittens?"

"Well," said Dick, "we will come and see him to-day, and then we shall be able to form an opinion on the merits of his performance. You will be there?"

"I am always there," was the answer. "I am his assistant—his valet, what you like. I know him; he is very great."

"The valet," said Dick, "has not Wampa's swagger; but he is not bowed to the earth with humility."

"I like the fellow," said Carl; "he is true to his master."

From thence they wandered on, presently coming to a wide street filled with mansions that were, for the most part, relics of bygone magnificence.

Some were inhabited, but others showed signs of neglect and decay.

There was one place, however, where there were indications not only of habitation, but of luxurious living.

Gaily-dressed people, bearing themselves proudly like the grandees of Spain, were going in and out, and several carriages were standing near the door.

"I wonder what place this is?" said Dick.

"An ambassador's, I should say," replied Carl.

"What makes you think so?"

"The air of business of some of these people. It is hardly the hour for paying visits of pleasure."

"True!"

"Shall I enquire who resides here?" asked Phil.

"Thanks, if you will," said Dick.

Phil walked up to an official-looking personage, who had just come out, and, raising his hat, said—

"May I ask who resides here?"

"The Duke of Lavante," was the reply.

DICK STRONGBOW:

The Diamond King,
AND WONDER OF THE WORLD.

The Prefect drew out a folded paper from his breast and spread it before him on the table.

No. 13.   Price One Penny.

"Pardon me again, but of what country is he?"

"Sweden   He is the ambassador here."

Dick had heard every word that was said, and the answer brought a flush to his cheek.

He did not know the title, but the word Sweden brought Lucella to his mind.

He had not forgotten her, it is true; but the memory of her had not of late been so vivid as it used to be.

With a thoughtful face he walked slowly on, his friends following.

"Shall we ever meet again?" he asked himself; "and if we do, what then?"

He looked up with a sigh, and in a careless, indifferent way glanced at a passing carriage.

Two ladies were seated inside it, and at the sight of them all his indifference vanished.

It was Lucella and her mother.

CHAPTER LXI.

DON TIMOLE TURNS UP—A LETTER FROM VIARDOT —BUTTERFLICK AND THE SPANIARD.

OSSIBLY the fair girl would not have seen Dick but for her mother, who, catching sight of him, started so violently that the attention of Lucella was drawn to her.

Looking into her face she saw the direction of her eyes, glanced at the same place, and beheld Dick. He was startled, but he did not lose his head.

There was a slight additional flush to his cheek, but nothing more to show his emotion.

Lucella, on the other hand, flushed a deep red, then turned deadly white.

Dick raised his hat, and the girl's head drooped rather than bowed in return.

Then the mother turned upon her, and Dick noted the knitted brow and slightly-moving lips of the elder woman as she muttered a reproof.

A moment later and they were gone.

"Did you see who was in that carriage?" asked Dick, turning to his friends.

"A marvellously handsome girl," replied Carl.

"A picture," said Phil.

"You do not know her, Carl?"

"No; I wish I did."

"How foolish of me!" exclaimed Dick. "How should you know her? Well, that was Lucella."

"Whew! what good or ill fortune brought her here?"

"How can it be ill fortune?" asked Dick, testily.

"My dear fellow," said Carl, laying a hand upon his arm, "it will be better for you to forget her. It is a hard thing to say, but these people are proud, and—"

He stopped, looked at Dick, and exclaimed—

"What a fool I am! I beg your pardon. As if you were not good enough for ANYONE."

"You are right in your way of thinking, Carl," said Dick. "It is too much for me to hope that I can ever be anything more to her than I am at this moment—a successful mountebank and adventurer."

"You shall not disparage yourself in that way, Dick. You are a man of whom any woman might be proud."

"The woman, but not her parents," said Dick, bitterly. "Let us get on."

They walked on, but had not got far when they encountered a swaggering form they knew well. It was that of Don Timole Murphaleo, who had adorned himself with a suit of clothes of such gorgeous colours that he looked like a walking rainbow.

On seeing the three friends he pulled up short and saluted.

"Sorry a bit did I expect to see you," he said "And what may ye be doing in this poor street, which, in comparison with Sackville-street, Dublin, is no better than a back alley?"

"We are strolling about, that's all," said Dick; "and you?"

"It's meself that has just arrived in state," replied Don Timole, with twinkling eyes, "in company with one Don Sebastian de la Tourville."

"I know him," said Dick.

"Aye! and it's that which gave me an introduction to him, sure," returned Don Timole; "for, hearing him mention your name, I made bould to say you were a friend of mine, and he invited me to stay with him."

"When did you meet him?" asked Dick, with slightly knitted brows.

"Maybe two hours ago," replied Don Timole, "and, being in sore straits, I told him how that thafe of a Carlist gang robbed us. He behaved like a prince, sure, saying, 'There's my wardrobe, and any friend of that same Strongbow is welcome to every rag of it.'"

"I don't know that you had any right to use my name," said Dick.

"Divil a right!" replied Don Timole, easily; "but there's nothing right in this thafe of a country, and ye won't be after expecting me to be better than the rest. I'd not have lied if the truth would have got me the clothes, but it wouldn't, and so I laid on a thumper."

"I don't like lies," said Dick.

"No! But you won't be afther betraying a poor divil," said Don Timole; "the man as stood up for you in your throuble?"

"But ARE you staying with Tourville?" asked Dick.

"I HAVE stayed with him," replied Don Timole.

"Are you with him now?"

"No; I only stayed long enough to get this suit of clothes, and if he kept money in the pockets I'd have nothing to complain of, but you see what a poor lot they are here. See!"

He turned his pockets inside out, and looked at Dick with a curious twinkling in his eyes.

Dick affected to be very stern, but he could hardly keep his countenance.

"And it's not a gintleman like you," answered Don Timole, "that can look on pockets like these and not feel inclined to put something in 'em."

"Here's a few coins," said Dick, giving him half a handful of loose change. "You are a strange fellow, and I am afraid you will one day get into trouble."

"It's trouble I've known since the hour my mother bore me," said Don Timole; "and if ever it laves me it's like an orphan I'll feel for the loss of it. But now, by your lave, I'll go and get something to eat, for I've a big hollow here that hasn't been filled up since yesterday."

He raised his hat, gave it a flourish, and strutted on, leaving the three friends struggling with their tendency to laugh.

"If trouble sat as lightly on all the world as upon him," said Dick, "it would be but a feather."

On their return to the hotel they found that Captain Granalo had called and left his card.

There was also a short letter from Viardot for Dick.

"*I thank you*" (she wrote), "*for many things. I am a happy woman, and I will be a faithful one to the man who has loved me so well. We may meet no more, and perhaps it will be better for one of us at least. Adieu!*"

"VIARDOT."

The rest of the party had returned also, and, barring one little dispute with a Spaniard, Butterflick reported all well.

"The senor," he said, "stood right in the middle of the path barring the way. We had given up riding, and taken to walking, as it was quicker, for of all the old knock-kneed varmints of horses ever put into a vehicle the one we had was the worst I ever saw. The driver said it was going in for the next bull-fight, which I believe is done here instead of sending the worn-out critters to the knackers."

"But the Spaniard?" hinted Carl. "He who straddled in the way."

"Oh! him," said Butterflick, with the air of recalling something he had forgotten. "Yes—he was standing making a letter Y, upside down, of himself, and I thought it wasn't perlite to a lady, so I moved him."

"How?" asked Phil.

"With this," replied Butterflick, raising his foot. "You see, I don't understand their gibberish, and not feeling like wasting time, I gives him a lift, and then says, 'Hadn't you better get out of the way, my lad?' He rose up quite stiff, he was that dignified, and come down ker-flop forrards on his face."

"And then?" suggested Carl.

"We passed on," replied Butterflick, "and he comes on arter us when he had got up. I heerd him rushing, and calculating the time to turn, so that I could give him one between the eyes, I give him it!"

"And down he went again, of course?"

"Yes, but not quite so stiff, but stiffish, and this time on his back. Then we went on again, and for some reason he didn't follow us no more."

"You don't know who it is, I suppose?" said Dick.

"Never set eyes on him afore," answered Butterflick, "and can get along if I never see him again."

"It will be better if you can get along without much of this sort of thing," said Dick, "for the Spaniard, like others born in hot climates, has a lot of revengeful blood in him, and seldom forgets or forgives an injury."

"If he comes in my way again," said Butterflick, airily, "he won't remember anything for some time. I can't get along with uppish people, and there's so much swagger about here that I am getting tired of it."

"Different people," said Carl, "have different ways. Haughtiness is natural to the Spaniard—and we must not be too hasty about it."

"Just what I told him," said Pardiggle Brown. "I noticed the fellow's eye just as Butterflick hit him, and if ever I saw the old 'un in a man's head I looked on it then."

"Brown," said his wife, "you have no real manhood in you."

"What I've got I want to keep there," replied Pardiggle Brown. "I'm not thinking to have it let out with a knife."

"I consider that Mr. Butterflick acted like a hero," said Mrs. Pardiggle Brown; "quite in the style a knight of old would have performed in a tournament."

"I'm blessed!" exclaimed her husband. "Who ever heard of a knight lifting up parties with his foot?"

"Well, it's done," said Dick, "and let us hope that no evil will come of it. We will have an early dinner to-day, as I propose that we all go to the grand circus to see the lion tamer perform."

"My eye!" said Muffins, "that's just in my line. I've never seen a lion that I knows on, 'cept in picters, and I think that a man who tames one can do anything."

"There are various ways of taming them," said Dick, with a smile; "but I won't say anything about our friend Wampa until I see how he does the trick."

CHAPTER LXII.

AT THE GRAND CIRQUE—WAMPA IN THE BOAST-
ING SEAT—DICK'S DARING VENTURE.

THE interior of the Grand Cirque was like a theatre, save that there was no actual stage.

One side of the circular building had been cut off, so as to have two huge cages placed there.

They stood side by side, and communicated with a sliding door.

Let us take a peep at what was doing prior to the admission of the public.

One of the cages was empty—in the other was a lion, a lioness, and two cubs, eagerly watching the movements of Wampa, who, with his assistant, was cutting up a joint of meat into pieces about four inches square.

When this was done the pieces were placed in a row upon a table outside the cages, in full sight of the animals, who began to roar and paw up and down the cage, the lion occasionally making a dash at the bars.

About this time the public were beginning to assemble, and the attendant was dispatched to see, from some point of vantage, what they were like as regards numbers.

While he was gone Wampa further goaded the animals by holding up one of the pieces of meat upon a pitchfork, and waving it to and fro in front of the lions, until their roaring was ear-splitting.

While he was engaged in this pursuit the attendant returned and reported that the people were assembling in considerable numbers.

"As I thought," said Wampa, tossing the piece of meat upon the table ; "the bare report that the great Strongbow would be here to compete with me has drawn. Ah ! my good Muro, it will be all money to me. I shall be a greater man than Carrugia was before his fall."

"But suppose this Englishman decides to enter the cage ?" said Muro.

"He will be eaten," replied Wampa ; "for the dose I shall give to Cæsar will only last an hour to-day."

"I see," said Muro ; "and you will time things so that if the Englishman cares to enter the cage he will find Cæsar ready for him ?"

"It is so," said Wampa. "You may feed the others while I prepare the meat for him."

Muro's first act was to open the door between the cages, and immediately he did so the lion dashed through.

Before the lioness and cubs could follow the door was dropped again.

Then they goaded the animals a little more, so that their roaring might be heard outside.

The object of this was obvious. It would give the hearers an idea of great ferocity in the animals.

And, as far as the lion was concerned, the opinion would be a just one. He was a most ferocious brute.

Wampa knew it, and he had a method of dealing with Cæsar which was effectual.

He was possessed of a potent drug, which, although it did not stupefy the animal, took the heart out of him.

The only danger about the use of it arose from the fact that an error of one drop might be fatal to the man who professed to "tame" the animal, for it lasted only a certain time, and the effect of it suddenly ceased, so suddenly that there was positively no warning whatever.

One moment the lion would be abject and cowering, the next he would be fully endowed with his native ferocity, and dangerous in the extreme to man.

Wampa was experienced in the use of the drug, and knew to a few minutes how long a certain quantity would keep in action.

So well acquainted was he with it that he could time his leaving the cage to a minute or so, and had often cut it so finely that he had barely left the cage when Cæsar would be raging around, thirsting for his blood.

His intentions towards Dick Strongbow were plain enough.

The idea of his avenging his cousin may be put aside as of no account. He simply wanted to make capital for himself.

In the defeat of Carrugia he, with a showman's keenness, saw a chance of making headway for himself.

Say that he could induce Strongbow to enter the cage, and pay the price of his temerity, what a glorious advertisement it would be for him !

Here, at home, the death of a man would have stopped the performance with the lion.

Not so in Spain.

Human life, when lost in sport, is not of much account there, and on the dead body of the audacious Englishman Wampa would take his stand as a hero. If Dick Strongbow refused to emulate his "daring," then the advertisement would be about as good.

What the conqueror of Carrugia refused to attempt he, Wampa, was ready to do daily.

Oh ! there was money in it, and he commended himself for his shrewdness as he carefully cut an incision in one of the pieces of beef and slowly counted out the drops of the potent drug wherewith he poisoned it.

When all was ready he looked at his watch and bade Muro order the doors to be opened.

Then he cast the drugged piece of meat to the eager lion, and removed the table and all signs of the feeding.

The attendance was very heavy that day.

Judicious advertising had brought a multitude to see Wampa perform, and to get a glimpse of the great Strongbow, who was to be there as a spectator and possibly as a rival.

The body of the place consisted of all cheap seats ; the upper part was for those who could pay a higher price, which was generally the case with the nobility alone.

They had been chary of patronising Wampa hitherto, but on this day the upper tier was more than three-quarters filled, and the two or three private boxes—hitherto empty—were taken.

In the box near the cage there were two ladies. The face of one, evidently a person of high birth, was concealed by a mantilla. The other was her attendant, pretty but bold, and in no way disposed to conceal the charms of her face and figure.

Facing this box was another on the other side of the cage, and this had been taken by Dick Strongbow, who, at the hour appointed for the performance, put in an appearance with his friends.

Mrs. Pardiggle Brown was gallantly put in front, and Butterflick sat beside her.

Immediately behind, keeping a jealous eye on his better half, was Brown, and the others stood in the shade.

From their position they could see the lions fairly well, and when Cæsar came to the front and began to rest his nose against the bars Dick laughed softly.

" He has taken his dose," he said, " and it makes him uneasy. We shall soon see the great Wampa masquerading before the public."

The lion Cæsar was pacing restlessly in his cage, lying down for a short time at intervals, and rubbing his nose with his huge paws.

These symptoms Dick Strongbow watched very closely, but he made no comment upon them.

The place rapidly filled, and the audience were tiptoe with expectancy.

For some time they stared about, as if looking for a particular object, and presently their eyes were fixed upon Dick's box.

They had found out where he was, but they were uncertain of their man.

Butterflick, as he looked big, was the choice of the public, and many hands were raised and and fingers pointed towards him.

The entrance of Wampa drew all eyes upon him.

He was attired in tight-fitting clothes of a dark blue colour, and around his waist was a coloured sash.

In his hand he carried a strong, pliable riding-whip.

Before beginning to perform he looked at his watch, and then entered upon a speech prior to his performance.

It was to the effect that real strength lay in the power of man over wild beasts, and those who succeeded in this direction were leaders amongst men.

He challenged all the world to do what he was about to do—to enter the cage of an untamed lion, whose ferocity was boundless.

He defied any other man to do it, especially the noted Englishman, Strongbow, whom, he was assured, had honoured him with his presence there that afternoon.

This challenge was eagerly taken up by the audience.

As Spaniards they were desirous of lowering the colours of a foreigner, as they naturally decreed Dick to be.

To them the reasoning of Wampa about REAL strength was very acceptable.

For a few moments every eye was fixed upon the place where Dick stood.

He came quickly forward, leant out of the box, and cried aloud in Spanish—

" I accept the challenge of this man."

" Dick—Dick !" cried Carl, from the back of the box, " what next ?"

But his remonstrance was drowned in the loud plaudits of the general audience.

They saw there was a possibility of something very exciting to be obtained for their money.

But, in the box where the two ladies were, the one wearing the veil was visibly moved.

She took out a piece of paper from her pocket, and, having scribbled a few words thereon, gave it to her attendant.

Wampa was now ready to begin.

Another glance at his watch told him it was time to enter the cage, and, descending the steps, he u bolted the door and stepped in.

At the same moment almost the attendant of the lady opened the door of Dick's box, slipped the small piece of paper into his hand, and vanished without a word.

" What's this ?" asked Dick, looking around in amazement.

" A strange time for a billet-doux," said Carl.

Dick unfolded the paper, and read as follows—

" *You must not go into the lion's cage.* " L."

Dick had no need to ask who had written the letter, but he had no idea who the veiled writer was.

Nor could he see her now, for shortly after the attendant left her she deserted her box and returned no more.

" It is a wish I would gladly gratify if I could, but I cannot," thought Dick.

He folded the paper, put it into his pocket, and turned his attention to the cage.

Wampa was going through an ordinary performance with the lion, the beast crouching and quivering before him, obeying sullenly the words of command as it stared half stupefied at the " Monarch of Tamers."

It was soon over, and Wampa backed out of the cage, not sorry, it seemed, to finish with a whole skin.

Another glance at his watch showed him that in five minutes the poison would have lost its effect, and it would be dangerous for any living man to enter the cage.

One effect of the poison was that it acted as an AFTER stimulant, giving additional strength to any animal to which it had been administered.

Dick lost no time in getting down to the side of the lion-tamer by the simple way of simply dropping out of the box to the floor beneath.

His appearance in this way was unexpected to Wampa.

He stared hard and drew back a pace.

" Give me the whip," said Dick.

" Senor," said Wampa, " one moment. There is no hurry. I wish to say a few words to the audience."

" The whip !" said Dick, again.

As Wampa still hesitated he seized him by the wrist and closed his iron fingers upon it.

With a howl Wampa dropped the whip, and Dick picked it up.

" I shall enter the cage," he said, to the audience, " and will soon come back. ON MY RETURN I CHALLENGE THIS MAN TO RE-ENTER IT."

Wampa's face turned to a yellow hue, and his eyes seemed to bulge out of his head with sudden alarm.

He saw that a new peril was in store for him.

If Dick should come out scot free the lion would be in far too dangerous a state for him to encounter.

With a light step Dick ascended the steps, unbolted the door, and entered the cage.

With his eyes on the beast he pushed the door to with his foot.

Then with whip ready he advanced slowly.

The lion shook itself, like one dispelling the effects of sleep, and reared its head proudly and angrily.

Then, crouching for a moment, with eyes that were brilliant with the lightning of wrath, it gave vent to an awful roar and made its spring.

CHAPTER LXIII.

THE EYE OF MAN AND BEAST—DICK HEARS NEWS OF MORELLE AND PAN—THE COUNT.

 OW often has the life of a man depended on his nerve and presence of mind?

Had Dick quailed for an instant before the lion he would have been a dead man; but he stood firm, and kept his eyes fixed upon the glowing optics of the savage beast.

A man looking at a wild beast will not cause it to retreat.

One must let the animal see that there is courage behind the look—that the man has absolutely no fear, then the victory will be his.

It was only for a few moments that Dick and the lion remained gazing at each other. The brute was about to spring, and when at last it bounded forward it was only in a half-hearted manner, so that all Dick had to do to avoid it was to step lightly aside.

The lion in professional parlance "missed its tip," and as it passed Dick it received a cut upon its haunches the like of which it had never known before.

Dick put all his strength into the blow, and it raised a blue ridge on the skin of the beast. A roar of pain from the terrible mouth of the lion followed, and then it threw itself down upon the floor of the cage to lick out the sting of the whip.

Dick smiled, for he knew that the victory had been won. A touch of his boot sufficed to make the lion shift his ground, and step by step he made it move round the cage until it crouched in a corner —subdued—abject in its bearing towards him.

The plaudits of the spectators filled the circular hall, and high above them was heard the roar of the delighted Butterflick.

"Bully for the captain!" he shouted; "there's not another lion-tamer in the world can touch him. Hoor-o-o-o-o-ar!"

His stentorian voice was heard all over the theatre. Even the lion was moved to raise its head and stare about as if in search of the owner of it.

But it soon forgot him as Dick came forward, and stooping down, thrust his face close to that of the beast.

Eye to eye now indeed, and the huge brute was terribly cowed.

It grovelled and whined in the most abject manner.

That was enough for Dick; he had won the victory, and rising, he backed out of the cage, closing the door behind him.

Walking to the "Monarch of Lion-tamers," who was fully as much cowed as the beast, Dick said—

"It is now your turn to enter the cage again."

"Mercy! spare me," whimpered Wampa.

"Did you spare me?" demanded Dick, sternly; "was not your object to see me killed? Did you not time my entrance into the cage when the drug had ceased to act and the furious beast was ready to tear me to pieces? You fool. I knew the trick, but I was not afraid."

"If you expose me I am ruined," said Wampa.

Dick turned from him in disgust and walked back to the side, where he climbed up into his box and motioned to his friends to leave.

"It is time for us to go," he said; "we can safely leave Wampa to the audience, who will be sure to settle with him."

He was right. The cries for Wampa to go again into the cage increased in force, and as he stood, sullen with fear, between the people and the lions, their demands became thundering.

"Coward—coward!" was the cry.

In vain he held up his arms for them to be still, that he might speak. The cry was "To the cage— to the cage!" and at last he wheeled round and fled.

The disorder in the place was now very great, but it ended in noise. Nobody was disposed to do injury to Wampa's stock-in-trade—the lions in the cage—and after a considerable amount of yelling the audience dispersed to carry the news of Wampa's defeat from one end of Madrid to the other.

It was not the sort of tidings they cared to carry, but there was no shirking the truth. Wampa, for some reason the public could not quite understand at first, had refused to enter the cage a second time. Why?

The truth in this case, as it often does, soon leaked out, and before the day was over there were a thousand tongues busy with the talk of a drugged lion for the Spaniard and a really savage one for the Englishman.

There, as here, the people have a sense of justice, and, despite the fact that it was to the disadvantage of their countryman, they utterly condemned the conduct of Wampa.

It was hardly likely that he would exhibit in Madrid again.

Meanwhile Dick and his friends, all elated with the outcome of the adventure, had returned to their hotel.

Mrs. Pardiggle Brown asked her husband why HE had not gone into the cage, like a man, and he replied—

"If I had been fool enough I should have come out nothing like a man, if ever I had got out at all. That lion would have made a door-mat of me."

"Oh! if I only durst do such a thing," said Muffins to Butterflick, "I think I should die happy."

"You would die, in course," said Butterflick; "but if you ever came out of that cage alive, old Sally, your mother, would be proud of you."

"Old Sally isn't my mother, you know," hinted Muffins.

"My lad," said Butterflick, tenderly, "she might have been. Rum things happens in this world. You never can tell what's going to turn up."

On his return to the hotel, Dick was made the recipient of quite an ovation.

The news of his triumph had gone before him.

and his entrance into the place was the signal for a reception on the part of the proprietor and the attendants he was not prepared for.

The host, addressing him as "Milord Prince," said he was honoured by the presence of such a guest, and hoped he would stay to lend lustre to his modest domicile.

The garcons were in a state of perspiring excitement, and fluttered about him like so many butterflies.

They seemed to have no eyes or ears for anyone else in the party.

About an hour before their return a letter was brought, addressed to Dick, in a delicate female hand.

He knew who it was from before he opened it; it was from Lucella.

"*Let this be your last risk,*" she wrote. "*Surely you have done enough in this way? Is there nothing higher to aim at? Forgive me! I do not wish to pain you; I desire only to see you great.*"

There was no signature to the letter, but he knew who it was from, and he placed it with the other relics of his love.

It was hard for him to have given his heart to one so high above him, and harder still to know that she returned his love, with a barrier that appeared to be insurmountable between them.

Dick thought it over a great deal that night, and eventually he came to a resolve to put himself in a proper position with Lucella and her parents, or end it for good and all.

"On the morrow I will visit the count," he said. "To-day I have bearded one lion in his den, why not another?"

The evening was destined to be a lively one, for many people of position called to do him honour.

Those of birth simply left cards, but the mayor and certain members of the corporation had to be seen and thanked for their commendations of Dick's valour.

Why they should take this trouble he did not at first perceive, but ere they went away they spoke of a great local festival, to raise funds for the city charities, and if Dick would only consent to exhibit there in some way they were sure he would be a great draw.

It was to take place in two days' time, and he told his visitors that he would, if possible, attend in the cause of charity, and show the Spaniards what a strong man could do.

But he warned them that he was a little uncertain about his movements, and if he left them suddenly it would be because urgent matters drew him away.

The urgent matters were, of course, connected with Morelle and Pan. Up to that time he believed they were in Madrid.

A visit from the chief of the police, however, dispelled that illusion.

He put in an appearance at a late hour—a fine-built man, in the uniform of a general—a most imposing personage, but affable on the whole.

"It is to my friend Don Sebastian de la Tourville that I am indebted for the permission to call upon you," he said. "From him I received commands to watch one Morelle and his companion."

He had been shown up to a room where Dick and Carl were alone. The others were scattered about the hotel.

Butterflick, with Phil and Pardiggle Brown, in the billiard-room; Mrs. Brown in the drawing-room; and Muffins in the kitchen with the servants, who were making much of him.

"I have to thank you for your courtesy," said Dick, handing the prefect of police a chair. "It has put you to much trouble, I fear."

"None at all. It is so easy to trace a foreigner here. Madrid is not Paris or London. Our visitors are few."

A bottle of wine being suggested, he offered no objection, and it was ordered, with cigars.

Manillas and a bottle of port were brought and placed upon the table, which Dick had drawn up to the open window.

The prefect drew out a folded paper from his breast and spread it before him upon the table.

"Morelle and Pan," he began, "giving no name, but heard so to address each other, are in the Prada-alley, keeping aloof, living quietly. That is the first report."

He folded it up, put it aside, and drew another from his breast.

"This," he said, "is the second and final report of my agents. Morelle and Pan, last seen in the quarry, but heard of bearing south; cause of hasty departure, Morelle having shot Parnello the assassin."

"They are gone then?" said Dick.

"Yes, gone, but be not disappointed or alarmed. They will not be lost sight of. It is impossible for them to get out of the country unseen. In two days' time you will be made acquainted with their destination."

"And for that information I must wait here."

"It will be better so, senor."

"In that case," said Carl, smiling, "you will be able to do your best, Dick, to add to the funds of the charities."

"What is that?" asked the prefect, quickly.

They told him of the visit of the mayor and some of his councillors, and their declared object in coming to see Dick.

"How is it," he asked, "your adage—your saying in England—Charity shall begin at home. It is so here. The mayor will give to charity—a little, when he has given to himself—much. I know him, but you had better go. It will please the people."

CHAPTER LXIV.

BUTTERFLICK GETS INTO TROUBLE WITH A FENCING-MASTER—THE STRANGE DUEL IN THE SQUARE.

HE billiard-tables of Madrid are like those of Paris. They are made for the cannon game only; there are no pockets.

This was not a very serious matter for Pardiggle Brown —who had never played a game in his life—but his companion, Butterflick, said it would be impossible for him to play on such a table.

"I'm used to a bagatelle table with pockets," he

said; "give me nine holes and I can do something, but this—I call it fool's play."

Nevertheless he and Pardiggle Brown started a game, and Phil sat upon a lounge looking on. Ere he had made half-a-dozen strokes, Butterflick had cut a slit in the cloth three inches long.

"Did you ever see the likes o' that?" he asked; "the cue regularly slipped off the ball."

"It's all right," said Phil, "you want nine holes to play with, and if you are smart you will soon have them—on the cloth.'

"It seems to me," said Butterflick, "that the safest thing to do is to play with the thick end of this 'ere stick."

And reversing the cue, he proceeded to play with the butt-end of it, to the great enjoyment of several Spaniards who were looking on.

There was one portly person, quite a big grandee in his way, who showed his mirth in a manner which Butterflick considered offensive.

But having been cautioned by Dick not to enter lightly into any quarrel, he bore it very well for the time. At last a louder burst of laughter than any preceding it took him over the border.

"You laughed, senor," he said; "may I ask what for?"

"Pardon," said the Spaniard, "I speek little English."

"Durned little, I should say," replied Butterflick, "but you larf a lot in Spanish. Take my advice and soften it."

Butterflick, as he spoke, made a vicious dig at his ball and sent it flying off the table.

This the Spaniard considered to be especially funny, and he laughed louder than ever.

The others laughed too, but in a way not so offensive. Taking them collectively they were not objectionable.

Butterflick walked across the room, picked up the ball, and replaced it upon the table.

"Now," he said, to the Spaniard, "let me see what you can do with it?"

"Pardon," replied the Spaniard; "I do not play."

"You play the fool," retorted Butterflick.

"Senor!"

"The fool—the derned fool—the lopsided, one-eyed fool."

"Senor, you are rude.'

"I shall be glad to take a lesson in perliteness from you. Git out of the way."

Butterflick pushed him aside, and the Spaniard laughed no more.

He lost some of the colour in his face, and a few words were hissed out from between his set teeth.

Then he stalked out of the room.

"Settled him," said Butterflick, looking round at the company. "If there's one thing I do hate it's a dern fool."

Phil Norton laughed and Pardiggle Brown smiled, but the Spaniards looked grave.

"Will the senor pardon me," said one of the bystanders, "but he is not settled. Varlos, the fencing-master, is not so easily quelled."

"So he's a fencing-master, is he?" returned Butterflick. "That makes no difference. I've upset him."

Nothing more was said about the matter, and they went on with the game.

When they had cut five holes in the cloth between them they thought it was time to give up.

The marker—there was only one—was scoring for two players at the other end of the room, and not suspecting mischief, simply came up and took his fee when they left.

As it was getting late they retired for the night. Butterflick occupied a double-bedded room, in which his adopted son, Muffins, also slept.

Muffins was by this time in bed, and Butterflick, seeing he was asleep, turned in too.

If there ever was such a thing as a thorough good sleeper, Bill Butterflick was the man.

Having got between the sheets he went off, according to custom, and at once entered upon the task of cracking the ceiling with his snoring.

It must be confessed that he did not QUITE succeed, but no man ever went nearer completing the job. If the ceiling was NOT cracked nobody had a right to blame Bill Butterflick.

Muffins snored also—a compound snore between a cornopean and a penny whistle.

In the rooms on either side were two Spaniards, who either were not good sleepers, or they found it impossible to get repose with the concert provided for them free of expense.

They first signified their objection to it by tapping at the wall.

Neither of the sleepers heard, but slept on, rising gradually into higher flights of nasal excellence.

At last both the Spanish gentlemen determined to come out and say something, and unhappily for themselves they chose the same moment for so doing.

By that time everybody in the hotel was in bed, or supposed to be so, and the lights were out.

The consequence was that they ran against each other in the dark, knocking their heads together as they stooped to find the handle of the offenders' door.

Being in an exceedingly irritable mood, they did not wait to ask each other any questions, but aimed a blow at each other with telling effect.

One felt as if he had endeavoured to impede the flight of a cannon-ball with his eye, and the other experienced the sensation which a rash man would probably feel if he tried to make a railway buffer of his nose.

Unaccustomed to pugilistic work, they both retired to their rooms with the precipitancy which thoughtless people attribute to fear, and, having locked themselves in, they vituperated the snorers in the choicest Spanish for awhile, before they finally went to bed.

Butterflick heard nothing, saw nothing, until the morning, when he was awakened by being shaken, and, opening his eyes, he saw Muffins by his bedside.

"What is it, my son?" he asked.

"That Irish chap, Don Timole, called to see you," replied Muffins.

"And what may he want?'

"He wouldn't say. He says it is private, and nobody else is to know anything about it."

"I know," said Butterflick; "he wants to borrow a few pounds to carry him through until his remittance arrives. It's an old story, but as he isn't a bad sort of fellow I'll oblige him just for once."

Don Timole was below in one of the ante-rooms.

He still wore the apparel he had borrowed of Don Sebastian de la Tourville, the only change in him

"Seven to one!   Are you not ashamed of yourselves?" she said.

being that he wore his hat more on one side than ever.

"You are an early visitor," said Butterflick, as they shook hands.

"It's on business or an early nature I'm here, i' faith," replied Don Timole ; "but it's soon done if you'll name your friend."

"Which friend ?" asked Butterflick. "I've several."

He was puzzled, and still more so by the smile that expanded the face of Don Timole.

"And that's your experience of life, Butterflick," he said ; "not to know what I mane ?"

"I'm blessed if I do."

"Then it's myself as has come from Varlos, and it's satisfaction he wants right away."

"Varlos—Varlos ?" said Butterflick. "Oh ! I remember now. It was that fellow who grinned at me. Well, what sort of satisfaction does he want ?"

"He, being the party insulted, chooses swords."

"Naturally guessing that I'll be in a fix there. But may I ask how you come to be here as his friend ? You've been well treated by us."

"By accident," replied Don Timole, coolly. "Hearing a jintleman raving about being insulted I offered to help him, not thinking that it would bring me back to ould frinds. But it's no offence on my part, I'm sure."

"Then Varlos isn't your friend ?"

"I niver set eyes on him till last night."

"I'm danged," cried Butterflick, "if you are not a rum 'un. You'd have got level with old Sally, and it's a pity you weren't arter her afore I went wrong. So you want a friend. Well, I don't know o' one I'd care to bother over this paltry business, except my son Muffins."

"He's but a bhoy."

"He's a man in some things, and he'll see me through this job. Although I'm no more of a hand at using the sword than I am at working a steam-engine, I won't shirk it. But I make one stiperlation afore I fight."

"What's that ?"

"If we can't get on with swords that I've the second choice o' weapons."

"Oh ! that's granted shure," said Don Timole, readily ; "but you'll get through with swords right enough, and if ye get pinked it's myself that will help to give you a dacent funeral."

"I'm obliged, and thanky," said Butterflick ; "and now I'll fetch my boy down, so that this job may be got through with right away."

It is needless to say that Muffins was fairly staggered when he learned what was required of him ; but he took upon himself the position of second to his adopted father without hesitation.

The meeting between Muffins and Don Timole was a veritable burlesque of the real thing.

They bowed and kept up a portentous gravity while settling preliminaries that was very edifying.

Varlos, it seemed, was anxious to conclude the affair at once, and was waiting in a quiet square hard by, where they could fight, as he grimly said, long enough without interruption.

His eyes lighted up with an evil look when Butterflick appeared.

He meant to kill him, and had brought a very keen pair of swords with him.

Don Timole, as in duty bound, acquainted his principal with the condition Butterflick had named, and Varlos made no objection to it.

"By the saints !" he said, with suppressed ferocity, "he will find one kind of weapon all that is required."

Muffins, now that the eventful moment was at hand, began to feel a little queer in the region of his waistband.

What would be his after-feelings if his adopted afther should fall ?

"Dad," he said, "I wish you wouldn't fight. You know nothing about swords."

"You leave that chap to me," replied Butterflick. "If I don't bounce all the fight out of him from now till Christmas call me a fool."

Varlos had taken off his coat, and motioned for Butterflick to do the same.

"Not me," replied that worthy fellow ; "if I can't hide you with my coat on I'll go under. Now then, hand me my toasting-iron !"

"You have your choice," said Varlos.

"Either will do," said Butterflick. "Are you ready ? Whoop—la ! here's at you."

"Stop !" cried Varlos. "I not fight that way."

Butterflick was slashing and cutting at Varlos as he would have done with a riding-whip, which of course was absurd in a fencing-master's eyes.

The weapons were simply pointed, and had no cutting powers.

"I believe a man can fight as he pleases," shouted Butterflick. "Whoop ! mind your skin, old chap."

"Stay," cried Varlos, backing, and defending himself as well as he could ; "you are mad—you will only break the swords. Ah ! it is so, fool."

Butterflick with a heavy slash had brought the weapons together, and broken the sword of Varlos short off by the hilt. The fencing-master danced about cursing and raving like one demented.

"Now you go easy," said Butterflick ; "ye will want all your breath for the second part of this show. The choice of weapons is mine now."

"I care not what it is," hissed Varlos. "Give me something that I may kill him."

"Once more," said Butterflick, soothingly, "go easy."

All this time they had been undisturbed in the square.

The houses around gave out no signs of life, the majority of them being empty, and in those inhabited the occupants had not risen.

"You've got your coat off," said Butterflick, "and you've got the weppins. I've fixed 'em. Up with your dukes."

As Butterflick spoke he raised his clenched hands and began to spar with more vigour than science.

"Hurroo for ye, Butterflick !" cried Don Timole. "It's a broth of a bhoy ye are. Give him one on the breathing trumpet."

"Keep off," cried Varlos. "This is folly. I fight not in this way."

"But I do," said Butterflick. "You've had your innings with your weppins, and I'm having a go with mine. How's that for a start ?"

And lunging out his fist, he dealt Varlos a terrific blow between the eyes, that sent him down upon his back as if he had been thrown from the roof of a house.

"Time !" cried Butterflick. "If he isn't up in half-a-minute, Don Timole, you've got to throw up the sponge."

"It can be thrown up at once," replied Don

Timole, who was kneeling beside his principal, "for, by the blessed pig of Anna Maria O'Brien, ye've killed him."

CHAPTER LXV.

THE SECOND PART OF THE DUEL—VARLOS FEELS AN IRON HAND—DON TIMOLE'S SUAVITY.

IGNS of awakening in the square began to increase. From the windows of the upper rooms of half a score of houses curious faces, mainly those of women, peered forth with staring eyes fixed upon the burly Englishman and the agile Varlos. Muffins and Don Timole, standing aside looking on, scarcely counted a part of the show.

Varlos soon showed signs of coming round, and staggered to his feet, with the assistance of Don Timole.

"I shall not fight with such weapon so low," hissed Varlos. "Fist indeed—English knuckles! No!"

"Look here," said Butterflick, "you had first choice, and I stood to it, and if you are going to shirk the job when it comes to my turn do you know what I'll do?"

"No low fist," repeated Varlos.

"I'll take you by the neck and legs and snap your back across my knee like a rabbit," continued Butterflick. "I hate a shuffler. Up with 'em."

"I know it not—the box," cried Varlos.

"And I knowed it not—the toasting-iron," said Butterflick, mocking him. "Here's at you—one for your eye."

Butterflick was not the most scientific of boxers, but for a man of his size and weight he was pretty smart. Lunging out his huge fist, he struck Varlos —not on the eye, for he turned his head aside, but near the ear—and down he went again.

Knocked out.

It is a phrase with a new meaning. Pugilistic persons in the old days were often knocked out, but not, except by accident, in the modern style, which we believe was introduced by that unmitigated ruffian—Sullivan, the American slogger.

Butterflick, by accident, performed the feat which all latter-day pugilists aim at, and knocked out his man.

He laid upon the ground insensible, and perhaps nobody there was more astonished than the striker.

"Here! get up," he exclaimed; "you can't have had enough of it already."

Don Timole came forward to pick up his man, and he saw that there was no shamming in the matter.

"The saints be praised!" he said; "ye've settled the dirty thafe."

This was, perhaps, a comment not to be expected from the second of a fallen man : but Don Timole's heart was probably with the victor. His share in the business arose out of a natural love of fighting.

Anything in the way of a shindy was meat and bread to him.

The spectators at the windows were calling to those within the houses to come and see the fight. More windows were opened, and from the doors many men rushed out to learn what it all meant.

Varlos, reclining on the knee of Don Timole, was recognised by two or three, and they began to mutter among themselves.

He was no great favourite with the people around, but he was a Spaniard, and the others were "foreigners."

"Say," cried one, in his own tongue ; "what is this—three to one?"

"Three to one!" replied Don Timole, in the same language. "You fools! don't you know a British duel when you see one? Swords first and fists afterwards."

Varlos was now coming to the second time, and, opening his eyes, he stared about him like a man who had been drugged.

A dim idea of recent events returned to him, and he fixed his eyes on Butterflick, shuddering.

"No more iron hand," he murmured.

"What did he say?" asked Butterflick.

Don Timole translated the words.

"All right," replied the victor ; "if he gives in I've done."

"Up goes the sponge, shure," said Don Timole, with an upward action of his hand. "Varlos, ye're a poor fighter, but, if ye was born without an inside it's not myself can put it into ye. Stand up, there."

He put the defeated man upon his feet, and Varlos, in the careful, gingerly way one handles a very sore place, placed his hand on his jaw.

"His hand," he said to his countrymen, "travels like a cannon-ball. It smashes—crushes ; my jaw is in pieces!"

Butterflick was moving away with Muffins, and Don Timole, having seen his man come out of his swoon, prepared to follow him.

"It's a poor figure you've made of yourself," he said ; "and hang your impudence for asking me to stand by you! You'd best be civil, or I'll be calling you out for it."

With this parting shot Don Timole swaggered off after Butterflick, whose arm he took in his own easy, graceful style.

"Ye're a man afther my own heart," he said, "and it was as good as getting a thumping legacy to see ye knock the speerit out of the worm."

"I hardly touched him," said Butterflick. "I don't understand it."

"You hit him on the point, dad," explained Muffins.

"Hit him where?" asked Butterflick, staring.

"On the point of the jaw," said Muffins ; "it's where they knock a chap out. I've settled lots of fellers with it in the old days."

"Oh! have you indeed?" said Butterflick, looking doubtfully at him. "And where did you pick up the trick of it?"

"Oh! knocking about," replied Muffins ; "hearing people talk, seeing it done. I don't like it, but it's useful when you have a go with a chap bigger than yourself, and he isn't up to it."

"Could you knock a man out?" asked Butterflick.

"Yes, if I got the chance."

"Could you knock ME out?"

"I think I could, dad."

"Well, things have come to something," said Butterflick, "when a boy like that tells a fellow of my size that he could knock him out!"

"You asked me, dad," said Muffins, apologetically.

"It don't matter—you've said it," returned Butterflick; "and I say that boys ain't nowadays what they were. Why, you ain't got out of the spanking age! The world's turned topsy-turvey!"

"Whichever way it is," said Don Timole, "it's the right time for breakfast, and if ye're agreeable we'll have some."

"Certainly," answered Butterflick. "I'll peck a bit with you. Where are you hanging out?"

"Your hotel is handy," said Don Timole. "It would be a pity to have to walk so far as mine, and I'm doubtful if the cooking is as good. Butterflick, having seen you through this little affair of honour, I'll breakfast wid you. If there's one thing that's a part of Don Timole Murphaleo which is a credit to him, it's the noticeable fact that he never deserts his friends."

Butterflick looked at him with a puzzled face.

There seemed to be something about his cheery and FAITHFUL companion which he could not quite understand.

But he was too hungry to go into the question then, so they entered the hotel together.

CHAPTER LXVI.

THE DUKE'S LETTER—DICK GOES TO THE EMBASSY—A SOMEWHAT STORMY INTERVIEW.

HE Duke of Lavante will be glad if Mr. Strongbow will make it convenient to call upon him at the Swedish Embassy. The duke will be there this day from two till three o'clock, and will, during that time be at the service of Mr. Strongbow."

"Now, Carl," said Dick, as he read the letter aloud, "tell me what it means."

"I don't like it," replied Carl.

"But why should he send for me if it is to say something agreeable?"

"About Lucella, you mean?"

"Yes."

"My dear fellow, prospective fathers-in-law await a word from prospective sons-in-law. They do not send for them—at least men like the duke do not—to ask their intentions; and furthermore, you and Lucella cannot as yet be said—"

"No, certainly not," hastily interposed Dick, "we have scarcely exchanged a dozen words. But, Carl, old fellow, I have THOUGHT so much about her that it seems as if she were part of myself. I have had day dreams of her which have been very real."

"I understand," said Carl, sympathetically, "and it is a pity."

"You think he intends to say something disagreeable."

"These men of title are very proud."

"Yes, but the true gentleman is never rude, and avoids giving needless pain. But it is useless to speculate on what this letter means. I will call at two o'clock and hear the best or worst."

Dick made no further reference to the matter that morning.

After breakfast, which they partook of alone, they strolled about Madrid, avoiding places where Dick might be recognised.

He did not succeed in entirely escaping the attention of the public.

Occasionally some passer-by would stare at him, stop, turn back, and take another look at him.

Sometimes he would get a favourable word or two, such as "The saints preserve your strength, senor;" but it was as often a muttered curse or a scowl, for the Britisher was not very popular in Spain just then, owing to certain speculative men in this country having advanced money to Don Carlos.

But on the whole the walk was a quiet one, and after an early luncheon Dick set out for the Swedish Embassy.

He was evidently expected, for an officer, standing on the steps, saluted him and exclaimed—

"Mr. Strongbow, I believe?" in most excellent English.

Dick bowed in assent.

"His grace is disengaged," said the officer, "and will see you at once."

"I am at his service," replied Dick.

The embassy was an old mansion, which had once possessed rare beauty, and was still, within and without, architecturally splendid.

It was of Moorish design, and the excellent taste of its present occupier had led to its being harmoniously furnished.

But Dick had no eyes for the building or its contents. Dick sat down upon a chair on the other side of the table, and the duke resumed his seat.

His mind was busy with thoughts of Lucella and the coming interview.

He accompanied the officer through several chambers ere they reached an inner court—open to the air, with a small fountain bubbling up cool water—very grateful in that climate in the middle of the heated day.

It was here they found the duke seated on a lounge, with a round table at his hand, on which were a number of letters and papers.

"Mr. Strongbow," announced the officer, and disappeared behind the heavy curtains that covered the entrance to the court.

It was one of the features of the interior of the house that there were no doors. All the communicating openings between the chambers were covered with tapestry of modern manufacture, but in full accord with the ancient stonework of elaborate design abounding throughout.

The duke rose from his seat—dignified, but without any sign of hauteur.

"Mr. Strongbow," he said, "you are more than kind to come so promptly in response to my expressed wish to see you. I trust it is an augury of a pleasant interview. Be seated."

After one moment's silence, his grace, speaking calmly, opened the conversational battle.

"Mr. Strongbow," he said, "I have sent for you to make a request, which I trust you will accede to. It is not the first time I have had occasion to com. municate with you, although this is our first personal interview. On the previous occasion when I felt it necessary to write to you, I found your conduct, on the whole, satisfactory."

"To have satisfied your grace in one thing is gratifying to me," replied Dick, quietly, "and I trust I shall be able to see my way to act so as to continue to deserve your commendation."

The duke cast a quick glance at Dick. By the slightest possible bending of the brows it seemed that he did not exactly like this answer.

"To come to the point at once," he said, "my request, Mr. Strongbow, is that you leave Madrid as speedily as possible."

"May I ask why?" enquired Dick.

"Mr. Strongbow," said the duke, rising, and walking slowly to and fro, "surely you will not press me for an answer? It is the old story of a handsome—and, I must say, engaging—man, and a weak, foolish girl. Need I say more?"

"Your grace probably supposes that I am here with some design?" said Dick.

"I can but assume so," was the reply.

"Your grace is right," rejoined Dick, "but it is a design that in no way concerns you. When I came hither I had no hope, no thought of finding you here. It was quite another matter which brought me to the place."

"May I ask what that matter is?" asked the duke, with a slight smile that betrayed incredulity.

Dick rose from his seat, with his face slightly flushed. They stood facing each other, both in their respective ways commanding men.

"I am here," said Dick, "on the track of a man who holds the secret of my birth."

Again the duke smiled, but he strove to hide it by passing his hand across his mouth.

"What is the romance of your birth?" he asked.

"My mother," said Dick, "was a circus rider, and my father an English gentleman."

"Of the name of Strongbow?"

"Strongbow is not my name."

The duke turned quickly upon him.

"You live under an alias," he said. "I hardly expected it."

"I gave the name one night on impulse to an enquiring stranger," said Dick, "and ever since I have borne it, and shall be content to bear it while I live, so long as I get at the true story of my life. Duke, I would not exchange the name of Strongbow for yours."

"It is an exchange that could not possibly take place," said the duke, coldly. "You are right to be proud of your name, for it is widely known. What satisfies the ambition of one does not, of course, meet the desires of another. As a showman—"

"Stop, sir," cried Dick. "I am not ashamed of the fact of my having been a public performer, but I am no showman in the sense you imply."

"You draw a nice distinction," said the duke; "you admit your mother—"

"We will leave my mother out of the question,' interposed Dick, "and confine ourselves to your request. You ask me to leave Madrid, and I will do so. It was my intention to leave."

"When will you go—to-day?"

"No."

"To-morrow?"

"I cannot say."

"This is quibbling!" said the duke, with some show of heat. "You say you will go—"

"In my own time," said Dick, "or rather when the object of my life permits. I may have to go in a day or two, or it may be a week or a month—"

"Enough, Mr. Strongbow," said the duke, "I see you are not disposed to be compliant, and I must look to my interests in another way. You have only yourself to blame."

"Am I to understand this is a threat?" asked Dick.

"You may take it as you please," was the answer; "as for my daughter Lucella—"

He stopped and bit his lip. It was evident that he had, in the heat of the moment, been betrayed into speaking of Lucella contrary to his intention.

"Aye," said Dick, "your daughter, Lucella. Duke, I may anger you by what I am going to say, but I cannot keep it. I love her, and what is more—one day I look to win her."

"YOU WIN HER!" cried the duke.

"Yes—why not?" asked Dick, proudly; "what have I done to debar me from hope? Is there aught dishonourable in my career—"

"But, my dear fellow," said the duke, endeavouring to speak calmly, "think of the social gulf between you."

"It at present exists only in your eyes," said Dick.

"And furthermore, Mr. Strongbow, as I must call you, not being honoured with your name—"

"An unworthy sneer, duke."

"And furthermore, may I ask on what grounds you think my daughter encourages your ambition?"

"One ground," said Dick, "is my presence here to-day by your desire."

It was a good answer, and it hit home. The duke walked to the far end of the court and back again ere he made reply.

"Mr. Strongbow," he said, "you have the advantage of me in every way. I admit that my daughter, by her demeanour at home, does encourage you—that in blind folly she looks down to you with the eyes of infatuation. It is not love, Mr. Strongbow, and an alliance would only bring misery to you both. I would cast her off, and when she realises the position she has lost she will hate you. The alliance would be a curse."

"I think, with your grace's permission, I will terminate this interview," said Dick. "It has brought no satisfaction to either of us, and I will respectfully take my leave."

"One moment," said the duke. "I will give you a week, if you will promise to go then."

"I will promise nothing," answered Dick.

"Then the consequences be upon your own head," cried the duke, as he turned his back upon him.

Dick, with anger in his eyes, swung round upon his heel and strode away.

The duke stood listening to his footsteps on the marble floor until they had died away in the distance, and then threw himself into his chair, clasping his head with his hands.

" Defied by both—but it shall never be !" he muttered. " Marry a showman—Lucella, the daughter of the Duke of Lavante—never ! I'll employ the knife of the assassin first. Nay—I will kill HER—my only child—as I would to save her from dishonour !"

CHAPTER LXVII.

DICK AND LUCELLA—SEVEN TO ONE.

'LL woo and win her," thought Dick, as he strolled back to the hotel, " Nay, if she will come with me. I'll bear her off. A humbling of his pride will make a better man of him. Infatuation—not love—he called it. What if it should be so ? Shall I sacrifice Lucella to avenge myself on her haughty father ? Heaven forbid !"

He was both angry and troubled. Dick was the soul of honour, and if Lucella did not love him with a love that would last he would leave her for good and all.

But how was he to know ?

He had never even had what might be called an interview with her.

Hitherto he had held aloof, not seeking her, as a less honourable man might have done ; but the interview with the duke had destroyed his delicacy in this respect.

" I will see her once," he said, " and hear from her own lips what there is in store for me. What matters to me whether her father is a duke or a peasant ? I love her. That is enough for Dick Strongbow."

Of the interview all he said to Carl about it was that he had judged aright—it was not favourable—and proceeded to carry out his resolve to speak to Lucella as soon as an opportunity presented itself.

At night he went out alone and walked down to the Embassy, where he took up a position so as to see who went in and out.

Prudence dictated to him that he should as much as possible keep out of sight.

He did not like the idea of it, for he felt mean, and he soon abandoned the position he at first took up.

It was a doorway on the opposite side of the road, and as he emerged from it the officer who had received him in the afternoon came down the flight of steps.

He descended leisurely, being engaged in putting on his gloves and looking about him.

The street just there was fairly well lighted, and he soon espied Dick, who had seen the officer as he emerged from the house.

There was a moment's hesitation on the latter's part, and then he crossed the road to where Dick was standing.

" Pardon me, my young friend," he said, with easy familiarity, " but are you wise ?"

" If I am," replied Dick, with a smile, " it would be foolish of me to talk about it. A man is but a poor judge of his own wisdom."

" That is something akin to evasion," said the officer ; " you know what I mean. The duke is angry."

" I regret to hear it," said Dick, politely ; " it would be to the advantage of a man of his years to keep his temper."

" He is justly angry."

" That is possible—but what concern is it of mine ?"

" If he sees you here," said the officer, " he may send out some of his servants to remove you."

On hearing this Dick fairly laughed.

" I appreciate your kindly intention," he said, " but do you know how many men it would take to remove me ? I do not wish to boast, but if any of the duke's men have the temerity to attack me, I will make straws of them."

" It is my duty to report that you are here," said the officer.

" Is not this a public thoroughfare ?" demanded Dick. " And why should I not be here ? I thank you for your friendly hint ; but I will not budge of my own free will."

" In that case," said the officer, " I must call those who will see that you go."

He bowed to Dick, who returned his salute and walked across the road.

Pausing at the bottom of the steps, he looked back at Dick, who was sauntering up and down.

With a motion of his arm he asked the question—

" Will you not go away ?"

And Dick responded with a gesture—

" No !"

After that there was no more to be said on either side.

The officer went up the steps and disappeared within the house. In a few minutes he returned with half-a-dozen men at his heels.

They were, as far as Dick could see, unarmed, but they were all big men—not one under six feet.

He awaited their coming across the road, led by the officer, who once more tried persuasion in preference to force.

" My orders," he said, " are imperative. If I caught you prowling—"

" What ?"

" I beg your pardon. If I saw you hovering about here I was to have you removed."

" By what law ?"

" None that I know of, save the will of my leader, the Duke of Lavante."

" Remember," said Dick, quietly, " that it is not I who break the law, but you. If a hand is laid upon me I will not be responsible for the consequences. I care not to be assaulted by any man."

" I can only obey," replied the officer. " Will you leave here ?"

" No !"

" Then you must be made to do so. Men, you know your duty !"

They were not particularly eager to advance, but as six big men were opposed to one none of them cared to show the white feather, so they came forward in a body—slowly.

But ere they could reach Dick a white form emerged from the house, sped across the road, and glided between Dick and the men.

It was Lucella, who wore an evening dress of Indian muslin and a white silk shawl drawn over her shoulders.

No hat was upon her head—only the splendid crown of her rich, wavy hair.

Never before had she been so beautiful in Dick's

eyes. He could, for the moment, only stand still and look upon her as some fair vision.

"Go back!" she said. "Seven to one! Are you not ashamed of yourselves?"

"My lady," said the officer, "it is the duke's orders that this man be removed."

CHAPTER LXVIII.

A KNOTTY PROBLEM.

BESEECH you," said Dick, advancing, "not to stand between us. I am grateful to you for your consideration, but I do not fear these men."

"Fear! No, that is not in your nature," Lucella said, as she raised her eyes, so full of tenderness, to his; "nor would you fear if you saw death. But no servant of mine shall degrade you with his touch. "Back all of you. Disobey me, and to-morrow you shall be dismissed from the embassy."

They looked at each other and still hesitated; but an imperious gesture from her settled the question.

"My lady," said the officer, bowing, "we must obey you, but I have to remind you that I must report the matter to his grace."

"Report what you will," said Lucella; "but away with you at once. I will follow."

As the men turned to cross the road she glided up to Dick and whispered—

"You came to see me?"

"Yes," he answered, in a voice trembling with emotion.

"Be at yon statue at the top of the street in two hours," she said. "I will come there for a few minutes only. It may be the last meeting we shall have in this world. Do not fail."

He would have vowed that nothing should keep them asunder; but she took his answer for granted, and, hurrying with a light footstep across the road, she glided up the steps, past the sentries, and disappeared in the house.

Dick had no longer any excuse for lingering there.

His object had been attained. He had seen Lucella, and, with a good fortune bordering on the miraculous, obtained an appointment with her.

But how came it about that she would see him there?

Modest, simple maidens do not make appointments after this fashion. Was it boldness or innocence, or was she in deep distress, and stood in need of his assistance?

"Whatever may be the mainspring of her action," he mused, "I will be there. Oh! Lucella, never so dear to me as at this moment, if—if— Ah! with you I shall care for little else. Let ALL go—name, wealth, everything—rather than lose you now."

He had three-quarters of an hour to spare. There was time to go to his hotel and back.

It was something to do, and better than mere sauntering about. Anything to kill time.

A cigar and a chat with Carl would steady his tumultuous thoughts; but other company he did not care for just then.

He hastened back to the hotel, and was passing through the hall when the chief garcon presented himself before him with a note on a salver.

"From the prefect of police," he said.

Dick took the letter and thrust it into his pocket.

"It will do to read," he remarked, "AFTER I have seen Lucella."

He bounded upstairs to the sitting-room he occupied, and found nobody there.

He rang the bell and made inquiries of the garcon who responded.

All his friends were out, and none had left word whither they had gone.

It was unfortunate, and he must spend the time alone. So he ordered a bottle of light wine and a cigar, which were brought to him.

"Will the senor have another lamp lighted?" asked the garcon.

There was one upon the table, and Dick assured him it would suffice. The garcon bowed and left the room. After he was gone Dick brought out the prefect's letter, and mused as he turned it over and over in his hand.

"To read or not to read? What is here? Tidings that ought to take me away at once? If so, shall I —can I go?"

He hesitated a little more, but finally broke the seal. Inside was a short pithy communication.

"*The two men are on their way to England. They have by some means got hold of the travelling tickets and passports of two tourists. They go to England.*"

"To England—to London, where I may lose sight of them and never find them again."

There was a time-table lying at hand, and, opening it, he speedily found what he wanted to know.

The mail started at eleven o'clock. It was, for Spain, a quick train, and by catching it he could get ahead of Morelle and Pan.

Once ahead of them he would arrive in England first, and then it would be an easy matter to await their coming and put men upon their track.

Instinctively Dick guessed what they proposed to do. Gonzalo's papers were there, and it was to get them, and perhaps destroy them, that Morelle had ventured back to the old country.

"What can I do?" Dick asked himself. "Lucella here—my good name yonder. Which has the greater demand upon me? Love and honour call me—one from the north, the other here. Which am I to obey?"

CHAPTER LXIX.

DICK AND LUCELLA'S INTERVIEW—A WOMAN'S TRUST AND MAN'S HONOUR — FATHER AND DAUGHTER.

IF a man has to make a choice between two things of vital interest to himself, he invariably selects that in which the heart is the more closely concerned.

Dick was a strong, resolute fellow; but he was only mortal, and Lucella carried the day.

"I will see her and tell her all," he thought.

"It is well for her to know that I have no right that I am aware of to any name."

He wrote a short letter to the head of the police, thanking him for his courtesy, and despatched it by a special messenger.

He also wrote a few lines to Carl, to give him an idea of his whereabouts.

"There is no knowing what may happen," thought Dick, "especially as his grace does not look upon my suit with a favourable eye."

A few minutes before the appointed time he sauntered out and proceeded quietly in the direction of the Swedish Embassy, which he would have to pass. Prudence again prompted him to keep in the shadow of the houses as he went by.

But there was nobody in sight—neither servant nor guard—nor any light visible; all within had apparently gone to rest.

The statue Lucella spoke of stood at the top of the thoroughfare in which the embassy was situated.

It was a bronze figure of some Spanish potentate on a broad pedestal, with several steps for a base. On one side fell the light of an adjacent lamp— the rest was in shadow.

Dick was the first to arrive, being, like a true lover, before his time, and he sat down on one of the dark sides of the statue.

He thought of many things in a few brief moments, his mind being in a state of abnormal activity—of his early days with Gonzalo, his schooling in Germany, his after adventures.

With incredible rapidity the panorama of his eventful life was passing before him, and he had got as far as his early adventures in the Transvaal when the rustling of a dress fell upon his ear.

It was a slight sound, but it sufficed to wake him from his dream. Springing up, he saw Lucella, in a shrinking attitude, before him.

His impulse was to take her in his arms, but the look and bearing of the beautiful girl induced him to restrain his ardour for awhile.

"I am here," she said, "at a great risk, and I must not be long away."

"How shall I thank you for coming at all?" he replied; "you—the daughter of a proud duke! I —a man without a name!"

"I have been told your story," she said, hastily; "but it is nothing to me. You are not responsible for your birth. It is enough that you are brave, noble, and great in your life and actions."

"Who has told you my story?" asked Dick.

"My father."

"May I ask for a brief outline of that story—as told by him?"

"Can you ask me to repeat it," said Lucella, raising her lustrous eyes to his, "when I tell you that I care nothing for it—that it has not lessened you one iota in my—my—estimation?"

"Estimation is a cold word, Lucella," said Dick. "Does it not seem strange to you that I should be so familiar?"

"No," she answered, simply. "I have always thought of you as Dick. I heard it was your Christian name long ago, you know. But let us sit down."

She set the example, and Dick took a place by her side. He could no longer resist the desire to put his arm around her. She did not shrink from his touch, but allowed him to draw her close to him.

"Lucella," he said, "our being here is a confession of mutual love—is it not, dearest? From the first we were drawn to each other. It was to be."

"Do you believe in fate?" she asked.

"In some things," he replied. "I believe in there being a destiny for many of us. Rather let me call it a bearing in a certain direction. Yet we have only to accept things as they are, and just now they appear very pleasant to me."

Lucella laughed softly.

"And how long will you find pleasure in my society?"

"Always—while life lasts!"

"Dick," she said, "it would be foolish of me to say that I do not love you, for I do. But we must be prudent in our love. We must wait awhile."

"For how long?"

"I cannot say, dear. But I feel that it will not be for ever. I am not a love-lorn maid who talks of dying for love, and pines away because there is an obstacle in the way. No, Dick. If I thought that we should always be kept apart by my father I would go with you now."

"Lucella!"

"No, Dick. I know what is in your heart, but do not speak it. I cannot—will not—run away with you like a weak girl, for I am a woman— strong in will as you are strong in these arms of yours. I will not marry another, and if you are really true to me, as I feel you are, I will one day be your wife."

She held up her face to him, and he kissed her tenderly, reverently.

"Darling," he said, "it was in my heart to ask you to fly with me, but your better principles have prevailed. I have yet something to do—ere we can be man and wife."

"I know," she said, gently; "your good name is what you seek to restore. Hear me on that point once and for all. If you fail I will still be your wife. It is you I love, and I am not concerned in who may have been your father and mother."

"But it is of moment, Lucella."

"Yes, but not of sufficient moment to come between us. One thing I must ask of you. Should you succeed in finding that you are rightfully possessed of a great and honoured name, you are never to bear it."

"Not bear it?" exclaimed Dick, astounded.

"No. As Dick Strongbow I learnt to love you, and as Dick Strongbow you must be my husband. In your country it is easy to legitimately change your name, or to get a legal title to it. Do what you like to clear your father's or your mother's name, if there should, as I do not believe, be any taint upon either; but, having done that, become Dick Strongbow again, and live so. Now I implore you to go away from Madrid, as there is danger in the very air."

"Am I threatened?" asked Dick, quietly.

"You know you are," she answered, "but you will not heed that."

"And be laughed at as a coward, Lucella?"

"Nobody who knows you," said Lucella, "will laugh at you, Dick, and cannot you afford to laugh now at what men may think? There are two sorts of bravery—the physical and the moral. You have shown the physical so as to place your courage beyond suspicion. Let me now see your moral strength."

DICK STRONGBOW:

The Diamond King,
AND WONDER OF THE WORLD.

The brigand leader flourished a long rapier as he cried, "March!"

No. 14.   Price One Penny.

"When shall it be ?" asked Dick.

"At once. To-night if you can, to-morrow for certain. Get back to England and prosecute your search. Write to me here—openly, boldly."

"Will you get your letters ?" asked Dick.

"Assuredly. My father with all his pride would not descend to meanness ; and my mother—she thinks better of you than she did."

"Is she a friend ?"

"Hardly that as yet, but no longer a foe. Dick, I have been too long away. Good-bye."

"Lucella !"

She stood up, and he held her for a moment close to his heart. Their lips met, and then she tore herself away, Dick making no attempt to detain her.

"So strong, so gentle, and so nobly true," she murmured. "Ah ! Dick, in all the physical strength you have shown, you have never exhibited anything half so creditable to you as your bravery to-night. Good-bye, dearest—ere long we shall meet again."

He could only murmur a response, for his strong nature was stirred to its very depths, and the desire to keep her by him was almost overpowering.

But honour and true love kept him rooted to the spot, and he let her go.

He did not know, or even guess, that if he had endeavoured by force or persuasion to get her to elope that she would have yielded to him and fled from home.

Better as it was, for his forbearance put the final rivets to her love. He was her beau ideal of a man before—he was her idol now.

"The bravest and best of men," she murmured, as she glided up the steps of her home. "Heaven speed the hour of our re-union !"

The door of the house was closed, but it opened to her hand. She had come forth by that way and left the fastenings unsecured.

The curtain of the court which her father used by day was raised, and there was a light within.

Lucella had to pass that way, and on seeing the court open she paused for a moment with a fast-beating heart.

She knew what that parted curtain portended— her father was within, awaiting her coming.

Indeed, she could hear him moving inside, and, after a moment of irresolution, she went boldly forward.

The duke was there, with a despondent look on his face, that was more striking than any show of anger.

Lucella paused in the doorway, and their eyes met. He stood by the fountain with his hands clasped behind him. It was a dramatic scene.

"Lucella," he asked, "where have you been ?"

"To meet the man I love," she replied.

"To dally with a low-bred, nameless dog !"

"No—to meet a man of truth and honour, one of the very few. If he had asked me to-night to fly with him I should have left you, although it would have torn my heart-strings ; but his love is so deep that he spared me."

"This is a bitter confession to me, your father," said the duke.

Lucella looked at him closely for a moment, then glided forward and put her two hands upon his breast.

"Father," she said, "I love Dick, and Dick loves me. Nothing can part us, and no man or woman will make us false to each other ; but, for all that, until YOU say 'Yea' we shall never be husband and wife."

She raised her hands to his neck, drew his head down, and kissed him.

"Good-night, dearest !" she said.

And ere his lips could frame a reply she was gone.

CHAPTER LXX.

LEAVING MADRID — BUTTERFLICK'S GALLANT ADIEU—PARDIGGLE BROWN GETS OUT OF THE FRYING-PAN INTO THE FIRE.

"OFF to England—to the old country !" said Butterflick. "Well, that's a movement which suits MY complaint. How do you feel about it, Muffins ?"

"I think," said Muffins, slowly, "that I shall like it very much. I want to look round where I used to live, and give the street-boys all the plum-duff they can eat, just for a treat."

"My son," said Butterflick, "your sentiments are a credit to your parents. Old Sally would be proud of you."

"Perhaps we may meet her at home," said Muffins, innocently.

"Save my life ! don't mention it," cried Butterflick, alarmed. "Although Old Sally is a most excellent party to view from a distance, I don't want any closer acquaintance. Like some picters I've set eyes on, the furder she is off the better she looks."

Dick had lost no time in announcing his immediate departure, and everything was got ready with the celerity of the practised traveller.

Eleven was the hour named for departure by train.

At half-past ten Don Sebastian de la Tourville appeared. He was in a perturbed state of mind for a Spaniard.

"Is it possible, my brave young friend," he said, "that you are going ?"

"It is not only possible, but a fact," replied Dick, with a smile.

"But why this haste ?"

Dick smiled again.

"Sudden pressure—a call from the old country," he said. "Perhaps one day, Don, I shall see you there ?"

"You may, as a refugee," replied the Don, with a shrug. "I have money, and I am having it invested in your country. In case of another civil war here I shall come over to live with you."

They shook hands, and the Don took leave of all except Mr. and Mrs. Pardiggle Brown, who intended to stay in Madrid a few days longer.

It was just ten minutes to eleven when two other friends were announced—Captain Granalo and a lady—his wife, Viardot by name.

"I am glad you have come," said Dick, who received them alone—Carl and Phil Norton were looking to the packing. "I was thinking of you this morning."

"And we shall think of you always," said Viardot. "Shall we not, my love ?"

Captain Granalo twirled his moustache, and declared that, next to his wife, Dick should have all his thoughts.

"For you must know," he said, "how much we owe you."

"If I have ever done you a service," replied Dick, "it was by accident."

"Ah! that is your modesty—your kindliness," said the captain. "But we have no time to discuss it. We know—so do you. Senor, you will take away with you our lasting love and good-will."

"And nothing shall I bear away from Madrid with greater pleasure," replied Dick, "save, let me say, one thing."

"Is it so?" said Viardot, quickly. "You have seen her—she whom you loved so long?"

"Yes," replied Dick; "we have seen and talked with each other. All is well."

"Tell her—whoever she is," said Viardot, "that I kiss her on both cheeks and wish her well."

Dick promised to do so, and also to write and let them know all about her when he got to England. So they parted.

And now there was nobody else to see, and the time for departure had arrived.

Muffins, who, as usual, had ingratiated himself with the kitchen, having been kissed and cried over by the female servants and shaken hands with the men, was with his father exchanging a few words with the Browns in the hall.

That some lingering spark of jealousy was in the mind of the husband was so apparent that even Butterflick perceived it.

Always anxious to make people happy, he drew Pardiggle Brown aside and said—

"Look here, old man, you and I have had slight ructions, but let us part in peace now."

"Certainly," said Pardiggle Brown.

"The cause of our coolness, which was trumpery—"

"Temporary, I suppose you mean," hinted Brown.

"Certainly—same thing," said Butterflick. "The cause was, as usual, a woman."

Pardiggle Brown breathed hard.

"A woman—your wife," pursued Butterflick; "a most estimable woman, I've no doubt, but not my sort, so there never was any need for you to be jealous."

"Not your sort?" snarled Pardiggle Brown. "What do you mean by that?"

"Not my pattern," replied Butterflick, innocently. "Bless your heart! I couldn't cotton to her if she had a million of money."

"Ho! indeed," said Brown; "and what's put it into your thick head that she's ever cottoned to YOU?"

Butterflick looked at him with a countenance somewhat changed in expression.

"What did you say about my head?" he asked, haughtily.

"I said it was thick," replied Pardiggle Brown—"THICK! Why, darn you! coming and talking about my wife, as if she—"

"Now, look here," said Butterflick, "I came orrard as a man to put you at ease about that wife o' yours, but you don't seem to have got no intellects to grab the situation. I don't blame you for THAT. But don't you cheek me, or I'll test the hickness of YOUR head by knocking it against the doorpost."

"What are you two confiding to each other?" asked Mrs. Pardiggle Brown, sweetly.

"Nothun, marm, of wital importance," replied Butterflick; "we are squaring up, so as to leave free of debt in a friendly sense. Brown, here's my hand. Lay hold."

Brown took hold of the large hand held out to him, and Butterflick gave him a grip that made him wink.

"That's right, Brown; now we are friends for ever. Mrs. Parwriggle—"

"Par—DI—ggle," interposed Brown.

"Certainly," said Butterflick, "same thing a hundred years hence. Mrs. Pardiggle Brown the best of friends must part, and you and I must tear ourselves in sunders."

"I am sure, Mr. Butterflick," she replied, "I shall always be grateful to you for your care and attention. You are one of the few gallant gentlemen of the age—quite a relic of the days of chivalry."

"I does my best to go easy with ladies," said Butterflick. "Never in my life have I laid a rough hand on one meaningly. Even old Sally will support me in that. Mrs. Parwriggle—I mean Rarpiggle—Pardiggle—dash it!—Brown, I take my leave of you. I shall often dream of thee."

"Will you—true?" Mrs. Brown exclaimed, delighted.

"Bound to," answered Butterflick "Most men would, having once seen you. You are a woman who couldn't easily be forgotten."

"Go away, flatterer," she said.

Pardiggle Brown, who was looking gloomily on, was sensibly relieved by the appearance of Dick Strongbow. With Carl and Phil Norton he was descending the stairs.

His adieux were soon over. He said he would be glad at any time to see them in England or elsewhere, and trusted they would meet again.

Carl and Phil also said something equally polite, and then the party stepped into a huge sort of waggonette, waiting to convey them to the station.

Butterflick, who took his seat on the box, kissed his hand to Mrs. Pardiggle Brown as the vehicle started, and that was positively the last salute.

"A charming man," said Mrs. Brown.

"I differ with you," snarled her husband.

"Dear me!" exclaimed Mrs. Brown. "I thought you were such friends."

"Friends, indeed," said Brown, "after the way he went on with you! Mrs. Pardiggle Brown, you ought to blush for yourself, and you would do it—if —the paint would let you."

Mrs. Pardiggle Brown, bottling up some affectionate feminine reply, went upstairs to the sitting-room, and Brown sallied forth to walk himself into a cooler state.

"Anyway," he said, as he reached the street, "I've got rid of the fellow, and needn't fume about it any more. Them Spaniards know how to behave themselves. I haven't seen one look a second time at my wife."

Now Brown had not left the hotel ten minutes when a gentleman came hurriedly in and asked for Butterflick. On being told that he had left with the majority of his friends the visitor stared aghast.

"By my sowl," he said to himself, "this looks like desartin' an ould friend, and I'll call 'em to account for it."

"And so they are all gone?" he said to the attendant who had answered his question.

"All but Senor Pardiggle Brown and his wife."

The visitor, in whom the keen-eyed reader has probably recognised Don Timole Murphaleo, instantly brightened.

"Begorra!" he said, "thin I'm not quite desolate. I'll see them."

"The senor is out, but the senora is at home."

"It's the senora I'll see," said Timole. "If yer tell me the number of her sitting-room I'll find her. You needn't announce me."

The number was given to him, and, with the springy step of a true gallant, he ascended the stairs.

It was fully an hour afterwards when Pardiggle Brown, thoroughly cooled down and anxious to make amends to his wife for his decidedly rude remark about the paint on her face, returned to the hotel.

Without making any enquiries he went straight up to his sitting-room, and had his hand upon the handle of the door when he suddenly stopped short.

What is this he hears?

A man's voice and the laughter of his wife!

"Who the deuce has turned up now?" he gasped. "Am I never to be free of these butterflies dangling about her?"

With a wrench he opened the door and walked in.

Mrs. Pardiggle Brown was seated on a couch, and leaning over the back of it, fanning her, was Don Timole Murphaleo, quite at home.

The old feud had been forgotten—joy and peace reigned between them.

"Begorra!" said the Don, calmly looking up; "it's the old man, and ye didn't expect him back for an hour. How do you do, Brown? And it's meself that wishes you blooming health. Hope you enjoyed your walk."

"Sir," replied Pardiggle Brown, "to what am I indebted for the honour of this visit?"

"To love and friendship, shure," cried Timole, advancing and smacking him upon the shoulder; "it's basely and meanly we've been desarted, so we'll stick to each other and go back in company to the land of the Saxon. Maybe we'll have a run to Dublin City. Begorra, Brown, but there's fine times in store for us together."

"Excuse me, sir," said Brown, with strained politeness, "but—"

"Be aisy, Brown," interposed Don Timole, "it's the missus and me have settled the programme, and when a lady has got a hand in it, ye'll niver want to change it. I've ordered a room to stay wid you while you are here, and it's the merest trifle I'll ask of you. Be my banker till I get back to Dublin, when I can raise a thousand or two on a bit o' land my father owned there. Cheer up, Brown. It's fine times we've got ahead of us."

"This," thought Brown, as he sank down upon a chair, "is the bitterest pill of all. Can I swallow it? I think not. If this ruffian persists in clinging to us I may take his life. Let him beware."

"Ah! Brown," said Timole, placing a hand upon each of his shoulders, "it's the kindness of your eye that overcomes me. We'll travel together, and I'll give you an I.O.U. for fifty to start with. You'd better keep back thirty on account of rint and board, and give me twenty for odd cash and incidentals. There's grand times a-coming for us both. begorra."

CHAPTER LXXI.

THE PASSENGER BOAT—A WEARY MAN AND HIS BAG—MORELLE AND PAN WITH THEIR BOOTY.

UNDER a dark-midnight sky the boat for France touched Dover pier. For the time of year the passage had been rough, and many of the passengers, as they hastened to the train in waiting, showed that unsteadiness of limb which betrayed a disagreeable run across. The foreigner had suffered, of course, so had the Englishman, for sea sickness is not confined to one nation or people.

Among those who had suffered most was a stout gentleman of sixty or so, who carried a small black bag in his hand.

From the tenacity with which he held it, in spite of his sufferings, it seemed to be very valuable.

So thought two men who accompanied him across, and who, being hardened to the sea, escaped the terrible malady.

Jacob Morelle and Pan were on board, and on the look out for any chance to add to their diminishing stock of money.

As with all criminals, money lightly gained had been lightly spent, and when they landed at Dover they had not three pounds between them.

But they had their tickets to London, and so far were safe. In the metropolis, however, they would be able to do very little with what they had, and more must be obtained somehow.

"Seems to be a likely one, don't he?" said Pan.

"The best here," replied Morelle. "Hang back a bit. Don't let him see us."

The passengers were not very numerous, and there was ample room in the train. The aged traveller, weary with his short voyage, looked out a compartment he could have to himself, and stepped in, closing the door behind him.

"Now wait until the train is about to start," said Morelle, "and then you jump in. I'll follow Sham being the worse for drink."

In a few minutes the train was ready to start. All but Morelle and Pan had taken their seats.

"Are you going on?" asked the guard as he passed.

"Yes," replied Morelle.

"Then jump in, if you don't want to be left behind."

Morelle opened the door and they jumped in, closing it after them, so that the guard did not see the other passenger, who had wearily curled himself up in the far corner.

He half opened his eyes, and, seeing others in the carriage, raised the bag, which was lying on the seat by his side, and put it across his knees.

The action was significant, and confirmed the opinion of Morelle that he had either money or jewellery in the bag.

The ruffians each took a corner near the door, and the train moved on. In a few minutes it had left the town behind and was rushing through the darkness. With half closed eyes Morelle watched his intended victim, who shifted about uneasily, and for the first mile or two made strenuous efforts to keep his eyes open.

His hands held the bag with a tight grip, and when he presently fell asleep he did not relax his hold.

It was the mechanical grasp of one accustomed to travel with valuables.

Morelle was in no hurry to act. He was too old a hand in crime to be precipitate. He knew he had a good hour for his work.

Pan had learnt to obey him, and waited for his cue. It did not come until a third of the journey had been performed.

Then Morelle opened his eyes and sat up. Pan did the same.

They looked at each other, then at the man in the corner. No doubt he was asleep.

Morelle leant over and whispered—

"You do the TRICK. I will look to the bag, and throttle him if he wakes. Now."

They rose up, and without a sound crossed over to the unsuspecting man.

.   .   .   .

In due time the train arrived at Ludgate-hill, and the passengers, who had given up their tickets at Blackfriars, went their way.

Pan wanted to get out at Blackfriars, but Morelle said—

"No. It's a chance if anybody else gets out there, and we should be noticed."

It was sound advice, for as it happened nobody got out on the Surrey side of the river, and two men with one small bag between them would assuredly have attracted attention.

As it was, in the livelier station at Ludgate-hill nobody took any particular notice of them.

"Now," said Morelle, "we will walk as far as Oxford-street, and take a cab there. On the way I will make up my mind what we are to do."

It wanted two or three hours to daylight, but the streets were not very dark, and a great many people —mostly connected with the newspaper world— were abroad.

As they passed down Farringdon-street Pan said—

"I should like to feel that bag; it seems heavy."

"No feeling in the open air," replied Morelle. "There are eyes everywhere in this city, and the least action of an unusual nature stands the chance of being seen and a note made of it. Up this way by the market—it's quieter.

———

CHAPTER LXXII.

MORELLE AND PAN FIND OUT THAT THE WAYS OF THE WICKED ARE HARD—MORE "BAD LUCK" FOR THEM.

HE term "evening paper" is applied to any daily publication which may be issued after early morning. Very often, when there is any exciting intelligence abroad, the first edition of the evening papers is out at ten a.m.

It was so on the morning of the arrival of Morelle and Pan in town.

They had breakfasted, and were rambling down the Strand, with the ultimate object of "glancing casually at Danes' Inn," when the first street newsvendor—a shoeless and hatless boy of twelve— came dashing along, yelling—

"Another hawful railway murder! Gentleman robbed, murdered, and thrown out of the carriage! Body found in a tunnel!"

Pan looked very white and queer. Morelle showed no emotion, but stopped the boy and quietly bought a copy of the paper.

He glanced carelessly over it, folded it up, and put it away in his pocket.

"Let us go down to the Embankment," he said; "we shall find a seat there. What a cowardly brute you are!"

"It took me by surprise," replied Pan; "we ought to have got rid of the bag."

"An ordinary black one," said Morelle, contemptuously, "left at a coffee shop in charge of the proprietor, who is told that it contains specimens of ore from the Cape."

"I would not have left it with him."

"Better there than here. Now walk steady."

"I'd like to have a drink," muttered Pan.

"Come and have one," growled Morelle.

They entered a public-house and had some whisky—Pan asked for a double dose—and then they crossed the road, and by way of Arundel-street reached the Embankment.

In one of the pretty pieces of garden which embellish that splendid place they found a seat and took possession of it.

"Fill your pipe, smoke, and look at your ease," said Morelle, "while I see what is in the paper."

He glanced it over—there did not appear to be more than twenty lines—and passed it to Pan.

"He's not dead, it seems," he said; "but he is insensible, and the doctors have no hopes of him."

"Not dead," exclaimed Pan, "after all—"

"Silence, you fool!"

"Who is to hear what I say?"

"It is idiotic to run the risk."

Pan turned to the paper and read the report, half of which was sensational headlines.

It related to the discovery of the body of a gentleman—stout, middle-aged, and dressed in dark clothes—in a tunnel on the London, Chatham, and Dover Railway.

He had no wounds, but appeared to have been garroted, robbed, and thrown out of a carriage of a passing train.

"Nothing yet about the bag," thought Pan. "Perhaps it may never be heard of."

They sat there for about an hour, and then Morelle, who felt sure that further particulars of the affair would be out by that time, went back to the Strand.

He was not disappointed. Further intelligence had come to hand.

The guard of the Continental Express had seen the gentleman, and recognised him as a passenger who had got into the train at Dover, WITH A SMALL BLACK BAG IN HIS HAND.

"Confound these guards!" muttered Morelle; "they see everything."

He was a little disquieted now, although there was the comforting assurance that the "victim of the outrage" was still insensible and sinking fast.

"Pan may be right," Morelle muttered, as he sauntered back. "I ought not to have left the bag there; but what could we do? Our pockets would have been inconveniently filled with the jewellery. Shall we go for it at once? No—I think not. It might raise suspicions, as I said we should not be back until the afternoon."

And now the ball of excitement had been set rolling. Every half hour or so one of the papers came out with fresh details about the horrible outrage.

The victim went on dying until one o'clock, when, according to the reporters, he suddenly rallied, and hopes were entertained of his recovery.

As these press bulletins were read by Morelle—here and there as they wandered about—a conviction settled upon him that he had not been quite so successful in the dastardly affair as he thought.

If the maltreated man recovered sufficiently to give a description of the guilty pair there would soon be a hue and cry after them.

It was then three o'clock, and he thought he might safely go back to the coffee-shop where the bag had been left. It was in the Gray's-inn-road, and had been selected especially because of its quiet look.

He and Pan set out for the place, the latter with a foreboding heart shown in his face, Morelle keeping up appearances as well as he could.

Nothing unusual attracted their attention until they were close to the coffee-shop, but there Morelle, who was a little in advance of Pan, saw somebody standing by the door.

He seized Pan by the arm, wheeled him round, and marched him back. At the corner he looked back and saw the man still standing there.

"He didn't notice us," said Morelle.

"Who? Not Strongbow?" asked Pan, breathlessly.

"No—he can't be here yet. You saw that man by the coffee-shop?"

"I saw somebody standing there—a quiet-looking fellow."

"A detective, if I know the cut of one, and I ought to," returned Morelle. "We are blown upon."

"But who could have done it?"

"The bag did it. The fellow who keeps the shop must have read the papers, and as such men are always on the look out for a chance of getting somebody into trouble—just for what is to be made out of it—he has suspected us."

"And they've opened the bag?"

"Not yet. I reckon they are waiting for us to return, when we shall be asked to do it. It's all over, Pan; we've worked for nothing."

"Was there ever such accursed luck as ours?" groaned Pan, with a martyr's expression on his saturnine countenance.

"We must disguise ourselves as soon as we can and get out of the way," said Morelle.

"Where shall we go? Into the country?"

"No, not unless you want to be taken before the day is out. When in trouble there is no place like London. We had better go down near the docks, hide awhile, and see how things go. Then, when a favourable opportunity arrives, we must shift for some foreign land."

"What fools—what fools!" moaned Pan, as Morelle turned his steps towards the East-end, the safest hiding-ground in the wide world.

CHAPTER LXXIII.

HOMEWARD BOUND—THE BREAK DOWN—IN THE POWER OF DANGEROUS MEN.

SPANISH railways have never been numerous, and what there were at the time of our story were not under the best of management.

The pace at which trains travelled was comparatively slow, and time was very badly kept.

A train only an hour behind its appointed time was looked upon as fairly punctual.

The train in which Dick Strongbow and his friends were travelling did the first thirty miles without performing any eccentricity worthy of notice.

It was behind hand, of course, and here and there the passengers had bumping evidence of a rough road, but there was no mishap up to then.

But evil was doomed to happen that day.

As the engine was speeding at the rate of twenty miles an hour through a gorge between some hills, it suddenly left the track, skidded over some rough ground, jerking the carriages after it, and finally came to a standstill.

The passengers did not number a score in all. There was plenty of room to be shaken about in the carriages, and shaken they were, but beyond black eyes, bleeding noses, and sundry bruises on prominent parts of the body, no great harm was done.

It was barely past noon, and a very hot day. The train had come to rest in a perfect natural oven, and the first thought of the passengers when they found no great injuries had been sustained was to find some cool retreat. Dick and his party took matters quietly, notwithstanding the fact that the delay arising from the accident might be very serious for our hero.

He made enquiries of the driver, and learnt that the next station was ten miles away, the intervening country being very sparsely inhabited.

What was to be done?

The engine could not be sent back for assistance, having got off the rails, and no means were handy for replacing it. The station they recently left was five miles behind them—a miserable place, where neither a fresh engine nor carriage could be obtained.

No good purpose would be served by going there.

The driver would not leave his engine, nor the guard his train, which carried the mails. These officials decided to await the coming of assistance, which would be sure to be sent when it was found the train did not arrive.

"And how long shall we have to wait?" asked Dick.

"Oh! for hours, anyway; perhaps all day, or till the next train comes," was the answer.

"And when will that be?"

"In the evening."

The next station was called Ravinelle, and thither Dick suggested going.

This idea found favour with his friends, and commending their luggage to the care of the guard, they were about to start when one of the passengers gave them a warning.

"You had better remain here. The country is still infested with little bands of the broken army of Don Carlos."

"We are not afraid of small bands," said Dick, drily, "and if we meet them will make them smaller."

The passengers commended him to the care of the saints, for which they were thanked, and the small body of adventurers went their way.

"This work's jolly hot," said Butterflick, as they walked on the track, using the sleepers as they would stepping-stones in a brook. "I'd give a sovereign now for a pint of good old ale."

"I sigh for lager beer," said Carl, "and the shade of the Linden-trees."

"It's no use wasting your breath in sighing," said Phil Norton; "but keep on steadily. We shall get out of this gully before long."

The railway track took a sweep to the right, where they hoped to find open country; but alas! it was not so.

For miles ahead it could be seen, with breaks here and there, winding among the hills apparently interminably.

It could not be called a mountainous country but the hills were very fine, and assumed picturesque shapes which under other circumstances would have been pleasing to the eye.

Upon the present occasion the travellers did not appreciate their beauty.

They had no food with them, and only a little

wine, which required water to be mixed with it for "a fair all-round drink," as Butterflick said.

Presently they looked about for a spring, and eventually saw one a short distance from the railway, sending out a tiny stream from the side of a hill.

It seemed to be only a few hundred yards away, but the clear atmosphere deceived them. It was nearly a mile, and on a closer view proved to be a very considerable jet of water, flowing from a small cavern, and forming a brook that was soon lost in the rocky ground.

It was a cool, inviting, shady spot, and the same thought was in the minds of each: "Why not rest here until the heat of the day has somewhat abated?"

Muffins expressed it first, in his simple way.

"I do jest feel tired. Shouldn't I like to sit a bit."

Then all sat down laughing, and for a while talked together, but the heat of the day had a soporific effect upon them, and one by one they fell asleep.

They were awakened at the same moment with a rattling sound. Springing up, they found themselves surrounded by a circle of rifle muzzles aimed at their heads.

These arms were held by ragged, unwashed, determined-looking ruffians, under the command of a gigantic fellow fully six feet three inches in height.

"Stand all," he shouted, in Spanish, "or you will be shot."

Only a fool or one tired of his life would have disobeyed the order. The one chance of life open to Dick and his friends was to obey.

"Disarm these men," was the next order.

Two of the ruffians laid aside their weapons and removed the arms of the prisoners. They touched nothing else.

"Cover them!" shouted the chief to some of the men whose weapons were drooping.

They were all levelled at the prisoners again. Thirty muzzles looking at them like so many evil eyes.

"Senors," said the chief, "you will consider yourself my prisoners. I see you are not my countrymen, but aliens, and as such must pay toll for passing through MY country. You are English."

"All but one," replied Carl. "I am German."

"Ah! then," said the ruffian, "your name is Fritz, and all the rest of these are Smiths."

Nobody contradicted him, because they saw that the brigand—as they judged him to be—was joking. He appeared to think himself a very humorous fellow, and grinned at his own feeble jests.

"Senors," he said, "you will fall in and go with me."

He indicated the spot where they were to stand, and his men immediately surrounded them.

Not a word had the prisoners as yet exchanged.

The expression of Butterflick's face was a study. He looked like a man who had been awakened from a pleasant dream to receive an order for immediate execution.

Dick and Carl walked together, then came Phil and Butterflick, with Muffins next.

"March!" said the brigand leader, flourishing a long rapier.

Their road lay away from the railway, among the hills, over rather rough but easily traversed ground.

The brigands talked together in an undertone, which gave Carl and Dick an opportunity of speaking to each other.

"We would not be warned," said Carl.

"No," replied Dick; "it was all my fault. But I am headstrong, and was so eager to get on."

"This fellow will look for ransom."

"And ask something heavy if he finds out who we are. We had better take him at his word, and all be Smiths."

After a walk of three miles or thereabouts they came in sight of a cluster of houses, several of considerable size, but the majority mere peasants' huts.

Scattered about were a number of armed men of the same type.

They came hurrying up to make enquiries, which were asked and answered in a "patois" our friends did not understand.

By the sound of it Dick judged it to be the Romany or gipsy tongue.

"Ah! Carl," he said, "I fear we have fallen into the hands of some of the cruellest ruffians in Spain."

"What makes you think so?"

"Their tongue. I have read of the gipsy brigand. He bears the worst of characters."

They were conducted into a yard attached to one of the larger houses. It was surrounded by a high wall, and offered little chance of escape. The only means of exit was by the entrance-gate, which was guarded by armed men.

The chief remained there awhile, talking with some of his followers, and then came to the prisoners. Singling out Dick with his eyes he said—

"You appear to be leader here—is it not so?"

"Well, yes, I suppose so," was Dick's answer.

"Will you follow me?" said the brigand. "I desire to speak with you."

CHAPTER LXXIV.

THE BRIGAND PROVES TO BE A STRANGE FELLOW —DRINKING TO GOOD LUCK.

THE chief led the way out through the gate and turned aside into the house by a wide doorway. Every few steps down which they traversed stood an armed man, and in a room which the chief entered were half-a-dozen more, lying about on what had once been splendid furniture, but was now soiled and torn.

All sprang to their feet, and at a signal from their chief left the room. The door closed, and Dick was left alone with his captor.

"If he only knew," thought Dick, "how easily I could kill him he would stop that satisfied grin."

"Senor," said the chief, "we have been unceremonious with you, but our needs must be our excuse. Probably you take us for brigands?"

"What else am I to think?" asked Dick.

"You are right," said the chief, "we are brigands; but our object now is not plunder. You must ransom yourselves with a pardon."

"A pardon?"

"Not yours, but the king's, my friend. Brigands we are, but it is a poor business. The Carlists have left us nobody to rob, and therefore we

desire to go into the cities. That cannot be done without the king's pardon."

The situation was a novel one. Dick could not help responding to the brigand's smile.

"But how am I to obtain it?" he asked.

"Write for it," returned the brigand. "Say that you will pay his majesty any reasonable sum if he will but pardon Gastra Fuello and his men. His majesty has need of money, and will be glad to sell that which costs him nothing."

"But why should I do it?" asked Dick.

"To save your lives," was the reply, "for if the pardon does not come in a week you will be shot."

He spoke so coolly that it was quite clear he meant it. Dick saw that this jester could be very serious at a pinch.

"There is a table," said the brigand; "write to anyone you know who will see that the letter is delivered to the king. Offer his majesty all you can —all you are worth—for life is precious."

"I have only one friend who could do this thing," said Dick; "a lady."

"Ah! lovely woman—all the better," chirruped the brigand. "Devoted to you, if I mistake not. Ha! ha! What would the world be without the pretty creatures?"

Dick bit his lip. He was sorry he had spoken of a lady friend—by whom he of course meant Lucella —for he could not have her name jestingly spoken of by the ruffian without feeling an irresistible desire to knock him down.

"I am not sure the lady would be the friend to apply to," he said. "I have another friend—a gentleman."

"His name?"

"Don Sebastian de la Tourville."

"Well, write to him. I have heard the name," said Gastra Fuello. "If he has any power the thing can be done quickly. There, at my secretaire, you can write."

The secretaire was rather a rickety table, with some coarse writing materials upon it.

The paper and envelopes, however, served, and Dick, sitting down, wrote to his acquaintance, asking him to call upon Lucella, who might gain the ear of the king.

He offered to pay nothing, but simply asked for the pardon of the brigands for the sake of his friends and himself.

He said all that was necessary, sealed the envelope and handed it to the brigand, who had been lolling in an old easy chair smoking cigarettes

The letter was addressed to the hotel which Dick had left that morning, and outside were instructions for it to be delivered immediately.

A stamp of the foot upon the floor brought in a man, to whom the letter was given with instructions to hasten with it to Madrid.

"You have a good mule," said the brigand, "do not let it lag."

The man departed, and Dick, who had had enough of his present company, asked if he could return to his friends.

"Not yet," was the reply. "I want a companion, and you are a man of mettle, I can see. Among the crew I govern I have no kindred spirit. We will drink and smoke together for awhile."

He opened a box by his chair, took out a bottle and two metal goblets, and placed them upon the table.

Dick held Gastra Fuello as a shield and retreated down the narrow path.

He also brought out a handful of long, thin cigars, with straws running through them.

"They are better than they look," he said. "Try one."

Dick thought it better to humour him, and sat down, taking a cigar at the same time. The brigand chief uncorked the bottle and filled up the goblets.

"You have a toast at home," he said. "I've heard it. 'Here's luck' Let us drink it now. Luck to both of us! May the king pardon me and I spare you! An excellent toast! Here's luck."

Dick drank it with a grim smile, and smoked on for a time in silence. The brigand talked, drank, and smoked very fast. Ere long he began to brag.

"I am a strong man," he said; "a giant, a fox, a lion. I can shoot the eagle as he flies, wrestle like a gladiator, and fight like a whole regiment. Did you ever see such an arm as that?" he asked, bending his elbow so as to make the most of his biceps; "feel it."

Dick complied, and said it was a good muscle—above the average.

"It is the weakness of your race," said the Spaniard; "you are puny. You have no muscle."

"None to speak of," replied Dick, "but I am fairly strong."

"You?" said the brigand, staring at him with drunken gravity. "You are a babe, a suckling. I could break you into pieces."

"I hope you won't try it," said Dick.

"All in good season, my dear," said the brigand, banteringly; "if you behave yourself I will be very kind until the time comes to set you free or kill you. You do not drink much?"

"I take very little," answered Dick. "I have not the head for it."

"Ha—ha! what poor things you Britishers are," said Gastra Fuello, contemptuously; "all talk, no show. See here."

He turned an ordinary chair with its back towards him, picked it up between his finger and thumb, and held it at arm's length.

"What think you of that, my boy?"

It was a respectable feat in its way, and Dick said so truthfully.

"Can you do it?" asked Gastra.

"I can try," replied Dick, modestly.

"Let me see you."

Dick could have lifted five times the weight the same way, but he thought it advisable for once to do a bit of shamming. After several apparently strenuous efforts he gave up the job.

"I would rather leave these things to you," he said.

The brigand was immensely pleased with himself, and it may be said with Dick also. He was delighted to find one of his race who could be astonished at anything done by a foreigner.

"It isn't like you fellows generally," he said; "you think you can do everything."

"Oh! no," urged Dick.

"But I say you think so," said Gastra Fuello, with drunken obstinacy. "Don't contradict me, or I shall strike you."

"I hope you won't," thought Dick, "for I sha'n't be able to stand that."

He was anxious to get away and rejoin his friends, so as to guard them against admitting anything that might get them into trouble, but the brigand would not let him go.

"We'll have some fun to-morrow," he said. "In my band I've some splendid athletes—fine runners—good wrestlers. We will show you good sport. Have you any wrestlers among you!"

"We have done a little that way," replied Dick, humbly.

"To-morrow we will see what you are made of. Now for another bottle, so that we may drink good luck to us both again."

CHAPTER LXXV.

A DISCIPLINARIAN—THE CHIMNEY-LIKE TOWER—"DON'T SLEEP IN THE MOONLIGHT UNCOVERED."

GASTRA FUELLO opened the other bottle and passed it to Dick, who pretended to fill his goblet; Gastra did so in reality, talking in a boastful way until he was quite overcome with the drink. Finally, he sank back in his chair and went off into a dead sleep.

Dick took a rapid survey of the room, and a second box in the corner attracted his attention. He tried it, and finding the lid was unfastened, took the liberty to inspect its contents.

To his great joy he found the arms of which he and his companions had been deprived.

They were stowed away under some garments, evidently belonging to Gastra Fuello.

Dick speedily concealed the revolvers about his person, and resumed his seat to await the return to consciousness of the brigand.

This he knew might not come for hours, but happily he was spared the ordeal of a long waiting.

One of the men, who evidently knew the habits of his chief, came in and looked at him with a smile.

"Gone!" he said, "and so is the wine, I suppose."

There was a little left in one of the bottles, which he drank with gusto. He then motioned to Dick to follow him.

"I must put you back with the other birds and look after you," he said, "or my head won't be worth much this time to-morrow."

"What shall I do?" thought Dick; "it would be so easy to stun him with a blow—but no! That won't do. I can't get to the others alone. We must wait a bit, perhaps until to-morrow, when the sports are on. Athletes do not usually exhibit with arms in their hands. That will be the time."

Had Ajax not been despatched home to England he might have had an opportunity of distinguishing himself.

Dick was sure he would have been, even in his weakened condition, a fair match for the redoubtable ruffian. For his own part, he looked upon Gastra Fuello as a foeman altogether unworthy of his steel.

Being escorted back to his friends, he gave them an account of the interview with the brigand, and gladdened them with the tidings of his having recovered their weapons.

"It is one of those lucky chances," he said, "which come off in real life, although some people will not believe it."

As there might be prying eyes around, he did not then distribute them, but reserved doing so until night should fall.

"Perhaps we may be able to get out of this hole," suggested Phil.

"I think it will be better to wait until to-morrow," said Dick; "we shall then be in the open air."

"I wonder what's become of the people in the train?" mused Butterflick. "They'll have a long wait for us. Lord! what a country to live in."

"It's in a disturbed state now," returned Carl; "but it will pull round. It has been a grand country in its time, and will be again."

Hitherto the prisoners had been kept in the open air; but late in the evening, just before dusk, Gastra Fuello appeared with an armed guard, and announced his intention of putting them into sleeping quarters for the night.

He looked, as Butterflick said, "rather yellow about the gills" after his debauch, and he was in a short-tempered mood, which first showed itself for the benefit of one of his men.

Gastra Fuello, in bombastic tones, was ordering the prisoners to come up and fall into line when he observed one of his men standing at ease, leaning on his rifle and lazily watching the proceedings.

His chief fell upon him and BOXED HIS EARS.

It was a good, open-handed smack, that could have been heard a hundred yards away, and it made the recipient of it blink again. A suppressed howl bubbled from his lips.

"You dog!" said Gastra Fuello. "Who, in the name of St. Anselmo, gave you leave to loll about?"

"Chief—your pardon," replied the man.

"Stand straight," said Gastra Fuello. "Attention! Eyes right! Why, you fool, you've put them left! Take that."

Another box of the ears was administered, and the man groaned aloud.

"Chief," he said, "I put my eyes right. I'll swear it."

"They were left to ME," growled the chief.

"They would be so," pleaded the man, "seeing that we face each other."

"What," said Fuello, "dare you bandy words with me—you—you fool? Ha! Must I give you more?"

He struck that unhappy man on either side of his head half-a-dozen times, knocking it this way and that, while the poor fellow stood stiff at the "attention."

"You see," said the brigand chief to Dick, "I train my men well. I know English discipline, and I practise it. I box. I hit. I keep at the atten—shun! Fall in all of you."

Dick would dearly have liked to take the inflated wretch by the throat and shake the life out of him, but the time for such energetic action had not yet come.

So he fell in, smartly enough to all appearance, and his friends took up a position in Indian file behind him.

"March," said Gastra Fuello, "all one step—left by right—so. Ha! I know ze English discipleen."

"Yes, you do. Lord help you!" muttered Butterflick.

"Ha! you speak—you man of fat body," said Gastra.

"I was saying that if any man knows the British army drill you are that gentleman," replied Butterflick.

"It is so," said the chief, with a complacent twirl of his moustache.

He escorted them out by the gate, and, turning to the left, bore round towards a part of the building which none of them had been near before.

At one end was a round tower in which, deep set, was a small strong door. The brigand chief unlocked this door, and bade the prisoners go in.

"You have all of it to yourself," he said, "until to-morrow. At the way out, here by the door, are a dozen men on guard all night ready to shoot. If you can break down the door—try to get away. Ha! you understand?"

"No attempt of the sort will be made," said Dick; "but, permit me to remind you, we want some food."

"Bread, such as we have, shall be given you," said Fuello, "for it shall not be said that I wrestled or fought with starving men."

He had unlocked the door, and pushing it open bade them enter.

They did so, and found only a bare, cell-like chamber, with a narrow, winding staircase on the front side.

Gastra Fuello despatched a man for food and water, and waited until it was brought — half-a-dozen small loaves of black bread and a brown stone pitcher filled with water.

"You ought to sleep well," said Gastra Fuello, with a grin. "There is a chamber for each."

It was now dark. Night had come on and no moon had as yet arisen.

When the door closed Dick and his friends could not see their hands before them.

"This won't do," said Dick; "judging by what that fellow said we have the whole tower to ourselves. Let us make our way to the top. It must be cooler there."

"Before we start," said Phil Norton, "let us have a drink of water each in case of accidents."

In the dark the pitcher was passed carefully round, and each took a drink. Then the bread was divided, and they prepared to make the ascent.

"I will carry the pitcher and the rest of the water," said Dick. "Carl, find the staircase."

"I have it here," was the answer.

"Go up first—Phil next—Butterflick—Muffins with you—myself last."

"It seems awfully narrow," said Carl; "we had better have plenty of treading space between us."

"And Butterflick, old man," said Phil Norton, "a word with you."

"I'm ready," answered Butterflick.

"Don't you get up to any of your jokes by sticking fast half way. It would be awkward for you to stop up the passage."

"You get along," growled Butterflick, "there isn't much chance of you stopping up anything bigger than a gaspipe."

Carl, by this time, had gone a little way up the staircase.

His voice, in a muffled fashion, was heard calling to the others to be careful.

"Some of the stairs are broken," he said, "and the way gets narrower and narrower."

Phil Norton now began the ascent, and after him Butterflick, then Muffins, and Dick last of all, as arranged.

It was a desperately narrow staircase to be sure, but it was airy, thanks to many small ventilating slits in the wall.

Butterflick found it a tightish fit in places, but he did not, as Phil Norton had hinted at, stick fast.

At intervals they came to what might be called a landing, on which there was room enough for two.

Here, on each, they found a door which they could push open, but as they only communicated with other small cell-like chambers they did not wait to explore them.

Up—up, right to the summit of the tower they went, and there they found just room enough for them all to recline at ease on the leaden roof, around which was a parapet of stone.

"It's more like a chimbley than a tower," cried Butterflick.

"It certainly is a great height for its size," said Carl, looking over the parapet; "more than a hundred feet. I should say it was originally built as a look out."

"Fancy being up here," said Phil, "and a cannon-ball coming along and knocking out the middle of it! I wonder what the sensation would be to a man who felt himself going over with the top part of it."

Muffins shuddered.

It was an idea that was calculated to affect his vivid imagination.

"Don't talk in that way, Mr. Norton," he said, "or I sha'n't sleep."

They none of them made an effort to seek repose for a long time, but stood around trying to make out the scene below. The brigands had no fires outside or within that were visible, and they seemed to be very quiet altogether.

By-and-bye the moon rose, and then they looked upon a splendid scene, the rocks and hills and the tall building in which they were confined being bathed in silvery light.

Now they could see some of the brigands below. Gastra Fuello had not deceived them.

A dozen brigands with rifles were crouched on the ground below, close to the tower.

"I wonder how that party's getting on?" said Butterflick, suddenly.

"What party?" asked Phil Norton, and the others looked surprised.

"Why, the chap as that thief of a chief boxed."

"What makes you bother about him?"

"I was thinking that old Sally, who was as handy with her hands as any living woman, could not have laid on the smacks better."

"You feel sympathetic," said Phil.

"Well, it called up mem'ries of the past," replied Butterflick, with a sigh. "She used to tell me that one day I should find myself worse off than if living with her, and I used to say it warn't possible. But, by the last of the Moccasins—"

"Mohicans," suggested Phil.

"Moccasins," repeated Butterflick. "I know what I'm talking about. By the last o' them, she was right. Some women have got quite the gift of dipping into the future."

And Butterflick sighed as he settled down to get some sleep.

"Muffins, dear boy," he said, "if ever you marry—never mind what sort o' woman she may be—

stand by her. You took her for better or worse, and if you find she's got a bias toward wearing the breeches, LET HER DO IT. Then you won't in your old days stand a chance of getting chawed up by a wall-eyed brigand."

"I'll remember, dad," replied Muffins, dutifully.

This ready assent to do as he was told was a great comfort to Butterflick. It was extremely soothing, for he immediately began to snore.

"It's come to a question," said Phil Norton, "whether we are going to put up with that row or not."

All were more or less inclined to sleep, and were lying down, when Carl said—

"Cover up your faces. The moon has great power to distort them."

"Why not, then, when we are awake?" asked Dick.

"Because," said Carl, "the muscles are relaxed. I once knew a handsome woman who was made hideous by sleeping in the moonlight. Don't forget the attracting power of the moon. Remember how it fairly LIFTS the ocean and makes the tides. Cover up your faces, I say."

It was good advice, and they took to using their handkerchiefs for the purpose.

Butterflick being asleep, Muffins, like a loving son, performed the needful office for him, and a few minutes afterwards all were in the land of dreams.

CHAPTER LXXVI.

THE BRIGANDS' ARENA—BOASTING AND DOING —A FIGHT FOR FREEDOM.

FAIR woke the morn, the sun rising in a misty but glorious horizon. Half an hour after the great luminary was up the air was perfectly clear. Dick, the first to awake among his people, got up softly and looked down. The sentries were still there, or others who had taken their places, squatting on the ground, all with their muskets in their hands, and their faces towards the door of the tower.

Gastra Fuello was indeed a rigid disciplinarian.

While Dick was looking down he saw him come forth, and, after a glance round, walk to a spring that spurted its water between two rocks. Throwing down his hat he put his head under it.

The brigand chief was getting the benefit of the only pick-me-up available for a headache in that district.

He seemed to want a deal of picking up, for he rubbed his head and replaced it several times before the desired result was attained.

"The fool!" thought Dick; "so proud of the little strength he possesses, and yet squanders it for the pleasure of drinking."

After his reviver the brigand looked up at the

summit of the tower, and, seeing Dick, took off his hat by way of salute.

Dick returned the courtesy, and the chief came to the tower.

Halting immediately under it, he called out that they could come down one by one and refresh and cleanse themselves as he had done.

Dick at once availed himself of the opportunity, and having first wakened Carl and given him the arms to distribute, lost no time in getting down.

The chief let him out, relocked the door, and then, accompanied by an escort of six men, Dick was allowed to go and wash himself.

While thus engaged the men kept the muzzles of their rifles pointed towards him, which might have tried the nerves of some people, but Dick took it coolly, and, having bathed his head and hands, thanked the chief for the privilege.

Dick did not go back to the tower, but was taken to the open courtyard where he had been first confined.

One by one his fellow-prisoners, after a visit to the spring, joined him, Butterflick coming last.

He was so much behind the rest that Dick commented on it.

"You have had an extra wash, I suppose," he said.

"No," replied Butterflick, "I was the last left in that chimbley, and coming down I DID stick fast for awhile about two stories up. It was the most awful sensation I've knowed for years, but it happened near one of them port-holes, and the bit o' breeze brought on a sneeze which jerked me out of it. I slid down a dozen steps or more afore I stopped, and the man who says I ain't bruised and sore tells a lie."

They condoled with him, of course, but he was not soothed, and he went on expressing forcible opinions about the designer of that tower—who had been dead for centuries—until breakfast appeared.

More black bread and water, but it was better than nothing.

"Shut your eyes and eat it," said Dick, "it will help to keep up our strength. We shall want it to-day."

Breakfast over, they lounged about until a most excruciating blast upon a trumpet saluted their ears.

"Somebody's performing on a instrument they ain't up to," said Butterflick.

The performer proved to be Gastra Fuello himself, who appeared at the gate with a number of his followers at his back, and unlocked it.

"Come hither, my friends," he said, "it is time we departed."

"Do you not hold your revels here?" asked Dick.

"No, I prefer something safer—quieter," replied the brigand. "Nature has made an arena for me up yonder."

He pointed towards a mountain that rose abruptly behind the castle, presenting at first sight no appearance of a path.

But on looking closer Dick saw that a narrow way wound round it—a mere thread to the eye at that distance.

"At the other side," said Gastra Fuello, "there is a sweet little place, big enough for a performance by a small company, AND A SINGLE MAN CAN GUARD THE DOOR."

There was a deep significance in these words, or at least Dick thought so, although the brigand did not put any very great emphasis upon them.

Of course he meant that the narrow way leading to the cavern could be held by one armed man, which, of course, it could against a number unarmed.

It appeared strange that the brigands should take the trouble to go up the mountain to indulge in athletic exercises; but the secret of it leaked out in a few words that fell from the chief.

The chosen arena was a hallowed spot, where the Romany people of Spain had often foregathered to carry out certain mysterious rites, but whether of a religious nature or not was not clear.

To that spot they had to go, and as far as Dick Strongbow was concerned it was a most unfortunate thing.

The brigands mustered fifty or more, many of them new arrivals on the scene.

The latter took a keen interest in the prisoners, examining their faces closely, and asking questions of their fellow rascals.

There was one man in particular who was very much taken with Dick.

He looked at him again and again, with a puzzled expression of face, then asked some question of another brigand.

He spoke in the Romany tongue, and the substance of his enquiries was as follows—

"Who is he?"

"English, of course," was the reply.

"But his name?"

"It is Smith."

"Ah! then I know him not; and yet I have seen his face."

When the procession was formed—brigands fore and aft, prisoners in the centre—this man was just in front of Dick, who led his party, and the fascination still rested on him.

Every few moments he turned his head and stared at our hero, who put on a stolid expression of face—shrewdly suspecting that the fellow had seen him before.

This looking back soon brought the brigand into trouble.

First he trod upon the heels of the man in front, and shortly after he tripped over a stone and fell.

Gastra Fuello, seeing his chance, rushed up, and as a stimulant to rise with all speed kicked him in the ribs.

"Dog—pig!" he cried, "why do you lie there?"

"Chief, I fell by accident," replied the man.

"Ten thousand curses! I do not keep you in the band to fall," hissed the chief.

His overnight debauch had left him in a bad-tempered frame of mind, and his dark eyes glittered like those of a snake—with viciousness.

The troubled brigand looked back at Dick no more, but he was very uneasy, and kept jerking his head, as some people do when thoughts puzzle them.

The narrow path was soon reached, and ere they had travelled far the order was given to walk in Indian file.

Two could have walked abreast with ease, but for general purposes of safety it was considered better for them to proceed singly.

Half an hour's upward journeying brought them to a curious piece of table land projecting from the side of the mountain.

It was as much like a basket fixed on the wall as it could be, and to add to the similitude it was nearly semi-circular in form.

In size it could hardly be called an arena, being not more than a hundred feet across, and having nothing to prevent anyone falling off, it seemed hardly the place for athletic exercises.

But Gastra Fuello thought otherwise, and there they were.

His band formed round in a half ring, and the narrow path was guarded by two armed men. The prisoners were told to stand against the wall-like side of the mountain and await the orders of the brigand chief.

It was some time before he was ready to begin.

First of all he was, for some reason, very particular about the exact position his men took up, even to placing their feet against certain marks cut on the smooth surface of the table land.

Some of these marks were mere notches in the stone, others bore a rude resemblance to arrows, feathers, birds, beasts, and the human hand.

Whatever significance there might be attached to these signs or symbols was not clear to our friends, but without a doubt they were to Gastra Fuello things of deep import.

Having got his men into position he harangued them in a tongue the prisoners did not understand, but it was pretty clear by the signs he made that he was speaking about himself.

"He is going to annihilate all creation," said Phil.

"I'd like to try who's best man," returned Butterflick.

"Listen," said Dick, in a low tone. "I have taken stock of all things here, and our chance of getting away will be when that fellow and I try our strength. He will certainly wrestle with us all, for he believes himself to be a veritable champion. Now come a little closer."

They shifted up so as to be closer to him, and Dick went on—

"If he should wrestle with any of you first, let him throw you easily."

"I'm darned!" muttered Butterflick.

"It had better be done," said Dick, "and when it comes to my turn, you get as near as possible to those two fellows guarding the pass and lay hold of them—you understand?"

"Yes," they responded.

"Don't hesitate what to do with them," continued Dick. "Pitch them over. They won't be missed by the honest world. Then get down the pass as quickly as you can, and leave the rest to me. Don't wait. I sha'n't be far behind."

"I think I see your plan," said Carl, softly. "It is a desperate expedient."

"Only a desperate expedient can save us," said Dick. "Don't waste your fire on those fellows until I tell you. Every bullet may be wanted."

Gastra Fuello had now finished his address to the men, who cheered—or, rather, howled—lustily.

Under cover of this noise the prisoners settled back in their old position, taking their cue from Dick, who put on a look of meek resignation.

Gastra Fuello turned round and favoured them with a sneer.

"I will now show you how strong I am," he said, "and afterwards you shall feel it for yourselves. It is my intention to wrestle with and throw you all."

He then took up a position in the semi-circle between his captives and his men.

After a lot of circus attitudinising, intended to show off his muscular limbs, he called one of his men from the ranks.

The man came very reluctantly.

He knew what was in store for him, and would rather have declined the honour.

But his chief thought only of himself and his name as a strong man.

He laid hold of the unhappy brigand, hoisted him with a great effort in the air, and held him in one hand over his head.

Vociferous applause hailed the feat, which, however, came to a premature conclusion by the arm of the chief giving way and the fall of the brigand from aloft.

He descended to the earth in the fifth part of a second, meeting it with a force that must have bruised him severely, and assuredly took away his breath.

Gastra Fuello, in his unreasonable way of doing things, vented this partial failure on the innocent sufferer, cursing him roundly, and finally bestowing upon him one of his favourite kicks, which further incapacitated the unfortunate man.

It was a ludicrous scene, and our people at home would have laughed at it.

Not so the Spaniards.

They looked on stolidly enough, and exhibited not the slightest emotion, sympathetic or otherwise.

Gastra Fuello next singled out another man, of lighter build than the last, and he exhibited so much reluctance to be practised upon that his chief laid hold of one of his ears and fairly hauled him out by it.

Whatever the prisoners might have felt with regard to the perils of their own position, they could not help being tickled by this exhibition, and they laughed aloud.

"Ah! you laugh," hissed the brigand, turning upon them, "at what?"

"Why, at that fellow," replied Dick, drily. "You do not think any of us would dare to laugh at you?"

"I should think not," said the brigand, grimly.

The second man was favoured with another performance.

It was puerile in Dick's eyes, simply consisting of tossing the man up in the air as women do a baby. Once more the captive spectators laughed.

"You see," said Gastra Fuello, "but you still laugh."

"Well," said Dick, "to tell you the truth we do not think much of the show. Naturally we do not wish to excite the ire of so powerful a man as you are, but we can't help laughing."

"I will remove the laugh from some of you," said Gastra Fuello.

He signalled to the second victim of his prowess to get back to the ranks, accelerating his movements with a kick which nearly sent the man flying over the edge of the table land.

Indeed he would have gone, but for one of his comrades, who checked him with his musket.

"It is your turn now," said Gastra Fuello. "I will take you one by one. Come out you that are the strongest."

He beckoned to Butterflick, who, like the two

brigands, did not quite relish it. He felt vicious towards Fuello, and was thirsting to give him a fall.

But the commands of Dick Strongbow were imperative.

He would have to obey them for the good of all, and sink his private feelings.

As a man of resource under the most trying circumstances, Butterflick had not many peers.

He knew he must allow himself to be thrown, but would it not be possible to bring that powerful brigand to grief at the same time?

Anyway he would try to do so.

Putting on a show of fear, that was a little overdone, and would have warned anybody less bombastic and self-satisfied than the brigand chief, he went out to meet the foe.

"Excuse me, sir," he said, "but how do you wrestle—Cumberland or Westmoreland style, or fling as you like?"

"I know no style," replied the brigand, haughtily. "I catch hold of a man and throw him—that's all."

"I hope you'll go easy with me," pleaded Butterflick. "I'm not so strong as I look."

"I will throw you," was the reply. "Look to it, coward."

He laid hold of Butterflick by the shoulders and pushed him violently back, intending, when he was beat, to get hold of his waist and throw him.

But Butterflick, acting under orders, went down at once, so easily that the brigand fell with him, and pitching forward, gave his head a hard whack on the ground.

"Coward—thief!" he hissed, as he struggled up, rubbing his head.

"How strong you are!" groaned Butterflick. "I'm like a baby in your hands. Half my bones are broken, I think."

He got up, rubbing himself and groaning, which acted as a sedative to the angry brigand, and calmed him.

"You are nothing—you are a child," he said. "I cannot wrestle with you. Go back."

"I never come across such a strong man in my life," moaned Butterflick; "oh! my back—oh! my bones."

It was a hard task for his friends to keep from laughing as he limped back to his place, rubbing his back, elbows, and knees as if he had been dropped out of a balloon.

The watchful eye of the brigand roved up and down the rest.

Dick leant wearily against the rocky cliff, and seemed to avoid his threatening eye.

This affectation of fear was the snare that caught the brigand, and involved him unexpectedly in a dreadful mess, from which he did not easily escape.

"Here, you braggart!" he cried to Dick; "stand out!"

"Why me next?" asked Dick. "I would rather not wrestle with you."

"But you must; I demand it. Try a fall with me, or I will seize you and throw you over into the depths below."

"Let me make an appeal to you—to be merciful," pleaded Dick.

"Bah! mercy is for women," was the answer; "come forward."

Dick showed the greatest reluctance, and parleyed yet a little longer.

"If you take one of my companions I will get myself ready. Do you not see how bad I am? Would you struggle with a sick man?"

"You are sick with cowardice," said the brigand. "Come on."

"I am ready," rejoined Dick.

As he glided past Carl, he whispered—

"You know what to do. I can fritter away about another minute—no more."

"All right," was Carl's answer.

Dick advanced to the brigand chief, who had struck one of his most impressive attitudes, and meant real business this time.

He was not going to be taken in any more.

In his heart he suspected Butterflick had played a trick upon him, but in the absence of proof he let the thing go.

But Dick should suffer.

He would get well hold of him, hurl him to the ground, and SMASH him. That's what he would do.

"I am ready," he said, fiercely.

"So am I," returned Dick, quietly. "Now then."

The brigand laid hold of him, and Dick apparently yielded to his grasp.

But only for a few moments.

Suddenly Gastra Fuello felt his arm jerked up in the air and something like a vice close upon his throat.

One grip took all the go out of him, and the fear of death arose before his eyes.

He gasped out something, but with the imperfect words upon his lips he was twisted round and seized by the nape of the neck in the tremendously powerful grasp of Dick Strongbow.

This was the signal for his friends to act, and they rushed upon the two brigands in charge of the pass.

These men, like their companions, were staring half petrified at the sight of Dick making a puppet of their redoubtable chief.

They were taken by surprise, their muskets snatched from their hands, and themselves forced over the parapet ere they could realise the full purport of the sudden change that had come o'er the scene.

CHAPTER LXXVII.

THE RETREAT FROM THE BRIGANDS—THE ALGUAZIL—A JACK-IN-OFFICE.

N O body of men was ever taken more completely by surprise than the brigands were that day.

The sudden daring and activity of our friends was as astonishing as the leaping up of dead men would have been.

Down the narrow pass retreated Phil, Carl, Muffins, and Butterflick.

Behind them came Dick, still grasping Gastra Fuello by the neck and waist.

He retreated backwards, with an occasional glance to the rear to avoid taking a false step, which would have precipitated him and his burden over the precipice to the depths below.

Dick judged rightly that the brigands would soon recover sufficiently to attack men who were inferior in numbers, and, as far as they knew, unarmed.

On seeing their chief, with his eyes starting out of

his head, being dragged away, they began to yell and get ready to shoot.

But Dick held Gastra Fuello as a shield, and retreated down the narrow path.

The brigands, yelling, followed.

Suddenly Dick stopped short.

"Gastra," he said, relaxing his hold upon his neck, but still keeping him fast, "please give a few orders to your men."

"Mercy!" gasped the brigand. "I choke."

"I will choke you effectually and throw you over the side if you do not do as I tell you," said Dick.

"I will do anything," was the gasping reply.

"Yah—yah!" yelled the brigands. "Shoot!"

But they could not shoot Dick without killing their chief, and the winding path had carried the others out of danger.

In obedience to Dick's commands they had gone slowly on, trusting to him to get away safe, and in the full belief that he would succeed in doing so.

"Call on your men to halt," said Dick.

"Oh! my neck," cried Gastra Fuello.

"Do as I tell you," said Dick.

"Halt! you fools," screamed the half-choked chief.

"Now tell them to pitch their rifles into the valley below," said Dick.

"They will not."

"Then over you go."

And Dick, just to give him a taste of what he might expect, did swing him over the side like a limp doll, and drew him back again.

"Away with your guns!" screamed Gastra, furiously.

A murmuring arose from the men, and none for a moment obeyed him.

"You hear!" yelled Gastra Fuello. "Down with them! They will not be lost."

The men, accustomed to implicitly obey him, did as they were told, and dropped the weapons over the side of the path.

With a rattle they went down, some striking the side and bounding out fifty or more feet away, others going sheer down, dart fashion, to the ground.

"Will want repairing, some of them," thought Dick, grimly. Then aloud, "Now their knives."

"They will not heed me," groaned the brigand.

"I give you two minutes. One—"

"Away with your knives, you fools!" yelled the chief.

Again the men hesitated, but a second command was heeded, and the knives followed the rifles.

The brigands understood the position, and fully comprehended that without their chief they were sheep without a shepherd.

The terror inspired by the amazing strength of Dick, which in their eyes was miraculous, had something to do with their obedience.

Dick's next movement was to let go of the waist of Gastra Fuello and quietly feel over his dress to see if he had any concealed weapons.

Finding he had none, he finished off with an extra nip of the neck that for a moment took away the ruffian's breath.

Then he laid him unresisting upon the ground and, drawing the revolver in his possession, quietly said—

"Whoever attempts to follow me will be shot down."

If all did not understand his words, the action

was sufficient, and when he quietly walked on none attempted to follow him.

It is astonishing what one resolute man can sometimes do with a number of half-hearted creatures.

In America and Australia illustrations of this can be found almost every day.

One man has stopped a train and robbed all the passengers, compelling them to give up their possessions by quietly informing them they would be shot if they disobeyed him.

Single men have even "hung up" and robbed a small town. In short, there are hundreds of illustrations of what daring and coolness can carry out.

We do not commend the conduct of the train-stoppers and town-robbers, but refer to them as proof of what a plucky fellow like Dick Strongbow can do.

Some people—half-hearted stay-at-homes—will say that such a scene as we have just described could never take place.

It not only could, but it HAS taken place. It is simply a description of a thing that was done.

Well, Dick went down the pass to join his friends, and ere he had gone far he saw them standing close together, gazing down at the level land below.

Following the direction of their eyes he saw at the foot of the pass about a hundred men in the uniform of the regular Spanish army.

They were being harangued by a fussy-looking old Spaniard in civilian attire. He was seated on a mule, that every now and then emphasised his words by kicking its heels in the air. It was rather a funny scene, but not exactly a pleasant one.

Dick guessed that these men had come to rout the brigands out of their stronghold, and by some means had become acquainted with their being up the mountain.

The fussy man in private attire was of course an alguazil, which is equivalent to being a magistrate or lord of the manor at home.

"Carl," he said, as he joined his friends, "I would rather have been without this friendly assistance just now."

"That's the sort of old fellow who may give us trouble," said Carl, "but we had better go down."

"Yes—not showing any arms, and with our hands up as a sign of peace. We are seen already."

Such was the fact, and the man on the mule was haranguing the soldiers more violently than ever, the signs he made showing that he was calling upon them to fire.

But there was an officer with the soldiers, who did not think it necessary to go to this extremity, and he was seen expostulating and pointing to the upraised hands of our friends.

"Hang it!" said Phil, "I don't like this business."

"No more do I," replied Dick, quietly. "There is such a thing as using common sense with cowardice. They think we are brigands, and if they fired could riddle us in five seconds."

"And I'm blowed if they ain't going to fire," said Butterflick.

Some of the muskets were indeed levelled at them, but the officer with angry gestures struck them up with his sword, and then, to the great amusement of our friends, went for the alguazil's mule, seized it by the head and jerked it right and left, shaking up its rider, and would have shaken

DICK STRONGBOW:

The Diamond King,

AND WONDER OF THE WORLD.

Peeping through the window Muffins beheld the alguazil and his clerk.

No. 15.   Price One Penny.

him off if he had not laid hold of the pommel of the saddle.

Taking advantage of this little performance, Dick hurried down the pass with his friends at his heels, and keeping up the sign of submission, reached the level ground.

The officer, seeing them, let go of the mule and came forward. At the same time the alguazil urged on his steed and took refuge behind the soldiers.

"Who are you?" asked the officer.

"English prisoners who have just escaped from the brigands"

"Ha! is it so? And where are they? How did you get clear of them?"

Dick, in as few words as possible, told his story, the officer listening with an astonished, and it may be said, doubting face.

"If the great athlete named Dick Strongbow had been with you," he said, "I could have understood these things being done."

"I AM Dick Strongbow," replied our hero, calmly. "If you doubt me, here is my revolver with my initials upon it. If you doubt me still ask me for some proof of my identity."

"An exhibition of your strength, perhaps," said the officer, laughing.

"Yes—if you wish it," replied Dick. "Shall I lift you with one hand in the air, or go over to that man on the mule, and upset steed and rider?"

"Oh! don't do that," said the officer, laughing; "that will be putting the fat in the fire. He is a great man in a small way, and is in command here. Heaven help him for a fool! Permit me to introduce myself to you, and then I will introduce you to him. I am Captain Ravielle."

They shook hands, and the rest of the party being duly introduced, Dick and the captain walked round to where the alguazil, in visible trepidation, was looking on.

The soldiers, with their rifles grounded, were standing at ease.

"Keep him off," said the alguazil; "see that he is not armed, and let him be guarded. These brigands are treacherous dogs."

"Your highness," said the officer, in a tone of voice that was covertly sarcastic, "this gentleman is no brigand. He has been a prisoner among them and has just escaped."

"I have only his word for it,' said the alguazil; "they are up to all sorts of tricks. Keep him off, I say."

"There is no help for it," said Captain Ravielle, dryly. "Keep aloof from him."

"Let them all be put under guard and conveyed to the castle," said the alguazil.

"Your highness," pleaded the officer, "that would be excessive caution."

"Are you in command here or not?" squeaked the old man. "I sent for you to obey me, not to give orders."

"You will have to go," said Ravielle, making a wry face; "it is merely a matter of form."

"A most inconvenient form," said Dick, "and one that may get him into trouble before long."

"I hope it will," said the captain, "but at present yield to him. I will see that you are as well lodged as the place permits."

The news that they were still prisoners was conveyed to the others, and their wrath was very great. But it was a case when yielding was the wiser

course, and under the escort of ten men and the captain they were marched off to the brigands' stronghold.

It was open to them, being absolutely unguarded, and Captain Ravielle, who had half-an-hour before explored it, put his "prisoners" into the room usually occupied by the chief.

"It is about the best den of the lot," he said, "and your occupying it will compel that old fool to take an inferior place. You have arms, I believe?"

"Yes."

"I will trust to your honour, Senor Strongbow, not to use them on my men except as a last extremity."

"You may safely do so."

"I don't anticipate the necessity of using them, for I shall quickly let it be known who you are. But there is no telling what that old idiot may take into his head to command. I will now return and see what can be done for the brigands. Unarmed, I reckon they will yield without a blow."

With a general bow Captain Ravielle left the room. He did not lock the door nor leave any guard behind him.

"Another act of the brigand farce," said Carl.

"When I looked at that old man on the mule," said Butterflick, "my gorge rose at him, and I wanted to hoist him ten feet in the air."

Muffins did not say anything, but he looked as if he and that alguazil might collide later on.

"Sometimes a fool does more mischief than an absolutely vicious man," said Phil Norton. "Now suppose this old fusser chooses to insist that we are brigands, and orders us to be shot—what then?"

"We stand a very good chance of being shot," said Dick; "but I do not fear it."

"The door is not fastened," said Muffins, as he opened it, "and I don't see anybody outside."

"For all that we will remain here," said Dick. "Captain Ravielle would get into trouble if we attempted to escape, and our doing it would imply guilt. We can remain here fearlessly like honest men. Of course, if the worst comes to the worst we will give a good account of ourselves."

CHAPTER LXXVIII.

A SPANISH JUSTICE—SHORT AND SWEET DEALING WITH THE BRIGANDS—DOGBERRY'S DECISION.

A N hour or a little more had elapsed when a commotion was heard outside. Butterflick opened the door a few inches and looked out. Through a window at the end of the passage he could see a number of men filing past.

"They've collared the whole crew," he said, excitedly.

It was so, and for awhile there was a noise in the castle, arising from the movements necessary in stowing away a number of prisoners.

When it had in a manner subsided Captain Ravielle came back to the room.

"We've got the lot," he said, "including the chief,

who gave in without a blow. What curs these brigands are."

"They had lost their arms," replied Dick.

"Well, if you had would you have yielded without a blow? Why, a man with a cartload of big stones could have kept us at bay for hours."

"How does the chief carry himself?" asked Phil.

"The biggest cur of the band," was the answer.

"I thought he was," said Phil.

"I came in to let you know the programme of the day," said Captain Ravielle. "His highness," with a laugh, "will partake of refreshment after his military exertions. Then he will have a smoke and sleep, and in the afternoon you will be brought before him. Our rations consist of bread and grapes, and a little wine. Such as we have you can share with us."

They thanked him, and he went out calling for one of his men, who appeared with some good bread, luxurious grapes, and two bottles of wine.

The officer from his own pocket brought out a handful of cigars.

"You will want a smoke after tiffin," he said. "I regret I shall not be able to join you. Until his highness decides that you are NOT brigands it would be high treason of me to make friends with you. Senors, for the present adieu."

He left them, and they partook of their humble fare with the appetites of men who have little on their minds to worry them or aught to fear.

After the meal they lighted the cigars, and found them better than one usually meets with in Spain.

It is a curious fact that Spaniards, who might be expected to get the best tobacco, usually have to put up with the most atrocious weeds, the pick of the growth at home and in their colonies being sent to foreign countries.

The alguazil was apparently in no hurry to get to business with his prisoners, for the afternoon was well advanced when Dick Strongbow and his followers were summoned into his august presence.

He was in a room—a hall it might be termed—barren of everything but a long oak table and a few rough seats.

A stranger had arrived meanwhile, a man as old as the alguazil and as weazen as an Egyptian mummy, who acted as magistrate's clerk.

The alguazil sat at the head of the table, and his clerk beside him. Behind his chair he had a guard of soldiers, and half-a-score others watched over the prisoners.

Captain Ravielle took a seat by the side of the alguazil, facing the clerk, who, with a pen in one ear, another in his hand, and half-a-dozen on the table before him, evidently meant business.

"Let the prisoners be closely watched," cried the alguazil. "We will now examine them. The boy first."

This was startling to Muffins, who certainly did not expect the honour of being the first put through the mill.

"Boy, of what nationality are you?" asked the alguazil.

The old man's English was not quite so good as written here. We leave out its imperfections to make it clearer to the readers.

"I didn't understand you, sir," replied Muffins.

"He's axing your age," whispered Butterflick.

"Oh!" said Muffins, "I'm not certain how old I am. Say anywheres between eleven and sixteen."

"That is an impertinence," said the alguazil to the clerk. "Put down 'answer, rude.'"

He was a veritable old Dogberry this man. Shakespeare's creation was not more incompetent for the post he held.

The clerk wrote down the answer made, and the alguazil put another question.

"What's your name?"

"Muffins."

"Muffins—that is one name; in your country you have two names always."

"He's Wicount Muffins," said Butterflick; "I'm his father, Lord Crumpets. We are a-travelling for pleasure, and I'll bet you five to one that before you are a month older you will wish that you'd slept in a bed of broken bottles afore you insulted us."

"That's a very long answer," said the alguazil to his clerk; "have you got it all down?"

"No, your highness, none of it," replied the clerk, confusedly. "I was waiting for the boy to speak."

"It's your duty to take everything down—every word," said his master, wrathfully. "The father says he is Lord Crumpets, and I believe he is a liar. Muffins—boy—where do you live when at home?"

"Anywheres," replied Muffins.

"He lives in Anywheers," said the alguazil to his clerk. "What part of England is that, boy? I never heard of the place."

"It strikes me," said Butterfiick, "that you ain't heerd much in your time. Did you ever hear of Old Sally?"

"Ole Sally?" mused the alguazil. "No—London and Man-ches-ter I have. Well, this boy—Viscount Muffins—is he rich?"

"He is," said Butterflick; "we've all got a pile."

"Ah! then," said the alguazil, cunningly, "this affair may be arranged by fining you."

"If you think that we are going to pay you black-mail," said Dick Strongbow, sternly, "you are very much mistaken. We are unjustly detained, and I tell you that ere long you will smart for it."

"I am ruler in this district," said the alguazil, "and fear nobody. Have you put what HE said down?"

The clerk thus addressed had not thought it necessary to do so. No question had been put to Dick, and he did not think his interpolation required any notice to be taken of it.

The day was hot, and the old man, overcome with the heat, had dozed off.

His august master stared at him viciously, and, leaning forward, rapped him on the crown of his bald head with his truncheon.

The startled old clerk woke up, and wildly began to write all sorts of foreign characters in the record book.

"Pig—idiot!" said the alguazil; "attend to business, or you will be fined and imprisoned for contempt of court."

Dismissing Muffins, the alguazil next beckoned to Butterflick.

"You say your name is Lord Crumpets?" he said.

"I said so, sartinly," replied Butterflick; "but you needn't believe it unless you like."

"I shall do as I please," said the alguazil. "I do as I like at all times."

"There's no doubt," said Butterflick, "that you are an ornament to this 'ere country—of the Chimpanzee style."

"You are putting all this on record, I hope?" said the alguazil.

"Every word, your highness," said the clerk. "You are an ornament to your country in the Chimpanzee style. Yes, it is all here."

"What is the Chimpanzee style?"

"I don't know, your highness; but it has a Japanese sound. The Japanese rulers are very wise."

"Oh! that's it. Lord Crumpets is a perfect gentleman; I am disposed to deal more leniently with him than the rest. Are you a lord too?"

The question was addressed to Dick, who simply answered—

"No."

"No title at all?"

"None that I know of."

"You have a name?"

"I call myself Dick Strongbow."

"Ha!" exclaimed the alguazil. "I have heard that name before."

The clerk laid down his pen, the ink blotting the book, and stared aghast at Dick.

"You know this man?" said the alguazil.

'He was the terror of Madrid," replied the clerk. "He appalled and scared the whole city; the streets cleared as he walked abroad. He is possessed by a devil."

This answer shows what talk may do, and how the reputation of a man may be worked up or down, as reports about him float through the country.

What the clerk said had been told him by an eye-witness of Dick's doings in Madrid.

"Save us!" exclaimed the alguzil; "but this man is possessed of a devil, and we have no priest here to exorcise the spirit. This is awful. What is to be done to him?"

"Put him back in his cell, and let the holy father be summoned to subdue the evil within him."

"It had better be done," said the alguazil.

And bending down, he whispered a few words to Captain Ravielle, who gravely bowed.

"I will myself guard over him," he said, "for, possessing a charm in the form of a bone from the little finger of St. Palestro, I do not fear his evil power."

"Remove them all," said the alguazil. "Never again will I hunt brigands without a holy father."

Accordingly Dick and the rest, who did not at all comprehend the reason of the sudden closing of the examination, were hurried out of the room by Captain Ravielle, who led them back to their place of imprisonment.

Closing the door he burst into a hearty fit of laughter, which lasted for a minute before he could speak.

Then, when he had told them the cause of his mirth, they laughed too.

"That is how legends get about," said Captain Ravielle. "One of these days you will be spoken of here as Jack the Giant Killer is in your own country. You will become a mythological personage. It is very funny."

"What will be the end of it?" said Dick.

'Oh! one of the priests will be sent for, and he will take the whole thing in its true light. He will calm the fears of the alguazil, and make friends with you. Priests, as a body, are very sensible fellows, and would be glad to get rid of the superstition of the people, but it isn't an easy matter. However, I am here to keep a close guard upon you, and, to kill the time, what do you say to another cigar? Perhaps I may be able to get a few bottles of wine. We came upon this expedition well provisioned."

While Dick and his friends were having a fairly good time of it, sterner business was being done in the hall in the presence of the alguazil.

One by one the brigands were brought in and examined.

They could not at all deny their guilt, and their separate appeals for mercy met with no response.

The last brought forward was the chief, who, so Ravielle stated, was the biggest coward of them all.

He implored, he bellowed, he craved for mercy, and on his knees prayed to the alguazil as if he had been an idol.

With such a man the alguazil was at home.

He was not afraid of him, and he played the stern judge fairly well.

In the then state of Spain short was the shrift for men of Gastra Fuello's class. When caught the trial was over, sentence passed, and execution carried out in a single day.

The alguazil had power to sentence the brigands to death, and that was his intention.

For them no mercy, no anything—nothing but death.

And it may be said they richly deserved it.

Thieves and murderers to a man, what else could they expect?

It was an hour before sundown when Captain Ravielle was summoned into the presence of the alguazil, and shortly after hurriedly returned to Dick.

"Follow me," he said. "I will put you into a quiet place to see it"

"See what?" asked Dick.

"The execution of the brigands. They are all sentenced. We have no prisons to keep them in— no time to waste upon them. They are to be shot. Already some of my men are digging the grave. It is only a trench in which they will be laid side by side."

Dick went with him. The others were desired to remain behind.

"I have the alguazil's permission for you to be present," he said to Dick.

"I do not take pleasure in seeing an execution," said Dick, "but I will be there. I want to see how far a brutal life will help a man in the hour of death."

"You may see strange things done and hear what you little expect," said Captain Ravielle. "Hush! There is the tattoo beating. The grave is ready. It is time for the execution to begin."

CHAPTER LXXIX.

EXECUTION OF THE BRIGANDS—THE WORST SPARED—THE ALGUAZIL'S RANCOUR AGAINST DICK STRONGBOW.

 GRIM scene in the light of the setting sun. Dick stood aside with Captain Ravielle, on the left of the soldiers. The alguazil and his clerk sat on a high rock, well out of reach, to see that justice was done.

The first man marched out was one of the rank and file. Dick remembered him as one of the men who had escorted him to the brigands' haunt when he was first captured.

The fellow assumed a bravado that carried him to the spot where he was to stand and receive the swift leaden messenger of death. Then his heart failed him.

He fell upon his knees, and with trembling hands upraised cried out for mercy.

The ministrations of an exceedingly shabby-looking priest were unheeded by him.

A signal from the alguazil was given and twelve men fired simultaneously. The wretched man fell back into the trench-like grave prepared for him and his fellows.

So one by one in quick succession out marched the doomed men.

Some wept, some prayed, others cursed, but not one met his end LIKE A MAN.

It was pitiful, and long ere the procession had come to its end Dick looked no more. It was not until Gastra Fuello, the last to suffer, was brought forward that he turned his eyes in the direction of the spot chosen for execution.

He was anxious to see how this big bully, the bravo who had ruled these men with a rod of iron, bore himself.

He could not bear himself at all.

He had to be CARRIED to the place of execution.

With eyes fixed, and a feeble moving of his lips, he was borne by half a dozen sturdy soldiers to the spot where he was to pay the debt he owed for all his crimes.

Once, twice, thrice they endeavoured to stand him upon his feet, but each time he sank helpless upon the ground.

"What is to be done with the cur?" asked Ravielle.

He looked up at the alguazil, who sat with staring eyes, almost as helpless as the man brought there to be shot.

"Give him some wine," hinted the clerk to his senior.

The alguazil caught the words and cried out—

"Yes, bring him some wine, and a little to me."

The wine was brought, when the doomed man and the man who had doomed him to death drank wine poured out of the same bottle at the same time.

They did not toast each other or anyone, but they drank, as it happened, together.

It gave strength to both, and the brigand made an effort to stand up. His eyes fell upon Dick.

"Ha! fiend," he shrieked, "you are more than man. I feared nothing till you laid hold of me."

Dick turned away.

He had no desire to triumph over the brigand, especially in the last moments of his life.

"Get it over," he said to Ravielle.

"I do not give the signal," he replied; "it must come from the alguazil."

He looked up, but the signal was not given.

The alguazil sat with his hands clasped before him, and his eyes looking ahead, as if thinking.

Suddenly he sprang to his feet and cried out—

"Take that man back to his cell."

A murmur of surprise ran round the soldiers; they forgot their discipline in the consternation of the moment.

Captain Ravielle was as much surprised as anyone, and stared hard at the alguazil, who was being assisted down from his seat by his clerk.

"Take him back, senor," he said—"he, the leader—and all his men shot?"

"It is my order," said the old man; "will you dare disobey it?"

"I dare many things, but I have no desire to disobey you," answered the captain.

To his men he said—

"Take that ruffian back to his cell."

Gastra Fuello was now almost himself again, and marched away with the men at double-quick time.

More than half the soldiers remained, resting on their rifles.

The alguazil walked or rather tottered up to Captain Ravielle and said—

"Here is a man who deserves death—Strongbow."

Dick started. He had good occasion to do so, so sudden was the attack made upon him.

"Senor," said Ravielle, "you must be mad."

"I give you fair warning," said Dick, "that I am a desperate man, and will not die without a struggle."

"I say that you are to be shot," doggedly returned the alguazil; "is not that enough?"

"No," said Ravielle, resolutely; "I refuse to obey your orders."

"Then I will command the men myself to do it."

"If you do," said the captain, coolly, "I will tell them to disobey you."

"You dare not!"

"I dare."

The alguazil looked from one to the other with an evil light in his small, mean eyes.

"I see," he said, slowly, "you have arranged it together to defy my authority. You shall both suffer."

Drawing a short cloak over his shoulders, he motioned to his clerk to follow him, and hobbled back into the castle.

"I fear," said Dick, "that you will get into trouble on my account."

"The venomous old fool had better look to himself," said Ravielle; "he is a jack-in-office, and may find himself grassed ere long."

He gave orders for some of the soldiers to lay the dead decently in the trench and fill it in. Then he walked back with Dick.

"I will guard you closely to-night," he said, "not to prevent your escape, but to see that no mischief may befall you."

"I am obliged," said Dick, "but I may tell you in confidence that we can protect ourselves. We are armed."

"Hey-dey! How came that about?"

Dick told him of the way he had succeeded in recovering the arms of which he and his companions had been deprived, at which the captain laughed.

"I am right down glad I did not stand by the old man," he said; "you might have shot both of us."

"I certainly would have shot somebody," replied Dick, grimly.

A few moments later Dick was housed with his friends for the night, all under lock and key, with Captain Ravielle on guard.

At a late hour he entered their cell, with a rifle for each and a bag filled with ammunition.

"If you want these things," he said, "use them. I have warned my men not to obey the alguazil, but I cannot trust them all, I fear. If they choose to attempt murder on his account, their blood be upon their own heads."

CHAPTER LXXX.

THE ALGUAZIL VENOMOUS—A SUMMONS TO SURRENDER—MUFFINS GOES FOR AN AIRING.

HE alguazil and his clerk sat in whispered consultation in the hall. Behind them, a few paces away, stood a number of soldiers, with eyes and ears upon the watch.

As yet these men had given no expression to their sentiments on the question of allegiance to the alguazil; but they were disposed to do his bidding simply because he was by law chief in command.

By doing so, they argued, they would be safe. If anything went wrong it would rest upon his shoulders.

Their captain was, in a sense, of secondary importance, for if they disobeyed the alguazil and got into trouble it would be through him, and he would be in trouble too.

Therefore he would be powerless to shield them from the authorities.

It was not clear why the alguazil had conceived such an antipathy towards Dick and his friends, but the fact was clear—he was deeply embittered against them.

We may go so far as to say that he had spared the life of Gastra Fuello to annoy Dick, and he would have spared the other brigands also if he had not been afraid of their numbers.

But he knew their nature.

They were not merciful or grateful, and would have cut his throat for sixpence an hour after their release without the least compunction.

"Say now, truly," he said to his clerk, "can it be done?"

"It can," replied the clerk. "The orders are to arrest all persons found in the haunts of brigands, and if you are satisfied of their evil character shoot them on the spot."

"Of the true character of these men I am quite satisfied," said the alguazil, with a smile, "so let the warrant for their death be written out."

The clerk took a piece of parchment from his portfolio.

It had some printing on it, and was, in fact, a royal warrant for the execution of malefactors, leaving a blank for the name or names.

"What names?" asked the clerk.

"Any will do," was the reply. "Who will gainsay my authority? I know them not, save as the companions of malefactors."

"There are Smiths, Browns, and Joneses in England," said the clerk.

"Mix them up," said the alguazil.

So the clerk mixed them—three Smiths, one Brown, and one Jones—and the warrant was ready as soon as the alguazil had attached his name to it.

"All that now remains to be done," said the alguazil, "is to name the hour of execution."

"Now—by torchlight," replied the clerk. "Get it over."

"Send for Captain Ravielle," said the alguazil to one of the men.

The soldier saluted and departed.

While he was absent the alguazil sat with his eyes shut twiddling his thumbs.

The clerk nibbled his pen, and seemed to be rather cooling over the business.

But he had the consoling reflection that he was but the servant of his superior, and he trusted that if anything went wrong he would, on that account, be exonerated.

The clang of a sword announced the return of the soldier.

The alguazil opened his eyes and found the man was alone.

"You could not find Captain Ravielle?" he said.

"Yes, your excellency," was the answer; "but he declines to come."

"Declines!"

"It is so, your excellency. He says that he no longer recognises your authority."

"Why, this is high treason!" said the alguazil. "Write it down—write it down."

The clerk entered the report in his note-book. The soldier still remained at the salute.

"You have something more to say?"

"Yes, your excellency."

"What is it?"

"Captain Raveille says you are a mad old fool."

"Make an entry of that," said the alguazil.

"Mad old fool," murmured the clerk, as he completed the entry.

"Anything more?" asked the alguazil.

"Nothing more, your excellency."

"It now remains for me, as the representative of our gracious king, to arrest the captain for high treason."

As the alguazil made this portentous announcement he rose up in his seat and signalled to the soldiers to draw nearer to him.

When they had gathered in a close semi-circle near him he proceeded to put a few questions to them.

"Are you loyal to our gracious monarch?"

Of course they said they were with much enthusiasm. A month before two-thirds of them had been howling mad in the cause of Don Carlos.

"You recognise his authority?"

"We do."

"And you acknowledge me as the chief representative of his authority here?"

"Yes—yes."

"Then you will at once proceed to arrest your captain for high treason, and having bound him securely you will bring him here."

They shouldered their arms and walked out. The alguazil rubbed his hands with satisfaction.

"We shall soon see who is master here," he said.

"We shall," replied the clerk, dubiously.

After a short delay the men came back, rather in a hurry and very mixed.

They had not the captain with them, and the alguazil frowned.

"You have not done your duty," he said.

"Your excellency," said one of the men, "our captain has shut himself in with the prisoners, and they are all armed. They say if we attempt to force the door they will fire into us."

"In that case," said the alguazil, "you—you—must go- and—and—be fired into. You had better also—fire—into them."

But the men looked doubtful, and one of them ventured to say that it was a dangerous business.

"That is nothing to me," said the alguazil; "you are paid for dangerous business. Go and do it."

They stood about shuffling their feet, none offering to go. The alguazil roared out—

"Take down their names. I will report them for disobedience to orders in the face of an enemy."

"The penalty for which is—death," said the clerk, impressively.

"Your excellency," replied one of the men, "we are but common soldiers and can do little unless we are led. It is the same all the world over. We want an example—an inspirator. Will you lead us?"

"No," replied the alguazil, hastily; "if I fall all authority may be at an end. You may take my clerk."

But the clerk urged that he had never handled a rifle in his life, and would on that account most likely prove more dangerous to friend than foe.

In any case he could only be a hindrance to the more experienced.

A brilliant idea entered the alguazil's head. He knew that soldiers loved plunder, and put a tempting bait before them.

"Your captain wears jewels," he said, "and so does some of the others also. IF THEY SHOULD BE SHOT IN THE FRAY ALL THEY POSSESS IS YOURS."

That settled it.

The thirst for plunder was as good a stimulant as any, and the men declared they would carry out the orders of the alguazil.

Dick and his friends were in the room once occupied by the brigand chief.

It was an apartment at the end of the passage, and had a very strong oaken door.

For windows it had two grated openings about seven feet from the floor.

Now none in that room knew where those grated openings looked upon, and it was then too dark to see.

The sun had gone down and a haze obscured the stars. As yet no moon had risen.

"It would be as well to know exactly where we are," said Carl, "which can only be done by somebody getting between the bars. How about Muffins, now. Is he thin enough?"

"But there may be a hollow or a precipice outside," said Dick.

"Master," said Muffins, "I shall be all right. I can get through the bars and hold on. You may trust me not to let go unless I know where I am going."

"Trust him," said Butterflick. "He's got the sperrit of his dad in him, and isn't likely to make a mistake."

"Did you never make a mistake?" asked Phil Norton.

"Never."

"What—not with Old Sally?"

"No," said Butterflick; "I knew where I was going, but she drew me on, in spite of my knowledge. She would have drawed you and half-a-dozen like you."

As nobody there had any personal acquaintance with Old Sally they could not controvert this assertion.

Butterflick laid hold of Muffins, hoisted him up, and asked him to try the bars.

He did so, and with no apparent effort got his head between them. Then, with great caution, he wriggled his body through, and sat down on the stone ledge of the window outside, holding to the bars.

"There's no ground outside here," he said, "but a flat roof. I can make out that much. I fancy the big hall is at the end of it. I can see a light there."

"Any windows?" asked Dick

"Oh! yes—little ones. Shall I go and have a look through them?"

"Yes, if you can do so safely."

Muffins slid down, and they heard him moving cautiously away. Throughout they could not see him, as they had no light in the room.

"If we only had a lamp of some sort, or candle," said Phil.

"There is sure to be something of the kind here," replied Captain Ravielle. "The peasants and brigand fellows about the hills burn big, coarse candles, which they make themselves out of fat and cotton or twisted linen."

"You think we might find some here?"

"Possibly."

Phil struck a match, and as it flared up Carl and Dick went for two boxes in the corner and overturned them.

Among the heterogeneous contents they found a packet of those very candles, kept there for the brigand chief's use.

"I'll fix 'em," said Butterflick.

The candles were lighted, and Butterflick, having dropped a little hot fat in two places on the table, planted the candles in the thick of it, and as soon as it was cold they were fixed.

"That's how we do it," he said. "Saves a deal of outlay in candlesticks."

At this moment a bang was heard at the door, and a voice in Spanish called upon them to surrender.

"You came on that errand before," said Captain Ravielle, "and had your answer."

"If you don't open we shall fire," was the reply.

"Your blood be upon your own heads if you do," said Captain Ravielle, solemnly.

"Let me put in a word here," said Butterflick. "I know enough of your lingo to understand what they are saying. I'll put matters straight. Hi! there, cut it, or by George I'll make holes in the foremost of you."

His stentorian voice, which he exerted to the utmost, had the effect of driving them back, although they did not understand him.

A few moments later they opened fire.

A bullet struck the door and penetrated the wood, but it stopped short at an inside plate.

The ping of it could be distinctly heard by those in the room.

"Keep out of the line of fire," said Dick, "and call that boy back."

"Muffins!" roared Butterflick.

There was no answer.

"Muffins, you disobedient beggar! don't you hear me calling you?"

If Muffins did hear him he made no reply.

"Give me a leg up," said Butterflick to Phil. "A man's voice is bottled up in this stone cupboard."

Phil gave him a leg up, and, grasping the iron bars, he drew himself level with the window.

"Muffins!" he roared through the bars, in a voice that went echoing away among the mountains like the rumbling of distant thunder.

Still no answer.

"Where can that derned boy 've got?" cried Butterflick in an agony "What's happened to him? MUFFINS! MUFFINS! Can't you hear your father's voice?"

He ought to have heard it certainly, but no responding cry came back; nor was there any movement of feet outside

All was still.

"He's been got hold of by somebody," said Butterflick, in agony; "and to think of my being shut up here! Open the door! I'm going out to see what's come of him."

CHAPTER LXXXI.

NO MUFFINS—BUTTERFLICK FIRES A STRANGE SHOT—A RETREAT.

UT Butterflick's request could not be complied with. To open the door would be to expose them to the fire of the soldiers in the passage, who could shoot them down like rats in a cage.

"Keep cool," said Phil Norton; "the boy will turn up all right"

"You've never had a son, and don't know a father's feelings," replied Butterflick, with a moan; "blessed if it isn't enough to drive anyone wild."

The report of two more rifles cut him short, and this time a bullet passing through an exposed part of the door, whizzed by Butterflick's head and flattened itself against the wall behind him.

"Come out of the line of fire," said Captain Ravielle.

"All right! One moment," replied Butterflick; "I'll just have a squint at 'em outside."

As cool as if looking through an ordinary keyhole he placed his eye against the orifice made by the bullet and tried to see what was going on without.

"The place is so blessedly full of smoke. I can't see anything," he said. "Stop a moment, though—it's clearing away. Whoop!"

He darted aside as three or four more rifles belched forth their fire. This time none of the bullets penetrated the door.

"I'd like to give 'em a return shot," he muttered.

"Don't try it," advised Phil Norton.

"Just one," said Butterflick. "I can pop one through the hole they have made."

"Mind the recoil," said Phil; "hold it quite close. Jam the muzzle into the hole."

"All right," said Butterflick, as he pulled the trigger.

Bang!

Notwithstanding the precaution he had taken there was a considerable "kick" by the weapon, and it jerked his hand up quite a foot. Dropping the revolver, Butterflick laid hold of his wrist.

"Not sprained, I hope?" said Dick.

"No, I think not. Kinder shut up a bit, like a telescope," replied Butterflick. "I'll soon have it all right."

He rubbed and pulled at it, and having seemingly got his wrist into working order, picked up the revolver and stood aside from the door.

"Derned if I didn't think it had slid my hand up to my elbow," he said; "but I think I made one of them squeal."

They all listened, but could hear nothing outside save a faint sound of shuffling feet for a few moments, and then all was still.

"Scared them away, if nothing else," said Captain Ravielle; "they won't try the door any more, but—"

He pointed significantly at the window, and they all saw that it was a source of danger.

As there appeared to be a flat roof just outside, it would act as a platform for the operations of the enemy, and shots fired through it would command the greater part of the room.

That the roof was accessible from some part of the castle was a foregone conclusion; but they had a faint hope that the soldiers might not remember it as a convenient place to continue the assault.

It was a hope which was doomed to be shortly dispelled.

Carl, who had been listening at the window, suddenly turned and put the light out.

"Silence," he said; "they are approaching."

They all held their breath, and by the sounds they heard on the leaden roof some persons were certainly assembling, and Dick reckoned there were at least a score slowly creeping up to the window.

"We can't hold out here," he whispered. "What think you Ravielle?"

The answer, to Dick's surprise, came from the other side of the room, near the door.

"Hush! do not talk, but come here."

Wondering what he was doing Dick went over to him, and found to his astonishment that the door was open.

Jupe crouched behind the wall waiting to strike.

"The fools!" Ravielle said, softly; "they did not remember that I had the key."

"What are you doing?" asked Butterflick.

"Going out," whispered Dick.

"You may go, sir, but I'll wait for my boy to come back."

"Don't be a fool," said Phil; "he CAN'T come back."

"Because he's dead?"

"Not he; that boy's dodged the blackguards. He's a true son of his father."

"Do you think he's safe?"

"Let us get out and see," said Phil; "go ahead!"

He gave Butterflick a jerk forward and got him outside.

The others were already in the passage.

Captain Ravielle gently closed the door, locked it, and put the key into his pocket.

"Now they may challenge and blaze away," he said.

As he spoke the firing began upon the leads, with hoarse shouting by way of accompaniment.

"Just in time," whispered Captain Ravielle, with a chuckle. "Now we must get right away from the place."

"Not without the boy," said Dick.

"Tell me where to look for him," said Ravielle, "and I will go for him."

They could do nothing of the sort, and it was clear to all, even Butterflick, that for the present Muffins could not be helped in any way.

"I don't think that the old fool will have him killed," said Captain Ravielle, speaking as he had done for the last half hour in Spanish; "if he has got hold of him he will most likely frighten the boy by shutting him up in some dark room."

"THAT won't frighten him," said Butterflick, with a chuckle, to whom the remarks were translated by Carl.

"Our friend is right," said Dick; "we must get away." Here another volley interrupted him. "There are many places outside where we can hold our own."

"The brigands' retreat on the hillside," suggested Phil.

"You forget we have no food or water," said Dick; "let us go and take our chance of finding a suitable place."

It was not at all to the taste of any of them to desert Muffins; but what were they to do? The boy had disappeared, and they had not the least notion what had become of him.

He had vanished, just as a sprite might have done, into the darkness of the night.

Two minutes sufficed to get the party clear of the castle, and as they were turning away towards the hills a third volley was fired.

"They think that ought to settle us," said Phil, "and I daresay they will soon be looking for our bodies."

"The mad fools," said Captain Ravielle, "to be led away by fear of an alguazil. Bah! I disown them, and every man shall smart for what he has done to-night."

———

CHAPTER LXXXII.

WHAT BECAME OF MUFFINS—THE ALGUAZIL AND HIS CLERK—MUFFINS AS GAOLER.

POSSIBLY some of our readers are desirous of knowing what became of Muffins, and as in duty bound we now proceed to gratify their anxiety.

Muffins was not dead, neither was he a prisoner at the time his friends were in the cell and escaping from it.

On reaching the leads he saw some windows lighted up, and, as we before suggested, rightly judged they belonged to the hall where the alguazil had been sitting in judgment.

He lost no time in getting to the nearest of the windows, and, peeping through, beheld the alguazil and his clerk pacing up and down conversing.

The action of the clerk showed that he was in some way expostulating with his master, while the alguazil remained as dogged as a mule.

"I'd like to give that old fool a scare," Muffins muttered, and, looking about for some way down to the hall, he saw a low, narrow entrance to a staircase, with the door hanging upon one hinge.

Muffins before going down peered into its dark depths, but could make nothing of it.

If he wanted to see exactly where it led to he must go down. Accordingly he went.

"I'll soon get there, and be quick back again," he thought.

The staircase was a winding one, and he had now no doubts about whither it led. The bottom of it communicated with the hall, and here there was no door.

Muffins peeped in, and saw the alguazil and his clerk pacing slowly up and down about ten paces from him. They were still talking, but in Spanish, which Muffins only imperfectly understood.

But he made out sufficient to understand that the clerk was expostulating with his master on the treatment of the prisoners.

The suggestion of the clerk was that trouble might come of it.

But the alguazil was determined to go on. He did not, so he said, care for any man in the land, save the king, whose commands he as of course prepared to obey.

Muffins did not know what to be up to, but he was determined to do something before he went back again.

After a short delay the two old men resumed their seats.

As they were settling down their faces were turned the other way, and Muffins, with a stealthy footstep, crept up to the table and dived under it.

He had now a view of four spindle legs, and the temptation to kick them was almost irresistible.

But Muffins withstood the longing, and having searched for and found a pin in his coat, he proceeded to operate in a milder form upon the calf of the clerk.

"I won't be talked to by you," the alguazil was saying. "I tell you— What's the matter with you?"

"A bite on the leg, senor," said the clerk.

"You look as if you were having it sawn off. Ah! what again?"

"They bite in most places," the clerk said, humbly, "but here they pierce—they—"

"Stuff and nonsense," said the alguazil, "there is nothing— OH!"

The old man threw up his legs in agony as Muffins favoured him with a sharp stab with his small but potent little weapon.

Muffins narrowly escaped a kick under the chin.

"Honoured senor," cried the clerk, "what ails you?"

"A murrain pulverise them," cried the alguazil, stooping down and scratching his leg; "they bite like vipers. They are brigands of their breed."

At this moment the clerk jumped out of his chair, uttering a wild scream.

It scared the poor old alguazil nearly out of his wits, but ere he could say anything he, too, had good cause to leap up.

"It's not fleas," he screamed. "I felt something like dog's teeth."

The clerk peeped under the table, and saw Muffins, with his back to him, squatted on the ground and presenting the appearance of some hideous idol.

He did not recognise the boy, but immediately assumed that it was some evil spirit beneath the table.

"The fiend!" he yelled, and, backing his chair violently, upset it, turning a somersault in the hall.

The alguazil at first could not move for terror, but on getting another stimulating prick from Muffins he, too, upset himself, but was up again almost as soon as he was down.

Muffins had been a street boy once upon a time, and was of course a past master in the art of making hideous noises.

He screamed, he whistled, he yelled like a demoniac.

Away went the alguazil and his clerk out by the upper end of the hall, and Muffins was about to go back the way he came when the clang of arms was heard and the soldiers trooped into the hall by another door.

He had just time to pop back under the table again to save himself from being seen.

From this position he could only see the legs of the soldiers as they walked past the table, but as they got further out he had a view of their whole figures.

They were making in Indian file for the staircase down which Muffins had just come to the hall.

The feelings of the boy on this discovery being made cannot be described.

Not only was his own retreat cut off, but he knew that the soldiers going in that direction meant mischief to his friends.

He would have given one of his ears if by so doing he could recall the time he had lost in playing his pranks upon the alguazil and his clerk.

But if he had given his head he could not have had his wish.

All the soldiers did not ascend the stairs. About half-a-dozen remained behind.

First of all they gathered in a group near Muffins.

He could have used the pin upon THEIR legs, but he made no attempt to do so. So close were they that he dare scarcely breathe.

Then a horrible fear came upon him.

What if he should cough or sneeze?

And with the thought came the desire to do both.

The awful preliminary tickling of his nasal organ indicated what was coming, and the memory of the time when he was inside the clock at the Cape and all that followed came back to him.

He sneezed then with wonderful good results, but he could not hope to do so now. He could not lift the table into the air, or blow the soldiers across the room, or do anything but sneeze and be found out.

Awful, overpowering, terrifying thought.

He battled with the sensation as one struggles for life, but he had to do it silently. He could move his arms, but that was all.

Suddenly, when the sneeze had travelled down to the tip of his nose and was on the point of discharging itself with a cannon-like report, the crash of firearms was heard.

The soldiers in the hall shouted, and a new alarm acting upon the nerves of Muffins the sneeze remained unexploded.

The men in the hall stood still listening.

Muffins sat under the table quaking for his friends.

Another volley and much yelling, and in a little while a third firing. Then came comparative stillness.

But it did not last for long.

In a few minutes the soldiers from above came bundling down the stairs as fast as the narrow way would permit, and held brief conference with their comrades in the hall.

Muffins succeeded in getting at the meaning of some of the words they uttered in their excitement, and he gathered the joyous tidings that his friends had made good their exit from the room.

Some awful cursing, happily unintelligible to Muffins, was poured by the soldiers upon the heads of the escaped men, and then in mad pursuit they rushed from the hall.

Muffins took time to breathe and recover his scattered wits ere he came out of his hiding-place.

Two lamps upon the table were alight, and he could see that he had the hall to himself.

So far he was comforted; but where were his friends?

He did not think they would go very far without him, but he hoped they would for their own sakes.

"I can dodge about all night," he thought, "and shall go back to Madrid."

Notwithstanding this determination, he had a very poor idea of the way he ought to take, and, without somebody to direct him, might have wandered for a long time ere he found the Spanish capital, if he ever succeeded in finding it at all.

But first he had to make his way out of the hall.

Here he was nonplussed, for he had lost all recollection of the way in which he had been brought in to be examined before the alguazil.

There were at least half a dozen doors in the

place, and only one, with the exception of the stairway leading to the roof, that he was at all certain about.

As the soldiers had gone out that way he did not intend to use it.

He had the strongest possible objection to running against any of the body.

It occurred to him that he might with greater security follow the footsteps of the alguazil and his clerk.

They had gone out by the door at the upper end of the hall.

He found it open, and passed into a passage where all was dark, groping his way along until he came on a turning to the left, and then he saw a feeble light in the distance.

He could also hear the familiar voices of the two old men.

They were talking aloud in a state of great excitement.

Creeping along carefully, so as to make no sound, Muffins came upon a chamber, of which the door opened outwardly.

Inside he could see the alguazil and his clerk squatted on a low wooden bench, quaking all over with fear.

It was a barren chamber otherwise, and looked as if it had been rarely used.

Muffins felt about the door, and discovered two things. There was a stout lock upon it, and the key was outside.

A smile, quite impish in its exultation, spread over his face.

Why should he not lock these two old men in for the night?

He immediately acted upon the idea, closing the door with a mighty bang and locking it in a twinkling.

Up sprang the two prisoners in alarm, and the alguazil shouted his loudest—

"Open the door, you fool; don't you know who is here?"

"What do you say?" cried Muffins through the keyhole.

"Who's that?" asked the alguazil.

"It sounds like the voice of that accursed boy," replied the clerk.

"I thought so," snarled the alguazil. "He shall pay dearly for his jest. Boy—boy! Viscount Muffins!"

"What did you say?" asked Muffins again.

"Open ze door at once," said the alguazil, in English, "or I sting—whip you."

"What's the odds you ever see me again?" asked Muffins.

"Ze what?"

"The odds. Will you like to bet a gooseberry to a ten-pun'-note that you ever get hold of me again?"

"If I do," replied the alguazil, "I vill skin you first, and zen HANG you."

"No doubt you would," replied Muffins. "Goodnight!"

"Ha!" yelled the alguazil, "vould you dare to leave me here?"

"Bet your life I will," said Muffins. "Surely you are not such a fool as to think that I would let you out? Sorry you ain't got a feather bed to lie on, but that ain't MY fault. I didn't furnish the place."

The clerk then whispered a few words to the enraged alguazil, who immediately changed his tone.

"Boy—boy!" he said, "don't go. Let me out. and you shall be pay—a sheeling, or ze same as two —a ducat."

"Certainly," replied Muffins, "of course I am sure to do it. You ain't at all innercent, are you for an old 'un. Bless you, I've not been took in on the soft lay for years. Anything else?"

"Two ducat?"

"Not enough."

"Ten ducat."

"If you said ten thousand," replied Muffins, "I should say NO. You've got to keep there until my friends come back for you. They've gone away to fetch the perlice."

"Gone avay!" shrieked the alguazil.

"That's so," said Muffins; "all is clear, and I'm off after them. Ta-ta, adoo! Fare ye well."

And away he went bursting with laughter, followed by the cries and yells of the enraged alguazil.

Muffins took the key with him to assure the keeping of the prisoners until wanted.

Smart boy that.

CHAPTER LXXXIII.

MUFFINS GETS AWAY—AN OLD FRIEND TO THE RESCUE—THE ALGUAZIL'S HUMILIATION— WHERE IS DICK STRONGBOW?

UFFINS, after wandering here and there for a while, found his way from the castle by the main entrance. Outside it was very dark, for a haze of mist obscured the stars, and he was in considerable doubt which way he ought to go.

He could hear the soldiers gathered together a short way off, eagerly talking, and he judged by the sound, which was of even volume, that they were gathered together in a group, and could easily be avoided.

Now more than that he wanted to know which road to take, and on that point he was at sea.

But the life of Muffins had been of a happy-go-lucky nature from the start, and he bore away to the right, resolved to take his chance of what might turn up.

Road, in the true sense of the word, there was none, and the way was rough. Muffins had to take every step with caution.

We need not detail all that he did between then and dawn. Suffice it to record that he put about two miles between himself and the castle, and just as morn was breaking he found himself in a narrow defile between two hills.

Then he saw signs of it being used as a road, and set forward with a brighter heart, but feeling uncommonly hungry.

He had not traversed far ere he heard the sound of advancing footsteps, and the regularity of the tramp, tramp, indicated that disciplined men were approaching.

Fearing that it was the soldiers from the castle, he hid himself behind a rock and cautiously peeped out, to see if his surmise were correct.

The men soon appeared in sight—a captain with a troop of soldiers ; and in the leader he recognised an old friend—Captain Gravalo.

The joy of Muffins was unbounded.

Leaping up, he took off his cap and waved it by way of salutation.

The captain recognised him instantly.

Having shaken hands with him, Gravalo told Muffins that he had come to rescue his friend Dick Strongbow from the brigands, and that other officers and similar bands of men were closing in upon the castle to give assistance, if required.

"The idea of ransom with Gastra Fuello was not to be thought of," he said. "He would in all probability have murdered you afterwards."

He was astonished and pleased to hear the turn events had taken, but he was bitterly angry with the alguazil.

"The arrogant old fool !" he said. "He must be punished for his proceedings. Luckily I have a warrant from the king in my pocket, which will enable me to do exactly as I see fit in dealing with this district."

Of course they had not been standing still while conversing, but were marching on towards the castle.

There was no longer any need to approach with caution, the brigands being dead save the leader, Gastra Fuello, whom Captain Gravalo intended to hang without delay.

They arrived within hail of the castle as the alguazil and his clerk emerged therefrom, just released from their prison by the soldiers, who up to that time did not know where they were.

The arrival of a fresh body of soldiers considerably astonished those who were already there, and seeing an officer with them they stood at the salute.

"It's only a captain," said the alguazil to his clerk. "I will soon take the starch out of this fellow Senor !"

He addressed Captain Gravalo, who looked at him with a frown, and asked him what he wanted.

"That boy there," said the alguazil, "is one of a nefarious band, who have infested this district for a long time. He has recently escaped from custody here, and I demand his return."

"All in good time," said Captain Gravalo ; "you are somewhat hasty in demanding. I have a warrant here which I will read to you."

He drew it out and quietly read it so that all could hear.

The power it gave him was absolute. So far as that district went, he was its temporary governor.

"And now, senor," he said to the alguazil, "I first of all demand of you the release of my friends, Dick Strongbow and his companions."

"I do not know such people," replied the alguazil, feebly. "There were some men here, but they left last night."

"Senor," said Captain Gravalo, sternly, "prevarication and lying will not help you. I know the whole story. Now as to Gastra Fuello—where is he ?"

The alguazil, who had not many roses in his cheeks after a sleepless night, turned saffron colour, and opened his lips, but no reply came forth.

"Where is he ?" Gravalo demanded of the clerk.

"He is released—on parole," he stammered.

"Released—on parole !" cried Captain Gravalo, indignantly ; "a murderous ruffian, the head of the gang ! You have destroyed all the tools and released the hand that guided them. It is treason to the people and our king."

"He gave me his word he would not go outside the castle," stammered the alguazil.

"Arrest that man," said Captain Gravalo, "and see that he is kept in close custody."

"Arrest ME !" screamed the old man ; "do you know who I am ?"

"You were alguazil—chief constable of this district," replied Gravalo ; "now you are a confederate of Gastra Fuello the brigand, and stand a very good chance of spending the rest of your years in prison."

"Mercy !" he cried ; "spare me. I am an old man. If I have erred in judgment—"

"Take him away," said Gravalo ; "as for you," turning to the clerk, "you have recorded certain proceedings which have been conducted here. You will keep the books safe and produce them at the proper time."

"Your excellency shall be obeyed," replied the clerk, immensely relieved to find that he was not to share imprisonment with his master.

The alguazil was led away moaning and wringing his hands, and Captain Gravalo gave orders for breakfast to be prepared.

"Our friends," he said to Muffins, "are pretty safe, although I would have preferred the final consolation of knowing that Gastra Fuello was in our custody. He is a dangerous fellow—a sneak, a coward, and a born assassin."

"Master can take care of himself against HIM," said Muffins.

The soldiers had brought their rations, and two extra men were bearers of food for their captain.

There was plenty for Muffins and to spare, notwithstanding the fact that he ate tremendously, having fasted for many hours.

Breakfast over, the soldiers were allowed to rest for awhile, and then several small parties were sent away to search for Dick and his friends, who might be wandering aimlessly about.

Muffins remained behind with the captain, and shortly after two other bodies of troops came in.

Much indignation was expressed at the conduct of the alguazil, and if some had had their way he would have been despatched with the aid of a piece of rope, but those in command knew better than to take the law into their own hands.

The morning passed away, and there were no tidings of the missing men. The search parties returned one by one, with the news that they had scaled peaks in various directions, and scanned the county round, but could see nothing of them.

It was very odd, and Captain Gravalo did not quite like the look of things.

"It is impossible," he said, "for them to have been very far on their way, and I relied on their being in the immediate neighbourhood on your account, Senor Muffins."

"I expect they think I am dead," replied Muffins, with a grimace.

"Anyway," said the captain, "it is strange. I wonder what has become of them?"

Muffins did not know—nobody knew, and guessing was a vain pursuit. It was annoying and rather distressing.

Captain Gravalo felt very uneasy on account of the missing men.

CHAPTER LXXXIV.

DICK AND THE PEASANT—THE ROADSIDE INN—
THE PRETTY LAVINE.

 ICK STRONGBOW and his friends were, after all, not far away.

The general opinion was that they ought not to go any distance until they had positive intelligence of the fate of Muffins. Butterflick was inconsolable.

But Dick Strongbow, although uneasy about the boy, was not troubled with very serious apprehensions.

"Muffins," he said, "belongs to a class of youth who have more lives than a cat. It doesn't matter what height they fall from, they are sure to alight upon their feet; and they can dodge every form of danger, from an open-handed blow aimed at their heads to an avalanche."

Dick's words were comforting, and Butterflick's sorrow sobered down.

Morning found the party in a valley westward of the castle about three miles, and here they discovered an old peasant living in an hovel, which for meagreness and poverty could hardly be surpassed.

The old man had risen with the sun, and came to the door just as the party reached it.

He stared at them more in curiosity than dismay.

"We are travellers," said Dick, in Spanish, "and are in search of food. Can you tell me where we can procure some?"

The old man smiled wearily.

"It is a question I ask myself every day," he said. "I go forth each morning not knowing where I shall earn a crust of bread."

"You have no employment, then?"

"There is no work for anyone, senor, except that which he finds by chance. The country is in a state of wild confusion. We are all poor save Dorello the innkeeper."

"And who is he?" asked Dick. "Does he live hereabouts?"

"His inn lies a mile from here," said the old man, "on the main road. Dorello is rich, but not out of his inn-keeping."

And the old man shook his head dolorously, as if the doings of Dorello were very bad indeed.

"Is he a brigand?" asked Dick, naturally undesirous of falling into another nest of ruffians.

"Oh! no, he steals not," said the peasant; "but it is whispered that he was a man trusted by Don Carlos. The Pretender made his inn one of his headquarters, and Dorello betrayed all he knew to the Royalists. You see?"

"Yes, I understand," replied Dick. "He was a

spy—a traitor; but if he can give us something to eat You will get what you want," said the peasant. "I am going in that direction myself, and will accompany you."

"I am afraid I must overlook that."

He walked briskly for an old man, and they set out for the inn.

The guide was garrulous, and told Dick a lot about this same Dorello, which was sufficiently interesting to listen to.

"His daughter Lavine," said the old man, "is charming. Her father thinks she ought to marry a duke, and the girl has some such thoughts also. Jupe woos her in vain."

"And who is Jupe?" asked Dick.

"A young servitor—a garcon at the inn—good-looking, but a fool. No brains, and what little thought he has is for Lavine."

Putting two and two together, Dick got at the position of the innkeeper whom the old man spoke of as Gippa.

He had made a little money by betraying the Carlists, and was, in the eyes of his poorer neighbours, passing rich.

He had a pretty daughter—and this was an interesting item of intelligence—who had a lover, a servitor of the father, whose attentions were not appreciated.

"But how comes it that this man Gippa, having money," said Dick, "was not robbed by Gastra Fuello, the brigand?"

"Brigands," replied the old man, "are always friends with those who live around them. They rob only those who come from OUTSIDE. You see, senor, it is good for brigands to have near them those who will lie to the gendarmes and put them off the scent, or hide them at a time of trouble."

Dick saw clearly, and likewise he also saw the inn, which stood alone on the road which they had now reached.

There were a few huts scattered about, but the inn, to all intents and purposes, was solitary.

It had an encouraging look about it, for it appeared also to be a small farm-house.

Pigeons were flying about and fowls strutted to and fro.

There was also a yard, with a mule looking over the gate.

On one side of the inn was an orchard of considerable extent.

"You see how he flourishes," said the old man; "it is the wicked who make the money."

"Well, my friend," said Dick, "never mind—if breakfast is to be got here you would like some?"

"Senor, I would gladly break my fast," answered the peasant. "It is now sixteen hours long."

Dick led the way to the hostelry, his friends following. The old peasant remained outside.

It was a place of the usual type found in Spain.

The door opened at once upon a general drinking room with a bar at the end.

Behind it, backed by flagons, bottles, and a few metal vessels, was a tall, thick-set man, with a somewhat forbidding but not unhandsome face.

"I salute you, senors," he said.

"Good morning, friend," replied Dick. "Can we have breakfast here?"

"Aye! what you will; but whence come you?"

"We are travellers and have been in the hands of the brigands—but we have escaped."

"Ah! then you have no money," said Gippa.

"But we have these arms," said Dick; "surely one of these rifles will pay for breakfast."

"Two might," replied Gippa; "but let us not talk of payment yet, senor. I know you are noble; I see it in your face. Welcome to what I have and pay me when you càn."

"There is a poor man who was our guide here," said Dick; "I promised him a breakfast."

"He shall have it," replied Gippa, "enough and to spare. Senors, this is no room for you. Let me show you to the guest-chamber."

Turning to a small door at the back of the bar, he called out—

"Lavine, daughter, come and take charge here."

In a few moments a girl of about eighteen appeared. As she stood in the doorway, with the dark background to show up her figure, the visitors were all struck by her appearance.

She certainly was very beautiful, and her eyes especially were magnificent in their size and brilliancy.

She cast a quick glance upon the visitors, favouring Dick with a prolonged look and a welcoming smile. He doffed his hat and bowed with courtly grace. It was an involuntary act of homage to beauty.

"These senors," said Gippa, "have been in the hands of Gastra Fuello, who has taken their all. But they have succeeded in getting arms and escaping."

"Pardon me," said Dick; "but, judging by what you say, I fear you are in ignorance of what has happened to the brigand band."

"I know nothing—have heard nothing," said Gippa.

"The band is destroyed—dead," said Dick. "All but their chief are shot, and he, I believe, is in prison."

"Why, that is rare news," said Gippa, "for, although we who live so near the thieves have to feign a friendship for them, we like them not."

He came round the bar, and, motioning to his guests to follow him, led the way up a staircase opposite the entrance.

The eyes of the Spanish girl were fixed on Dick until he disappeared.

"He is handsome," she murmured, "and I am sure he is noble. Is it possible that my FATE has arrived?"

Her dark eyes flashed, and the burden of a Spanish song broke in soft cadence from her lips. The girl was not only beautiful, but she was a dreamer. She was the soul of romance.

Living in a secluded spot, away from the world, she had little to do but dream and hope for the coming of a lover who was to be both noble and handsome.

The few books she had to read were all stories of peasant girls beloved by the rich and great, and her ideas of life were founded upon their teaching.

When a child she had thought of a coming lover, on the verge of womanhood she longed for him.

But he came to her of her own class. She aspired to the companionship of a nobler kind, as depicted in story books.

In Dick she saw such a one as she had dreamt of, and as she sat in the bar thinking of him who must needs come to break in upon her pleasing thoughts but—Jupe.

The fellow was good-looking enough, and his attire showed the pains he took to make the most of himself, but he was only a servitor after all.

He came up to the bar, and, leaning upon it, looked into the face that had such a potent power over him.

She did not see him at first, and it was not until a very pronounced sigh escaped him that she awoke to his presence.

"Well," she asked, with a frown, "what do you here?"

"Lavine," he answered, "you know why I am here. Because I cannot keep away from you."

"Why not go altogether?" she queried; "you know you waste your time."

"If I were transported a thousand miles from this," he replied, "I should find my way back, though I had to walk through fire and water"

"I hear so much of this," said Lavine. "Too much."

Notwithstanding that, she did not object to it at times. When there was nobody else at the inn the wooing of Jupe was better than nothing.

But now that her ideal in Dick Strongbow had come Jupe was very much in the way. He was decidedly objectionable and must be dismissed.

"Yesterday," said Jupe, "you were almost kind, to-day you are cruel."

"I get so tired of your sighs," she said; "of what use are they? I am not interested. They do not inspire me. I shall never love you."

"So," said Jupe, bitterly, "it is one of these strangers who supplants me. I have seen them. Two are handsome; but they are all poor. They are nothing—they have not a ducat."

"Because of Gastro Fuello, who takes all," returned Lavine; "but what of that? They have only to write to England and a ship will bring them gold enough to buy all Spain."

"It is weak to talk like that," said Jupe.

"You dare to say I am weak," cried Lavine. "Away! you small thing—you travestie of a lover—you poor little rabbit! To your work, and trouble me no more."

It was more her manner than her words that struck home. She was upon her feet, with clenched hands and flashing eyes. The words rolled like the waters of a cascade from her lips.

Jupe was dismayed. In that presence he was dumb, and with undignified haste beat a retreat.

CHAPTER LXXXV.

NOW DANCE WE A MEASURE—JUPE'S WILD EFFORT AT REVENGE.

THE guest-chamber was a spacious room, with a large, old-fashioned hearth in it. The furniture was old and scanty, but there was a table and seats for all, and the visitors asked for no more.

"Breakfast, senor," said Gippa, "shall be ready in the tick of a clock." It was not quite so speedy as that, but its production was very prompt, and they all did justice to it.

They all felt the better for it, and even Butterflick cast aside some of his anxiety about his adopted son.

"A boy of mine," he said, "CAN'T go wrong—it isn't possible."

Having lighted cigars, a discussion arose as to their next movement. It was interrupted by a tramping of feet outside, and Captain Ravielle, looking out of the window, saw a detachment of soldiers.

They were piling arms, and had evidently stopped to refresh.

"Friends," said Ravielle, joyfully, "stay here a moment; I will soon return."

He left the room and hastened below to the bar, where he found the officer in command of the detachment.

The story of the imprisonment among the brigands was quickly told, and the alguazil's conduct excited great indignation in the heart of the listener.

"The old fool," he said, "stands a very good chance of being shot. He must have been mad."

"With his own importance," replied Ravielle.

He invited the officer upstairs, to be introduced to the late captives, and after a chat and a bottle of wine a short conference took place.

It was the duty of the officer to go on at once to the castle, and he promised to look up Muffins and send back instantly any tiding she could gather of his whereabouts.

Ravielle offered to accompany him, and with the soldiers they shortly after departed.

Prior to leaving, the officer gave Gippa an assurance that whatever bill his guests might run up it would be met.

"You have a great man here," he said; "take care of him."

To Lavine this was a confirmation of her idea concerning Dick, and it acted as oil thrown upon the fire.

Here was the prince of her dreams come at last.

After such a night the wanderers stood in need of rest, but they did not ask for beds. It was too early after their escape to remove their clothes.

So they, like hardy travellers, slept when and how they could.

Phil Norton and Carl dozed off on three chairs each, and Butterflick, seated by himself in a corner of the room, with his back to the wall, was snoring in something under two minutes.

Dick closed his eyes and briefly forget the troubles of this life, but that was all.

In so short a space of time that he doubted if he had slept at all he was awakened by the twanging of a guitar.

Everybody knows that a short nap is generally very refreshing; one wakes from it with all sense of fatigue departed. Thus it was with Dick.

He opened his eyes, and all thought of further sleep was gone; but he sat still for awhile listening to the twanging of the guitar.

Presently a cracked voice broke in with a song, and his fancy that it might be Lavine who was the musician was dispelled.

"Who have we here now?" thought Dick.

Rising from his chair he went to the window, but could see nobody. The musician was immediately beneath.

His companions were all asleep, and the variety of nasal sounds they emitted might be amusing, but they were certainly not poetical. Dick thought he would find something more congenial below.

Was he thinking of Lavine?

It might be.

Her beauty would have drawn an anchorite into a flirtation, and hanging about in the old inn was terribly dull work, so he went below.

Lavine was standing by the door talking to a withered old man—the musician—who was seated on the bench.

She looked up quickly at Dick and asked him—

"Can you dance?"

"A little," he replied, with a smile. "I have picked up some of your dances during my stay in this country."

"Will you dance with me?" she asked, eagerly.

It was a bold question, but somehow it did not seem so, the request came so naturally from the girl's lips. Dick looked around.

There was nobody in sight but himself, Lavine, and the old musician, who was one of those itinerant minstrels found in every land.

The sun shone brilliantly, the air was still and warm, and it was just the time and place for a little romance with a pretty girl.

But it was a fatal mistake not to say—"No."

When he assented Lavine was intoxicated with joy. It must, indeed, be the man of her dreams, whom kind fortune had sent that way.

She produced two pairs of castanets, and gave one pair to Dick.

"I am ready," she said.

The old musician, with a leary smile upon his face, struck up a quaint, appropriate air, and the dance began.

Lavine could dance gracefully. She was a true daughter of Spain, and had acquired—goodness knows how—the art of an alluring coryphee.

Dick fell into the humour of the moment, and for a time forgot everything but his surroundings.

But there were jealous eyes upon the pair.

Jupe had been watching, and saw everything, or nearly everything, from the side of the inn.

Up to the time when Dick came downstairs he had not been quite sure which of the strangers had won the heart of Lavine, but that one HAD won it he was sure.

Here was proof of who it was, and the first thought of the maddened lover was to kill him.

The Spaniard is ever too ready to use cold steel, but never more so than when thwarted in love. Jupe had murder in his heart.

Crouching behind the wall, stiletto in hand, he waited to strike. But the opportunity did not readily come.

The dancers glided here and there, turned from this side to that, and changed places in a series of swift movements that foiled the would-be assassin.

He crouched like a tiger ready for his spring but it seemed as if the opportunity would never come.

At last the dance was over, and Dick, having given his hand to Lavine, gallantly led her to a seat fixed without the inn.

In doing so he brought himself very near to his foe, who rushed out, stiletto in hand.

A shriek from Lavine acted as a warning note to Dick.

He turned just in time to see the upraised hand, and, with a lightning-like movement, grasped the assassin's wrist.

DICK STRONGBOW:

The Diamond King,
AND WONDER OF THE WORLD.

Behind the wainscot Dick saw a bundle of papers.

No. 16.   Price One Penny.

A shriek of pain burst from the lips of Jupe.

The deadly grip put on by the enraged Dick threatened to smash the bones.

"You wretch!" cried Dick. "What have I done to you that you should seek my life?"

Lavine, panting with excitement, fixed her large eyes upon the writhing Jupe, marvelling why he should look so horrible when only his wrist was grasped by another.

If Dick had had hold of his throat she would have understood it.

At length—it was only a few seconds later—Jupe sank to the earth, having first dropped his weapon. He lay there holding his wrist and moaning.

"You coward!" cried Lavine. "Who has hurt you?'

Jupe turned up his pallid features, and, with a quivering face, replied—

"You do not know. He grips like a fiend."

"I am very strong," said Dick. "It is a gift I possess. See here."

He took her by the waist with his two hands and raised her as a child.

The old musician, who at the first symptoms of a row had bolted to the door of the inn, smiled once more.

"What a wonderful person you are!" said Lavine.

"But who is this man?" asked Dick.

"It is Jupe—a servant, a scullion," replied Lavine. "He has not only dared to love me, but to tell me so."

Jupe said something between his teeth which Dick did not quite catch, but he knew it was bitterly opprobious by the start that Lavine gave and the flush that overspread her face.

So he stepped up to Jupe, and, raising him from where he lay, cast him across the road as if he had been an empty sack. He fell in a heap upon the ground, and lay there moaning.

Lavine sprang forward, and, putting her arms about Dick's neck, kissed him. It was an act of impulsive homage to his strength.

"You are magnificent!" she cried; "the greatest man in Spain."

The appearance of Gippa from the inn relieved Dick from a very embarrassing position. The innkeeper gazed around with an enquiring look upon his face.

"I have been dancing with the senor," said Lavine, "and that dog Jupe tried to kill him."

"Sacramento!" hissed Gippa; "was the fool mad?"

"Master," cried Jupe, as he arose slowly and painfully to his feet, "I am not mad, but you and that jade of a daughter of yours are. She has been looking for years for a nobleman to come and marry her. Ha! ha! it is good—old Gippa's daughter!"

The innkeeper glared wrathfully at his assistant and put his hand into his sash, but Lavine stayed his hand.

"Would you kill a snarling cur?" she said. "Get a whip and beat him, then send him back to his work."

"I can go to THAT," said Jupe; "and you may trust me, Senor Gippa, when I say that the love I had for your daughter is GONE. Bah! I have been a fool. Now I am wise."

He walked away round the house in the direction of the inn-yard, and Gippa, bowing to Dick, said—

"Senor, it is for you to say if that fool is to be forgiven."

"I do not think he will attempt my life any more," replied Dick. "Let him be."

"Oh! how lofty and noble," cried Lavine.

"The senor is great," murmured the musician.

Gippa would have said something more, but Dick would not hear it.

"No harm has come to me through the fellow's audacity," he said; "he is the only sufferer. Let the matter end."

He would have gone in then, but Lavine would not part with him yet.

"Come with me," she said, "and see our vineyard. It is now in the height of its beauty"

Dick's judgment said "No," but another spirit in him prompted the word "Yes," and he assented.

Lavine put her arm through his as confiding as if they had been friends of many years' standing, and they sauntered off.

"Senor," said the musician, "they are a handsome pair."

"They are not a pair yet," replied the innkeeper, rather curtly.

"But soon they will be."

"I don't know. In my opinion my daughter makes too free with a man she did not know yesterday."

"Is it so?" exclaimed the musician. "I thought they were lovers."

"You had no right to think at all," replied the innkeeper, wrathfully. "Have you been paid for your work?'

"No," answered the musician; "they were too busy with their love thoughts to think of me."

"Come in and drink," said the innkeeper.

We must for a few moments return to Jupe, who, with raging fires of wrath in his heart, went off to the farmyard.

On one side of it was a row of stables, always open, but seldom used.

Save for the one mule of the place it rarely had an occupant.

Jupe sought this place of retirement to give vent to his fury, and, throwing himself down upon a heap of dirty straw, cursed Lavine and the handsome stranger with all the vigour of a son of Spain.

While he was thus engaged a face appeared at a loft hole in the ceiling, and two dark, enquiring eyes were looking down upon him.

That pair of eyes was fixed in the head of Gastra Fuello. The brigand was in hiding in the loft.

He heard enough to find out exactly how the land lay, and, dropping lightly down upon the straw touched Jupe upon the shoulder.

The startled man turned over and raised his face to the brigand, whom he knew by sight.

"Ha!" he cried; "you here, mighty chief?"

"Get up, and don't lie drivelling there," said Fuello. "I have need of a friend—so have you. Let us work for each other."

Jupe looked at him in wonderment.

What did that mighty chief mean? Help each other? How?

"I," said the brigand, "have lost my castle and my men, but I shall rise to power again if you will help me. I am hungry and want food. Get me something to eat and drink, and then we can talk over a scheme of revenge."

"I am your servant," said Jupe; "your slave!"

"But hark ye!" said the brigand, seizing him by the shoulders and twisting his face to the light; "do not think for one moment of betraying. You will fail, and I will punish you bitterly."

"Betray you?" said Jupe. "To whom?"

"To that Englishman."

"To HIM! I'd rather burn my hand off—die—than do it. Curse him! It was a bitter day when he came here"

The brigand released Jupe, who crossed over to the inn, and presently returned with some wine, bread, and fruit in a basket.

"Old Gippa is getting drunk to celebrate the betrothal of his daughter to the PRINCE—ha! ha!—who is some poor runaway dog."

"He is a dog who barks little but bites dangerously," said Gastra Fuello, as he uncorked a bottle of wine. "He has the strength of ten men."

"Of a hundred, I should say," replied Jupe, with a shudder. "See here—my wrist, with all his finger-marks—as black as night. His hold is terrible."

"Now," said Gastra Fuello, "as I can eat and drink and talk too, let us try to scheme something to bring this dog to destruction."

"What can we do?" asked Jupe.

"He may sleep here to-night," said Fuello. "Are there no ways of getting at him when he is unconscious?"

"Many, if he does not secure his door,' replied Jupe.

"You do this," said Gastra Fuello. "When it is known that he will stay—as he will, if he is not blind to the pretty Lavine's charms—you weaken the sockets of the bolts so that a jerk will detach them. All then I ask is for you to admit me to the inn to-night, show me where he is, and leave the rest to me."

"And the others?"

"If there is time I may settle them also, but let me kill the cock bird first. The remainder will be easy."

Jupe promised to do all that he was told, and when the brigand had finished his meal he took up the basket and returned to the inn.

Gastra Fuello climbed back to the seclusion of the loft to sleep away the time until night should come.

The hours passed, and the sun rose high in the heavens. The time for the siesta approached.

No other person came near the inn—all was quiet there. The tired wayfarers still slept on. Dick and Lavine did not return from the vineyard.

Gippa went to the door two or three times to see if they were coming, but could see nothing of them.

Had it not been the hour of siesta he would have gone in search of them, but the noonday repose was one of the few luxuries of his life, and he could not give it up.

"I will sleep first," he said. "Perhaps they will return."

He had his sleep, and, awaking about two o'clock, found Carl and Phil Norton in the bar.

They had got up, but Butterflick was still taking recuperative power from Nature.

"Where is our friend?" demanded Carl.

"He went out for a stroll," replied Gippa.

"Alone?"

"No, with a friend. My daughter is with him."

"Dick is getting himself mixed up with another flirtation," remarked Carl; "this time he may not find a Gravalo to put things square. Which way did they go?"

"To the vineyard," Gippa said; "it lies on the base of the first hill to the right. You will find him there."

"Here he comes," said Phil Norton.

A hasty step was heard outside, but it was too light for Dick's. It was that of Muffins, who came bounding into the bar.

"Whoop la!" cried Phil; "here's the lost lamb."

"They are all coming this way," said Muffins, breathlessly; "the officers and soldiers, and that—what's-his-name—old fool. Where's dad?"

"Getting forty winks," replied Phil. "First door on the top of the stairs. Wake him up. It's a pity he should have to wait a moment without knowing that his dear son is back again."

Muffins bounded up the stairs, and Phil and Carl hurried to the door.

There they saw a cloud of dust, which betokened the coming of the troops.

The uniforms of the men could be faintly distinguished, also the bent form of an old man upon a mule.

"The alguazil!" cried Phil, gleefully.

"The sword of Damocles has fallen," returned Carl. "Truly we are avenged. But where is Dick?"

"I'll go in search of him—I can reach that vineyard in five minutes."

Phil went off with rapid strides, and Carl, with a bright light in his face, returned to the bar.

"Give me a glass of wine—something good," he said. "I'll drink to our coming friends. All's well that ends well. But has all ended well?" he asked himself immediately. "Where is Dick?"

The steady tramp of the soldiers now fell upon his ears, and above he could hear Butterflick literally roaring with joy over the recovery of his lost son.

Only Dick was wanting to complete the happy party.

But ere the soldiers returned Phil came back with Lavine by his side.

The face of the Spanish girl was pale under the olive of her skin, and there was a set, determined look upon her face.

"She says that she does not know where Dick is," Phil said, "and that she has not set eyes on him for hours."

"And it is true," said Lavine, passionately. "Why should I lie? He is lost to me, because he is not mortal."

"Stuff and nonsense!' said Carl. "He is mortal enough to have travelled many thousands of miles with us. Where did you leave him?"

"He left me," said Lavine, clasping her hands like one in pain. "He was here, so, by my side. We walked and talked together, strolling through the vines. I went forward a little to gather him a beautiful bunch of grapes, noble and worthy of him. When I looked back he was gone."

"It is very strange," said Carl, amazed.

"Why should I lie, I ask again?" said Lavine, passionately. "Was he not my prince? Did I wish to lose him? Ask yourselves if it could be so. No, I wanted him to-day—to-morrow—always. But he is gone—vanished! He was too great, too noble to be mortal. Did you see him with a power beyond man toss Jupe like a toy across the road?"

"We have seen nothing," answered Carl, bewildered. "It is all new to us. Who is Jupe? Why should he throw him across the road? What does it all mean?"

"He was a spirit, not a man," murmured Lavine, covering her face with her hands. "He has been and is gone. I have lost him. Oh! my prince—my prince."

CHAPTER LXXXVI.

DICK'S DISASTER—THE SCORN OF LAVINE—JUPE IN TROUBLE AGAIN.

CARL soon decided what to do. He and a few more went to the spot where Dick had disappeared, accompanied by Lavine.

In the manner of the girl there was nothing to give rise to the least suspicion of foul play; but one can never be sure.

One thing was certain—the girl, in a romantic way, was completely "gone" on Dick, and there was just the possibility that, finding he did not reciprocate her love, she had used the knife with Spanish readiness.

But the girl showed no hesitation in accompanying them back.

Alone she would not have gone for the world, for she was superstitious, and the vanishing of Dick had smitten her with an overwhelming terror.

The whole of Dick's immediate friends, including Captain Ravielle and Gravalo, went off to the vineyard, which we have already sufficiently located.

Lavine led the way up to the vineyard, then she gave way to Carl, and, pointing to a spot where the vines grew thickest, said—

"It was there I beheld him. My prince—my king! It was there he vanished."

"There will be trouble with this girl, anyway," thought Carl.

They left her standing by the entrance to the vineyard, and spreading themselves out walked slowly through the vines, which grew thick and trailed upon the ground.

When near the place Lavine had pointed out an exclamation from Butterflick attracted general attention.

"What is it?" asked Carl.

"I heard his voice," replied Butterflick. "Stand still. Whoa! my son."

They all stood still, and the voice of Dick in muffled tones reached their ears.

"I am down here—not hurt, but I can't get out."

"Down where?"

They looked about them, and at first could see nothing, but presently Muffins, whose visual organs were of the best, espied a dark opening under one of the thickest-growing vines.

"Here it is!" he yelled, and plunging forward he had a narrow escape of going down also, for a portion of the ground broke away beneath his feet.

But for his watchful foster-father he would have disappeared as Dick had done.

It all came to this. An old well, long dried up, had been covered in and forgotten; the artificial crown of it had given way, and there he was in a hole about twenty feet deep, physically unhurt but far from comfortable.

As soon as they found out exactly how things were they sent Muffins off to the inn for a strong rope.

Lavine, on being informed of the nature of the accident, clasped her hands in thankfulness.

"He is spared for me, cara mia!" she cried.

"Derned if that young woman isn't bad!" said Butterflick. "What's the matter with her?"

"The complaint they all catch one time or other," replied Phil.

Carl, lying upon the ground, talked to Dick in his prison.

The facts of the accident were very simple.

"I was standing quite still," said Dick, "when suddenly the earth seemed to break away from me. I came down straight as an acrobat doing the drop, and lighted upon my feet. I know the trick of it, and it's not the first time I've found it useful."

Muffins was soon back with the rope, which was first tested and then knotted and attached to a short pole laid across the opening of the well.

Dick came up hand over hand with scarce an effort, which was another trick he had picked up in the circus in his old days, and received the congratulations of his friends.

Lavine stood aloof, and seemed to wonder why Dick did not rush up to her side and embrace her.

As it was he simply smiled, and, raising his hat, hoped his "inconsistent disappearance had not alarmed her."

"I scarcely noticed it," she replied, tossing her head.

"My lady is goin' on the other tack now," thought Butterflick. "She's riled. Oh! wimmin—wimmin, what conunderums art thou?"

It was not often that Butterflick burst into poetic language, but when he did it was in a manner which his friends called "up to high-water mark."

He felt that this last reflection of his was something out of the common, and he repeated it aloud, for the benefit of those around him.

"Oh! wimmin—wimmin, what conunderums art thou?"

"Why, what's the matter, dad?" said Muffins. "Not took bad, I hope?"

"I don't want none of your cheek," growled Butterflick. "All boys should be kept in their places."

They were moving away from the vines now, Lavine, with a disdainful face, falling back into the rear.

Butterflick, ever gallant, as we have seen, told himself off to play the part of cavalier.

But Lavine would have none of him, and in response to his first attempt to render himself agreeable looked so tigerish that he at once abandoned the task.

Dick, after a chat with Carl and the Spanish captains, looked back for Lavine, and asked her why she walked alone.

"Keep to your friends," she said; "I am nothing."

Now Dick, while down the well, had had time to reflect, and in that somewhat unwholesome seclusion had arrived at the conclusion that a flirtation with Lavine would not do.

It was not fair to the girl and might get him into trouble.

A chat with Gravalo confirmed this idea.

It was to the influence of Lucella that he owed the prompt assistance sent to him. She had considerable influence over the king, who was one of her admirers.

"But it is a case of hopeless love," said Gravalo. "Such a woman was not made for the sport of kings."

Dick was very sorry he had gone so far with Lavine, but he could see that if she found he was only amusing himself for the moment she would not, like the maiden in the song, fade slowly away with hopeless love.

She was far more likely to scratch him, for, pretty as she was, she was a bit of a vixen.

This idea of his was confirmed by her further acts of petulance.

On getting near the inn she glided swiftly to the front, and was the first to re-enter the door.

There she encountered the wretched Jupe, who, hearing the tramp of feet, was coming out to see who it was.

Without a word or any sign of warning Lavine boxed his ears on both sides.

Involuntarily Dick and his friends burst into a roar of laughter. Lavine turned upon them, proud, pretty, and with a fierce light in her eyes.

"You laugh," she said. "Ah! you are no prince."

"I beg your pardon," replied Dick; "I didn't mean to laugh at you. It was at that fellow. You made him so ridiculous."

Lavine's face softened for a moment, and she looked as if she would have said more, but, changing her mind, she threw her head up and marched indoors.

"The sperrit of old Sally," said Butterflick, "seems to be in more'n one of 'em."

"Ah!" said Captain Gravalo, "zat vas ze lady you loved in your youth."

"I don't know whether it was love 'zackly," said Butterflick, scratching his head. "I wus faithful to her because I didn't want her to be allus grabbing at my whiskers and similar recedings. In my opinion the party who marries that girl who's just shot herself inter the house had best start married life with his head shaved and keep it so."

The return to the inn with Dick safe and sound was celebrated over a bottle of wine and a cigar. Then the best dinner the place could give them was ordered, and Gippa was told to do his utmost on pain of being treated as a brigand.

"The fellow has been more or less in league with Gastra Fuello," said Captain Gravalo, "but we do not think it necessary to interfere with him, IF HE BEHAVES HIMSELF."

Gippa seemed to be aware of the position, for he bustled about and roared at his household to bestir themselves and "do honour to their noble guests."

Lavine, however, would do nothing.

"I will not wait upon the plebs," she said.

"Very well," replied her father; "then Jupe and I must do all. Jupe, you dog's son, see that there is a good fire—catch and kill the fowls, look up the eggs for the omelettes, and milk the goats. The senors above are not to be trifled with."

The place was all alive.

Soldiers in and out the house were lounging about smoking, laughing, and when they could bandying a few words with Lavine and a hideous old serving-maid who sprang up from somewhere.

But none went into the stables or thought of going up to the loft where Gastra Fuello, quaking from head to foot, lay hiding in the coarse hay.

CHAPTER LXXXVII.

FINISHING OFF THE ALGUAZIL—THE STOLEN FOWL—MUFFINS ONCE MORE GETS HIMSELF IN A FIX.

"F course it is not our intention," Captain Gravalo said, in his native tongue, "to leave this part until we have hunted down Gastra Fuello. He is not far away."

"There is one man I should like to show mercy to," said Dick.

"Ah! the alguazil, I suppose," interposed Ravielle.

"Just so."

"The old dog doesn't deserve it."

"Well, I think he is hardly worth punishing," said Dick. "You have cut his comb, and he will never crow or show fight again. Is so old a bird worth killing?"

"No, I suppose not," replied Gravalo.

"And you have the power to show him clemency?"

"Yes."

"Then let it be shown."

"But he must know that it came from you," said Gravalo.

So the alguazil was sent for and in due time brought into the room.

It was just before dinner, and Jupe was laying the cloth, shaking like an aspen leaf before so many grand senors, with the knowledge he had of the adjacency of Gastra Fuello.

The alguazil was completely cowed.

He had played the part of fool and rogue combined, but any man with a genuine heart must have pitied him.

Our friends formed a semi-circle by the window, and in a small way formed a very imposing court.

Butterflick, who had an end seat, was ultra magisterial, and his gravity was that of a Cæsar.

The scene was finished off by half-a-dozen soldiers, who kept guard over the alguazil.

The wretched old sinner thought he had come up for judgment, and he cast an imploring glance all round, finishing off with Muffins, who had to breathe heavily to suppress a grin.

In measured tones Captain Gravalo first of all expatiated on the enormity of his offences, and just as the old man was expecting to hear some fearful sentence passed on himself he was told that those he had persecuted had pleaded for a remission of punishment for him.

"On condition that you never do anything tyrannical again," Gravalo said.

The alguazil could hardly believe his ears.

It was altogether so far out of his line of action that he could not understand it at all. It sounded like a mockery—a preliminary jest to the coming punishment. But, convinced at last that he was forgiven, he fell upon his knees, and went into such a paroxysm of gratitude that Dick could not stand it.

"Take him away," he said to Butterflick, "and see that he has something to eat and drink before he leaves."

Butterflick rose up, and with one hand lifted the alguazil from his knees.

"Come along, old man," he said, "our cap doesn't care for grovelling. But it's all right as far as showing gratitude goes."

He took him down to the bar-room below, where he found the clerk also in waiting, and forthwith proceeded to press upon both an undue consumption of the strongest liquors obtainable in the place.

The old men showed no unconquerable objection to "taking their whack," as Butterflick put it, but rather exhibited a bacchanalian alacrity, which soon emptied two bottles of port.

By that time they had forgotten their troubles, and the alguazil, having buried his dignity for good and all, became very brotherly towards Butterflick and others around them.

He hoped they would come and see him and spend a week or so at his house by the Catalonia Hills—"not a modern place, but filled with all necessary comforts."

Finally he began to sing an old Spanish ditty, accompanying himself on the guitar, which he borrowed from the old musician, who still lingered about the place.

The clerk joined in, and their united cracked voices were enough, as Butterflick said, to "kill a cat."

Suddenly Lavine appeared in the bar and commanded silence.

"Away, you parchment-faced villains!" she said, "or you shall have your heads dipped in the well to cool them."

"Angel," said the alguazil, "be not angry with us. We shall stop but for a very little while longer."

"Let 'em have a bit of a fling to wind up with," urged Butterflick; "they'll be awful bad to-morrow, and that ought to console you."

"Away—away—elephant!" said Lavine, after casting about in her mind a fitting epithet to bestow upon him.

"Will you excuse me, missy," said Butterflick, "if I give you a word of advice? You've addressed me in your own lingo, which I don't clearly understand; but I've got at that word helephant, and I must say it ain't becoming from so pretty a one to a party who's old enough to be your father."

"Away—go!" said Lavine.

"I think I'd better see you off," said Butterflick to the alguazil; "it's time for you to leave. Your missus will be expecting you."

"One more bottle," said the alguazil; "I can pay."

But Lavine insisted upon them going, and they went, alguazil and clerk arm and arm and much in need of mutual support, singing in their cracked voices the ditty Lavine had so brusquely interrupted, and followed by the laughter of the soldiers.

So they disappeared from the scene and out of the history of our hero.

Butterflick went upstairs in time to join the guests at the dinner-table, which was now replete with the best the inn afforded.

Jupe and Gippa were both in attendance, and Jupe was in a terrible state of mind.

He had paid a recent visit to Gastra Fuello, who had smelt the dinner, and, notwithstanding the fact of his having had his appetite appeased within an hour, demanded that some dainty from the table be brought to him.

"A fowl, or something choice," he said, "and fruit for dessert. Diablo! shall I lie here with dog's food while my enemies feast in the style of kings?"

Jupe, in mortal terror of the man, was bent upon appropriating something.

Gippa, with a landlord's eye, and lack of faith in his assistant's general honesty, was keeping a sharp look-out upon everything.

At length Jupe saw his chance, his master's back being turned, and he slipped a whole fowl into his trousers' pocket.

It being garnished with parsley-and-butter sauce did not trouble him.

He had got his fowl—a dainty for the terrible Gastra Fuello—and he was satisfied.

Only one person saw him, and that was Muffins, whose eyes, from sheer force of habit, were everywhere.

Jupe had given himself airs with the boy, and Muffins bore him a bit of a grudge.

Thinking that he had appropriated the fowl for himself, Muffins was determined that he should not enjoy it.

A little later on Jupe managed to get some bread into the other pocket, after that some fruit, and then he appeared to be satisfied.

Now Muffins never or rarely drank wine, and the usual after-dinner sitting had no temptation for him.

Give him a handful of fruit and permission to leave the table and he was satisfied.

Dick, knowing his habits, told him, when the cloth was cleared, that he could go, and Muffins, with his pocket full of pears, went after Jupe, who had just been dispensed with.

Muffins had no definite intention with regard to the fowl which had been appropriated, but he meant somehow to spoil Jupe's enjoyment of the same.

Jupe, in a hurry, vanished down the stairs, and by a back way hurried off to the stables.

Muffins let him get across the yard and then darted after him.

A peep into the stables gave him a sight of Jupe's legs disappearing loftwards.

"Gone up, like a dog to its kennel, to enjoy it," he thought. "I'll get up behind him and bark."

It was a simple, boyish trick he deigned to do, but out of it came all the elements of a tragedy.

As he crept up the short ladder that led to the loft he heard voices above him. There were two men speaking in very low tones.

One was Jupe he knew, but who was the other? Who was the man for whom it was now pretty clear the fowl had been stolen?

Jupe did not want it for himself, that was pretty clear. Perhaps, after all, it was some beggar who had touched the heart of Jupe by one of the stereotyped piteous appeals.

Whoever it might be, Muffins was bent upon getting a peep at him.

"Or was it a her?" Muffins asked himself.

Muffins got his head above the floor of the loft, but even then he could not see who it was. There was a heap of hay, and the other person, who, of course, was Gastra Fuello, was seated therein.

Jupe had thrown himself down beside him, and they were both out of sight.

Muffins went up inch by inch, and on his hands and knees began to crawl across the floor.

When about half-way Jupe suddenly got up and uttered a cry of alarm.

The next moment Gastra Fuello was on his feet also, and saw Muffins, who for the moment was too much startled to move.

"Stop the hole there !" cried Fuello, pointing to the way Muffins came up.

Jupe sprang to the spot indicated, and, drawing his knife, stood ready to use it if need be.

"Ah ! you boy- you VIPER !" said Fuello. "What you do here ? Say no word, or I kill you Ah ! it is good. I have you !"

Fixing his eyes upon Muffins with a venomous glare, he slowly approached him with the stealthy tread of some wild animal, his hand upon his knife ready for use.

Muffins tried to spring up, to cry out, but could do neither.

CHAPTER LXXXVIII.

A PROMPT ACTION—THE BRIGAND'S DOOM.

ITH a ferocious hiss, scarcely human in its intensity, Gastra Fuello aimed a blow at Muffins which would have terminated his career but for a burst of laughter from the outside. It came from Dick Strongbow, who was in the yard under the loft window, he having with Carl come down to see if there were any mules in the stable which could be made available.

It was some jest of Carl's that set him off, and the laughter saved Muffins' life, for it not only aroused the boy from the spell which held him, but startled the brigand so that his aim was diverted.

He struck short, the point of the knife cutting a slit in his clothing but not touching the skin.

On the right of Muffins was a door, which opened into the yard. It was used to take in hay or grass when required, but, being several feet from the ground, was not available for ordinary purposes.

That door was closed, but not fastened. Muffins made a dash at it and got it open. With a yell the brigand sprang upon him and seized him by the throat.

Below Dick was moving across the yard. Carl had already gone back into the inn.

"Master !" gasped Muffins.

Dick looked up and saw the boy and man struggling together. The object of the infuriated brigand was to drag Muffins back a pace or two and kill him.

The wretched Jupe, fortunately, made no movement. He remained on guard where Gastra Fuello had told him to stay.

Dick acted with a promptitude that was almost entirely his own. His mind took in the entire situation at once.

To rescue Muffins by the ordinary way was impossible. To attempt to shoot the brigand might end in lodging a bullet in the boy as the pair struggled together.

One way of rescue remained, and Dick adopted it. It was all the work of the moment.

Close by, under the loft window, was the door of the stable, with a wide coping of stone strong enough to bear a man by the look of it. Dick grasped its edge and pulled himself up. Quick as lightning he was upon his feet, stretched out his hand, and grasped the leg of the brigand.

With a jerk he brought him and the boy down, catching Muffins as he fell. The brigand he allowed to slide.

A moment later and the coping gave way, so that Dick and Muffins fell also.

The former was prepared, and, an expert at falling, dropped down unharmed, but Muffins was a bit shaken by the jerk.

Gastra Fuello lay senseless upon the stony ground.

The noise of the falling stonework brought back Carl, who was speedily followed by Gippa and a number of the soldiers staring with surprise at the scene.

" Look to the boy," cried Dick.

He stooped down, and, lifting up the brigand with one hand, passed him over to the soldiers.

" Bind him," he said, " and call your officer ; also secure that man," pointing to Gippa. " We shall want to know how that ruffian became concealed on his premises."

Gippa began to protest, truthfully enough, that he had no knowledge of the presence of the brigand, but it was hardly to be expected that his listeners would believe him.

" You shall have a fair trial," said Dick.

" Master," cried Muffins, " there's another in the loft—that waiter fellow. He took a chicken to the brigand."

" Ha ! what do I hear ?" shrieked Gippa. " Who says chicken ? Jupe, you thief ! come down and be hanged."

Jupe had no thought of offering resistance.

He was too much staggered by the turn events had taken to do anything but come down and give himself up. Two of the soldiers took him in charge and bound him.

By the time this task was completed Gastra Fuello had recovered consciousness and taken in the whole extent of the disaster.

He was cowed and beaten, and began to whine for mercy.

" Senor," he said to Dick, " I was but joking with the boy. I would not have hurt a hair of his head."

Dick took no notice of the falsehood, and, the captain having put in an appearance, a hasty consultation was held.

" It would be folly to take him to Madrid," said Paulo, alluding to Gastra Fuello, " as he may escape by the way. These brigands are eels, and I have full powers to dispose of him."

"The other, too, must be imprisoned," said Ravielle.

Here Gippa began again, with tears in his eyes, to protest his innocence. He called on Jupe to do justice to him, but the malevolent fellow only grinned.

"Speak, you dog!" yelled Gippa. "Did I know anything of Gastra Fuello's being here?"

"Master," replied Jupe, "we will all suffer together."

"I think," said Dick, "that I may take it upon myself to say that the innkeeper is innocent. The reply of that rascal is evidence in his favour."

At that moment Lavine appeared, and, hearing Dick's words, cast a gratified glance at him.

"After all," she said, "you are noble, because you are just. Speak! you cur," she cried, turning to Jupe. "What had my father to do with Gastra Fuello being here?"

Jupe hung his head. He could not withstand the fierce glance of her eyes.

"He knew nothing," he said. "Fuello came here and demanded food and secrecy from me. I gave him both, because he threatened to take my life. I was afraid of him."

This was so palpably true that those who were in authority did not think it necessary to keep Gippa any longer in custody, so he was released.

"Senors," he said, saluting them, "you are just. I am grateful."

Lavine did not speak then, but came over to Dick and took his hand in hers.

"You are my prince again," she said. "You will go away and I shall see you no more, but I shall ever forget you."

There was something very fascinating about the wayward, pretty girl, and Dick, if he had been alone with her, might have been tempted to kiss the upturned face. But the presence of others was a bar to any such demonstration of admiration, and he merely smiled.

"You are a good girl, Lavine," he replied. "I hope you may find a true man to love you and be happy."

A slight gesture of indescribable pathos was her only response, and gliding back she re-entered the house.

Dick saw her no more.

And now the stern hand of justice was uplifted for the last time against Gastra Fuello. This time there was no escape. His doom was sealed.

There no need to call witnesses. He did not deny his identity, and his crimes were a matter of history.

A few whispered words of consultation were exchanged, and then came the sentence—

Death!

What else could the man of many crimes and a long list of deeds of robbery and cruelty expect? And yet when that sentence was pronounced he seemed to realise for the first time what was in store for him. No words of condemnation or exhortation were wasted upon him. He was simply told that he was to die, and at once.

Immediately four of the soldiers went in search of pick and spade, and then chose a soft spot by the roadside. There they dug his shallow grave.

He saw it done, standing with a guard near him, his lips bloodless, his eyes staring.

Ever so ready to deal out death to others, he was by a natural law, let us suppose, more deeply impressed by his own impending fate.

Dick and his friends remained to the end, keeping zealous watch and ward over him, lest he should break away from the guard of his fellow countrymen and escape again.

And when the time came for him to go and meet his doom what an awful spectacle he was.

The order to march he could not obey. His shaking limbs refused to carry him.

In obedience to a gesture from Captain Gravalo, the men laid hold of him and bore him thither.

The grave was reached, and they bade him try to stand up "like a man."

Then he found his tongue, and a shrill scream burst from his lips.

"It is a woman's cry," said one of the men, "and yet they used to call him brave Fuello. Bah! comrades, he is but a child after all."

They left him rocking on his feet, his eyes gazing at them and yet seeing no one, his lips working convulsively, but giving out no sound.

"Ready. One—two—fire!"

A dozen rifles rang out, and Gastra Fuello made no movement for a moment. Then he sank back in a heap and rolled into the grave.

They went up to him, and found him dead, riddled through and through.

"Even in this," said Captain Gravalo, "we have shown him more mercy than he showed to many. Comrades, fill in the grave and lay down the turf smoothly. If there be one about here who loves him well enough to put a cross over his grave it may be done. It is not our work."

*   *   *   *   *   *   *

The ground was smoothed over the grave of the brigand, and Jupe was taken away a prisoner.

He cried out for Gippa and Lavine to help him, but all within the inn was still. The door was closed, the blinds drawn.

On they went, the late prisoners, who had suffered so much and endured so bravely beside the leader of the troops, the men, save the guard over Jupe, marching at ease.

Cigarettes were deftly rolled, placed between the lips, and lighted by the Spaniards. The Englishmen, while in sight of the spot where death had set its seal, refrained for awhile.

As the cavalcade passed away, winding down the narrow road to where a jutting mass of rock shut it out from view, one of the blinds in an upper window was drawn a little aside and a pretty face was pressed near to the latticed panes.

Two dark eyes rested on Dick until he was lost to view, and then the face was withdrawn and a wail of sorrow floated about the chamber.

"Oh! my prince—my prince. To come only for awhile, then leave me desolate! But it was not to be. I have dreamt it all my life, and will dream no more."

A few minutes later Gippa from below heard the twang of the guitar and his daughter singing a love song of her native land.

The old man smiled grimly.

"So like a woman," he said. "They think of us when we are with them, but as soon as we are out of sight they forget."

But Gippa, wise man as he was, did not know everything. Many a light song has been sung with a heavy heart.

Dick acted with a promptitude that was entirely his own.

CHAPTER LXXXIX.

ON THE ROAD HOME—BUTTERFLICK AND THE GENDARME—DISCORD AND RESTORED HARMONY.

URING the next few days things moved swiftly with Dick Strongbow. He refused on behalf of himself and friends to go back to Madrid, pleading truthfully a strong desire to get back to England.

The luggage of himself and friends was all safe. It had been taken care of by the authorities who took possession of the brigand's effects.

No vast wealth was found in Gastra Fuello's stronghold.

The reports of his possessing such were unfounded.

As with all thieves and rogues, so it was with him.

That which came lightly went lightly. When by any lucky chance he got a haul he soon spent the proceeds in dissipation.

Gravalo and Ravielle accompanied the party to the nearest railway station, and there they took leave of each other with many a kindly word and messages to friends.

"We part now," said Ravielle, "but who knows when we may meet again?"

"The world is but a garden with a few hiding-places," said Dick; "men move in small circles after all."

Dick wrote a few lines to Lucella. The tone of them may be guessed at, and we need not record them here.

Once more on their homeward way the travellers went with light hearts.

Dick was somewhat thoughtful, but he was not sad. After so many vicissitudes and narrow escapes he had a strong faith in everything coming out right in the end.

Carl was thoughtful, too.

He was thinking of Clarice Lefrau, of whom he had not heard for a long while.

Carl did not talk about his love. Like Dick, he was not demonstrative about such matters, but he had not by any means forgotten the pretty French girl with whom he had shared such an adventurous time in the Transvaal.

Dick readily guessed what was in his thoughts, and one day, when they had crossed the Pyrenees and were travelling towards Bordeaux, he asked him what steps he had taken to hear from her.

"I told her to write to your chief office in London," replied Carl, "and possibly I may find a letter waiting for me there."

"Many, it may be," said Dick, with a smile.

They stayed one day in Bordeaux, and from there went on to Paris, supposed to be the City of Delight.

But our travellers did not care particularly about it. It was too frivolous.

The only thing that occurred to vary the monotony of the days there was a row between Butterflick and a gendarme.

Butterflick happened accidentally to collide with a member of this fraternity, who immediately began to jabber at him "like a parrot," as Butterflick said, and that burly individual, not being in the humour to argue in a language he knew nothing about, did his level best to end the controversy by knocking down the official.

A crowd gathered immediately, with every third person a gendarme, and the din was awful.

Butterflick was marched off to a palace of justice and charged with Heaven knows what, besides being a German spy and a public marauder.

But Dick came to the rescue, and, being told who he was, had a friendly hearing.

His exploits in the "Mother City of the World," as the Frenchmen modestly call their capital, had not been entirely forgotten.

He explained that Butterflick was his friend, a "rough but honest man," who lacked the refinement of the French, but did not mean any harm.

The gift of a few francs to the injured gendarme had also the effect of making him forget his sufferings. He was willing to forgive, and the affair was finally settled by the payment of a modest fine and an exhortation from the magistrate for Butterflick to cultivate the grace, elegance, and courtesy of the land in which he was a sojourner.

Butterflick did not understand a word of it, but he was much edified, and by way of response told the great man that "he wasn't at all a bad sort." To this he appended an invitation to come out and have a drink, which was either not understood or ignored.

Butterflick, however, succeeded in inducing the gendarme to partake of liquor with an unpolished son of Albion, which ended in their swearing everlasting friendship in their respective languages.

At parting the gendarme shed bitter tears, and vowed that his future life without Butterflick would be all darkness and misery.

From that time till their arrival in England the lives of the travellers were uneventful, and all went well.

CHAPTER XC.

IN TOWN—THE HOUSE IN DANE'S INN—A NEW TENANT—A RECOGNITION.

E had better go into lodgings, I think," said Dick, on their way up from Dover to London.

"Look here, cap," replied Butterflick, "you are one of the good sort, with no nonsense about you, but that's no reason why you should allus be hung up with the likes o' me."

"What nonsense are you talking, Butterflick?"

"Nonsense that I mean. Me and Phil Norton have been talking it over, and we've come to the conclusion that while in London we'll live near you, but not with you. In course Muffins mustn't desert his father, and we three will get on first rate. If you want us at any time why there we are—if you don't, we can go about and see the sights. I don't know much about London—nothin in fact—but my boy was born there, and he's up to all the moves."

"I can take you to the Abbey, and the parks, and the waxworks," said Muffins, proudly.

"Perhaps it will be as well to leave you free," said Dick, thoughtfully, "and I really have a desire to get about unobserved. Five in company might attract more attention than I desire"

Butterflick's idea was therefore adopted, and it certainly gave him much satisfaction.

"I'm a sensible man in the main," he said, "although my intellects was a bit shook up by Old Sally durin' the time we were together."

"I suppose there's no chance of meeting her in London?" said Phil, innocently.

Butterflick turned ghastly white, and a look of indescribable terror appeared upon his face.

"If I thought that," he said, in a hollow voice, "I'd rather go back to that brigand chap, Gastric Fool."

"After all these years," said Dick, "she would never know you,"

"I should know HER," replied Butterflick. "Dash it all, if I did set eyes on her, I should cut and run for it."

He was troubled for a time with reflections on the possibility of meeting with his spouse, although he soon became himself again.

On arriving in the metropolis he would not get quite out of the carriage until he had had a look round to see if she was waiting for him.

Convinced, after some persuasion, it was hardly likely she could in any case know of his arrival, he descended and made for a cab.

"Look after the luggage," he said to Phil Norton; "I'll lie low a bit."

Dick finally decided to go to the Westminster Palace Hotel, and they all went in that direction. On the road apartments were secured for Butterflick's party on a flat in Richmond-street. A month's rent in advance was paid in lieu of a reference. Dick and Carl then went off to the hotel.

They put their names down in the book as Jones and Smith—an innocent deception, and, from Dick's point of view, a necessary one.

It was afternoon then, and they ordered an early dinner. After it they went out to look at 47, Dane's-inn, where Dick believed he could learn something of his early life if he only knew how to get at it.

He found the dismal old place dark and deserted. There was not a light in any of the windows, and by the names on the different doorposts he saw it was entirely let out for offices.

"I suppose there is somebody in charge of the different houses," he said.

"Possibly," replied Carl; "I do not know your English ways."

Dick went up to No. 47, and rang a bell to which no name was attached.

Getting no response for a time, he rang again, and a minute afterwards a woman came up the inn with a beer-can in her hand.

Seeing Dick she hurried towards him, and made a bob by way of courtesy.

"All the gentlemen have gone, sir," she said, "but if you will leave a card or a message I'll see to it, sir."

"I am looking for an old friend of mine who lived here many years ago," replied Dick.

"What may his name be, sir?"

"Morelle."

The woman shook her head.

"I don't know it, sir," she said; "he must have left before my time."

"But don't you keep a record of those who come and go?" asked Dick.

"Me, sir?—no," replied the woman. "I might do nothing else. Many of 'em—artistes and littering gents—are in and out like a dog in a fair. Some pays and some doesn't. The landlord keeps an account of 'em—or rather I ought to say his agent, seeing as how the landlord is a lord."

"And what is the agent's name."

"Waffle, sir."

"Where does he live?"

"I can't say for certain, but it's somewhere City way. All I know of him is that he drops in once a week to get the rents and receive my report, unless it happens that there are rooms to let—then he's here oftener."

"Are there any vacant rooms?"

"Yes, sir. First floor front and back—wainscotted rooms, and as dry as a bone—with every convellience"

"I'll take those rooms," said Dick. "Will you secure them for me?"

He held up half-a-crown as he spoke. It glittered in the light of a lamp, and there was a responsive twinkle in the old woman's eye.

"It would be a pleasure to have sich a real gentleman in the rooms," she said. "The last as was there got me to do his washing, but never did I see the colour of his money."

"You will have three more to make up half-a-sovereign," said Dick, "if I get the rooms. I want them in memory of my old friend."

"You may consider 'em yours, sir," said the woman.

"What is your design in taking these rooms?"

"I mean to find out what part of the house Jacob Morelle occupied."

The woman had gone in and they were sauntering down the Inn towards the Strand.

"And having found out that?" queried Carl.

"Whoever has those rooms," replied Dick, "will have to be bought out."

"Why not buy the whole house?"

"It would be expensive, and might raise suspicions which would prove embarrassing. I went to get over the business as quickly as I can, Carl."

"Quite right. I wish I could help you."

"My dear fellow you can do nothing. And I've been thinking if you would like to run over to Germany—"

Carl interrupted him with a shrug.

"Not just yet," he said, "if ever I go. I left nobody behind I care a rap for; but I may have occasion to go elsewhere. All depends upon my getting letters at the post-office to-morrow."

They were in the Strand now, and the noise of the passing vehicles made conversation difficult.

Carl took out his cigar-case and handed it to Dick, who helped himself to a weed.

Carl also selected one, and as he was about to feel for a box of matches in his pocket a man came out of the thick of the passing crowd with matches in his hand.

He saw the cigars first, and was about to offer his wares for sale when he looked up at their owner's faces. They had not seen him, and it was fortunate for him they did not.

With a frightened face he wheeled about and vanished with the gliding celerity shown by the criminal classes when they fear pursuit.

It was Pan !

CHAPTER XCI.

THE DARK WAYS OF SINFUL MEN—MORELLE'S LAST HOME—"ON HIM RESTS ALL"

 AN—abject, ragged, poor, degraded—an object of pity to the ordinary wayfarer, who knew nothing of his history. Even Dick Strongbow, who knew the man so well, felt a twinge of compassion as he came upon him again in less than an hour.

It seemed as if Fate willed it so.

Stepping up to his side, Dick said, in a low tone—

"Pan, I want a word with you. Follow me."

Pan started violently, and appeared as if he would fall, but, recovering himself, he stared at Dick with the eyes of a frightened wild beast brought to bay and hopeless of escape.

He would have run away, but he could not. The master spirit had spoken to him, and he dared not, could not, disobey.

"I would be alone with you for a few moments," Dick said, and the hint was taken by his companion, who, after a few whispered words with Dick, left them.

Pan, like a fawning dog, followed Dick into a quiet byway, where our hero faced about.

"Where is Morelle?" Dick abruptly demanded.

"Can't you let him alone?" asked Pan. "He's low enough now."

"He is alive, then?"

"Yes, and that is all."

"I must see him. Where is he?"

Pan hesitated a moment before speaking, but an imperative gesture from Dick warned him to make answer quickly.

"It's an awful place—the worst of characters—a desperate, dangerous hole."

"What care I for your dangerous places?" answered Dick, with a gesture of disdain. "Is it far from here?"

"No."

"Then lead the way and I will follow you."

Pan walked on ahead, still crouching, passing through a maze of narrow streets, keeping always in the shadow, and crossing over whenever he saw a policeman standing or strolling along on duty.

Everybody but Dick and the officials seemed to be skulking about in those ill-lighted ways.

There the lowest types of humanity, the criminal and the lost of both sexes, were prowling, keeping out of the light with the instinct of those whose whole lives are darkness and despair.

Here and there the glare of a public-house lighted up the roadway, but even these were not illumined as similar houses were in the highways, where honesty showed its head.

These places were full—they always are, for even when famine lies like a cloud upon the land men and women somehow find the means to drink

But there were no sounds of laughter or riotous mirth in these dens.

Drinking went steadily on, but the talking was in a low tone or in whispers, for all were busy hatching fresh crimes to give them means of subsistence

Evil sat brooding over all.

Degradation of mind and filthiness of body were the common lot.

By-and-bye Pan came to a narrow passage, before which he paused.

Its depths were as dark as the yawning of that great cavern wherein the poets tell us the everlastingly condemned are doomed to live for ever.

"I'll make bold," said Pan, "to say a word or two more before I take you to him."

"Speak," replied Dick ; "but be brief."

"You don't mean to put the police on him, I hope ?" said Pan.

"I promise nothing," answered Dick.

"You may have 'em dodging us," said Pan, with a cunning look. "I don't care for Morelle, but I think of myself."

"Pshaw ! man, go on," returned Dick. "Do you think that the police, with all the appliances of the law, could make your lot worse than it is ? To me death would be a thousand times more preferable than your existence."

"Ah !" said Pan, "you don't know. To the last liberty is sweet to us."

"Again I say I will promise nothing," replied Dick. "Until I have seen Morelle I know not what I shall do."

"He's lying in one of the worst dens in the whole of London."

"You suggested as much before ?"

"There are men in the house who think nothing of murder. They'd take a man's life for sixpence if they thought it wouldn't get them into gaol"

"Go on," said Dick, imperiously. "Do you think I am likely to be afraid of these human RATS ?"

"Promise that you won't harm ME !" whined Pan.

"Go on, I say !" was all the answer Dick would give him.

Pan turned down the dark way, and, guided only by his shuffling footsteps, Dick followed him.

He knew there was peril in this venture, but he was bent on learning at any cost whether Morelle could help him towards a solution of his parentage.

He had a strong feeling upon him that the hour for the solution had arrived.

He heard a door open and Pan softly say—

"Wait here a moment. I'll see if we can get up to him without being noticed."

"Don't attempt to play any tricks upon me," said Dick, warningly.

"Why should I ? What's the use ?" asked Pan. "No man could harm you. You've got the luck of getting the upper hand of us all."

Dick heard him go into the house, where all apparently was still. The darkness was profound.

A few moments elapsed, and then an awful scream, followed by the fall of a heavy body in one of the lower rooms, momentarily startled Dick.

He listened, but could hear no more. Whether a crime had been committed or the sound had emanated from some simply drunken wretch he could not tell.

Wasting no time in speculation, he listened for the return of Pan, and presently heard him come shuffling back again.

"You may come in," he said, in a whisper. "Some of them are out—'tothers are busy."

"What was that cry I heard?" asked Dick, softly.

"How am I to tell?" replied Pan. "It wasn't in my crib, and it's no business of mine what goes on in other places. Every man looks after his own affairs. Maybe they've found a flat—some countryman who's been flashing a few pounds. If they've got him in there THEY'LL HAVE THE MONEY."

Dick felt hot and angry.

The idea of a helpless greenhorn being deluded into such a place and murdered for a few beggarly coins made his blood boil.

But he could not champion any man's cause just then. He had his own affairs to attend to, and as Pan once more stepped into the house he softly followed him.

"Stairs," suddenly whispered Pan, "and mind the holes. Keep close to the wall, for half the rails are gone."

The need of obeying this injunction was soon made apparent by Dick getting his foot into a hole on the third stair. Pan, with a full knowledge of the many little pitfalls of the den, went up without mishap.

Up, up three flights of stairs, and they were at the top. A faint light showed through the cracks in a door, which Pan pushed open.

It had no lock, not even a handle There was apparently no protection from intrusion.

What an awful place!

A dingy attic with rotting floor and broken ceiling, stained with the dripping of many a rainstorm. patches of plaster lying in places where they had fallen, the place uncleaned and unswept for many and many a day.

Fixed in an old medicine-bottle was a common rushlight candle, burning with the dim light that makes the gloom of a place more apparent.

Stretched on the floor, with only a handful of rags under his body and a bundle of coarse waste-paper for a pillow, lay a ragged form, with the head bandaged and the blood of some wound or wounds lying thick upon the wasted cheeks.

At a glance Dick saw that the clothes had not become ragged by wear alone. There was evidence of violence in some of the huge rents that exposed the torn linen and flesh beneath.

It did not seem to him to be possible that this was Jacob Morelle, but he it was, lying with staring eyes, and drawing the short, sharp breath which so often precedes dissolution.

"How came he in this fearful state?" asked Dick.

"He mixed himself up with a lot below," replied Pan. "I told him not to do it, but he would, and there was a row over a 'joint,' and they all went at him."

"'A joint'—what is that?"

"'A joint's' a job where a lot of 'em go in for a little business, and settle up fair and square when it's done."

"By business you mean murder and robbery?"
Pan nodded.

Dick took up the candle and held it over Morelle's face—a more ghastly object he had never looked upon.

"Has a doctor seen him?" he enquired.

"A doctor! HERE?" replied Pan. "Oh! no."

"But he's very bad."

"I can see that." said Pan; "and he'll die. I wasn't coming back any more when I met you to-night."

"What would the others do?"

"They'd get rid of him somehow. Shove him into an empty house—down in a cellar, perhaps. He'd be found, of course, but who'd know anything about him? Who'd bother?"

"It would get into the papers."

"It might; but cases of this sort don't excite much attention. It would end by the police making a record of it."

"What has he had to take lately?"

"Nothing that I know of. He's had nothing from me; I'd nothing to give him."

"Go and get some brandy," said Dick, giving Pan a shilling. "If you are not back in a quarter of an hour I shall communicate with the police. You understand?"

"I'm fly," replied Pan. "I'm not going to get into trouble if I can help it. I'll cadge, or anything that way, but no more crime."

"I should think that you have had your full share of it," quietly rejoined Dick.

Pan stole away stealthily as before, and Dick stood by the injured man watching for some change in him.

Apart from his ghastly appearance he saw that his hours were numbered. He had the indefinable look of a dying man. The shadow of the grim destroyer was upon him.

"If I can only bring him back to consciousness for a few minutes," he thought, "I may learn the precious secret. If I fail, it may be lost to me for ever."

And as he stood there watching, the conviction that all his hopes in this direction rested on that man grew stronger and stronger.

CHAPTER XCII.

DEATH OF MORELLE—PAN UPON THE STAIRS— THE ROOM IN DANES'-INN.

FULLY twenty minutes elapsed ere Pan returned, and he came back breathing like one who had hurried

"I had to look around a bit before I could get it unseen," he said, producing a small flat bottle. "There are so many who, if they knew I had a shilling, would have wanted me to stand treat."

"What!" exclaimed Dick; "even if you had told them it was for a dying man?"

"What's dying men to THEM?" asked Pan, scornfully. "Nothing! All they think of is a living man and what's to be got out of him"

Dick took the bottle, and, pulling out the cork, knelt down beside Morelle. Between the parted lips he poured a few drops of the coarse, fiery liquid and waited.

After a few moments he administered a little more, and so on, five or six times in succession.

Then the light of consciousness began to return to his eyes, and he moved a little, moaning.

"Master," said Pan, "may I have a drop of the stuff? Just a sip? I dursn't touch it until I had your leave."

The admission was a tribute to the power Dick had over the man, and he handed him the bottle.

"Only a little," he said; "I may want some more for Morelle."

Pan with his thumb marked a place on the bottle down to which he would go, and with a few sips disposed of the portion he had elected to take.

"It makes one forget if only enough of it can be got at," he said; "but it don't often nowadays run to that."

Morelle's eyes were moving and his lips quivering. He was coming back to a knowledge of things around him.

Dick gave him a little more brandy, and shortly after he spoke, in the tone of a querulous old man.

"Is that you, Pan?" he said.

"Yes," was the answer.

"What's come to me?" asked Morelle. "And who—who— Ah! Dick Strongbow."

His voice suddenly leapt up to a scream, and then as suddenly died away again.

"You—you HERE?"

"Yes," said Dick; "I have come, Morelle, to ask you to do me justice. Tell me truly what you did with the paper Gonzalo entrusted you with. Did you destroy it?"

A distortion of the lips, probably meant for a smile, was the only reply.

"Morelle," said Dick, "I hesitate to pain you by telling you the truth, but I must do so. You are a dying man."

"I know it," feebly answered Morelle; "I'm done for. I am now experiencing what a man feels when he's been maltreated to death. You want to know about that paper, do you?"

"Yes; you are aware how important it is to me," replied Dick. "I urge you to let your life close with a good deed."

"Promise me one thing," said Morelle, "and I'll tell you all?"

"I will promise to perform anything reasonable and in my power," said Dick.

"It's easy enough," answered Morelle. "All I want is the nest here to be broken up. You will do it as an act of justice to the world, but I want it done because they lied about 'the joint.' It was downright mean and miserable of 'em. It was shabby!"

Dick was somewhat amazed to hear the man of many crimes expressing with his feeble, dying breath indignation against "shabby treatment" on the part of his companions in crime.

But it is a strange and true thing that there is honour among thieves and even murderers, although it is an honour that is warped to the use of villainy.

"I promise," said Dick, "that every effort shall be made to deal out justice to them."

"I'm satisfied," said Morelle; "YOU'LL DO IT."

And this was another tribute to Dick's worth. Morelle knew his word was sacred and it would be kept.

"You will find the paper behind the wainscotting of the rooms I used to live in at Dane's-inn—ground floor. I read 'em first and put 'em into a place I know of there. You can't get at it without pulling the boards down. I nailed it up. The ready money's all gone, but—left—"

He stopped short with a choking sound and convulsively rose up a few inches, then fell back exhausted.

Dick gave him a little more brandy, but it had no effect, then more and more, until the bottle was empty, but, panting and staring, he remained in the last stage of exhaustion.

"Run!—more brandy," cried Dick; "here is money. Treat your friends, but get some for him. Quick! I must have a few more words with him."

Pan seized the bottle, and, kicking off the unlaced boots he wore, so that no sound might be made by his footsteps, hurried from the room.

Again and again Dick urged Morelle to speak, but he made not even a sign of response. The last moments of the wretched man had come.

Let us turn aside from the spectacle of the death of such a man. It is not for the eye to look on or pen to depict.

Speedily Pan came dashing back with unwonted vitality in his famine-enfeebled limbs. The brandy-bottle was full again.

"Take it away," said Dick; "it is not wanted. You are too late. Show me a light."

As he went slowly downstairs he turned his face up towards Pan, who stood upon the landing.

In one hand he held the feeble light, and with the other he was raising the brandy-bottle to his lips.

"Drinking to drown HIS thoughts," said Dick. "What a hell some men make for themselves upon earth! Whatever sins you have been guilty of, Pan, the price in full is now being paid by you."

. . . .

Dick was up early on the following morning, in a restless frame of mind.

Previous to going to rest he had communicated with the police about the death of Jacob Morelle, and had received an answer that the case should be attended to.

He had done all that lay in his power, and now his thoughts turned to his own affairs.

He wanted to get possession of that room at Dane's-inn without delay.

It happened to be a part of the house which he believed he could readily get possession of, provided he was allowed by Waffle, the agent, to take it.

On turning out of the hotel alone—Carl was still asleep in the full enjoyment of a luxurious English bed, and Dick had seen no need to disturb him—he ran against Muffins and Butterflick.

Naturally Dick marvelled as to the cause of the appearance of his friends.

"Muffins," said Butterflick, "speak up. You are more an orator than I am."

Thus urged, Muffins gave vent to a burst of eloquence.

"Captain," he said, "we saw Ajax last night."

"Indeed!" replied Dick. "I hope he is well."

"Well and hearty, cap," replied Butterflick, "and happy as a bird. What do you think has happened to him?"

"Come into some money?" suggested Dick.

"No, better than that."

"Got a good berth of some sort."

"He's got that," said Butterflick. "They've made him hall-porter of the Royal Openhanded Insurance Company. Two pounds a week, clothing, home, and firing. But that ain't the best of the news."

"I am afraid I must give it up," said Dick.

"HE'S FOUND HIS WIFE," said Butterflick, with an expanded mouth, "and a nicer little party I I never see. There's a boy, too—a regular young Ajax, I should say—quite a man, although he is a baby. Ajax took us home to tea with him. A fine time we had with the family, hadn't we, Muffins?"

"I am glad to hear of this," said Dick, "for I believe that I was indirectly the cause of their being separated. So she's made it up with him?"

"They told me all about it," said Butterflick, "and it drawed a thimbleful of tears into my eyes, I can tell you. The Royal people put him into livery, you must know, cap, and he was standing at the door on duty when she and the young 'un went by. Mrs. Ajax being a neat and tidy party, given to hard working and saving, and all round a good sort, she looked uncommon nice. 'I say, old girl,' cries Ajax—"

"No, dad," interposed Muffins. "He said, 'Oh! Gabrielle, my wife'—he told us so."

"Well, the meaning is the same," said Butterflick; "and don't you cut in with your jaw when you are not axed to."

"But, dad, you asked me to tell the story."

"And who's a-stopping of you now?" demanded Butterflick. "Well, cap, as I was a-saying, they see each other, and Ajax holloaed out SOMETHING that pulled her up. She'd made up her mind not to live with him agin, but she wasn't proof agin that uniform."

"Mrs. Ajax said she didn't see the uniform, but only her husband," said Muffins.

"That may be your yarn and hers," returned Butterflick, "but don't you tell me. All wimmin-folk grovel afore uniforms. They catches 'em like bird-lime, and it was his blue coat with gold braid that pulled her up short. Anyway, they've made it up, and it's real business."

"You bring good news," said Dick, "and I will take an early opportunity to call and congratulate them. Meanwhile I am going for a walk down the Strand to see a place I'm thinking of taking. Will you come with me?"

"Cap—WILL we come?" exclaimed Butterflick. "Now, Muffins, if you've finished your yarn, we'll not keep the cap waiting about the street like a dancing man."

"I haven't had much of the talking," muttered Muffins, "and I'm quite ready."

"You answer me like a son, proper," growled Butterflick, "or I shall be reading up Solomon's rules and regerlations for the spanking of children, and act on 'em."

"If you do," said Muffins, "I'll run away to sea."

Butterflick growled out something not quite intelligible to either listeners, and, Dick having by this time got under weigh, they walked off towards the Strand by way of the Embankment.

It was too early for the ordinary City life, although there was, as there always is in London, any amount of bustle in the streets; but they were not prepared for the crowd they found forming up about Dane's-inn.

"What's the matter?" Dick asked of a man who was standing on the kerb.

"A bit of a fire," he replied. "They've gone for the engine."

"A fire—where?"

"Dane's-inn—No. 47."

Dick, attended by his two followers, dashed into the house and cast a hurried glance around him. The door of the room he wanted was adjacent, and with a slight pressure of his knee he burst it open.

Once inside the apartment he literally went for the wainscotting, and, having found a weak place near the hearth, began to pull it down like a breaker-up of houses working by contract.

The insidious smoke sent Muffins and his adoedpt father into fits of coughing that were very trying, but they stuck to their post and bravely looked on, unable to do anything more.

Dick forgot everything but his quest, and he looked, as he always did in times of excitement, like a young giant.

Suddenly a cry was heard outside—

"Way, there, for the firemen!"

"Put your back against the door and keep them out, Butterflick," said Dick.

"I'll try, but the smoke 'll come in. Ugh—ugh! I reckon another minute will settle us."

Crash!

"Open, there!" shouted somebody outside.

"Throw up the window," said Dick to Muffins, "and get outside. Hurrah! I have them."

In a niche in the wall behind the wainscotting he had been tearing down he saw a bundle of dirty papers.

Seizing these he thrust them, as they were, into his pocket, and, Muffins having by this time got the window up, he ran towards it.

"Get out sharp," he said. "Butterflick, this way."

"I'm a coming," muttered Butterflick, who was stopping the door from being opened with his foot. "You fools outside there, give me time to draw back the bolts."

"All right," responded a deep voice, "only be smart about it."

Butterflick turned his head, and saw that Muffins and his captain had got out of the window into a small yard or court at the back of the house.

He ran after them, and precipitated himself through the window with such violence that he fell in a heap upon the flags below.

"Dad's killed hisself," cried Muffins.

"That's a lie!" growled Butterflick, as he got up half dazed by his fall. "Cap, where are you?"

"Here," replied Dick, from a small doorway. "Come on, my boy. We must get away from this sharp."

Dick, for the first time for many a day, felt nervous. He had no fears of any physical punishment to follow the undoubtedly unlawful raid he had made upon the rooms.

It was the safety of those precious papers he had in his mind.

The passage in which they found themselves belonged to some house at the back of the inn, and at first Dick was afraid of getting into trouble for intruding.

They might even be suspected of attempted robbery or burglary.

But Butterflick was the means of dispelling the idea. After a curious sniff or two he made the following announcement—

DICK STRONGBOW:

The Diamond King,
AND WONDER OF THE WORLD.

Ere the Frenchman could do mischief Dick laid hold of him by the ear.

No. 17.

Price One Penny.

"We are in a public-house," he said, "and that door on the left goes down to the cellar. I fancy the one ahead leads into the bar."

The latter was a green baize-covered door, with a small oval window, and, as Butterflick suspected, the bar was on the other side of it.

No idlers were there, everybody having rushed out to see what sort of fire it was in the inn. The barman was standing on a tub by the window, trying to get a peep at what was going on without absolutely deserting his post.

So deeply engaged was he that he did not observe the three strangers going out one by one. They reached the street at length safe from all chance of detection.

Quite a crowd had gathered about the gates of the inn, but there was no particular excitement. Tidings of the fire being of no great moment had already spread around.

"The old woman who looks arter the houses set fire to her night-cap," said a man in Dick's hearing; "it's nothing."

It was more than that, as the reader knows, but it was not a serious conflagration, and all danger to the other houses was over.

But there was one thing which was exercising the minds of the firemen and the public.

Who was it that had torn down the panelling of the lower room?

Happily the people at the gate had forgotten all about Dick's entrance—the old housekeeper was too dazed to remember, and the firemen had not seen him.

So all chance of trouble about the matter was at an end.

But Dick did not know this, and he thought it prudent to get away as soon as possible.

Bidding Muffins and Butterflick to go home by way of the Embankment, he sauntered off as far as Somerset House, and from thence took a cab to the hotel.

Carl was up and breakfast was awaiting him.

"I thought you had gone out for a stroll," he said.

"Yes, a lucky stroll," replied Dick, and then he told him all about the morning's adventure.

"It certainly seems providential," said Carl. "You say you felt a strong desire to go there this morning?"

"I felt as if I were drawn there," answered Dick.

"How very strange!"

"It is; and here are the precious papers." Dick took the packet out of his breast-pocket, and laid it upon the table. "There are not many of them. I hope, Carl, you will forgive me if I don't read these until I am alone."

"My dear fellow!" said Carl, warmly, "you need not have even mentioned it. You know I am not at all curious about affairs that do not concern me."

Dick suitably acknowledged this expression of correct feeling, and, breakfast being over, Carl rose to depart.

"It is my turn to take a walk," he said. "I think like other dandies, I ought to show myself in the park. How shall I dress, Dick?"

"In anything but a stove-pipe hat," replied Dick, "I abhor the thing."

"The waiters will look upon us as genteel cowboys, I fancy," said Carl. "Well, I have no objection."

"Nor I," replied Dick, carelessly.

He got up, rang the bell, and ordered the table to be cleared. While this was being done Carl went off to get some English apparel and afterwards "show himself in the park."

At last Dick was alone, and his first act was to lock the door.

"I must have no intruders upon me while I read the story of my birth," he said; "whatever it may be I will give it welcome. Anything is better than the doubt that has lain upon me these many years.

He drew out the papers once more, and, having removed a piece of tape that bound the package, took the topmost one and began to read.

CHAPTER XCIII.

THE PAPERS—DICK LEARNS THE STORY OF HIS BIRTH—FOR A LITTLE WHILE ADIEU.

HE first paper which caught Dick Strongbow's eye was an official-looking one, which a glance showed was a marriage-certificate written in French. It was dated twenty-five years ago, and showed him that a Reginald Bourville, second son of the Squire of Haviland Hall, in the same parish, was married to Varcia Gonzalo — the place of marriage the town of Marseilles, the church that of the Saint Sebastian. Dick's eyes glistened as he reviewed this confirmation of his hopes that he was a legitimate son.

For the Squire of Haviland he cared nothing. It was enough that his mother was an honest woman, and had his father been a labourer he would have equally rejoiced.

The next paper was a letter from the Squire of Haviland Hall—an answer, as it appeared, to one sent by Reginald announcing his marriage.

It was short and to the point.

The squire repudiated the marriage, and cast off his son, but only for a season.

"*If your elder brother dies*" (it ran in one paragraph), "*you will inherit the estate, because it is yours by right of birth; but unless that untoward event should happen in my life do not come near. Should he survive me, and you survive him, he leaving no heirs, your offspring shall inherit all.*"

The letter was not an unreasonable one. The father was angry about the marriage, which may have disappointed some hope of an apparently more advantageous union.

The next papers were letters announcing the death of the squire and a reference to his will, which distinctly pointed out that if the son of his son Reginald, of whom it seemed he had heard, did not receive the education of a gentleman, and prove it at the age of twenty-one, he should not come into the property.

It was to pass to the Crown.

This clearly showed that the elder son was dead and the second one—Dick's father—also at the time the will was made.

It also accounted for Dick having been educated and kept from circus life by Gonzalo, who no doubt hoped to live and finally present Dick to the trustees of the estate as a fit and proper person to inherit it.

As was set forth in the early part of our hero's adventures, Gonzalo died ere the time of the fulfilment of his plans took place.

The wise old circus-rider had, however, taken what he thought were ample precautions to secure Dick's rights by placing all the papers in the hands of Jacob Morelle.

Now this man was the solicitor of the Bourville family, and was, in conjunction with an old friend of the squire's, trustee of the estate.

In case of the death of either, the surviving man was to be sole trustee.

The friend of the squire died, and Jacob Morelle had everything in his power.

How he abused his trust we know in part. As Dick read on he saw that the villain must have helped himself to a considerable sum of ready-money lying in the bank—the accumulation of rents of the estate—but he could not touch the estate itself.

That he went as far as he dared, and finally fled to avoid exposure, was clear. Dick saw how the man went from one course of villainy to another, until he died a miserable outcast in a haunt of criminals.

With him Dick had done for ever.

He cared nothing for the money the fraudulent scoundrel had robbed him of, nor much for the estate that he had now reasonable hope of becoming possessed of.

He knew who he was and what he was, and that sufficed.

But why had Gonzalo concealed his real status from him? That was easily worked out.

A circus-rider's idea of a gentleman is limited.

Gonzalo did not know exactly what would be expected of Dick. All he could do was to give him an education and trust to his coming up to the required standard.

And that he would be more likely to do so if kept in ignorance of what was expected of him was pretty sure.

And it was furthermore the intention of Gonzalo to have Dick judged without his knowledge if possible, so that in case he did not come up to the mark, and should be rejected, he could be kept in ignorance of it.

There was a letter among the rest, sent to Jacob Morelle, plainly setting this forth, and one of the final passages brought a smile to Dick's lips.

It ran as follows—

"*I do not wish him to become one of my people, but if he is ever driven to it* HE WILL MAKE A NAME."

"Poor old Gonzalo!" said Dick, as he retied the papers together and carefully placed them in his pocket. "He was a thorough good fellow and a clear-headed one, although he was only a circus-rider."

Dick's first care was to find out a good firm of solicitors who would undertake the task of proving his claim to the Haviland estate, which it seemed was situated on the southern borders of Leicestershire.

After due enquiries he found a firm in Lincoln's Inn who could be trusted to do all that was required with efficiency and despatch.

They told Dick that the estate had been in Chancery ever since Jacob Morelle fled from England, and it was therefore in safe and experienced hands.

There had been no claimant for the property. Dick was absolutely the last of the Bourvilles.

He was now pretty much alone in London. Phil Norton had gone off to see some distant relations, and Carl was in France, spending a happy time with the fair Aimee, to whom he was shortly to be married.

Muffins and Butterflick were enjoying themselves in their way, and in a sense were not continuous companions for Dick.

He saw them every day or two, and was much entertained by the fact that Butterflick was a child in the hands of his adopted son, who "showed him the sights of London."

Butterflick took much to the wax-works at Madame Tussaud's, having discovered in the effigy of Fair Rosamund a distant likeness of what Old Sally "might have been if she hadn't been a living Winchester Repeater, allus loaded and allus going off!"

But, much as he seemed to revere the memory of that estimable woman, to mention the bare possibility of his meeting her again was sufficient to make his hair stand up with fright.

"No—no, my son," he would say to Muffins, "it's better as we are. Some people love each other best apart, and that's the case with me and Old Sally."

Whether he will ever meet her is, of course, hard to say.

Up to the present Old Sally has not yet shown herself to be in the land of the living.

During the time necessarily spent in proving Dick's identity he wrote many times to Lucella, and received letters in reply from her; but not a word did he say about his claim to the Haviland estate until it was finally established to the satisfaction of the law officers that he was the man.

That done, he took another step which was necessary for him to do, if he were to retain the name that made him famous.

He changed "Bourville" for "Strongbow," paying the usual sum to the Crown, and circulating the fact through all the requisite legal channels.

Then and then only he wrote to the Duke of Lavante, asking for an early marriage with Lucella.

The answer was that the duke and his family were coming to England shortly, when Dick's desire should be fulfilled.

DANGER AHEAD;

OR, DICK STRONGBOW'S LAST JOURNEY.

CHAPTER I.

A TELEGRAM—MUFFINS AND BUTTERFLICK.

"TELEGRAM, sir."

The servant handed the dull-red envelope to Dick Strongbow, who had just finished breakfast and was enjoying a morning cigar.

Dick's rooms were in Victoria-street, whither he had moved about a month before, there to await a communication from his prospective father-in-law, the Duke of Lavante.

He had been forewarned of its coming, and here it was at last.

Dick opened the envelope, read the contents, and, turning to the servant, said—

"No answer."

When the door closed upon the attendant he read the telegram again.

"*Be at the German Embassy at two.*"

That was all, but it was very different to what Dick expected, and rather puzzled him.

He expected to receive a message from abroad, but here was the duke in England. What had brought him hither, and to the German Embassy, too?

It was clear that he was not here in an official capacity, but had probably come over in a hurry.

"Well, it is useless speculating," said Dick, "but I think I had better look up Muffins and Butterflick, to prepare them for immediate action if it should be necessary."

Dick had received intimation more than once that, when called upon, he would have a task to perform that might tax all his strength and mental powers, but of the nature of that task he knew nothing.

All he was clear upon was that when the task should be successfully performed there was a prize awaiting him in the form of the lovely Lucella for a bride.

She was well worth winning, especially to Dick, who adored her, and had the satisfaction of knowing that he was loved in return.

Doubt about his ability to carry out whatever was set before him to do never entered his head, for he was not only physically strong, but had a heart as sound as a perfect bell.

It never rang out the false note of fear or beat in the least degree the quicker at the thought of peril.

Those who know what Dick Strongbow has been in the past need not be told this, but perchance there are some to whom he now comes as a stranger,

and to these must be given a slight sketch of his character.

Endowed with enormous strength, not made apparent by any unnatural development of body—handsome, brave and generous—he was a model man, who would have made his mark at any time, in any age, and in any country.

Possessed of wealth, he could have lived at ease, but, loving one of the fairest women on earth—Lucella, a Swedish girl, daughter of the Duke of Lavante—he was ready to make any sacrifice and go through any peril that man could hope to surmount to win her.

Why the duke should have thought it necessary to put him through such an ordeal we shall presently see, but it may be here stated that a task of no ordinary magnitude was prepared for Dick.

Butterflick—the burly, good-natured, simple miner—with his adopted son Muffins, had taken rooms in a street on the south side of London that was near the gasworks. There were big, strong men at work there, with whom Butterflick fraternised, and he, having seen so much of the world, was a great favourite.

He told good yarns and was very liberal with his money, which did not, by any means, reduce his popularity.

Muffins was in the hands of a private tutor, who was doing his best to educate him, but not with conspicuous success.

The name of this gentleman was Mr. Flutterby Fowler, a B.A., of Brasenose, Oxon—a little man of very mild appearance, who spoke clearly, but scarcely above a whisper—just the sort of man some people endeavour to impose upon, not always with success.

Dick, on calling at the apartments of his friends, found Muffins and the tutor poring over a book that seemed to have had the effect of making every hair of the boy's head stand up, while it had bathed the forehead of the tutor in perspiration.

"I am sorry to interrupt you," said Dick, as he shook hands with Flutterby Fowler and nodded to Muffins, "but I have something important to tell Butterflick. Where is he?"

"Gone to see one of the gaswork men," replied Muffins, "who has hurt his foot and is laid up."

"Do you expect him here soon?" inquired Dick.

"He has ordered a beefsteak-pudding for dinner," replied Muffins, "and he will come home sharp for that."

"It is his favourite dish," said Flutterby Fowler. "Somewhat heavy to a man of my build, but sustaining to muscular men."

"How is your pupil getting on?" inquired Dick.

"On the whole, fairly well," replied the tutor;

"but, alas! he doesn't take kindly to our old friends, the classics."

"I should like 'em well enough," returned Muffins, with a sigh, "if I knew what they were. But I don't, and I don't believe anybody else does. A lot of crack-jaw stuff."

"Well, Muffins," Dick said, smiling, 'you will soon be eased of your lessons, as I think we may have to go abroad again directly."

"Where to?" asked Muffins, his eyes brightening.

"Ah! that I can't tell you until later in the day," replied Dick. "After dinner you and Butterflick had better come on to my place as soon as you can."

"We can be there by two o'clock, sir," said Muffins.

"Three will do," returned Dick. "Of course, Mr. Fowler," he added, addressing the tutor, "this is no notice, but you will not be treated unhandsomely."

"May I have a word with you in private?" said Mr. Fowler, who had suddenly become very pale.

"I want to go out for a moment," cried Muffins, jumping up, "so you can talk here. Good-bye, sir. We'll be at your place at three."

"He's gone," sighed Flutterby Fowler, as the door closed on Muffins—"anything to get away from his books—and he won't come back until the pudding is on the table."

"I am afraid that the life he has led with me has unfitted him for the part of a student," replied Dick. "But about yourself, Mr. Fowler—I suppose you have a proposal to make to me?"

"I have, and a strange one," answered the tutor. "It is this—do not dismiss me, but let me go abroad with you."

Dick smiled, and was about to speak, but the tutor rapidly went on—

"It may appear absurd to you," he said, "but, believe me, that boy will learn better in a casual way than he will by steady application."

"That I can understand," returned Dick; "but it is yourself I am thinking of. How do you think a rough, adventurous life will suit you?"

"It is impossible to say, for I have never tried it," replied Flutterby Fowler; "but whatever it may prove to be I must adapt myself to it."

"Do you think you can do so?"

"I can try."

He spoke very quietly, and Dick, regarding him more intently than he had ever done before, saw that there was some real grit about the little man.

Still, he looked far from strong, and there would be great inconvenience in being hampered with a sickly man.

Putting this thought into a delicate form of words, he suggested as much to the tutor.

"All I can say is," said Flutterby Fowler, "that the moment you find I hinder you, what you have to do is to leave me behind. Wherever it may be—even if it means leaving me to die—I won't complain."

"Very well," said Dick; "I like your style of talk. If I can arrange it you shall be one of the party."

And they shook hands upon it, thereby sealing a bargain destined to be of great import to both in the future.

CHAPTER II.

TWO ASTONISHED YOUNG MEN—AN INTERVIEW WITH THE DUKE—A STRANGE COMMISSION.

HEN people take it into their heads to contest an incontestable fact, they play the part of a fool, and we feel sure that none of our readers will attempt to argue with us when we say that ever since the Germans thrashed the French they have exhibited a somewhat bumptious spirit.

It is so, without a doubt, and it is exhibited nowhere more emphatically than among those who are the servants of the German Embassy in London.

It was, at the time of our story, particularly strong in the demeanour of two young gentlemen who wore the livery of what we should call here "the boy in buttons."

They might have been twins, but were not so favoured, having been simply selected for their office, like the servants who stand behind the carriages of the rich and great, "because they matched."

In cheek and all-round bounce they were twins, but in nothing else.

Neither of these young gentlemen had a personal acquaintance with Dick Strongbow, and when he, at the appointed hour, presented himself at the embassy, they were disposed to treat him in an offhand, not to say insolent manner.

Dick wore his usual free-and-easy dress—a little out of place in London, perhaps—but that was a matter in which he did not feel any concern. Anyway, he behaved himself like a gentleman.

"Will you kindly tell me," he said, "if the Duke of Lavante is here?"

They stared at him, then at each other, and laughed softly. After that they resumed the conversation his arrival had interrupted, conducting it in their national tongue, of which Dick had a pretty good knowledge.

"Yes," said one, "he was a boy of the butcher trade—tall, fat, and strong. 'How now,' said I, 'can you fight?' 'Yes,' he replied, 'I can eat you.' Then I knocked him down, turned him over, and rubbed his nose in the mud."

"And after *that?*" asked his companion, delighted.

"After that," said the braggart, "he cried for his mother, but she did not come, so I said 'Hey! there, get up and run to her,' giving him a kick with my boot."

"Pardon me," interposed Dick, suavely, "but I am waiting for an answer."

"It is so with all these Anglians," continued the victorious youth—victorious, it may be said, only in his story. "If you knock them down they cry for their mothers."

"As you will not answer me," said Dick, "I shall go in and inquire of somebody else."

He endeavoured to pass between them, but immediately they turned on him, one striking at his face and the other kicking at his legs.

"Get out, you dog!" they cried.

Dick's blood was roused, but he could not fight with boys. Nevertheless, it was necessary to teach the cubs a lesson.

So he took each by the collar, dragged them outside, and then, in the presence of a startled audience, composed of some stray members of the British public, swung them up and down and to and fro, as if they had been rag-dolls, until their brains were in the mixed condition of curds and whey.

Finally he deposited them in a sitting position upon the pavement, and coolly walked into the embassey.

In the hall Dick encountered an official-looking personage, who had just descended the stairs, to whom he addressed himself.

"I am here by appointment to meet the Duke of Lavante. Will you kindly tell me if he has arrived?"

"You are Mr. Strongbow, I believe?" said the official.

"I am."

"Please to step upstairs with me. His excellency is awaiting your coming."

As he spoke he cast a quick glance around, as if puzzled to know what had become of the two attendants, who were cooling off upon the pavement. But he failed to make any remark, and conducted Dick to a room upon the first floor.

It was a comfortable, yet plainly-furnished apartment, such as would be used as an ambassador's waiting-room.

The duke was there, reading a daily paper, and he rose at once, giving Dick a hearty greeting.

He looked anxious, and, Dick thought, a little older than when last they met, but his manner was composed and dignified.

"We are not to be disturbed, colonel," he said to Dick's guide.

"I will see that your excellency is not intruded upon," was the reply, as the colonel glided out of the room and closed the door.

"Strongbow," said the duke, "be seated. I am glad to see you."

Dick sat down, pleased with his reception. The duke drew a chair close to him, and in a quiet, confidential tone, continued—

"Strongbow, I have to propound a great task to you, which, if you happily succeed in performing, will give you a first rank among the travellers of the world. It is not for myself that I ask it to be done, but for my king, whom I believe you hold in grateful remembrance."

"I do—with good reason," replied Dick.

"It is he who is responsible for the choice of you. I ought to say," said the duke, "that he does not know that you are affianced to my daughter, and I have kept it from him, knowing that he would see in it an obstacle to sending you on this mission. But I am his servant, and it is my first duty to serve my king."

"It is good to be loyal to such a man," said Dick.

"Yes," answered the duke, "and I, being a loyal man, am willing to make some sacrifice for his sake. I know your worthiness for the task about to be set you, which, if happily carried through with success, will give the crowning touch to the honour of our family by enrolling you among its members."

"Tell me what it is," said Dick, "and let me set to work at once. What man dare do I will attempt, for Lucella's sake."

"You have no need for payment," rejoined the duke, "and I know, therefore, that for her sake you undertake it, and for that alone. It is simply this. Make your way to the north-west region of Persia, to the town of Astrabad, and there give this letter to Longimans, the beglerbery or governor of the place. He, in return, will hand you a small package, which you will bring back to England, and on your arrival signify your coming by wiring here."

"And is THAT all?" asked Dick.

"All and enough," replied the duke, "as you may probably discover. It is not easy for an Englishman to travel in Persia, especially in the direction of Afghanistan, without his being subjected to many obstacles. There are the chances of a prison and, I ought to tell you, a secret or violent death."

"From whom?" asked Dick.

"From the authorities and the Russian agents, who infest the land. But the dangers to you will not be so great in the going as in returning."

"May I ask why it should be so?"

"They will make sure you have some object in view before they attempt to destroy you. If you can succeed in blinding them you may not be hampered very much either way, but that you *will* have obstacles put in your way is certain. My advice is for you to travel openly, like an ordinary traveller, with two or three attendants, if possible, and let it be known that you intend simply to write a descriptive book of the country, without any political bias. They will not mind that at all."

"I can manage the attendants easily," said Dick. "Muffins, the boy who has been with me for some time, and Butterflick, will gladly go with me, unless there is more than ordinary risk in their doing so."

"There will be little for them," said the duke "They will be treated as small fry, not worth the killing."

"I also designed taking a tutor with me," continued Dick. "He is at present engaged in educating Muffins."

"What sort of a man is he?"

"A little man, not of notable appearance—indeed, some would think his looks were mean—but he has a lot of grit in him."

"I should say the very man," replied the duke. "He is not at all warlike in appearance, you say?"

"Quite the contrary."

"Nothing of the British officer about him?"

"The veriest savage would not suspect him of any martial proclivities whatever."

"Good," returned the duke. "Now as to route. You start from here and get to Marseilles with all speed. From there you will go to Beyrout, and then your troubles will begin, for you will have to cross Syria into Persia, making your way to Ispahan. Now comes the most dangerous part of your road. From Ispahan to Astrabad your path will bristle with perils."

"I have the way in my mind's eye," said Dick, "but the details of the journey must be worked out as we go along. Money, of course, I must take with me."

"Yes," replied the duke, "and a fairly liberal supply, for bribery is the great open sesame of Persia. I ought to tell you that his majesty insists upon paying the expenses of the journey."

"I really would—" Dick began, but the duke stopped him.

"It is right and just it should be so," he said,

"and it would not become us to haggle with a monarch who is in a position to pay. It is a condition of your going that will be insisted upon."

"As you please," said Dick. "How much money shall I take with me?"

"Two thousand pounds," replied the duke, "and, as time is precious, I took the precaution to have the money ready for you. Here it is in English notes, exchangable anywhere in the world where the currency is known. I would advise you to sew it up in the lining of your coat, removing the notes as you need them."

"Good practical suggestion," said Dick, "and now, if you have no further commands for me, I am ready to go."

"I have no more," returned the duke; "you will be better able to work out the matter as you go along. It is impossible to say what means of getting about you may not be obliged to have recourse to. Your judgment, especially when you are on the spot, will be always better than any advice I could offer you."

The duke arose and held out his hand.

"Good-bye," he said, "and may we see you safe back again."

"One word," said Dick. "Does Lucella know I am going?"

"Yes."

"And she approves?"

"No—not as a woman; but she has no fears. She says you will surmount all difficulties and come back to her. Her faith in you is unbounded."

"May I ask if she is in London?" Dick faltered.

"Yes," replied the duke, "and I have arranged for you to have an interview with her. But let it be brief. Stay in this room and I will send her to you. Good-bye once more. I shall not return."

He left the apartment, and Dick paced up and down to still the emotions that were surging in his heart.

Presently a light footstep fell upon his ear, and the beautiful Lucella rushed into his arms.

CHAPTER III.

DICK MAKES PREPARATIONS TO START — JOY OF FLUTTERBY FOWLER — A SECOND TELEGRAM.

OVERS' interviews ought not to be intruded upon or the vows of faithful hearts made public property.

We therefore pass over the interview of Dick with his lady-love, and come to the time when he had parted from her and was on his way from the embassy. It seemed from what he had heard that the duke and his daughter were guests there during a brief stay of two days in London. Their visit had not been announced in the papers, and they would depart, giving no sign.

Their coming had been to see Dick Strongbow alone.

As he walked down the hall the two young servants who had favoured him with their insolence were standing there in a deeply abject condition.

By some means they had learnt that Dick, after all, was a very important personage, and they expected a wigging if nothing more.

But he passed them as if they had never met before, and so on out of the house, much to their relief.

"The good goblins keep him from coming here again," said one.

"He is the son of an evil spirit of the forest," replied the other.

Dick, without thinking of the pair into whose hearts he had instilled a little wholesome respect for his great muscular powers, hailed a cab, and ordered the man to drive him home.

Flutterby Fowler was walking up and down outside, the victim of great anxiety. As Dick jumped out of the cab and gave half-a-crown to the driver he looked at him keenly.

"Anything the matter, Flutterby?" asked Dick.

"Nothing—only I thought I would like to know," was the wistful reply. "Do I go or not?"

"You go," replied Dick. "We take the next tidal train for Dover, and from thence to France. After that we shall see anon."

"That is good news," said Flutterby Fowler. "But in an hour! How about luggage?"

"We must travel without any," replied Dick; "buy what we want as we go. You will need a pair of revolvers. Have you such things?"

"Bless me! no."

"Get them at once."

Dick slipped a note into his hand, and saying, "Be back here as soon as you can," entered the house.

The burly Butterflick was alone with Muffins. In two minutes they were acquainted with as much as they cared to know.

"Go and pay your rent," said Dick. "Pack up what you do not want, and send it on here. I will, in the meantime, make arrangements for everything to be stored in a London furniture warehouse."

"Good luck to us all! but I'm glad of this," returned Butterflick. "A life of ease is all very well for a week or two, but some people have got to keep on moving or die. I'm one of 'em, and there's another thing, Mister Strongbow, that makes it fit in with *circumstances*."

He looked at Muffins, who had risen, and was waiting to start for home.

"You can go on, my boy; I'll follow you in a wink or two."

Muffins left the room, and Butterflick, advancing on tip-toe to Dick, whispered in his ear—

"Old Sally—you've heerd of her—my wife as was?"

"Yes, a time or two," replied Dick, with a smile.

"Well, I'm blessed," said Butterflick, "if I don't think I saw her yesterday."

"Never!"

"Her, or her double, at the foot of Westminster-bridge, a-shaking her fist at a man who had collided with her."

"What! after all these years?" asked Dick.

"Years aint anything to her," said Butterflick. "She isn't altered a bit—thin as a rake, wispy as a

Dick Strongbow swung them to and fro as if they had been dolls.

snake, and a fist that's like a small cannon-ball. It was her. I saw her as you might see a flash of light on a dark night in a quiet street, and I bolted."

"Well, Butterflick," observed Dick, "she will have some trouble in following us where we are going. I suppose it's one of the most outlandish places on earth."

"Sally would find it if she had a mind to," said Butterflick.

He departed shaking his head ominously. Notwithstanding the many years which had intervened since he last saw his shrew of a wife, her influence was over him still.

Such is the potent power of woman over man.

Ten minutes after he was gone the servant brought Dick another telegram.

It was from the same source, and ran as follows—

"*Lose not a moment. It is a race between you and another to—you know where.*"

CHAPTER IV.

CROSSING THE CHANNEL—A LITTLE MAN WHO MAY BECOME A BIG ENEMY.

 UR Channel boats are very fine vessels, especially when the shortness of the voyage is considered. You have all the comforts of a liner on board, and, if the weather is unfavourable, many of the discomforts also.

Dick and his three followers were among the passengers on board the Falcon, and there was a choppy sea, which soon upset the equilibrium of some of the more sensitive of the passengers.

Among the first to go under was Mr. Flutterby Fowler.

He frankly confessed at starting that he had never been to sea, and he was afraid it would not be kind to him. His apprehensions on this score were fully justified by events.

Within five minutes of starting Flutterby Fowler found out that something was going wrong with the double smoke-stack of the engine. There was a great deal of wobbling going on, and the two huge iron funnels kept multiplying themselves into four in the most unaccountable manner.

Then the head of the vessel rose up strangely into the air, at times assuming a position verging on the perpendicular.

Passengers also waltzed about—or appeared to do so—and while reflecting on this extraordinary state of things Flutterby Fowler suddenly arrived at the conclusion that he was ill.

"I am going to suffer," he said, "and I must seek some quiet corner to lie down in."

"Don't go below," urged Dick—"you will only eb worse. We shall be there in an hour or so."

"If I went below," murmured Flutterby Fowler, "I—I— Excuse me."

And then he vanished somewhere in the direction of the head of the vessel, and for the time was seen no more.

Dick walked slowly up and down, smoking a cigar and thinking.

Muffins and Butterflick also strolled about, but apart, and the former, with his hands in his pockets, put on the air of an old traveller, who had been accustomed to travel first-class all his life, and thought nothing of it.

Among the passengers was a Frenchman who was *not* seasick.

Whether he looked upon it as a rare thing and something to be proud of we cannot say, but proud he was, for he strutted about with a grandiose air, evidently thinking himself far and away above the other human beings aboard.

"He thinks he's a prize magnum bonum," said Muffins, "and the rest of us very small pertaties."

He certainly looked upon Muffins as a mere seedling, for, on their colliding by accident when the steamer rolled, he pushed him violently aside, crying—

"Out—away—you little, miserable John Bull!"

Muffins had some of the old, resentful fire of the street-boy still left in him, and could not brook an insult, especially from a Frenchman.

But, not being physically in a position to do battle with his foe, he used what is probably an arab's keenest weapon—his tongue.

"If you don't behave yourself," he said, "I'll set one of the performers in a German band upon you. It seems to me that you are groaning for another licking."

"Get out of sight—go away—die!" replied the Frenchman.

"Why aint you careful," demanded Muffins. "smoking a cigarette with that 'bacca in it? Are you tired of your life? Do you want to die afore you reach that miserable country of yours?"

The Frenchman lunged out his foot at him, and, with the true courage of his nation, kicked the boy in the stomach.

Poor Muffins was fairly doubled up, but he was still defiant.

"Do it a—again, will yer?" he gasped.

"I kick you—ovar—bo-ord," cried the Frenchman.

He was proceeding to further maltreat and assault the lively Muffins when Dick Strongbow, who had come up behind, laid one of his powerful hands upon the Frenchman's shoulder.

"Hey! my friend, it isn't manly or fair to assault a mere boy."

"I kill him—you—all!" hissed the Frenchman, as he wheeled round to kick Dick.

But ere he could do any more mischief Dick laid hold of him by the ear.

The deadly strength of the nip took away the breath of monsieur, and in his agony he danced upon his toes with the inimitable grace of a monkey upon a barrel-organ.

But only for a moment or two.

Dick, having administered the punishment, let go, and walked on, motioning to Muffins to follow him.

It had all transpired so quickly that none of the other passengers paid any particular heed to what had passed.

The majority of them were too much engrossed in their own sufferings to pay any heed to the business of others.

"Ah! you Engleseman," he hissed. "Your card, sir."

"I do not carry cards," coolly replied Dick, "but my name is Strongbow."

"Ah! no cards—so low—only plebs haf no card. Here is mine."

He drew a piece of paper out of one of his waistcoat pockets and flourished it before Dick, who took it and read—

" *Vicomte de Falma.*"

"Yes," he said, "I see you are a man of position. What then?"

"You pull my ear!" hissed the vicomte—"I challenge you to fight."

Dick laughed grimly.

"My dear fellow," he replied, "do you think I am such a fool as to mix myself up with one of your affairs of honour—so childish that all the world laughs at them?"

"Ve shall see," said the Frenchman. "It is enough. Go—I vill be avenged."

The affair seemed to be a trivial one, and Dick at any other time would have laughed at it.

But now he was vexed, as the quarrel might seriously impede his journey.

"Monsieur," he observed, "this is ridiculous. Of course, if you insist upon fighting I must fall in with your humour, but remember this—IF I FIGHT I KILL!"

He saw something in the eye of the Frenchman which led him to indulge in what, at any other time, would have been a bit of bombast unworthy of him.

It had exactly the effect he desired. The vicomte paled and shrank back. When Dick had finished with him he was positively trembling.

"I am a man," said Dick, "who never cares to do anything by halves. If I go out to fight a duel with a man I expect it to be a real fight—no more, no less. None of your beggarly scratches and honour-satisfied affairs will do for me. Stay! why not now? See, I have the weapons ready." He opened his coat, exhibiting the butt-ends of a pair of pistols in his belt. "Take your choice, monsieur, and let us blaze away at each other as we are."

But monsieur was not fond of real fighting—that was plain. Nor did Dick, indeed, expect he would show any inclination that way. As he surmised, the Frenchman drew out of it with a bit of bluster.

"I am no bull-ee," he hissed, "nor butcher of accursed Anglais—but a nobleman of France. I retire now, but we shall meet again."

The whole affair was so very absurd that Dick treated it as a joke, but, trifling as it seemed, it was destined to have great influence on his future.

The vicomte disappeared, and Dick bade Muffins go and sit down by the paddle-box, so as to be out of the way.

Butterflick at this moment rolled round the funnel, and appeared before them. His quick parental instinct saw that something was the matter with his adopted son.

Dick departed, and the pair sat down together.

"Muffy, my boy," he said, "what's the matter with the governor?"

"Nothing's the matter with him," replied Muffins. "A beastly Frenchman kicked me here," indicating the spot, "and Mister Strongbow pulled his ear—that's all."

"Kicked you, and calls himself a man, perhaps," growled Butterflick. "Where is the mannikin?"

"That's the chap, over there," answered Muffins, "with his head in the air and a-smoking his cigarette."

"I'll pull his other ear to make matters square," said Butterflick.

"Oh! don't. The governor won't like it, perhaps," urged Muffins.

"I'll do it quietly, my son," returned Butterflick. "Kicked, did he? It makes me ill when I think of such creatures walking about in coat and trousers."

The vicomte, unconscious of impending evil, was airily smoking his cigarette, when he felt something like the buffer of an engine strike him in the back, and he was projected forward over a camp-stool upon his hands and knees.

His first idea was that something serious had happened to the vessel, but on looking up he ascertained that all was safe.

Nor could he see anything to account for the violence he had suffered, unless it emanated from a big, burly man who was smoking a short pipe and calmly watching the flight of half a score seagulls in the wake of the steamer.

"*Sacre!*" he said. "If it is he, shall he not suffer?"

But on second thoughts he got up again, and did nothing more than sit down in the middle of a long seat by the side of the vessel.

Butterflick, the burly man with the pipe, promptly came and sat down beside him.

"Fine day, mister," he said.

No answer.

"Don't you parley voo onglay?" asked Butterflick.

The indignant vicomte got up to go away, but the shoulder-of-mutton hand with which Butterflick was blessed closed upon the tails of his coat and drew him back again.

"Why can't you be sociable," he said. "I said it was a fine day, monseer, and if you say it aint you are a liar! Now, then."

"I decline to converse with you," replied the vicomte. "Shall it be for me to call for help?"

"If you do," said Butterflick, coolly, "I will chuck you into the sea. Why don't you get higher up? Give a man room."

As Butterflick had half the seat to himself this may be considered to be a very unnecessary demand on his part.

The vicomte did not stir, so Butterflick, with a gentle but irresistible pressure, urged him along sideways.

"You've got to go," said Butterflick, "and if you utter a word I'll overboard with you. What do you mean by kicking a boy where you might have killed him?" A push. "It's like you French frogs; you can't use your hands like men. Get further, will you? Do you want ALL the seat?" Another push. "We had one of your cut in the Durban camp. HE kicked a man's front teeth out, and we stretched his neck for him. It's a contamination to sit near you. Higher up."

And as they had now arrived at the end of the seat Butterflick gave him a final push and shot him off upon the deck.

Several of the passengers saw it done, and wondered what it all meant; but as Butterflick—satisfied with having avenged the injury done to Muffins—got up and sauntered off they did not interfere.

The vicomte sat quite still for the third of a minute or so, with an expression on his face which fully justified the opinion of Voltaire about his countrymen.

"Half monkey and half tiger," was his verdict

upon them, and those who have had much dealings with the sons of France will understand how true it was then and is so now.

At length the vicomte arose, and with trembling hands lighted another cigarette.

What torture he would have inflicted upon both Dick and Butterflick we cannot say, but it would probably have satisfied the veriest savage on earth.

And the hatred he felt was the sort of stuff to keep, for he was a venomous coward, and his breed never forgives.

He was, however, spared further molestation on the way to Calais.

Punctual almost to the moment the steamer put into harbour, and the more lively among the passengers went at once ashore.

After a short delay the sufferers from *mal de mer* began to appear on deck, among them Mr. Flutterby Fowler, who tried to put on a jaunty air.

"Not at all a bad trip," he observed to Dick. "The steamer behaved admirably."

"I should say so," said Dick, with a smile. "Shall I assist you ashore?"

"Thanks, no. I never was better in my life," answered the little man.

He screwed himself up to "walk the plank"—that is, up the landing-stage—cast a shuddering glance at the sea, and with quick, nervous steps reached the quay.

"There is no time to be lost," said Dick; "the train is due. If you want anything to eat we must wait until we get to Paris."

"I can wait longer than that," replied Flutterby Fowler. "I am not a believer in having too many meals—ahem! Really, there are few things more enjoyable than a short trip across the sea."

The usual host of touts were howling at the passengers, with the idea of luring them away to one of their hotels or getting the job of carrying their luggage, but, with Dick and Butterflick in front, and Muffins and his tutor behind, they soon got through them, and in a quarter of an hour were on their way to Paris.

Preceding them went a telegram to the following effect :—

"*Four Englishmen—three men and a boy—travelling without luggage. Appearance suspicious. Let them be watched.*"

It was sent by Vicomte de Falma, who was, in an official sense, much bigger than our friends suspected.

CHAPTER V.

A DIFFICULTY ABOUT A PASSPORT—DICK IN CUSTODY —BUTTERFLICK IN THE HANDS OF THE PHILISTINES.

"YOUR passports, messieurs."

It was an unusual thing to inquire for them at the Paris railway-station, and Dick Strongbow asked the gendarme why it was done.

"Your passport," was the rough reply, "and do not utter the question of a fool."

It was a very good thing for the gendarme that Dick Strongbow felt the necessity of restraining himself, for the desire to lay hold of the very protuberant nasal organ of that personage and wring it soundly was very strong.

But he remembered his mission, for whom it was undertaken, and the reward of success, therefore he restrained himself.

"Dick Strongbow," said the gendarme, who, of course, was speaking in his native tongue. "Dick. Dick !—it is no name at all."

"It is mine," briefly replied Dick.

"It is what you call a name of the gutter," coolly pursued the gendarme, "such as is given to thieves and rogues in your country."

"Is the passport correct?" demanded Dick.

Instead of replying to him, the gendarme turned round, and beckoned to someone standing a little distance away.

In response another gendarme put in an appearance, and to him was handed Dick's passport.

"For scrutiny," said the first, curtly.

Facing the party in the carriage—our friends were by themselves—he then said, roughly—

"Next !"

Butterflick had his ready, and handed it to the gendarme, afterwards quietly moistening the palm of his hand, preparatory to hitting that official between the eyes if he made any doubting references to his respectability,

But happily nothing of the sort was done. The passport was handed back to him without a word.

Muffins and his tutor were similarly favoured.

"Your friends can go on," said the gendarme to Dick Strongbow, "but you must accompany me to the prefect."

Dick got out of the carriage quietly, and his friends followed him.

"Let us get this tomfoolery over as quickly as possible," he said, "as time is precious to me."

The prefect, or his representative, was handy—in a room in the station, as it turned out.

With all the ostentation of guarding a dangerous character the two gendarmes placed themselves on either side of Dick and marched him down the platform.

Butterflick was in the mood to attempt a rescue, and but for Flutterby Fowler he would have done something rash.

"What are you going to do?" the tutor asked him, as he doubled his fists and drew back his right arm for a blow.

"Going to give them talking parrots a blow each under the ear," he replied.

"Don't be foolish," urged Flutterby. "This is only one of the fads of this fussy country."

"But I could do it in a moment," said Butterflick.

"And after it is done—what then? There will be two score people on you, and the chances are you will get six months' imprisonment."

"Don't be a fool, dad," said Muffins.

Butterflick dug his hands deep down into his pockets and gave out a sound very much like a small engine letting off steam. Flutterby Fowler took one arm and Muffins the other, and in this order they followed Dick to a room near the booking-office.

Dick and his two attendants passed through, but the door was promptly shut in the faces of his friends, and the click of a spring lock showed that it was fast.

Butterflick backed a little and shook off his two

companions, but they laid hold of him again and held on tight.

"Why don't you keep quiet?" urged the tutor. "You will only make matters worse."

"I could *walk* through that door," replied Butterflick. "Just let me put my foot against it, and see what happens."

"Madness!"

"I don't call it manly to stand here and let them popperjays drag him about as if he was a pickpocket."

"You *are* a duffer, dad!" said Muffins. "Do you think that master would be quiet if he didn't think it was the right thing to do? Can't he take care of himself?"

"I suppose he can," sighed Butterflick. "But I feel a longing to have one of them chaps in a quiet corner for a few minutes. He'd want binding up and a bit o' glue rubbed about his j'ints when I'd done with him."

Dick Strongbow, on being ushered into the room, found himself face to face with one of the usual type of French police-officers—a man about fifty, close-cropped hair, thick moustache, well gummed at the ends, and dark, cunning eyes, set rather close together in his head.

"Is this the man?" he asked.

"Yes, monsieur."

"Name?"

"It is given as Dick Strongbow on the passport."

On hearing the name all the colour fled from the cheeks of the official, and with a hasty hand he struck a bell.

Another gendarme promptly appeared from an inner room.

"Full guard," cried the official.

A word was spoken without, and half a dozen other gendarmes promptly filed into the room.

"Guard that man closely," said the chief officer, with a visible quivering of the lip.

Dick smiled. He fancied he understood the cause of all this fuss. The chief officer had evidently some knowledge of him, but he waited for developments, not speaking a word.

"Prisoner," said the officer, "you are given here as one Dick Strongbow. Are you related to a man of that name who was in Paris two years ago?"

"I am that man," quietly replied Dick.

"Before proceeding," said the officer, "I must carry out the law of France and have your hands secured."

"It is no law of France," replied Dick, "and you know it. Why all this childishness? If you put the handcuffs upon me I could snap them asunder as if they were thread. But keep your mind easy; I have no intention of being the *first* to enter upon violence. Tell me why I am brought here."

"We have information that you are a suspect."

"Suspected of what?"

"That is not for me to say. It is enough that you are a suspect, and you must clear yourself."

"Well, go on."

"In the first place," said the official, "why are you again in Paris?"

"I am simply passing through," replied Dick, "on my way to Marseilles."

"And why to Marseilles?"

"To take ship from there."

"Where to?"

"You must excuse me," said Dick, "but that is my affair. I can go where I please, I suppose, and you may rest assured that I shall not again return to this country simply to enjoy your courtesy."

"You must be frank," remarked the officer, "being a suspect."

"Suppose I say I am going to America?" asked Dick.

"In that case your ticket will be taken for you if you have the money. After that you will be seen on board and watched until the vessel sails."

"I am not going to America," said Dick, "so we need not proceed with the subject."

"Where to, then?"

"That is my affair."

"You will not answer?"

"No."

"I am only obeying instructions," said the officer, in a hesitating, furtive manner, "and it is my duty to give you time to reflect."

"In other words," observed Dick, coolly, "you intend to send me to a prison?"

"To a place of detention, monsieur."

"It is the same," rejoined Dick. "I recognise that any resistance I could offer would only be to the injury of these men near me, and I yield—but, trust me"—here he laid his knuckled hand upon the table and looked the shrinking official full in the face—"those who are responsible for my detention will have to pay dearly for it."

"Monsieur, do you threaten me?" began that officer.

"You? Hardly," replied Dick, with contempt. "You are but the tool of somebody behind the scenes. Now what is to be done with me?"

"If I thought monsieur would not break out," said the official, "it would suffice for him to be incarcerated in the next room until I receive further instructions."

"I give you my word," replied Dick, "that until to-morrow I will be passive; but, meanwhile, may I see my friends—one of them, at least?"

"There is no objection to one," was the answer.

"Then let somebody go outside and ask for Mr. Fowler," said Dick.

Instructions were given to a gendarme, who left the room. He was presently heard asking for "Monsieur Fowler," and the tutor was ushered in.

"I wish to see my friend alone," observed Dick.

"There is the room at monsieur's disposal," answered the official.

Dick walked in, and Flutterby Fowler followed him. The room was empty, and Dick closed the door.

"Fowler," he said, "this is an awkward business, and I don't quite understand it. Possibly it is only the fad of the authorities, or it may have a deeper meaning."

"I think we have to thank our friend the Vicomte de Falmer," said Flutterby Fowler. "A few moments ago I heard two of the gendarmes talking of him as somebody of importance connected with the police."

"If it is nothing more than that," returned Dick, relieved, "I do not care. What can the man do? But still a delay of any length would be serious. Will you look up the Swedish ambassador here and ask him to communicate by wire at once with the Duke of Lavante? He must know how I am hin dered here. Meanwhile you had better put up at some place near the station, where I can communicate with you."

"There is an hotel outside which will serve us, I think," said Fowler. "I caught a glimpse of it while I was waiting."

"Go at once, and make such arrangements for Butterflick and the boy as you may think necessary. Above all, keep them out of mischief."

"I'll do my best," said Flutterby Fowler, dubiously, "but that Butterflick is a walking bombshell, always ready to go off. I had great difficulty just now in stopping him from bursting in the door of the place and coming to your rescue."

"Tell him," said Dick, "that he will have plenty of opportunity by and bye to exercise his muscular power. For the present we must hold a candle to the nameless one and be quiet."

Flutterby Fowler promised to do his best to look after him, but as it happened it was already too late to keep the excited Butterflick out of mischief.

Being left alone with Muffins, he sat down on one of the few seats scattered about for the use of waiting passengers, and, pulling out his pipe, filled it and prepared to smoke.

As he was in the act of striking a match a very small porter, with moustaches so big that they seemed to drag his head forward, came up and deliberately blew it out.

He followed up the act by saying something in French which Butterflick did not understand.

Anyway, if action and expression were to be taken as indicative of his meaning, he was very offensive.

Like all big men possessed of courage, he had the strongest possible objection to striking one smaller than himself, so he pushed him away, saying—

"Go along with you. Don't play boy's tricks with me, or I shall box your ears."

Whether the porter understood him or not matters nothing. He certainly took up a lofty position, and when Butterflick lighted another match he blew that out also.

The next moment his ears were boxed.

Butterflick had a heavy hand, and on the impulse of the moment he struck more heavily than he would have done in a calmer moment.

The blow fairly sent the porter spinning, accompanied mentally by a brilliant display of stars, squibs, and crackers.

Having been spun round once, he fell upon his side, and set up an awful caterwauling, which brought quite a little host of officials of all sizes to the spot.

Butterflick stood his ground and wanted to explain matters.

"Here," he said, "just listen. He blowed out a match, and I told him—"

But they would not listen.

Was it not enough that one of their compatriots had been smitten by an alien hand?

Did they not behold him with one cheek of the colour of the peony and the other as yellow as if he had laid in an extra stock of jaundice.

A crime had been committed, and the offender must suffer.

"Arrest him!" was the cry, and in a body they went for Butterflick.

Muffins endeavoured to give aid to his adopted father, but was immediately bowled over, and fell with a wild-eyed station official on the top of him.

Butterflick uttered a loud "whoop," and, like an old war-horse, charged into the thick of the foe.

The blows he dealt were too much for them, but numbers prevailed, as one might expect, and, with a dozen cat-like men clinging to him, he fell heavily just as Flutterby Fowler came out to instruct him in the art of keeping the peace.

CHAPTER VI.

A CURIOUS SHIFTING OF THE WEATHERCOCK—ON THE WAY TO MARSEILLES—GRIF THE STRONG MAN.

 OOR Flutterby Fowler stared aghast at the scene, which appeared to be of a more sanguinary nature than it really was, owing to the frightful chattering and caterwauling of the excited Frenchmen.

That matters were very serious was evident, but something had to be done, and Flutterby ambled up to play the part of peacemaker.

But he could not make himself heard.

Indeed, as soon as he opened his mouth a fierce gendarme, who had been hovering round the struggling men, ready to do his part in worrying a prisoner, saw his opportunity, and seized the tutor by the throat.

"Sacre!" he hissed, "how so many more? Come —I have you!"

But now a sudden change came over the scene.

An authorative voice was heard calling upon the gendarmes to desist, and Flutterby Fowler, in a very rumpled condition, was released. Butterflick was also at the same time allowed to get up.

Then it was seen that Vicomte de Falma had put in an appearance. He wore an official coat of some sort, with so much lace and frippery about it that he might have been mistaken for a mountebank.

But he was a man in authority, as was evinced by the respect, not to say terror, exhibited towards him by the gendarmes and porters.

"How now!" he cried. "what is it that I hear so much? Ah! my friend of ze steamboat, you are rumple, you are disorder. Say who has done it, and he shall suffer."

Butterflick was so much astounded at this unexpected friendly greeting that he could only stare at the vicomte like one in a dream.

But Flutterby Fowler put in a word.

"I fear," he said, "that my friend is of an excitable disposition and has got himself into a wrangle. But he is a well-meaning man."

"He is great—he is good," returned the vicomte. "So light of heart—so full of fun! I laugh as I tink of ze fun he haf wif me. Monsieur, I salute you."

Butterflick looked about him for a few moments, then hard at the vicomte, and finally, in a breathless state, exclaimed—

"Well, I'll be jiggered!"

"And where is our young friend," pursued Vicomte de Falma; "he vith the fingers so to pinch—all in fun? How is it zat he is away? Shall he be ill?"

Flutterby Fowler took upon himself to explain the position, which caused the vicomte to open his eyes in real or affected surprise.

"All wrong—must be," he said. "I put him right. Stay here."

He crossed over to the officer, and went in as if he had a full right to do just as he pleased in the place. Flutterby Fowler, hardly crediting the evidence of his own senses, stood near Muffins, who was almost as dazed as himself.

Butterflick was the victim of a multiplicity of sensations such as he rarely experienced before.

As for the gendarmes and the other officials, they stood about in twos and threes, exchanging the glances of men utterly confounded.

Presently two began to talk in their native tongue, which Flutterby Fowler was master of. He listened to their comments with absorbing interest.

"How came he here?" asked one.

"By special train—soon after the other," was the reply.

"Was he alone?"

"No—the Russian Turcomatz is with him."

"He—and why him? He is no more than a spy."

"Ah! you must ask De Falma so much, if you dare. He gave word for the English to be arrest—so—and now he is astonished."

"It is true, my friend."

"But it is not for us to say, 'Why is it so?'"

"Oh! no; we are dogs that must bark and bite only when we are told."

The appearance of De Falma with Dick Strongbow turned Flutterby Fowler's attention to them. The Frenchman was profusely apologising for the inconvenience he had caused.

"All a mistake of fools," he said, "but ve haf so many. It is your nature—you John Bulls—to forgive. Pardon us."

"I am willing to overlook the matter," replied Dick, coldly, "provided I can at once proceed on my journey."

"You can go at will," said De Falma, eagerly. "Ah! you go to—to—"

"Marseilles."

"Yes—so—and it shall be. Your passport I give you. I have put a leetle mark in ze corner dere, and none vill dare to detain you."

So far all was satisfactory, but Dick, failing to comprehend the entire affair, was not so gracious to De Falma as he might have been expected to be.

But this the Frenchman did not appear to see.

He accompanied them to the door and saw them on the way to the station of the southern line of railway, overwhelmingly polite to the last.

They had a little hasty refreshment before starting, and, furthermore, took a basket with them. A deal of polite attention was shown to them by the officials, and they were ushered into a compartment of the train which they found to be untenanted.

Furthermore, although there were a great many people going by the train, none approached the especial compartment which they occupied.

Some, in passing, glanced at it, and one man pulled up as if he meant to go in, but immediately went forward again.

"Now I would give something to know what all this means," said Dick.

"It is strange," remarked Flutterby Fowler—"one moment treated as pickpockets, the next as some great magnates of the land."

"And yet it is not real courtesy."

"I fear not."

"What, then, is it?" asked Dick.

To this question Flutterby Fowler had no answer ready. A moment later and the door was opened by a gorgeous creature who might have been a general in our country.

"Are the messieurs comfortable?" he asked.

An answer in the affirmative having been given the door was closed, and the train moved on slowly, but afterwards quicker. Never, however, did it exceed twenty miles an hour.

"I have been thinking over something I heard," said Flutterby Fowler, "which may possibly give a key to the mystery of this overwhelming politeness. We owe it possibly to a Russian named Turcomatz. Do you know him?"

"Never heard of him that I know of," replied Dick.

Flutterby Fowler then gave him the details of the conversation he had overheard, and Dick agreed with him that they owed the sudden change of treatment to the Russian.

But why he should interest himself in them passed their comprehension.

Butterflick's opinion was that all Frenchmen were mad, and he based a long argument, mainly listened to by Muffins alone, on the recent arrest of Dick Strongbow.

"Which no sane country would have thought of doing," he said. "Why, if he'd minded to do it, he could have pulled the station down on top of the lot and smashed 'em."

Muffins was not sure his master could have done quite so much as that, but he was certain that, had he chosen, he could have "given fits" to all the officials that had been arrayed against him.

In the midst of this argument the train stopped at a station, and, the door being violently opened, a stout, tall man, with an unmistakable circus air about him, got in.

One of the porters came running up, and told the man that the compartment was engaged, and received a curse by way of an answer.

"I have paid," he said, "and who shall say that Grif the strong man shall not have a seat for his money?"

"Oh! but monsieur," said the porter, with a shrug, "it is not to be. Our orders say—keep the compartment for those in it. Come, descend—retire—be gracious."

"I shall not come out," was the fierce reply. "If it is my company to be objected to let the strangers retire."

"Pardon me," said Dick, who had been listening quietly, "but I understand your language, and it isn't pleasant to hear."

"I care not for that," replied the new-comer.

"But why do you intrude?" asked Dick.

"Because it is my will."

"And suppose it is my will that you go out?"

"Ah! then I shall stay. It will be all the same. For am I not Grif the strong man, and who shall move me?"

In a moment Dick, without any warning, had the arms of the mighty Grif pinioned to his side with that terrible grip which had daunted and cowed so many before.

The Frenchman, just for the portion of a moment, seemed disposed to resist, and then he caved in

DICK STRONGBOW:

The Diamond King,
AND WONDER OF THE WORLD.

Turcomatz poured a small quantity of some dark fluid into the glass.

All the colour fled from his cheeks, and his eyes, by degrees, began to protrude out of his head.

He would soon have been a most unsightly object but for the prompt action of Dick, who, with no great visible effort, lifted him from his seat, and projected him from the carriage like a wad out of a popgun.

He certainly lighted upon the platform on his feet, but immediately fell upon his hands and knees.

In this position he, as a strong man, was a most pitiable object, and the porter who had been remonstrating with him seemed to be quite overcome.

He stood near the fallen man, with his hands raised and his eyes rolling, muttering some incomprehensible words, until Grif slowly got upon his feet and turned his pallid face towards the compartment from which he had recently been projected.

"Monsieur," he said, "I thought there was only one man in the world who could have done that, and him I have never seen. He was in Paris a year or two ago, and his name was Strongbow."

"My name," replied Dick, serenely, "is Strongbow."

"Ah! is it so?" said Grif, rising and gazing at him eagerly. "Oh! how shall it be I not know it before? Ah! I haf seen ze great Strongbow, and am happy. Here, let me be put into a dog-box, and I shall be content."

Where the porter finally placed him Dick did not take the trouble to see.

But the little incident stirred the old blood within him, and obliterated for the time the memory of the recent humiliating scenes.

They all, indeed, laughed over it, and the rest of the journey to Marseilles was performed without any incident worth narrating.

Nor did anything worthy of note transpire during the time that elapsed from then until one sunny morning they found themselves on the shore near the Syrian city Beyrout.

CHAPTER VII.

BEYROUT—UPSETTING THE TOUTS—IN A MURDEROUS DEN.

STRANGE place it was to the eyes of the travellers, for none of them had ever been in an eastern Asiatic city before.

Beyrout has a mixed population of Mahommedans, Christians, Maronites, and Jews.

The Jew we have, indeed, everywhere, although he varies very much in appearance and disposition, according to the country and clime which is favoured by his presence.

The Jew of Beyrout is rather of a low order, and in our own country would be included in the list of crimps who infest every port in the kingdom and make a prey of poor Jack and the unwary freshlanded passenger.

It was inevitable that our friends, when they landed, should be waylaid by some of these pests, and two of them were especially pertinacious in their attention.

In outward appearance they were all that could be desired.

As far as their garb and physique went they might have sat for the models of some of those goody-goody pictures of the East which are seen in magazines for infants.

Either of them might have passed for the good Samaritan, fresh from having done a deed to be proud of, but it was all outside show.

Inwardly they were as vile and rapacious as man could possibly be, even in the East, which is going a long way, and they fastened upon our friends, metaphorically, like leeches.

"Good hotel—good bed—good food—all day—altogether!" said one, in Butterflick's ear.

"Oh! my young friend—oh! stranger from afar," purred the other, as he walked by Dick's side, "is there a fair spot in Beyrout I cannot show you? Kind master, come with me and see what a palace I have prepared for you."

Now Dick in all cases prefered trusting to his own judgment in the selection of an hotel, and being an utter stranger in Beyrout he was especially wary of being taken in hand by strangers.

He therefore told his persistent attendant that he had no need of his services, and would rather choose for himself.

Then the gentle Jew became abusive, and used certain expressions towards Dick which led him to deal him a comparatively light blow and knock him down.

Butterflick, at about the same moment, having had enough of his man, seized him by the collar of a sort of tunic he wore, twisted him round, and by means of the skilful introduction of a knee into his back brought him down with a force that shook all the touting gabble out of him.

It was hardly an auspicious beginning to their sojourning in a strange land, and so Dick thought.

The moment he had upset the tout he felt that he had been hasty.

Not a sound did either of the Jews make after they were down, but both lay quite still upon the ground, with their glittering eyes fixed upon the men who had put them there.

Muffins laughed to see them so quiet, but Flutterby Fowler thought he had never seen anything so strange.

There was something exceedingly repulsive and ominous in the appearance of the men.

It reminded him of certain insects which, when touched with a stick, stretch themselves out and lie perfectly still until they get an opportunity to sting and eject poison into the body of their foe.

Dick, however, sauntered on into the heart of the city, with its narrow streets and flat-topped houses, arranged so as to serve for sleeping-places at certain seasons.

Here and there one or more of the inhabitants stood at the doors, and a few chance wayfarers crossed their path, but the place had in the main a deserted look.

"Ah! now I begin to understand the records of the East," said Flutterby Fowler. "Look at that man there—he who is standing by the door with his turban in his hand. Did you ever see anything so abject and miserable?"

"I am principally concerned just now," replied Dick, "to know where we shall put up for the night. I find, on looking at the map, that we have a sandy track to cross, besides a portion of the mountains of Lebanon to pass over, and I must get at some means of being conveyed beyond them."

Here a curious sort of signboard caught Flutterby Fowler's eye.

"This should be an inn," he said. "Let us see what is on the board."

There were only two words, but they were full of promise to them.

"Englis otell."

"It is inviting," said Dick. "Let us go in and see what it is like."

The outside was anything but agreeable to the eye, for, like most places in the East, the windows, such as they were, formed but a small portion of the front of the house.

Inside they found themselves in a square room, rather dark, but lighted at the upper end by means of a gap in the wall.

A man attired as a Turk was seated on the floor, with the stem of a hookah between his lips.

He made no attempt to rise, and it would never have occured to them that he was the landlord but for his asking "what could be done for the gracious lords?"

A place to sleep in and a room where they could get something to eat was what they required. The host had all they asked for, so he said, but first "my lords" would eat while their chamber was being prepared.

He showed them into a barn-like place, at the back of the house, which he seemed to be proud of.

But the accommodation was most meagre, consisting of a few plain tables and rough seats.

"It must serve for the time," Dick said; "and for food—what have you?"

He had goat's flesh, and fowls, and most excellent bread, and wine almost too good to drink. Dick bade him prepare what he had with all speed.

Barely had he left the room when who should come in but the two Jew touts, as quiet and composed as if they had not recently been subjected to unceremonious treatment.

Advancing with many bows, they drew up near Dick, and, presenting their open palms—none too clean, by the way—asked for "their pay."

The coolness of the proceeding would have been amusing at another time, but Dick was not in the humour for fun, and sternly bade them go about their business.

Unruffled, they made their next appeal to Butterflick, who, but for the restraining influence of Flutterby Fowler, would have there and then done them violence, but, subduing his wrath, he simply told them he had nothing that day for them.

A like appeal to the tutor and Muffins having failed, the importunate scamps returned to Dick Stongbow with unabated mendicity.

"My lord, being good and great," said one, "he will give us three shekels each."

"What is it they want?" growled Butterflick— "three shakings?"

"Shekels—shekels," softly explained Flutterby Fowler. "Do not be so hasty—restrain yourself. Our friend Strongbow will, if necessary, take action."

Dick, it seemed, found it necessary to take action forthwith.

Rising, he seized each of the importunate ones by the front of his tunic, and shook them until the rattle of their teeth was like the distant sound of a corner-man with the bones.

They offered him a little resistance at first, but soon yielded themselves up to their fate.

Having shaken them until they were on the verge of a fit, Dick dragged them out of the room like a pair of limp dolls, and finally cast them into the street.

This summary mode of disposing of a pair of touting leeches was witnessed by half a score men of various tribes and nations, who, when the fallen ones were left in a heap in the middle of the road, gathered about them, eager to know the full particulars of their ejectment.

What they asked and what they finally were told we need not go into, but it sufficed to create quite a *furore* among the rag-tag and bob-tail of the place.

A mob speedily gathered in the street, and, pressing into the house, presented their eager faces at the door of the room in which our friends were partaking of dinner.

But beyond that they did not go, and if Dick so much as turned his eyes for a moment in their direction the foremost speedily gave place to the others.

"It is Anak himself restored to life," they said. "A mighty man, with arms of brass, has come among us."

Suddenly the eager observers were thrust aside, and a tall, bearded man strode into the room.

He was attired in the ordinary apparel of a European traveller—a suit of light tweed—and wore a grey, broad-brimmed felt hat, which he removed as he entered and bowed to our friends.

"What an accursed country for prying this is!" he said. "Why does the landlord permit that lot of vermin to hang round the door? Hi! there, away with you. In my country," he added, addressing Dick, "they would get a taste of the knout."

"From your reference to that instrument of torture," said Dick, "I judge you are a Russian."

"Yes," he replied; "I am one of the Czar's dogs who has bolted away from the kennel. Of a truth it is a sorry country to live in, and one who owns it as his place of birth has little need to brag about it."

"Whatever one's native land may be," said Flutterby Fowler, "it's hardly right to run it down. That ought to be left to strangers."

The Russian turned a frowning face upon the little man, and did not for a moment say anything. His brow clearing, he laughed softly.

"You are right," he said, "but you speak as an Englishman. Were you a poor devil of a Russian like myself, driven by oppression and cruelty to wander in other lands, you would not be disposed to brag about the country of your birth."

"I am not given to bragging about anything," replied Flutterby Fowler, stiffly.

"Indeed! Most men are—out of Russia," said the stranger. "But we have little to brag about. See here. I had a home in Russia—a good one being well born—the Czar robbed me of it—no matter how and when. At this moment I am a trader between Beyrout, Teheran, and Astrabad, carrying my life in my hands nine-tenths of the year—"

He was going on about his hardships when Dick checked him.

"Excuse me for a moment," he said. "You trade between here and Teheran, and on to Astrabad?"

"I do," was the reply, "and have done so for years."

"You know the country well?"

"Too well, for it is a country infested with petty thieves and murderous robbers. One must be well-armed, and sleep with both eyes open, if one goes, as I do, alone."

The host of the inn now appeared with some food and wine, which had evidently been ordered by the Russian when he came in.

He fell upon both with the appetite and thirst of a man who had fasted for awhile.

Meanwhile the landlord had driven the mob of curiosity-mongers out of the house, but the murmur of voices in the street, discussing the deed of the "man with arms of brass," reached the room, like the buzzing of bees.

Dick beckoned to Flutterby Fowler to draw aside for a moment.

The action was apparently disregarded by the Russian, nor did he betray any interest in the short, whispered conference that ensued between them.

"What think you of this fellow?" asked Dick.

"He appears to be honest," replied Flutterby Fowler, "but—"

"One could hardly hope to find an honest trader in the East," said Dick, "and in my opinion he is not a trader at all."

"What is he, then?"

"A spy upon us."

Flutterby Fowler stared hard at Dick. The suggestion was a startling one, and with no apparent foundation of probability.

"I can hardly see how it can be so," said Flutterby.

"And I only instinctively feel it," replied Dick. "Now, I think he intends to accompany us on our mission, fooling us to the the top of our bent, and at the right moment thwart us. You must remember, Fowler, that I only imperfectly understand what I have to do myself, but I have been warned that there is danger of a secret foe, and the man I have to fear—if I should for a moment entertain fear—is HERE."

"Well, have nothing to do with him," suggested Flutterby Fowler.

"On the contrary," said Dick, coolly, "I shall make a fool of the man who would make a fool of me."

"It is a daring thing to do," observed the tutor.

"Why?"

"He may be one of many—he may have emissaries —friends."

"Numbers are nothing," said Dick. "I speak to you in this matter because I can rely upon your intelligent assistance." Flutterby Fowler's face beamed. "It won't do to ask Butterflick to dissemble, because he would over-do it. Your office will be to keep him in order, in case he should seek an open rupture. Leave the rest to me."

They returned to the table, where the Russian, having just finished his meal, was lighting a huge cigar.

"Ah!" he said, "one enjoys tobacco after food, and what a man a full stomach makes one. You are travellers, I presume?"

"Yes."

"For pleasure?"

"Partly. I may say, with no idea of profit.

Now I have just been consulting with my friend here "—Flutterby Fowler bowed to the Russian, who grandiosely acknowledged his salute—"and we thought we might trespass upon your kindness for a little advice."

"Yes, certainly. Why not? I am at your service," replied the Russian.

"Our intention is to cross Persia to the very place you named—Astrabad," said Dick. "At first we thought of going by the way of Ispahan, but that would be away from the usual route."

"A long way out."

"Yes. So we have finally elected to go by Teheran, and, if it would not be trespassing too much upon your kindness, might we ask for some information how to get there?"

"By camel and on foot, with a proper guide," was the reply.

"And where is that guide to be obtained?"

"My friend," said the Russian, "there lies the difficulty. Nineteen out of twenty of the ordinary guides are but the agents of brigands and cut-throats. They will lead you into the jaws of a murderous community."

"But do you not know of a guide?"

"Of one only," replied the Russian, laughing.

"And he is—"

"Myself. Listen, friend; I am accustomed to travelling the road alone, but I don't like it. I shall be only too glad of such good company as yours, and it will be ample repayment for me."

"You are sure," said Dick, "that we shall not incommode you in any way?"

"I say your company will be a boon to me," cried the Russian.

"When do you start?"

"To-morrow, and now let us drink to our good luck in another bottle of wine. Ho! there, you dog of a landlord. Bring in some more of the decoction you playfully palm upon us as a fine vintage, and be quick. My friend, your name?"

"It is Strongbow," said Dick.

"What! he of the strong arm?" cried the other.

"The same."

"Ah! man, you must be terrible company to travel with."

"Why?" asked Dick.

"Why, one might quarrel," replied the Russian, "and then where would a wisp of a man like myself be?"

"Well, if a quarrel arises," said Dick, smiling, "it will not begin with me. You must be the author of it."

"Ah! then," replied the other, "I am safe. Name your friend?"

"Flutterby Fowler."

"And the boy, and his—his—"

He stopped, and Butterflick finished the sentence for him.

"His father by proxy—that's what I am—and if ever a father had reason to be proud of his son I'm the man."

"I should say so," said the Russian, pleasantly; "he seems a likely boy. Mother living?"

Whether the question was honestly asked or meant as a joke at Butterflick's expense it is not easy to say. The face of the Russian was quite expressionless as he put it.

"Whether his mother is living or not," said Butterflick, "don't matter—she won't have him if

I can help it. Her name is Old Sally. Perhaps you've heard of her?"

The Russian shook his head.

"The lady is unhappily a stranger to me," he replied. "And now I know you all—Strongbow, Fowler, Butterflick, Muffins—good.

"Which reminds me that I don't know your name," said Dick.

"Ah! no. I had almost forgotten it," replied the Russian. "My name is—*Turcomatz*."

CHAPTER VIII.

A VALUABLE CAMEL—TURCOMATZ DOES A VERY STRANGE THING.

NLY two of the four friends recognised the name of the Russian—Dick Strongbow and Flutterby Fowler—and neither moved a muscle.

"Well, as we all know each other," said the former, "we may consider ourselves friends."

"Certainly," replied Turcomatz, with an easy smile. "And now we will go into details. You carry little luggage?"

"None to speak of," Dick replied.

"A wise arrangement; but for all that we must take with us certain necessaries—some provisions, a few skins of water, and a tent. The latter will be more needed by day than night. When crossing the sandy wastes we must rest at noon."

"If you will kindly make all necessary arrangements," said Dick, "I shall only be too happy to fall in with them."

"Good," responded Turcomatz, rising. "We will start at eve. The night is the best time to travel when there is a moon; it is now at the full."

He rose up and strode out of the room, twirling his moustache like a thoroughly self-satisfied man.

Butterflick was dozing, and Muffins was amusing himself in the vain effort to squash the nimble Eastern flies that buzzed around and lit every moment or so upon his face.

It was not until the footsteps of the Russian had died away, and Dick heard his voice outside, that he spoke, and then he did so in a drawling tone, without showing any emotion.

"As I expected," he said, "the man who is dogging us has managed to keep at our heels."

"He must have come by the same vessel," replied Flutterby Fowler.

"Not necessarily so," rejoined Dick. "I think he got here before us. Well, he is but one man, and he risks much in playing his tricks upon me."

There was the question of how far those tricks might go, to be sure, and the need of being ever on the watch was apparent.

Flutterby Fowler and Dick arranged that in all times and all seasons one or the other should keep a careful eye upon him.

Turcomatz came back shortly, and announced that he had succeeded in hiring a camel.

"It is one I have had before," he said, "and it is the hardiest of that hardy tribe of animals I have ever met with. He will go without food and drink, at a pinch, for a month."

This was a palpable exaggeration, but Turcomatz had already shown he was inclined to look at things through a magnifying glass.

"Will you come and see him?" he said. "He is in a stable outside, lying on the straw, in the full enjoyment of a good full stomach, which, by and bye, please the pigs, will be reduced by travel."

Dick said he would take his word for its being a good animal, but the others might go and see it if they pleased.

Glad of any relief from the gloom of the inn, Butterflick, Muffins, and Flutterby Fowler, escorted by Turcomatz, left the room.

The Russian led them out of the house to a building on the other side of the street, and in a hole of a place, with no light save that which came through the doorway, they found the wonderful camel.

"Get up, my child," said Turcomatz, giving the beast a sounding kick in the ribs; "let us see your beauty. Ah! my faith, there's a creature—swift as the wind, graceful as a gazelle."

The camel was about as unpromising-looking a brute as Flutterby Fowler had ever set eyes on.

In addition to the charms of natural ugliness which all camels possess to a superlative degree, he had a specially ungainly look about the legs, and his hump stood up on his back like a beehive with the crown dented in.

He turned a pair of very malicious-looking eyes upon the company, and drew back his lips like a hyena about to indulge in one of its blood-curdling laughs.

But no sound escaped him, and Turcomatz, having given him a command, accompanied by a second application of his foot, the beast fell awkwardly upon its knees, and with a series of jerks resumed a recumbent position.

"Oh! what a picture—what a treasure!" exclaimed Turcomatz. "The marvel to me is that some caliph has not sent and snapped him up. Now, my children, let us go."

They turned out of the stable, and on returning to the street found that an Eastern musician had posted himself before the inn.

He had an instrument made of pieces of wood, arranged on strips of cloth or tape. He beat upon them with two sticks, extracting sounds something like the drawing of corks, as an accompaniment to a noise he was making with his mouth, which, by the aid of a powerful imagination and a charitable disposition, might be assumed to be singing.

Flutterby Fowler was a student, and the sight of the musician naturally attracted him.

A group of listeners had already gathered round the man, and he joined them, so did Butterflick, but Turcomatz strolled into the inn.

Muffins would have waited if there had been anything worth hearing, but he really could see nothing in the strange musical performance, and after listening to it for a few moments he also adjourned to the inn.

The host and two or three idlers had come out to enjoy the music, so Muffins on entering found the place deserted.

Walking softly, because he was in no hurry, Muffins crossed over to the corner of the room where Dick Strongbow was, and then he suddenly stopped short.

A strange scene was being enacted within.

Dick, owing to the heat, perhaps, had dozed off, and before him, on the table, was his half-emptied glass of wine.

Turcomatz stood by the table intently regarding Dick for a few moments, after which he passed his hand lightly over his breast and waist.

"You have given way to the heat of the day, my friend," he said, softly.

Dick did not stir.

Then Turcomatz took out a phial from his pocket and carefully dropped a small quantity of some dark fluid into the wine.

Muffins dodged behind a rough bench in the ante-room and watched the Russian go out again.

Then he darted into the other chamber, and seizing the glass emptied its contents upon the floor.

Muffins, during his varied life, had heard of men being drugged, and he had no doubt that Turcomatz had put the liquid into the glass with a similar motive; but he thought he would make no fuss about it then.

Leaving Dick still asleep, he hurriedly returned to the street, and was fortunate in getting back to the crowd, which had now gathered to listen to the musician, unseen by Turcomatz, who had rejoined Butterflick and the tutor.

Muffins slowly edged his way round, displaying a lot of sham anxiety to get a view of the performer, until he was espied by the Russian.

"How now, my young friend," he said. "Where have you been?"

"Oh! hereabout," replied Muffins, carelessly. "Isn't it a beastly row?"

"It is interesting as a study," said Flutterby Fowler. "Music varies with every age and all people. There is a certain harmony in this man's music."

"So there is in the clucking of an old hen," growled Butterflick. "It would do him good to put a pail of water over him."

"Ah!" said Turcomatz, gaily, "you are better acquainted with the Italian opera, it may be."

"Not me," said Butterflick, "but I like a good rousing song as well as any man. As for that squeaking, it's enough to curdle your blood. I've had enough of it."

He took himself off into the inn, and shortly after the rest followed.

Turcomatz, on entering the room, cast a quick glance at Dick's glass, and, seeing it was empty, smiled.

"Number one is safe," he said. "All goes well. If he will only take his physic properly I shall win the prize and laugh at the mighty Strongbow."

CHAPTER IX.

THE START—TURCOMATZ CURSED BY THE BEGGARS.

VENING came, and the party were ready to start. The tent had been procured, and, with a few cooking utensils and stores, made into a big bundle, which formed an additional hump upon the camel's back.

A number of idlers were there to see them start, and among these was the usual proportion of beggars, which, in the East, means three-fourths of the company.

They cried out for backsheesh, and told stories of horrible affliction, which Turcomatz derided.

He bade them stand back, and struck two or three of them with his heavy fist. Then they rained down curses upon him.

"Go, die like a dog in the desert!" shrieked one. "Rot in the sun and be food for flies. The curse of Ishmael be on you!"

Dick had received a lot of small change from the landlord, which for the most part looked like odd bits of brass, and these he good-naturedly threw among the crowd.

As they scrambled for the pieces they heaped blessings on his head. They wished he might prosper and grow rich, and live for ever, with other good things which so many of us hope for and never get.

"A fig for their curses!" said Turcomatz. "I have been cursed before—I always am when I start upon a journey—because I will not be robbed by them, and the louder they curse the more I prosper."

"It shall not be so now," shrieked a wild-eyed man, with one arm the natural size and the other shrunken to the proportions of that of a child. "You are proud and boastful, but you shall fall. All your food shall become ashes—your drink turn to gall. Away, you murderous dog—away!"

"Let us go on," said Turcomatz.

Butterflick had volunteered to be the first leader of the camel, and, giving the rope which served as a halter a jerk, he bade the brute "come up."

The camel did not seem inclined to "come up," but, by sundry movements, clearly expressed its intention to lie down.

Thereupon Turcomatz applied his ready boot, and the beast set out at a shambling, lopsided walk.

The party was accompanied to the outskirts of the town by all of the little crowd who were able to hobble after them.

The lame and the halt continued to curse Turcomatz and call down all sorts of evils on his head, and he, in reply, laughed at and derided them.

When he would have struck some of them Dick stayed his hand.

"Let the poor wretches be," he said. "Their lot, in any case, is a hard one."

"I'd make it harder for them if I had my way," hissed Turcomatz, between his teeth. "Who in the name of that tyrant hound, the Czar, can listen to them with patience?"

But they were shaken off at last and the town left behind them.

Their way lay along a well-defined road, which, however, was deserted, for the darkness of night was rapidly falling.

"I don't know how it is," said Flutterby Fowler, after a short silence, "but the curse and the blessing have alike always been considered potent in the East."

"Who says so?" demanded Turcomatz.

"Oh! writers generally agree upon that head."

"Writers are fools," laughed the Russian. "Are you such a child as to think there is anything in the mutterings of those sore-spotted beggars? Bah!"

"Oh! I say nothing," replied Flutterby Fowler.

"but I think I would rather have their blessing than their curse."

"Because you are a weak, timorous man."

"Yes, I am both, I suppose."

Here a slight interruption to their progress was made by an attempt on the part of the camel to return to Beyrout.

The brute began to back, and with swinging movements of its head swayed this way and that, to the great discomposure of Butterflick, who was jerked here and there like a dancing doll.

Turcomatz was getting ready to use his foot when Dick motioned for him to keep quiet, and, stepping forward, he took hold of the halter.

With one tug he stopped the antics of the camel, and a second one brought it almost to its knees.

Astonished to find its master in a single man, it started on again, and in Butterflick's hands became as docile as a lamb.

"You are strong," said Turcomatz, as if he had just discovered a secret.

"Fairly so," replied Dick, carelessly. "I have some reputation in that direction."

"I am no child," said Turcomatz, "but I could not have done that. Bah! what is mere muscular strength? It is the mind that governs."

"And that you possess," observed Flutterby Fowler.

"I also have some reputation—in that way," replied Turcomatz, drily.

"Oh! we are none of us fools, if it comes to that," remarked Butterflick; "which you may find out if you try to come any tricks."

"I—a trick?" exclaimed Turcomatz, indignantly. "I, who am your guide?—who provides you with a pear' of a camel—a creature of priceless worth?"

"Butterflick," said Dick, "you must not say such things. You don't mean to offend, but people are apt to object to your open way of speaking."

"I'm done, sir," growled Butterflick; "if I've offended I'm sorry."

"It is enough," said Turcomatz; "but to be suspected of a trick—"

"I assure you," interposed Dick, "that I do not think you are at all likely to impose upon me."

"I am satisfied—comforted," said Turcomatz.

After an hour's journey the road began to be less distinct, although the moon had risen and was throwing its bright, white rays upon the earth.

Turcomatz explained that they would soon leave the public highway, which wound about, and take a short cut to the mountains, through which he would lead them by a path unknown to all save a few traders like himself.

Now all this time Muffins had had no opportunity to tell Dick what he had seen in the room at the inn, but he intended to do so as soon as he got an opportunity.

It was presently given him by Turcomatz, who, going upon another tack, fastened on to Butterflick, with a view to strengthening their "friendship."

Flutterby Fowler also joined them, and Muffins was left behind with Dick Strongbow.

"Master," he whispered, "I've something to tell you."

"Yes? Is it anything particular?" returned Dick.

"It is—that Russian chap tried, I believe, to poison you."

"Muffins, you have been dreaming."

"Maybe, sir; but let me tell you about it. Can you hear me, whisperin' so low?"

"Perfectly."

Then Muffins told him what he had seen, and, although Dick outwardly showed no emotion, he was a bit taken aback by the intelligence.

"You are sure you are not mistaken, Muffins?" he said.

"Quite. I see him do it with my own eyes."

"I don't suppose you saw it done with those of other persons, Muffins. Perhaps it was a joke. Anyway, don't take any further notice of it. Leave it to me."

CHAPTER X.

CHANGING THE DRINKING CUPS—STRANGE CONDUCT OF TURCOMATZ.

FOUR hours elapsed ere a halt was decided on, and it would not have been called then but for the fact that Flutterby Fowler was giving out.

He made no complaint, but kept steadily on until he began to rest here and there, and all his brightening up and dogged determination could not conceal the fact that he was pumped.

The camel also, considering his unrivalled staying powers, displayed a remarkable readiness to lie down, and when they had all settled on the sandy soil Turcomatz proposed a drink.

"Just one cup of wine to our future good luck," he said.

Without waiting for assent he rose up and walked over to the camel. Loosening a portion of the bundle upon its back he succeeded in extracting therefrom a bottle of wine and five tin cups.

He was some time in temporarily replacing the covering, and when he turned round Dick saw that he had a single cup in his left hand. The others he held in his right one.

The cup from his left he placed before Dick, and having uncorked the bottle he filled it with wine.

A second one he filled for himself, and then attended to the rest.

His own cup he had placed upon the ground where he had been sitting, close by Dick Strongbow, and it flashed upon Dick that it would be a good experiment to change them.

Taking advantage of the back of the Russian being momentarily turned, he effected his object, and took a sip of wine from the cup not originally intended for him.

Turcomatz resumed his seat and pledged him.

"A good life, a long life, and increasing strength to you," he said.

"I shall be content with the former," replied Dick, "provided the latter remains."

"It may not always do so," Turcomatz remarked. "Here, in this accursed country, one is apt to experience sudden weaknesses, unaccountable to even the most experienced."

"And does it last?"

"Not always, although sometimes it does. But

Dick tackled one and Rutterthick was responsible for the other.

the old tone comes back on return to your native land."

He tossed off his wine as he spoke, and as all had now rested the journey was resumed. Dick was moving towards the camel, without any idea of interfering with it, or even to touch it, when the animal fairly sprang up ere he could reach it.

"Oh! he knows his master," said Turcomatz, laughing.

On resuming their way the Russian settled down by Dick's side, beguiling the time by telling him stories of the Syrian people, and once more he dwelt upon the peculiar weakness which was likely to overcome one not accustomed to the climate.

Suddenly he stopped short and put his hand to his side.

"What is the matter?" asked Dick. "Are you unwell?"

"Oh! it is nothing—a mere stitch," he replied. "I am accustomed to it. Saints above us! what has come to me?"

He staggered forward a pace, and fell into a sitting position upon the ground. Dick again asked him if he was not ill.

"I am smitten," he answered, "as one accursed. I am as weak as a child."

"And yet you laughed at the curses of the poor and afflicted," said Flutterby Fowler, solemnly.

"It isn't that—it can't be," replied Turcomatz.

"Perhaps it is the peculiar weakness you were speaking of?" suggested Dick, coolly.

He had no pity for the man. How could he have when it was but too clear that he was suffering from a dose of some villainous compound which he intended for Dick.

"Strange, very strange," murmured Turcomatz. "I—I—"

He stopped again, and stared about him as if in a dream.

Then he looked into Dick's face and laughed—vaguely, strangely.

"By order of the Czar," he said, slowly, "and when it is his orders who is to say nay? *Curse* him!"

He laughed again and twisted his moustache, then with an effort he got upon his feet.

"I am better now," he said. "It was a passing attack—a grip; one has to get used to it. Still, if you would walk slowly—"

"Choose your own pace," said Dick, "or wait a little longer if you wish it."

"No, no," replied Turcomatz; "unless walked off now it will remain for ever. You are never the same man again. I must have put down the wrong—What am I saying? Go on, please—slowly—I will follow you."

"Shall I remain with you?" asked Flutterby Fowler.

"No, no—go on," was the nervous reply; "I shall be better alone—a passing weakness."

"Shall I hoist you on the camel?" asked Butterflick. "An extra load would not hurt him."

"I beg of you to go on. I shall soon overtake you."

So they went on, and he remained behind, but not to immediately follow them.

Once more he threw himself down upon the ground, and lay there quite still until their forms were misty in the distance.

"I gave myself the stuff!" he growled. "What careless dog ever played such a trick as that upon

himself? Anathemas on it! I say. It is a filthy mixture. How it claws at one's vitals and unnerves one. And such a dose, too—for a strong man."

He lay there muttering for awhile, and then a tendency to sleep came over him.

He battled with it fiercely at first, and tried to get up, but the inclination to lie down was overpowering, and sinking back he stretched himself out at full length and slept.

Meanwhile Dick and his friends went on for a good mile without halting. Then the camel was stopped, and they looked back.

"He is not coming," said Flutterby Fowler.

"That is his look-out," replied Dick, grimly.

"He is a strange fellow, and I do not like him, but to see him suffer so—"

"My dear Fowler, he deserves it. That suffering he intended for me."

Then Dick explained the whole affair, which so amazed the listening tutor that he could only give vent to his astonishment in a series of ejaculations until the story was finished.

"You see," said Dick, "it is clear he meant to hocus me with something to take away my strength. What his object was I don't know. That may become clearer by and bye. At present it has failed, and I have the whip-hand of him."

"Do you think he will die?" asked Flutterby Fowler, in a low tone.

"If he does who is to blame?" answered Dick. "But he will not die—indeed, I think I see him coming."

They looked in the direction they had travelled, and the outline of an advancing figure was seen, but it slowly melted away, and all was vacant as before.

"Odd," muttered Dick. "I don't understand it."

"This is an uncanny land," remarked Flutterby Fowler; "the land of enchantment and of evil spirits."

"I don't pin much faith to that idea," said Dick.

"There is the figure again!" hastily ejaculated Flutterby Fowler.

Butterflick and Muffins, who had been whispering together by the camel's head, heard the exclamation, and looking back they, too, saw the figure.

It came on for a time, and then seemed to melt away as before.

"That's the Russian chap having a lark with us," observed Butterflick. "He looks to me like a man of tricks. That illness of his was all a sham."

"It wasn't the Russian," put in Muffins. "It was somebody taller and slimmer."

"Stay here," said Dick. "I must go back and investigate this matter. If it is simple foolery I will speedily put an end to it."

"It is no foolery," replied Flutterby Fowler. "On my word I am not alarmed, for I do not fear the spirits of darkness—their powers are limited—but I beseech you not to go back, or at least let me go with you."

"No," said Dick, with a smile. "I can hardly accept you as a protector. Remain here with Muffins and Butterflick. I shall come to no hurt."

Dick had no fear of any real peril, and he was not superstitious, but he prepared for emergencies by getting his revolver ready for action as he left his friends and quietly walked back in the direction where the strange figure had presented itself.

He reached the very spot as near as he could judge, and looked around him, but saw nothing.

The moon shone brilliantly, and he could see clearly a considerable distance—say, a furlong. Beyond that the gloom began to show its power, and approaching the horizon it was quite dark.

Dick hesitated a moment whether he should return.

What was this drug-dealing Russian to him? Whatever his fate might be he richly deserved it.

But his better nature took the lead, as it always did, and he started off to find the man. When another hundred yards or so had been traversed he came to a halt again.

Something living was approaching.

He could see it in the distance, but it bore no resemblance to a man, for it was travelling on all fours.

CHAPTER XI.

IT IS TURCOMATZ—PITCHING THE TENT—CONTENTS OF TWO POCKETS—AN EXCHANGE OF LIQUIDS.

THE strange sight might have daunted the boldest of men, especially at that hour and with such lonesome surroundings, but Dick was not afraid of man or beast, and quietly drawing his revolver he awaited the coming of the creature.

It had a waddling movement, swaying from side to side, which was soon accounted for. It was no beast at all, but Turcomatz!

As the form of the man crawling on all fours grew out of the gloom Dick burst into a hearty fit of laughter, which had the effect of pulling the Russian up short.

"Come on, man; it is I—Strongbow," said Dick.

He went on as he spoke up to the side of Turcomatz, who was sitting panting on the ground.

"I thought you were many versts ahead," he gasped. "What have you come back for?"

"To see if I can help you," replied Dick. "Why, man, what is the matter with you?"

"Didn't I tell you that people were taken with all sorts of things in this accursed country?"

"Ah! yes, to be sure. I had forgotten. Come, let me help you."

He took him by the arms and raised him as if he had been a featherweight.

"You are mighty strong," said Turcomatz.

"Yes; I can put a grip on a man that makes him feel like a rope of sand," replied Dick.

The Russian shuddered.

"I know what you mean," he said. "I feel like that to-night."

"By the way," asked Dick, "why did you crawl? You are not weak enough for that."

"No," said Turcomatz, "but I heard the cry of Guetras on the march, and as they have a terror of anything on all-fours by night I shammed being a wild beast."

"What are the Guetras?"

"They are a class of what you would call Parsees. Those who prowl about these deserts would rather cut your throat than leave you alive."

"Brigands?"

"In a way. But they are not to blame. They are men of the yeoman class, cultivators of the land, who have been sweated of everything by the Shah's

agents and turned adrift. Many of them have even lost their wives."

"It's enough to make anyone murderous."

"Oh! there are pretty goings on in the Shah's country, as you will see by and bye."

"You must be a daring man to risk your life trading here," said Dick.

He looked down at the face of his companion as he spoke, and saw that a decided expression of uneasiness had settled upon it. It was some moments ere he offered to make reply.

"I what you English call dodge them," he said, "and when I can't do that I bribe them. A lying promise of bringing back gifts has also saved my life more than once."

He walked—or rather crawled—so slowly that Dick felt it would be impossible to travel on with him for awhile, so on reaching his friends, who were more surprised than pleased to see Turcomatz with him, he announced his intention of pitching the tent.

"Not for me," said Turcomatz. "I don't mind being left behind again. As soon as the sun rises"—he stopped short, his head drooping—"as the sun "—another nod—"rises, so—"

He was asleep again.

"Get the tent up quickly," said Dick to Butterflick. "This man is queer. Something odd is the matter with him. You need not worry about the camel. It won't run away."

The cheerful brute did not exhibit the least intention of doing anything of the sort.

Squatting on the ground with closed eyes, it gave itself up to ruminating, accompanied by that to-and-fro movement of the lower jaw so strongly suggestive of a cow chewing the cud.

Butterflick was a good hand at pitching a tent—he had put up many a one in his old mining days, when prospecting—and it was soon ready.

Dick took up the insensible Turcomatz and carried him inside. A moment afterwards he was heard calling for Flutterby.

The little man went up to the mouth of the tent, but it was so dark he could see nothing.

"I want a light," said Dick. "There are some candles among the stores. I think the man is dead."

A suppressed exclamation of horror escaped the tutor as he hastened to obey. Assisted by Butterflick, he soon had a candle, with which he returned to the tent.

Lighting it, he saw Dick kneeling by the form of the Russian, stretched out stiffly upon the ground.

There were really no signs of life in him.

"As I brought him in he suddenly stiffened out," said Dick.

"It is very strange," observed Flutterby, holding the candle over the still face.

"There is no doubt he is suffering from some subtle poison," rejoined Dick, "which he intended for me. But I don't feel quite sure he is dead, because the face keeps its warmth."

"The eyes are too tightly closed," said Flutterby Fowler. "He is alive. It is a state of absolute inanimation, that is all. He will come out of it."

"It may seem mean," mused Dick, "but in dealing with rogues one must not be squeamish. I must see what this man has about him. Hold the light a little higher."

Flutterby Fowler complied with the request, and

Dick, after a close look at his clothes, to see if there was any peculiar way in buttoning them, proceeded to open his waistcoat.

As he suspected, there were inside pockets—one right and another left.

From one he took the small phial which Muffins had seen the Russian use, and, holding it up to the light, saw that it was three-parts filled with some absolutely colourless liquid.

"This is the stuff," he said. "Have you any knowledge of the nature of poisons?"

"Hardly any, except by reading," replied Fowler.

Dick handed him the bottle. He uncorked it and put his nose to the mouth of it.

"No smell, and, I should say, no taste," he observed, carefully putting just the tip of his tongue to the bottle, "but none the less dangerous, I fear."

"There is a small bottle containing cayenne pepper among the stores," said Dick; "I brought it for my own use. Empty the pepper out and I will take charge of this poison. We can put water in its place."

Flutterby Fowler went off on this errand, and Dick, having stuck the candle in the sandy ground, proceeded to examine the other inner pocket.

He found nothing in it but a small piece of parchment neatly folded.

But the inside explained the use of it.

There were about a dozen lines in French—the language of diplomats—addressed to the Shah of Persia or any of his high officials into whose hands it might fall.

"*To my beloved brother, the mightiest of rulers, Shah of of Shahs, King of Kings, and all who are servants in the land blessed by his rule:*

"*Be gracious to the bearer of this, for he is one of my faithful children, whose name is Count Salvormarck, and to him is given the power to do all things that will bind together the fortunes of myself and my brother the Shah. Greeting and love to all.*"

Then followed the signature of the Czar, with the seal attached, and a cabalistic mark beneath, evidently part of some secret code of communication.

"I need not look any further," thought Dick, as he carefully replaced the valuable document. "One day this may be useful to me—meanwhile it remains with its owner."

Flutterby Fowler now came back with the small bottle of cayenne pepper. Its contents were emptied out, and the poison, as it was supposed to be, poured into it. Dick took charge of that.

Finally a little water was obtained from a skin of it borne by the camel, and the phial carefully rinsed.

Then, with the same quantity of the harmless fluid poured into Turcomatz's bottle as there had been of the poison, it was restored to its resting-place, and the two friends left the tent.

"Lie down and get some sleep," advised Dick. "I think we may consider our guide safe for some hours."

CHAPTER XII.

FLUTTERBY FOWLER GOES FOR A STROLL—HE MEETS A STRANGE FOE—BUTTERFLICK SHOWS HE CAN SHOOT.

WHETHER there were Guetras or Parsees about or not, none came to disturb the repose of our friends. All, save Dick, slept well till sunrise, but he only permitted himself to doze occasionally.

Of the patient within the tent nothing was heard during the hours of darknesss, but as the sun rose he began to give out signs of returning animation.

Dick peeped in once or twice, but did not go inside until he heard him feebly call his name. Then he went to him.

"How long have I been here?" he said. "I've got a sensation of having slept for years."

"Only one night," replied Dick. "When you went off we laid you down and left you. It was impossible to sleep near you. How you Russians snore!"

Dick assumed an air of jocularity to throw him off the scent, and Turcomatz was hoodwinked.

After having surreptitiously felt his waistcoat to see if the precious bottle was safe he smiled back.

"And you, too, have slept?" he said.

"Yes—fitfully," replied Dick, "but my friends thoroughly. I'd as lief have a brass band blowing near me as to lie awake close to such a fellow as you again."

Turcomatz laughed, stretched his limbs, and yawned. He seemed to be almost, if not quite, himself again.

"A sound sleep does me good," he said, "and I am hungry. If I might be excused, being a convalescent, will the genial Butterflick prepare breakfast?"

"He is already at it," responded Dick, peering out of the tent. "Will you be able to travel with us to-day?"

"As well as ever," replied Turcomatz, "for these strange attacks can always be cured by a sound sleep. Now and then," he added, with a sly glance at Dick, "the sleep is like a fit."

"Yours was very much like one," said Dick, "but we could not help you, and so left Nature to do its work."

"It is the only way. The slightest disturbance might be fatal."

"You were not disturbed."

Turcomatz appeared to be immensely relieved, and became quite gay. He even indulged in scraps of song, and in a general way conducted himself like one who has passed safely through a peril of no ordinary magnitude.

Outside another person was in a bit of a fix, and it was no less a person than Flutterby Fowler.

While Butterflick and Muffins were preparing breakfast he strolled off a little way, looking about him in search of anything geological that might be interesting.

Geology was one of his fads, but he could, under the circumstances, only indulge in it on a small scale.

As he strolled on he suddenly became aware of something that looked like a rag or cloth lying on the sand ahead.

It was moving, too—heaving up and down—which certainly was very strange, for there was not a breath of wind.

"Some mystery of the desert," he thought, and, bent on solving it, he hurried in the direction of the strange object.

Then there suddenly sprang up from a hollow in the sand a fierce-looking warrior of the desert, such as Flutterby Fowler had often seen in pictures and admired.

Now that he had a good view of one in real life he thought he was a most objectionable person.

Uttering a curse, the fierce Syrian drew his sword and made preparations for the swift decapitation of the tutor.

Flutterby Fowler had a revolver somewhere about him, but in the excitement of the moment he forgot it, and fell back upon the noble art of self-defence, which is an instinct with all who are British born.

Putting up his fists he danced about with such amazing agility that the desert savage in vain tried to get a fair cut at him.

It was like trying to hit a gnat, dancing in the evening light, with a walking-stick.

But in the end the warrior would have prevailed only for the intervention of another.

The shot of a revolver was heard, and the Syrian gave a bound in the air, falling heavily on his side, then rolling upon the sand, where he lay quite still.

"Pinked him as neat as wax," cried the voice of Butterflick. "Give in with that dancing, will you, Mister Fowler. The show is all over."

"Butterflick, my friend," said the little tutor, faintly, "I'm glad it's you. How did you come—and—and what's the matter with the man?"

"The man won't have anything the matter with him again," replied Butterflick, coolly, "and you would have been at rest about this time if I hadn't happened to look after you and see that chap spring out of the ground. Don't you go wandering about alone again. You aint big enough to do it."

"Is he dead?" asked Flutterby Fowler.

"As mutton," said Butterflick, looking at the fallen man critically. "Fine old chap for a darkey, but too fond of using his toasting-iron."

"Really," observed Flutterby Fowler, "this is very dreadful."

"It is," said Butterflick, "but not uncommon. Here's the hole he seems to have popped out of. Ketch hold of his heels—we'll lay him in it."

"It is awful," exclaimed Flutterby Fowler.

He took hold of the heels of the dead man, and gingerly helped to lay the Syrian where he had sprung from.

Butterflick took the sword and a pair of old-fashioned, silver-mounted pistols as trophies of war, and marched back with Flutterby Fowler, who felt sick and faint.

It was the first time he had experienced an adventure of this description, and being a very sensitive man it somewhat upset him.

Muffins was pouring the coffee into the tin cups when they returned, and Flutterby Fowler was congratulating himself on the boy's knowing nothing about the recent tragedy when Muffins scattered that idea to the winds by coolly remarking—

"A good shot that of yours, dad."

"It was, my son," replied Butterflick. "I kivered him just above the waist, and, lowering for the up-jerk, he received the lead in the middle of his breast."

Butterflick took up two of the coffee mugs and carried them into the tent, when Flutterby Fowler went up to Muffins, and softly said—

"Weren't you shocked, my boy?"

"At what?" asked Muffins.

"To see a man lose his life that way."

"No—he would have taken yours. I've seen lots of men lose their lives, Mr. Fowler, and so may you before you get home. You won't think so much of it by and bye."

"I suppose one gets hardened to anything," sighed Flutterby Fowler, "but it certainly is very dreadful. Still, we ought to be grateful to Butterflick. He shoots extremely well—and I must practice, I suppose—but if ever I hit a man with a bullet I shall never forgive myself."

Good, gentle little man! But the time is coming when you will lay aside your delicacy and defend your own life at the cost of others, and not be sorry for it afterwards.

Not a bit of it, but rather feel proud of your deeds, just as other men are.

CHAPTER XIII.

THROUGH THE MOUNTAINS—A ROAD OF FLOWERS—THE RUSSIAN MAKES ANOTHER EXPERIMENT.

URCOMATZ gave an explanation of the presence of the Syrian. He said he was either one of the lone robbers who prowled by themselves, or belonged to a large band sent out to watch for expected prey. According to the custom of his class when alone, he had scooped out a sleeping-place, so as not to be a conspicuous object to anyone travelling at sunrise.

As these desert cut-throats are very particular about their religion, even when on a marauding excursion, it was probable he was at his morning devotions when Flutterby Fowler came upon him.

Turcomatz had quite recovered.

He was so buoyant, so elastic, that he danced in an elephantine manner upon the sand after break-fast.

"We will march on to-day," he said, "and by noon shall be among the mountains, where there is shade."

The adventure of Flutterby Fowler induced them to keep a sharp look-out for the band his assailant might possibly be connected with.

There was no doubt he had a knowledge of the whereabouts of the travellers, and intended to spy upon them.

Dick was of opinion that he was the spectre-like form he had seen the previous night.

A swift-footed son of the desert could easily have played the part, but there was no proof of it, and he left the matter as it was.

While the sun was at a moderate height in the heavens they made rapid progress.

The camel, by aid of the voice and boot of Turcomatz—principally the boot—actually bestirred itself, lopping along in fine style, and by eleven o'clock they had reached the hills.

It was getting hot enough for anything or anybody then, and they were glad to lie down and rest under the shadow of some crags that looked like petrified clouds.

There was nothing of the steepness of ordinary mountains about these Syrian hills.

Instead of being formed by violent volcanic action they looked as if they had bubbled up out of the earth and got fixed there.

Butterflick compared them to " boiling glue " that had suddenly stopped bubbling.

A dreary day, a dreary night, then another dreary day, and these hills were passed, after which they were in Persia—in the country of the Shah.

We have, at a bound, flown over this part of the journey, because nothing of note occurred that would interest our readers. On the eve of the second day they camped on the Persian side of the hills and looked over a land of fertility.

But not of cultivation. No.

Here and there were signs of habitations, but Turcomatz, as cheerful as before, said they were only ruins.

"You see," he said, "it is thus—a fool who knows nothing finds a land that is fair, and he says, ' Here will I raise corn and gather herds together.' He does so. Then comes to him an agent, with some dogs of cut-throat soldiers at his back, and says, ' The Shah has need of half your possessions,' and takes them."

He laughed—the joke was so good—and went on—

" In a little while comes another agent with more soldiers—old friends, perhaps, in new uniforms—and he says, ' We have need of the other half of your possessions,' and takes them. After these come the robbers—"

"I thought they had been before," interposed Dick.

" Not professionals—amateurs these," said Turcomatz. " The real robbers strip the fool of his coat—everything—and say to him, ' Fly; we will take care of your wife!'"

" And suppose he doesn't fly ?" asked Butterflick.

" Why, then he has to DIE," said Turcomatz, with a chuckle.

Butterflick looked at Turcomatz with a speculative expression in his eyes, then rolled up his sleeves, and, thrusting his hands into his pockets, walked up and down.

" I feel," he said, " that we've got into a land where an honest man has a right to punch nine out of ten of the heads he meets."

" It is hardly worth while," rejoined Turcomatz, " unless you want to lose your own after a few preliminary tortures special to Persia.

" Our way now," he added, " lies north-east. Beyond yonder forest we shall find a road that will remind you of civilisation. It was made long before the present line of effeminate Shahs—in the days when the Medes and Persians humbled old Nebuchadnezzar, and sent him out to eat grass. It will be a grand day when the last of the Shahs is gone and our father, the Czar, rides down it on his way to India. Wild talk, you say, but it will be."

There was something very insolent about him at that moment, but it quickly disappeared. He seemed to have forgotten for awhile that he had expressed a hatred of the Czar, but it was in the minds of Dick and Flutterby Fowler, and they exchanged a smile.

" Rise up, old crawler," said Turcomatz to the camel; " we shall soon part with you for the more tractable horse. We may find some travellers who will exchange with us," he said, turning to Dick. " Up, old sluggard, and away."

They crossed a wide stretch of park-like land, where flowers of every imaginable hue grew in profusion, and passed through the forest he had pointed out.

It was filled with cedar and other trees that were for the most part strange to the travellers. Turcomatz knew little about them.

" I do not deal in wood," he said, sententiously, in answer to the question.

On the other side of the forest they came to the road he had spoken of, broad and well-defined by broken walls on either side. Between them the flowers grew thick and strong.

Here and there they had been trampled down by some single wayfarer passing along. This was the road of the Medes and Persians—long neglected, but marked out still by the ruined walls built by men who had been dead thousands of years.

Straight before them it stretched into a rich country, then it wound about, hidden here and reappearing there, until it was finally lost on the horizon.

" It is a long road," said Turcomatz, " but as you traverse it you will find much to amuse or disturb you. Beware how you walk. There are several varieties of snakes about, and the bite of two or three is fatal. From their fangs a remarkable poison has been abstracted."

" What is its action ?" asked Dick.

" I do not know it myself," replied Turcomatz, looking him straight in the face, " but the legend goes that one drop will make a child of the strongest man for a day, two drops weaken him for life, and three drops kill. Y—u—up, you hump-back atrocity; let us get on. What was the old cry of your thieves of the highway—' Hurrah for the road !' Ah! that is it. Hurrah for this road, as it leads us to fortune—honour—everything !"

His manner was so wild for the moment that one might have suspected he had gone mad or had been drinking.

He was not under the influence of either one or the other, as he showed by his suddenly becoming quiet and turning a laughing face towards Dick.

" I am merry," he said, " for it is good to be with friends whom you can trust. Eh ?"

" It is," replied Dick, as he lighted a cigar.

" And you and I are friends?"

" Oh! most excellent."

Then Turcomatz once more burst into song, and, taking Butterflick by the arm, hoped they were good friends too."

" Middlin'—middlin'," replied Butterflick, naïvely.

" Oh! but we must be more than that," said Turcomatz; " warm friends, close companions, boon comrades. Heigho! when we halt by and bye we will drink together."

Dick marked these words. He thought there was something significant in them, but he knew there was no danger.

The sting had been taken out of that little bottle, and any experiment Turcomatz might attempt to make with it would fail.

But that was what the Russian had in his mind.

When the halt was called it was his hand that got out the drinking cups and the wine.

He talked incessantly while he did it, and was very slow in getting Butterflick's cup ready for him.

His own he placed upon the ground, and then, with many effusive expressions, poured out some wine for Butterflick.

Dick, meanwhile, seated himself near the other cup, and when the back of Turcomatz was turned coolly put into it one drop of the liquid he had in his possession.

Turcomatz kept his eyes upon Butterflick, bidding him hold his cup ready. Then he picked up his own and half filled it with wine.

"Together," he said. "To the very dregs."

Butterflick tossed his off and the Russian also.

Then he turned to attend to the rest, and saw Dick smilingly waiting to be served.

CHAPTER XIV.

THE BITER BIT—A NOON-DAY SLEEP—WHERE IS THE RUSSIAN?

 ICK STRONGBOW lighted a cigar, and Turcomatz took one he offered him. The Russian was in the highest spirits.

"Life," he said, as he put a match to the cigar, "is full of strange surprises. A man is but as grass. To-day he is full of sap and life—to-morrow he is withered by the sun."

He turned and looked at Butterflick, who was calmly smoking his pipe.

Muffins lay on his back among the flowers, and Flutterby Fowler was reading a small book he had taken from his pocket.

"Now take our burly friend there," he said. "What do you think of him? Strong and firm as the oak to look at—"

"And he IS strong," interposed Dick.

"As strong as I am?" asked Turcomatz, with a cunning smile.

"Stronger."

"Permit me to doubt it."

"Butterflick," said Dick, "our friend here thinks he is stronger than you are."

"I'd like to wrestle with him," replied Butterflick.

"I am ready," rejoined Turcomatz. "I know your English wrestle—Cumberland, Westmoreland—back heel, hipe, lock-leg—I learn them all; but I am not a delicate master of the art. If I throw at all I may throw heavily."

"All right," said Butterflick, indifferently; "if you don't care I don't."

"It is possible I may hurt you."

"Well, I won't grumble if you do. At the same time I warn you to look out for a cropper."

"I am ready," said Turcomatz. "Do you take off anything?"

"No," answered Butterflick; "just as we are."

He laid down his pipe, and Turcomatz carefully placed his cigar upon a stone. Then they advanced towards each other, and Butterflick threw his arms, wrestling fashion, round his opponent.

"Take your grip," he said; "I don't want the pull of you any way."

"I have it," said Turcomatz. "Ah! Ready! Oh! Holy Mother of Russia, what is it now?"

He was down, thrown to the earth with a force that would have cracked an image of stone.

Butterflick, with a surprised face, stared at him as he laid panting and wild-eyed upon the ground.

"Zounds, man," he exclaimed, "YOU wrestle? Why, you've only got a baby grip."

"I am not well," gasped the Russian. "I know not what it means. Am I among magicians?"

He turned his face, now bedewed with cold perspiration, towards Dick Strongbow, who was looking down upon him with a calm, critical eye.

"Tell me," he groaned, "are you a mortal man?"

"Yes," replied Dick; "but that question might be more reasonably put to our friend Butterflick, who made no more of you than he would have done of a bundle of straw. What madness induced you to pit yourself against him?"

"I don't understand it," said Turcomatz. "There's something wrong somewhere."

"There must be," replied Dick.

They had all gathered about the Russian now, who lay upon the ground, making no effort to rise.

"Go on as before," he said, "and leave me here. Go a little way and wait."

"But you may die," rejoined Dick. "Here, let us put you on the camel."

"No, no—leave me."

"I shall not listen to you. Put him on, Butterflick, and secure him so that he does not fall off."

Turcomatz would have resisted if he could, but he was past that. Butterflick lifted him up as if he had been a sick child and set him astride the camel. That done he bound him to the packages on the beast's back, which he feebly protested against in vain.

"At least," he gasped, "go on and heed me not. I do not understand it at all. I am weak—sleepy. Oh! our Father the Czar, if you could but see me now—"

He stopped short and his head fell back, lolling a little aside, so that it rested on the hump of the camel, and there he lay like one exhausted with fever.

"Muffins," said Dick, "you lead the camel. Butterflick, see that he doesn't come to any harm by getting one of those bands twisted round his neck."

He beckoned to Flutterby Fowler, and they walked a little way ahead together.

"What think you of that?" he asked.

"I do not understand it all," said the little man, in an awe-stricken tone of voice. "How much did you give him?"

"One drop—only one."

"It must be a very potent poison."

"Terrible, and I don't like using it even upon him, scoundrel as he is. But I wished to make sure of its being what he covertly stated it to be. One drop takes away strength for a time, two weakens for good, three kills."

"What will you do with him?" asked Flutterby Fowler.

"I have not yet decided," answered Dick. "For the present we will take him with us. He has a pass from the Czar that may be useful. By and bye, when he is sound asleep, I will borrow it of him."

DICK STRONGBOW:

The Diamond King,
AND WONDER OF THE WORLD.

Putting up his fists he danced about with amazing agility.

No. 19.   Price One Penny.

"In my mind," said Flutterby Fowler, glowing with indignation, "hanging is almost too good for him."

"And yet we cannot take his life in cold blood when he is so helpless," returned Dick. "Possibly we may be able to get rid of him in some way."

They walked on for an hour or more, and there was no change in Turcomatz. He lay upon the back of the camel in an exhausted condition, but awake.

Occasionally he opened his eyes and stared about him in an unutterably miserable way, but as soon as Butterflick came under his observation he closed them again.

On, on they went, until another halt was imperative, and this time they drew aside from the road and camped in a grove of date-trees.

The fruit was ripe and tempting, and they all partook of it but the helpless man, who, when offered one, tightly closed his lips, refusing it.

So they left him in peace, and, stretching themselves upon the sward, by the advice of Dick, they tried to get some sleep.

The heat and the shadow of the trees acted as a sedative upon all but Dick, and soon he was the only one of the party awake.

Turcomatz slept with an apoplectic insensibility, giving out gasps and snorts of the most hideous description.

Dick rose up, and, after testing him in various ways, came to the conclusion that he was really asleep, when he unfastened his waistcoat and took out the pass of the Czar.

"It is a legitimate robbery under the circumstances," he said. "Why should I show consideration to a man who would have been so merciless to us?"

He placed it in a small inside pocket constructed in his own coat.

It was arranged with a double flap, so that anything in the way of papers could be hidden away and escape ordinary inspection.

Then he too began to feel the influence of fatigue and the heat, and, having chosen a soft bank, he stretched himself upon it and fell asleep.

The sun was past the meridian, and slowly it bore down towards the west.

Hour after hour passed, and none of the party on the ground stirred. They were in such a sleep as the lotus-eater enjoys after partaking of his dreamy plant.

The first to awake was Flutterby Fowler.

He yawned, stretched his limbs, opened his eyes, and turned over upon his side. He was in that pleasant condition of mind and body experienced by a healthy man who half awakes from a sound sleep.

"Just forty more winks," he would have said to himself if he had been at home and in bed.

But he was not there, and by degrees it dawned upon him that he was in a very different situation.

Rousing himself, he had a glance around, and, recalling recent events, sat up.

Close by him were Muffins and Butterflick, sleeping the sleep of the weary. A little further off was Dick, as quiet as if the breath of life had left him.

Then he looked for the camel and Turcomatz. They were not there.

With a cry of astonishment he sprang to his feet. He awoke the others, and they sprang up also.

"What is it, Fowler?" cried Dick.

"The camel—Turcomatz!" was the answer.

A search showed that neither were near them. They darted out of the grove and looked up and down the road.

It was barren of all living things.

"Find the tracks of the beast," said Dick.

They examined the road, but could only trace them the way they had come.

The camel must have departed another way.

They found its footmarks in the grove and outside too, showing that it had gone in and out many times, but of tracks leading away from the spot they could find no sign.

In two directions there was a belt of hard, rocky ground, which would leave no trace observable to the ordinary eye.

One led backward, nearly in the direction of the way they came; the other led into the interior of the country.

The camel must have taken one of these roads.

But which? They puzzled over it for a time, but were obliged to give it up.

"It does not matter to us," said Dick. "Our way lies ahead, and we must be getting on. All our stores of food are gone, but we have our arms and a few cartridges. Perhaps they will serve us until we find something to help us on our way."

"It's a horrible fix to be in, isn't it?" asked Flutterby Fowler.

"Say rather an unpleasant predicament," replied Dick; "but I have been as badly placed—and worse—before. We will go on with light hearts, with hope leading the way. Pluck and resolution always win the day."

CHAPTER XV.

THE STRANGE CITY—THE WOMEN AT THE WELL—THE RESULT OF A PANIC.

SOME eight days later our four travellers came in sight of a city that was like one of those magical places we read of in Eastern tales.

At a distance it looked especially beautiful. Right and left spread long lines of square-topped houses, with here and there a fantastic building higher than the rest. In terrace fashion they rose up—to the very summit of a high hill—and there, like a crown, rested a huge castle or palace.

The whole thing was as pretty as white stone, gorgeous-coloured ornamentation, and gilt could make it.

There were domes that shone with gilt as if they had been solid, burnished gold.

Tall towers—slender in column and covered with elegant stone tracery—solid-looking square buildings with massive arched doors and windows, halls that were pierced as if for musketry, fantastic building work everywhere—it was a sight to bring the travellers to a halt, so that the eye might feast upon its Eastern glories.

The eight days had been days and nights of care and watchfulness.

As they travelled along our friends had to draw aside from the road and even hide from the bands of men on horseback they occasionally saw approaching.

The latter act was dictated by prudence and not by fear, for Dick was too good a general to risk a fight which would not be of service to the mission he had in hand, and these bands bore in their persons and accoutrements the unmistakable brand of brigands or marauders.

For the most part they rode like men in a hurry, but whether flying from pursuit or bent upon some murdering and plundering business it was not possible to tell.

Avoiding them was a necessity of the time, and our friends had succeeded in doing it.

Of the camel and Turcomatz they saw nothing, and the conclusion our friends came to was that the brute had made up its mind to go home again, and had set out on a backward journey.

Of the fate of Turcomatz under such circumstances they did not care to speculate.

He might escape with his life by a miracle, or something near it, but the probabilities were that he would die where he was.

It was a grim picture to think of—the scheming Russian borne back a corpse, and the speculations of the natives as to the author of his fate.

But it was all imagination, and Dick observed that it was an idle way of passing the time. "Fix your thoughts ahead," he said.

And so they came to within easy distance of the city, and halted to look at it.

A cautious approach would have been advisable under ordinary circumstances, but Dick felt strong in the possession of the pass of the Czar addressed to the Shah of Shahs.

"The powerful arm of Russian protection overshadows all the East," he said.

"Then I'm bothered if I think much of the East," retorted Butterflick.

Muffins and Flutterby Fowler were both footsore, but they made no complaint, and the prospect of a rest in that charming place quite delighted them.

So on they went, and as they drew near to the city they began to find signs of life.

First of all they came to a well in a hollow, where several women, with veils over the lower parts of their faces, were filling tall stone jars with water.

Some of them had little children by their side, and they were chattering and laughing together when Dick and his followers appeared.

At the sight of them the women appeared to be petrified with astonishment, and the little children buried their faces in the dresses of the women, screaming and bellowing in the most awful manner.

Dick made signs that he did not mean to harm them, and sent forward Flutterby Fowler to try his knowledge of Eastern tongues upon them.

But the moment he began to advance the women cast down their stone jars, and, seizing the children, flew frightened towards the city.

"Well, I'm blessed!" commented Butterflick, "if they musn't be poor-hearted women to be afraid of men. They want a few lessons from Old Sally."

"Yes, mother would wake 'em up," observed Muffins, with a sly glance at Butterflick.

"We must get on before these women have time to alarm the city," said Dick.

They quickened their footsteps almost to a run, but the women had got well ahead of them, and were seen to dash through a gate in one of the walls on the left.

"To the right," observed Dick.

He saw in this direction that the walls of the city were broken down, and, there being no gate to pass, they were less likely to be observed.

The road was a fairly good one, and they hastened along it, listening for the clamour which they expected would arise when the alarmed women began to tell some extravagant story of the strangers approaching.

When within a couple of hundred yards of the ruined wall they came upon an old man tending half a dozen goats, cropping some scanty herbage that grew on the semi-barren soil.

On seeing them he threw up his arms, and, falling flat upon his face, lay stretched out like one dead.

"They have never set eyes on a European before," said Flutterby Fowler.

Dick merely observed "Hurry up," knowing that if once a panic fairly set in he and those with him would not be able to cope with it.

The broken wall was reached, and clambering over some loose stones they entered a portion of the city which showed that it had, for some reason, been a long time deserted.

The houses were in ruins and the streets overgrown with weeds.

As they hurried on in the direction of the inhabited portion of the city they passed ruins that exhibited signs of being once magnificent structures.

But everywhere the destroyer had been at work, hastening the labours of time.

Suddenly Dick stopped short.

"Listen!" he said.

They stood still, and heard a clamouring of voices and beating of cymbals ahead. The noise had aroused the inhabitants of the city.

"Fowler," said Dick, "are you any hand with the Persian tongue?"

"I can read it," replied the tutor.

"Have you ever spoken it?"

"Not with a native."

"Then that won't do," said Dick. "Confound these women! Like all the Eastern race, they see everything through a magnifying-glass. Goodness only knows what story they have gone back with."

That the alarm was now getting general they could hear, and they also saw that in the great castle on the summit of the hill a commotion was going on.

Little dots, which were the heads of men peering over the walls, were bobbing to and fro, and a flag, evidently a signal, was run up on the top of one of the numerous towers.

"We must face it out," said Dick. "I'll trust to the good luck that has never deserted me."

They were going on rapidly all the time, and now the ruined part of the city had come to an end.

A squalid street—alas! how different to what it appeared in the distance—came into view.

In the doorways—dark and wretched in spite of the glorious sun—men and women and children were seen standing.

As Dick advanced into view these groups vanished one by one, uttering strange cries. It was curious, almost ludicrous, to see the effect the coming of strangers had upon them, but at the same time it was serious and aggravating.

Presently a small square was reached, and at the entrance of it Dick stopped and looked around him.

There were several grave-looking men near, walking about in twos and threes, calmly and solemnly discussing some general subject.

An absence of excitement gave rise to hope in Dick's heart.

"Stay here a moment," he said; "I will go forward and try to make friends with them."

Apparently neither he nor his companions had been seen, and when Dick was perceived by two Guetras or Parsees it was obvious that he was not a welcome visitor.

They drew back, staring at him more in indignation than in fear, but still the latter was in evidence.

"Do either of you speak English?" asked Dick.

They said something to him in Persian which he failed to understand, and it was palpable that they did not comprehend him.

He addressed them in French, with the same result, and was about to do so in German when, with an unlooked-for and sudden ferocity, they sprang upon him.

CHAPTER XVI.

OVERPOWERED BY NUMBERS—A PRISON—THE BUILDING ON THE SUMMIT OF THE HILL.

DANGEROUS thing it is to assail a strong man when he is in an irritable mood, and Dick just then was not at all disposed to put up with rough treatment.

As the two Parsees sprang upon him he seized both by the throat. One he shook like a rat, the other he bent backwards, and finally cast him to the ground with a force that must have utterly dazed him.

But, quickly as this had been done, the alarm raised by the other Parsees was quicker.

If one of them had possessed a magic wand he could hardly have filled the square more quickly with a host of men, who fell upon Dick and his friends, as they rushed to the rescue, like a legion of devils.

Dick was a mighty man, but he was mortal.

Though for awhile he threw men about, and scattered them as autumn leaves before the blast, he had to succumb in the end.

Whatever the weaknesses of these people, lack of courage was not one of them.

Though the blows some received were fearful, and more than one man fell never to rise again, they still pressed forward, until Dick, exhausted, was overcome and made a prisoner.

"Let us be wary of dealing with him," said one; "he is not a man, but a god."

They put no bonds upon him, but, forming in a circle, gently pressed him forward.

He looked around for his friends, but could not see them. Casting his eyes upwards, he observed that they were being conducted to the castle above.

He raised his hands and then dropped them in token of submission.

"Of what avail to resist now?" he asked himself, bitterly.

He walked slowly at first, and the crowd of men around him accommodated their pace to his.

When he found his strength returning, and he walked quicker, they did so also.

One thing he noticed, and that was the men were chary of touching him.

Though they kept around him as a guard, a superstitious fear seemed to have assailed them, and contact with a man of such might they most strenuously avoided.

The way up to the summit of the hill was by a series of zigzag paths cut out of the solid rock.

This road was lined with houses and buildings of various descriptions—from the mere stone hovel of the humblest to noble, temple-like structures that were masterpieces of the builder's art centuries ago and are masterpieces now.

Dick saw and noted these things without taking any real interest in them.

All his thoughts were centered on his position and his prospects.

The clouds had gathered thickly enough about him at the very outset of his journey, or what may be considered as such.

All other perils which had beset him sank into insignificance compared to that which encompassed him now.

The worst of it was that not even his great strength could avail him.

Had it simply been a question of a struggle with half a dozen or a dozen men he would have faced them bravely, fought them, and possibly won.

But it was not a mere matter of battle.

He had in a moment of haste assailed two men—possibly of position—and to have carried that resistance further would have been to rouse a whole country against him.

And such a country!

Governed by a tyrant, in a semi-wild state, unknown—or practically so—to Dick, he had need be something more than human to be able to traverse it and live.

While these thoughts troubled him he found himself at the gate of the palace, which he judged it to be by its appearance.

A splendid archway of Moorish architecture reared itself high overhead, and the gates of cedarwood were studded with nails of gold.

They swung back heavily on their hinges, and with his escort he passed through.

That his friends had gone before him he had good reason to believe, but he could see nothing of them in the great hall in which he found himself.

Ranged round it were a number of armed men, and at the upper end was a high chair or throne, with a canopy above it to represent a blazing sun.

The throne was empty, but standing on either side of it were about two score men, who wore dresses of white fine cashmere robes, much in vogue among the Eastern tribes.

Around their waists they had rich-coloured sashes, to which were attached swords with gleaming jewels in the hilts.

It was a magnificent array, but not pleasant to one in Dick's position.

But he held his head up, and looked proudly and defiantly at them all. Whatever might befall him, there would be no yielding on his part.

He was sore at heart for the sake of his friends, whom he bitterly regretted he had been induced to bring with him.

But it was to present the appearance of being a traveller only that he had brought them with him, and now a few timorous, squalling women threatened to upset everything.

Whatever curiosity the men around him might have felt, they did not exhibit it in their faces. There was no more expression in their dark countenances than there would have been in figures of bronze.

He was marched up to within a few yards of the throne, and then a halt took place.

Not a word was spoken, and but for the occasional light rattle of a sword-sheath, as some of the warriors restlessly moved, no sound broke that impressive silence for fully a quarter of an hour.

It was trying to the nerves, but still Dick knew that much would depend upon his bearing.

To have exhibited fear or anxiety would have been to gain the contempt of all assembled there.

So he stood erect, with folded arms, calmly gazing about him, taking no apparent interest in anything around, and showing a stoic's indifference to the presence of danger.

At length the silence was broken by a fanfare of some wild music, the like of which he had never heard before; then the two curtains beside the throne were parted, and a white-bearded man of patriarchal appearance entered.

He had an escort of armed men, who broke into two lines and ranged themselves down the hall as he ascended the throne.

Slowly and with great dignity he assumed his seat, and addressed a few words in a low tone to a scholarly-looking man who stood on his right.

He, in his turn, looked down on Dick Strongbow, and addressed him in passable English.

"Who and what are you?"

"A stranger travelling here, meaning no harm to any, and one who expected more hospitable treatment than I have received," Dick replied.

This answer having been interpreted to the old man on the throne, another question was put.

"As a traveller how comes it, then, that you assault and terrify our women?"

"Pardon me," replied Dick, "but I did not assault or terrify anyone. It was by chance we came upon them."

"You dared to address them?"

"No; they began to cry out, and I made signs that I meant no harm."

So the questions and answers went on until Dick had told his whole story.

He was sorry, he said, that he had shown violence to anyone, but he had been first attacked.

"It may be so," replied the interpreter, coolly, "but if one meets with a wild beast he does not wait to be attacked."

"May I ask," said Dick, "if I am in the country of the Shah?"

"You are in a country ruled by the Vizier Ab Ogah," was the answer.

"Does he owe allegiance to the Shah?"

"That is not a question for you to ask," was the reply. "Your name?"

"Dick Strongbow."

"Who are those men with you?"

"One is the companion of many travels—the other has not journeyed with me before."

"And the boy?"

"A servant of mine."

Another colloquy in an undertone took place between the interpreter and the old man upon the throne. When it was ended the latter signalled to Dick's escort, who closed round him once more, and by signs intimated that he was to leave the hall.

At first he was hopeful of being dismissed and sent on his journey, but when he was escorted by the way the vizier had come he knew that hope must be abandoned.

Through many passages and halls he was conducted until they came to a more meagre portion of the building, and from that to a corridor where there were doors, the nature of which could not be mistaken.

Outside there were huge locks and bolts, and, one of them being opened, Dick was suddenly thrust into a cell-like place and the door closed behind him.

CHAPTER XVII.

DICK STRONGBOW V. IRON BARS—BONE AND MUSCLE WIN THE DAY.

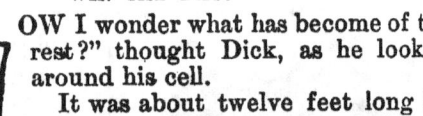

N OW I wonder what has become of the rest?" thought Dick, as he looked around his cell.

It was about twelve feet long by seven feet wide, but not so barren as similar places at home.

Even there the ancient builders had shown their love of art, and on the ceiling and walls the sculptor had left some record of his genius.

At the upper end was a grated window about two feet square. The bars that crossed it were very thick, and looked strong enough to resist any ordinary force that man might bring to bear upon them.

But Dick, in giving them a shake, found they rocked a little. In looking closely at the stonework he saw that it had a tendency to crumble.

"Old Time has done me service so far," he said.

He could see that the removal of the bars would not be so difficult a task as it appeared. Indeed, he felt sure that he could remove them after a few minutes' shaking to and fro.

But the question was, would it be prudent to wait until dark.

He resolved, in any case, to wait until the evening, and then make his effort. Possibly his friends were confined in some adjacent cell with a similar window. If so, he would soon be able to find them.

The bars, though not so tightly fixed as they once had been, would still have held out against any ordinary man. It was Dick's enormous strength that gave him the chance of breaking out.

He thought of the possibility of being hauled again before the vizier, but he resolved to risk that, and if he found himself condemned to death he would give them a test of his powers.

He was visited once in the afternoon, but only by a gaoler to bring him some food.

The man said something to him in Persian, but Dick shook his head to signify he did not understand.

The man then bent his head and gave his neck at the back a chop with his hand. Having done this, he looked up and nodded significantly.

Finally he pointed to the window and slowly dropped his hand.

All this pantomime was interpreted by Dick to mean that he was to be beheaded after dark, but he simply smiled in acknowledgment.

The gaoler bowed, repeated the chopping action, as if he enjoyed it, and left the cell.

Dick found that a very palatable dish of meat and rice had been brought him. It was better than anything he had tasted for a long time, and he enjoyed it as well as he could, under the circumstances, be expected to do.

"Richard himself again," he said, stretching out his arms.

He judged by the angle of the sunbeams which streamed through the window that it was about four o'clock. If he was to be executed after sundown he had three hours to spare.

Not much for what he had to do, so he formed the resolve to begin at once.

After listening intently for sounds outside, and hearing nothing but the murmur of town life below and the occasional clank of some soldier on a distant part of the city walls, he went to work.

Seizing the bars with both his hands, he jerked them quickly to and fro.

Every movement broke away some of the stone-work, and in less than the three minutes he gave himself he found they could be dragged out of their sockets.

Each bar was distinct from its fellow, and he resolved to keep one as a weapon. In his hands it would be very formidable.

Drawing himself up, he carefully put his head out of the opening and looked around and below.

There was nothing to trouble him on either side, and such of the people as he could see beneath him were little more than ants in appearance.

Then out he crept, and dropped upon the hard rock a few feet away without sustaining any injury, although he was obliged to alight upon his hands.

But Dick had a good many little tricks of the circus at his finger-ends, and at a pinch could be as much at ease upon his hands as on his feet.

Having righted himself, he quickly scanned the castle walls above him, but saw no sentry or sign of human being.

Then his eyes roamed to the right and left, and he found, as he expected, evidence—in the form of barred windows—of other cells adjoining the one he recently occupied.

Anon came the question—"Were they occupied, and, if so, by whom?"

Dick had to proceed on his tour of discovery with caution. Any other person save his friends, on finding him outside, might give the alarm, and if Dick personally succeeded in getting away the others would have to suffer.

Keeping close to the wall, and crawling on his hands and knees, he got to the next window, where he stopped and listened.

Somebody was inside, croning a sort of chant or song. The voice was not European, and Dick went on.

The second cell was empty—not so much as the rustle of a dress told of an inmate—so he pursued his way to the next, and the next, until at length he came to a window larger than the rest, and there he found those he sought.

They were conversing together inside the cell close to the bars—not of themselves, but of him.

"You talk of his doing wonders, Mr. Fowler," Butterflick was saying. "I tell you that he didn't half lay on. He seemed to me to be treating 'em tenderly."

"You, of course, are the best judge," replied Fowler, "but to me it seemed the work of a giant. Still, he certainly said it would be wise if we were moderate in showing a hostile spirit."

"He should have seen the governor among the diamond-diggers, shouldn't he, Muffins?" said Butterflick.

"Rather," replied Muffins; "that *was* a treat. Why, he threw some of the men up so high that they looked like dolls in the air."

"Dear me—marvellous!" exclaimed Flutterby Fowler.

Dick thought it was time to make his presence known, and so cut short the kindly exaggerations of Muffins and his adopted father.

Raising his head until it was almost level with the window-sill, he said, quietly—

"Not a word—not a sound; keep quite still. I am here."

There was little need for the injunction to be still, as the simple sound of his voice, so unexpected, fairly deprived them all of breath and motion.

He raised his head above the window-sill, and they saw his face.

"It *is* him!" gasped Butterflick, "and not his ghost."

"Steady, all," said Dick, "while I remove these bars."

"Can I help you?" asked Flutterby Fowler

"Murder! man," replied Butterflick; "no more than a bluebottle could."

"Be quiet, please," said Dick.

He quickly examined the bars, and by their appearance he thought they seemed firmer than those in his own cell, but as a set-off the window was wider, while, the bars being larger, a greater leverage could be obtained.

He had just laid hold of them when a fanfare of music was sounded somewhere inside the castle. The sound of it reached them all, and Dick, guided by experience, judged that the vizier's court was assembling again.

That the music portended little good to him or his friends he did not doubt. What he had to do must be done quickly.

Then Flutterby Fowler saw something occur that staggered him and—as he verily believed at the time and afterwards—made his hair stand up. The memory of it haunted him in his dreams.

He saw Dick seize the bars, and, with an effort that made the veins upon his forehead stand up like cords, twist and wrench out three of them, crushing and splitting the stonework as if it had been sugar-candy.

"The thing's done," he heard Dick say, in a quick, gasping voice. "Come out—all of you—quietly."

Fowler, on getting outside, saw Dick sitting on the ground with his head between his hands and his elbows on his knees.

"You have hurt yourself, I fear," he said.

"It is nothing," replied Dick, in a whisper. "I shall be better in a minute."

They stood by for a little while, and then he looked up, his face deadly pale.

"I am right now," he said. "You are alarmed, Fowler—but needlessly, I assure you. These efforts overcome me for a while, but the reaction sets in and I am strong again."

"It is most wonderful," said Flutterby Fowler. "How can flesh and blood and muscle stand the strain ?"

"Because the splendid machinery with which I am blessed is perfect," replied Dick, raising his arms in exultation. "Oh ! what a glorious sense of power comes over one as strong as I am when called on to do his utmost. But steady—down, all of you. We must look for a means of safe descent to the level ground below."

CHAPTER XVIII.

THE ESCAPE FROM THE PALACE—AN ANXIOUS TIME—HORSES—FLUTTERBY FOWLER RIDES AND SUFFERS—THE LONE HOUSE.

HILE all this was going on a native sentry, by the main gate of the palace, had been keenly listening to certain faint, unwonted sounds that reached his ears.

They were scarcely perceptible, and had nothing to do with anything below. They were, in fact, the sounds of breaking which inevitably accompanied Dick's efforts and the murmur of the voices of his friends. The sentry was a dull fellow—a shepherd of the plains—who who had been called upon, conscript fashion, to give five years' soldier's service to the vizier.

He was a dreamy, silent man, who had acquired the habit of dull speculation in the things he saw and heard, so he speculated on the noises that floated to his ears, and not having the wit to guess their import he decided to gain the evidence of his eyes.

Dick was hidden from his view by an abrupt turn of the palace walls, about midway between them, and from the same cause the sentry was hidden from them.)

But they could hear the clanking of his arms as he strode leisurely along, and knew a danger was approaching.

Dick bade his friends lie close to the wall, while he advanced to the corner and awaited the coming of the sentry.

There was no alternative, it seemed, but to kill the man, and a more unwelcome task could not have been offered to Dick. Still, it was his life or theirs, and there was no time for reasoning.

On came the unsuspecting sentry, expecting to find nothing more than that some animal had strayed to the summit of the hill and had been scratching at the walls.

He swung heavily round the bend, and then—there was a hand upon his throat.

What an awful grip !

The man swooned instantly, and as he fell in a heap at Dick's feet he loosened his hold.

A glance at the quiet face, handsome and picturesque in its way, was enough.

"I cannot kill him," said Dick to his companions, who had crept up. "Remove his arms, and gag and bind him as well as you can, Butterflick."

Assisted by Muffins, this work was soon done, and Dick, raising the man, walked back and thrust him through the cell window, then dropped him on the floor as if he had been a doll.

"It is marvellous—amazing," said Flutterby Fowler.

Then he felt his own muscle, and a very dissatisfied expression passed over his face.

To take the public road from the great gate would be courting discovery and possibly recapture.

But Dick had now made up his mind to temporise no more.

"If we are discovered," he said, "and attacked, fight it out."

He gave them each one of the bars, and bade them avoid using firearms until very closely pressed. Then he began the descent of the rugged hill.

It was little more than a barren rock on the summit and in places very precipitous.

The surface was also much broken up, but this was an advantage, as the huge lumps of rock scattered about offered them cover from observation above and below.

They had descended about a hundred feet when they came to a place scooped out of the solid rock.

It was neither a cave or a cell exactly, and appeared to have once been favoured with a spring, but it had long been dry.

Possibly it had not been a natural spring, but a sham one got up by priests, who supplied the water from above at given times.

With its original nature we have nothing to do. Dick espied it and thought it would serve for shelter.

"While daylight lasts," he said, "we must hide. Hark ! they have discovered our escape."

That something was wrong above was clear. Voices, the rattle of arms, and the blowing of trumpets were heard, while the sounds of alarm soon found a response below.

They heard the great gates open, followed by the tread of hurrying feet. From the vicinity of the cells came cries of surprise mingled with terror.

There was no scattering of men about the hill, as one might naturally have expected. No ! The pursuers kept together, and Dick shrewdly guessed the reason why.

Only in force would they attempt to recapture a man who had made straws of iron bars.

The city below was like a huge hive stirred with a stick. The rushing to and fro was continuous, and there was a clatter of arms as various parties of armed men started in pursuit of the fugitives.

The prevailing opinion appeared to be that they had descended the hill and got clear away, for by the time darkness had fallen there was quietude below and above.

It was then that Dick and his followers came out of their retreat and began their descent down the zigzag way.

Eve is the hour of the Eastern man's rest, and laughter and song were heard in the houses as they passed.

Flutterby Fowler saw Dick do something that staggered him.

But only dogs were abroad, prowling about for the offal which at this time of the day is cast into the streets.

All was not so quiet in the city proper, for, like other places, it had its loose characters, and there were a few abroad—roystering young blades and generally questionable characters.

They avoided two or three parties of this description by stepping into gateways, but at last ill-luck brought them face to face with three men, who suddenly emerged from a café.

Even these they might have passed unnoticed but for the light that streamed from the open door. It seemed to reveal the attire of our friends.

"The escaped prisoners!" yelled the foremost man.

Dick sprang upon him and hurled him through the doorway. In quick succession the other two followed him, so that they all lay in a heap upon the floor.

"Skittles!" exclaimed Butterflick, delighted.

"Hurry on," said Dick, "through the ruins and into the open country. It is our only chance."

The shouting inside the café was prodigious, and cries were heard in every direction as men hurried up to learn what was the matter.

Dick, as swift of foot as he was strong in the arm, led the way, and the others kept up with him as well as they could.

He would soon have distanced them had he not heard sounds of distress and accommodated his pace to theirs.

The ruined part of the city was reached, and with the starlight for their only guide they hastened on. Presently Dick saw the gap in the wall by which they had entered and dashed through.

Across a broad patch of half-cultivated ground he hurried, and soon struck the road. All held their peace, as breath, in the case of three at least, was getting scarce.

It was certain they had thoroughly outpaced their pursuers, for the clamour of pursuit was far behind them, but one would hardly look for it on foot beyond the walls.

Dick dropped down to a walk, and little by little the breathing power of all returned. Flutterby Fowler, the last to come round, declared that he had never run half so fast or so far before.

Dick enjoined silence for the present, and, the road being covered with a soft, sandy substance, they made little noise as they strode along.

Presently they heard the jangling of the arms of horsemen.

"A pursuing party returning," said Dick. "Now, if they are not too many and we are bold enough, might we not possess ourselves of horses to ride?"

"I'm game for anything under a dozen," said Butterflick.

"And I am prepared for anything and everything," said Flutterby Fowler, brandishing his iron bar.

Muffins said nothing, but he moistened his right hand and grasped his weapon with the air of an ancient knight who meant to win or die.

"Butterflick and Muffins, that side of the road," said Dick ; "Fowler, you stop with me this side. Do nothing until you see me make my rush ; then go for a horse, lay hold of the bridle, and knock the rider out of the saddle."

The jangling drew nearer, and mingled with it they could hear the voices of men talking angrily.

As the party came into view Dick could see there were six riders, and they were eagerly disputing something he, in his ignorance of the language, could not understand.

"Leave the first two to me," whispered Dick to Flutterby Fowler ; "you take the third. Hit him hard—don't be squeamish—and be sure you don't give him time to draw. If you do you will be a gone coon."

Jingle, jangle, with wordy wrangle, on came the men.

"They are talking of us," whispered Fowler. "I heard the word 'English.' I think they are disputing whether we have got clear away or are still hiding in the city."

"They will soon know all about it," said Dick, grimly.

When the two foremost men were abreast of Dick he leaped out upon the first man.

Seizing him by the foot, he shot him out of the saddle, so that he fell to the ground several feet from the horse.

The next man received a similar attention so soon afterwards that he practically fell at the same moment.

Both laid where they fell—unconscious.

Meanwhile Flutterby Fowler had gone for his man and made a hash of the job.

He aimed a blow at the soldier, but missed him and struck the horse upon its haunches.

The result was that it kicked, plunged forward, and fell in a heap with its rider and the gallant Flutterby.

Butterflick, more expert in war, had unhorsed his man, but Muffins failed.

For the two rearmost men were quick to see that something was wrong, and turning their horses' heads they put them at the wall lining the road, over which they leaped and disappeared.

"Come here—take these horses," cried Dick to Muffins. "Quick!"

Muffins ran up, seized the bridles, and Dick went to the aid of Flutterby Fowler, who was rolling about the ground with his dismounted enemy in close embrace.

"Give in," Dick heard him say, "or you shall have no quarter."

In reply the Persian tried to bite, and did succeed in getting hold of the brim of Flutterby Fowler's soft felt hat.

Dick stooped down, and pinioning the Persian's arms to his side lifted him up from the ground.

Flutterby Fowler, clinging to him like a wild cat, had to be lifted too, until Dick cried out—

"Let go. I have him, Fowler."

Then the little man relaxed his hold and dropped upon the ground, panting.

"Remember," he said, "I didn't give in to him."

"It's all right," said Dick ; "look to his horse. It's getting up."

The horses, although noble-looking creatures, were very docile. A grasp of the reins sufficed to hold them.

Dick took the man he held to the roadside, and cast him as far as he could over the wall.

Then he returned for the one Butterflick had unhorsed and was holding.

It was better than killing them, and they were totally incapacitated for anything but staring wildly about them for fully ten minutes afterwards.

"Can you ride, Fowler?" asked Dick.

"I can try," was the answer.

"Then up you go."

He gave him a leg into the saddle, and then went over to the two horses held by Muffins.

"Get up," he said, relieving the boy of his task.

Muffins, nimble as a monkey, slipped into the saddle, and Dick mounted also.

Butterflick had got into his seat somehow by this time, and was "whoaing," his horse like an experienced rider.

"Follow me," cried Dick, "and stick to the saddle as if you were born in it."

The horse he rode was a magnificent, cream-coloured one, with a long mane and tail of pure white. The other horses were coal black.

Away they went, Dick leading, all exultant in their having so far made their escape, but, as far as Butterflick and Fowler were concerned, feeling very precarious in the region of the saddle.

Butterflick leant back until his toes were under the horse's neck and his head not far from the tail. Flutterby bent his legs up the other way, and utilised the mane as a steadier.

Both had their eyes half shut and their teeth set. They meant to stick where they were unless moved by an earthquake.

Dick, of course, was a splendid rider.

When on a horse he looked like part of it, and Muffins was one of those boys who had the aptitude of a jockey in his veins.

To him the ride was an exhilarating thing.

Two miles of ground or thereabouts was covered, and then they drew rein by Dick's command.

"Be silent," he said, "and let us hear if we are pursued."

There were many voices in the distance, but none of them loud enough to tell of immediate danger.

No sound of horses' hoofs reached the ear; but this was not an assurance of safety, for the soft road deadened the sound of the unshod feet of the animals.

To put a good distance between them and the strange city was Dick's first object, and once more they rode on.

But a few miles more had been traversed when a groan from the rear startled the leader.

He pulled up his horse and asked what was the matter.

"It's Mr. Fowler, sir," replied Muffins.

The tutor was lying on the neck of the horse, and both his legs were dangling down one side of it.

"Don't mind me," he said, faintly, "but ride on. I shall be able to overtake you presently."

"But we cannot go on without you," replied Dick. "Are you in any pain?"

"Yes, but not of a vital sort," answered Flutterby Fowler. "You see, I am not used to riding, and the saddle is so confoundedly rough that—you understand."

"Yes," answered Dick, checking a tendency to laugh, the more readily because he knew that the tutor's injuries, though common to all riding novices, were painful.

"I think I could ride side-saddle for a little while longer," observed Flutterby.

"Very well," said Dick; "every mile is, of course, important. We will go on until we come across some place of shelter. I will lead your horse while you keep hold of both crupper and pommel, and then no harm will come to you."

Screwing up his lips, Flutterby Fowler prepared for the further torture of the journey.

He must have suffered, but no sound escaped him, and he did not so much as open his lips.

The rest were silent, too, for safety's sake, and so they rode on for a few miles more, when they came to a building standing aside from the road, with a window lighted up.

"It is a lone house," said Dick, "and there can be little to fear. If we are refused shelter we can only go on. I will see what sort of hospitality we may expect."

Giving the bridle of the tutor's horse to Butterflick, he turned the head of his own towards a path that led from the road to the building.

It was well kept, and as he drew near the house Dick saw that it was of greater extent than he supposed it to be. The frontage was not considerable, but its length went back for sixty feet or more.

It was an unglazed window through which the light shone, and Dick, hearing talking in a low tone going on, thought it would be permissible for him to look in before knocking.

He saw in a room richly hung with tapestry about a dozen fellows of somewhat villainous aspect, gathered in a circle, in the centre of which was a heap of spoil—silk and jewels.

He inferred from their manner that they were discussing the division of the same, and feeling this was hardly the place he required, he was about to leave when a horse in a stable at the back whinnied.

Immediately Dick's horse responded with a loud neigh.

After that any attempt to get away, with Flutterby Fowler in his tender condition, was not to be thought of.

The men were already on their feet, and Dick, taking the bull by the horns, did not wait for them to come out, but loudly knocked at the door.

CHAPTER XIX.

THIEVES' HOSPITALITY—A TREACHEROUS PLOT—THE BITER BIT.

"HAVE you any place where I could sleep?" calmly asked Dick of the first man who presented himself in the doorway.

The others, to the number of nearly a dozen, crowded behind him, looking out loweringly upon the visitor—an ugly crew.

The man turned to those behind him and said something in an undertone. Immediately afterwards one of the rearmost of the gang was pushed to the front.

He came unwillingly enough, and when he reached the doorway his face was black with a scowl, and his hand rested on a huge knife in his sash.

"You are English?" he said.

"Yes," replied Dick.

"How came you here?"

"I am travelling with some friends."

"How many?"

"We are four in all."

"And what do you want ?"

"A place to rest in for a few hours."

These questions and answers were rapidly exchanged, and then the man who spoke English made a remark to his friends, who growled back a reply.

Once more he turned to Dick.

"We are all poor men," he said, "and cannot afford to take in strangers for nothing."

"I can pay," replied Dick, whose money, thanks to his secret pockets, was still safe about him.

"Well, we will see. Let your friends advance."

Dick hailed the others, and they came slowly down. Meanwhile some of the gang had returned to the interior of the house. Dick guessed they had gone to clear away the valuable things he had seen them inspecting, and he subsequently discovered he was right.

A glance at the rest of the party seemed to satisfy the men, for he who spoke English bade them dismount.

"Enter," he said. "We will see that your horses are well cared for."

Four of the men came and took the horses, and our friends were ushered into a room which Dick recognised as that which he had looked into through the window.

But all the silks and jewels had disappeared.

"The best we can give you," said their guide. "Remain here awhile and we will bring you something to eat."

He and two or three who had followed him vanished, and our friends were left to themselves.

The faces of Butterflick and Flutterby Fowler wore a dubious expression, which Dick readily understood.

"You wonder at my stopping here ?" he said.

"Well, I do—a little," replied the tutor. "I don't like the look of these fellows at all."

"No, more do I," said Dick ; "but there was no help for it It was the neighing of the horses that betrayed me. We could not have got away."

"You could—but I could not," returned Flutterby Fowler, sadly. "I feel sorry that I ever thrust myself upon you. Why not have gone on and left me? Better one should perish alone than all."

"We aint dead yet," interposed Butterflick. "I feel I am about equal to half a dozen of them chaps, murderers as they look."

"Well said," replied Dick. "I am not at all sure they mean us mischief. But we shall see."

"There's two of 'em talking outside," said Muffins, who was standing near the window.

"You have good ears," whispered Dick to Flutterby Fowler; "go and listen. Perhaps you will understand their language. It is quite unknown to me."

"I will," said the tutor, "and you had better keep on chatting with Butterflick."

Dick Strongbow saw this was good advice, and entered into a conversation with Butterflick on matters of a light nature.

Butterflick was keen enough to take the cue, and, Muffins joining in, they kept up a conversation on nothing in particular for five minutes or so.

Meanwhile Flutterby Fowler, crouching near the window, listened to the men talking outside.

They stood a few feet away, speaking without reserve, feeling safe in using their native tongue.

After awhile they departed, and Flutterby Fowler came back to the middle of the room.

Standing with his back to Butterflick and Muffins, he looked Dick quietly in the face.

"They were talking about the horses and ourselves. master," he said. "We are to have supper directly."

"It can't come too soon," rejoined Butterflick. "What say you. my son ?"

"I could eat anything," replied Muffins.

Dick saw there was something behind the words of Flutterby Fowler, which was reserved for him alone. and he drew a little aside, the tutor following him.

There being no chairs, Butterflick and Muffins, both rather tired, were lying upon the floor, stretching themselves out, with their hands clasped behind their heads.

"Had you better not sit down ?" said Dick.

"I will," returned Flutterby Fowler, "but I am terribly sore. Who would think that riding was such a trying ordeal to the novice ?"

"You will be all right to-morrow, Fowler. The soreness will soon wear off."

"We are to have bread and wine," said Fowler, in a low tone, "and the wine will not be good."

"Drugged ?" queried Dick, sententiously.

"Yes, and when we are asleep they will cut our throats, take what we have got, and clear out," said Fowler.

"This, then, I judge, is not their house ?"

"No ; it belonged to a family whom they have murdered, and the bodies of the unhappy creatures are in the stables outside."

Dick shuddered, but it was more with loathing than fear.

"The brutes !" he said, after a pause. "Can we eat the bread of such people ?"

"It is not their bread," replied Flutterby Fowler, "and I fear we must have something."

"You are right," said Dick.

"They will bring in water and wine," Flutterby Fowler continued.

"Water be our drink," said Dick, "and the wine we must dispose of somehow. Give a quiet hint to Butterflick and the boy, and leave the rest to me."

Flutterby Fowler, descending to the floor with extreme caution, stretched himself out beside Butterflick and gave him the required caution, adjuring him to show no signs of suspicion.

"We are fly," was Butterflick's answer.

Dick walked slowly up and down the room, revolving in his mind what he had heard.

It was disquieting anyway, but he was not by any means dismayed. If he judged these men rightly they were no more than a gang of cowardly murderers, who would not stand the test of a struggle with anyone bold enough to resist them.

His plans were soon formed.

A portion of the wine must be disposed of somehow, and the whole party must shortly afterwards sham a heavy sleep.

He, being looked upon as the leader of the party, would be selected for the first victim, and a grim smile passed across his face as he thought of what he would do to the man who attempted to take his life.

The sinister-looking ruffian who spoke English soon reappeared, bearing a tray, on which was placed some black bread, a jug of water, an uncorked bottle of wine, and four metal cups.

"You English must have strong drink wherever

you go," he said, with a feeble attempt to be jocular. "It is all we have left, but you are welcome to it.

"I thank you," replied Dick. "The wine is sorely wanted."

"The house is small," said the man, "and there are many of us. If you must sleep here I will bring some cushions for you."

Dick thanked him, and as he was going out of the room began to pour out the wine.

"Quietly empty the cups out of the window," he said to Flutterby Fowler.

It was done, and having trimmed off the outside of the bread, because it had been touched by the hands of murderous ruffians, Dick gave them a portion each.

The water, at least, was good—cool and sweet—and with the bread sufficed for their immediate requirements.

While eating it Flutterby Fowler emptied the remainder of the contents of the bottle out of the window, taking care to let it trickle down the wall, so that it did not make any sound.

He had barely done this when their attendant and the leader of the gang appeared, each bearing an armful of cushions, which they arranged pillow fashion along one side of the wall.

"It is a poor accommodation," said the chief, "but we leave the recognition to you. Pay us what you please to-morrow."

Once more Dick thanked him, and, the two ruffians having retired, Dick gave the word to occupy their positions.

"We must talk for awhile," he said, "and drop off one by one."

This they did, with the result that presently Muffins and Butterflick really fell asleep.

Both being worn out, they began to snore, the elder performer being especially gifted with nasal power.

Flutterby Fowler could not have slept easily even without the natural anxiety which kept him awake.

The aches and pains that assailed him after his horse-exercise made a latter-day martyr of him.

But in due time he feigned sleep, enduring his anguish with a stoicism that few, judging by his physique, would have given him credit for.

Dick lay very quiet, with eyes so far closed that he seemed to be asleep, but from between the eyelids he could well see all that was in the room.

The lamp was still burning.

It was not a very strong light from our point of view, but it illuminated the room fairly well.

There were two doors to this apartment—one communicating with the outer passage and the other leading to the interior of the building.

The latter as yet had not been opened, and Dick knew nothing of what might lie beyond it.

Some time elapsed—possibly about half an hour—and then Dick heard a sound like that of persons whispering behind this door.

There was also a faint chink of steel.

"Now must I, if ever, rely upon these strong arms of mine," thought Dick.

The door opened an inch or so, and through the interstice thus made he could see a dark, glittering eye.

Butterflick and Muffins were now in the full heat of a snoring competition. Flutterby Fowler lay as still as a mouse.

Another inch and two eyes were seen beyond the door, also a dim outline of evil, eager faces.

A hand appeared, and the door was opened sufficiently for a man to enter.

Then the English-speaking ruffian glided in.

He stood just within the room, with his hand behind his back, looking around him as if he had stepped in to see that his guests were safe and well.

Then he pushed the door wide open.

A motion of his hand warned the others not to be hasty in their advance, then with a swift, quiet step he advanced upon Dick.

He knelt down, and his hand was raised to strike, when Dick leaped up and seized him by the throat.

One nip and his worthless life was taken out of him, and Dick was upon his feet.

Fowler, forgetting his anguish, rose up also.

Dick dashed the body of the man he had slain in self-defence into the thick of the startled crew and then went for them.

"Bring the lamp here," he cried to Flutterby Fowler.

His voice aroused Butterflick, who started up, and with the ready comprehension of an experienced traveller grasped the situation.

"Here's among you," he yelled, as he threw his burly form into the thick of the struggling mass in the inner room.

Muffins awoke also, but Flutterby Fowler bade him stand back, and with marvellous composure walked to the doorway, holding the lamp above his head.

He there beheld a scene he would never forget to his dying day.

On the opposite side of the room was another doorway, through which the cowardly ruffians were endeavouring to force their way.

What was in their minds we cannot say, but they probably looked upon Dick as something more than mortal—a mighty genie in disguise, come to punish them for their sins.

Dick used no weapon but his arms and hands.

Such terrific blows as he dealt them had rarely been seen by human eyes. Down they went like oxen in the shambles, dead or insensible, until two-thirds of their number were on the floor.

The rest got out of the room somehow, and, yelling with terror, disappeared by a back way out of the house, when they were seen no more.

But they were heard for awhile, uttering cries of alarm as they sped across the country, seeking refuge from that terrible man, like wild beasts hurrying to their lair.

CHAPTER XX.

AFTER THE STRUGGLE—THE ROBBERS' VICTIMS—
TEHERAN IN SIGHT—THE CROWDED ROAD.

LEANING against the wall, momentarily pumped out by the tremendous effort he had made, Dick received the congratulations of his friends.

"I knew we were safe in your keeping," said Futterby Fowler, "and therefore I felt no fear."

"It isn't only his

own strength that comes in," remarked Butterflick, "but he gives strength to others. I feel, when in a row, with Mister Strongbow near me, that I am a giant too."

"We must get away from here," Dick said, as soon as he could speak clearly. "Better sleep anywhere than in this dreadful place. But first let us secure those who still remain alive. Butterflick, you are good at the work ; bind their arms and legs."

Butterflick and Muffins, assisted by Flutterby Fowler, who held the light, secured the limbs of the prostrate men.

They did not examine them, to see who were living or dead, as it was not a congenial task, but secured one and all.

While this was being done, Dick, as was his habit after a great effort, kept as quiet as possible, during which time his exhausted strength returned to him.

Reaction with him was marvellously rapid, and by the time the work of securing the prostrate ruffians—with strips of linen and their own sashes—was done he was almost himself again.

"Bring the light," he said ; "we must find the horses now—and, Muffins, one of those cushions will be useful to Mr. Fowler. Trot it along. We shall not ride far," turning to the tutor, "only until we get out of the foul atmosphere around this place."

They found the way out to the back and turned to a big building behind, which they rightly judged was the stables.

Opening the first door he came to, Dick was about to enter, but hastily closed it again.

"Not there," he said.

The next door was the place they sought. It was a long stable with a dozen stalls, and in addition to their own horses there were half a dozen others of a heavier build, such as might be used for farm work.

They were not, however, so heavy as our English horses employed for the same purposes.

"A well-to-do family lived here," said Dick, "a father, mother, and three children, all lying in the adjoining shed—a horrible sight. Butterflick, set the other horses free. If left behind they might starve. Our own appear to have been fed, the rascals looking on us as dead men and our horses as their property, I suppose."

He prepared a saddle with a cushion strapped upon it for Flutterby Fowler, and as soon as possible all were on the road again.

Butterflick and Muffins, refreshed by their short nap, were ready to ride on all night, and Flutterby Fowler was too eager to get away to think of sleep. Dick, at a pinch, could be indifferent to it.

Two hours' riding carried them sufficiently far away from the dreadful place, and then, having found a spot sheltered by trees, they tethered their horses and threw themselves down on the ground.

Oblivion came to them almost instantly, and undisturbed they slept till sunrise.

And now came several uneventful days, or what they considered so.

Guiding their course by the sun, Dick bore away in the direction of Teheran, halting here and there at some lone house to purchase food for themselves and horses.

Their arrival always caused alarm, and more than once the doors were barred against them ; but they invariably succeeded, by making peaceful signs and exhibiting money, in getting the good-will of the people.

Two small towns came in their way, but these they rode through in the night.

The villages, for the most part, were a number of scattered houses, deserted in the daytime by all save the women and children, who hid away until the alarming strangers had passed by.

Flutterby Fowler got used to the saddle, and the horses, by careful management, were kept in good condition.

On the evening of the eighth day they saw before them, at the end of a wide, fertile plain, a great city, and they knew that Teheran was in sight.

"We must enter it to-morrow on foot," Dick said.

They camped in a rice-field, where a line of trees shielded them from the high road.

The horses were relieved of their saddles, and, with a pat for a good-bye, set free to roam where they willed.

Delighted with their freedom, they kicked up their heels and galloped away.

The time had come when Dick would have to use the pass that belonged to Turcomatz, for on entering the city he would certainly be called upon to give some account of himself.

He had full reliance on its potency, because he knew the Shah was afraid of his neighbour the Czar, as a little tyrant is always terrorised over by a big one.

They arose early. partook of some simple food they had with them, washed and made as good a toilet as they could on the banks of a small stream, and then set out on the high road.

Ere they had got far they found themselves journeying with others, some on foot, some in carts drawn by bullocks, and all in holiday attire.

The women had their faces veiled from the throat to the eyes, and many a glance of mistrust was cast at the travellers as they strode along.

By and bye the number of wayfarers increased, and personages of greater importance than the peasantry mingled with the throng.

Haughty men in authority galloped by, not deigning to draw rein even for the children who were in the road.

It was for those on foot to get out of the way or take the consequences.

There was much crying out of mothers as these horsemen passed, but no accident happened, although some of the youngsters had a close shave.

"Some great event is taking place to-day," said Dick.

"Probably the feast of the Sun," replied Flutterby Fowler ; "the Persians worship the orb of day."

Thicker and thicker grew the wayfarers, until there was quite a crowd, and progress became a matter of difficulty.

But one of the gates of the city was at hand, and there it was quite a crush, such as one might expect at the pit doors of a popular theatre.

Any attempt to inspect those who entered the place would have been futile, and without let or hindrance our adventurers went through with a rush into Teheran—the chief city misruled by the Shah.

———

CHAPTER XXI.

THE SHAH AND HIS WIVES—THE PRIESTLY LISTENER—
DISAPPEARANCE OF FLUTTERBY FOWLER — DEATH
BY FIRE.

OVELTY is charming even to the most exceptional traveller, and the sight of the streets of Teheran had an inspiring effect on our friends after their experience of the country.

The whole place was alive, for it was a great day at Teheran. The Shah, after a sojourn abroad and a long retirement in his palace, was coming out to show his august person to the people.

It was Flutterby Fowler who gathered this much from the talk he overheard among the crowd.

Dick's lip curled with contempt.

"One would think they were here to greet a benefactor and a friend," he said, "instead of the foulest tyrant that ever blotted the earth's surface with tyranny and cruelty."

"He is more a monster than a man," returned Flutterby Fowler.

They were standing on the rough footway—for Teheran, as yet, is not paved like the more civilised cities—unconscious that two sombre-faced men, clad in the long robes of the priests of the Temple of the Sun, were listening to them.

Evidently, by the angry gleam of their eyes, they understood what was said.

After a few whispered words one of them glided away, and the other remained to keep watch over the men who had unconsciously been guilty of the highest of high treasons by speaking insultingly of the one most puissant Shah.

Some great pageant was approaching, for now a number of soldiers were engaged in clearing the street, not with "By your leave" in words, but with blows, as one would drive ahead a pack of wild dogs.

Whips were cracked and sticks plied with vigorous hands upon the shoulders of men and boys and such women as there were in the streets, while the soldiers were crying out something which Dick could not understand.

"What are they saying?" asked Dick.

"Faces to the wall," replied Flutterby Fowler. "The wives of the Shah are coming."

"I have read somewhere that it is death to look upon the wives of the Shah," said Dick. "I suppose, for the sake of peace, we had better comply with the rule."

It was explained to Butterflick and Muffins what the hubbub meant, and as the people around them were all turning their backs to the centre of the street they did the same.

"They couldn't make more fuss if my old Sally was coming," said Butterflick; "but she wouldn't want me to clear the way—she would do it herself."

On went the horde of street-whippers, belabouring whoever came within their reach, whether they were obeying the order or not.

Dick's eyes flashed full of scorn upon a people who could endure such treatment and come hither in their thousands to fawn upon the man who tyrannised over them.

A clatter of horses' hoofs, more blows, and shrieks, and curses that were but whispers, and the wives of the Shah were past.

Immediately after there was a commotion near where Dick was standing, and he was severed from his friends.

He caught a glimpse of Muffins and Butterflick being thrust against the wall of a house, and the latter hitting out, to the serious derangement of the tall head-gear of many grave Parsees, but Flutterby Fowler he had lost sight of altogether.

A moment later and the Shah himself, on a cream-coloured horse, led by two men in gorgeous uniform, came riding by.

In close attendance upon him were a horde of generals and high officials, on all of whom the people might lawfully feast their eyes.

Dick did not envy the Shah.

On his dark, sallow face was stamped the most unendurable of all human feelings—satiety.

All pleasures had been weighed in the balance—weighed pretty frequently, too—and found wanting.

His face was but an index to the countenances of the men behind him.

Not one was illuminated with a single ray of joy.

After the Shah was gone the greater part of the crowd melted away, and Dick had an opportunity to look about him for his friends.

Butterflick and Muffins, both in a heated condition, were there, but Flutterby Fowler had vanished completely.

A question to Butterflick elicited an important fact. He had seen the tutor struggling with half a dozen tall men, who had fallen foul of him for some reason.

"I couldn't get at 'em," said Butterflick, "or I would have helped him. But I thought he was holding his own. He hit out like a Tom Thumb of the ring."

Dick was dismayed by this intelligence, but he conceived the idea that the tutor had simply got into trouble with some of the Shah's street gendarmes, who would lock him up for a while and then set him free.

He looked about for some place where he could make inquiries, and, espying a café a little way up the street, resolved to go there on the chance of finding some attendant with whom he would be able to converse in French, English, or German, all of which languages he was master of.

It was a very different café to those of Europe. There were no chairs, but divans, with box-like tables before them, on which were placed cups of coffee.

All sorts of pipes—except the English clay and briar-root—were in active service, for the café was pretty well filled with grave Parsees, who, owl-like, are deep thinkers but very poor talkers.

Dick, on entering, was encountered by an attendant, who bowed low, and asked him "what my lord needed. Speak, for his servant is here to obey."

The air and words were Eastern, but the accent was German, and Dick addressed the man in that tongue.

His face flushed with pleasure, for he was indeed a true son of the Fatherland.

"Ah! mein herr," he said, "it is good to hear the sweet old tongue."

Dick explained to him the loss of his friend and asked him what he thought of it.

"I cannot say here," replied the attendant, casting a quick glance around. "There is an inner room at the back. If you go there I will come to you soon."

And what had become of Flutterby Fowler ?

As Butterflick had seen, a struggle took place between him and a number of tall men, by whom he found himself surrounded.

But it was no vulgar street row, no simple encounter with the street gendarmes.

The men who laid their hands upon him were the emissaries of the priests of the great temple of Teheran, which spreads its massive form and rears its fantastic head high above the heart of the city.

There were eight of the men, and their orders had been to secure both Flutterby Fowler and Dick, but the little man offered them such a sturdy resistance that Dick, fortunately for the emissaries, was unassailed.

No man raised hand or voice on behalf of Flutterby Fowler, although, having been secured with bonds, he was dragged, like the carcase of a dog, through the crowd.

The people, on the contrary, made way for the men with an alacrity that showed they were known and feared, and, half dead, Flutterby Fowler found himself being taken through a low doorway—one of the side entrances to the temple, of which more anon.

Flutterby had no idea whither he was being borne or for what reason he had been subjected to such an outrage, but he knew it was a very unpleasant thing.

"Whatever comes, even though it may be death," he said, "I will meet it like a MAN."

He could hardly believe, however, that anything serious was intended; but thought it possible that he might unconsciously have infringed some rule of the tyrant Shah "for the proper government of his people."

They carried him down a dark passage and then up an incline to a door, where the leading man knocked thrice.

The door was opened, and a flood of light fell upon the hapless prisoner. Before him stood the two priests who had overheard the remarks exchanged by Dick and the tutor.

Flutterby Fowler did not know the men, nor could he form half an idea of what interest they had in his career.

But he understood their tongue, and this is what he heard—

"One only—where is the other?" demanded the elder of the priests.

"This one alone, oh mighty Aldrac, taxed all our strength," replied the foremost man. "He is small, but he has the spirit of a giant."

"Base dogs, were there not enough of you for two?" snarled Aldrac, the priest. "Bring him hither."

Flutterby Fowler was now carried by his arms and legs, and a moment later found himself in a small but gorgeously-furnished temple.

At one end there was an altar with a shining image of the sun above. At its foot was a sort of iron grill, standing upon iron supports, with the materials for a wood fire laid beneath it.

Three other priests stood back, statue like, by the wall.

In a moment it flashed upon the tutor that the latter arrangement was intended for him, and from his head to his feet he turned cold as ice.

His fears were too soon verified, for the men who bore him carried the hapless tutor to the grill and bound him fast to it, hand and foot.

A wave of the hand, and a command "Go, get the other, you dogs !" and the men disappeared.

The priests and their victim were alone in the temple for a little while, the former standing by the altar chanting in a low tone.

Suddenly one of them turned, and, pointing a finger at the silent, despairing Flutterby Fowler, hissed out—

"Whoever revileth the chosen—the King of Kings, the Shah of Shahs—shall perish by fire."

In a niche to the left of the altar there was a lamp burning, and under it a bundle of torches.

Obeying a signal from the priest who had hissed out the doom of the prisoner, one of the others took a torch, lighted it, and, advancing to Flutterby Fowler, stooped down to kindle the wood beneath him.

"I want all my strength now," he thought. "Be strong, my beating heart. Show your contempt for these cowardly torturers by dying mute. Oh ! tongue, be *dumb*."

CHAPTER XXII.

IN THE NICK OF TIME—ALDRAC THE PRIEST MEETS WITH HIS DESERTS.

 OW often have the lives of men hung upon a thread and yet a timely intervention has saved them? It was so with Flutterby Fowler when the high priest of the Temple of the Sun was on the point of setting light to the materials beneath him.

The side door opened and an aged priest came tottering in, holding up his hands.

"Hold—hold !" he cried, in his native tongue, which Flutterby Fowler, as we know, could understand. "What is this ye are doing ?"

"It is a Frank who has spoken ill of the Shah of Shahs," was the answer.

"Who heard his tongue ?"

"I, Aldrac the priest, as I walked abroad."

"It is impossible."

The manner of the old man was very emphatic. Aldrac and the other priests stared at him in trembling surprise.

"You are fools," proceeded the old man, who by his air showed that at least he was in supreme command. "Your ears lie to you. Release the stranger or beware the vengeance of your master."

Demurring no longer, Aldrac hastened with the task of setting Flutterby Fowler free, and the little man stood up, wondering what good fortune had sent him this timely help; but too cautious to exhibit it in his face.

Maintaining a rigid silence, he looked round him with a composure which, under the circumstances, was very creditable to him.

DICK STRONGBOW:

The Diamond King,

AND WONDER OF THE WORLD.

A desperate struggle took place between Butterflick and the Priest.

No. 20.   Price One Penny.

"Will it please my lord," he said, in trembling tones, "to pardon the act of one who is at the best a blind fool? He hath mistaken you for another."

"I desire at once to be restored to my friends," replied Flutterby Fowler, "who by this time must be marvelling at my absence."

"The friends of my lord are here," said the old man. "Lo! another fool caused them to be seized, but when he of the royal mien produced the Great Pass from the most puissant Czar the eyes of all were opened."

Flutterby Fowler was beginning to see what had led to his release. The pass of the Czar taken from Turcomatz had done good work.

Maintaining his composure, he simply desired to be taken to his friends, with whom he " would confer on the subject of the outrage he had endured."

Aldrac stood quite still, his eyes alone moving as he glanced from one to the other in doubt and dismay.

"Oh! Murak," he cried, "hear me."

"Speak, Aldrac," answered Murak, "but use your tongue sparingly, for the precious moments fly."

"Forgive me, oh! Murak," said Aldrac, "if I doubt the story that you bring, but this man here is no son of the Czar."

"What matters who he is if he comes with the word of the Czar to save him from the clutches of madmen and fools?"

"He is English, oh! Murak, and the Czar loves not his race."

"Peace!" replied the old man, sternly. "It is well for you that the Shah of Shahs does not hear you. My lord, wilt thou follow thy servant?"

Flutterby Fowler's feelings during this controversy were none of the pleasantest, but, as he had hitherto done, he maintained an external indifference, like one strong in the sense of right and sure to triumph in the end.

Bowing slightly to Murak—who was almost abject in his bearing—he walked out of the temple by the door which stood open.

Murak followed, and was about to close the door when Aldrac came creeping up.

"May I crave leave to make amends to the son of the great Czar by being his servant?" he said.

"It is a timely thought," answered Murak, " and may save thy life. Conduct him to the western chamber, and there leave him."

Aldrac, bending almost double as he passed Flutterby Fowler, took up a position in front and led the way through a long passage to a room of considerable dimensions, but almost barren of furniture. There was an altar at one end.

Here Dick Strongbow, Butterflick, and Muffins were sauntering up and down. As Flutterby Fowler entered they turned quickly towards him, but his staid demeanour and a wink of deliberate intensity gave them the cue to make no demonstration of welcome.

Even Muffins had grasped the fact that in the presence of a Persian priest it was necessary to be cautious.

"I understand," said Dick, gravely, "that you were brought here. It is a very serious mistake."

"For which that man will have to answer," replied Flutterby Fowler, pointing to Aldrac, whose face plainly showed that at last terror had fairly laid hold of him.

"Oh! my lords," he said, "if I erred it was in love of my master. Is it a sin to be faithful to those we serve? Surely, if I had known that thou wert from the great Czar, I would not have defiled a garment of thine by placing my vile hands upon thee."

"Tell him," said Dick, loftily, "that I can promise nothing. And, now we are together again, we must depart at once."

By this time the aged Murak had arrived. He came tottering into the room, and, bowing thrice before he spoke, thus addressed Dick—

"May I crave of my lord a few moments of his time ere he departs? I would see him alone in the adjoining chamber, which is mine own, and none set foot therein unless they are great."

"What good purpose can our interview serve?"

"That my lord will see. I beg him to come, for his sake and mine."

"Let there be no more treachery," said Dick, sternly, " or, by the strong hand of a great ruler, all shall suffer. Lead on, old man, and you, Butterflick, keep guard over that fellow "—pointing to Aldrac—"while I am gone."

"I'll see to him," replied Butterflick, taking up a position at the side of the dismayed priest. "If he attempts to budge an inch I'll wring his neck."

Dick and the old priest left the room, and the door closed behind then.

"Now, Mr. Flutterby," said Butterflick, "what game have they been up to with you?"

Flutterby Fowler, who had taken down a sword from the wall, where it was hanging, and was examining its superb make, answered quietly enough—

"Oh! that bearded idiot intended to roast me alive."

"Did he, now? Dern his cheek!" said Butterflick. "Muffy, my son."

"Yes, dad."

"Bring that 'ere box yonder over here. It's open, and there don't seem to be anything in it."

The box he named was a strong chest, somewhat heavy, but as it stood only a few feet away Muffins managed to drag it to where his adopted father and the priest were standing.

Aldrac's restless eyes wandered from the box to Butterflick, and back again, in quick succession, but not a word escaped his lips.

"Get in," said Butterflick. "You are just the make and shape of a Jack-in-the-Box. It's dull work standing here doing nothing, so jump in. Give him a prod with that sword, Mister Fowler."

Flutterby, who owed Aldrac a bit of a grudge, complied with his request, and the dig he gave the priest sufficed to send the point of the sword through his robes. He started violently, but made no movement towards the box.

"Now, Jack, will you get in?" said Butterflick. "Just another touch, Mister Fowler."

As Flutterby Fowler touched him again, less gently than before, Aldrac, with a hissing sound, turned upon him, drawing a dagger from the concealment of his upper garment.

This was what Butterflick wanted. He had excited the priest to resistance, and with a joyous laugh he went for him.

One blow dashed the weapon from his hand, and a second one between the eyes sent him staggering back into the box.

He fell in, head and shoulders first. Butterflick

coolly seized his legs and turned them over as if they had belonged to a doll.

"Down with the lid, Muffy," cried Butterflick

Muffins ran round to lower it, but Aldrac fought and kicked like a wild cat, overturning the box in his struggles.

His head and shoulders came out, but Butterflick jammed down the box over him, pinning the furious priest to the floor.

"Keep guard over the door, Mister Fowler," gasped Butterflick; "I mean to get him in, dern him! He's a born Jack-in-the-Box. I'll have him in, and shut him up, alive or dead. Who's he to burn men alive?"

He relaxed his pressure on the box, and Aldrac immediately tossed it off him and endeavoured to rise, but Butterflick threw his whole weight upon him and held him fast.

"When I undertake a job," he said, "I carry it through. Muffy, right the box. I've got him."

Muffins turned the chest over, and stood ready to drop the lid at the right moment. Then ensued a desperate struggle between the priest and Butterflick.

The latter was by far the stronger man, and strength prevailed.

Limp and exhausted, Aldrac was at length got into the box—knees and nose together—and the lid jammed down.

It closed with a click, that showed it fastened with a spring.

"There! I've carried my point," said Butterflick, as he tried the lid and found it fast. "I've made a Jack-in-the-Box of him, and there he'll stop till some of his pals let him out."

"Won't he smother in there?" asked Flutterby Fowler.

"Not a bit on it," replied Butterflick, examining the lid; "there's two holes in the top. It's a sort of eel-box, and he's a eel—listen to him wriggling. Now what shall we do with him?"

"There's a bit of a trapdoor over there, dad," said Muffins, pointing to the far end of the room.

"Just see what it is, Mister Fowler, will you?" asked Butterflick, who had seated himself on the chest.

Flutterby Fowler and Muffins walked to the end of the room, where there was an iron ring in the floor.

With their united efforts they succeeded in raising a slab of stone. Beneath it was a flight of stone steps, and below they could hear the rush of water.

"A stream or river runs along here," said Flutterby Fowler.

"I can see a boat," cried Muffins, eagerly. "It's tied to the steps below."

"What a horrible place!" exclaimed Flutterby Fowler, shuddering.

"It's good enough for this warmint," replied Butterflick, coolly. "Stand clear—we'll put him into the boat and set him afloat."

"But, Butterflick—"

"Now you leave him to me, Mister Fowler. Hang it! is a man like this to get off scot free? Not if I knows it. Anyway, we give him a chance for life, and that's more than he intended to give you. Don't bar the way, sir, as the job's got to be done."

Flutterby Fowler stood aside. Why should he show any compassion for the wretch who would have roasted him alive? And was Butterflick not giving him a chance of escape?

"Do as you like with him," said Flutterby.

Butterflick dragged and pushed the chest to the top of the steps, and from thence expertly worked it down to a broadly-built boat at the bottom.

There were a pair of short paddles in it, which he left there, and loosing the rope he gave the boat a push out.

It was a dark, noisome place, the full width of which could not be made out from where they stood. By the span of the arch Flutterby Fowler judged it was at least sixty feet wide.

The swiftly-moving water caught the boat and carried it away into the darkness beyond.

In all haste they hurried up again into the light of day, and, the stone being replaced, they reached the other end of the room just in time to receive Dick Strongbow on his return.

CHAPTER XXIII.

THE BEGGARS OF TEHERAN—THE JOURNEY RESUMED—A HALT AT A VERY STRANGE INN.

DICK was alone, and there was a smile of triumph on his face, which showed that the interview with Murak had not been an unpleasant affair

"We are free to leave now," he said; "I have passes that will carry us safely through the kingdom of the Shah. But where is the priest?"

"He's gone on a trip," replied Butterflick, evasively, "and he won't be back in time to bid you good-bye."

"It is well he is not here," answered Dick, "for Murak is gone to prepare a fire for him. I endeavoured to turn him from his purpose, but the old man was resolute. The way out is close handy—down this passage and through the priests' door."

A minute later they were clear of the temple and hurrying down a street at the back of it. For some reason, they could not account for, it was completely deserted.

"It's a skewrious thing to me," said Butterflick, "how often you do a kindness to a man when you mean to give him a hoist another way. Fancy my having taken all that trouble to save a Jack-in-the-Box from being roasted!"

Dick turned an inquiring look upon Flutterby Fowler, who explained what had been done with Aldrac. Dick laughed grimly.

"Where there is running water there is an outlet," he said, "and the malicious brute may be spared. But it is a matter that need not trouble us. Our first care is to get clear of Teheran and take the chance of what lies beyond. The way lies north-east from here."

Street after street they passed through without seeing any sign of life save the forms of lean, snarling dogs prowling about in search of food. They were the only scavengers of the place—as they are in many Eastern cities—brutes that never gave vent to an honest bark, but snarled from morn till night.

But they are harmless if let alone, and beyond intensifying their growls and snarls as they passed by they took no notice of our friends.

We may as well state here how it came to pass that Dick became the instrument of the release of Flutterby Fowler.

Dick, Butterflick, and Muffins, when in the *café*, whither they had gone on leaving the crowd, had not long been there when suddenly a whole troop of armed men poured into the room. At the head of them was an officer, who, in passable French, demanded the name of Dick Strongbow.

By way of answer Dick produced the special passport he had in his possession, and on seeing it the officer at once cahnged his tone.

He apologised for having been "misled" by an informant, who had told him that some dangerous characters had come to Teheran, revolutionists from Europe, who were bent on taking the life of the Shah.

In proof that he had not fallen into error without just cause he stated that the priests of the temple had arrested an Englishman and taken him to the Temple of the Sun for examination and, if found guilty, "for punishment."

A few words convinced Dick that it was Flutterby Fowler who had fallen into the dangerous clutches of the fanatical priests, and he acquainted the officer with the fact, plainly stating that if anything happened to his friend very serious results might ensue.

The officer at once hastened to the temple—which was, happily, only a few yards away—and having gained access to Murak, the chief priest of the temple, told him of the "error" into which Aldrac had fallen.

Dick and his companions had accompanied the officer to the temple, and the haughty bearing assumed by our hero had its weight with Murak, who hastened to save the helpless victim from a dreadful death.

The rest, of course, we know. It was a short and lively experience of Teheran, which none had any desire to repeat.

But that was not the sole reason which led Dick to hasten his movements in leaving the city. He feared most the obsequiousness of his new-found friends, who might mention the arrival of the Russian emissary to the Shah.

An introduction to that potentate might lead, and probably would, to the discovery that the real Turcomatz was not before him.

After that the end was pretty sure.

An autocrat so absolute as the tyrant of Persia usually dispenses with any form of trial, and keeps a headsman on hand ready for immediate action. A Shah is high-class company, risky to cultivate.

It was not until they got to the outskirts of Teheran that they met any of the inhabitants, and, their way lying through the beggars' quarters, they were saddened and horrified with the sight of such awful monstrosities and cripples as none of them had even conceived in a nightmare-dream.

It is impossible to describe half of them, nor would it be of any service to the reader if we did so. Perhaps the most horrible of all was a distorted, hump-backed dwarf with one eye, and a plain fleshy protuberance where the other ought to have been.

Crooked features, withered limbs, and a hundred other awful distortions of the human form divine crawled about in the sunlight, mumbling for alms and shrieking out curses when their prayer was denied.

"It is like the pictures of Dante's 'Inferno,'" said Flutterby Fowler.

They were almost clear of the town when a figure, presumably that of a woman, judging by the attire, rolled hedgehog fashion out of the door of a house, and, unfolding itself, disclosed a body without neck, the head being stuck upon the trunk in a sickening, horrifying form.

The hands, each with more than its complement of fingers—how many extra none of them attempted to count—were thrust out, and a hoarse, rattling voice shouted—

"Backsheesh!"

Dick cast a coin upon the ground, and the hideous figure closed upon it just in time to save it from a one-legged youth with an enormous head, who hopped out of the same house and pounced down on the woman in an effort to get the money.

The sight was too much for all, and they fled, Dick, the strong and brave, setting the example.

On they ran, till they had left the city behind and stopped not until a grove of palm trees at the bend of the road hid it from view.

"Why is every city of the East filled with these monstrosities?" asked Flutterby Fowler, as he wiped his perspiring brow.

"There certainly seems to be some special curse upon this part of the earth," replied Dick, "and yet it is here that wisdom was born."

"It is a puzzle," said Butterflick.

"Why it's fifty times worse than anything we have at home," remarked Muffins, "for I am familiar with all that can be seen there."

"Let us hasten away and forget the city of the Shah," said Dick.

So resolute were they to bury it in oblivion, if possible, that they spoke of it no more, but kept on until they came to a house by the wayside.

A woman was milking some goats close by, and on seeing the strangers she rose up and put her hands before her eyes.

"Tubal, Tubal!" she cried, "the evil spirits are here."

"Not so, my good woman," returned Flutterby Fowler. "We are but travellers who have need of food, for which we will pay."

Tubal—whoever he was—did not appear, probably objecting to encounter anything uncanny, and it was some time before the trembling woman could be induced to look upon the strangers.

When she did so it was still in doubt, until she saw a piece of money held up before her eyes.

Its magical effect was instantaneously visible. However ignorant and superstitious people may be, they do not believe in shadows from another land walking about with current coin in their pockets.

Recovering herself, she gave them milk and procured some bread from the house.

Dick spoke to her in English, French, and German, but she only shook her head, so Flutterby Fowler tried her in her own tongue again.

"Which way lies Astrabad?"

"No," she answered.

"You do not know it?"

"No."

"Ah! I forgot. Your name for it is Azerbrijan. You know that?"

"Yes, yes," she answered, eagerly. "Great city—far—so many days."

She threw up her hands, opening and closing them twice, thereby showing that she meant it would take twenty days to reach their destination.

"Persian pace," said Flutterby Fowler; "we ought to do it in ten."

He next asked her if there was an inn on the road where they could stop.

A nod of the head and an outstretched finger was the reply.

"How far?"

She held out one finger and laid another upon the middle of it. Half a day's journey.

"Two hours for us," said Flutterby Fowler.

They thanked her for what they had and left her. The minute after they disappeared a lithe-limbed, swarthy man, with an evil face, crept out of the house.

"Ah! Ela," he said, "you are in luck. Rich man has been kind to you."

"It is so," she answered.

"Give me the money," growled the man.

"Not so, Tubal," the woman replied; "go get some for yourself. They sleep to-night at the inn kept by your cousin Jah. Is it not enough to have our share of the wealth when the bed of death has fallen upon them? Hasten—the road winds. You have but half the journey to traverse across the plain. Go—prepare in time."

Tubal tightened the sash about his waist, and drawing a deep breath started off at a trot, getting over the ground at a rate that would ensure his being the first to arrive at the inn, provided he did not, like the hare in the fable, take a nap by the way.

Unconscious of having left an ungrateful woman behind them, and having a cut-throat hastening to arrange for their destruction—true Persians both —our friends proceeded gaily on their way.

They had, as far as they knew, a clear field before them and no pursuers.

Should they be fortunate enough to obtain horses they would be in Astrabad in three days—condemned to keep on foot it would be done in ten.

"And then for a short interview with Longimans," said Dick, cheerily; "after that home."

"I wonder what have become of that Turcomatz chap?" asked Butterflick.

"We will leave all our wondering until we get home again," replied Dick, laughing.

In something less than two hours they sighted the inn, having met only two or three dejected-looking peasants by the way.

On every side they saw the half-tilled soil and the neglected buildings and woods—the brand-mark of the tyrant curse over all the land.

The inn itself was a huge, rambling building, very old, and bearing on it the general marks of being inhabited by an impecunious landlord.

As the four travellers drew up at the door a tall, saturnine man came forth, and stared hard at them without any greeting.

"Speak to him," said Dick Strongbow to Flutterby Fowler.

The man turned quickly upon him, saying—

"I understand your tongue—I have been in your land with the Shah, when he paid his first visit to you. Ah! how you grovelled before him, you purse-proud people. He was a fool and arrogant before, but you made him worse—worse!"

"We, personally, know nothing of what you speak," returned Dick. "Are you the landlord of this inn?"

"I am the dog," was the rejoinder, "sentenced by the Shah to keep watch over this kennel."

"We have need of a place of rest and food," said Dick, "for which we will pay."

"Enter," responded the Persian, relaxing a little; "such as I have is yours."

He stood aside and they passed into a class of interior with which they were now becoming familiar.

The great idea of all houses in Persia seemed to be to get shade from the sun. Light was quite a minor consideration.

A big, square room, with one unglazed window high up in a corner, half a dozen bench-like seats, a mat or two, and a hookah. This is what first met their view.

"There are other chambers," said the host from the rear; "this is the common one—for servants."

The superior room to which he showed them was little better, but it was not so barn-like, and there was a table on which meals could be served.

"My lord, supper is being prepared," said the landlord, who every time he spoke became more obsequious.

He seemed desirous of eradicating the first impression made by his churlish bearing.

"Bring us some wine—not uncorked," said Dick; "we have a fancy for drawing the corks ourselves."

"It shall be as my lord wishes—I but live to obey," said the host, as he glided from the room.

Two bottles of wine and drinking-cups were soon placed upon the table, and on being tasted it proved to be good Burgundy.

"I brought it from France," said Jah, "when I travelled with the Shah. Such customers as I have cannot afford to pay for so good a drink."

Supper came in due time—a pair of fowls, rather skinny, but neither old nor tough, a dish of vegetables, mostly artichokes, and some bread and fruit.

To old travellers, hungry after a long journey on foot, it was enough, and more than enough.

Ere they finished the meal night had fallen, and two lamps were lighted in the room.

There did not seem to be any other guests in the house, nor were there any casual visitors to the inn.

As far as they could see, the landlord and themselves were the only occupants of the place.

After a hearty supper signs of being in want of sleep arose. Dick and Butterflick smoked, while Flutterby Fowler and Muffins nodded and dozed. When the pipe of one and the cigar of the other were finished Dick gave the signal for bed.

Jah was close handy, ready to escort them to the upper part of the house, and they now learnt, for the first time, that only one chamber had been prepared.

"My guests are few," said Jah, "and the other rooms are in disorder. But there are four beds side by side."

Dick was not averse to the arrangement. It was better for them to keep together, and the chamber into which they were shown was of considerable size.

It was an oblong square, with the usual open window high up at the end of the room. The ceiling, to Dick's surprise, was of wood.

Side by side four beds were placed—they were only mats on the floor, with a roll of linen to serve for a pillow.

The heat of the night was very great and no coverlet was needed.

"The door," said Jah, "has two strong bolts. It will be well to draw them, for there may be prowlers abroad."

There was an apparent honesty in the man which ought to have satisfied them, but Dick did not quite like it. It appeared to him to be somewhat forced.

But he said nothing to disturb his companions, who were "yawning their heads off."

With all speed they stretched themselves upon their beds, and Butterflick was asleep ere Dick had drawn the two bolts of the door.

A glance round showed there was no exit to the room, and Dick laid down upon the outside bed, which had been left for him.

It was the coolest position in the room, being nearest the window.

The lamp left by Jah for their use was a dismal affair, and Dick blew it out.

But the room was by no means dark, for a bright moon was shining outside, and sent its rays slanting through the window.

Dick noticed the window particularly. It was at least three feet deep and two wide, an extra size for a Persian building of that class.

He lay for awhile watching the light shining through it, but fell asleep at last.

For awhile he slept, how long he knew not, and then awoke with a start.

Why he had done so he could not tell, for he had not been touched, nor had he heard a sound.

Instinctively he turned his face to the window, and in a moment was sitting upright, staring hard at it.

When he went to sleep it was three feet deep at least and two wide.

Now it was not more than a foot and a half deep, but the width was unchanged.

What was the meaning of that?

As he asked himself the question he saw the depth of the window still more sensibly shorten, as if closing up.

Was he awake or dreaming?

CHAPTER XXIV.

THE FATAL BED—DICK'S STRONG ARM ONCE MORE REQUIRED—PUNISHMENT OF JAH.

MORE amazing phenomena than the change in the shape and size of the window Dick had never met with.

On going to bed he had noticed that it was like the majority of windows in the country—a simple opening in the wall without any glass or shutter—and he remembered clearly its shape was that of an upright, oblong square.

Now it was, although still an oblong-square, horizontal.

As he lay quite still, with his eyes fixed upon it, he saw the window narrowing, and convinced at last it was no illusion he decided to get up and see the cause of the peculiar change.

But first he thought he would wake his friends, so as to have them prepared for any emergency which might entail a quick retreat from the place.

The appearance of Jah, their host, had not been inspiring in a confidential sense, and Dick knew—from reading authentic books on the subject—that the inns of the East, especially in Persia, had a bad record.

The rich traveller had to run the gauntlet of all sorts of tricks and traps, and neither his money or his life were safe unless he was wary and well armed.

A touch roused Flutterby Fowler, and a word of caution kept him quiet.

Butterflick was also aroused without any trouble, but Muffins was a sleeper of a different mould.

Nobody in the world sleeps so soundly as a tired boy, and it was not until his adopted father had stood him on his feet and given him a good shaking that he was made at all conscious of where he was.

He opened his mouth to yawn, but before he could employ it for speaking purposes Butterflick had his hand over it, and whispered in his ear—

"Not a word—summat's wrong."

Muffins shivered a little from the chill which is felt in any climate by a sleeper awakened from sound repose, and nodded his head to imply that he understood.

So Butterflick released him, and the trio stood together watching Dick Strongbow, who had walked softly across the room to the window.

They saw him raise his head, look steadily at the ceiling of the room for a moment or two, and then hurriedly advance towards them.

"We must get out of here at once," he said; "this is a murderous den."

"What's the matter?" asked Butterflick.

None of the trio realised the nature of the peril, which Dick explained in a few words.

"The ceiling is a solid mass, worked by some sort of machinery, and is slowly descending. If I had not awakened it would have crushed us as we slept."

He could not have had listeners with stouter hearts, but this terrible piece of intelligence made them shiver. There was something particularly atrocious and cowardly about the whole thing. Such a death as they had been threatened with might well inspire the hardiest of men with horror.

"Unbolt the door," said Dick, quietly. "Step outside, but go no further until you hear from me."

Flutterby Fowler drew back the bolts and pushed open the door. Unlike interior doors at home, it opened outward.

The passage without was quiet, and lighted by a lamp sufficiently to show them that nobody was there.

A window at the side let in the rays of the moon also, so that they had a clear view of the narrow passage from end to end.

Close by the room they had just quitted there was another open door, through which Dick could see a flight of stairs leading to some chamber above.

It flashed upon him that there he would find the nefarious operator of the machinery by which the dreadful ceiling was put in motion at work.

"Remain here," he whispered, "and be ready for *anything*."

Not another word was necessary. The only answer they made was to get their weapons out for action, and Dick, with light steps, reached the staircase without making the least sound perceptible to human ears.

The steps, like the greater part of the house, were of stone.

All the better, for boards creak and yield under ordinary pressure.

As he began the ascent he heard a slight humming, like the whirring of a distant mill-wheel—confirmation of his having correctly surmised that the evil-doer was engaged there.

Thirteen steps brought him to the door of the chamber above, and that was open too, giving him a view of Jah and the machinery by means of which the ceiling was being lowered.

It was very simple—a thick wooden screw running through the floor to the ceiling below, and a huge wheel horizontally fixed upon it.

Apparently, when set in motion, it spun round and round for a considerable time without further aid, for Jah stood by watching its rapid evolutions, with his hands behind his back, like some workman keeping his eye upon the movements of machinery under his charge.

He stood with his profile towards Dick, and the malevolence of his nature was expressed by the movement of his features.

Although the wheel worked rapidly the screw turned slowly. The soft, buzzing noise came from the former—the latter, well greased, made absolutely no sound.

Dick was not by nature cruel or revengeful, but he had the resolute courage which brooks no injustice, and he could, at a pinch, be as stern as any judge.

As he stood there he asked himself, "What is the fitting punishment for this monster?"

The answer which came back to his mind was, "The fate that he decreed for you."

A few swift steps, or rather bounds, and he had the startled Jah in his grasp, holding him in that fearful grip which had never yet failed to unnerve the man subjected to it.

Jah was powerless and speechless, limp and helpless, with the terror of the mouse in the claws of a cat.

Not a word said Dick, but lifted up the would-be murderer and carried him downstairs.

"Open that door," he said, in a low, clear voice.

Butterflick and Muffins had heard him speak in that way before, and they knew that he was in one of his moods which allowed of no trifling.

Flutterby Fowler, startled, slipped back, but he made no effort to save the wretch, whose fate he promptly realised.

The door was opened.

Inside all was dark, for the massive wooden ceiling was now below the window, shutting out the light.

It was, indeed, coming down past the door, so that anyone desiring to enter would have to stoop.

As men cast a bundle of straw or sticks into the furnace, so Dick cast Jah into that room and closed the door.

There was no lock, but, as he had suspected, there were bolts outside as well as within, and with a steady, unfaltering hand he shot them into the sockets.

"Our sojourn here is at an end," he said; "let us go."

Leading the way, he descended the staircase—the others followed with the feeling of a dreadful stillness upon them.

From aloft there came the faintest of buzzing sounds.

The wheel was still revolving, and he who set it going alone knew if it would stop ere the life was crushed out of him.

At the foot of the staircase stood a hand-lamp, which Dick raised from the floor.

With its aid he found a back door, which he opened—outside was a stable-yard, with the customary buildings.

He entered one of them, and inside were two horses standing ready saddled, as if in expectation of some rider.

They were, indeed, prepared for a periodical messenger of the Shah, bearing letters to men in authority about the country.

Adjoining this stable there were other houses, but the doors were locked, and ere Dick could force them open a clattering of arms and the beating of horses' hoofs upon the road were heard.

"Listen," he said; "all keep still for a few moments."

The sounds drew nearer—they were, in fact, very near when first heard—and as they stood listening a voice was heard shouting in the front of the inn.

"He calls on Jah to open in the name of the Shah," said Flutterby Fowler.

"Then we must be gone," replied Dick. "We must ride double. Butterflick, you take Muffins; Mr. Fowler will mount with me."

The horses—two strong, thick-set animals—were brought out, and, Butterflick having mounted, Muffins scrambled up behind him.

Dick then got into the saddle, and, stooping, lifted up Flutterby Fowler with scarcely an effort, and so assisted him to his seat.

"What amazing strength!" sighed the little tutor. "I wish I had a tenth of it."

"You have a strength of your own," replied Dick, "weak as you deem yourself. All quiet, now. We must ride across country a bit ere we take to the high road."

The main party of the new arrivals, evidently soldiers, were now at the door of the inn, and the demand for immediate admittance was getting more and more imperative.

A dozen voices were shouting, and the door was beaten with the butts of rifles or something of equal substance. The din was prodigious.

In the midst of it Dick guided his horse out of the stable-yard to a stretch of open ground which skirted the main road.

A short ride took them out of sight of the inn, and as there were no fences or hedges to bar their way they had little difficulty in taking to the public track again.

"I wonder if they will miss these horses?" said Butterflick, as they rode along side by side.

"I should say they will," replied Dick, "for they are superior animals, and were certainly saddled in readiness for somebody—probably couriers."

"In that case," remarked Flutterby Fowler, "we may be pursued."

"That is true," rejoined Dick; "and what we have to do is to put as wide a tract of road as possible between them and us. But we must ride with care, for the horses are carrying double."

CHAPTER XXV.

THE PURSUIT BY THE SHAH'S MESSENGER—A RUSE TO
AVOID CAPTURE—A CLOSE SHAVE.

OWEVER kind a rider may be to a horse, there is a limit to its powers, and after an hour's trot along the ill-kept road the gallant steeds began to show signs of fatigue.

Dick reined up, and gave orders for all to dismount.

"We must walk the poor beasts for a few miles," he said, "or they will be prostrated."

Relieved of their burdens, the animals again moved along briskly, and inspired by the conviction that to linger was to get into trouble with the enemy the party of four strode along briskly.

As yet no sound of being pursued had reached their ears, but they could not shut their eyes to the great probability of soon having the soldiers on their trail.

In a little while the darkness of night would pass away, and daylight would come, with its advantages and disadvantages.

One of the former was—they would be able to make out the country better; the chief of the latter being that their pursuers would be able to see them from a considerable distance, the country just there being flat and free from woods of any extent.

Flying from any foe was distasteful to Dick, but first and foremost he had his mission and its reward in his mind's eye.

Secondly, he valued the lives of his companions and his own too much to cast them away recklessly.

The moon went down about four o'clock, and after that, until the dawn arrived, the darkness was greater than they had before experienced in Persia.

At length, while they still walked to husband the strength of their horses, the "oosha," as the Persians call it, flashed into the sky.

It is a sudden ray of light that sweeps from the east to mid-sky and then dies away, leaving all as dark as before.

The "oosha" is the herald of the morning sun, and known by the worshippers of our great luminary as "the mother of the young god."

To see it once, as it exhibits itself in the East, is to remember it for a lifetime.

A minute after it appeared the light of day began to unfold and spread far and wide, like a fluttering mantle worn by the sun, which soon appeared, and day was there.

No song birds, as in our own country, welcomed the birth of another day. All was still.

Far and wide no habitation could be seen, but ahead was a line of broken hills with mountains beyond.

"There is our place of refuge," said Dick, "but we lack one thing—food. You have a knowledge of all things botanical, Fowler; look round and see if there is anything for us to eat."

There was coarse grass for the horses and water

for all, but at first it appeared as if they would have to go on their way without breakfast.

At length diligent search rewarded the efforts of Flutterby Fowler, who, in a damp hollow close to a spring, discovered some fungi, which he said was good to eat.

"It is not very palatable," he said, "but it is nourishing and supporting."

The food was indeed anything but toothsome—Butterflick said it reminded him of damp sawdust—but they ate their fill from sheer necessity, and stored away in their pockets some of the fungi, for use, if needed, later in the day.

The rugged country was about five or six miles off, as near as they could judge, and Dick suggested they should walk the first two miles and ride the rest.

Of course what he suggested was acquiesced in, and the wisdom of the idea was proven ere long.

They had walked the specified distance, and were getting into the saddle, when Muffins, looking back, saw a white cloud in the road behind them.

"Master," he cried, "what is that?"

"Horsemen," at once replied Dick, "and riding furiously. They are in pursuit of us. Now ride your best," he said, addressing Butterflick. "If we can reach yonder hills we may find safety. If overtaken before we attain them it will be simply a question of fight or yield."

"Your pass—will not that serve you?" asked Flutterby Fowler.

"The pass of Turcomatz," returned Dick, with a smile, as he put his horse into action, "must not be used too often. We have stolen two horses—don't forget that. On the whole I prefer trusting to our noble steeds and our own wit."

The horses, having had an easy time of it for the last two or three hours, started off again as if fresh from the stable, but of course they laboured under the great disadvantage of having two riders instead of one.

It is true that Flutterby Fowler and Muffins were of light build, but in a race every pound counts.

Only sturdy steeds could hope to bear them to a point indicated by Dick.

It was a part of the road where it suddenly bore away to the left and was lost among hilly ground.

The probability was that there the geographical necessities of the place caused the highway to twist and turn snake fashion, and this would be of great advantage to them.

Dick had a scheme in his mind which he intended, if circumstances permitted, to carry into execution. It was one of those simple ruses which are often more successful than the most elaborately-conceived plan.

It was merely, on reaching the broken ground, to pull up and dismount.

Then he would send the horses forward, who, rejoicing in their freedom, would gallop on at a pace that the pursuers could not emulate; but they would most probably follow, leaving the four travellers in comparative safety.

Butterflick and his adopted son Muffins rode behind, and the latter, from his post of vantage, occasionally reported the progress of the pursuing party.

One of the Priests lighted a torch and advanced towards the doomed man.

At first, it will be remembered, he saw nothing but a cloud of dust raised by the hoofs of the horses, but ere they had gone far he beheld dim forms, like spectres in a mist.

"I can see the soldiers, master!" he cried.

"Clearly?" asked Dick.

"No. They are like people in the thick of smoke."

"Call out as they get clearer."

On sped the horses at a wonderful pace, considering what they bore. Half a mile had been covered when Muffin's voice was heard again.

"The figures are getting blacker, master, and I can see something glittering."

"Swords or lances," said Dick to Flutterby Fowler. "They are gaining upon us."

"Will they overtake us?"

"I cannot say. Much depends on their seeing us. Get on, good horse. Keep an eye on Butterflick—we must not get too far ahead of him. 'All or none to be saved' is our motto."

"Master," again cried Muffins, "I can see the men quite plainly now. They're soldiers."

"All right, Muffins," sang out Dick. "I was afraid they were something lighter. How far are they off, Butterflick?"

"A good distance," answered Butterflick, cheerily. "You get on, sir; I'll keep up with you, or this horse will know the reason why."

Dick fixed his eyes on the point of the road which he hoped would bring them safety. It was about a mile ahead—not far in one sense, but it takes a good horse to get over that bit of ground with nearly twenty stone upon his back.

"Be thankful, Fowler," he said, grimly, "that you are to-day as light as a feather. What is your weight?"

"Not more than seven stone," answered Fowler; "I am a bag of bones."

"Hurrah! for bones," cried Dick. "Muffins, are they gaining?"

"Coming on fast, master; I can see their faces almost."

"Do they see us?"

"They are shouting and waving swords, master."

"It will be a close shave at the best," muttered Dick. "Hold on, Fowler."

"I am holding on to the best of my ability," answered Flutterby Fowler, "but I have never ridden at this pace before, and every bound I feel as if I were going to fly into the air."

"Press hard with your knees, shut your eyes, and cling to me," advised Dick. "On, good horse, on."

A horse knows when it has a rider in the saddle, and when it has one is ready to do its best. The steed Dick was riding raised its head, stretched its neck, and snorted as it flew over the ground.

Again, the spirit of emulation is strong in horses, and when one sees another going on ahead the rearmost one does its level best to keep up with it, so Butterflick's animal strained every nerve not to be left behind, and succeeeded in keeping within easy hail of its companion.

And now the nature of the ground at the roadside began to change.

The grass disappeared and tall, ill-favoured weeds took its place. The way was marked by huge stones, accidently or designedly placed, and the road to be traversed assumed a more rugged form.

Dick asked no more questions nor even looked back.

The race was now to the swift, and he who would ride in such a place with safety must be careful in guiding his horse.

On—on, with the hoofs fiercely beating the ground and the riders clinging to their seats as drowning men cling to planks in the surging sea.

Behind came quite a little horde of mounted men.

Presently their voices, furiously shouting, reached the ears of the men ahead, and rapidly grew louder.

Only a quarter of a mile to the place where the road suddenly broke up into tumbled masses of rocks and stones.

"Will the horses do it?" Dick asked himself.

The beautiful head of the animal he bestrode was beginning to droop, but it required a practised eye to see it. Its spirit was not yet broken or its strength dissipated. At length they came to a spot where the road slightly dipped, and down this they went at a break-neck pace.

The slightest stumble on the part of either horse would have been fatal. But they were too sure-footed to make a mistake, and winged their way without the semblance of a slip or fall.

"How far are they away?" cried out Dick.

"Three hundred yards, sir."

"Too near," Flutterby Fowler heard his leader mutter.

A yell from Muffins startled them all, but it was not a cry of fear.

"Whoop!" he cried, "one of 'em is down. They're a-tumbling over each other like skittles."

Dick looked back, and saw that the incline had worked havoc with the soldiers.

One of the foremost horses had fallen, and three or four others tumbled over it. The remainder were being reined up, and all for a time was confusion.

"Good luck to the horse that fell," said Dick, exultingly; "we have a few minutes more to spare."

As he spoke they passed between two high rocks, and the road took a sudden turn. Fifty yards ahead it wound again. Dick had rightly gauged the nature of the highway he would meet with among the hills.

Once, twice, thrice they turned, and then he reined up and dismounted, taking Flutterby Fowler with him.

A blow with his hat, sufficient to scare but not to hurt, sent his horse forward.

Butterflick was not slow to follow his example. He and Muffins tumbled to the ground, and the second horse was sent after the first.

"This way," said Dick, softly.

He scrambled over a stone between two boulders, and behind them was shelter from the observation of passers-by for them all.

"This will serve us as well as any other place," he said.

Then he threw himself down, and, his example being followed by the rest, they lay there panting, awaiting the inevitable coming of their pursuers.

CHAPTER XXVI.

AN OLD ACQUAINTANCE REAPPEARS—THE VIZIER'S TRAIN.

 ERY little time had they to wait. The heavy beating of hoofs on the hard road soon fell upon their ears, and Dick, bidding the others lie close, took off his hat and peered out of his hiding-place to see the soldiers go by.

They were riding at a fair pace, but not so fast as before. The recent tumble had taught them to be careful.

Foremost was a young officer in command, and close behind rode two other men, both in civilian garb—one a Persian and the other—

Dick felt his breath stop short, for he was completely taken by surprise. The other was the Russian —Turcomatz.

It was not at all likely he could make a mistake, although the glimpse he caught of him was very brief, the soldiers rapidly closing up behind him.

The heavy face, the thick-set form, the dogged look, were all the characteristics of Turcomatz, and Dick, as he drew back, felt that the Russian was still the bane of his journey through Persia.

"Fowler," he said, in his quiet way, "an old friend of ours is with these fellows. Guess who it is."

"It can't be Turcomatz," returned Fowler.

"It IS Turcomatz, and how the fellow got here is a puzzle to ME."

Dick sat down, feeling like the others, in need of rest.

A broken night's sleep and the hard gallop had tired them, and, as Dick shortly after remarked, there was no hurry.

"Our horses," he said, "will probably break away from the road and betake themselves into the fastnesses of the hills, and those fellows will ride on and on in a vain pursuit."

"Think you that Turcomatz knows who he is pursuing?" asked Fowler.

"Of course," answered Dick; "he is sure to have a description of us. What a leech the vagabond is. It was misdirected mercy for us to spare his life."

"He would have taken ours," said Butterflick. "Dern him! The next time, master, we get hold of the vagabond, you leave him to me."

The sound of the horses speeding along the hard road died away, and Dick cautiously scaled a rock hard by to take an inventory of the country around.

It was of a most hopeless aspect, for the hills were bare, with the rounded tops peculiar to all high lands of the East.

"Just as if Nature had been san'-papering 'em down," Butterflick remarked.

No sign of habitation or chance of getting food anywhere.

"The question is," said Dick, when he rejoined his companions—"is this the only road through the hills? I think not, and I propose that we take a bee-line, bearing north through the rough ground. If we find nothing in the way of a path to reward us by sunset we can return to this road."

"There's another question," added Butterflick, turning up one of his feet—"boots. I've holes in the bottoms of mine each as big as a crown piece."

All had the same thing to trouble them, but, as Dick said, if they reached Astrabad they had the means of getting them restored. After all, food and water were the main things to be desired.

Of the former they had sufficient for the day, but of the latter they had immediate need.

A ride along a dusty road is provocative of thirst. The skin of their bodies was dry and their lips parched—so an immediate search for water was imperative.

Starting on the route mentioned by Dick, they clambered over the broken ground with eagle eyes, roaming in every direction for the signs of moisture, and presently the botanical knowledge of Flutterby Fowler brought them what they needed.

He espied a plant growing under the shelter of a huge stone, which he declared would not exist without frequent "ablutions."

From this small indication of water he tracked down another of the species, and by degrees led them to a rift in the face of a hill where the soil was damp.

Within that rift, in a crevice where the sun's rays never penetrated, they found a spring of water feebly bubbling from the earth.

"In the wet season," said Flutterby Fowler, "this spring creates a tiny brook, which disappears in the warmest parts of the year."

Dick bade the others drink first, and, insisting upon it, Muffins, being the youngest, was desired to slake his thirst. So he took a long draught, which, he said, was sweeter than any wine he had ever tasted.

When they had all drunk of the water they ate half of the poor food they had brought with them, and, by Dick's advice lay down in the shade to get a few hours sleep.

"After that," he said, "we will eat what we have left, take a good drink, and go on our way."

The spot he chose was on the dryer side of the rift, where there was a rough semblance of a shelf of rock. It was a hard resting place, but beggars and tired men are not often disposed to grumble at their beds, however humble they may be, and contented with the advantages of the present they stretched themselves out and slept.

An hour passed, and no living thing, save a few stray insects living in the holes and corners of the rocks, came near them.

The sun got higher and higher, pouring down its wealth of warmth upon the earth, turning the ground under its influence into the semblance of the floor of an oven.

There was no reek, as there is in our own fields and meadows at home, for the land outside the rift was as dry as a freshly-burnt brick.

The spring bubbling out its meagre waters permeated the ground around, but evaporated as soon as it came under the influence of the great luminary.

A hideous vulture sailed across the sky, saw the sleeping men, hung steadily on its wings for a moment peering down, found out they were living beings and not carrion, and passed on.

Another passed, and the sleepers still lay as quiet as the mummied figures in a pyramid, save for a slow, gentle heaving of the breast.

Then a naked-footed man came up to the rift, looked in at the spring, and clasped his hands in thankfulness.

He, too, was parched, as the travellers had been; but his thirst, as yet, was not to be slaked, for suddenly his eyes lighted upon the sleeping strangers, and he staggered back as if an arrow had pierced his heart.

For a moment or two he remained gazing at them, and then, muttering something in the Persian tongue, he leapt out of the rift and sped away.

CHAPTER XXVII.

DICK IS TAKEN CAPTIVE—MATTERS ARE NOT SO BAD AS HE THOUGHT—THE VIZIER AND HIS STORY.

NCONSCIOUS of approaching peril, Dick Strongbow and his friends slept on—dreaming of home, perhaps, or perchance, in the depth of their slumber, not dreaming at all.

The minutes fled by until nearly half an hour had passed, and then sundry armed men in the dress of the natives of the country began to encompass our friends.

Stealthily as Indians they gathered, until the narrow rift in the hill-side was full of them.

Then, at the signal of one who appeared to be leader, they pounced upon the sleeping men and secured them.

For making them captives they had come prepared, and thongs of leather were secured about their wrists and feet before they were well awake.

Resistance was useless, save in Dick Strongbow's case, for he could have snapped his bonds like threads, but finding himself in the presence of an armed force he peacefully yielded for the time.

His first care was to glance round to see if Turcomatz the Russian was present, but that astute person was not of the party.

So far it was a relief.

"Keep cool," said Dick to his friends. "We shall learn presently what this outrage means."

Addressing the man in command of the party—a tall, dark personage, possessed of a superior air—he asked him, in the several languages he was able to speak, who he was, and by what authority he had arrested him?

No answer was vouchsafed him, but a sign was made for Dick and his friends to fall in close together preparatory to marching away.

"I will see which way he takes," thought Dick. "If he goes back towards the road we have deserted I must make some effort to escape. If the other way, I must wait the issue of events."

Butterflick looked at him for guidance, but a simple depression of the eyes was a sufficient instruction for him, and the lowly miner remained as gentle as a lamb.

Mumns, a philosopher beyond his years, was resigned, because he had such faith in "master" that he felt he would be sure to get them out of the hobble. Flutterby Fowler kept a smiling face.

The party did not go back to the old road, but took an opposite direction, picking their way over the rough ground until they came to a perfect little oasis in the mountains, where about two score tents had been fixed.

In the centre was one of larger size than the rest, and of better material, for the majority were of simple canvas, and that was of silk.

At the door of it, which had a flap of the silk raised and resting on two poles fixed in the ground, two swarthy Nubians stood on guard with drawn swords.

They remained as still as statues, and, beyond a roll of the eye, took no notice of the captives as they drew up and were ranged by the officer in front of the tent.

Having done this, he marched past the guard and disappeared within the shade of the silky covering.

So strong was the light without that it appeared to Dick that something akin to darkness was within the tent, but it was merely the gloom of the deep shade, natural in a place that admitted no ray of the sun.

A murmuring of voices was heard, and anon the officer, reappearing, motioned for Dick to accompany him within.

Dick obeyed with his quiet stride, so indicative of fearlessness and strength, and found himself in the presence of a white-bearded potentate, who squatted on a carpet in the centre of the tent.

Ranged in a semi-circle behind him were half a dozen closely-veiled women, evidently the wives, or some of the wives, of the Persian chief.

"You are English?" he said, in clear accents, speaking in the dear, old, familiar tongue.

"I am," replied Dick.

"What are you doing here?"

"Travelling, to find a friend known to a friend of mine."

"Who is that?"

"Hamanodob Longimans, the Grand Vizier of Astrabad."

This answer startled the aged listener, who raised his head a little, and stared at Dick with a surprise rarely seen on the face of an Oriental.

"You jest," he said, "knowing who I am."

"Indeed I do not," replied Dick, "for I have no conception who you are."

"I am the Ab Ogah, the Grand Vizier you seek," said the old chief.

It was now Dick's turn to be surprised, and he showed it plainly in his face.

There was a silence of a few moments, and then the vizier, for it was indeed he, motioned for the officer to leave the tent.

When he was gone the vizier bade Dick sit down beside him, at the same time taking a dagger from his girdle.

"I have been warned of your coming in a dream," he said, "or in some way. What matters it? Know ye a certain duke of the Court of the King of Sweden?"

"The Duke of Lavante?"

"The same."

"He is my friend," said Dick, "and I am to marry his daughter if I but perform my mission and safely return."

"Your mission is—*what?*"

"To receive something from you and bear it safely back."

The vizier raised his dagger, and with a stroke of it was about to cut asunder Dick's bonds, but he paused.

"I have been warned or dreamt of the man who

was to come to me," he said—"a man of strength and fame."

"I am he," replied Dick; "my name is Strongbow."

"Let me see you break your bonds," said the vizier, "so that by the sign of your strength I may know you are the man."

Dick raised his wrists, and with a jerk snapped the leathern bonds as if they had been threads.

There was a slight shout from all the women seated behind the vizier, but otherwise they did not exhibit any cognisance of what they saw.

"Verily," said the vizier, "you are the man."

He clapped his hands, and two men, clothed in short white dresses, came hurrying into the tent.

A motion of the hand sufficed to tell them what to do, and two hookahs were brought forward from the rear and placed before Dick and the vizier.

With the aid of a tinder-box—how strange it was to see them use that ancient thing—they lighted the pipes, and, bowing low, departed.

"That which you seek," said the vizier, "is not here, but at Astrabad, whither I am returning after visiting my people to administer justice. Ere we talk more let us await the coffee."

"I have friends without," suggested Dick, "who may be suffering some anxiety."

"They are already free," answered the vizier, sententiously.

The appearance of the two slaves with coffee stopped the talking for a little while, but after they had again retired it was resumed.

"Know you what it is you are to take charge of?" asked the vizier.

"I can but guess," answered Dick. "Something of value, I assume."

"It is the most valuable diamond in the world—the Ab-Gonab, the king of jewels," said the vizier. "The Shah hungers for it, other monarchs seek it, notably the great White Czar of Russia, to whom our ruler—may the sun shine upon and scorch him—promised it a year ago."

"Then it is the property of the Czar?" said Dick.

"As much his property as the rest of Persia," replied Hamanodob, "for all things in this land are his—the men, the women, the horses, the cattle, the gold, the jewels. They are his because he is king, and takes what he will."

"Is it possible people endure such tyranny?" exclaimed Dick.

"When the people are broken enough they bear anything," answered Hamanodob; "but they do not give their all even at his bidding, for those who are wealthy hide much, and the jewel you are to bear away has been lost for a hundred years.

"It was my grandsire's," continued the vizier, with sudden warmth, "and his father's before him, but the Shah at the same time coveted it. He sent his emissary to our house demanding it, and it was given up."

"Given up?" echoed Dick.

"Aye," replied the vizier, "but the emissary, on his way back to Teheran, was waylaid and murdered—by robbers, it was said—and from that hour to this no eye but those who hold it have beheld it."

"I understand," murmured Dick.

"See here, my friend," said the vizier, laying a hand upon Dick's arm, "it is ours—mine. Why should we have been robbed of it? But, on the other hand, we could not sell it, for purchasers of such things are scarce."

Dick took two or three quiet pulls at his pipe, reflecting at the same time on a phase of the subject which had occurred to him.

"You have, I presume, been looking for a purchaser of the diamond for years?" he said, at length.

"It is so," answered the vizier; "that is as much as I dare do. I had an agent abroad who was instructed to make inquiries."

"And you have found one in the King of Sweden?"

"Again it is so."

"But the question of the money?" said Dick. "I do not understand that. Who is to bring it to you?"

"Nobody will bring it to me," replied the vizier, smoking calmly; "not a coin of it will ever enter this country."

"Of what use will it be to you, then?"

"It will be of no use to me."

Dick's puzzled face brought a faint smile upon the features of the vizier.

"Let me tell you all," he said, "for I know you are to be trusted. I have a son—an only son—whom I love. He is in your country, where I have obtained permission for him to be educated."

"Yes, we have other foreign princes there," observed Dick.

"The great Shah, in his wisdom," said the vizier, with a curious, semi-sarcastic grin on his face, "granted permission for him to go, so that he might bring back with him some of the secrets which make your people great. He will not return, even though he has to live there as poor as one of the dogs of our streets."

A sudden passion lighted up the face of the old vizier, and his right hand was raised and his voice quivered as he went on—

"What matters if I never have my old eyes gladdened by the sight of him again so long as he is happy and free? I can bear it for a few short years, and then I shall be dead. I am great and powerful now, but only by the will of the Shah, who, if he desired, could to-morrow send one of his accursed assassins to take my life—and none of my people here would dare to raise a hand to help me. We go through existence with our lives hanging on a thread. We know in the morning, when the sun rises, that we live, but none of us know if we shall see it set."

"Truly a dog's life," said Dick.

"It is only by lying and fawning—by robbing the people for the good of the Shah—that we live on," pursued the vizier. "If he—the potent, the mighty—demands so much money, we have to get it from the poor and the rich alike. To get it we have to screw and threaten and torture. A man may toil for his children, and when lying on his death-bed see all that he has acquired taken away—for the good of the Shah."

"And how is it the people endure these things?" asked Dick.

"Centuries of slavery have broken their spirit," was the reply. "They have no faith or trust in each other—no hope, no anything, but to drag on their miserable lives, seeing no chance of peace but in death.

"And now, oh friend from the great and free

nation," added the vizier, "you know all—the why and wherefore that you are here. As your friends have trusted you to come to me, so I have hope in you to return with the precious jewel, the price of which, placed in the safe hands of bankers, will give my son the means of living among you free, at rest, and in peace. Come, now, and let us get on to Astrabad."

"You have spoken freely to me," said Dick, as he arose and glanced back at the women behind him; "may I ask if there is any other here who knows the reason of my coming?"

"Not one."

"These women here—"

"They know no tongue but their own, and little of that. Our women are, to our shame, mere puppets —dolls—chattering, senseless toys, with but two thoughts in their minds—to hold the favour of their husbands and to have no lack of sweetmeats. Years ago I could have done something to make them more like the women of your famed land—but I dared not. One movement to alter aught that exists here would have caused my head to be forfeited. If you have rested enough we will start upon our journey to Astrabad."

CHAPTER XXVIII.

A CHANGE IN THE LOT OF OUR FRIENDS—ASTRABAD AT NIGHT—THE VIZIER'S STRONG MAN.

IN five minutes the whole camp was in motion.

Dick rejoined his friends outside, who were walking about in a state of wondering delight, and, having briefly explained to them that they were among good people, and had no cause for fear, they watched the preparations for departure.

The striking of the tents was accompanied by the striking of many engaged in the operation. Blows were, it seemed, necessary, being looked for by the swarthy soldiers and attendants, who were undoubtedly as lazy and spiritless a body of men as one would care to see.

"How suggestive of the taskmasters and slaves we read of in old stories of the East," said Flutterby Fowler.

"It beats me that some of 'em don't turn round and hit back again," growled Butterflick. "Why, if my son Muffins here took all that licking without at least landing them bullying officers one on the shins I'd disown him."

"Oh! I'd do it right enough, dad," replied Muffins, confidently.

The vizier remained in seclusion until the last moment, and Dick understood his policy.

However confidential they might have been in private, in public an appearance of distance and reserve must be maintained.

For the women of the potentate there were palanquins, with curtains all round, into which they were smuggled as if they had been human curiosities being taken from one place of exhibition to another.

The vizier mounted a cream-coloured horse, richly caparisoned, and for our friends four others, as noble in appearance, but less richly garnished, were brought forth.

It was with deep emotion that Muffins found himself being assisted into the saddle by three Nubian slaves.

One held the horse's head, a second grasped the stirrups, and a third bent his back, to be used as a stepping-stone by Muffins.

They were all similar honoured, but Dick and Butterflick declined the use of the slave's back. Flutterby Fowler and Muffins only employed this means of rising to their seats as a necessity.

Evidently the vizier had made it known that the strangers were to be treated as honoured guests, for the soldiers on surrounding them showed by their deferential bearing that they were a guard of honour and not an escort of prisoners.

"This life suits me," said Butterflick, as they started a little in the rear of the vizier and his wives, "and if I thought it was going to continue I wouldn't mind spending a few years in this benighted country. Whoa! you restless beggar— what now?"

Butterflick's horse, without any warning, began to prance in a somewhat embarrassing manner; but it was only in play, and a little experience of it sufficed to make it almost enjoyable.

Muffins thought it delightful when his steed followed the example set it by its fellow horse.

"It's as good as a see-saw," he said, but Flutterby Fowler was some time before he became reconciled to it.

Dick sat his horse with the easy grace of one who had been a rider from childhood, and as a perfect horseman gained the respect of the men around him, who belonged to a race that may be said to live in the saddle.

When his horse curved, reared, or ambled sideways, neighing in the delight of exercise, every motion was responded to by him with the easy bending this way and that which shows a man at home in the stirrups.

But we cannot divert on the delights of the journey.

After a ride of three hours they came in sight of the towers of Astrabad, and shortly after sundown passed through a gateway in the walls of that ancient city.

The vizier's army had been heralded, and the quaint streets were lighted with little, twinkling lamps, hung from the windows and doorways.

In places ropes were swinging across the street with half a dozen lamps shining like jewels of various colours, and the people were abroad to do homage to their governor.

There was no noise, no bustle, no crowding, or hurrahing, or laughter—none of the good-humoured disorder of a crowd such as we see at home.

Silent as mutes the people stood in rows, bowing as the vizier passed, and but for the clattering of arms and the sounds of the horses' hoofs, as they struck the hard ground, one might have thought it was a city of shadows—a haunt of the spirits of the dead.

To the visitors, or some of them at least, it was like a dream.

The many-coloured lamps, the glittering cavalcade, the dumb people, were things that we read of in the stories of the Arabian Nights and wonder if they could have ever existed.

But here they were clear to the eye—indisputable facts.

"It is worth all we have gone through to be here

to-night," said Flutterby Fowler to Dick, by whose side he was riding.

"It is charming, and would be enjoyable," replied Dick, "if one did not know what lies beneath this glitter."

After a ride through half a dozen streets they came to the house of the vizier—a vast pile of masonry, three hundred feet long and about half that height, with towers and battlements and windows deftly mingled together in picturesque confusion. A veritable maze of the builder's art.

The mansion gates were swinging back as the cavalcade approached, and the horses bore their riders under a huge archway of carved stone to courtyard beyond.

The vizier and his wives disappeared immediately, and Dick and his friends were assisted to dismount and taken charge of by an officer, who conducted them to a suite of rooms of barbaric splendour.

Massive masonry, rich tapestry, and velvet lounging cushions were the chief features of the place where they were to pass the night.

After a short delay food and wine were brought in, and, if the former was a series of strange dishes, everything was palatable, and the wine was good. So they ate and drank their fill, and, worn out with the day's exertions, went to rest.

At an early hour—it was barely light—Dick was aroused by a hand being laid upon his shoulder.

Awakening, he saw the officer who had looked after their comforts the previous evening, who motioned for him to follow.

The others lay asleep in different parts of the chamber, and leaving them in the full enjoyment of dreamless slumber Dick went out softly with the guide.

First he was led to an open room—that is, a chamber, or marble court-yard, as some might call it —with a small bath filled with water as clear as crystal in the centre. Towels and bathing requisites were in charge of a Nubian who stood beside the bath, his figure perfectly reflected below.

For all the sign of life given out by this still figure the man might have been a statue.

Leaving Dick there, the officer retired, and our hero, only too glad of the opportunity to enjoy a bath, undressed and plunged in.

The water was not absolutely cold, and a pleasant perfume was mingled with it which made it peculiarly refreshing.

After a few minutes' plunging and rolling about Dick emerged, and the Nubian, who had stood unmoved until then, suddenly became a thing of life.

He cast a towel as big as a sheet over Dick, completely enveloping him from head to foot.

Swiftly his nimble hands were plied, and the process of drying was soon performed.

Then Dick, with a grateful sense of comfort, redressed, and bestowed upon the Nubian a few coins of Persian money he found in one of his pockets.

The gift, though small in Dick's eyes, was a great one to the Nubian. In his gratitude he bowed his head to the earth.

A few moments later the officer returned and conducted Dick to an adjoining chamber, where he found the vizier alone.

"My friend," he said, when the officer had disappeared, "it will be necessary for you to remain there at least two days ere the jewel can be recovered from its hiding-place, and it will be better if I give out that you have come here at my bidding to amuse me.

"Be not angry," he added, as Dick's face flushed; "we Eastern fools never send for men to make us wise, but to kill the time that hangs like lead on our hands. You are here, and I must give a reason, or suspicions will arise."

"I am agreeable to do what you will," answered Dick.

"Now be it known to you," continued the vizier, "that I have one of my people—Gahzreal by name —who is a performer of feats of strength and distortions of the body? He is a poor fool in my eyes, but my people think much of him, and he is proud. Now if I, knowing that you are so strong, might give out that you are brought hither to rival him—"

"I understand," interposed Dick. "Let it be so; it will pass the time. I, Dick Strongbow, will meet Gahzreal."

"Friend," said the vizier, laying a hand on Dick's arm, "you have strength and wisdom and prudence —you must conquer in all things. I sent for you early lest my people should wonder. For the time, farewell."

When Dick went back to his friends he found they had risen and departed.

Rightly judging that they, too, had been summoned to bathe, he was not uneasy about them, and in a little while they came back, looking and feeling as well as men could desire.

"Blessed if ever I bathed in scent before," said Butterflick; "it aint in my line. I bought a bottle for Old Sally once of a man in the train—lavender-water, he said it was. He axed fourpence for it, and I gave him tuppence, but it warn't o' much account."

After a breakfast of coffee, bread, and fruit they strolled out of their room, and presently found their way to the courtyard.

It was almost deserted, but there were two persons who appeared to be peculiarly interested in our friends.

One of them was Gahzreal—Dick guessed at once he was the man—a tall Persian, with long, powerful arms; the other a priestly-looking man, who was in conversation with him.

The latter appeared to be somewhat excited, and was either railing at Gahzreal—who affected a profound indifference to his speech—or endeavouring to urge him to do something.

In one corner of the courtyard was an old well of the class one sees in the East.

There was a fringe of stonework on three sides, and on the other a flight of steps leading to the water below.

Dick, amused by the excited harangue of the priestly-looking man, sat down to watch the scene.

"What's the matter, Fowler?" asked Dick.

"As far as I can make out," replied Flutterby Fowler, "he is telling that fellow that you have come here to ruin him, and I should say our excitable friend has some interest in you."

"That man is one Gahzreal," said Dick, "and I am going to have some fun with him by and bye. I will tell you all about it presently."

"He is urging Gahzreal to come over and insult you," remarked Flutterby Fowler, after a pause.

"Oh! is he?" answered Dick, quietly. "I advise him not to do so."

"He says he will do it himself if the other doesn't."

"Very good—let him come."

And, indeed, after another long speech the excitable one left Gahzreal—who, with a contemptuous curl on his lip, disappeared through a doorway—and came bouncing up to Dick.

What he said we need not record.

But he made a long speech as he danced before Dick, and, meeting with no response, got bolder and bolder, until at last he was mad enough to make an attempt to push him into the well.

He failed, of course, for Dick was prepared for him.

Without any appearance of haste or excitement Dick got upon his feet, seized the excited man with his powerful hands, hoisted him in the air, and after shaking him a bit, when he screamed with terror like a wild cat, dropped him feet foremost into the well.

CHAPTER XXIX.

DICK AND THE STRONG MAN OF PERSIA.

THE well was not deep enough to drown the insolent Persian, but in any case Dick would not have allowed him to pay the penalty of his rudeness with his life.

Passing round to the side of the opening, our hero descended the steps, and with one hand dragged the fellow out of the water and carried him up to the courtyard, where he laid him down upon the stones.

"You are not much hurt," he said, "and if you lie there for a while you will soon get dry."

The fellow did not answer him. He was far and away too much scared for speech. All he did was to lie gasping and staring at the author of his overwhelming confusion.

Dick, having brought about this satisfactory state of things, walked away with a smile upon his face and disappeared, followed by his friends.

The drenched Persian had the whole place to himself, but several minutes elapsed ere he ventured to get upon his feet.

After one glance round, to convince himself that Dick had gone, he darted through the doorway by which Gahzreal had disappeared, and, having threaded his way through several passages, eventually came to an apartment where the Persian strong man was lying on some cushions at his ease.

"What ho! Nugah," he cried, "where hast thou been?"

"Into the well—even into the well," answered Nugah, "whither I was cast by the unbeliever."

"Ho! he cast thee there? How was it done? With his foot?"

"Nay. As I live and had a father," answered Nugah, "he took me up as a child and threw me in—I was as a straw in his hands."

Gahzreal laughed contemptuously.

"Why tell me a lie? Am I a babe, to be scared with such a story?" he asked.

"Gahzreal," said Nugah, "hearken unto me. Am I not thy agent—thy friend? Do I not pave the way for thee to walk into rich places?"

"It is so. Well?" assented Gahzreal.

"As I do so, is it for me to lie to thy disadvantage?" demanded Nugah. "Shall I say aught to make the unbeliever greater than thou art?"

"Thou hadst better not," said Gahzreal, with a frown.

"For all that," returned Nugah, "I say that he is as a giant to a child compared to thee. Have naught to do with him. Say that thou art sick, and will have no strength to perform before the vizier."

Gahzreal sat up and stretched out his right arm—a muscular one, as arms go.

"Look at that," he said. "Hath the unbeliever such muscles as these?"

"I know not what he hath," answered Nugah. "Whate'er it is, I bid thee shun him, or thou art lost."

"Pah!"

"It is so, and the vizier will be angry because thou art prevailed against by an unbeliever. He will have thy head struck from thy shoulders."

"Away—out of my sight!—thou half-drowned dog," cried Gahzreal, furiously. "Thou who drinkest strong wine in the morning—"

"By my mother's grave I have touched none of it this day!"

"Thou liest, Nugah!—I can smell it, mixed with the water of the well. Go to! Thou didst tumble in because thou wert drunk, and I say to thee—begone, or I will pound thy drenched body to a pulp. Away!"

Gahzreal made an apparent effort to rise, and Nugah, having no desire to be pounded or beaten in any way, vanished from the room.

The Persian strong man threw himself down, and, laughing heartily, yelled after his agent to put on the clothes of a woman, and no longer disgrace the form of man.

There was no answer, for Nugah had fled and hidden himself away, to await what he knew must come—disaster.

An hour after noon was the time appointed by the vizier for the exhibition of the feats of Gahzreal, and a sort of herald went abroad proclaiming the fact, inviting all who so desired to compete with him.

A response was hardly to be expected, for Gahzreal had the reputation of not only being unconquerable, but needlessly cruel to those who were rash enough to pit themselves against it.

More than one cripple in Astrabad and the region round about bore witness of his merciless treatment.

He was, in a sense, admired, but not loved.

The people were glad, of an opportunity of witnessing his feats, for there was so little to relieve the monotony of their dreary lives, but they would have rejoiced at his overthrow.

When, therefore, it became known that an "unbeliever" was going to enter the lists with Gahzreal, the slow stream of Astrabad life was stirred to its depths, and all sorts of stories were set afloat about the "stranger."

The soldiers who had escorted Dick and his party from the mountains to the city had a good word for him.

"He is of noble bearing," they said, "and snaps leathern thongs like twine—but it cannot be by strength, because he is slim, therefore it is by magic he does it."

All the town were invited by proclamation to attend in the grand square outside the castle of the vizier.

For his accommodation a stage or throne, apparently kept for such occasions, was put together on

DICK STRONGBOW:

The Diamond King,
AND WONDER OF THE WORLD.

Dick dropped the unfortunate man plump into the desert well.

No. 21.

Price One Penny.

the right-hand side of the castle gate, and another erection was placed a few feet away for the performers.

Around the two platforms, in a semi-circle, the soldiers would stand, and the people outside, in an erect position also, were allowed to see the whole of the entertainment for nothing.

CHAPTER XXX.

THE CONTEST.

ONG before the appointed hour the people were thronging into the square, not in the boisterous, merry way of an European crowd, but in a silent, stealthy way, as if they did not consider they had an entire right to be there.

On their first coming they flocked right up to the castle gate—for the soldiery had not yet come out—and there they stood, men, women, and children, under a broiling sun, discussing the coming treat.

"Ah !" said a white-bearded old man, " Gahzreal is blessed by the priests, and so prospers, while he breaks limbs and backs as he wills."

"The unbeliever he will kill outright," remarked another aged man.

"It will be a sorry sight," remarked a woman, closely veiled, save for one eye, " for they say he is passing fair to look upon."

"What is that to our women ?" demanded the old man, sternly.

"Our women are but women, after all," was the characteristic reply.

The old man frowned, but he said nothing more.

With the exhibition so near at hand it would be unseemly for him to wrangle with his favourite wife, whom he had graciously permitted to come and see the show.

Nevertheless, he began to think that the death, of, or a misfortune of great magnitude to, the unbeliever, would be to him rather agreeable than otherwise.

By and bye the gates of the castle opened and the soldiers appeared.

At the first glimpse of them the people began to fall back—not in undue haste, but in a silent, methodical way, without pressure from the guard.

So the semi-circle was formed, and the expectant people, packed close together and baking under the sun, patiently awaited the opening of the performance.

Nothing could be done, or even attempted, until the vizier appeared, and he, like all Eastern potentates, was in no hurry.

Punctuality is a thing unknown in Persia. The Shah keeps the people waiting hours for him, and sometimes a *whole* DAY, just to let them know that he is boss of the situation and can do exactly as he pleases.

It was quite three o'clock when the vizier, with his retinue, slowly filed upon the platform, and behind them came the four strangers who were gracing the castle with their presence.

There was some doubt in the minds of the people about the man who was to compete with the mighty Gahzreal. The men fixed their eyes on Butterflick, but the women declared for Dick Strongbow.

" He alone of all the unbelievers here hath beauty and grace," they reasoned.

Last of all came Gahzreal, accompanied by Nugah, his agent, who was still in a very troubled state of mind.

They had in attendance upon them some men, carrying weights and iron bars and chains, wherewith Gahzreal was to delight his audience.

Dick, standing on the left of the vizier, smiled as he saw that only old, time-honoured tricks were about to be performed.

It is true that he would have to wrestle with Gahzreal, but he knew that it could only end in one way, for he had taken the measure of Gahzreal, and could make light of him as an antagonist.

Gahzreal, left to himself in the centre of the platform—his agent and servitors having retired to the side, where they squatted down, so as not to impede the vision of the spectators—took up a weight and tossed it into the air.

A subdued murmur of applause passed round the square.

Gahzreal looked at the vizier for some sign of pleasure or approval, but saw only a stolid-faced old man indifferent to the feat.

"That's good child's play," said Butterflick to Flutterby Fowler. "I'll back my boy Muffins to do as much."

" Don't back me, at any rate," sighed the little tutor.

The next feat was the tossing of *two* weights in the air, one after the other, and keeping them going. The people visibly warmed under it, and the applause became most marked.

Then Gahzreal took up an iron bar and bent it across his knees.

This produced some hand-clapping, and the performer, turning to the vizier, invited Dick to come and do what he had done.

Quietly Dick descended from one platform and mounted the other.

Taking up the weights, one after the other—there were six of them—he tossed them like pebbles in the air, and, deftly catching them as they fell, laid the whole upon the platform.

Gahzreal was standing near Nugah, and a wrathful feeling came over him as the agent gave vent to a groan.

"Dog, be quiet !" he said.

"But it is ruin for you and me," whined Nugah ; " the people will stone us."

Gahzreal did not answer him, for his attention was now taken up by Dick, who, having picked up one of the iron bars, gave it a twist or two, and broke it in twain.

A perfect hurricane of applause came from the crowd.

The vizier signified his unqualified approval by a raised hand. Gahzreal turned green with envy.

Once more Nugah groaned.

Unable to bear the irritating influence of the sound, Gahzreal turned upon him, laid hold of his garment by the waist, dragged him to his feet, and kicked him off the platform.

This variety in the entertainment met with popular favour. Somebody was hurt, and that was sufficient to raise the spirits of the lookers-on.

The general applause was most fervent, and Gahzreal bowed as if he had done something good and clever.

Dick now, with his handkerchief, tied all the weights together. Their united weight was about fifteen stone.

It was not much for him to lift, and he raised them above his head with scarce an effort.

Gahzreal, being invited to do the same, succeeded in getting them as high as his shoulder, and there stuck fast.

In a fit of anger he cast them upon the platform, and signified by motions that the feat was new to him and required practice.

The vizier was displeased, and, through one of his officers, desired Gahzreal to "try again." The face of that dismayed performer was a study.

Sinking upon one knee he craved a boon. "Would the mighty, the peerless, the all-potent vizier permit him first to get the wrestling through?"

The vizier was indifferent to what was done, for he knew that the end would be the same, and not all the tricks of cunning for which Gahzreal was famous would help him.

"Let the dog do as he wills," said the vizier.

The Persian athlete expressed his thanks by bowing to the floor of the platform, against which he knocked his forehead thrice, and then, rising to his feet, motioned for Dick to advance.

Carelessly throwing his hat down, Dick walked up to him, and they closed.

Persian wrestling is not unlike the French. It consists of a deal of clinging and wriggling, and a lot of trickery more than strength.

Gahzreal clung to Dick, and sought by sundry devious ways to throw him, but he might as well have endeavoured to upset the London monument.

Having allowed him to have his own sweet way for awhile, Dick suddenly put forth his strength.

With one wrench he dislodged Gahzreal from him, then he was twisted round, and, with a contemptuous kick, sent flying from the platform.

It was an exact imitation of the treatment he had bestowed upon Nugah, and the joke was readily seen and appreciated.

The spectators laughed heartily, and as the unwonted sound fell upon the ears of the astounded Gahzreal, who was lying upon his back in the square, he called down upon his conqueror a series of ills such as only the Eastern mind can conceive.

But to call is one thing, to ensure their appearance another. Dick was unharmed. Without any show of triumph he replaced his hat and awaited the return of his opponent to the platform.

But Gahzreal came not.

The star of the East had a full knowledge that to attempt to recover his lost laurels would end in further humiliation, so he accepted his defeat, lying still upon his back, crying out that "he was overcome by magic, and would not deal with one who called evil to his aid."

"What is it the dog says?" demanded the vizier.

The words of Gahzreal were repeated to him, and the vizier laughed scornfully.

"He is a fraud and a liar," he said. "He hath been overcome by one who is his superior. No more. Let him be taught the beauty of truth by receiving forty stripes with a rod."

A signal from an officer sufficed for Gahzreal to be secured.

As the soldiery lifted him up he began to cry for mercy, and Dick, hearing from Flutterby Fowler, whom he had rejoined, of the sentence passed upon him, ventured to ask for pardon for the defeated one.

"Let him stand upon the platform, then," cried the vizier, "and publicly proclaim that he has lied, that no magic has been brought to bear upon him, and that he hath been defeated by the better man."

CHAPTER XXXI.

AFTER THE CONTEST—MUFFINS IN TROUBLE.

WITH as much good grace as he could call to his aid, Gahzreal mounted the platform somewhat stiffly, and before the people proclaimed that he had been honestly defeated.

Nay, more—he was but a poor child in the hands of so great a man, who now had the honour of being the guest of the most potent and most gracious vizier Astrabad had ever known.

In acknowledgment of this act of humility the people howled at him, and none howled louder than Nugah, who had abandoned his old employer for good and all.

The show was over, and if there had not been much variety there was considerable excitement and a crowning sensation. The people were overjoyed.

The vizier beckoned to Dick, and as he rose to leave gave him a friendly hint.

"Stay awhile with the people," he said; "it may be an act of grace that will do you a good service."

"Assuredly," replied Dick, "in this and in all things I am at your disposal."

"Furthermore," continued the vizier, "while they pay their homage to you I *have work to do*."

A meaning look was given as he passed on, attended by his officers, and, descending from the platform, entered the castle.

The great gates closed behind him, and the soldiery broke up, being free for awhile to enjoy themselves with the populace.

Then had Dick to pay the penalty of being a hero.

As the waters rush in from behind a broken sea-wall so the populace swept down upon him.

A palanquin—where got from he could not even guess—was borne up, and he was urged to take his seat therein.

"Let us bear him round the city," the people cried

Dick was much amused, and he fell in with their humour, taking a seat inside.

There was room for one more, and after some demur Flutterby Fowler accepted the offer of the extra seat.

Butterflick and Muffins elected to follow behind and see the "fun."

"I didn't think these people had a ounce of life in 'em," remarked Butterflick, "but you never can tell what's in a body till you've roused it. Muffy, my boy, I found that out years ago, when I first upset your respected mother, Old Sally—a wee thing was she, but with a heart in her that a rampagious lion or a buffler might be proud of. It's a wonderful world."

The palanquin started, borne on the shoulders of men who had fairly fought for the honour, and Butterflick and Muffins fell in behind.

Out of the square into the narrow streets went the procession, and ere long our burly friend began to feel that he had had enough of it.

A thirst that arose from the heat and dust assailed him, and he began to back out of the crowd.

But in this compact mass it was no easy task to get free. In the struggle he and Muffins were separated.

The boy had had enough of it too, and he, being more expert in clearing a crowd, succeeded in getting close to the doorway of a house while yet the panting Butterflick was but midway.

Standing on the step, Muffins grinned with delight to see his adopted father in a state of profuse perspiration, expostulating and imploring to be allowed to get through without hurting anybody.

As he spoke to the people in an unknown tongue he was not hearkened to with the attention he would otherwise have been.

On the contrary, there was an eager desire of the populace to keep up with the palanquin, and the press forward was greater than ever.

Muffins laughed aloud, but suddenly his mirth was checked by his being seized from behind, while a big hand was placed over his mouth.

He was drawn backwards into the building behind him and the door closed.

Inside it was dark, or it seemed so after the light of day, and the boy, fairly terrified by his position, struggled and kicked to get free from his assailant.

But in vain.

He was dragged down the passage, and, a door at the end of it opening, he was thrust into a chamber where two priestly-looking persons were seen sitting at a table.

From them he twisted his head round, and saw that his assailant was Turcomatz, the Russian.

Now indeed his heart sank within him, for he knew that he was in bad hands, and might look for scant mercy.

"Stand there," growled the Russian, planting him before the priests, "and answer the questions put to you."

"I will answer nothing," replied Muffins.

"Hey, what! art insolent?" cried Turcomatz. "Come, we must tame you. Now, then, speak."

He laid hold of Muffins by the ears and lifted him from the ground—once, twice, thrice.

Only those who have suffered the exquisite pain arising from this form of brutality can fully appreciate what the boy endured.

While undergoing the torture he was powerless, but immediately he felt himself firm upon his feet, although bound, he managed to turn upon the Russian and give him "a shinner"—a kick into which he threw his whole spirit.

Muffins had been silent under his suffering, but Turcomatz set up a howl that startled the two priests sitting at the table, hitherto calm and outwardly unmoved spectators of the scene.

Muffins darted towards the door, but the Russian was long of reach, and grabbed him by the collar.

Holding the boy at arm's length, he said—

"Answer—answer, or you will die. Do you hear?—die!"

"I can die," cried Muffins, "but I won't answer

anything. Help, help!—murder! Dad—master—Mister Fowler—help, help!"

"Stop his cries," said one of the priests to Turcomatz. "He wastes his breath. The walls of this house are thick enough to stifle thunder."

He spoke in English, much to Muffin's astonishment.

"Very good," he replied, "I won't waste my breath, and you may spare yours. I won't tell you anything."

"Boy," said the priest who had not hitherto spoken, "it is not much we ask of you. The questions are harmless."

"Very well," returned Muffins, making an effort to appear quiet and dignified, "put 'em. I don't mind answering if I don't betray other people's business, but it looks bad your dragging me in here in this style."

"It is because you will not see I am your friend," said Turcomatz, assuming a soft, winning tone. "Come, I did but lift you by the ears to show my friends how brave you British boys can be. Listen to their questions and answer them."

"Oh! only to see how brave we are," said Muffins, drily. "Werry good—proceed."

"You are staying at the castle with the vizier?" said the priest who had previously addressed him.

"I think I may say yes to that," replied Muffins, "seeing that everybody knows it."

"And your master, the great Strongbow, is on terms of friendship with him?" was the next question.

"They don't appear to be enemies at present," replied Muffins, cautiously.

"What the priest means," said Turcomatz, "is—"

"Thanky for nothing," interposed Muffins; "I can understand him without your assistance."

"Why, you—"

"Friend," said the priest, "leave the boy to us. He means well, and he is right in being faithful to his master. This great Strongbow and the vizier are much together—eh, boy?"

"I can't say," answered Muffins, shaking his head; "and, if they are, what then?"

"You are to answer questions, not to ask them. So they are together. When does your master go away?"

"Is it to-morrow?" asked Turcomatz, eagerly.

"No," replied Muffins; "he's taken his apartments for three years, and signed the lease."

The priests both looked at Muffins in surprise Turcomatz burst out in a fury.

"He is joking with us!" he cried—"'making game,' as they say in his country. Many people take a house for three years—it is the common way of hiring one abroad."

"Oh! indeed, our young friend jests. Well, we shall have our joke by and bye. Boy," said the priest, sternly, "answer me truly. Has the vizier placed anything in charge of your master?"

"Any what?" asked Muffins, now putting on a vacant stare.

"It would not be much—a small packet, or a—Come, boy, speak."

"I have spoken all I intend to say," doggedly replied Muffins.

Turcomatz laid his heavy hand upon him again, but the priest bade him be still.

"Not yet awhile will we be violent," he said.

"Come, boy, tell us. Have you heard any talk about a jewel?"

"When?" asked Muffins.

"To-day—yesterday."

"Not that I know of."

"He lies," said Turcomatz, furiously. "This Dick Strongbow confides in him and the burly ruffian who calls himself his father. Out with it, you whelp of the lion! Tell us all you know, or, by the Great White Czar, I'll rend your heart out."

"One moment more," said the priest; "another question, and if he will not answer then he must be tortured. Boy, was not your master with the vizier this morning early."

"I sha'n't answer you," replied Muffins; "and now you can do your worst. If you cut me into strips I won't speak. Try it, the whole three of you. As for you, you poison-giving hound, why I—"

And Muffins, in a white heat, went at the Russian like a young bull in the arena half maddened by the matadors.

CHAPTER XXXII.

THINGS TAKE A BETTER TURN FOR MUFFINS—THE DESERTED THOROUGHFARES—OUTSIDE THE CITY WALLS.

HETHER it was the pluck exhibited by Muffins that influenced the priests or a feeling of ordinary humanity we know not, but for for some reason they felt called upon to check the struggle between the boy and Turcomatz.

"Stay your hand, friend," said one, "and let us try what persuasion will do for us."

Turcomatz put his back to the door, and Muffins, panting, stood in the middle of the room facing the priests.

Adopting a softened tone they endeavoured to get something out of him, but they failed.

"I don't know anything," he said, "and if I did I would not tell it."

At length they gave him up, and, turning to Turcomatz, one said—

"The boy knows nothing. We have wasted our time. Let him go."

"That is folly," answered Turcomatz. "He will raise his friend, the great Strongbow, against us. He will go to the vizier and tell him what he has suffered here."

"It is nothing," commented one of the priests. "We have only questioned him, and he knows us not. There must be no blood shed."

"But something must be done with him," urged the Russian.

"There is a back way from this house," said the priest. "Let him be unbound and sent forth. No more. Dissent again and we will have naught further to do with you and your mission."

Turcomatz bit his lip and frowned, but he endeavoured to hide his chagrin by seeming to assent to the release of the boy.

"So let it be," he said. "I will take him back to his people."

"And yet me thinks," said the priest, looking keenly at him, "it were better that I should set the boy free. Stay here until I return."

Muffins could hardly believe his ears, and he was inclined to fear treachery, but he obeyed the beckoning finger of the priest and followed him from the chamber.

It was quite a maze of passages through which he led the boy, ending at last in a low door, very strong, and bound with iron.

Drawing back a number of bolts, that were strong enough to resist an ordinary battering-ram, the priest threw open the door, revealing to the glad eyes of Muffins an open street beyond.

But ere letting him go the priest had a word to say.

"Boy," he said, "your life is given you. If aught should happen when you may be able to make some return for it, do not forget."

Muffins looked at him wonderingly. He did not seem to clearly comprehend.

The priest explained his meaning more fully.

"Anon thou mayest or may not see us in the presence of the vizier. Should it be so, be blind."

"All right," answered Muffins, "I'm fly. I don't feel any malice towards you, though I don't see why you should have allowed that brute to lift me by the ears."

"Ah! it was your endurance that pleased us,' replied the priest. "You come of a sturdy people—a free race that can suffer without a murmur. Go—I know that thou wilt not betray one who has been your friend."

"No, I won't," said Muffins; "but I mean Turcomatz to smart for it. If master gets hold of the beggar he'll make rags of him."

The priest drew aside, and Muffins lost no time in getting into the open air, more than thankful for his escape.

The street outside had an old, worn-out look, and was evidently a thoroughfare sparsely populated.

A cripple hobbling about on crutches was the only person in sight.

The strong door closed behind the boy, and he had a look around him to get the bearings of the place.

But he was completely puzzled, and knew not whether to go to the right or left.

In his extremity he thought he would inquire of the cripple, and ran up to him to ask a question or two.

But all the response he could get was a hand extended for alms and a few muttered words in Persian, which Muffins could not understand.

He had some money in his pocket, and in pity gave a coin to the cripple, on whose face flashed the light of joy.

Without staying to listen to the whole of his muttered thanks, Muffins went on ahead, determined to take his chance of finding his way back to the abode of the vizier.

He wandered on until he came to a turning, down which he went, and arrived a minute later at a blank wall.

It was a blind thoroughfare.

Turning back, he entered the next, and went on until he came to another turning, which also ended in a blank wall, seemingly a continuance of that which he had already encountered.

It was very disheartening, especially as he was

beginning to feel tired and the evening was now approaching.

In a little while it would be night, when he knew it would be dangerous for him to be abroad alone.

Astrabad, like the other cities of the Shah, was infested during the dark hours with a variety of ruffians, who went about on the look-out for somebody to rob or murder, or, if necessary, to do both.

And these blind streets seemed peculiarly adapted for the doing of dark deeds.

Back Muffins went again, and tried yet a third thoroughfare. Here again he found the wall, but this time there was an opening in it, where there had once been a gate.

A portion of it still hung upon the hinges, but the rest of it was gone.

Glad of any way out of the maze of deserted streets, Muffins passed through the opening, and found himself outside the city.

It was the wall that ran round it which formed the termination of the streets.

On either side of him it ran, with towers and buttresses at intervals, and before him was a country which he had not seen before.

"Now, where am I?" Muffins asked himself—"on which side of the city? What a beastly fix to be in, and my legs aching as if they would drop off. I wish I was out of this place altogether. I wonder if master has missed me, and what is he doing? Dad must be nearly out of his mind."

Unable to locate himself, Muffins sat down to think a bit, and the more he thought the less he saw a chance of getting back before night set in.

As for returning by the way he came, he was determined not to do that, for the wretched, deserted streets had inspired him with a feeling of loathing and horror.

CHAPTER XXXIII.

ANXIETY OF MUFFINS' FRIENDS—THE SEARCH FOR THE MISSING ONE—A SOUND THRASHING.

OW where the tarnation is that boy?" muttered Butterflick.

The procession had gone round the city and returned to the gates of the vizier's palace, when Dick was allowed to dismount from the palanquin, and, with Flutterby Fowler, be at peace again.

The people, having displayed their enthusiasm, subsided quickly into their old phlegmatic condition and quietly dispersed. The three men were left alone.

"Where, in the name of Old Sally, can he have got to?" asked Butterflick.

"I thought he was with you," replied Dick.

"So he was," rejoined Butterflick, "but I missed him half an hour ago. We got separated in one of the rushes of them 'ere niggers. I wasn't particularly uneasy, thinking he could take care of himself. but now he's gone and got lost."

"In the usual way," said Dick, gravely, "Muffins would not lose himself, especially as he could easily have followed us."

"Perhaps he has returned to the palace," suggested Flutterby Fowler.

"Hardly likely," said Dick, "but we can inquire."

They inquired of the guard at the gate, receiving an answer which quenched their hopes in that direction.

It was now apparent to them that Muffins had gone astray.

"We must seek him," said Flutterby Fowler. "I would suggest that we go in different directions and devote an hour to finding him. If not successful we had better reassemble here, and then take counsel as to what we ought to do."

"As good a thing as we can do," said Dick.

They accordingly separated and went different ways, so as to each have a portion of the route taken by the procession to search.

We will follow Dick Strongbow.

He took a northern line, and searched here and there until more than the hour had elapsed. He was about to return when a little knot of beggars, eagerly conversing, attracted his attention.

One of them was a cripple with two sticks, who was relating some story, occasionally interrupted by his companions.

Dick had by this time acquired a slight knowledge of the Persian tongue, and was able to pick out a word or two here and there.

The cripple was talking of a boy who had given him a silver coin—a fortune, which would keep the beggar for a week or more in rice, coffee, and tobacco.

He seemed desirous of putting his friends on to a good thing, for more than once during the time Dick stood near listening he pointed in the direction of the spot where he had met his generous, youthful benefactor, and the way he had gone.

Dick made no attempt to converse with the man, mistrusting himself in the use of the language, but set out at once in the direction indicated.

It was time Muffins was found, as the night was approaching, and Dick would be expected before dark by the vizier at the palace.

Dick was armed, and had no fears for himself, but he knew that a boy with money about him might become an object of unpleasant attention from the cut-throats of the place.

Hastening on, he presently came to the street which led down to the old gate in the city wall.

It was his intention to pass to the left, but one of those mysterious inward suggestions, which we have all experienced at one time or another, checked his footsteps and induced him to turn in the right direction.

It was well he did so, for Muffins at that moment was in the hands of Turcomatz the Russian, who had succeeded in tracking and pouncing upon him.

Luckily he had no knife or pistol about him, but in place of them he had a stout whip, with which he was striking at the boy, who, pent up in a corner by the wall, could only dodge half the blows, and in vain endeavoured to escape.

Muffins could be silent under suffering if he wished to, but he saw no reason for being mute now, and was yelling his loudest.

And it was not so very loud after all, as he was getting into an exhausted condition, but Dick heard him and knew his voice.

Dashing away from the old gateway, he saw the

peril of his *protege*, and with the rush of a wild steer went for Turcomatz. He seized him just as Muffins, pretty well played out, fell exhausted upon the stoney ground.

The moment Dick's hand was laid upon Turcomatz the Russian knew in whose grasp he was.

All his heart went out of him like a puff of smoke, and abject fear laid hold of him.

"Mercy!" he gasped.

Dick's answer was the wresting of the whip from him and a blow that sent the Russian to his knees.

"Get up," cried Dick.

"I can't," yelled Turcomatz.

Dick laid hold of him by the collar of his coat, and, half raising him, beat the cowardly brute as if he had been thrashing corn with a flail.

He beat him until he was smarting from the nape of his neck to the calves of his legs.

He beat him until every nerve of his body was on fire with pain, and finally threw him to the ground with a force that made his bones rattle again.

"If you were worthy of the death of a *man*," he said, "I would shoot you. Lie there, and grovel like the cur you are."

"You've killed me—curses on you!" groaned the Russian.

Dick turned to Muffins, who had now so far recovered as to be able to sit up; but he looked very pale, and was as near exhausted as he could be.

"Has he hurt you much, Muffins?" asked Dick.

"Not much, master, thank you," replied Muffins. "I'm pumped a bit, that's all."

"No bones broken?"

"Oh! no, master."

"Come along, then; we must be getting back," said Dick. "Let me help you?"

He took the boy by the arm and raised him up. Muffins screwed himself together, and started off to walk with an air of jauntiness; but he soon subsided into a crawl.

"I shall be better by and bye, master," he said.

"Get on my back, Muffins, and I will carry you," replied Dick.

"Master, on *your* back?"

"Do as you are told."

Dick bent down and Muffins, mounting a big stone, clambered upon the back of his generous master. After a glance back at the Russian—who lay like one dead upon the ground—he started off at a smart walking pace.

The pair disappeared through the gateway, and for a long time the Russian did not stir. But at length he began to move, and with many a groan struggled into a sitting position.

"What an accursed hand he has. It strikes with the force of a demi-god, and he turned that stick into a rod of lightning. It not only struck, but *scorched* me."

He sat there awhile, rubbing himself with the care of a man who deals with tender spots upon his anatomy, groaning and muttering vows of vengeance, which he would assuredly fulfil if ever he got the chance to do so.

It was not until the sun touched the horizon, warning him of the impending night, that he got upon his feet.

It cost him a sharp twinge or two to do it, and every movement he made was like the wrenching of broken bones.

But by degrees he crawled back to the gate, and

entered the city just as the darkness—which, in that latitude, promptly follows the going down of the sun—fell upon the scene.

CHAPTER XXXIV.

LAST HOURS IN THE VIZIER'S PALACE—THE DEPARTURE AT NIGHT—A TORN HANDKERCHIEF.

GREAT was the joy of Butterflick on recovering his long adopted son, and overwhelming was his amazement when he heard that Dick Strongbow had brought the boy all the way home upon his back.

"And he travelled a good six miles an hour," Muffins explained to Butterflick and Flutterby Fowler. "He pegged along just as if he had nothing on his back."

"What marvellous strength!" exclaimed Flutterby Fowler. "I cannot realise it."

"You could if he gave you a nip," said Butterflick, with a grin. "He's never given me one, but I've seen men go to *dust* the moment he laid hold of 'em, and I know what the feeling must be like."

Dick was away from them that evening, and they saw nothing of him until the following morning at breakfast-time, when he announced their departure during the following night.

"It is necessary," he said, "to get away without exciting observation. My mission here is now fulfilled. I have nothing to wait for but the close of day."

He was silent for a moment, and then, lowering his voice, he went on.

"I have in my possession," he said, "a small leathern bag. It is here, in my breast pocket—the inside one. It contains a diamond of enormous value. Now, should anything happen to me—death by sickness or violence—you, Butterflick, are to take charge of this treasure and carry it back to the Duke of Lavante."

"I'll do it if I live," replied Butterflick.

"And then, again, if anything occurs to shorten *your* life here, Flutterby Fowler will take charge of it. Last of all it must come to Muffins, if need be. But I do not anticipate the charge coming down to him."

"If it does I'll carry it through somehow, master," said Muffins.

"Well spoken. I believe you would do it or die in the attempt. Now there is nothing more to say or do but to pass the time as pleasantly as we can."

"I should like to ask one question," said Flutterby Folwer. "Is this jewel the famous Persian diamond that has been so long missing?"

"It is. How did you know anything about it?"

"By reading. It is an historical jewel, and I have been inclined to look upon the story as a fable."

"It is a solid fact," said Dick. "Here, you shall see it. It is something worth looking upon."

He brought out the bag, and, having unloosened the string that fastened the mouth of it, turned into the palm of his hand a diamond, by far the biggest and brightest any of them had ever seen.

"It is of the purest water," said Dick, "as rare in colour as in size, and when this was cut the man who performed the work was a master of his craft."

He laid hold of Muffins by the ears and lifted him from the ground—Once, Twice, Thrice.

Replacing the jewel in the bag he restored it to his pocket, saying—

"You now all know what I came hither for, and for who it is intended you also know, as far as the Duke of Lavante goes. More you need not be acquainted with."

"Shall we see the vizier again?" asked Flutterby Fowler.

"No," answered Dick. "I am here as an entertainer of his highness, and as such have been paid and dismissed. It was necessary that the farce should be played by us for the vizier's sake."

He took out of his pocket a handful of gold coins, ill-made according to our notion of coinage, but very pretty to the eye withal.

"They have been sweated out of the people," said Dick, "and to the people they shall be given back. But it must be done discreetly. To-night, at the hour of nine, horses will await us at the gates, on which we are to mount and ride away. As we go through the city I will drop a coin here and there, until all are expended, and let us hope that the finders will be those who need them most."

"And out of your generosity," said Flutterby Fowler, "will arise a story that on a certain eve it rained gold in Astrabad. These Eastern people have the knack of creating a legend from everything. They will begin with a description of someone in need of gold, and he will consult a magician, who will tell him that the heavens shall pour down gold, which will fall upon the streets, and only those who are worthy of such help shall find it. Oh! they will make a very pretty yarn of it."

"They seem to be given to lying," remarked Butterflick.

"It is hardly lying," said Flutterby Fowler; "it is only the way of the people. They poetise everything."

"Well, if any man at home told me it had rained gold I should punch his head," returned Butterflick.

"And you would be justified in doing it," said Flutterby Fowler, "for, not being of a poetic mind, he would be guilty of telling a lie."

"But why should a poet have a license to lie more'n other people?" demanded Butterflick.

"I don't know, but the poets have it," answered Flutterby Fowler, "and it's a license sanctified by ages, which no Act of Parliament can take away."

"I thank goodness I'm not a poet," said Butterflick, fervently, "seeing that it's a fancy name for a born liar."

Dick and Flutterby Fowler laughed, and Muffins regarded his adopted father with a pitying air.

"You aint up in these things, dad," he said, "and you had better leave poets alone. They never did you any harm."

"I'd like to come across a poet writing his rubbish about *me*," said Butterflick. "I'd make him skip."

It would have been useless to attempt to bring about in him a better feeling for the poets, and nobody attempted it.

Retiring to one of the small courts where there was plenty of shade, and a cool, sparkling fountain playing in the centre, they lounged an hour or two away with smoking and chatting about home.

Dick had been so far successful in his mission that he had every right to be elated, but he was not unduly so.

He knew that the homeward journey might be every whit as perilous as the outward one, perhaps more so.

It did dawn upon him that he had done an unwise thing in sparing the life of Turcomatz, but he hardly regretted it.

He could not slay even the bitterest of his enemies in cold blood or unfair fight.

And there was the chance that Turcomatz had had enough of him, and would not cross his path again.

The reputation of the Russians for doggedness is pretty general, and it was not by any means certain that Turcomatz would hold aloof and leave them in peace to pursue their homeward journey.

"If he persists in crossing my path again," thought Dick, "he must die."

The night came in due course, and at sunset our friends partook of a meal that was quite a feast.

The vizier did not come near them, but the attendants had evidently been commanded to serve the guests well.

Indeed they did so gladly, for had not that mighty Englishman, Dick Strongbow by name, vanquished as a child the hitherto unassailable Gahzreal?

This once great man had vanished with Nugah, his agent, probably to do what other fallen stars do— work the provinces under another name.

After the repast the officer who had attended upon the party from the time of their arrival ushered them to the gate, where five horses were awaiting them and their conductor.

He went with them as an escort to the gate by which they had first entered the city of Astrabad.

It was guarded by a dozen men with an officer, to whom the pass of the vizier was shown. The guard were all eager to get a good look at Strongbow, and, as they were led to believe he was only a public performer, they asked him to stay awhile and give them some exhibition of his strength.

Feeling it would be better to keep up his assumed character, Dick did as they desired, and broke stout ropes bound round his chest, and bent an iron bar, and did other things that immeasurably delighted them.

At last they let him go, and he had much difficulty in persuading them to keep the few coins out of their miserable pay they were anxious to bestow upon him.

The leave-takings over, they were enabled to leave the city behind them. There was light enough for them to see the road by, and, the horses being fresh, they got over the ground at a rattling pace.

"Hang it!" said Dick, suddenly, "I forgot all about dropping that money in the streets."

"There's a good legend lost, then," remarked Flutterby Fowler.

"It will save some of them poet chaps from telling a thumping lie," said Butterflick.

"For all that I will find a use for it," said Dick. "I do not desire to carry away with me one penny of the Shah's blood-money."

On they rode, keeping to a highway that was strange to them, but which they had been told was the shortest cut to the mountains. It was the road which their pursuers had taken on the memorable day when they first fell in with the vizier.

Anon, as they rode along, they saw a light ahead, and presently came to one of the meagre farmhouses of the district.

It stood back a short distance from the road, but Dick, as he reined up his horse, could see into a sparsely-furnished room, where a man was standing with bowed head, weeping.

Dick's heart was touched by the sight of the man —he hardly knew why—and he desired Flutterby Fowler to go and ask him what was the cause of his distress.

Fowler dismounted, and walked down the sandy footpath to the house, but he halted by the open window, where he stood in an attitude of listening.

In a little while he came back again.

"Here is a splendid opportunity for the use of that money," he said. "The old man is bewailing the loss of his wealth. It seems he had a hoard, which the Shah's agent heard of, and swooped down upon. He is imploring some good geni to return it to him."

"I will be that geni," said Dick, as he tore his handkerchief in two and placed the money in one portion of it. "Place this quietly on the window-sill, where he is sure to find it, and come away."

Flutterby Fowler executed his commission so quietly that he did not disturb the old man in his bewailing, and, the road here being covered with soft sand, the horses moved away without making a sound that reached the old man's ears.

When they were at a safe distance for speaking Butterflick asked if "them poet chaps would, after all, get a chance of lying?"

"I presume so," replied Flutterby Fowler. "The old man is sure to notice that the good geni placed the money there."

"Well, it's your affair and not mine," said Butterflick. "After all, perhaps, it don't matter so long as the old man gets the money. That's the main thing, I reckon."

It was a good act, a kindly act, but it brought evil to the four adventurers for the next day Turcomatz was riding by in pursuit of them, and saw the half of the handkerchief in the old man's hand as he stood by the door.

It was of pale-blue silken material, and the Russian knew it. He stopped and asked the old man where he got it from.

"I found it by my window this morning," was the cautious reply. "Perhaps the wind blew it there."

Turcomatz rode on with an evil smile upon his face. Up to that time he was not sure he was pursuing the right road, but the sight of that piece of silk was reassuring.

He was on the track of a man who had outwitted and beaten him, and the hatred he felt towards him was very bitter indeed.

CHAPTER XXXV.

A WOLF UPON THE TRAIL—THE OLD STABLES—A TALK AT THE FOUNTAIN—MUFFINS AROUND.

 UIET persistence is one of the characteristics of the Russian nature. The blood of the people runs slowly in their veins, and it takes a long time to rouse them, but when thoroughly stirred up their anger is slow to subside.

Turcomatz was a true Russian. He had gone through the quiet, persistent period, and was now on the verge of madness with the bitterness of his feeling.

He had so far been foiled in his mission, which was simply this.

His august, imperial master coveted the diamond which was in the possession of Dick Strongbow. It was known to exist, and to be in the hands of the Vizier of Astrabad.

But where it was hidden was a secret.

Now, between the Shah of Persia and the Emperor of Russia there was an understanding that if ever that diamond was found it was to become the property of the latter, on condition of payment of certain monies and protection to the Shah in case he should go to war.

Various attempts had been made to induce the Vizier of Astrabad to give it up, but the old man had always protested he knew nothing of its existence—that the story of it was, in his belief, a myth, a fable.

Had he been weak enough to produce it his august master would have had him instantly executed on some pretext, and his repeated denials of all knowledge of it preserved his life.

For to slay the vizier would be equivalent to burying the secret of the hiding-place of the diamond for ever.

Somehow the knowledge that the King of Sweden was after the jewel had come into the possession of the Czar's agent, and Turcomatz had undertaken the task of watching for anyone who was sent to the country to fetch it away.

By means of spies, who swarmed everywhere, it was discovered or surmised that Dick Strongbow was the man selected for the task, and Turcomatz was forewarned of his coming.

All that follows we know.

Up to a certain point the wily Russian was successful. He succeeded, as he thought, in ingratiating himself with Dick and his friends, yet the result of his labours hitherto had been a thorough and complete failure.

He had no great hope now of obtaining the diamond, but he was resolved upon revenge, and, having traced him to the house where the money had been left for the unfortunate farmer, he was sure of the homeward track he had taken.

So far—good. But he would have to be wary in his movements, as he knew that if Dick Strongbow discovered him to be in pursuit his chances of living long were infinitesimally small.

The unfortunate part of the business, as far as Turcomatz was concerned, was that he had lost his precious pass, for, although he was known to some of the priests in Astrabad, he was, in a general way, a stranger in the country.

He could not secure the assistance he needed, and what he could do now would have to be done alone.

"By the might of my country," he muttered again and again, as he rode on in pursuit, "I will have his life, if nothing else."

The horse he bestrode was a good one, and he did not spare it. For hours, with a brief halt now and then, he proceeded, until he sighted a village ahead, where he was pretty sure to find them resting.

It was the first place where they would be likely to make a halt, and instead of entering it he stopped short at a peasant's hovel to make inquiries.

There was only a woman at home, but she could give him the information he wanted.

The four strangers had arrived, and had put up at the only inn in the place.

"It is that big house there," the woman said, pointing towards a rambling building in the centre of the village. "It was once the country house of the vizier, but it is falling to pieces, and so it has become an inn."

Turcomatz brought out a piece of money and held it before her eyes.

"Serve me well," he said, "and this is yours. I would know how long these strangers propose to stay here. Go now and inquire, but do not betray me, or your life will be forfeited—for I am the servant of the great high priest."

He opened his tunic, and showed her a silver plate, fashioned in the form of the sun, as it is pourtrayed by the faithful worshippers of that luminary.

The woman tremblingly bowed and said—"I am the true servant of my lord. With or without his gift I will serve him."

"Go then," he answered, "and return speedily."

The woman departed, and Turcomatz, having stabled his horse in a shed at the back of the humble abode, unslung a rifle he had hitherto carried on his back and sat down near the door to await her return.

She did her work speedily, returning with the information that the strangers intended passing the night at the inn, so as to give their horses a much-needed rest.

They had endeavoured to get other animals in exchange, but none were to be had that they would accept.

Turcomatz gave the woman the piece of money—the value of which was about equivalent to an English shilling—and bade her exhibit the wisdom of the wise by preserving a silence about his coming should anyone visit the hovel and ask her questions.

Then, it being afternoon, he stole out, and, having made a detour, bore down upon the inn, using everything in the way of trees and bushes as cover, so as to get to the point he aimed at unobserved.

In some of the outhouses of the inn—not a quarter of which were in use—he knew he could find a hiding-place, from whence he could watch the movements of those going in and out, and he trusted that an opportunity would be found to vent his malignity on the man who had so successfully foiled him.

Having once been the country house of a vizier, the stabling was of course of the most extensive description, and two-thirds of it had long been neglected.

Doors stood open or hung upon one hinge, or in some places had disappeared altogether; and the inn itself, built for the accommodation of a host of servants, was only occupied in one wing near the high road.

The rest was left, like the stables, to ruin and decay.

Turcomatz succeeded in gaining one of the outhouses which commanded a view of the occupied part of the inn, and for the greater ease of movement he unslung his rifle and placed it and also a revolver in a corner of the dismal place.

It was now about half-past four in the afternoon.

The heat of the day had passed, and those who had been sleeping or keeping in the shade when the sun was high were abroad again.

A servant came from the inn and filled a huge earthern jar from a well in the yard. As she was poising it on her head, preparatory to returning, a man-servant appeared, and the two stood chatting together for awhile.

Turcomatz could not clearly hear what they were saying. Perhaps it was of no moment to him, but with the instinct of the true spy he thought it would be better to get nearer and listen.

There were inner means of communication from one stable to another in the form of openings—some with doors and others without.

None of the doors were fastened, for what need was there of using bolts and bars when no horses were ever seen there now?

By passing through half a dozen stables Turcomatz got to a window exactly opposite the well, and, crouching just beneath the opening, listened with all his ears.

The man and the woman were still talking, and their theme, as he expected, was the four strangers at the inn.

"Ah! they are great and generous," the woman was saying, "for he of the handsome countenance gave me these pieces of silver, and I have two others, one from he of the broad face and the other from the small man."

"It is noble to give so freely," returned the man. "I, too, have received a piece of silver. It is enough for a man. I am not a woman, with bright eyes and lips that are as the leaves of roses."

The woman laughed softly.

"Be not jealous," she said; "they made no love to me. See, now, we are rich enough to marry and be our own masters, Is it not so?"

"Aye, aye!" replied the man, cheerily; "but get you in and look well to these strangers, for if they give freely at coming they will give more when they ride away."

The girl, with the jar of water deftly balanced upon her head, returned to the house with the man at her heels, whispering things that the Russian did not care to hear, as they did not bear upon the matter that interested him.

Slowly he sauntered back through the stable, halting here and there to peer through the openings that served to let in light and air.

When half-way back he saw Muffins sauntering up the yard, having apparently been strolling round the house.

He had his hands in his pockets, his hat on the back of his head, and he was whistling cheerily.

"Ah! my young friend," muttered Turcomatz, "there is a little debt to settle between you and me. If I can kill the lion I will not spare the cub. Whistle while you may."

He remained cautiously looking out, and watched Muffins as he walked up the yard.

The boy halted by a window of the inn and said something to somebody within. Dick Strongbow appeared.

"What is it, Muffins?" he asked.

"I have something to tell you, master," the boy replied.

"Is it important?"

"I don't know, but I think so."

"Come in," said Dick.

Muffins turned back and passed through the door-way.

"Why not *now!*" hissed the Russian.

He would never get another chance so good, perhaps.

Dick was there in the room—the window was low. A quick aim through it and he would be a dead man.

The Russian dashed back to where he had left his rifle and revolver, laid hold of the latter, cocked the trigger so as to be ready to fire, and rushed out with murder in his small, cunning, gleaming eyes.

CHAPTER XXXVI.

THE SHOT—DICK FALLS—THE RUSSIAN'S FLIGHT—HIS HIDING-PLACE.

ICK STRONGBOW was alone in the room—a poor-looking place, but cool and comfortable, it being on the north side of the house, and well shaded from the sun.

He had been resting, and was thinking of the joy of a safe return home and all the pleasures that would follow.

Once again in the old country his wanderings would be at an end, and with wealth and the sweet Lucella for a wife he could settle down and enjoy a well-earned rest.

Muffins was several minutes in finding the room, for he had entered the house by a different door to that by which he had left, and, having taken a wrong turning, he lost himself for a brief space of time among the many passages.

But resuming his way he hastened into the room with a face lighted up by excitement.

"Master," he said, "I've found something. It may not be our affair, but it is strange for such things to be left in one of these rotten old stables."

"What has been left?" quietly asked Dick.

"A rifle," replied Muffins, "a breach-loader, and a revolver with it. Both of the newest make. I'd been searching outside, and seeing there was no door to the stables I entered. In a corner stood the weapons, ready for use."

"Point out the place to me," said Dick. "Can we see them from the window?"

"I'll look, master," replied Muffins.

He stepped up to the window, and was about to look out, when the muzzle of a revolver flashed before his eyes.

Involuntarily he dropped upon his hands and knees.

"Look out, master!" he screamed.

Dick, who had turned his back for a moment, wheeled round, and saw the muzzle of the revolver pointed straight at his breast.

Behind it was the malevolent face of Turcomatz.

He had no time to get out of the way.

The trigger was pulled and a broad flame flashed before his eyes.

He felt himself struck in the centre of the fore-head. Staggering back, Dick tripped on the rough floor and fell.

Muffins, in an agony of terror, sprang to his feet, laid hold of the revolver, and yelled murder.

Turcomatz did not wait to struggle to obtain possession of the weapon.

Letting it go, he fled away, panting with exultation.

Taking the route he had observed in approaching the inn, he dodged his way back to the hovel of the peasant, and, rushing in, sank upon a rough seat near the door.

The woman was busy preparing some food for the evening meal. She looked up with a terrified face.

"What ails my lord?" she inquired.

"Woman, listen," said Turcomatz. "It was decreed by the High Priest of the Sun that one of the strangers should die. He is dead. In obedience to the command of my master I have slain him, and here I must hide."

The woman covered her face with her hands and began to weep.

"None of that," said Turcomatz, roughly. "It is not for you to judge the work of the High Priest. Point out to me where I can hide."

"Though poor, there has been no blood upon this house before."

"What of that? The blood is none of your shedding. Be dumb, you fool."

"But if they seek you here there is your horse—"

"Say that I left it here, and did not return. Woe to you if you betray me, for have you not already taken blood money?"

The woman took the piece of silver that represented her present, walked to the door, and cast it away with all her force.

"I will have none of it," she said, "but as you are the servant of the High Priest I will hide you."

She left the room, and after a short absence returned with a spade, with which she began to break up the flattened earth that formed the floor of the room.

In a little while a wooden trap was revealed. This she raised disclosing a ladder.

"Go down," she said, "and lie close. I will replace the door, cover it with earth, and no man shall find you."

But Turcomatz hesitated.

It seemed to be nothing more than a dark, dismal hole below.

"I might stifle," he said.

"Men have lived there for a week and not died," the woman answered. "I hid my son there when the Shah sent out to collect all the young men of the country to serve him in a petty war with the tribes of the Khan. I told them my boy had died of fever, but, alas! they found out afterwards, and he was given to the Czar, because his mother loved him."

"What! found him here?" exclaimed Turcomatz.

"No, after he came forth," she said; "but say, will you go or nay?"

"It will be better to do so, perhaps," muttered Turcomatz, "for one is not safe now that accursed boy has seen me. But hark ye, woman, if ill befalls me you will have to render an account of yourself before the altar of the Sun."

"I will not betray you," said the woman, with a set face.

So Turcomatz, with doubt in his heart, went down

step by step, and the trap-door closed over his head.

A feeling of being enclosed in a living tomb came over him, and on the last step he sank down shivering.

He could hear the woman replacing the earth upon the trap-door, beating and flattening it down.

How like filling in a grave it seemed to him!

He rose up hastily, and began to reascend the ladder, but felt ashamed of his cowardice, and again returned to the floor of his hiding-place.

It was darker than the darkest night down there—dark as a tomb could be—absolutely black, without one scintilla of the blessed sun to break the crushing intensity of feeling that arose out of a sense of being where NOTHING existed.

In all his life Turcomatz had never before known anything approaching the horrible sensation he now endured.

"What if the woman has fastened the trap-door down and left me here to *die* ?" he asked himself.

He fought with the terror this thought inspired, and to kill the dreadful time began to measure the extent of his hiding-place.

Groping about until he reached the damp, cold wall, he felt his way around it—no, not around, for it was about eighteen feet one way, then six feet across, and down again to quite a narrow bend.

"Bones of my people !" he cried, "*it is shaped* LIKE A COFFIN !"

In mental terror he fell forward upon his face, and lay there panting for awhile.

Rising, he saw there was a light—a dancing *ignus fatus* kind of star, that skipped here and there and then suddenly disappeared.

It was a phantom of the brain.

"I'll get out of this," he hoarsely muttered ; "I can't stand it."

Crawling back to the ladder, he ascended, and tried to raise the trap-door above.

But it was fast.

"Betrayed !" he shrieked. "I am a dead man."

In his agony he momentarily lost his strength, and rolled limp and helpless down to the floor again. Then he lay still and listened.

"In a little while," he said, "and she—the hag—will return. I shall be taken and charged with murder. But I care not—anything is better than this hellish hole. It will be something to see the light of day again."

It was strange that he should have so soon become unstrung, but the fact may be accounted for by the strain which had been upon him for some days past, culminating in the shooting at the inn.

He felt that he had triumphed, but it was no triumph.

Nay, more—it would be the bitterest thing he had ever known if he were indeed condemned to die like the toad embedded in coal.

In the fearful excitement that was upon him he lived a day in a minute.

No words of ours could pourtray the workings of his usually sluggish but very cunning mind. It moved swiftly, it raced as a river long pent up in some canyon by rocks and stones suddenly breaks out into a free course.

And it took all with it—common sense, judgment, reassuring power, everything. Clear to an extent, his mind was in the main chaotic.

But the strangest thing of all was the way in which hunger and thirst suddenly assailed him.

Without warning the two desires for nourishment came upon him. His fevered blood dried about his lips, which cracked, and a longing for food, almost too intense to bear, came upon him.

Then he thought of the time which had elapsed since he had eaten or drank anything.

Since early morning, or stay, was it yesterday since he had tasted food or moistened his parched lips? He could not, in the seething of his mind, make sure.

CHAPTER XXXVII.

THE LAST MINUTES IN THE HIDING-PLACE—RELEASE—
IS THIS A SPIRIT?

 T last he began to cry out for help—to implore the woman to raise the trap-door and set him free.

"I cannot bear this dreadful darkness," he yelled; "it is not of this world."

But he cried in vain.

There was no sound above, and the trap-door remained fast.

A frenzy of fear laid hold of him.

Standing on the topmost rung of the ladder but three, he bent his back and endeavoured to force the door upward.

It yielded a little, and with one exultant cry he renewed his efforts.

The trap-door lifted an inch.

"Free !" he shouted, and with one tremendous effort sought to force up the door.

But he forgot the strain upon the ladder on which he stood.

It could not bear it, and with a cracking sound it parted in twain.

Down he went with the shattered ladder, and lay upon the ground, conscious that he had been injured and was bleeding somewhere, but could not locate the spot.

Indeed he made no effort to do so, but lay quite still, dumb with terror and despair.

After awhile—he knew not how long—a smarting in his right leg indicated the spot of the wound.

He put his hand to it, and found that his nether garment had been ripped up and a gaping wound torn in the flesh beneath.

The blood was not flowing quickly, and the artery was therefore untouched. So far he was safe.

But with increasing agony came a returning sense of the hopeless nature of his position.

Instead of bettering the time by repenting of his sins, he cursed all things that led him into this position.

The Czar came in for the first full share of his anathemas, then the Shah, and afterwards all the men in authority in Persia.

After that he favoured the country with a few withering utterances, but when he came to Dick Strongbow he stopped.

He could not curse him he believed to be dead, for in a little while he might join him in the great fathomless beyond—the unseen world of the future.

He shrank from the uncanny task of cursing the man he had murdered.

He had to give it up altogether after awhile for want of breath, and rising to his feet he once more felt his way round his prison tomb.

There was no particular object to be gained by it. He did it mechanically, and when he came to the broken ladder stopped again.

And now it seemed to him as if there were some light in the place, and raising his head he saw that the trap was raised and the woman peering into the depths below.

He could only dimly see her, for night had come on, but a little light was a great deal to him then, and he could have shouted for joy if he had not nearly lost his voice.

"How is it with you?" the woman asked.

"Let me come out," he hoarsely answered. "How long have I been here?"

"The sun set half an hour ago," she answered.

"No more? Then I have been here an hour at the most?"

"No more."

"Get me a ladder and let me come out."

"Where is the ladder that you used?"

"Broken."

The woman muttered something—what it was he could not catch—and went away.

The few minutes she was absent seemed very long, but not so long as before.

She brought with her a short, heavy ladder, which she lowered, and Turcomatz, with trembling limbs, crept up to the room above.

"Your enemies," said the woman, "have been here and are gone. Knowing how awful it is to be down there, I raised the trap to see how you fared."

"I cannot go down again, though it cost me my life to remain above," replied Turcomatz, wiping the perspiration from his brow.

"Perhaps there is little need; but you cannot remain here," said the woman.

"Get me my horse," he said, "and bring it round to the door."

"Nay, I cannot," was the reply; "it is taken away."

"Who has taken it?"

"Your enemies. One a burly man, who spoke loudly in the English tongue, which I understand not, but he seemed to curse you."

"That was Butterflick," muttered Turcomatz.

He shrank from an encounter with the miner—he would have shrank from an encounter with a child just then—and it was equally distasteful for him to stay where he was.

He must get out and away—anywhere—so as to be able to feel safe and lie down and rest.

"Did they say why they took the horse?" he asked, wearily.

"I know not, save that they may have thought it was yours," was the answer; "but get you gone. It will be better for you not to stay, since when you are in hiding you scream and shout for help."

"You heard me, then?" he said, ferociously.

"One might have heard you from the bowels of the earth," answered the woman. "It was by good fortune you were silent when they were in the house. They promised to return again."

This was enough for Turcomatz.

He must be gone, and, opening the door, he passed into the night.

Barely had he left the place when the whole manner of the woman changed.

"Let him beware," she softly said, her eyes filled with the light of exultation; "the wolf may find the hunters yet. As for his horse, why should I not lie to him and make it mine? By the day he, the murderer, will be well away, and then I can seek my prize in the pasture land where I have tethered him."

Meanwhile the Russian had gone along the road, choosing the direction of the village.

Seeing no one abroad, he thought he might venture to pass through.

So he went on, and presently came within sight of the inn, when into the middle of the road there glided, without a sound, the tall, graceful form of Dick Strongbow.

"His spirit!" yelled the Russian, as he fled madly away.

CHAPTER XXXVIII.

NO GHOST, BUT LIVING FLESH AND BLOOD—THE PUNISHMENT OF TURCOMATZ.

 VERY few emotions can rival that which is felt by nervous persons when they fancy they see a spirit from another world, and Turcomatz, being in a highly-strung condition, was completely staggered by the sight of Dick Strongbow.

But it was no ghost he looked upon. It was Dick in the flesh—thanks to the sharp wits of Muffins.

The boy, when he found the revolver lying near the rifle in the stables, opened the breaches of both, and saw the revolver was loaded.

Although he did not understand why they should be there, he thought they might possibly be indicative of coming mischief, so he whipped out his knife, cut open the upper part of the cartridges, extracted the bullets, and replaced the lower halves, containing the powder, alone.

It was the wad that held the powder in its place which struck Dick upon the forehead, and, although it gave him a stinging blow, that for a moment or two reduced him to a semi-unconscious condition, it did him no material harm.

Muffins was about to explain what he had done when the Russian appeared at the window and fired at Dick.

Apparently he had succeeded in his project and fled.

As soon as Dick recovered from the blow he had suffered from, Muffins hastily explained what he had done, and we may be sure he received, as he deserved, hearty thanks for the foresight he had shown.

Dick went in search of the Russian, but, failing to find him in the immediate neighbourhood of the inn, gave up the idea of settling with him for the time, but he resolved, if ever they met again, to put it out of his power to repeat the dastardly offence.

And now they had met again, sooner than Dick expected.

Standing at the door of the inn, to enjoy what coolness there was in the evening air, he was amazed at the sight of his enemy approaching.

Then it flashed upon him that Turcomatz must

DICK STRONGBOW:
The Diamond King,
AND WONDER OF THE WORLD.

"Get up," cried Dick. "I can't," yelled Turcomatz.

No. 22.   Price One Penny.

believe he was dead, and he arranged a surprise for the Russian.

It was a complete and unqualified success.

Turcomatz made no attempt to flee—he could not —but stood quite still, until he felt the powerful hands of Dick twist him round and pin his own to his side.

"If you utter a word I will kill you," said Dick, quietly.

It was a needless threat, for there were no words left in the terrified man.

He realised now that his attempt on Dick's life had failed, and he was in the power of a man whom he had deeply wronged.

Pushing his prisoner before him, Dick re-entered the inn and returned to the room he had recently left—that in which he had been fired at by the Russian.

Butterflick was there, dozing in the heat of the room. He woke up on hearing footsteps, and stared, as well he might, at the sight of captor and captive.

"Stand there," said Dick, thrusting Turcomatz against the wall. "Move if you dare. Butterflick, see if he has any arms about him."

"Certainly, sir," answered Butterflick, readily. "Now, young man, you stand easy, or I shall be obliged to be rough with you."

"Mercy!" gasped Turcomatz.

"Oh! yes, why not?" said Butterflick, in a bantering tone. "Every consideration shall be shown you. Knife, revolver, purse, and a few papers—that's all, Mister Strongbow."

Dick had turned to the table, on which stood a flask of wine, half-emptied, and a drinking horn.

Into the latter he poured a little of the former, and faced Turcomatz.

"You have asked for mercy," he said, "and I will show it to you. I will spare your life—on one condition. You see this?"

He drew a small phial from his breast and held it up before the Russian's eyes.

"Do you know it?"

The lamp in the room burned dimly, but it gave light enough for the Russian to see and recognise the phial.

He made no answer.

With great deliberation Dick uncorked the phial, and carefully let fall three drops of its contents into the horn.

"If you drink this," said Dick, "you may go free. If you refuse I will take you outside and shoot you as I would a hyena."

"To drink that," replied Turcomatz, with a hoarse rattle in his throat, "is to be a child for life."

"A live child is better than a dead man," remarked Butterflick, with a grin.

"It is your own medicine for others," said Dick. "Come, I have no time for fooling. Drink this—I shall not wait three seconds longer."

Turcomatz, with a groan, laid hold of the horn, and tossed its contents into his mouth.

"Swallow it!" cried Dick. "Throw your head back and open your mouth."

Turcomatz obeyed, and Dick seized his nose with a terrible grip. The Russian gave one gasp and the medicine was down.

"And now," said Dick, "I must see you housed for the night."

"Cannot I go my way?" asked Turcomatz.

"No, not until the morrow," answered Dick;

"the potion must have time to act. Come and help him along, Butterflick."

There was need of it, for the mere thought of the future before him was sufficient to reduce Turcomatz to a state of feebleness.

Butterflick laid hold of his arm, and, partly dragging and partly pushing him along, followed Dick to the stables in the rear and shut him in one where the door could be made fast.

They heard him moan as they drew the bolts and went round to the window, which was too small to permit of his escape by that way, and there Dick gave him a last word.

"You will remain quiet until the sun is well up to-morrow," he said. "If I am disturbed by you I will take steps to make you quiet altogether."

The only answer was a sound between a groan and a growl, but immediately after the Russian was heard no more.

"I could not act as executioner even to that man," Dick said to Butterflick, as they returned to the inn, "but as I have seen illustrations of the potency of the poison I took from that villain I think I am sufficiently avenged."

"He will still be living," remarked Butterflick, "and may do a lot of mischief yet."

"He will not have the nerve to attempt it," said Dick; "and now, as this phial has, like the bull of the Borgias, brought punishment to its inventor, I think an end may be put to it."

Taking out the phial, Dick dropped it on the ground and set his heel upon it.

"So perish all fiendish inventions and discoveries of man," he said.

"You were speaking of a bull—what sort of an animal was it?" asked Butterflick.

"At the time of Cæsar Borgia," answered Dick, "when the torture of men and women was the daily pastime of the rulers of Rome, a fiend, to curry favour with the emperor, invented a brazen bull. It was so constructed that when a man was placed within its hollow body, and a fire lighted beneath, his cries of agony passed through an arrangement in the throat of the beast, producing a sound like the roaring of a bull."

"Mercy on us!" exclaimed Butterflick, "what a devilish invention."

"It was," said Dick; "but the inventor paid the price of his cruelty, for Cæsar Borgia, who was possessed of a fiendish humour, resolved to test the efficacy of the invention by roasting the inventor, who was accordingly placed inside his own instrument of torture and roasted to death."

"Dern me!" said Butterflick, "but it served him right. And if they had sent that chap Cæsar after him—"

"Just so," said Dick; "but if he escaped that death he was eventually assassinated—poisoned by his sister, who was more cruel than he."

"And yet those were the 'good old times,'" growled Butterflick. "Well, I calls ancient history a swindle."

Dick smiled, but did not answer him. He had nothing to say against Butterflick's estimate of the "good old times," the age of perpetual war and of unlimited cruelty and wrong.

———

CHAPTER XXXIX.

ENTRANCE INTO TEHERAN—MUFFINS AND BUTTER-FLICK GO ON AN ARCHÆOLOGICAL EXPEDITION—BATS.

HEY did not wait for the full day, but at the first glimpse of dawn they were away. Dick and his friends started when the "oosha"—the mother of the young god—flashed in the sky.

Crouching in his prison, Turcomatz could hear the horses' hoofs and the cheery voices of the riders as they bade adieu to the people of the inn, whom they had treated with great liberality.

Blessings were heaped upon their heads, sufficient, and more than sufficient, to neutralise the curses of the Russian.

But he might curse as he chose—he was henceforth powerless for evil. The wasp had lost his sting; he was like Samson, shorn of his hair—weak, helpless, nerveless, impotent to do evil.

It was an hour ere the keeper of the inn found him in the stable, and few who saw him creep away, after he had been well belaboured with a stout stick, would have recognised the once bold Turcomatz.

Shrunken in form, broken in spirit, he wandered out of the village, not knowing whither to go—unless he returned to Astrabad.

"And what will they think of me there?" he asked himself. "No, I cannot go."

Leaving him to his well-merited fate, we will follow Dick Strongbow, skipping over a few uneventful days, and coming to the time when Teheran was almost in sight.

There, if anywhere in Persia, they would be in peril—not so much of their lives, for the pass made out for Turcomatz would protect them from the possibility of their being taken before the Shah by some officious personage.

They had to fear the priests of the Sun more than any others, for, although Murak was their friend, they had to fear those who were friends of Aldrac.

What had become of that venomous priest they only partly knew. It was possible, but hardly probable, that he had survived the watery underground journey on which he was despatched.

If not, he would be missed, and his disappearance laid at the door of Dick Strongbow. If he had survived, then a meeting with him might have a very serious following.

Their horses had been ridden hard, and the travellers would in any case have to rest in the city of the Shah three or four days for the animals to recover their strength. The question was—how and where was the time to be spent?

"Well, without any settled plans I have hitherto managed to come up the right way," said Dick, "therefore we will trust to our old assistant, whom some would call Chance."

They camped out that night in an open plain, here and there cultivated in an imperfect way.

Around them were grass and water, and they had food for themselves, so, lacking nothing, they passed a quiet time.

By noon on the morrow the spires and minarets of Teheran were in view.

A prettier scene one would have been puzzled to find. In outward appearance it was the true land of magic, mystery, and song.

Here, indeed, might dwell the genii with magic powers, lanterns, and rings. It was, to look at, the true home of Aladdin, Ali Baba, and the other heroes of the Arabian Nights.

But our friends had heard that under the fantastic gilding lay corruption. The tyrant Shah, with his unscrupulous satellites, vampire-like, sucked the life-blood of the people.

The stories and magic, so dear to the people, were simply the offspring of hope. They never took the form of reality to the crushed people.

At the gate of the city Dick was, as he expected he would be, stopped and questioned. Flutterby Fowler, as the best up in the native language, answered all the questions in one.

"We are travellers, come to see the greatness and the glory of the country of the Shah, desiring but to rest in the Jewel City of the World a day or two, and then go upon our way."

This answer and a discreet bribe secured their admission to the city.

Quarters were secured at a café or inn, where the stabling abounded, as it usually does in Persia, when there is stabling at all.

The reason is that any man who desires to accommodate the public for his own benefit must be ready to make room for a certain number of military horses when requested.

His pay for this accommodation is limited to curses for the inferiority of all he provides. Even thanks are never vouchsafed him.

Travellers are always welcome at Teheran, as their coming is rare, and they are generally men who are able to pay.

Dick showed that he was one of the class to be welcomed by ordering everything of the best and making the mind of the host easy with a liberal deposit.

That night there was a tolling of bells heard in the city, and the people flocked into the streets.

One of the numerous religious festivals in connection with the worship of the sun was to begin on the morrow, and the Shah was expected, if he could make up his august mind to be agreeable, to show himself to a grateful people.

Anyway, it was something for the down-trodden inhabitants to see the gorgeous cavalcade of Shah, ministers, military chiefs, and troops. It relieved the monotony of their lives and gave them an interesting subject outside their daily wrongs to talk about.

So the bells tolled, and the people came out to hear them.

There was one bell in particular, blessed with a sonorous note, that could be heard far and near, and Flutterby Fowler, who was a student of all things out of the common, asked the host where it was.

He was told that it stood in a tower in an adjoining street, and it had been there about four thousand years.

Some allowance must be made for the natural exaggeration of the Eastern mind, and by striking a nought off one would get near the age of the ponderous piece of bell-metal

Flutterby Fowler was also informed that the tower and belfry were open to all visitors, and the tolling would cease about nine o'clock.

Flutterby Fowler wanted very much to see that bell, as it would give him something to write about in the book of travels he meant to publish when he got home, and he expressed his determination to visit the belfry.

Dick Strongbow offered no objection to it, nor even to Muffins going with him, so about nine o'clock the pair set out, with one of the servants of the inn as dragoman, to guide them to the place.

In the well-filled thoroughfares, where the people quietly streamed up and down, they passed without much observation, and the tower, on being reached, proved to be in structure akin to many old towers we have at home.

There had been a building attached to it once upon a time, but it was now in ruins, and little beyond fallen heaps of masonry remained to show that it ever existed.

Flutterby Fowler did not pause to examine anything outside, although a bright moon gave him an excellent opportunity to do so, but, accompanied by Muffins, passed though an open door and ascended a flight of crumbling stone stairs.

The dragoman, for some reason he did not explain, proposed to remain below.

Why he did so was made apparent afterwards.

The bell was a huge affair, weighing many tons, and by its make—examined by Flutterby Fowler —it was apparent that it was of the kind familiar to us at home.

It had probably been cast about the fourteenth or fifteenth century.

Muffins looked at the bell as he would have regarded anything out of the common, as a sort of curiosity, and when Flutterby Fowler struck it with the handle of his pocket knife, he put his ear to it and listened to the soft, lingering vibrations with the same interest as an extra-sized Jew's harp would have inspired.

"Where does the sound come from?" Muffins asked.

"It would require a long explanation, Muffins," replied Flutterby Fowler, "but I may say in a general way that it is the result of— Mercy on me! what is that?"

A huge bat came fluttering in at the window, and Flutterby Fowler, who had the very common hatred for these uncanny creatures, took off his hat and struck at it.

Muffins also had a dislike for bats, and, diving under the bell, he lay there, a witness to a very strange scene.

From the open air, through a glassless window, bats of great size began to stream in.

The evening's prowl in search of food was over, and they were returning to their usual resting-place.

Taken by surprise at finding an aggressive stranger there, they blundered about, uttering curious little squeaks, and in a venomous fashion dashing at Flutterby Fowler, who fought them as a man fights for his life.

Some of the largest fastened upon the tutor's clothes, and clung there like huge cobwebs, inspiring him with a loathing and terror which drove him nearly wild.

He staggered about, fighting the foe, who, beyond clinging to him, did no apparent harm, until he came unexpectedly to the flight of steps, down which he fell headlong.

Muffins heard him gasp and scream as he rolled to the bottom, and then the voice of the dragoman was lifted up in a sort of wail of anguish.

To describe the feelings of the boy at this outcome of the archæological researches of his tutor would be difficult.

In all his life he had never before felt anything akin to it.

The feeling was worse than that he experienced on a memorable occasion when he hid in a clock-case and witnessed the bringing in of Butterflick, drugged and prepared to be murdered.

He could not move, but simply lay there until he heard Flutterby Fowler calling from below—

"Muffins, come down!"

"I'm coming," gasped Muffins, as he crept out and made a dash for the staircase.

Immediately the belfry was again filled with the sounds of squeaking and fluttering wings.

Muffins slipped and fell, travelling downstairs on his heels and spine.

Half-way down he met the dragoman, who, urged by Flutterby Fowler, was slowly coming up to the rescue.

The impetus of the boy took the Persian off his feet, and in a moment they shot down to the gateway at the feet of Flutterby Fowler, who was wiping his perspiring brow and confounding all bats—past, present, and to come.

"That fool," he said, pointing to the dragoman, who was dolorously rubbing the most prominent part of the body, "tells me that the tower is infested with bats, who eat people alive."

"When bell sound they go out," moaned the dragoman; "no think they come back again so soon."

"Muffins," said Flutterby Fowler, "we will go home. I have had enough of archæological research in this country; it's rotten and bad from commencement to end."

"But would they have eaten us up?" asked Muffins, as they got into the open air.

"Well, no, perhaps not—I don't know," answered Flutterby Fowler. "It's difficult to say; bats vary so in different countries. There's the vampire bat of the Brazils—it will suck your blood and fan you with its wings to keep you asleep. There's the— Muffins, what is that on my back?"

"A bat," replied Muffins, "hanging on like old boots!"

"Knock it off!" cried Flutterby Fowler, in terror. "Hit it on the head and stun it."

Muffins, who had now recovered his nerve, struck the bat with his clenched fist, and it fell to the ground, where it lay still. Flutterby Fowler took out his penknife, opened a blade, and passed it through the short neck of the hybrid creature.

That settled it, and, spreading out its wings, he saw that it measured about eighteen inches.

"I'll stuff this and take it home," he said. "If I do, people will then believe in the existence of such creatures. Perhaps I may send it to the British Museum. 'Presented by Flutterby Fowler, Esq., on his return from Persia,' will read well on a card. I am not sorry, on the whole, I came here to-night, but I do not think I shall come again."

CHAPTER XL.

DICK IS SUMMONED TO THE PALACE—THE WILY VIZIER
IS ASTONISHED.

URING the absence of Flutterby Fowler and Muffins a visitor called upon Dick Strongbow in the person of a chief officer of the grand vizier.

By what means the great functionary had heard of Dick's arrival is unknown, but that he had received information on the subject was clear.

The chief officer brought an imperative summons for Dick at once to appear before the grand vizier and the Shah.

As it was a summons that could not be ignored or evaded, Dick, with characteristic boldness, expressed his willingness to accompany the officer to the palace. Turning to Butterflick, who was in the room at the time, he said—

"Should it be the pleasure of the Shah to detain me, you know what to do."

Then, as the chief officer faced about to lead the way out of the room, Dick quietly placed the small bag containing the precious diamond upon the table, laying a finger upon his lips to express caution on Butterflick's part.

The rough miner was equal to the occasion. He simply nodded, and with affected cheerfulness bade his chief good-night.

"I shall be in bed when you return," he said, "for I'm fairly tired out."

But after the door had closed upon Dick a change came over Butterflick.

Having secured the diamond in an inner pocket, he strode to the window, which commanded a view of the street, and saw the forms of Dick and his escort fading away in the gloom.

The hair of the miner bristled with wrath, and, although he uttered no sound, he confounded inwardly the Shah and all his belongings, with an intensity that was full and complete.

Leaving him there, pacing up and down like an angry lion, we will follow Dick to the palace of the Shah, which stood in the heart of the city.

It was one of many owned by the most potent, puissant Shah of Shahs, kings of kings, et cætera.

Instead of guiding Dick to the main entrance, guarded by a troop of horsemen, the officer led him through a small doorway, which stood open apparently to receive them, for immediately after they entered it was closed, and Dick, looking round, saw a negro, who must have been standing behind it, shooting the bolts into position again.

This was ominous, but as Dick had been allowed to retain his arms—a brace of revolvers—he did not yet look upon himself as a prisoner.

Yet he congratulated himself upon the forethought which had led him to leave the precious diamond with Butterflick.

Through many passages and up two winding sets of stairs the chief officer, uttering not a word, escorted Dick, until he came to a chamber, the door of which was heavily curtained and guarded by two Circassian mutes.

In this apartment was the grand vizier, an old man with a flowing white beard.

He was seated on a divan smoking a fragrant hookah, and he was alone.

The chief officer received a sign and retired, leaving Dick with the grand vizier. The old man motioned to Dick to sit down beside him.

"I speak your tongue," he said, "enough for us."

"I am pleased to hear it," replied Dick, "for I am but a very imperfect master of yours."

"Stranger," said the grand vizier, "what is your name?"

"Dick Strongbow."

"Ah! then it is the same whose coming here was foretold for days by our seers and prophets."

Dick happened to be looking straight at the old man's face at that moment. The light of a huge lamp, swinging from the ceiling, shone full upon it, revealing a cunning twinkle in the deep-set eyes.

"Ah! I know the sort of seers and prophets you mean," thought Dick—"priests and spies."

"You come as a friend," continued the grand vizier. "That also was foretold."

"Yes," replied Dick, "although I had no voice in my coming. You sent for me, and I had to obey the call."

"So that you might fulfil your mission here," said the grand vizier, turning his eyes upon Dick. "I am ready to receive the great diamond entrusted to you by the vizier of Astrabad."

Dick's face expressed the utmost surprise. He had prepared himself for all forms of attack.

"You speak in riddles," he said; "I have no diamond upon me."

"But it may be in your trunk at the café."

"I have no luggage at all."

The grand vizier look puzzled, and Dick thought he understood the expression.

The grand vizier was under the impression—thanks, possibly, to imperfect information—that he was travelling alone.

"What were you in your own country?" asked the grand vizier, after a pause.

"A strong man—gave exhibitions of feats of strength," replied Dick, "and at Astrabad I struggled with, and overcame, one Gahzreal."

"Is it so?" said the grand vizier, slightly raising his eyebrows. "I have heard of him. He has no equal among our people. So you overcame Gahzreal?" he asked, doubtfully. "He was the bigger man."

"For all that I overcame him," replied Dick, quietly. "I speak of it so that you may know me. I do not wish to boast."

The grand vizier stroked his beard and was thoughtful for a few moments. Then he spoke again.

"I must put your words to the test," he said. "First of all you must prove to me that you have not the diamond with you."

"Search me," replied Dick, coolly. "I have nothing about me but a little money and these poor weapons."

As he spoke he drew out his purse and the pair of clean-made, shining revolvers.

On seeing the latter the grand vizier paled under his dark skin.

"I knew not," he said, "that you carried those instruments of death; but I sent a fool to fetch you, and he shall pay for his carelessness with his life."

"Why should he?" asked Dick; "no harm has come of it. See this"—he opened the chamber of a revolver, and proceeded to draw out the cartridges, tossing them upon the floor—"they were not brought here to use upon *friends*."

He emptied both weapons, and, tossing them upon the divan, opened the short jacket he wore, and said—

"Now, if you find that I have aught here, be it jewel or anything else, let my life pay the forfeit."

His air was not servile, but quietly proud, and the grand vizier was favourably impressed.

"I believe now," he said, "you are but a poor showman after all, and as such I will be kind to you. Take up your weapons and replace the cartridges. To-night you shall stay here, and to-morrow you shall go upon your way."

"Why not now?" asked Dick. "Who am I to sleep in the palace of the Shah?"

"It is because the Shah has need of you that you will remain," said the grand vizier. "He is of a sad mood, for life has nothing now left for him. He has exhausted its pleasures—everything—unless, as it may happen, he may find some new joy in witnessing feats of strength. But mark this, if you have lied, if you have not met Gahzreal, but prove a weakling, it will fare ill with you and me."

"Let me give you a proof," said Dick. "I can lift you as if you were a child."

"Do it," replied the grand vizier, laughing incredulously.

He was a stout old man, weighing fully eighteen stone. What man could lift him like a child?

Dick stepped behind the divan, quietly took the old man by the arms, and raised him up once, twice, thrice.

"You are a man of truth," he said, in accents of astonishment, "and if you do not please the Shah then there is nothing left for him but to die. Come, let us go to him. But be wary in dealing with him, for he is short of temper, and has an executioner within the sound of his voice."

CHAPTER XLI.

DICK AND THE SHAH—AN UNTOWARD COMMAND—THE SENTINEL ON THE RAMPART.

IS Majesty the Shah of Shahs sat in one of his magnificent rooms with all the weariness of greatness and a life robbed of its sweetness upon him.

Like a great Eastern monarch of many centuries ago, he had tried all the pleasures of life, and found in them nothing but vanity.

The sun when it rose gave him no joy, and its setting marked but another day that had dribbled away. Was there no man in all the land who could bring back the light of happiness to his saddened face?

To him entered the grand vizier, deferential, humble, almost beseeching in his manner, bowing thrice ere he ventured to speak.

"I crave an interview, oh! gracious lord of us all," he said.

A bowed head implied that he had permission to say what had brought him into the august presence of the tyrant.

"First of all, oh! my lord," said the grand vizier, bowing, "I would tell you that the man who was reputed to have brought the great diamond from Astrabad is here."

A faint light flashed in the depths of the dark eyes of the Shah and then died away.

"It is well," he murmured.

"But, oh! my lord," said the grand vizier, bowing almost to the carpeted floor, "the report was false; the messenger lied. The man is but one Strongbow, a juggler, an exhibitor of feats of strength—a puppet."

"Ah!" exclaimed the Shah, with a frown.

"I would have sent him here," pursued the grand vizier, "but for the thought that his foolery might serve to wean your mind for awhile from the affairs of State. He is a gifted man—a giant—not in statue, but in strength. But just now he did lift me from the floor, making no effort, but raising me as if I had been a child."

"I would see that done," said the Shah, gravely.

He implied indirectly that the grand vizier was telling a lie, and he was desirous of his being convicted of it.

"My lord," said the old man, "he is without."

"Let him be admitted."

"But ere he enters, my lord," interposed the grand vizier, "I would crave pardon for any errors of ceremony he may commit, for he comes of a people who are rude of speech and faulty in manner. It is not that he purposes to offend, but he is ignorant of our refinement."

"I have been among his people," observed the Shah, "and have not found them rude. Their manners of greeting differ from ours, but they are more hearty—they have more fire. Our people sleep—his countrymen are awake."

"I will bring him to you, my lord," said the grand vizier, backing out of his statement imputing rudeness to a people who certainly showed the Shah all the courtesy he deserved—and a little more.

Dick, who was chafing outside the royal chamber, was ushered in and bowed before the monarch, who scanned him closely, but did not respond to his salute.

A motion of the hand signified that the Shah was willing to see some feats of strength, and, first of all, that his ponderous grand vizier should be lifted "like a child."

With unbroken gravity that mighty potentate who, next to the Shah, was the most powerful man in the kingdom, seated himself upon the ground, and Dick, with a strong tendency to laugh outright, lifted him three or four times in his easiest manner.

The Shah, in a stolid way, was delighted, and desired the feat should be repeated.

"It is great and good," he said to Dick. "You enjoy life?"

"Yes, my lord," answered Dick.

"So did I at your age," said the Shah. "Now do something more—amuse me."

"Send for an iron bar and I will bend and break it," replied Dick.

"Impossible!"

"My lord, I will try."

The grand vizier went to the door, and dismissed one of the attendants in search of the bar.

He speedily returned with one about an inch thick.

Dick bent it this way and that two or three times, and then with a sharp jerk divided it in two.

"Give me that bar," said the Shah.

The pieces were handed to him, and he examined them closely, thinking he might find some signs of the bar having been prepared for breaking.

But he could find none.

"All Englishmen are not so strong as you are," he said.

"No, my lord," answered Dick, "and I owe it not to myself, but to my father and early training. My mother belonged to a circus."

He purposely humbled himself before the Shah, who, if he had entertained any idea of his real position, would have detained him or sacrificed his life on the mere suspicion of his having deceived him.

That Dick had excited a considerable amount of interest in the breast of the potentate was certain, and it soon began to take a form unpalatable to our hero.

The Shah expressed his desire that he should remain and become part of his Court, and such a desire was equivalent to a demand.

Wisely abstaining from exhibiting his feelings on the subject, Dick expressed his thanks.

As an illustration of the joys attending the service of the Shah, Dick, ere he left the presence of the tyrant, had an illustration of his power.

The grand vizier was desired to send in a man whose name Dick did not catch.

In a minute or so a priestly-looking man appeared in the chamber, attended by a Nubian with a naked sword.

The grand vizier followed them, but remained at the bottom of the room near the doorway.

Behind him Dick caught a glimpse of armed men.

But in one sense there were but four persons in the chamber—Dick, the Shah, the Nubian, and the prisoner.

"You have brought a story here," said the Shah, "and it is a lie. Confess now it was told to deceive me."

"Oh! master of the earth, and son of the moon and stars," answered the prisoner, "I brought what I was bidden to bring—no more."

"Kneel," said the Shah, sternly.

The man knelt as humbly and submissively as if he were about to receive a favour.

An almost imperceptible sign from the Shah sufficed for the Nubian, and in a moment the sword had descended and the head of the man rolled upon the floor.

It was done so quickly that it came upon Dick like a flash of lightning from a summer sky.

He had no time to interfere even if he had been disposed to do so.

The moment the executioner had done his awful work the Shah rose, and walked unconcernedly to the door of the chamber.

Dick instinctively followed him, repressing a strong desire to shoot down the tyrant at all risk.

Whatever the fault of the man who was slain, he had been given no opportunity to defend himself, and Dick furthermore suspected that the lie he was supposed to have told concerning the great diamond was the truth.

"What a curse there is on such wealth!" he thought.

The Shah was greeted by the grand vizier with a bow, and, the armed men outside parting, his gracious majesty passed through them and walked away to another chamber.

Thither Dick did not follow him, but remained behind, wondering what he could do to get out of the place and away from it.

The grand vizier took possession of him, having, in some inscrutable way, discovered that it was the Shah's desire to retain Dick in his service.

A suggestion to go back to his hotel and return on the morrow from Dick was met with a decided refusal.

"The Shah's servants," said the grand vizier, "cannot leave the palace without special permission."

"At least I may walk where there is air," protested Dick; "this place stifles me. There is an odour of blood in the place."

"Hush! it is treason to talk thus," returned the grand vizier.

"I am not used to the ways of such a place," replied Dick, sharply. "What man's life is safe here?"

"None but those who are obedient," said the grand vizier. "Do not forget that with obedience there is safety, but out of rebellion comes death. If you would walk in the night go up yonder staircase. It leads to the summit of a tower. It is a sight to look upon our city from thence."

"If I must remain I will sleep there," rejoined Dick.

"As you will," answered the grand vizier. "We rise early to greet the sun. The tocsin will warn you to hasten down and join the worshippers."

Dick did not say yea or nay to this, but, turning, left the presence of the great man, and ascended a staircase which had been pointed out to him.

It was of a winding nature, carpeted a portion of the way, but presently was bare stone.

Up, for sixty feet or more, went Dick, until he came to a small door, which he pushed open, and stood upon the summit of the tower.

It was one built upon the outer walls, with a sheer descent of sixty feet to the ramparts and thirty more to the street—ninety feet in all. But little prospect here of escape.

The scene below was a grand one, for the moon was shining with surpassing brilliancy upon the city, so quaint, so beautiful, so full of misery.

And in the shadows cast by the luminary there were coloured lights in twos and threes that twinkled jewel-like, while in one place two rows of lamps stretched along in an irregular line for a considerable distance.

Dick judged that these were shining in the principal street, where there was a bazaar and such places of entertainment as the people favoured.

But how quiet everything was.

The hum of a great city was not heard there. With slippered feet the men walked abroad, and the women were all at home.

Talking is not an Eastern weakness, and whispering is the general tone.

But for the figures moving below it might have been a city of the dead.

Dick had not come there to survey the scene, however, and he quickly turned his attention to way out of what was really his place of confinement.

He had no means of lowering himself, and the walls of the towers afforded no foot or hand-hold.

It was hopeless to attempt to escape from where he stood.

Below, on the wall or rampart between the tower and another about thirty feet away, a sentinel paced to and fro.

The man was alone, and armed with a long firelock and sword.

A man might drop from the rampart and possibly escape great injury, especially if he knew how to fall.

And Dick, in the old circus days, when he was a boy, had acquired the art.

He was ready to risk a drop from where the sentinel moved to and fro rather than remain where he was.

But if he escaped injury he had other dangers to surmount.

It would not be easy to get out of the city at night, and in the morning he would be missed and searched for.

"But I must risk all that," he thought. "And now to find my way to the rampart. I am sorry, my friend," he said, apostrophising the sentry, "but I fear I must be somewhat rough with you."

But first to find a way to the man.

He turned back and descended the stairs to the corridor, where he had parted with the vizier.

It was deserted, but there was a lamp burning with a dim light which enabled him to see the curtained doors around him.

There were five in all, and two windows on the right filled with a horny substance in the place of glass, through which he could see nothing but the subdued light of the moon.

With his knife he speedily cut a hole, and through it caught a glimpse of the street below.

So he was on the outer side of the palace, and the way to the rampart must be on the other side of the staircase.

On the thickly-carpeted floor his footsteps made no sound. Noiselessly he sought the door, and found it.

It was heavily barred top and bottom, and there was a lock in the centre, but the key was in it.

With his strong hand he slowly turned it, holding it so that there was no click of the spring.

Next he tried the topmost bolt, and found it moved easily in its socket. He drew it back, and performed a like operation with the other.

The door of itself swung open an inch or so.

Through the opening Dick saw the sentry advancing towards him with measured tread.

He was a tall, powerful man, with a face almost as dark as that of a Nubian, but the features were of Arab cast. He looked like what he was—a son of the desert—brave and strong, and no mean foe to encounter.

There was no parleying with such a man.

What had to be done must be done well and swiftly.

Dick allowed him to come quite close to the door, and then he swung it open, dashed out, and struck the startled man with his clenched fist fairly between the eyes.

It was a terrible blow, and the man went down as if he had been struck with a bullet.

Dick's first thought was—"Have I killed him?"

Stooping down to see if the man breathed, he in his turn was taken by surprise, the man grasping him by the throat with the grip of a vice. With a skull as thick as that of the rhinoceros, and hardy as a man in full training, he was but partially stunned, and, recovering rapidly, with his native ferocity he attacked his unexpected foe.

CHAPTER XLII.

THE MISSING LEADER—HELP FROM THEIR HOST— WAITING OUTSIDE THE CITY.

"DON'T like this—eleven o'clock, and the chief not back," said Butterflick.

Flutterby Fowler and Muffins, whom he addressed, looked uneasily about them, but neither could give the speaker any relieving suggestion.

"I should say that the Shah has detained him," feebly remarked Flutterby Fowler.

"That's a dead sure thing," muttered Butterflick.

"What can we do for master?" asked Muffins, with tears in his eyes.

"Nothing, my son—nothing," answered Butterflick, "but just wait and see what turns up. He's the sort, in my opinion, that's bound to come out all right."

They were in the room where Dick Strongbow had parted with Butterflick. It was a chamber on the upper floor—a private room, which the landlord had set apart for the travellers.

Their host was an Albanian—so Flutterby Fowler said—a man who would not have all his sympathies with the Persians.

Indeed he had shown they were not, by his readiness to take in the guests, who were of a race not much loved in that country, thanks to Russian influence.

The question arose in the mind of Flutterby Fowler if he could not be induced to help them towards the elucidation of Dick's lengthened absence.

He had an opportunity of testing him a few minutes later, when he came into the room to announce that he should close the place for the night, and if they required any further refreshment it must be at once supplied.

Flutterby Fowler informed him, what he already knew, that Dick Strongbow had been summoned to visit the Shah and had not returned.

A shrug of the shoulders from the Albanian in part expressed what he thought about the matter.

"Those who visit the Shah," he said, sententiously, "sometimes stay long."

"You do not think that the call was a friendly one?" suggested Flutterby Fowler, anxiously.

"Do great men send for little ones at night to show their friendship?" asked the host. "Be frank with me; tell me if you have any cause for fear. I do not wish to know exactly what it is."

"Well, there is a cause," answered Flutterby Fowler.

"Enough for me to know that," rejoined the host.

"Now as to yourselves. Do you expect to be called also?"

"We cannot tell."

"Hear me, then. Listen to my advice and act upon it," said the host. "If your friend and chief does not return in two or three hours you will never see him again. For yourselves the only chance of safety is in flight."

"Our horses are beaten—worn out; they must have rest," said Flutterby Fowler.

"Other horses you can have," said the Albanian; "not quite so good as yours, perhaps, but they will serve your purpose, so that you can get away from here. In an hour I will have them without the city walls."

"But how are we to get there? How can we pass the guard?" asked Flutterby Fowler.

"Leave that to me," answered the host. "Now, as to pay for what you have had here, let that go; I shall make something by the exchange of horses, and that will suffice. Once outside the city walls wait there until Orion lies low in the southern sky, then go your way, for your friend will be lost to you; but, should he happily return here meanwhile, I will bring him to you. I go now to make preparations for your departure."

When he was gone the three followers of Dick Strongbow, with a sickening feeling in their breasts, discussed the situation.

There was no doubt that their host was right. If Dick did not speedily return he had fallen a victim to the Shah's tyranny, and it was their duty to ride away with the precious diamond for which he had risked so much.

"He made it clear to us," said Butterflick. "It's our duty—we must go."

"But without him," groaned Flutterby Fowler, "we shall be as children here."

"Anyway," said Butterflick, "if it comes to a pinch we can die like men."

At the end of about half an hour one of the servants of the hotel entered the room and quietly intimated that he had been deputed to lead them to his master.

It was nearly midnight, and the continued absence of Dick Strongbow was very ominous of evil. It really seemed as if he had at last fallen a victim to his foes.

"But I won't quite give in," said Butterflick, resolutely. "I can't think that they have circumvented him—not in fair fight, anyway."

The man who acted as their escort laid a finger upon his lips to imply that silence was necessary, and they passed out of the hotel into the now deserted street.

On their way to the city walls they had once to take refuge in a dark gateway, on the instigation of their guide, so that a night patrol of semi-savage armed men might go by.

That was the only interruption to their journey, and when they reached the gate by which they were to pass through they found guards lounging about, without any apparent eyes or ears for them, save in the person of one who, by his dress, was captain of the guard. He opened the gate and allowed them to pass through.

A short distance away they found their Albanian host standing with three horses.

"Your own saddles and bridles," he said, "and the beasts are the best I could procure on so short a notice. Mount, and remain in the saddle ready to start in case of any alarm. You must look to yourselves. And now adieu."

He bowed, and glided away with his servant at his heels, and the three friends, wretched enough in all conscience, were left to themselves.

"I think," said Butterflick, "that there ought to be a general law made to bust-up all such countries as this. If a Shah could be got into a mining district they would soon put a stop to his nonsense."

"Speak low," advised Flutterby Fowler; "the human voice travels far in the silence of the night."

"Dad," said Muffins, speaking in a broken voice, "I don't think I can go along with you. I will wait behind for master. They couldn't think of hurting a boy."

"Wouldn't they?" replied Butterflick, drily. "I shouldn't like to trust 'em. No, my son—you'll have to go along with me, for what good would you do, if you stayed here to be roasted or toasted, or whatever it is they might have a fancy to do with you."

"Perhaps if I remained," suggested Flutterby Fowler, hesitating, "it might be of advantage."

"Good heavens! man," exclaimed Butterflick, "what could you do? They'd EAT a whippersnapper like you."

"Ah! yes, I am a whipper-snapper, as you call it," sighed Flutterby Fowler, "but, of course, I hadn't the arrangement of my growth, or I should have been bigger."

"That's Orion, aint it?" asked Butterflick, pointing at the glorious belt of stars.

"Yes—beautiful anywhere, but especially so in this clear atmosphere," replied Flutterby Fowler.

"Listen!" said Muffins, "there's a noise over yonder in the city."

They sat still in their saddles, listening, and their horses being remarkably quiet they could clearly hear a murmur of voices and a dim sound of clashing of arms.

"There's a fight going on, anyway," said Butterflick, distending his nostrils like an old war-horse who hears the roar of a distant battle-field, "and if the master is in it there's somebody suffering."

"What can even he do against so many?" asked Flutterby Fowler.

"What can HE do?" exclaimed Butterflick. "Well, it's a pity that you aint seen him as me and Muffins have in the old days—eh! my son?"

"Ah! Mr. Fowler would have got a staggerer then," replied Muffins.

"Shall I tell you what the master is?" pursued Butterflick. "He's lightning bolts among ordinary men. He's an avalanche, an earthquake, a—anything that most men can't be."

"The sounds have ceased," said Flutterby Fowler. "The fight, whatever its nature may have been, is over."

They were all silent again, listening, and the minutes dragged slowly by.

Hope waned in spite of their efforts to keep its fires burning. Each in his way pictured Dick in every form of trouble which a prisoner in the hands of the Shah would be enduring.

Oh! it was a weary time, this waiting, and when their horses began to show some signs of impatience they walked them slowly to and fro on the soft, sandy soil.

And Orion gradually settled down as the great

earth revolved upon its axis—silently, steadily, with unvarying pace, as it has done for thousands upon thousands of years.

They talked but little now.

All their thoughts were within the city, now so still that it might have been one huge tomb.

A few lights which had been visible on the city walls disappeared, and the sensation of chilliness which is felt everywhere on earth when the night is far spent came upon them.

"Orion is getting low," said Flutterby Fowler at last. "We ought to go."

"Not yet," pleaded Muffins.

"My son," said Butterflick, "the first thing we have to think of is duty. I've been thinking that if Mister Strongbow cannot save himself we can be of little help to him, and duty is duty, you know. He said—'If I am in trouble, you get along home without me'—not in them same words, but of that meaning."

"I think we might be going on slowly," said Flutterby Fowler.

"As you like, sir," answered Butterflick.

"I can't go," cried Muffins.

"But you must," returned Butterflick.

He laid hold of the bridle of the boy's horse and led it beside his own as they began their journey away from the city.

Muffins all of a sudden burst out sobbing, and Butterflick affected to be angry with him.

"Blubbering's no good," he said, huskily.

But for all that he had tears in his own eyes, which were hidden in the gloom.

With bent heads they all began their retreat, the horses showing a tendency to increase their pace as they journeyed along, and presently they broke into a trot.

"Oh! pull up," cried Muffins.

"We ought not to," answered Flutterby Fowler. "Orion is very low—the dawn will soon be here."

"It's all over with him," muttered Butterflick. "We had better—"

"Stop!" almost shrieked Muffins; "I hear a horse approaching."

They reined up then, and sat still.

Yes, Muffins was right.

The dumb sound of the feet of a hard-ridden horse striking the soft road fell upon their ears.

But who was the rider?

Was it their dearly-beloved leader or a stranger?

Was it friend or foe?

CHAPTER LXIII.

THE FLIGHT FROM TEHERAN.

THE doubt the trio of friends felt was not of long duration, for the horseman bore down upon them so swiftly that in a few moments he was in sight.

"It's master, I think," said Muffins, straining his eyes.

There was a moment's silence, and then with one breath all cried out—

"It is he!"

Dick, sitting straight in the saddle, dashed up, and removing his hat gave it a twirl over his head.

"Here!" he said, speaking low, "and safe for the present; but ride on—no talking. We must get all we can out of the horses to-night."

They needed no second warning. To have wasted a moment would have been mad folly, but as they dug their heels into the horses' side it required all their self-control to keep from shouting aloud.

The animals had been idle for hours and were eager to get away. Breaking into a smart gallop, they got over the ground at a pace which seemed to imply that they had a share in the joyous spirits of the terror.

"I have had a narrow escape," said Dick. "Perhaps the closest shave of my life. But I am clear of Teheran, and our late host will do his best to stop pursuit—for his own sake as well as ours."

"It's all right, sir," returned Butterflick. "Already I sniff the salt water of the English Channel."

"You must have a good nose, dad," remarked Muffins.

They all laughed softly at the boy's little joke, for when the heart is light the risible muscles are easily affected.

"Twelve miles from here," said Dick, "we can get a change of horses, or if too closely pursued a friend of our host will take care of us."

They had now left the city well behind, so after a mile of hard galloping Dick drew rein, and the rest of the party promptly followed his example.

"We must be wise in using our horses," he said; "let us give them a rest. All still for a minute or so."

They stood like statues, quiet, and with their ears stretched to catch the slightest sound.

Had they been in the desert the stillness could not have been greater.

"Pursuit," said Dick Strongbow, "is inevitable, for I was chased to the very gates, and had only just got through when I heard an authoritative voice calling upon the guard to detain me. What happened in the Shah's palace I must tell you another time."

"I hope you shot the tyrant," said Butterflick.

"No," replied Dick, with a smile; "I am no assassin-avenger of a nation's wrongs. I was not ill-treated, and but for his majesty's desire to detain me as one of his people nothing would have happened. In endeavouring to escape I had a tough struggle with a sentry."

"I'm sorry for that fellow," said Flutterby Fowler.

"So am I," returned Dick, "for he was a plucky rascal, and was as wiry as a tiger. We had a rough-and-tumble scramble on the rampart of the palace, and it ended in our falling over into the street. He fell undermost, and was killed."

"Save us!" exclaimed Butterflick, "how far did you fall?"

"Something over twenty feet—I can't tell exactly—and the clatter of our fall aroused the other men on guard. At first I was half stunned, and could not get away until they saw me. Then I had a run for it to the café. As I drew up at the door, which was closed, I saw our host coming down the street.

"'Great sir,' he said, 'you must not linger here.'

"I assured him I had no desire to do so. 'All I want is my friends and a clear route outside this city.'

"Then he told me you were already gone," continued Dick, "and he would have a horse ready for me in a minute. There was no time to lose, for, although I had evaded my pursuers, they were scouring the city for me, and we could hear the alarm being sounded in the distance.

"Well, to make a long story short," said Dick, in conclusion, "my friend procured a horse, and in his company I hastened to the gates. By some means—most likely the magic means of money—I found I was allowed to pass.

"'Good-bye,' he said, as he slipped a piece of paper into my hands. 'Here you will find a list of places where you will be safe on your backward route. Lose no time, and if it ever comes to being taken captive—*die first*.'"

"That was significant," said Flutterby Fowler.

"It was," replied Dick; "and now, our horses having rested, we will get along."

Once more they started on their way, and rode for an hour and a half, occasionally halting to listen, but hearing nothing.

With increasing distance from Teheran they gathered strength in the feeling of safety, and by and bye came to one of the many villages dotted along their road home. This was one of the halting places Dick had been told of, and at the inn they got a change of horses.

A drink of wine, the payment of a few coins, an exchange of good words, and they were on the road again.

"How strange to receive help, and us strangers," said Flutterby Fowler. "Why, you have not even a password."

"It is not necessary," replied Dick. "I was assured by our friend the Albanian that the horses and the particular saddle we are using would be sufficient to carry us from place to place back to Syria."

"There must be a sort of Freemasonry among these people."

"Assuredly so."

All seemed well now, but Dick was too wise to indulge in a feeling of absolute security.

"Though they may be delayed for hours, or even days," he said, "they will pursue us."

"Surely they will not think it worth their while," observed Fowler.

"In an ordinary case, no," answered Dick, "but the fact of my being taken into favour by the Shah and fleeing from his munificent hospitality will rouse suspicion. I fooled them, Fowler, by palming myself off as a poor stroller—an exhibitor of feats of strength—and for a man of that stamp to be indifferent to the bounty of the Shah will open up a wide field of speculation in the heart of the grand vizier. He had correct information of my mission here, but I hoodwinked him."

Three stages were ridden that night, or rather during the night and the early part of the morning.

The slip of paper given to Dick by the Albanian was a neat little map, hand-drawn, but very concise and clear.

The distance from one halting-place to another, the nature of the houses to stop at, and other things, were plainly described. If not overtaken by their pursuers, three or four days would see them clear of the Shah's dominions.

Of the several places they halted and rested at during the day we need say little. Here and there they took short naps, as for the present lengthened repose was not to be thought of.

What struck them all forcibly was that their hosts were of varied nationalities. Here it would be a Turk, there a Jew, at another place an Armenian, but never a Persian, which showed that there was a banding together of people who were not natives—probably more in self-defence than offence.

Everywhere was the same readiness to do all that was required, and none would take more than a modest remuneration for their assistance.

"Enough, and no more," they said.

A proper sleep was imperative on the second night of their journey, for Muffins and Flutterby Fowler, particularly the latter, were worn out.

They halted, not at an inn this time, but at a farmhouse, where they found warm welcome from an Armenian and his family.

A good supper was put upon the table and beds placed at their disposal.

All went to rest, but Dick, before going, had a quiet talk with his host, who promised that a watch on the road should be kept by one of his sons, and an alarm given on the approach of any suspicious party.

"We are accustomed to watch," said the host, significantly. "From a room of one of our barns we can see far and wide."

Dick could have passed another night without sleep, but he thought it was advisable for him to get some rest.

The beds were all in one room, for the accommodation of the farmhouse was limited.

Butterflick, Muffins, and Flutterby Fowler lay like logs in dreamless sleep, and Dick, as soon as he stretched himself upon his simple couch—a wooden frame with a sack support for the blanket that was his mattress and covering together—sank into oblivion.

CHAPTER XLIV.

THE LAST PERIL IN PERSIA.

NE touch of the hand upon the shoulder and Dick was awake. By his bedside stood his host.

"It is late," he said, "the sun has been hours in the sky, and my son, who has ridden out to explore, has brought back news."

"Yes," said Dick, rising, "what is it?"

"A party of the Shah's horsemen camped last night seven English miles from here. They will come by and bye."

"We must begone," cried Dick.

His companions were still sleeping, but the voice of their chief soon aroused them. Then came the hasty toilet, and they would have gone at once, but the host said there was no hurry. They must eat first.

"The Shah's horsemen," he said, with a quaint smile, "ride swiftly when they are near his eye, but they lose their activity when he no longer sees them. They will be here at noon, and will rest in the heat of the day. Be sure we shall give them something comforting, so that they sleep sound."

The import of this remark was clear, and in it

was evidence that Dick and his friends had by sheer good luck fallen upon the men who could and would assist them by any means in their power.

As breakfast was approaching termination their host's son, a fine lad of sixteen, came in to announce the approach of the soldiers.

"But they are far away," he said, "and ride slowly—for they find it is good for themselves and horses that they travel easy."

Horses in exchange for those which had been ridden the day before were ready at the door, and once more there was a leave-taking, with many grateful acknowledgments of kindness received.

Moreover, their host would take nothing for his hospitality.

"You may give my son a few scudi," he said, "to pay for the sleep he has not had. But for me —no, not a coin."

The boy was in the saddle upon the back of a small pony. It was his intention to show the party a short cut, which would lessen their journey by several miles.

"And it is in the cool of the woods," he said, "therefore better than the scorching sun."

Instead of returning to the highway he led them across two fields, where, by leaping a small water-course, they could reach the wood he had spoken of.

There was no regular path through it, but the boy said he knew his way.

"It is one road to-day, another to-morrow," he said, "for we leave no real track for the Shah's men. They say there are robbers hereabouts," he added, simply—"men who waylay the tax-gatherers and the great men who bleed the poor. Indeed, many such have been stopped and robbed, but there it ends."

"The robbers have never been found?" asked Flutterby Fowler.

"No," replied the boy, looking straight ahead, "for you see they leave no regular track in the woods."

Flutterby Fowler was about to make some severe remarks on brigands in general when he caught Dick's eye, and the whole truth flashed upon him.

To the secret brigandage of Persia they were indebted for their safety.

It all stood out as clear as a sign-post at noon.

The Albanians at Teheran and all with whom they had recently been in contact were nothing more ... less than a secret society, banded together—as Robin Hood and his merry men were of old—to wring from the despoiler part of his spoils.

Into the ethics of the designs of this body Flutterby Fowler did not care to go. Whatever they might be to a certain portion of the population of Persia, they had been friends to Dick Strongbow, and there his reflections on them ended.

"There are two sorts of brigands in this country," he thought—"one we encountered as we entered the country, the other we find on leaving it. One class were jackalls, the others—well, I'll think as kindly of them as I can."

The boy who had "lost his rest" seemed none the worse for it, being evidently used to that kind of thing.

Two hours' ride through the wood did not make any mark upon him, and when he brought them to the high road again he looked as though a few hours more would not have hurt him.

"You are now in the Great Path," he said, "made by people who lived before Shahs were thought of. It will take you back to the mountains that border Syria."

"It is the road we traversed on our arrival," replied Dick.

Now that it came to parting, the boy, like his father, refused payment.

"Give me no money," he said, "but let me have something by which to remember you."

Dick brought out one of his revolvers, and asked him if he would accept that. The eyes of the boy glistened.

"It is a great gift," he said. "I have seen one before, and handled it—a friend of mine has it. He can make his cartridges, too, and will make some for me. Oh! it is a precious gift."

"Take it, then," said Dick; "and I would give you the other but for the possibility of my needing it."

"One is enough," replied the boy; "the joy of having two would kill me."

They shook hands with him all round, and with his precious revolver in his belt he rode away as proud as a peacock, for he could now—in the possession of a revolver that would shoot six times by touching the trigger—be a hero among his fraternity.

"It is almost, but not quite, like seeing home again," said Dick, glancing down the broad, well-defined road, made, perhaps, before the days of King Solomon.

Once more the way was carpeted with grass and flowers, scarce ruffled by the scanty traffic of man or beast. Again they were in the rich wastes of Persia.

"Our horses," said Dick, "are to be left stabled at the spot where the road and mountains meet, from which I imagine we shall find a parting hospitable abode."

They rode easily that day, for there were no more horses to be obtained in exchange, and towards evening came to a slope in the road which suddenly brought the mountains into view.

They all remembered the day when they looked upon the road from the mountain, wondering what lay before them, and it was with a sense of deep gratitude they thought of their having survived the many perils of their journey.

But from this feeling of security they were suddenly aroused by an exclamation from Muffins, who was pointing the way they had come.

All eyes were turned in that direction, and they saw a troop of horsemen approaching at a hand gallop.

"We must get on," cried Dick—"it is our last ride for our lives."

Down the gently-sloping road they urged their horses at a gallop. There, miles ahead, lay a narrow pass through the mountains.

Could they reach it ere their pursuers overtook them?

This pass was not the one by which they had come. To reach that they would have to ride across country. To do so they would also have to run the risk of being cut off by the enemy.

Their one chance of safety lay in keeping to the old road, and as they galloped on Dick saw ahead of him two low buildings of modern structure. They appeared to be nothing more than places for the stabling of horses or the storing of fodder, and the possibility of their being inhabited did not occur to him.

But as they approached these buildings a man came out of a low doorway, and, shading his eyes from the light of the setting sun, scanned the party closely.

He remained there until they were close upon him, when, simply waving his hand as a sign for them to pass on, he re-entered the building and disappeared.

As they rode by Dick and Butterflick's experienced eyes saw that the walls of these two structures, so innocent to the casual observer, were pierced for rifles, and at each of the holes they saw a portion of a swarthy face and gleaming eyes.

"A queer lot," said Flutterby Fowler to himself. "I wonder they did not molest us."

They were now within two hundred yards of the mountain gorge, which was bordered on each side with heaps of rugged stones which had from time to time rolled down the mountain side.

Dick looked this way and that for the place in which he was to tether the horses, but nothing in the way of hut or house could he see.

Suddenly it flashed upon him that he had passed the spot where he ought to have left the horses. The two low buildings by the side of the road were to have been used for that purpose.

But he had left them behind, and unless there was time to go back the horses would have to be cast loose.

Reining up, and signalling to his companions to do likewise, Dick looked back, and saw the soldiers of the Shah sweeping down the slope.

They had sighted their prey, and were waving their swords and shouting after the style of the Eastern warrior when he scents blood in the air.

"They will soon be upon us," cried Flutterby Fowler.

"Perhaps," replied Dick, quietly.

"But unless we hasten it is certain death for us."

"Wait and see."

When Dick waited the others could do no less, and if there was a slight fluttering in the heart of Flutterby Fowler nobody need marvel.

Dick brought out his revolver, Butterflick did the same.

"It is as well to be prepared," said the former, "but I do not think we shall need them."

"I'm blessed if I can understand what he is thinking of," muttered Butterflick. But it was not for him to doubt, and in faith he remained.

Yelling at the top of their voices, the pursuers came sweeping on, until they were between the two buildings, and then a fusilade was opened upon them.

In two seconds half the saddles were empty, and the remaining horsemen endeavoured to rein up and flee.

In the shock of surprise they could not face even Dick and his three followers.

But the doom of every man was sealed.

Flash after flash was seen, and the accompanying report fell sharply upon the ear. One by one, in rapid succession, the soldiers fell—some dead, others mortally wounded.

Then from the rear of the building a number of men on horseback swept out, and rode hither and thither capturing the riderless horses.

"We may let ours go," said Dick; "they will not be lost."

They rode on a little further, not sorry to hasten from the scene of slaughter, and, dismounting from their horses at the entrance to the mountain gorge, they set them free.

Old stagers in their way, they galloped at once back to the buildings, where, doubtless, they had been stabled before, and the four travellers on foot plunged into the narrow way between the hills.

———

CHAPTER XLV.

A TERRIBLE BLOW.

HOMEWARD bound! What a delicious sound there is in those two words.

So Dick thought as he lay alone in the shadow of a friendly Arab's tent.

On their way across the desert the four travellers had fallen in with a party of Nomads, who at first looked at them askance, but were induced by signs of friendship to fraternise with them.

The Arab party consisted of three men, with their wives and families, and with the hospitality of the true Arab they had given up one of their tents to the poor wayfarers to sleep in; and Dick, lying awake after a splendid night's rest, was thinking of the coming joys at home.

He was in that very delightful state which often follows after complete repose. He felt as if he would like to lie there and think, if not for ever, at all events for a lengthened period.

It is really a most enviable feeling, and is rarely experienced by the ordinary run of people.

Sometimes after a fever and when convalescence sets in it is known, but hardly ever in the daily run of our busy lives.

Lying on his back, with his head resting on his arms, Dick dreamily looked in the direction of the other tents, pitched—with a delicate sense of being unobtrusive—by the Arabs a hundred yards away.

From one of them a woman and two children were approaching, possibly, as Dick thought, to awaken him and his companions.

The sun was just about to rise, and daylight, for all practical travelling purposes, was there.

Dick had no idea of checking their approach by announcing that he was already awake, for he knew that the first word he uttered would dispel the delicious langour that was upon him.

So he lay still and awaited the coming of the woman and children.

But suddenly a sound on the outside of the tent attracted him.

It was not much for the ear to catch, but the morning was so still that it fell with a curious distinctness upon his ear, although it was nothing more than the sound of a soft, unshod foot upon the sand.

He began to wonder what it was in that lazy, pleasant way, and continued to wonder until he heard a scream outside.

Then in a moment he was upon his feet, and saw what that soft sound meant.

Facing the woman and children, just outside the tent, was a full-sized lion, about to spring upon them.

Dick looked round for a weapon of service at this moment of peril.

His revolver was hardly the thing, and with his bare hands he could not hope to emulate Samson by tearing the jaws of the beast asunder.

Close by where he was standing was a big wooden mallet, shaped like the "beetle" used for driving wedges and splitting logs of wood. The Arabs utilised it for knocking in pegs to keep up the tent.

Seizing it, Dick raised it above his head, and brought the lumpy weapon down upon the head of the lion with a crash, shattering its skull and laying it dead at his feet.

This deed was witnessed by the Arab men and the other women, who had espied the peril of the woman and children, and were rushing up to help them in their extremity.

When they saw the act Dick had performed they uttered a shout that awoke the other sleepers in the tent and brought them outside in various stages of rumpled hair and unseemly disordered attire.

Dick had put all his strength into the blow, and the huge mallet, made of some hard wood, was broken.

But it was the head of the slaughtered lion that excited the most profound astonishment among the Arabs.

They looked first at the skull, beaten in as if it had been struck by a thunderbolt, then at Dick, afterwards at each other, and finally threw up their hands and raised their eyes.

The rescued woman meanwhile lay prone at Dick's feet, expressing her gratitude by her extreme humility.

" Well, I'm derned!" exclaimed Butterflick, after he had looked at the lion. " I reckon, Mister Strongbow, you never struck anything a harder knock than that."

" I gave the brute the best I could."

He had now to receive the homage of the Arabs in turn.

They could not speak to him, except through Flutterby Fowler, as interpreter, and he wisely let them have their say without any unnecessary remonstrance.

They compared him to everything that was great on earth.

An impromptu poem was sung in his praise by one of the women who had witnessed the scene, and all the others at intervals joined in a sort of chorus.

When it was finished he was led away to one of the other tents, so that his eyes might not be affected

by the process of skinning the animal he had slain.

A lion's hide is valuable to the Arab, and they were very expert in removing it.

In a quarter of an hour it was skinned, and the carcase covered with sand to foil the myriads of flies which had, with most unaccountable rapidity, gathered at the spot.

" You will become a desert hero," said Flutterby Fowler to Dick. " Your deed will be the theme of their nightly talk for a long time, and the legend of it will pass from father to son for many generations."

" It is lucky I happened to be awake," said Dick, " or they would have had another song to sing. Now, Fowler, we have fallen in with these people, and as I do not happen to be a perfect desert guide, and have not much faith in any of you in that capacity, see if you can induce them to guide us to Beyrout."

The Arabs wanted but little inducing.

As soon as they knew what was wanted of them they declared their readiness to go to the far corner of the earth as servants of the man who could break the skull of a lion as if it were the egg of a bird.

They would consider it to be a honour to serve him for ever.

Making some allowance for Eastern exaggeration, they were honest in their gratitude. Congratulating himself upon the good fortune which had earned the service of the very people he needed, Dick expressed a desire to go at once, and ere the sun had risen an hour the Arabs were making a bee-line, with their wondrous instinct and knowledge of the desert wastes, for the city by the sea.

*   *   *   *   *   *   *

It was not until the city was in sight that the Arabs left Dick and his friends. Being pure Nomads, they had no liking for stone buildings, and had seldom ventured into the streets of thickly-populated places.

The parting was of a friendly nature, but the Arab is never demonstrative. He is as subdued in speech as the Indian of fiction, but he is none the less grateful for a kindness.

The final words spoken, our friends approached the city. Apparently all was smooth sailing now, but it was not to be so entirely just yet, for as they drew near to a small doorway in the walls an Arab, armed with a rifle and bayonet, stepped out, and called on them to stop.

The check was unexpected and irritated Dick, who drew his revolver and presented it at the head of the Arab.

" Stand aside," he said, in a determined tone, " or it will be the worse for you, my friend."

CHAPTER XLVI.

HOME AT LAST.

T HE Arab did not like the look of Dick's weapon nor his bearing. Lowering the point of the bayonet, he asked, in his native tongue—

"Who are you to come here?"

It was Flutterby Fowler who answered for them all.

"We are travellers, homeward bound for England. We have done no harm to anyone."

Then the Arab asked if they would consent to be taken before the governor of the city, and a ready reply in the affirmative was given. An explanation and a bribe, Dick suspected, would enable them to go free of further interference.

His anticipations were fulfilled. The governor, like all Eastern potentates of a minor degree, was open to "persuasion," and in their interview with them, which took place within an hour or so, he consented, on payment of a sum equal to about twenty pounds English money, not only to free them from further hindrance, but to assist them in leaving his arid country with the least possible delay.

"And this," said Dick, as they left his august presence, "is, I hope, the last bit of bother we shall have on our way home."

It was the last.

With two days' rest a trader bound for England was found, and, the captain consenting to take them as passenger-friends, they gladly took leave of the scene of all their troubles and adventures, and with a favourable wind set sail for the Old Country.

. . . .

Home again at last.

With a sense of deep thankfulness our travellers once more set foot upon the land where, with all our little errors of misgovernment, freedom in its truest form on earth is to be found.

They landed in the port of London, and Dick at once wired to the Duke of Lavante at the Swedish Embassy, requesting his message to be forwarded if his grace were not there, and giving his own address at Morley's Hotel, Trafalgar-square.

So quickly does the wire do its work that Dick, who left his friends behind to look after the little luggage and some boxes of knick-knacks they had gathered together at the different ports they touched at on the way, found that the telegram had been delivered and an answer in the form of the duke in person awaiting him.

The nobleman had secured a private room, and the meeting was a joyous one.

"I need not ask if you have been successful," said the duke; "I can see it in your face."

"The diamond is here," replied Dick, as he placed it in the duke's hand.

"Nobly done," was the hearty rejoinder, "and now I have a jewel to give you in return. Lucella is here. We have been to and fro, eagerly awaiting some tidings of you—come now, and receive your reward."

. . . .

Having waited so long, Dick Strongbow was not disposed to defer his marriage. Indeed, there was no need to do so when all concerned with it were of one accord.

Moreover, it was his desire that it should be as quiet as possible, and there again the duke and Lucella agreed with him.

Exactly one month after his return from abroad the wedding took place at St. James's, Piccadilly, at an early hour and without any fuss.

Among the limited audience witnessing it were his old friends, who afterwards joined the bridal party at a quiet breakfast, prepared at the restaurant bearing the same name as the church, which is just opposite it, as half the world knows.

The honeymoon was spent in a tour through Wales and Scotland, and the beauty of these portions of our kingdom led Lucella to ask an oft-repeated question—

"Why should Englishmen go continually abroad when they have so much to charm them at home?"

On their return they settled down in a delightful residence at Hampstead, near to the busier life of town, yet possessing many of the charms of the country.

Dick Strongbow has taken naturally to the life of a quiet gentleman, and few who meet him casually suspect that he is the hero of the startling adventures with which his name is associated.

Muffins and Butterflick reside at Putney, occasionally going on a trip to see their old leader.

Flutterby Fowler gave up the former as a pupil, and, having obtained through the Duke of Lavante a splendid appointment as English tutor to a great family in Sweden, he went thither, and, judging by his letters, is contented with his lot.

Of Turcomatz nothing more was heard, until one day an English traveller, recently returned from Persia, lecturing on Teheran, described a terrible figure of a childish beggar-man he had seen crawling about the streets and begging of the passers-by.

By his description of it Dick, who out of curiosity went to hear the lecturer, concluded it was Turcomatz.

From the King of Sweden our hero has received many presents, but the one persistently offered him —that of a title—he will not accept.

"No," he says. "As Dick Strongbow I have lived, and as Dick Strongbow I will die, leaving children, I hope, to inherit a name I have never disgraced."

Respected and honoured by those around him, loved by his wife, and already blessed with three little ones, we wish him long life and happiness to

THE END.